TEN POINTS FOR STYLE

ALSO BY WALTER JON WILLIAMS

Novels:
Ambassador of Progress
Knight Moves
Hardwired
Voice of the Whirlwind
Angel Station
Days of Atonement
Aristoi
Metropolitan

Collection:
Facets

Divertimenti:
The Crown Jewels
House of Shards
Rock of Ages

TEN POINTS FOR STYLE

The Crown Jewels
House of Shards
Rock of Ages

Walter Jon Williams

This is a work of fiction. All the characters and events portrayed in this book are fictitious, and any resemblance to real people or events is purely coincidental.

Published by arrangement with:
Tor Books
Tom Doherty Associates, Inc.
175 Fifth Avenue
New York, NY 10010

ISBN: 1-56865-166-X

Printed in the United States of America

CONTENTS

THE CROWN JEWELS

TO JOHN AND BETH

And about time, too!

"No crime is vulgar, but all vulgarity is crime."

—Oscar Wilde

ONE

Drake Maijstral walked on soft leather buskins down the center of the Peleng City ballroom and never made a noise. He was light-footed by trade.

Above him, ideographs for "long life" and "welcome, travelers" floated below the high ceiling. The glowing holos lit the room more brightly than usual, mainly to provide sufficient light for the large number of media globes that also floated over the assembly. Individuals, human and not, found themselves reacting to the unexpected brightness in accordance with their character and purpose. Some did not wish their business to be known, and these shrank into the shadows and mumbled with their faces turned to the wall. Those wanting to be seen promenaded beneath the hovering globes or floated on a-grav fields toward the ceiling in hopes a globe might condescend to interview them. Some promenaded in the light, but being self-conscious, blushed. Others tried their best to behave normally and ended up asking themselves what normal was, particularly under these conditions.

Maijstral did none of these things. He had been schooled in ways of maintaining assurance under unusual conditions, was used to a certain amount of media attention, and though his business was not entirely legitimate, he felt no urge to hide in corners and mumble.

The formal stance adopted by most of the guests featured the shoulders pulled back and hips tucked under a slightly curved but nevertheless rigid spine. The pose was natural to a Khosalikh but required training in a human. That Maijstral managed to add a supple grace to this posture was to his credit. He was only a few inches above the human average, but he looked taller. Also to his credit was his dress, which managed to make the most of the monochrome scheme demanded by High Custom—black being the mourning color of most of humanity, and white of the Khosali. He wore little jewelry save the silver pins used to hold back his long brown hair, and the large diamond on one finger. His eyes were a pleasant and unassuming green, and half-closed lids gave the impression of laziness. He appeared to be in his midtwenties.

Maijstral approached a tall, elegant, somewhat older man, who walked the ballroom unaccompanied. The man had a glass stuck in one eye, and was one of three hundred humans who bore only a single name. His skin was black, his ruffles and boots scarlet.

"Etienne," said Maijstral.

"Maijstral. How delightful."

Formally they sniffed each other's ears. A waxed mustachio point jabbed Maijstral's cheek. "Still in mourning, I see," said Etienne.

"My father's still dead," said Maijstral.

They spoke in High Khosali. Most humans managed the strange intonation and nasal vowels easily enough, but it took training to make proper use of the shifting syntax wherein the structure of each sentence makes a comment on the previous sentence, paragraph, or idea, and in one difficult parsing even makes a relation of the subject of the conversation to the state of the universe as a whole.

"I remember hearing the news about your father a year or so ago. There's no hope of recovery, I assume?"

"I'm afraid not. He sends me frequent letters complaining about his condition."

"The dead can be a burden, I'm sure. But mourning suits your figure well, Maijstral."

"Thank you. You look elegant, as always. Though I'm not sure the eyeglass suits you. I don't think you're old enough for such a major affectation."

Etienne lowered his voice. "It's cosmetic, I'm afraid. Pearl Woman challenged me on Heath Minor and ran me through the eye.

My boot slipped, damn it. There are still a few bruises around the implant." He paused a moment, as if troubled. "You hadn't heard?"

"I'm afraid not. I've just ended a long passage, and I haven't caught up on the news."

"Ah." Etienne seemed comforted. "Take my arm and walk with me. The citizens seem a bit shy."

Maijstral fell into step with the other man. Locals parted before them in a certain awe. "I am not surprised," Maijstral said. "How long has it been since members of the Diadem visited here?"

"Forty standard. And from the looks of this burgh, I can see why."

Maijstral was diplomatically silent. It is a credit to his teachers that he did not so much as glance upward to see if one of the media globes had overheard this remark. Etienne went on, his parsing indicating irritation.

"It's not so much the reception as the degree of eagerness, if you know what I mean. Too much reverence."

"They will soon learn to relax in your company, I'm sure."

"My dear Maijstral, I don't *want* them to relax. I'm not supposed to be a neighbor, I'm supposed to be a god."

Anyone, Maijstral reflected, who has got a rapier through the eye and then discovered that an old acquaintance hasn't even heard about it might be forgiven a certain amount of peevishness, even inconsistent peevishness. Maijstral shrugged.

"In that case reverence is only your due," he said. "Relish it, it is the coinage of godhood." Spoken in the difficult parsing relating the subject matter to the condition of existence.

Etienne wasn't so peeved he didn't know when someone had scored a point, but his recovery was graceful. He bowed to a tall blond woman who was approaching them at a lazy walk. She was elegantly dressed in blue and silver, and looked younger than her thirty-two years.

"Ah. Nichole. Maijstral was just asking about you."

Her scent was familiar and struck him like a silken glove. "My lady. I am ravished." Maijstral brushed her knuckles with his lips before sniffing her ears. She was taller than Maijstral, and pale. She, like Etienne, bore only a forename. She smiled at Maijstral whitely.

"Drake. Such a joy to see you after all this time. Mourning looks well on you." She spoke Human Standard.

"Thank you. And thanks again for the kind note on the death of my father."

"How is he, by the way?"

The media globes were beginning to jostle one another above Nichole's head. Etienne made his excuses, sniffed ears, and departed. Nichole took Maijstral's arm. Her nearness to him conveyed old intimacies, suggested new hopes. Linked, they strolled the length of the ballroom. At least fifty men turned red and mentally assassinated Maijstral on the spot.

"Etienne seemed disturbed I hadn't heard of his duel."

"His share was going down, you know. This mandated an *affaire de coeur* with a protégé of Pearl Woman, an *affaire d'honneur* with the Pearl herself, and then the new eye. A silly business. The second duel among the Diadem in a twelvemonth. Pearl Woman was furious."

"He told me his boot slipped."

"Perhaps it did. One hopes it will cure him of martial ambition. Dueling is habit-forming, though luckily suicide is not."

Even the Khosali, who had reintroduced to humanity the twin fashions of dueling and suicide, had mixed feelings about this part of High Custom. There is a Khosali saying, "Any fool can die in a duel." (They have a similar saying about suicide.) The tone of Nichole's comments (though spoken in Human Standard, which does not have the contextual modes of High Khosali) somehow managed to convey the essence of the Khosali expression without actually saying it.

Nuance, nuance. The globes, such as heard, loved it.

"How is Roman? Is he well?"

Maijstral smiled. "Roman is Roman. He'll be pleased you asked after him, but he will be secretly pleased."

As they spoke they watched each other, listened, touched. Explored, in their minds, possibilities. Each in search of a conclusion, a resolution.

"He's much the same, then. And yourself?"

Maijstral cocked his head while considering the question. "Well enough, I suppose."

"You're too young for ennui. That's more my line."

"Did that sound like ennui? I intended rather a becoming modesty."

"You're not a modest man, Drake. Don't assume virtues you don't possess." Said lightly, but still with a touch of vinegar. She had changed in four years.

"I have to assume at least a few," Maijstral said, "else I'll have none at all."

She put her free hand on his arm. "Now *that's* more like the Drake Maijstral I remember."

The second hand on his arm was an external sign of an inner process. She had come to a resolution regarding Maijstral, a resolution similar to that which he had reached himself some moments before. It was perhaps impolite, and certainly assumed much, for him to reach such a resolution so soon.

She looked at a group of Khosali standing a short distance away. "Are those Imperials snubbing us? They stand facing the wall."

"That is Baron Sinn and his friends. He was always deep in conspiracy with my father. I suspect he is a spy. He probably regrets being here at all, considering the media attention this is getting."

"What is there here worth spying on? A provincial planet, sufficiently far from the border to have little military value."

"He must earn his wages somehow."

Trumpets sounded from the a-grav orchestra suspended near the arched ceiling. People began sorting themselves out into couples and lines. "Ah," said Maijstral, "the Pilgrimage to the Cinnamon Temple. Will you partner me?"

"Delighted, sir."

The Pilgrimage was originally a sprightly dance called Going to Market, but eight hundred years before, during the reign of an elderly, arthritic Emperor, the pace had been slowed down and a more stately name applied. The change proved to have unexpected benefits. Because the dancers changed partners frequently, the slower tread gave everyone in the line the chance to sniff ears and exchange introductions and witticisms—and if you were short of witticisms, you could repeat the same one over and over without fear of being a bore. Cinnamon Temple was, therefore, the perfect get-acquainted dance.

The trumpet call repeated, and the dance began. Maijstral advanced toward his partner and sniffed.

"Will you come see me tomorrow?" Nichole asked.

"I'd be delighted," he answered. She was circling him, stately, her arm crooked to hold an imaginary market basket.

"Can you come at sixteen? I have to witness an Elvis impersonation at eighteen, and you can be my escort."

Maijstral did a caper. "I'll dress formally, then."

"God knows what it will be like." Nichole sighed. "He probably won't even be able to get 'Heartbreak Hotel' right."

Maijstral faced the man on his right and introduced himself. The dance spoke on.

* * *

"I don't like it, Pietro. Baron Sinn being here."

Pietro was a young man, gangly, of medium height. His partner was a few years older, with dark, short-clipped hair and a serious mien. Pietro was the taller, but only by virtue of high-heeled boots.

"I don't like it, either, Miss Jensen," Pietro said. "Perhaps he intends to interfere in the auction."

"Damn it. We can't outbid him. If only Tartaglia were here. I sent him a message, but no reply as yet."

"Oops. Sorry."

"You shouldn't dance in heels unless . . . Oh, hell. Later, Pietro."

"Baron, a word." Sinn was a Khosalikh; tall, with a pointed face and ebony skin beneath his dark fur. His interrogator was a human; short, fair, with intense blue eyes that glittered like diamond-bearing sand. She was in her fifties but looked ten years younger.

The Baron touched his warm nose to her cheek. "Countess."

Her ears pricked downward. "There may be a complication. I noticed that Maijstral is here."

"He has the contents of a planet to choose from, ma'am. I would not be concerned. The chances of our interests being similar are not great."

"Perhaps the simplest way is just to ask."

"I don't wish to betray our intentions to such an uncertain character. We shall simply watch, and wait."

Her mouth hung open, her tongue lolled. A Khosali smile. "Still. I haven't seen him in years. Will you join me, Baron, at the bottom of the set?"

"With pleasure, Countess. Take my arm."

"Drake Maijstral, sir." Mutual sniffs.

"Lieutenant Navarre, sir. I see we're both in mourning." He was a tall man, copper-skinned, about thirty, in uniform with a mourning cloak.

"I'm afraid I don't recognize the uniform. A local unit?"

A dismissive laugh. "No. I'm from Pompey. I just inherited some property here, and I have to inspect it."

"Substantial property, I hope."

"Oh, no. Just a house and some land. A lot of bric-a-brac—my uncle had eccentric tastes, but he wasn't rich. I'm selling it all."

"I hope you don't think me impertinent for asking."

A shrug. "Not at all. What else is there to talk about, between strangers?"

". . . Yes. My boot slipped, damn it."

"It was such a beautiful eye. I think it was your eyes that made me fall in love with you, years ago when I was a child."

"Er. Yes. To be sure."

"Drake Maijstral, sir."

"Pietro Quijano, sir. Say, are you *the* Drake Maijstral?"

"Ah . . ."

"Oh. I'm terribly sorry, sir. These are new shoes."

"Think nothing of it, sir. The answer to your question, I'm afraid, is yes."

A pause. "Sir? What question was that?"

"Hello again, Nichole. That was a lovely turn you just did."

"I had to try something new. I've done this dance so many times. . . ."

"Now who's filled with ennui?"

A wry laugh. "I just danced a measure with the most appalling woman. Countess Anastasia. You blanch, Drake."

"She must have arrived late, else I would have seen her." Maijstral's hooded eyes could not entirely conceal his disquiet. "A spectre from my youth."

"She must have found out that Baron Sinn was here. I don't suppose she came to see you."

"My father was terrified of her, and with reason. Truthfully, so was I." He craned his head down the set. "Possibly she won't notice me."

"I wouldn't count on it, Drake. I would guess that woman notices everything."

"Hullo, Pietro."

"I'm having a good time, Miss Jensen."

"I'm glad to hear it."

"Here we are, involved in a serious intrigue, and with all these famous people around . . . it's just like the Magic Planet of Adventure."

"The what?"

"Didn't you watch Ronnie Romper as a child? I did."

"Of course. I'd forgotten."

"Do you know who's here, Miss Jensen? Drake Maijstral. *The* Drake Maijstral."

"I'm sorry to be dense, Pietro, but I'm not sure who you mean."

"Don't you follow sports? The Khovenburg Glacier? The Inside Straight Affaire?"

"Ah. I remember now. Which one is he?"

"Over there. Talking to the onion-head. I was thinking. . . . He might help us with our, uh, problem."

"Oh." A tone of surprise. "That's a good idea, Pietro."

Two beats' pause. "Is it really?"

"Yes. Bad luck. My boot slipped."

"Drake Maijstral, sir."

A high-pitched voice composed of glorious harmonies. "Count Quik." The Count was a Troxan, less than four feet tall, with a large, round head composed of translucent layers of alternating brain tissue and cartilage. There were no external ears, as the structure of the head produced a resonance that had much the same purpose. Maijstral had to make approximations during the get-acquainted sniff.

"On unbusiness I am inning this system," the Count explained. "Humanity is me interested. I big tour taking am. Am on Earth big finishing, acquaintance making."

Maijstral wondered if teaching implants for Human Standard had never been developed for Troxans. "That sounds delightful," he said. "I have never been to Earth."

"You touring should. Home of Elvis and ancient Greeks."

"It's near the border, too, and I'm heading that way. I should make plans. Yes. Definitely."

"Lieutenant Navarre, ma'am."

"Nichole. The Pompey High Seas Scouts, I see."

"You recognized the uniform? I'm astonished at your breadth of knowledge, ma'am. Have you been to Pompey?"

"Alas, no. But I've always liked a man in uniform."

"Drake Maijstral, madam."

"Amalia Jensen, sir. Are you the Maijstral of the Mirrorglass BellBox?"

"I'm afraid that was Geoff Fu George, madam."

"I beg your pardon."

"Think nothing of it. The comparison flatters me."

Briskly, "I was wondering, though . . . perhaps we could discuss business."

"I am rapt attention, madam."

"An antiquity. About to be sold at auction. I'm afraid I might be outbid."

"I shall be happy to hear you. Please continue when next we share a measure."

"Delighted."

"Such a shame. I hope you've acquired a new pair to go with the new eye."

"Maijstral, sir."

"Paavo Kuusinen." He was a slight, cool man, entering middle age.

"That coat is cut Empire-fashion. Are you with the Sinn party?"

"I travel alone, sir. On business."

Maijstral could think of no reply to that, and the man's manner discouraged intimacy. He danced on.

"Drake."

"Nichole."

"Do you know that four hundred lives are lost annually on Pompey, in accidents relating to the sea?"

"Ah. I see you have been talking to the man in uniform."

"He is full of facts, Maijstral. How long has it been since I've actually heard a fact? Not a supposition, or a rumor, or a piece of gossip, but an actual clear-cut fact? Four hundred lives. A fact."

"It is a fact that you are beautiful."

"It is a fact with which I am distressingly familiar."

"Pietro Quijano."

"General Gerald. Marines. Retired." The General was a broad-shouldered man, erect, his face set in an expression of permanent fury.

"Your servant, sir."

"Ridiculous business, this dance. I've sniffed so many dirty necks tonight it's scandalous. Yours could use a little wash, by the way."

"Ah—I'll attend to it straight away. I say, do you know who I just met? Drake Maijstral. You know, the Khovenburg Glacier. The Swiss Cheese Incident."

"Maijstral? Here? Where?"

"There. In mourning."

"Hah! An outrage. And here, in this company."

"Oh. Sorry, sir."

"You shouldn't be wearing heels, young man. You don't need the extra height."

"Oh." Beat. "Do you really think so?"

"Nichole."

"Paavo Kuusinen. Your servant, ma'am."

"Are you traveling from the Empire?"

"Yes, ma'am. Is it that obvious?"

"If you wish to remain anonymous, you should have that coat altered."

"I am chagrined. I am a student of human nature, and I had hoped to blend in, the better simply to watch the rest of humanity at their games. My tailor assured me this was the latest style."

"Our fashions no longer come from the Empire. There are some here who would count that a loss."

"Drake Maijstral."

"General Gerald. Marines. Retired. Come after anything of mine and I'll kill you."

Astonishment. A caper terminated at the halfway point. "I beg your pardon, sir, but I have no intention—"

"I don't give a damn about your intentions. It's results that I'm after. Move in my direction and I'll kill you, or have it done. That's fair warning."

"Fair enough, sir."

"I don't need your judgments as to my fairness either, damn you. Go sniff that lady's neck and get the hell out of my sight."

"Miss Jensen, if all is as you say, my fee would be at least sixty. More if the job is difficult."

"Do you doubt my information?"

"Your information may not be up to date."

"Your price is . . . high, Maijstral."

"You aren't allowing me media rights. If you change your mind, the price will go down."

"Sorry. I'm firm on that point."

"Then I'm firm on my price. My apologies, miss."

* * *

"I saw that fight of yours. Damn bad business."

"Yes, General. Unfortunately my boot slipped."

"Hah. You're a liar, or perhaps an idiot. She dropped a foot on your instep, you lost your concentration, she caught your blade in forte and you were done for. A midshipman could have done better."

"Sir!"

"Don't play the outraged man of action with me. I may be past retirement, but I know better than to fall for tricks like that. I'd cut you to ribbons."

"Maijstral."

"Countess." There was a distressing wail in his nerves, a tendency in his limbs to tremble and betray his resolution. It is not pleasant to discover that a childhood ogre still has teeth, still possesses the ability to quicken the pulse, tighten the diaphragm, weaken the knees.

"Allow me to express my thanks for the kind note on my father's death."

"He was the worthy son of a great man. You could do no better than to emulate him." She spoke in High Khosali, her pronunciation impeccable.

Maijstral drew his ears back into the High Custom expression of qualified agreement. (High Custom demands mobile ears. Pity Count Quik, deprived of such a valued means of expression.)

"Given the nature of the times," he said, "that is impossible." He answered in Khosali Standard, which he suspected might throw her off balance somewhat.

Her eyes glittered like chips of polished blue stone. "Given *your* nature, you mean."

Maijstral shrugged. "Perhaps. If you like."

"You are here on business connected with your . . . occupation, then?"

He smiled. "Of course not, Countess. I am here to visit the zoo and see the methanites."

"The zoo." Countess Anastasia's face never seemed to change expression; she regarded him with an intensity he found not only frightening but somewhat embarrassing.

"Your father was a steady man."

"He moved steadily into debt."

"I could find you employment, if that's what you want."

"I prefer not to impose on old connections, Countess." Longing for the measure to end.

Ears turned downward, the Khosali mark of disdain. "Pride. Pride and unsteadiness. It is not a fortunate combination."

"It is not a fortunate time, Countess. To our mutual regret, I'm sure."

The measure ended, and Maijstral faced the man on his right. His nerves were still singing. Honors, he thought, were about even. Not bad for a man forced to relive the terrors of childhood.

"Baron Sinn."

"Ah. The spy."

"Beg pardon, sir?"

"General Gerald. Marines. Retired. You're the Khosali spy."

"You are mistaken, sir." Coldly. Drawn up to his full height, which was not quite that of the General's.

"You are a military officer, traveling under commercial cover, with two Khosali as military in appearance as yourself. If that ain't a spy, I don't know what is."

"I do not believe, sir, we have anything further to say to one another."

"You mistake me. I have plenty to say. But I'm willing to defer it, if you like."

"Ah. The last measure. I trust the room is brimming with new acquaintances."

Nichole looked at him with an amused smile. "You seem pleased with yourself, Drake. Did you conduct some piece of business?"

"I managed to hold off the awful Countess, and without being any more offensive than she."

"Ah. True cause for rejoicing." The dance ended and the set tapped their toes in a pattern of approval. (High Custom again. At least they didn't have to rotate their ears.) Nichole put her arm in Maijstral's and they began strolling through a dispersing, particolored cloud of couples.

"Etienne looks out of sorts," she said. "I wonder why?"

"Perhaps he's promised Countess Anastasia the next dance. May I offer you refreshment?"

"Thank you."

Media globes hovered nearer, their close-up lenses making soft whirs as they focused on the two faces. Somewhere in their controllers' headquarters, expert lip-readers leaned closer to their video screens. Their concentration on this single inconsequential conversation caused them to miss three choice syllables from General Gerald, who was looking after Maijstral with an expression of disgust on his high-colored face.

Maijstral fetched Nichole a sorbet and took a glass of rink for himself. He glanced over the crowd again, seeing the Countess in intent conversation with Baron Sinn. Both of them looked abruptly in his direction, then away. He wondered whether he had it in him to face the Countess again tonight, decided not.

"I think I shall retire, Nichole," he said. "I just arrived on Peleng this morning, and it was a long trip. I've missed siesta entirely. I came only to see you."

If Nichole was piqued, she didn't show it. In light of Maijstral's last remark, she mentally reviewed the resolution she had made earlier, then confirmed it.

"I will see you, then, tomorrow morning," she said. They exchanged sniffs. "I'm delighted you're here, Drake. Old friends always increase one's pleasure in new scenery."

"At your service, Nichole. As always."

The orchestra began to tune again. Floating holograms announced the Pathfinder. An eager young man tottered on high heels toward Nichole and bowed.

"Pietro Quijano, miss. Perhaps you remember. May I have the honor of the dance?"

If Nichole felt dismay at this apparition, she concealed it well. She smiled. "But of course." Media globes floated after them.

Maijstral finished his rink, abandoned by the media and feeling better for it. He strolled along the wall toward the exit, spoke briefly to Amalia Jensen, confirmed their earlier conversation, and promised he would be in touch. He strolled for the exit, and was about to walk through the cool hologram-patterned door when he was intercepted.

"Pardon me, sir." A man in uniform, Maijstral recognized, and a bearer of facts.

"Lieutenant Navarre."

"I wonder, sir, if I might beg your indulgence in the answering of . . . well, an insolent question."

Maijstral regarded him with his lazy green eyes. "Speak on, sir."

"The young lady you were just speaking to? An old friend, perhaps?"

"You mean Miss Jensen. We just met, on the Pilgrimage."

Navarre seemed relieved. "There is no attachment, then?"

"None, sir. The field is clear."

The man grinned. "Thank you, sir. Please forgive the impertinence."

"Your servant." Maijstral bowed and walked into the warm Peleng night. A media globe asked for an interview but was refused. He had all the publicity he needed.

TWO

If you have to be conquered by aliens from outer space, you could do worse than be conquered by the Khosali. The Khosali have conquered dozens of species and have had lots of practice at it, and this ensures that a minimum number of lives will be lost during the conquest and that the readjustment can begin right away.

There wasn't much of a fight when the Khosali conquered Earth. Humanity had barely got off its little rock in space, and when a hundred thousand alien warships suddenly appeared around the planet, their missiles and beams trained on the inhabitants, only a few hundred humans, crewing military battle stations, chose to resist, and once these were disposed of, the sensible majority sensibly surrendered.

Most Khosali conquests work that way. They've encountered only a few alien races that weren't as sensible as humanity, and these were, with regret, extinguished down to the last individual, and sincerely mourned afterward. The Khosali, admirable as they may be in other respects, do not see the humor in other species' independence. The whole point of the Imperial System is universal allegiance to the Emperor, and without that everything goes down the drain.

The Khosali, as conquerors go, are fairly enlightened. They

don't interfere with local institutions or religions if they can help it; their taxation is, on the whole, light; they import tens of thousands of teachers and missionaries to elevate the subject race to a useful near-equality and an appreciation of High Custom. When a race is sufficiently advanced, members will begin appearing on the Imperial Council and in positions of importance throughout the Empire.

There will, of course, be a few changes. There are garrisons; the news gets censored—Khosali are stuffy, but not stupid. High Custom defines what the Khosali consider best about themselves: their formality, their elegance, their rigid idealism. The Khosali consider High Custom a universal, but the reality of High Custom is that it's a test. If an alien can master the intricacies of High Custom, she proves herself someone the Khosali can talk to and deal with. That's what the missionaries and teachers are really about; they're fishers of men, dipping their hooks into the oceans of alien races, searching for those capable of standing as intermediaries between the Khosali and their own race, capable of communicating with both, interpreting one to the other.

Such lucky individuals often find themselves ennobled. Silly, really, but the Khosali insist. What's an Imperial System without a hereditary aristocracy? Earth had gone through one convulsion after another trying to get rid of its own hereditary nobility, and now they were back, counts and barons and dukes and all the rest, and to make it even more ridiculous, most of them turned out to be aliens.

High Custom might not be a universal, but the behavior of aristocrats certainly is. Earth's new aristocracy proved itself capable of grandness, enlightenment, inspired rule, the cultivation of worthwhile art and talent. Witness the achievements of Viscount Cheng or Solomon the Incorruptible. The aristocrats also proved capable of brutality, shortsightedness, dissipation, avarice, and gay folly—witness Robert the Butcher or Mad Julius. Humanity rejoiced or suffered under conditions created and maintained by its new nobility; much that was grand was contemplated, much that was ignoble was suffered. It was all quite predictable.

What was less predictable was the volatile mixture of human and Khosali. Each race bore traits the other considered admirable; each found the other frustrating.

Humanity, once it got to know them, found the Khosali high-minded but dull. The black-furred, long-nosed, square-shouldered conquerors revered the Emperor, practiced moderation, were fond of parades and military music, raised their offspring to be courteous, well-behaved, and productive citizens. They tended toward stuffiness and fussiness and were masters of niggling detail and Imperial regulation. There was nothing really objectionable in any of this—everyone has an uncle who behaves just that way, and he's a fine enough fellow at heart. But you don't invite your stuffy uncle to your good parties, now, do you?

The Khosali in general do not find irreverence amusing; neither are they inclined to trust frivolity, irresponsibility, freakishness, overt creativity, or individuals born with the gift of laughter and the sense that the world is mad. They don't trust people who whistle in public or make bawdy jokes or get drunk at sporting events. High-minded Khosali believe such individuals would be mightily improved by putting their shoulders to the wheel and taking the Emperor Principle seriously for a change.

Their sense of humanity, sad to say, is that they're all like that. Frivolous and amusing, possibly, but not to be taken seriously. Their stereotype of humanity is unjust—there are of course zillions of individuals who would fulfill every Khosali idea of a responsible citizen, and a lot of them found their way into Imperial service and won commendations from dutiful and exacting superiors. Some were more fanatical Imperialists than most Khosali—look at the excesses of Robert the Butcher, who indiscriminately slaughtered hundreds of thousands of humans in the name of the Emperor, something no Khosali governor ever contemplated.

Our own stereotype is likewise incomplete. There are Khosali who behave with frivolity and irreverence, and a lot more who would be frivolous and irreverent if they ever got the chance. In their secret souls, the Khosali dance drunkenly in the moonlight and sport with wet-muzzled damosels. They just don't talk about it much.

For the Khosali are not without their own secret depravities. They have a large popular literature involving rebels and tricksters, and possess a sneaking admiration for those who can flout convention and actually get away with it. They are kinder to their wayward cousins than the cousins probably deserve, and are no less vulnerable to charisma than humanity.

There is a place for waywardness in High Custom, and anyone who has ever seen a Khosalikh do an Elvis impersonation can scarcely disagree. There are places in High Custom for drunkards and charlatans and fools, provided that their behavior is suitably outrageous and performed with sufficient style. Style is largely the point—no one enjoys a drunkard who is not witty or a charlatan whose schemes do not entertain. There's a lot more to High Custom than ear-sniffing and stately dances.

If you can do it with adequate style, the law will even let you steal for a living.

Maijstral left his flier on the lawn of his rented villa and walked through the sonic screen that served for a front door. On his way he unlaced his jacket as far as the design would permit—an unwritten rule of High Custom insisted that clothing should not allow itself to be put on or removed without the help of a servant. Most used robots these days, at least in the Human Constellation.

Maijstral, however, had a servant, a Khosalikh named Roman. Roman was large, even for a Khosalikh, and very strong. The annual rings around his muzzle showed his age to be forty-five. His ancestors had served Maijstral's for fifteen generations, and Maijstral had inherited Roman from his father. He used Roman on errands of a physical and sometimes sinister nature, the character of which Roman often disapproved. Roman's disapproval, like much else, was kept to himself. He prided himself on being a loyal and incorruptible family retainer, even though the family in question was sometimes the despair of him.

Roman appeared from the hallway and glided toward Maijstral, moving with a silence and stately ease that Maijstral admired for reasons both professional and aesthetic.

"Is Gregor back?"

They spoke in Standard. Roman's voice had a suggestion of still waters about it. "Not yet, sir."

"No problems, I trust."

"I wouldn't expect any."

Roman unlaced Maijstral's jacket, helped him off with his buskins, and collected his gun, his knife, his collar and cuffs, doing it all with a supreme competence and economy of gesture that were as familiar as an old sofa. Maijstral felt his tension ease. Roman was the sole fixture in his scattered, uncertain life, less a servant than a sign of home, and home was a place where he could unbend. He dropped onto a sofa and put one foot up, wiggling his toes gratefully in fuzzy gray socks.

Holographic works of art rotated slowly on pedestals set into the walls, casting gentle light on Maijstral as he stretched on the couch. He looked at Roman.

"Nichole was there. She asked after you."

"I trust she is well." Maijstral looked at him. Roman's eyes were glittering, his nostrils a little dilated. Secret pleasure, Maijstral thought, happy in Roman's predictability. No doubt about it.

Nichole had always been one of Roman's favorites.

"Yes, she's very well. A little . . . jaded, perhaps. I'm escorting her to an Elvis recital tomorrow. That'll put me in the public eye again. Good for business."

"A letter has arrived, sir. From your father."

Maijstral's heart felt a touch of resigned despair. His father's communications had two themes, and both of them were sad.

"I will read it."

Roman brought it on a tray from the sideboard. It had been sent VPL, which meant it was written on paper, sealed in an envelope, and delivered by hand. All at great cost. Maijstral opened the letter and read it.

> "I do not understand your migration toward the border. Surely you will spend the season on Nana, in connection with your eleemosynary duties. If you are on the border before the season begins, you must pay respects to the Countess Anastasia. Perhaps you will be able to assist her in some endeavor relating to the Cause. If necessary, the Kapodistrias plots might be sold.
>
> "I have been approached by Lord Giddon, from whom some years ago I borrowed the sum of 450n. I must have told you about the obligation, and am dismayed that you have not met it. If you had not frozen my access to family funds I would not have mentioned this, but the situation demands that you uphold the family honor and redeem the debt. If you are temporarily short, the parcels on Kapodistrias might be sold.
>
> "I hope you will attend to this forthwith.
>
> "Your reproachful father,
>
> "Ex-Dornier, etc.
>
> "P.S.: The maintenance on my coffin will be due in two months. I hope I will not once again suffer the embarrassment of its not being met in time."

There it was, both themes at once, and in detail: the Cause, and old debt. Both interlinked for as long as Maijstral could remember.

He replaced the Very Private Letter in its envelope and held it out to Roman. "Burn it, please," he said. Roman moved silently toward the disposal. Maijstral frowned and tapped his teeth with his diamond ring.

The debt to Lord Giddon was new to Maijstral, but not unexpected—old lenders turned up with fair frequency these days. The parcels on Kapodistrias were hopelessly mortgaged; Maijstral's father had done it himself years ago and forgotten it since. His memory for money matters had never been good; death had worsened his recollection. There was no money for Maijstral's eleemosynary duties, none for Lord Giddon, none for Maijstral himself.

Maijstral's mode of life was expensive; his household was small, but moving in the highest circles cost. He looked at his ring, held the stone up to the light. It was a very good forgery; he'd pawned the real diamond two months before in order to finance this journey. Not even Roman knew the original stone was gone.

Perhaps he should take the Countess Anastasia's offer. He considered himself in that light: a pensioned dupe in a hopeless cause, uttering sentiments in which he did not believe. Someone, in short, very like his father.

No. Not that.

Roman returned with a glass of cold rink. Maijstral took it and sipped thoughtfully.

Roman's ears flicked back at the sound of another flier humming to a stop on the front lawn. He turned, looked through the polarized windows, and announced, "Gregor." He stiffened slightly as he spoke. Roman disapproved of Maijstral's irregularities, and considered Gregor one of them.

"Good." Maijstral wiggled his toes again, thoughtfully. "I can tell him about our commission."

Gregor Norman entered, pulling a dark blue cap off a mass of bright red hair. He was twenty, lanky, and intense. He was dressed entirely in dark colors and his coat had a lot of pockets, most of them filled with electronic gadgets. He smiled. His words came rapidly, and he spoke with a cheeky accent. Definitely Non-U.

"Mission accomplished, boss. Only too."

"Only too" was a form of slang of which Gregor was fond. It was shorthand for "only too easy" or "only too likely" or "only too happy" or any other handy phrase beginning with that versatile pair of words.

"Good. The media globes broadcast me with Nichole tonight, and the panic should start first thing tomorrow."

Gregor laughed. He was feeling pleased with himself. He had committed four acts of breaking-and-entering in the last four hours, and he'd done each seamlessly and without a hitch, leaving scores of little electronic gadgets behind in each case.

Roman looked from one to the other. His nostrils flickered. "You mentioned, sir, a commission."

"Yes." Maijstral rose, put his feet on the floor, and leaned toward the others. "Sit down, Gregor. I'll tell you about it." He knew better than to offer a seat to Roman—it was not a servant's place to sit in the presence of his employer. He waited for Gregor to seat himself and then went on.

"A woman named Amalia Jensen wants us to locate an artifact within the estate of one Admiral Scholder, HCN, retired, deceased. There's going to be an estate auction in a few weeks and Miss Jensen fears she might be outbid."

Roman's ears pricked up. "The current owner, sir?"

"Scholder's heir is his nephew, a Lieutenant Navarre. I met him tonight. I don't think he's very interested in his uncle's estate—certainly not in its security. He seemed to find the whole situation fraught with personal inconvenience."

Gregor grinned again. "They might not notice for weeks that the thing's missing." His fingers were tapping his thighs in some private rhythm. Usually some part of him or another was in motion.

"That's a good point. We should continue with our other plans. But tomorrow, Roman, I'd like you to initiate some inquiries about Miss Jensen. I doubt she's an agent or a provocateur, but one never knows. And she declined to give us media rights, which I suspect means there are undercurrents here we don't know about."

"Yes, sir."

"She also had a companion, a young man named Pietro Quijano. He might be a part of this and he might not. At any rate he might be worth an inquiry."

"First thing tomorrow, sir."

Maijstral turned to Gregor. "I'd like you to fly over to the Scholder estate and take a look at it. Check for—well, you know."

Gregor gave a breezy, two-fingered salute. "Only too, boss."

Maijstral thought for a brief moment. "Oh. Yes. Our other business. If any of your surveys turn out to be of property owned by a General Gerald of the marines, disregard it. He's filled with unnecessary complications."

Roman gazed at him levelly. "May I inquire their nature, sir?"

Maijstral took a breath while he considered what manner of lie to offer. "Security matters relating to the defense of the planet," he said. "I would prefer not to be involved with counterspies. It would be contrary to the image I wish to present here."

"Certainly, sir. I understand."

Maijstral put his feet up on the couch and pillowed his head on his hands. "And while you're off having fun, I'll be laboring at the Elvis recital."

"It must be hell, boss."

Roman's diaphragm spasmed once, then again, the Khosali equivalent of a deep, heartfelt sigh. *Definitely* Non-U.

Maijstral's irregularities were sometimes completely incomprehensible.

THREE

The Elvis was human and dressed in white and sequins. His movements—the way he leaned into the chrome microphone, the pelvic thrusts, even the gesture used in wiping sweat from his forehead with a red silk handkerchief—all were highly stylized, as ritualized as the steps of a Balinese dancer.

A holographic band stood in partial shadow behind. Stacks of obsolete and highly unnecessary amplifiers were placed on the wings of the stage, and the sound was arranged to boom from them as though they were real.

"Hunka hunka burnin love" sang the King of Rock and Roll. The screaming of debutantes centuries dead wailed up around the stage in answer to the meaningless pre-Standard lyrics. The Elvis leaned forward, mopped sweat from his brow, and presented the handkerchief to one of his assistants in the audience. The assistant brought it to Nichole, the guest of honor, who bowed and accepted it graciously, momentarily illuminated by spotlights. The audience offered polite applause.

"Now what the hell do I do with it, Maijstral?" Nichole asked, drawing her hand across her mouth so the ever-present media globes could not read her lips. "I'm not going to sit here all night with a wet rag in my hand."

Maijstral looked at her with sympathy. Her costume, a bluish thing composed of several semitransparent layers of pseudocarapace, did not allow for pockets. "I'll take it, if you like," he said. "Or I can tie it around your arm."

The spotlight on Nichole faded. Her diamond earrings and necklace dimmed. "I'll send it to Etienne," she decided. "It suits his coloring better." She signaled one of her coterie and whispered instructions. Etienne, in the next box, yawned behind his hand. He had decided to be bored by Peleng.

Before the concert Maijstral and Nichole had an enjoyable luncheon, discussing their lives, their times, old friends. He had discovered she had a tendency to assume he knew more about Diadem affairs than he really did, but he managed, he thought, to cover his ignorance fairly well. He really didn't keep up with gossip.

Maijstral leaned back and felt his chair adjust to his contours. He glanced across the hall and saw Countess Anastasia sharing a box with Baron Sinn. She gazed at him intently with her ice-blue eyes. A brief alarm sang in his nerves. He bowed to her, and she nodded back.

She calls me irregular, he thought. It was the Khosali who made Elvis a part of High Custom and left Shakespeare out. Probably, he reflected, because there were too many successful rebellions against monarchs in Shakespeare. And Elvis was a mock rebel who became, in the end, a pillar of the social order.

Maijstral liked Shakespeare a good deal, having read him in the new translation by Maxwell Aristide. The comedies, he thought, were especially good. This was, he supposed, an indication of his low taste. Most people found them unsubtle.

The lobby bar was padded in red leather and featured more polished brass than was necessary even for ornamentation. Media globes bounced uncomfortably along the low ceiling and stared at the intermission crowd. Half the audience, having stayed long enough to make certain they were noticed, took the opportunity to slip away from the incomprehensible performance.

Maijstral sipped his cold rink. His lazy eyes passed slowly over the crowd, taking in clothing, accessories, jewelry. Making mental notes.

"Yes," he said. "A playwright, a very good one. The Constellation Practices Authority rediscovered him and had Aristide translate him."

"I shall look for it, sir," said Pietro Quijano. His brow wrinkled and he tugged at his lower lip. "Do you think it's political, sir?"

"Nothing overt that I could see. But the Khosali buried him for some reason, so who knows?"

Pietro tugged at his lower lip again. Maijstral followed the direction of his gaze and saw Amalia Jensen talking to Lieutenant Navarre. Navarre nodded and smiled in answer to something Miss Jensen said. Pietro's frown deepened. Maijstral finished his rink.

"If you will excuse me, sir," he said, "I should see if Nichole needs refreshment."

"Certainly," Pietro murmured, and then he tore his gaze away from Jensen and brightened a bit. "She was a most stimulating dance partner, sir. Please give her my compliments."

"Of course."

Maijstral made his way to where Nichole was giving an exclusive interview to one persistent media globe. "We're old, dear friends, of course," she was saying. "I'm afraid it would be inappropriate for me to comment further." Said with a hesitation, a little flutter of the eyes. Nuance, Maijstral thought. Once he'd thought her very good at this, but in the last four years she'd become an artist.

After the interview the globe drifted away and Nichole took Maijstral's arm. Maijstral gave her Pietro's message. "A dreadful dancer," she said. "He kept tripping over his own damn boots."

"You made him look good, I'm sure."

Her eyes glistened. "I'm sure I did." She tapped his arm. "Do you see our High Seas Scout friend over yonder?"

Maijstral gazed once again at Lieutenant Navarre, who was still intently listening to Amalia Jensen. "Certainly."

"Would you do me the favor of asking him to sup with me this evening? I'd do it myself, but the globes are sure to notice, and they'll never leave off harassing the poor man."

Nichole, Maijstral reflected, would never have asked a man on this kind of errand four years ago. This was the sort of thing she had an entourage for. He reflected again on his earlier resolution and was thankful it appeared to complement hers.

"Of course," he said. "What time?"

"Thirty or so." Nichole smiled. "I'd invite you, but I'm sure you'll be off on business."

He answered her smile. "I'm afraid it would be inappropriate for me to comment further."

"As I thought." Knowingly. She patted his forearm. "I'd love to see you tomorrow, though. Luncheon again?"

"Delighted."

She glanced up and saw more media globes moving in. Her face did not exactly fall, but grew more controlled, less spontaneous. Less delighted. "Please fetch me some champagne, Drake, will you?" she asked. Her voice was silky. Maijstral sniffed her ears—this was a High Custom event, after all—then bowed and withdrew.

"Not much pelvis," said a high, wonderfully resonant voice. "Troxans cannot Elvis do well."

Maijstral bowed in Count Quik's direction as he strolled by the tiny round-headed alien. Amalia Jensen's laughter hung in the air. She was finding Lieutenant Navarre amusing. Maijstral glided toward them and touched the copper-skinned lieutenant on the arm. "With Miss Jensen's permission, a word, sir."

Miss Jensen gave her consent. Maijstral gave Nichole's message. Navarre looked confused.

"Oh. I'm flattered. And delighted. But I'm afraid"—he looked toward Amalia, who smiled, more at Maijstral than at Navarre-—"I'm committed for this evening. With Miss Jensen. Please give Nichole my sincerest regrets."

Maijstral glanced up at a clattering noise and saw Pietro, standing about ten feet behind Navarre, trying to extricate himself from the rubble of a spilled drink tray while a hostess looked at him with purse-lipped annoyance.

"I'll convey your apologies," Maijstral said. "I'm sure Nichole will understand."

He walked to the bar and asked for champagne. Receiving his glass, he turned to stare into the intent eyes of the Countess Anastasia. Looming over her was the bulk of Baron Sinn. Maijstral's blood turned cold—that old reflex again—but he smiled and exchanged sniffs.

"Champagne, Countess?"

"I have sworn not to drink champagne within the boundaries of the Constellation," she said, "till the Empire be restored."

"I fear you will have a long wait," Maijstral said.

"Your father—" she began. Anger surged in Maijstral's heart.

"Remains dead," Maijstral said. He sniffed her and excused himself.

The woman had always got to him, damn it. He had to wait some moments before Nichole was sufficiently clear of media globes to convey Navarre's regrets, and he used that time to calm himself. Nichole, when she heard the message, was astonished.

"He turned me down, Maijstral! What am I to do with myself this evening? It's one of the few free moments allowed in my schedule."

"I would offer to keep you company, but . . ." Maijstral's heavy-lidded eyes gave the impression of slyness. "I really do have other plans, my lady."

"I don't suppose I could watch."

Maijstral kissed her hand. "I'm afraid your presence would attract unwelcome attention."

Nichole sighed. "I hope you'll send me the vid, at least."

"Perhaps I'll be able to send you something interesting before you leave. My general run of jobs aren't very enthralling, though."

She pointed at the white stone on his finger. "I can always recognize your videos by the ring. When I see it, I cheer."

Maijstral smiled. "The ring is my trademark. They alter my face and body in the vids, but I need something noticeable to keep my place in the standings."

"Do you like the way Laurence is playing you, by the way? He *looks* more like you; but I thought Anaya seemed to capture your personality better."

"Truth to tell, my lady, I never watch them." Nichole gave a skeptical laugh. Maijstral looked at her. "I've lived through it once," he said, "I have no desire to see an imitation."

"If you insist, Maijstral."

Maijstral touched the clusters of diamonds hanging from one of Nichole's ears. His eyes widened with professional interest. "These are lovely, by the way. Are you certain you should wear them in such dangerous company?"

"If I can't trust you, Drake, who can I trust? Besides, they're not mine—the Landor Company lets me use them in return for a credit. They might even be delighted should they disappear—it could attract attention to their wares."

"We might discuss that," Maijstral said.

"Luncheon. Tomorrow."

He kissed her hand again. "Of course." The screams of a holographic audience began to echo from the theater, the signal that the second half of the performance was about to begin.

Nichole linked her arm in his. "I'll simply have to resign myself to a lonely evening tonight. No one would credit it."

"Cherish it, my lady," Maijstral said. "An event of such rarity must be savored."

"Pah," Nichole said as they began to stroll toward their box. "It just means I'm getting old. Or passé." But she seemed pleased.

One of the consequences of the odd and complex relationship between humanity and the Khosali is that, deplore us though they may, many Khosali find irreverence and irresponsibility interesting, and the human style of irreverence and irresponsibility of particular fascination. A human will perform what the stodgy Khosalikh only dreams about. Humans dance till five in the morning and show up late at work, suffering from hangovers. Humans write satires about Imperial officials and farces in which scores of people end up hiding in closets or under the bed. Humans engage in passionate relationships with people to whom they are not married, sometimes proclaim these relationships actually improved them, and frequently (and most tellingly) fail to kill themselves afterward in a display of proper social atonement. Some even commit the profounder sin of living happily ever after. Though the Diadem was created for human consumption, their joys, scrapes, and follies have a small but devoted following among the Khosali.

Even when the Khosali influence over humanity was at its height, the conquerors often had the unsettling impression that the humans were laughing at them behind their backs. Little did the Khosali know but that when Earth's children served up the punch line, it was going to be a doozy.

The punch line was, of course, the Great Rebellion, in which we got rid of the Imperial System, the Imperial caste, and the unfortunate Pendjalli Emperor, Nnis CVI, whose luckless person was seized at pistol-point in his very own palace by Scholder's Death Commandos. As part of the peace treaty, a pledge was extorted from poor Nnis to let the Human Constellation alone, a pledge which thus far he has been scrupulous to honor. This was the only rebellion, let alone the only successful one, to be perpetrated by a subject species once it had got over the trauma of its initial conquest. The whole precedent-breaking affair was such a shock to Nnis that he moulted and retired prematurely to his cryogenic vault, whence he still lies, heirless and alone.

The Emperor's termination of the war doesn't keep individuals on both sides of the border from wishing things were different. To the dismay of human ideologues, there is a large human minority in the Empire who live seemingly happy lives under the Imperial system and have no desire to immigrate to the Constellation. And on the human side, a large Khosali minority seem to lead contented and productive lives in the Constellation, expressing no more than a sentimental longing for the Imperial System.

And of course there are the troublemakers. The Human Constellation is blessed with a small but noisy Imperial party who claim the revolt was a mistake. For the most part they are a despised and ignored group of (largely human) malcontents, but they did win nineteen percent of the vote in the last election on Baroda, a figure so disturbing that the victorious Symbolist-Commonwealth party decided to do away with elections altogether until the Barodans developed a more refined sense of social responsibility.

On the Imperial side of the border there are a number of voices loudly proclaiming the Constellation an insane aberration, proclaiming as well the necessity to reincorporate the Constellation within the borders of the Empire. Thus far the City of Seven Bright Rings can afford to ignore these noises, as they come mostly from the humiliated descendants of those leaders who lost the revolt in the first place—many Imperial military positions are hereditary, which is offered by human partisans as a major reason for the revolt's success. The Reconquest Party's constant agitation serves, however, as a continuing pretext for the Human Constellation's rate of taxation, which is far higher than was the Empire's due to the necessity of keeping a large fleet in being to prevent an Imperial resurgency.

For the most part, however, the Reconquest Party is ignored. Nnis does not wish another war—the first was shocking enough—and for the most part the rest of the Empire has not yet recovered from the surprise of the human action. New possibilities have been awakened here, and other subject races are beginning to realize it. Odd though it may seem, revolt hadn't even been *considered* before.

Despite the revolt and its consequences, High Custom continues on both sides of the border—there is no acceptable alternative, no agreed-upon human standard of behavior. There is, however, a constant search within the Constellation for a true culture based on universal human principles—the report of the Constellation Practices Authority has been widely anticipated for the last generation, and is said to be in the final stages of the preparation. Until the CPA finishes its work, however, Imperial law and custom prevail in most of the human sphere. Even Imperial titles and grants of nobility are used as a matter of courtesy, though they have no official basis in law. The high Imperial caste has been thrown on its own resources for the first time in its history, and its members rise and fall by their own abilities. It is something they'd got out of the habit of doing. Within the aristocracy there is still a prejudice against working in trade, but some have been reduced to it. Many lost souls wander from place to place, living in High Custom as much as possible, looking for a home.

There are a lot of wanderers. After all, if through a fluke of ancestry you were saddled with being Baron Drago, Viscount Sing, Duke of Dornier, Prince-Bishop of Nana, and Hereditary Captain-General of the Green Legion, you could hardly ignore it, and neither, you would discover, would anyone else. It could hardly have escaped your attention that you were the hereditary exemplar of a social system that had no function or even relevance, that existed only because of cultural inertia—and *then* what would you do? Yearn for the past? Try to reach an accommodation with the present? Try to create a future more agreeable?

You might even decide to steal for a living. Who knows?

A new set of holographic representations rotated in the niches. The day art was pleasantly different from the night pieces—brighter, more cheerful.

"Trouble, boss." Gregor's eyes twitched as he sucked on a smokeless hi-stick. "We were followed today. Roman and me both."

Maijstral's ears were still ringing from the aftereffects of the concert. He frowned as Roman began to work on the complicated knotting of his jacket. "Police?" he asked.

Gregor grimaced. "Can police afford Jefferson-Singh high-performance fliers?"

Maijstral's brows lifted. "Indeed?" He looked over his shoulder at Roman.

"Both shadows were Khosali," Roman reported. "Mine was female, about twenty. I didn't notice her until after I had begun my inquiries about Miss Jensen. Then I gave her the slip."

"I spotted mine right away," Gregor said. He shook his long hair out of his eyes. "He was another Khosalikh, a male. A big bastard, too, which was how I saw him so quick. He was easy enough to lose, though."

"Thrill seekers, possibly," Maijstral said. He shrugged out of his jacket, and Roman took his pistol and began unlacing the side seam of Maijstral's tight trousers. "Perhaps they want the credit for catching us. Or maybe they just want to watch us work."

"Mine didn't look like he was out for fun," Gregor said. "He looked like he wanted to dismember me with his bare hands."

"Maybe police after all."

"He had that look. But I think he may have something to do with the commission." He sucked on his hi-stick again. "Tell him what you found out, Roman."

"Miss Jensen is the local head of Humanity Prime," Roman said carefully. His ears trembled with the repressed urge to turn downward in disapproval. "Mr. Quijano is the treasurer."

"I see," Maijstral said. Humanity Prime was a group formed to assure human domination of the Constellation, and its membership ran from perfectly respectable citizens to denizens of the gutter. The more respectable among them supported good works such as the Constellation Practices Authority, issued propaganda questioning the absurdities of High Custom, called for larger human families so as to keep the aliens outnumbered on human turf, and promoted expansion toward new worlds. They made a point of keeping up-to-date on the latest advances in Imperial weaponry and tactics, and supported the Constellation military in its never-ending quest for funding and expansion.

The less reputable elements of Humanity Prime were something else again, and included paramilitary groups formed to resist alien attacks and groups that spread scandal about prominent nonhumans —"inhumans" being their preferred term. Their activities included active harassment, the sending of thugs to disrupt Imperialist activities, and sometimes actual violence.

Humanity Prime's main branch never ceased to deplore such crude tactics, and to explain that they were not representative of their goals or membership. But somehow the parent organization never seemed to withdraw the charters of any of their groups who brought them disrepute.

Maijstral's own ears almost twitched downward. He'd had his own problems with humanity's partisans in the past.

"You think a Khosali group is monitoring Jensen and her contacts?" he asked.

"That may be possible, sir," Roman said.

Maijstral left his trouser laces dangling and went to the front window, holding up his pants with his left hand. He touched the polarizer control and gazed out into the late afternoon. The sun cast blue tones onto the grove across the sward, giving the chrome-yellow leaves a greenish cast. "Are they still out there?" Maijstral asked.

"In the grove, sir? Yes."

Maijstral indulged his irritation. "Blast them, anyway. What could they want?"

Roman's voice was hesitant. "If I may offer a suggestion, sir?"

"Certainly."

"Jensen's group is almost certainly aware of your family's history. They may intend to embarrass you, and will have informed the police of your commission. You may be walking into a trap."

"So the Khosali in the grove may be our friends?"

"That doesn't make any sense, Roman." Gregor's voice was loud in rebuttal. Roman's nostrils flickered. "If that bastard who followed me around this morning is a friend, I'll eat my boots. And if they don't like what Jensen's up to, why don't they just warn us instead of keeping us under surveillance?" He snapped his used hi-stick in half, then doubled the fragments and snapped them again. He looked around for a place to put them and found none, so he stuck the fragments in his pocket. "They want the damn artifact, if you ask me. They're going to try to snatch it from us as soon as we've got it."

Maijstral considered the alternatives and found Gregor's case more convincing. But there were still questions here, unknown factors, unknown quantities. He was not yet at the stage in his career where he could make many mistakes.

"We'll advance our schedule," he said, and polarized the window again. He turned to his servant. "Roman, I'll require you to be very busy tonight. You're going to pay some calls."

Maijstral hung suspended in tenuous a-grav darkness above the house of the late Admiral Scholder. His own private media globes circled around him, recording everything—Jensen might change her mind about media rights. He had neutralized the outside alarm—a simple hemispheric cold-field—and was now contemplating his options for gaining entrance.

Skylights, doors, or windows? If he wanted to be dramatic he could cut right through a roof or wall.

His heartbeat was fast and smooth. His muscles moved easily, without wasted motion. Fortunately all the alarms and guards were automated. Even at the thought of a live guard, his mouth went dry.

"Sentients are unpredictable," he had always told Gregor. "Always go for the automated systems. You can trust them to act as they're supposed to." He was never certain whether Gregor believed him or not. Whatever, it was something he needn't worry about right now.

He decided to go for one of the skylights.

Maijstral dropped weightlessly toward the roof, a wispy opaque night-cloud. He was, even at this moment, perfectly aware of the traditional bulk of High Custom scowling at him from out of the night. For even here he fulfilled one of High Custom's many roles, that of Allowed Burglar.

High Custom allowed a person to steal for a living, provided he followed certain rules: he must do the job by himself; the person from whom he steals has to be able to afford the loss; there can be no serious violence—bopping the odd guard over the head is allowed, but crushing his skull is not. The object stolen had to be of artistic, sensational, or piquant interest (no large quantities of cash or uncut stones, say, although there was nothing in the rules against pocketing same if they happen to be in the same vault as the Costikyan Emerald); the stolen objects had to remain in the burglar's possession through the midnight of the day following the crime; and the burglar must never deny what it is he does for a living—if he is going to steal, he must let everyone know it, and carry his card when working.

Most importantly, an Allowed Burglar had to practice his craft with style, with grace, with *savoir faire.* Style counted a full ten points in the ratings, and no wonder. Allowed Burglars were supposed to be a part of High Custom, and if they didn't fit well with the rest of the wayward elements, the gentleman drunkards, the glib, subtle charlatans and bright-eyed tricksters, what was the point in allowing them to take other people's property in the first place?

Maijstral hovered above the skylight without touching it and deployed a pistol-shaped detector, scanning it over the skylight and its frame to make certain there were no electromagnetic emissions. Amalia and Pietro had done some research on security in the Scholder manse and found nothing troubling, but Maijstral believed in double-checking all research. It was his skin on the line, not Jensen's.

A trap. All Roman's hesitations and uncertainties flickered unbidden through Maijstral's mind. He gnawed his nether lip and replaced the detector on his adhesive darksuit. His hand was shaking slightly as he brought out a miniature a-grav unit and stuck it carefully to the skylight. Before he took out his pencil-sized cutting tool and began slicing, he took a moment to stabilize his breathing and calm his nerves. The room below *might,* of course, be packed with police.

Most likely, however, it was just a room. Maijstral tried to maintain that thought.

Maijstral finished his cut and the skylight floated gently into the air. The a-grav unit would move it toward a preset place on the grounds and set it down. Taking a breath, Maijstral reversed himself and floated headfirst into the room.

His head and shoulders thrust through the skylight, he turned his head carefully left and right. The atrium was two stories tall, with a roof access and a balcony around three sides. Slipcovered furniture crouched in darkness. A wide flagstone fireplace yawned against one wall. The view from the back of Maijstral's head was absorbed by detectors and projected onto the optical center of his brain; his vision was nearly a 360-degree globe, but he turned his head to get the advantage of parallax. IR and UV scanners looked for characteristic police emissions. Audio pickups listened acutely for the fall of dust.

He slid into the room on midnight holographic wings. Starlight shone on his fake diamond. Jensen's researches suggested that the household's main defenses were alarms triggered by the minute compression waves caused by a body moving through space. This was a very expensive system—in order for it to work, the signals put out by an entering thief had to be distinguished from those created by heating and cooling units, thermal changes in the structure of the house, and those of family pets and robots.

Maijstral's darksuit was equipped to deal with such alarms automatically, taking a half step back in time and pulsing out waves that precisely interfered with the waves he made as he moved. This was widely regarded as impossible, both that and a miracle of modern physics.

Maijstral's darksuit was of the best.

Maijstral's target, the artifact he was after, gleamed in silver solitude in a niche by the fireplace. Silently, Maijstral made a circuit of the room in search of other items of value. The place seemed to be filled mainly with souvenirs of the Rebellion, weapons, medals in cases, portraits of heroes. A cool shock wave moved through Maijstral. Admiral Scholder, he realized, was the same young Lieutenant Scholder whose Death Commandos had stormed the City of Seven Bright Rings and seized the Emperor in the last battle of the Rebellion.

Well, well, Maijstral thought. He was tampering with History, no less.

The souvenirs had little value except to military history buffs, so he floated to the artifact and gazed at it, his visual scanners magnifying its image. The target was the size of a melon and vaguely saddle-shaped, a pleasant-appearing geometry made of silver and engraved with fine, precise lines. Maijstral saw the Imperial seal—the scrolled *N* for Nnis CVI interwoven with the skuhl vines of the Pendjalli, ideographs for "good luck" and "happiness," all encircled by the figure of the Zoot Torque—Maijstral realized that he was looking at something looted from the Imperial precincts themselves.

Interesting.

Maijstral made an electromagnetic scan and found a constant low-wattage background emission characteristic of, among other things, certain alarm systems. He looked more carefully and discovered that the object was itself giving off the radiation, not anything it was connected to. Odd, he thought. He wondered if the thing would scream "Help, help" if he picked it up, like something in a fairy tale.

It wouldn't be the first time. Alarm systems had lately begun displaying a regrettable tendency toward cuteness.

He scanned the pedestal very carefully and found nothing resembling a trap or alarm, and then gave a mental command to his darksuit that opened a collapsed ruck on his back. Time to finish the job and get out.

His gloved hand reached for the object, closed around it, and perceived its considerable weight. He picked it up and in one swift movement dumped it into his rucksack, which automatically closed around it. He began floating past the level of the balconies, toward the skylight. The object was a cold weight between his shoulders.

A door opened to an inner room. Maijstral's heart crashed in his chest. His inertialess drift ceased immediately. His scanners deployed at the speed of thought.

A small domestic robot entered the room on muffled wheels. It wheeled to a rack of de-energized Rebellion-era weapons and deployed a feather duster.

Maijstral calmed his nerves. The robot didn't even see him. Cloaked in his darksuit, he began floating gently toward the skylight again.

The robot finished knocking dust off the beam guns, then began rolling roward the niche. It paused and began to shriek in a hysterical feminine voice.

"Help! Help! We've been robbed."

A masculine voice answered from within the house. "What's that, Denise?"

"Intruders! I think he's still here! Bring Felicity and your guns!"

A different female voice. "We're coming, Denise! Any intruders are going to get what's coming to them!"

This conversation would probably have gone on for some time—the people who wrote security programs for domestic robots really should have been doing soap opera scripts for the Diadem—but

Maijstral silenced the robot with a quick blast from his disruptor, something he would have done more quickly had he not somehow missed the pistol on his first grab. A streaming sable cloud, Maijstral arrowed through the skylight and fled across the sward outside, followed by a bouncing trail of media globes.

His darksuit informed him that his black boxes, placed outside the perimeter, were doing a good job of repelling the mansion's efforts to cry for the police. He passed through the cold-field, his suit neutralizing it automatically, and then fled to where Gregor waited in the flier, manning his own larger black box that was scanning all neighborhood communications wavelengths. Gregor looked up with a grin as Maijstral settled into the driver's seat.

"What is that you're always telling me about automatic guards being safer and more predictable?"

Maijstral punched the power button and the flier hissed into the night on its silent repellers. The artifact pressed against his back. Media globes trailed like firecrackers on a puppy dog's tail.

The recordings of this commission, Maijstral decided, were decidedly *not* going to be sold to the broadcasters.

Maijstral's character was formed, entirely by accident, when he was sixteen. His character was *supposed* to be formed by then; he was a senior classman at the Nnoivarl Academy, one of the best-regarded schools in the Empire, which promised to develop character or kill the boy trying—but, in common with his classmates, he had learned a lot about High Custom, languages, and the Khosali liberal arts, and damn-all about anything else. His acquisition couldn't really be called *character,* but rather a surface veneer, handy in many situations, however much lumber it may be in others. Still, many get by with nothing but polish their entire lives, and if their character isn't tested they'll never know the difference.

Drake Maijstral's particular bad luck was to get his character tested before he was ready for it. That's usually the way with character tests—one never realizes what they are until they're over, and by then it's too late to prepare.

As a senior classman preparing for his exams he had been allowed a certain amount of liberty—he could leave the academy without permission, and travel in civilian rig. He took full advantage of his newfound freedom, particularly in the matter of the Honorable Zoe Enderby, the bright-eyed daughter of a local nobleman whose thirteen-year-old brother was at Nnoivarl. She was four years older than Maijstral and her character seemed fully formed. He had met her at a fencing match, and her brother was not on the fencing team. Later in his life this was the sort of contradiction that might make him pause. Not at sixteen.

It was midmorning. The place smelled of paint thinner—the Honorable Zoe was apprenticed to a local artist. Subdued yellow light, filtered by the tropical growth overhead, danced in mottled patterns on the windows. Maijstral was in one of the Honorable Zoe's dressing gowns, frowning into a magazine and smoking a cigarette. (He was smoking that year.) Zoe was in another room, talking to her mother on the telephone.

"Darling. I've brought you something."

Maijstral hadn't heard him come in. It occurred to him that he should have locked the door behind him the night before, that he had, with his long hair and Zoe's dressing gown, had been mistaken for her.

"I'm sorry we fought. Look."

Poor boy, Maijstral thought. He stood, turned, and saw Marc Julian, the assistant captain of the fencing team, standing in his stiff, grey Nnoivarl uniform, a package in his long arms. Julian was also Count Hitti, but titles weren't used in the school.

"Beg pardon, Julian," Maijstral said. "I think it's Zoe you wanted to speak to, wasn't it?"

The polish was, as has been noted, already there. Maijstral left the astonished boy standing agape in the front hall and went in search of Zoe. He went into the bedroom, informed her of Julian's arrival, and began practicing a new card trick (he got whatever distinction he possessed at the academy by doing magic stunts). By the time Zoe said good-bye to her mother and went to the hall, Julian was gone.

Zoe wanted to tell Maijstral about Julian over breakfast, but Maijstral allowed as how everything was clear enough, and she didn't have to say anything if she didn't feel like it. He really didn't want to hear the story anyway. He stayed the morning, dressed, and went back to the academy to study for his philosophy exam.

A later Maijstral would have never looked back. But this young Maijstral was trying very hard to convince himself he was in love, and in any case he wanted to make the most of the few weeks before he had to return to Dornier and the Human Constellation.

Maijstral was never positive, later, if Julian had help. Maijstral had been leaving his exam cubicle, walking with his friend Asad. Both of them were confident of having done well, were laughing—and suddenly Maijstral's feet were tangled and he lurched sideways. Something shoved him between the shoulders and he tumbled into the proud back of the boy ahead of him.

"You struck me, Maijstral." Marc Julian's eyes gleamed with dull content beneath the tassle of his uniform cap.

"Sorry, Julian," Maijstral said. "Someone gave me a—"

"You'll not get away with that." Coolly. "Zah will act for me."

Maijstral straightened. "And Asad for me." Maijstral was equally cool, and he was quick to note that Zah was right there, the captain of the fencing team, and had been behind Maijstral the whole time.

Maijstral felt Asad's comradely hand on his shoulder. Far from being comforted, the touch startled him, serving to remind him that behind this polished ritual was a deadly reality toward which he was now committed. His reflexes made him turn away and light a cigarette as he walked, as if he had nothing else to do.

Duels were forbidden between students, but they happened anyway. By way of precaution, the practice was for upperclassmen to vet the encounters of the juniors, but if upperclassmen wanted to fight each other, there was no one to interfere. The worst that would happen was expulsion.

"Julian wouldn't accept any explanation," Asad said later, in Maijstral's room. "He insists on the fight."

Maijstral nodded and blew smoke. "Very well."

"It will be pistols, of course. He'd cut you to ribbons if you fight with steel. I'm going to talk to Joseph Bob about the loan of his matched set of chuggers."

"Fine. Would you like some brandy, first?"

Asad shook his head. "No. Best go now. The fight will be tomorrow morning."

Maijstral was startled. "So soon?"

Asad gave an uneasy laugh. "Best get it over with, eh? Don't want it to interfere with your studying."

The door closed behind Asad. Maijstral poured himself brandy, lit another cigarette, and went to his terminal. He accessed Julian's pistol scores and a coolness brushed his nerves. For some reason he thought of one of the Honorable Zoe's paintings, a formal piece with a dull-red sun and gleaming nickel-iron asteroids.

Asad was back in a few minutes. He gave an admiring laugh. "You're a cool one, ain't you? Studying for your exams like nothing's happened." Maijstral turned off the display.

"Hullo, Asad."

"Joseph Bob is testing the pistols now," Asad said. "We'll be using the explosive ammunition. It's fairer that way—Julian's the better shot. If you follow my advice, you'll fire as soon as I give the signal. If you hit him first, you can take off an arm or leg, and he may not get a shot off. He's better, so if he fires at all he's likely to hit you."

"I'll bear that in mind." Pouring brandy.

"Pity we ain't got access to psych dueling here. You could pick his mind apart. He's got no defenses at all there."

"I was just thinking that. Would you like a game of cards or something?"

"Damned cool, Maijstral." Admiring. "Maybe a short game, then. None of your trick decks, though."

They played Cheeseup for an hour. Asad won forty marks, then stood and said he had to leave. He had some studying to do for his history exam.

"You'll take my marker, yes? My father's damnably late with my allowance." Over a year, truth be told. Lucky his credit was still good.

"I'll take it. Thanks."

"I'm sure my father will redeem it, if . . ." Best leave that unsaid. Asad smiled uneasily.

"I'll pick you up at six-eighty, then?" He grasped Maijstral's shoulder. "See you then." Maijstral didn't want Asad to leave. He didn't want to be alone with his thoughts.

Maijstral heard the door close. For a long time he watched the brandy tremble in the decanter. There were only two fingers left, he noticed, and he decided he'd better not drink them.

He could protest all he liked, he decided. He could make any number of declarations about how stupid duels were and how ridiculous High Custom was and that wouldn't alter a thing. If he ran away, no one would speak to him.

Explosive bullets. Take off an arm or leg. Or blow his lungs out through his ribs.

He practiced card tricks. His fingers bungled every stunt.

That night he didn't sleep, just lay sweating in his bed and stared at the ceiling. He ran through his entire supply of cigarettes. Two hours past midnight, he knew for certain that there was no way he was going to face Julian's pistol.

He began wondering what he was going to do about it.

* * *

Maijstral crouched silently by Joseph Bob's door and looked at the access plate. He tried to breathe slowly and naturally. To his amazement he seemed cooler than when he'd been writing his exam.

He took one of his playing cards and inserted it between the door and jamb. He'd spent the last forty minutes trying to crack the dormitory's computer security, and he thought he might have succeeded in unlocking the bolt by remote control. But he still had to move the bolt, and that might make noise.

The bolt clicked. Maijstral's heart stopped. He waited for several moments, his ears straining. Nothing.

He swung the door in and heard Joseph Bob's breathing. Maijstral crept on bare feet into the room. He was wearing night goggles that he'd borrowed from the gym—runners training at night used them—and he could see the pistol case sitting on Joseph Bob's desk. Maijstral pushed the door almost shut, then stepped to the desk.

Joseph Bob rolled over and muttered something. Maijstral froze, his pulse crashing in his ears. Joseph Bob sighed and began to breathe heavily. Maijstral relaxed slightly. Clearly the Earthman's sleep pattern had been disturbed, and Maijstral would have to be careful. Each motion taking eons, he reached out and opened the pistol case.

The antique chuggers lay on red velvet and were seen clearly in his enhanced-light goggles. Maijstral licked his lips and reached for the first one. The front sight was a bead poised atop a delicate piece of silver scrollwork. Maijstral covered the sight with a handkerchief, clamped a small pair of pliers on the sight, gave it a slight wrench to one side. He took off the cloth and inspected his work. There was no obvious tampering. He repeated the procedure with the other gun and closed the case.

He was surprised, now that he had time to think of it, how cool he was. It wasn't until he left the room that he began to be afraid. What if Julian fired on instinct and didn't use the sight? Was he that good? Maijstral might only have ruined his own chance.

He didn't sleep at all that night. It took him both fingers of brandy to get him bathed and dressed for the occasion. He tried to tie his hair back, but his fingers wouldn't let him. Asad, when he arrived, did it for him.

Maijstral was dressed entirely in dark colors—a bit of white could show as an aiming point. When he arrived at the dueling ground—a spot of turf behind the Chapel Garden—he saw that Julian had dressed similarly.

Maijstral said nothing at all. He jammed his chin down on his high collar so that his jaw wouldn't tremble.

"Remember," Asad said, "keep the left arm back and out of the way. Stand with your side toward him to narrow the target. Cover your upper body with your bent right arm. And shoot first if you can." He squeezed Maijstral's arm. "Good man."

The thing went quickly. Zah called out "One, two, three," and dropped a handkerchief. Julian's pistol fired before Maijstral's mind could entirely absorb the meaning of the falling white lace. Behind him, Maijstral heard a crack as the explosive bullet detonated against the garden wall.

Maijstral looked in surprise at the startled figure over his sight. Julian's face was red; his jaw worked. Maijstral remembered the way Julian had looked when issuing the challenge, and murder entered Maijstral's heart.

He tried very hard to determine how his front sight was off so that he could kill Julian, but he wasn't very good with the weapon and his bullet blew a small crater in the stonework of the old chapel. Then Asad was pounding Maijstral on the back, and Julian was wiping blood off his chin where he'd bitten through his lower lip.

Maijstral reversed the pistol and handed it to Asad. "Give Joseph Bob my thanks," he said. He tried to smile. "Would you like to see a new card trick? I learned one last night."

"Damned cool," Asad said, and rushed him away.

Relatively few people have such a firm grasp of their own nature as Maijstral on his seventeenth birthday. He was a coward and knew it. High Custom did not allow for cowards—thieves, yes, and confidence men—but Maijstral had a good idea of how to cope with it. He had to know High Custom inside and out; he had to be able to manipulate it to his own advantage. He had to glide smoothly through the High Custom world, frictionless, wary of traps.

"Any fool can die in a duel." That was the Khosali proverb. Maijstral was determined not to be that kind of fool.

FOUR

General Gerald was prepared to repel boarders. Crouched in battle armor in the corner of his living room, he smiled at his own strategy, his own cunning. Remote sensors in various parts of the house fed data through his armor and into his optical centers. He scanned them with chill, happy obsession. Maijstral might win—the General was willing to concede that possibility—but he would know he'd been in a fight. Maijstral was going to be in for the battle of his life.

He knew that no thief of Maijstral's caliber could possibly resist the gauntlet the General had flung in his face. He had threatened Maijstral with death knowing that Maijstral couldn't possibly pass up that kind of challenge. Hah, Maijstral would think, this old fogey thinks he can tell *me* what to do. And then Maijstral would decide to teach the old man a lesson and sneak into his house to steal something.

Little did Maijstral know that Gerald was ready for him. He had anticipated his enemy's reaction and was going to spring an ambush.

It was General Gerald's misfortune to have spent forty years as a warrior without a war. He had never once been in combat. For decades he had practiced for the inevitable Imperial resurgency, honed his skills, studied enemy tactics, waged endless campaigns for funding and battled the Empire only in simulation and exercises . . . and overnight, it seemed, General Gerald found himself facing retirement without the cowardly Imperial fleet having once shown up for the long-awaited Armageddon. It was more than a patriot could stand.

So now the General waited in his old armor, surrounded by weapons laid out in a semicircle, smiling as he scanned the remotes and felt the suit blowing cool air on his brow. He pictured Maijstral's entry in his mind, the thief moving in through windows or doors or even through the chimney, unaware that the General had just spent a fortune on detection apparatus and confident that his darksuit would hide him from the avenging ex-marine crouched in the corner. General Gerald would open the conflict with a snare rifle, try to catch the thief in its coils. Maijstral's darksuit could probably make itself frictionless and thus slip the bonds, after which the thief might well strike out with a chugger or a stunner, which the General's armor would, of course, repel . . . and then the battle would broaden, higher and higher energies brought into play, disruptors and mappers and spitfires, and then maybe it would even come down to hand-to-hand at the end, General Gerald with his trusty cutlass against Maijstral and his stiletto.

The General pictured his victory, Maijstral prostrate, the General triumphant, the room flaming (what the hell—the house was insured). The first time Maijstral had ever been caught and apprehended, a first-class thief brought down by the General's foresight and cunning.

Maijstral, the General thought. The Allowed Burglar wasn't quite the Imperial Admiral of the Fleet, but in the latter's absence he would just have to do.

Peleng wasn't any fun at all.

Sergeant Tvi of His Imperial Majesty's Secret Dragoons looked at her communications display in speechless despair. The Scholder manse was calling for help. Unmistakably. The Imperial Relic would not be reclaimed tonight.

Tvi's diaphragm gave a spasm of irritation. She banked her Jefferson-Singh speedster and rose high into the traffic lanes, imitating an ordinary commuter. She glanced over her shoulder at her darksuit and equipment and considered tossing them.

No, she decided. She might yet get a chance to show what she could do.

Sergeant Tvi was, to be blunt, a scapegrace. Her parents had been stodgy Imperial servants, existing in perfect descent from long lines of other Imperial servants, each priding himself on his exemplary dullness. Tvi's childhood had been a tedious one, full of boredom and fantasy. If she hadn't had a good imagination she might well have died of ennui. Trapped in one Imperial backwater or another, her horizons limited by the acidic atmosphere of Vanngrian or the endless bleak deserts of Zynzlyp, Tvi had followed the burglar standings, the confidence-racket broadcasts, the exploits of the Human Diadem, biographies of Elvis . . . if only, she'd thought, if only she had the chance, she'd show Geoff Fu George or Baron Drago a thing or two.

Her career as a burglar, unfortunately, had not been graced with success. Two standards ago, she'd had the misfortune to get caught on her first job, and her only refuge from Imperial law had been the Secret Dragoons.

As she had contemplated the service from her prison cell on Letharb and listened to the reproaches of her parents, the new work had sounded interesting, even attractive—the chance to visit far-flung worlds, participate in intrigue intended to further the designs of the Empire, find Romance, Excitement, Danger. Instead, however, she'd been assigned as a junior security officer at various consulates in the Human Constellation, a job that consisted for the most part in dealing with various human cranks, Imperialists mainly, who insisted they knew of plots against the Empire and exactly what she should do about them. Countess Anastasia was yet another in a long line of maladjusted human contacts, and Tvi had begun to despair of the whole race. Were these the same people who had produced Mad Julius and the incomparable Soderberg Vampire?

After Baron Sinn had claimed her for a special mission, her chances had seemed a bit brighter. The situation had been promising. She would be engaged in a race against the clock with the Fate of the Empire at stake, and her competition was none other than Maijstral—he was in the top half of the standings, and furthermore had style and promise. And now it appeared that Tvi had arrived too late.

Damnation. Now things would most likely be turned over to that unspeakable thug Khotvinn, and she'd find herself playing second fiddle in some sordid job of skulltapping or breaking-and-bashing.

Drat. Peleng was no fun at all.

* * *

Behind Sergeant Tvi, Paavo Kuusinen's matte-black speedster rose into the sky. The Khosali commando's flier was a clear blip on his screens.

Kuusinen had followed Nichole's advice and got a new jacket cut in the local style, the better to blend in. He was, as he had told Nichole, a student of human nature; he was also, as he told Maijstral, visiting Peleng on business.

That afternoon he had been combining both occupations—he was trying to follow Maijstral. To his surprise he'd discovered that Maijstral was being followed by someone else, the Khosali female. Maijstral had dutifully given her the slip earlier that evening, losing Kuusinen at the same time, and Kuusinen had since been following the Khosali in hopes she'd locate Maijstral again. Instead, the small female had gone off on a pointless excursion into the outback only to turn around abruptly and head back to Peleng City.

Did these people have *any* idea what they were doing? Kuusinen was beginning to suspect not.

The whole situation was quite bewildering. All he wanted to do was keep an eye on Maijstral, and to his amazement half the Imperial Diplomatic Service seemed to be engaged in the same errand.

There was clearly a mystery here. And, Kuusinen decided, he was just the man to unravel it.

Countess Anastasia contemplated her stiff-shouldered image in the reflection of her apartment window. She was dressed in a soft black dress that left her shoulders bare, and billowed around her ankles in a cascading wave of darkness. She touched the skirt, picked at an imaginary bit of lint—how *dare* common detritus adhere to her clothing.

Neuralgia danced in her spine, and consequent irritation whispered in her mind. *Maijstral,* the whisper said, and her ears flicked downward. She really did disapprove of the man.

"That Gregor person was asking about Jensen and her cohort. Maijstral's given us the slip. Your burglar Tvi reports that alarms are going off all over the Scholder house. How much more do you need in order to act?"

Baron Sinn's sharp-faced silhouette appeared next to hers in the reflective surface. He, too, was smoking, the cigaret hanging from the end of his muzzle. It was a vice he normally avoided, but which he indulged in for Anastasia's sake, an old-fashioned courtesy she seemed to appreciate. "I have only two personnel," he said. "Maijstral has servants here, and connections. If he has the Imperial Relic he's probably gone to ground."

"Damn him, anyway. Why didn't he take the bribe?"

"Perhaps he does not share his father's convictions."

Anastasia sneered. Smoke streamed from her nostrils in elegant little white traceries, and she admired the effect in the glass. "He simply takes pleasure in being wayward," she said. "That's why he took up burglary and that unspeakable Nichole woman, just to annoy the family. I always told his father to be firm with the boy."

"Too late now, my lady."

Her lip curled. A bit of tobacco, she noticed, was adhering to one bright tooth. "It's never too late for firmness, my lord Baron." It was one of the rules by which she lived, but the maxim was spoiled by her having to pick the tobacco fleck off her smile.

Sinn remained silent.

"That Nichole," Anastasia told the glass. "Nichole and the Diadem. The height of Constellation culture. People whose sole profession is to be gossiped about. Can you imagine it?"

Sinn moved the cigaret to the corner of his mouth with his lolling tongue. "We were speaking, Countess, about Maijstral and this Jensen woman."

"Firmness," she said, remembering her earlier tack. Neuralgia stabbed her neck. "If Maijstral is in the public eye, and might be missed, Jensen is not. If Maijstral has no one to deliver the Imperial Relic to, then . . ."

"Quite so."

Baron Sinn looked at the human woman and restrained his diaphragm from an irritated spasm. She was an ally, he reminded himself, and even if she was a grotesque crank she was a *rich* grotesque crank who had personally financed Imperial Party activities here in the Constellation. . . .

He dropped his cigaret into an ashtray. "Very well," he said. "I'll have to call Khotvinn into it. We'll pick up Jensen as soon as she's alone. She seems to be entertaining someone named Navarre right now—he's in the service and we don't want complications."

Anastasia stalked to him and put her arm through his, her palm stroking the smooth dark hair on his upper arm.

"Lovely," she said. Her mouth open, her tongue lolled: Khosali good humor. The glitter in her eyes was appalling. "Firmness at last."

Politics, the Baron quoted to himself, oft consists in ignoring facts.

He considered himself a practical person and rarely resorted to maxims. It was a measure of how she strained his nerves that he was thinking in clichés at all.

Lieutenant Navarre thought of Amalia Jensen as his flier arched across the night sky. An interesting woman, he decided. Dedicated to preserving the Constellation in her own chosen fashion, and with the facts and intelligence to back up her opinions, she'd proved a most stimulating companion for the evening. Head of a political organization, a third degree black sash in pom boxing, an expert conversationalist . . . Odd, given all that, she'd turn out to be a garden person. Her house was filled with plants and flowers, all lovingly tended.

Still he was a bit uneasy about turning down an invitation from Nichole. How often did a man, particularly an officer from Pompey, get a chance to be photographed with a member of the Human Diadem? Unfortunate that he'd not been in a situation in which he could escape the commitment with grace.

The communicator on his flier gave a discreet chirp, and he frowned. Who would be calling at this hour? He pressed a button and answered.

"Navarre."

"Sir? This is Officer Pankat of the Peleng Police. Apparently your late uncle's house was broken into tonight."

Navarre was astonished. "Really?" he asked. And then, *"But why?"*

"Upon the success of your actions in the next few hours," Baron Sinn declared, "may depend the Fate of the Empire."

Well, thought Sergeant Tvi, how much better than this can it ever get? *The Fate of the Empire*—her heart beat faster as the words rang in her mind like bells. This was a definite improvement on spending one's life in the civil service, gazing out the window at the endless deserts and intractable inhabitants of Zynzlyp. Even Khotvinn's dark, looming presence—he was a head taller even than Sinn—seemed less than its usual sinister self.

"Khotvinn will be under your orders," Sinn went on. "If there is trouble, he is trained to get you out of it."

"I don't anticipate trouble, my lord." In what Tvi hoped was a tone of quiet confidence.

Sinn looked at her, his gaze commanding. "Anticipate every possible trouble, Tvi. Then you will be able to cope with each problem as it arises."

Why did officers always talk like this? Tvi wondered. Nothing a subordinate said was ever quite right. Even expressions of confidence triggered a lecture. Her reply was dutiful.

"Yes, my lord."

Countess Anastasia stepped from the back of the room and laid a hand on Baron Sinn's arm. The Baron stiffened.

"Let no one get in your way," the Countess said. Unlike the Baron, she spoke High Khosali. "This is no time for hesitation or foolish regard for life. There must be no witnesses. You must be prepared to take harsh action." She held up a clenched fist.

Tvi remained silent. She didn't have to take orders from the Countess, but the Baron's group was dependent on the Countess for support on this planet, so there was every reason to treat her with courtesy.

The Fate of the Empire! Tvi thought again. Now there was something worth listening to boring speeches for. She wondered if, in future generations, there would be video programs about Tvi of the Secret Dragoons.

The Countess went on about firmness and the necessity for action. Tvi knew that when her superiors shifted into High Khosali they were trying to inspire her, and she could successfully drowse through it with her eyes open. She therefore stood in a respectful attitude, her ears cocked forward as if she were listening, and in her mind pictured Video Tvi and watched with cool pleasure as the heroine stole documents, battled spies, saved the Emperor's coffin from sabotage. . . . Then she looked at Khotvinn.

The big Khosalikh was standing with his eyes gleaming, the fur on his shoulders standing. The monster was absorbing the Countess's words with evident pleasure and anticipation, just waiting for the moment when he could crack bones, snap necks, bruise flesh. In their few days' acquaintance, Khotvinn had always given Tvi the impression of something that might choose to live in a cave. Now that impression was enhanced. Tvi's mind snapped to attention. Someone like Khotvinn wasn't in her mental script. The Khotvinns of the videos always sought employment in the service of villains, and were usually massacred by the heroine just before intermission.

Khotvinn was going to take watching. Tvi knew that now, and knew it for certain.

In her darksuit, Tvi flowed like black glass over the rolling yellow hills on the outskirts of Peleng City. Her sense of smell, enhanced by her darksuit attachments, brought her the scent of night-blooming bellseed flowers.

Khotvinn stood by the flier like a monument. Tvi had decided not to use him on her reconnaissance—she considered him clumsy, and was certain that he had let himself be seen tailing Maijstral's assistant the day before. Tvi lighted and switched off the suit's holograph projectors. Khotvinn gave no sign he noticed her presence.

"Navarre's flier is gone. There are no security arrangements on the house that I can detect."

Khotvinn was matter-of-fact. "Then let's go." His accent was provincial and hard to understand. He flexed his shoulders in a stiff, businesslike way, and Tvi wondered where Sinn had found this one. Half the Secret Dragoons joined the military from jail, and Khotvinn might well be some murderer recruited from the prison planets for the unpenitent, one of those who hadn't had the decency to commit suicide when caught.

She wondered how he could possibly have understood the Countess's speech. Tvi doubted he could *speak* High Khosali if it were put to him.

"Not yet," Tvi said. "Wait for light."

Khotvinn flexed again, impatient, but said nothing at all through the long purple dawn. He didn't seem to be much good at conversation.

She sighed. In the vids featuring Allowed Burglars, assistants were polite, amoral technophiles who followed orders with clear-eyed efficiency, always ready to pull some new black box out of a hat. Disappointingly, Khotvinn was out of the wrong mold.

Tvi waited till she saw a few early fliers carrying people about their business. Then she put on a battered jacket over her darksuit and motioned for Khotvinn to join her in the flier. It rose into the morning sky.

"I've got a plan," Tvi said. "Just follow my lead."

Khotvinn gave no sign that he had heard. Tvi chose to assume he had.

She didn't bother explaining her plan to him. She had tried to picture this discussion to herself, and the picture hadn't scanned. "We're going to pretend to be broadcast repair personnel, Khotvinn." Then, tactfully, "Do you know what broadcast repair personnel *are?*" No, best let her do the talking. Khotvinn was supposed to be strictly backup, in case of emergencies.

She'd do it all herself. She was Tvi of the Secret Dragoons, on her first real mission, and the Fate of the Empire . . . oops.

She had overshot Amalia Jensen's house. She turned the flier in a long loop, making it seem as if the oversight had been a deliberate attempt at reconnaissance. Khotvinn said nothing, assuming he'd even noticed. She dropped the flier onto Jensen's flat roof.

The edge of the roof was decorated with long planters and bright blossoms. A robot was moving from flower to flower with a watering can.

The robot was an ordinary all-purpose domestic, combining the functions of maid, butler, doorman, telephone answering machine, and cup-bearer. It rolled toward the flier. The watering can, Tvi noticed, was painted with little yellow daisies.

"May I help you, lady and sir?" the robot asked.

What Tvi planned to say was this: "We're from Peleng Independent Broadcasting. We've had reports of interference in your neighborhood, and we'd like to check out your sets." What she said instead was: "Khotvinn! What in hell are you *doing?"*

For the giant had leaped from the flier, not even bothering to open the door, and felled the robot with a single kick. It went sprawling, its arms flung out, the water can clattering across the roof. Khotvinn leaped into the air, then landed on the robot with both feet. More clattering.

Tvi was jumping too, for the black boxes in the back seat. She triggered them—just in time, she suspected—and saw the little gauges flicker as they began intercepting communications. The robot was alerting the household even as Khotvinn picked it up and began smashing it against one of the planters.

"Sir!" the robot chirped. "Can't we just talk about it like reasonable beings?" Tvi knew exactly how the robot felt. Khotvinn tore one of its arms off.

Panic thudded beneath Tvi's ribs. The Fate of the Empire, she recited to herself. Et cetera. *Do* something.

She jumped out of the flier and dashed to the roof entrance, then pressed the down button. "ACCESS DENIED," the door reported in four commonly-used scripts.

"Thagger," Tvi swore. She was going to have to get in the house some other way.

Khotvinn tore off the robot's remaining arm and began beating the machine with it.

Tvi snapped on her darksuit and pulled its hood over her head, giving her mental control of its devices. She triggered the hologram and, a miniature black cloud, floated away from the mayhem on the roof and dived over the edge of the building. She reached for a microcutter on her belt and began slicing at the first window she came to. As she popped the window out and began to drift through it, she realized she was entering Amalia Jensen's bedroom.

Darksuits are useless camouflage during the day. The black holographic cloud obscures the figure, of course, but it may be argued that a black cloud floating through someone's window may call more attention to itself than a person doing the same thing. And of course if you happen to be halfway through a window, your darksuit could be projecting the chorus from *Aïda* and you'd still be an easy target.

The first glimpse Tvi caught of Amalia Jensen was as the human female popped out from behind her waterbed and lobbed overarm a heavy vase that caught Tvi squarely between the ears. Stars exploded in Tvi's vision. She decided to get out of the window as fast as possible, and accelerated straight across the room. Unfortunately her depth perception was still numb and she smashed headfirst into a closet door.

Jensen, seen by Tvi through her rear projectors, continued to hurl weighty household objects into the darksuit screen. A heavy ashtray caught Tvi between her shoulders. A vase detonated over her head.

Enough was enough. This was Khotvinn's department.

Tvi flew down the hallway to the living room and unlocked the roof entrance. The amplified scent of flowers warred with pain in her skull—the place was full of plants. Khotvinn came slowly down the a-grav elevator, a robot arm in one hand.

"What took you so long?" he snarled.

Tvi willed her hologram projectors off and pointed numbly toward Jensen's bedroom. "That way," she said. Khotvinn flung the robot arm into a corner—there was a crash that echoed endlessly in Tvi's skull as the arm destroyed a porcelain planter—and then the giant began to lope at a ground-shattering trot toward the bedroom.

Unfortunately Jensen had changed position. She came flying out of a connecting bathroom, a green-and-white-striped towel blossoming from one hand. The towel draped nearly over Khotvinn's head just as Jensen's foot planted itself in his midsection. The air went out of Khotvinn in a rush.

There followed a good deal of confused thumping and thrashing. Jensen was aided by another small household robot that clung to Khotvinn's knees and tried in a fairly incompetent way to harm him. Tvi wasn't certain what she was watching, not being an aficionado of the martial arts—a proper burglar disdained violence—but it seemed as if honors were about even. Both fighters were breathless and bloody before Jensen broke off the combat and retreated back into the bathroom. Khotvinn, ignoring the clawing robot and a bottle of shampoo that bounced off his chest, marched in pursuit.

Tvi leaned against an overstuffed chair, holding her head. "Hey," she said as the thrashing started again, "use your stunner, why don't you?"

The household robot came flying out of the bedroom door and smashed to bits on the opposite wall. Amalia Jensen, crouched low, followed the robot out of the door—apparently she'd just ducked from the bathroom into the bedroom—and began backing toward Tvi. Tvi reached for her stunner.

Then Khotvinn appeared, brandishing a towel rack. Jensen reached for a flowerpot and let fly. Tvi lowered her weapon. The wide-beam stunner would get them both if she fired it.

The combat demolished most of the living room. Tvi floated up near the roof in her a-grav harness, trying to get in a clear shot, but Khotvinn kept blocking the way.

"Earth slime!" Khotvinn bellowed.

"Inhuman scum!" Amalia Jensen retorted through bloody lips.

Fate of the Empire, Tvi thought resignedly, and wondered how well her black boxes were doing without supervision.

Do something.

She floated over Khotvinn, grabbed his scruff with one hand, and yanked back, turning her a-grav up to max. Khotvinn flew backward, his arms windmilling, and landed on a glass table that shattered with a sound that rattled in Tvi's head like snapping thunder. Jensen cackled triumphantly and prepared her coup de grace. Tvi, now having a clear shot, fired and dropped Jensen in her tracks.

"No!" Khotvinn roared. He was having trouble disentangling himself from the table frame. "She was mine!"

"Idiot," Tvi said. Her skull was splitting. "You were just supposed to stun her. Pick her up and let's go."

"No fair," Khotvinn muttered sulkily.

Fate of the Empire, Tvi thought. Next time the Empire offered her its fate, it could jolly well go hang.

FIVE

Roman flew alone in Peleng's ruby morning sky. He found it encouraging that he hadn't been followed today—perhaps the two Khosali tags were thrill seekers after all, and had got bored.

He had spent the previous evening being a decoy, trying to give the impression that he and Maijstral were having an ordinary evening. He had taken a bouquet of flowers to Nichole at her residence. It had been delightful seeing her again, as she was one of Maijstral's friends of whom he could actually approve. At Nichole's, Roman had left word with the household robots to expect Maijstral later that night, laying a false trail just in case the small female Khosalikh who had been following Roman all evening should ask. . . . Roman had then ordered a meal for three from Chef Tso's Exquisite Mesa Catering, and picked up the laundry. At some point during these more mundane errands, Roman's tail had vanished, just dropped from sight.

This morning Roman had performed various evasions and escapes just in case, but he'd become certain before very long there was no one after him. Buoyed by the knowledge, he finished his evasions anyway, for form's sake. He hoped the rest of the day would be as free from aggravation.

Seen through the viewscreen of his flier, Peleng City's low pastel buildings, all surrounded by bright ornamental trees and blossoms, resolved from an early morning mist. Roman's heart gladdened. He put the flier on a landing spiral that would place it on the flat roof of Amalia Jensen's small white house. His ears turned down as he thought of Humanity Prime, and then his diaphragm spasmed once in resignation. If Maijstral was going to engage in an irregular occupation, he would inevitably deal with irregular people—Roman could only wish there were more like Nichole and fewer like Jensen and her friends.

The flier settled on the roof like a leaf on a spotless green lawn. The edge of the roof was decorated with planters and bright blossoms. Roman felt buoyed; he liked having living things around him. Enjoying the plants in spite of himself, Roman got out of the flier and headed toward the roof entrance. The first thing he saw was a dead robot.

Suspicion hummed in his nerves. He checked that his gun was loose in its holster and wished he had brought some of his darksuit attachments that would allow him to see behind his back.

Carefully Roman examined the robot. The machine had been torn apart—arms and legs ripped off, command unit excavated and thrown across the roof. The destruction was wanton, far more than would have been necessary to disable the machine. And whoever had done it had been very strong.

Indignation began to gather. There was an offense here, and not to Amalia Jensen, but rather to the honor of Maijstral's employer.

Roman drew his gun and clicked its setting to "Lethal." The green light on the roof elevator showed it wasn't locked. He stepped to the elevator and pressed the down button.

The living room was a mess. Furniture was overturned, papers scattered about, planters were smashed. Bright blossoms lay dying on the carpet. Roman's nostrils flickered in disapproval.

In the hallway another robot lay in pieces. One of Jensen's shoes lay in a corner, its mate nowhere to be seen. There was some blood on a heavy vase, evidence it might have been used as a club. Roman looked closely. There was short, dark hair on the vase that seemed consistent with Khosali fur.

Roman stood for a moment in the midst of the devastation and pondered events. He had come to tell Miss Jensen that her commission had been successful, if a bit messy, and to make arrangements for the sale and the delivery of the artifact. Getting involved in vandalism and violence was not a part of his job.

But something had happened here, something that possibly was related to Maijstral's commission. He decided he should try to find evidence of this, one way or another.

He had barely commenced his search when he heard the sound of a flier dropping to the roof. His gun at the ready, Roman slipped into the kitchen, where he could get a view of the elevator.

The elevator went to work silently, its a-grav field bringing the passenger down. Roman, his ears pricked, heard Pietro Quijano's voice.

"Miss Jensen? What happened to Howard? Oh."

Howard, Roman presumed, was the name of the robot on the roof. He clicked his pistol to "Stun," then put it back in its holster.

"Miss Jensen?"

Quijano almost jumped out of his skin when Roman glided silently out of the kitchen. Hoping to ease his mind, Roman smiled at him, tongue lolling from his long muzzle. Quijano glanced anxiously to the elevator and door, looking for a place to run.

Quijano spoke Human Standard through clenched teeth. "Who are you? What happened here?"

"I was hoping," Roman said, moving closer, "you would be able to tell me the answer to that last question."

Quijano looked relieved. "Are you police? Is Amalia—Miss Jensen—is she all right?"

"I don't know." Roman glided closer to Quijano, his feet moving noiselessly across the rubble. "It looks as if she has been abducted. Would you have any idea why?"

Several complex expressions passed through Pietro Quijano's face. From these, Roman gathered, Quijano had, first, a very good idea what might have happened, and secondly, that he had no intention of conveying this information to anyone he didn't know and trust, even someone he assumed to be a policeman. Perhaps especially a policeman.

"No," Quijano said. His eyes were darting toward the exits again. "I—I don't think—I don't know at all."

"Are you sure?" Roman said.

Quijano looked at Roman sidelong. He took a breath and braced himself, apparently taking heart from the fact that Roman hadn't actually attacked him. He stood with his arms akimbo and looked belligerent. "Say. I don't believe I know you. And if you're from the police, shouldn't you show me your identification?"

Roman gave a passable imitation of a human sigh as he tried to put the young man at ease. "You're right, sir. I've been neglecting the formalities."

He might as well admit he had run out of ideas.

Roman reached inside his jacket, brought out his gun, and shot Quijano at close range, terribly overstimulating his nerves. Roman caught the unlucky man before he fell, then slung him over his shoulder and carried him to the elevator. Once on the roof, Roman told Quijano's flier to head home on autopilot, then dropped Quijano into the back seat of his own machine.

Quijano looked up at him glassily. He seemed terribly disappointed at the way the cops were behaving.

Roman had decided to let Maijstral handle this. That's what criminal masterminds were for—to deal with the big picture.

"They stole *what?*" Lieutenant Navarre gazed in bemused surprise at the insurer and the man from the auctioneers'.

The auctioneer flipped through his catalog. "Here it is, sir. 'Engraved silver cryonics container, with power source, Imperial seal, functional, c9, wt 16sm, 18x17ng.' "

Navarre still felt bemused. He took another few steps into the large room, ignoring the trophies and battleflags, his gaze moving from one object of interest to the other—open skylight, stunned robot, empty niche. Skylight, robot, niche. Again, looking for some reason behind the thing. Skylight, robot, niche. Fixing everything in his mind.

"What was it worth?" he asked.

"We were, hm, going to start the bidding at twelve novae and hope to get, mm, sixteen or eighteen."

"It wasn't worth much, then."

The auctioneer's voice was defensive. "Sir. It was probably the most valuable, mm, single object in the house. The militaria is worth more as a collection, which is why we're selling it in large lots, but none of the single items are remarkable. The fact of the container's being loot from the Imperial quarters might have increased its value to some collectors."

"It's not exactly beyond the reach of collectors, either," Navarre said. "Sixteen or eighteen novae—the disruptor that was used to knock out the robot probably cost at least five, and the black boxes we found were worth more, maybe even eight or nine."

"They had an, hm, a homemade look, sir. They may have cost nothing if they were made from scratch."

The Khosalikh from the insurance company glanced over the

room, taking in the racked weapons, the decorations, the flags. "It may have been stolen by a traditional Imperialist," she pointed out. "The artifact came from the sacred precincts—selling it at auction would pollute it."

"Really?" Navarre was vaguely annoyed at himself for not perceiving this on his own—he liked having things in order. He fixed the fact firmly in his mind. Then he glanced up at the overhanging banners. "Then why didn't they steal the Imperial battleflags? They're loot from the sacred precincts as well."

"Perhaps, sir," said the Khosalikh, "the thief did not have time. The alarm seems to have been given fairly early."

"Perhaps."

"Drake Maijstral is on planet, sir." The auctioneer's tone seemed to hang the fact in the air, like one of the flags, without bothering to interpret it.

Navarre frowned. "This hardly seems in his class."

"True, sir. True. It had occurred to me that you might know him. I conceived it might be personal."

"It shouldn't be. I just met him the other night."

"Yes, but there is also . . . well, his family history, and yours."

Navarre frowned. "I shouldn't think so. He didn't seem to be the sort to hold a grudge that way."

The insurer sighed. "I'm sure you, hm, know best, sir."

Navarre walked to the skylight and squinted out into the bright yellow sky. Then he turned to look at the niche again, then the robot. Perhaps a different perspective would serve to clarify matters. Skylight, niche, robot. No help.

He realized he was standing between two portraits of his uncle: the young hostage-taker over the mantel facing the older Admiral Uncle Jack in his decorations and frown. Both looked fierce and determined, each in his own way. Navarre had always hoped his look of concentrated energy was as ferocious as Admiral Uncle Jack's.

A thought struck him. He turned his energetic scowl on the auctioneer. "By the way," he said, "was there anything *in* this container?"

The auctioneer hesitated. "We, uh, didn't, don't know. We didn't know how to open it." Navarre looked at him. "That's what the, hm, 'c9' in the description meant, sir. It's our code. It means there was a complicated lock on it, and it didn't come with a key, so we didn't open it for fear of damaging it."

Navarre intensified his scowl. "Suppose someone knew what was in it? That it was valuable, I mean."

"A cryonics container? What *could* there be in it?"

"Genetic material? Drugs? A piece of supercooled processing hardware?"

"Old wine."

"An antique, or perhaps a memento," the Khosalikh offered. "Something perishable that the Imperial family wished to preserve for sentimental reasons."

Navarre looked at her. "Such as?"

"The heart or other organ of one of the deceased household pets."

"Oh."

"The clever little foreclaws of a clacklo, for example," the Khosalikh went on. "I often wished I could preserve the claws of my little Peejee when she died, but I was young and my parents were afraid of the expense."

"You have my sympathies, ma'am," Navarre said.

The insurance investigator's eyes glowed. "You should have seen the little ways Peejee would invent to steal food. She would lay brilliant little ambushes around the refrigerator. She was so smart you could swear she was almost Khosali." Her nostrils dilated with emotion. "How I wish," she sighed, "I could have preserved at least some of her parts."

"I'm sure that would have been a consolation," Navarre said. He looked back at the empty niche. "But somehow I have a hard time believing that there are very many Imperialist animal lovers with the wherewithal to steal my uncle's silver jug."

"Quite, sir." The auctioneer frowned around him. "Perhaps we should increase security here, in case the thief or thieves return. It might be that the perpetrators were after something else, and only picked up the container on the way."

"Perhaps we should." Navarre did not like ambiguities, and the thought that there was still something here that someone might want made him uneasy. He glanced at the portrait of his uncle, the young man in tattered uniform holding a businesslike spitfire rifle on a startled-looking Emperor, the latter hiding in the harem and dressed as one of his wives. (That was the human version of the story. The Khosali version had the Emperor stunned and overcome while leading the defense in the uniform of an Honorary Life Guard colonel.)

"Blast it all," Navarre said. "What could have been *in* the thing?"

* * *

Roman's nerves sang of anger as he flittered through the sky. Wrongs done, insults given, actions demanded.

Maijstral, he knew, was careless in matters of honor. But he could scarcely ignore *this.* Roman's blood boiled on behalf of the Maijstral family.

This was an insult not to be borne.

As it drifted through the window of the small country cottage, the cool country air stirred Maijstral's unbound hair. The place was safe: Roman had rented it under a false name, and Maijstral felt free to relax and spend his morning in bed watching an old Western. He nibbled a bit of fleth and allowed the household robot to refill his champagne glass. "Thank you," he said, and began his third champagne of the morning.

Lying on the bed were a number of computer faxes that Gregor had given him. He really should have been working on them, planning his next job.

The next series of thefts would be easy. Two nights ago, Maijstral's presence had been splattered across every media broadcast in Peleng. Nervous owners of famous art treasures and gems, knowing his name, would naturally want to increase security while he remained on the planet.

That was why Gregor had been on a breaking-and-entering mission that same night—he had been planting microtracers on the equipment of Peleng's major security consultants. When the householders increased their security, the tracers would now lead Maijstral straight to their valuables. They would also make the job easier, since Maijstral would know in advance what manner of gadgets had been installed. Gregor had spent much of the previous day following his microtracers around Peleng and making note of their locations.

For a thief, knowing where to go was at least as important as knowing how to get there.

But instead of plotting his next job, Maijstral sipped champagne and watched his Western. Perhaps he was lazy. But he *had* been working late the night before.

The vid was one of his favorites, *Riders of the Plains.* He'd had a sentimental liking for it ever since he'd seen it for the first time at the age of seven.

Maijstral let the robot pour more champagne while he watched Elvis ride across the western prairie with his old friend, Jesse James. While playing idly on his electric guitar, Elvis tried to talk Jesse into going straight and giving up his life of crime. Elvis knew that Bat

Masterson had sworn to bring Jesse in dead or alive, but had promised Bat not to tell Jesse. It was a terrible moral dilemma.

What Elvis didn't know was that Jesse had chosen the outlaw trail because of his passionate affaire with Priscilla, Elvis's wife. Jesse knew that if he stayed around the ranch, Elvis would find out, and the knowledge would destroy him. The climax of the drama featured a violent multiple tragedy that ended with Jesse and Priscilla dying in one another's arms, and the truth finally revealed to a grieving King of Rock and Roll. At the very end, Elvis walked down a lonely trail, strumming despairing chords on his guitar, his own ultimate tragedy foreshadowed. It was a beautiful mythic moment.

Maijstral liked Westerns better than other forms of genre entertainment. He wondered why Shakespeare hadn't written any.

The robot chimed gently. "Visiting flier in our airspace, sir," it reported.

Maijstral frowned. No one knew his location but Gregor and Roman. Gregor was here, and Roman was supposed to be staying at Maijstral's other house, giving police, press, or other undesirables the impression that Maijstral was in residence. He told the robot to tell the house to give him an exterior view and a picture of whoever was in the flier.

The intruder was Roman. Maijstral's frown deepened. He knew that Roman wouldn't put in an appearance unless there was something seriously wrong.

He turned back to the vid. Elvis was talking about how much Priscilla missed Jesse, telling the outlaw that there would always be a place for him around the ranch. Jesse was turning away with tears in his eyes. It was one of Maijstral's favorite scenes, but there was no choice but to postpone the film's climax. He told the vid to turn itself off, then sprang out of bed and put on a silk robe. He brushed his hair back out of his eyes and went to meet Roman.

The Khosalikh was carrying Pietro Quijano over one broad shoulder. Maijstral told the house to ask Gregor to join them. This was going to be serious.

Roman's nostrils flickered as he saw Maijstral in his robe. He didn't approve of people who spent their mornings lounging in bed. Maijstral had probably been watching low entertainments, to boot. Hardly suitable in the light of the present affront to his honor.

Roman really knew Maijstral very well.

Maijstral helped Roman put Pietro gently on a plush couch—the Khosali difficulty in unbending is not due to temperament, but anatomy—and then stood while Roman explained what had just happened. Gregor entered in the middle of the story, and Roman had to begin again.

Pietro looked up at Maijstral. Rotating holograms—the day art —reflected in his eyes. He seemed desperate to say something. Maijstral leaned close. "Flig," Quijano said through thick lips. "Gleep."

Maijstral nodded as if he understood. "You pose a definite problem, Mr. Quijano."

"Neegle. Thrib."

"I'll have the robot bring you some champagne. It might make you feel better."

"Grl. Thag you."

Maijstral sighed as he moved off on his errand. "You're welcome, Mr. Quijano," he said.

No fun at all. Sergeant Tvi lay on her bed in Countess Anastasia's house, held a semilife patch to the bruise on her head, and closed her eyes. The indomitable chimes in her skull refused to stop clanging.

The Fate of the Empire. Romance, Excitement, Danger. She repeated the phrases to herself as she pressed another patch to her head. The point was, the danger wasn't supposed to come from your own side.

She'd reported Khotvinn's behavior to the Baron. Not that this had done any good—the Baron had just read her a lecture about how she had to explain things to subordinates in order for them to know their jobs properly, and how this was all a part of being prepared and anticipating difficulty.

Tvi concluded that the Baron had never actually worked with Khotvinn, or tried to explain anything to him. Officers, in her estimation, always had the perfect command of things they had never experienced.

The communicator in her room beeped. Echoes flooded her skull like a lunatic carillon. She touched the ideograph for "answer" and snarled.

The Baron's voice cut the air. "Time to relieve Khotvinn and bring Miss Jensen her second breakfast."

"Yes, my lord." Tvi covered her head with a pillow and whimpered to herself silently, a martyr of the Empire. Then obeyed.

She picked up Jensen's tray from the kitchen—the robot staff couldn't be involved in this, since their memories could be impounded as evidence if things went wrong—and then trudged up the stone stair to the attic room where Jensen was being held. The tray smelled of roast arnette. Tvi's mouth began to water.

A very popular children's puppet, a little over seven feet tall, waited at the top of the stair. It was human, with red hair and freckles and a perpetual grin. Its name was Ronnie Romper.

"Relieving you," Tvi said.

"About time," snarled Ronnie Romper. It snapped off the holographic device and became Khotvinn. Purple bruises showed through his dark fur, which was also mottled with semilife patches. He took off the holo projector and another gadget from his belt and handed them to Tvi.

"Your disguise," he said. "The restraint control."

"Thank you," Tvi snarled back. "So much." She clipped the projector to her belt, snapped it on, and put the manacle control on her tray. Khotvinn stomped down the stairs.

The door was secured by a heavy bolt that had been installed the previous night. Its alloy screws had chipped the dark wood of the door. Tvi shot the bolt back and entered.

The guest bedroom had been hastily filled with miscellaneous furniture brought from storage in the attic: a canopied bed with plump pillows and blue ruffles, a pair of chairs covered in peach brocade, a deep carpet of violet dewkin fur, a crystal lamp in the shape of a Khosali ballet dancer with a stained-glass shade on his head. The clash of colors and cultures made Tvi's headache worse.

Amalia Jensen produced another contrast with the frilly furniture. Her face was covered by semilife patches that were feeding her painkillers and sapping her bruises. She was lying on the ruffled bed in the black pajamas in which she'd been taken, her ankles locked together by restraints, and she glared at Tvi while sneering through a split lip. "Another Ronnie Romper," she said. She was speaking Khosali. "Why do you bother trying to look human? I can identify you both."

"Go ahead," Tvi said, answering in the same language. "What's my name, then?"

"Look. I suppose I can understand the need for disguises. But why did you have to pick something that *smiles* all the time?"

Tvi put the tray on an antique inlaid Troxan table and moved the table to the brocade-covered chair. She strolled to the corner of the room and sat on the other chair. "I'm going to close your wrists and release your ankles," she said, and picked up the control to Jensen's restraints. "Then you can move to the chair, sit in it, then I'll close your ankles and release your hands. Right?"

Jensen's eyes flickered over the room, taking in the bed, the chairs, the table. Measuring things. "Very well," she said.

Tvi knew someone preparing a desperate move when she saw one, and her diaphragm spasmed in resignation. She took her stunner out of its holster. "Right," she said. "Here we go."

She pressed the restraint controls. The snug bracelets on Jensen's wrists moved toward one another, as of their own volition, until they touched. Jensen swung her legs off the bed and walked stiffly toward the table. Her bruises were bothering her. She kept her eyes on Tvi's stunner. Standing by the table, she seemed to hesitate, then looked at the stunner again and sat down where she'd been told.

Tvi touched another button. Jensen's ankles came inevitably together. Her hands were freed. Jensen removed the food tray's lid and began to eat.

Tvi's upper stomach rumbled. No one had said anything about feeding *her.*

Jensen took a mouthful of roast arnette, winced, and concentrated instead on the softer vegetables. Tvi settled back in her chair.

"You must have got the wrong person, you know," Jensen said. "I'm not worth much ransom."

"You're not being held for ransom," Tvi said.

Jensen didn't seem terribly surprised. The human took another shaky forkful.

"Why then?" she asked.

"I daresay you would know best, ma'am," Tvi said. On the vid, Allowed Burglars were always polite. Style counted a full ten points, after all.

"Why am I still alive?" Jensen asked.

This wasn't bad, really, Tvi thought. A civilized conversation between a kidnapper and her victim. An occasion for her to play the suave mastermind. "No need for anything so extreme as murder, ma'am. You'll just be our guest for a few days."

"Until what?"

Tvi decided to feign a knowing silence. Much as she might enjoy playing the part of a cultured kidnapper, she hadn't actually been told the reasons for Jensen's abduction. She knew Maijstral was involved in it somehow, and that the Fate of the Empire was at stake, but other than that she'd been kept in the dark.

Amalia Jensen just shrugged. She swallowed her coffee. "Well," she said, "they probably haven't told you."

Tvi ground her teeth. This human was sharp. She decided to take another tack, another brand of sophistication. Elegant mercenaries were at least as much fun as elegant masterminds.

"That hardly matters," Tvi said. "I was paid well."

Jensen looked at her and put her forkful of pureed manna back down on her plate. "I could arrange that you be paid more."

"Miss Jensen. I seem to recall, not a moment ago, you said you weren't worth much ransom." Tvi's upper stomach rumbled. The roast arnette, she observed, was under a white sauce.

Jensen smiled thinly, then winced and dabbed her split lip with a napkin. "Things can be arranged. What would you say to forty novae?"

Tvi's ears pricked forward. That wasn't bad money, not really, assuming that Jensen could actually deliver and Tvi collect. But against the Fate of the Empire, she concluded, it was nothing. She waved a languid hand. "You do me a disservice, Miss Jensen, if you believe that a mercenary of my standing will change sides after already embarking on an adventure. I take pride in seeing my contracts through, you see."

"I apologize," Jensen said, smiling again. "I did not mean to impugn your professionalism."

"Apology accepted. After meeting Kho—my colleague, I can understand that you might mistake me. He is none of mine, I assure you. A creature of my employers."

"I understand." Tvi's lower stomach had joined her upper in a distressed chorus. She snarled beneath her human holographic smile.

Amalia Jensen seemed to perceive Tvi's rumblings. She held up the plate of arnette. "Would you like the roast?" she asked. "I'm afraid my mouth's a little . . . tender, this morning."

"I *am* peckish. If you wouldn't mind."

"Not at all." Jensen tottered to her feet, holding out the roast. Tvi rose to a half crouch, one arm extended. Jensen flung her plate at Ronnie Romper's grinning head and sprang, her hands clawed, her ankles still tethered together.

Tvi had been half expecting this—the Baron's lecture about preparedness hadn't fallen entirely on deaf ears, and Miss Jensen had turned far too pleasant all of a sudden. Tvi fired her stunner in the middle of Jensen's arc, and the captive's leap ended in a soft muddle on the plush dewkin carpet. Tvi's diaphragm pulsed with regret. White sauce ran down her neck.

Blast, she thought. Just when she was beginning to enjoy herself.

Pietro Quijano had spilled most of his first glass of champagne on his shirt, but managed to get down the second. His color and bearing had improved considerably. He was now able to sit up without danger of toppling over.

Gregor watched him from a straight-backed chair in the corner, his fingers tapping little rhythms on his knees. Roman stood silently in a corner, looming. Maijstral could tell he was seriously upset.

Maijstral walked into his room, and there tied his hair in a knot and pinned it on the back of his head. He changed into soft suede pants, pumps, a loose grey silk shirt, and an earring. If he was to have guests, he might as well look presentable.

He entered the parlor room and offered Pietro a piece of fleth from his plate. Pietro accepted. Maijstral chose a soft chair opposite Pietro's sofa and settled into it. Above him, a holographic representation of the Bartlett Head rotated slowly in its niche. Maijstral drew taut the drawstrings on his sleeves.

"Well, Mr. Quijano," he said carefully, "perhaps you can enlighten us as to recent events."

Pietro Quijano looked nervously toward Roman, then glanced at Gregor. "No idea," he mumbled, and held out his glass for more champagne. The robot purred from the corner and began to pour.

Maijstral began itemizing on his fingers. "Amalia Jensen appears to have been kidnapped," he said. "This kidnapping occurred less than two days after she commissioned me and my associates to acquire an artifact. My researches have noted the fact that Miss Jensen was quite visibly involved in politics here on Peleng, a ranking member of an organization that has branches throughout the Constellation. You are the treasurer for that organization."

Pietro was beginning to look uncomfortable. He bit a piece of fleth and chewed nervously. Maijstral rose from his chair, turned, and reached into the Bartlett Head. He drew out the silver artifact and, with the device in his hands, settled into his chair. Pietro's look turned to one of burning, undisguised eagerness.

"You recognize it, I see," Maijstral said. "Miss Jensen was kidnapped within hours of my acquiring this object. Since the object itself is not valuable, I assume it has some political or symbolic significance of which I am unaware."

He frowned down at the heavy silver container. He had examined it carefully after appropriating it, and knew that besides the Imperial seal, the container featured an engraving of Qwelm I, the first Pendjalli Emperor, receiving the submission of the first ambassador-delegate from Zynzlyp. It hadn't been much of a conquest—the sea-slug shaped Drawmii were so incomprehensible and unpredictable that it had never quite been determined whether they actually understood they had been "conquered," and therefore become members of a "Khosali Protectorate." But it had been the first Pendjalli conquest and the mythographers had, perforce, to make the most of it.

The other side of the saddle-shaped container showed the retiring Nnis CVI among his College, a group of renowned scholars he had gathered in the City of Seven Bright Rings to assist him in the abstract inquiries for which he was rather more famed than for his skill at governing the Empire. Maijstral looked closely. He recognized the face of Professor Gantemur, a human philologist who had passed plans of the Imperial Residence to agents of the Rebellion and subsequently been awarded the holdings of a number of prominent human Imperialists, Maijstral's grandfather among them.

Maijstral looked at Pietro. The young man's eagerness was almost palpable.

"Mr. Quijano, I must know what has occurred," he said. "My client has been abducted. It is possible that I—that we—are in danger from the same source. Within a matter of hours, this container will be legally mine, and I may dispose of it. Naturally, I would prefer to give it to Miss Jensen—that is my contract. But—" He held up a hand, and Pietro's face darkened. "If this object will bring me unwanted attention, I may have to get rid of it quickly."

"But," Pietro said, "you can't." He looked for support to Gregor. "He can't." Pietro asked, "Can he?" Gregor only grinned.

"On the contrary, sir." Maijstral was firm. "If Miss Jensen is not available, she cannot fulfill her part in the contract. I assume that whoever abducted her knows that, and will keep her incommunicado until such time as I have either left Peleng or disposed of the object in some other way. It is likely, if they find me, they will make an offer of their own. I may be compelled by circumstances to accept."

Pietro goggled at him. "Look," he said, "I'm the treasurer. I can pay you in Amalia's place."

"It may be," Maijstral said, "that I could place your bid among others in any auction taking place after Miss Jensen fails to reappear. But you *will* be bidding against others, Mr. Quijano."

Pietro appeared to cave in. He glanced toward Gregor again, then at Roman.

"I'll tell you," he said. "But your Khosalikh will have to leave."

Irritation snapped into Maijstral. A display of racism at this point was more than annoying. He glanced up at Roman's stolid, unmoving countenance. "Roman may stay," Maijstral said. "He is my oldest associate, and perfectly in my confidence."

Pietro shook his head. "This issue transcends mere personal loyalties, Mr. Maijstral." He leaned closer and lowered his voice, as if trying to keep Roman from overhearing. His tone was earnest. "The Fate of the Human Constellation," he said, "is in the balance."

Maijstral raised an eyebrow. "You don't say." This puppy was getting more annoying by the minute.

"Please," Pietro said.

Maijstral tossed the relic from one hand to the next. "And here I am asking a mere sixty. For the Fate of the Constellation."

Pietro was indignant. "You *agreed* to sixty!" Then he seemed to recover himself. "Trust me on this, Mr. Maijstral."

Maijstral sighed. There was a short silence, relieved only by Gregor's tapping on his knees. Finally Pietro spoke.

"Very well, sir. If you vouch for him. But I wish you would reconsider."

Maijstral glanced at Roman. "I will not." Another bout of irritation gripped Maijstral at the sight of Roman's stolid countenance. Roman was concealing some great anger, that was clear, and Maijstral assumed it was on account of this tactless young man. He leaned back in his chair and crossed one leg over the other. "What's in the jug, Mr. Quijano? The truth, now."

Pietro bit his lip. When he spoke it was a whisper.

"That container," he said, "is a cryonic reliquary containing the sperm of the heirless Pendjalli Emperor, Nnis CVI."

Maijstral looked at the object in his hands. He perceived Gregor's stunned look, Roman's jaw dropping, and he wished he had sent them both away, far out of earshot, far off the planet even.

The thing hummed in Maijstral's hand, a cold, impossible weight.

"Oh," Maijstral said. "The Fate of the Constellation really *is* at stake, then."

SIX

The cryonic reliquary sat on the table. It gleamed in the soft light of the room. Maijstral reached out his glass and accepted another fill of champagne. The group was on its second bottle. Maijstral told the robot to chill a third. He was going to need it.

He wanted nothing so much as to get rid of the reliquary without further delay. Drop it off a speeding flier into the nearest bottomless lake. Toss it into the heart of the first fusion furnace he stumbled across. Fire it into the heart of Peleng's sun.

It had come true, he thought. The worst nightmare of every thief. To have stolen something so valuable, so fabulous, that it would be desired by every soldier, every politician, every criminal, every diplomat, every murderous fanatic.

Poor Maijstral, thought Maijstral. And drank his champagne without pleasure.

Maijstral would not have been cheered by the idea that some people were in worse situations. Consider poor Nnis.

The current Pendjalli Emperor had spent his youth in the Imperial harem, a withdrawn, scholarly child, out of place in the competitive, none-too-gentle atmosphere of the place. He preferred catching insects and scrutinizing their genitalia under a microscope to the usual harem activities, which consisted largely of children engaging in intrigues that were imitations of those indulged in by their mothers, each child being pushed along in a typhoon of plotting and scheming and maneuvering, a miniature storm reflective of those external stresses created by the endless struggles of the best-born Khosali houses to make one of their offspring the favored child, the next heir. The Khosali Imperium had no rule of primogeniture, no regular system for determining the heir save the Imperial will itself.

If one were not a natural intriguer, childhood in the harem could be ghastly. Nnis was not an intriguer. He was, however, very good at bugs.

It was with considerable relief that Nnis learned he had lost the contest to a younger half brother. His bitterly disappointed mother, the beautiful and high-strung daughter of the Duke of Moth (pronounced Myth), lectured him for hours about his inadequacies. Nnis didn't care. He sniffed her ears good-bye and flew to Gosat on happy libelulla wings, where he spent the happiest three years of his life studying desert entomology. His studies were interrupted by the terrifying news that the Prince Royal had died in a freak ballooning accident, and that, as the result of a particularly successful bit of intrigue on the part of his mother and the Moth (pronounced Myth) clan, he had been anointed the next heir. Panicked by the prospect, Nnis dashed back to the City of Seven Bright Rings in order to inaugurate a counterconspiracy aimed at getting himself removed, only to find on his arrival that the Emperor had moulted and lapsed into coma. All was lost.

The Moths were smiling in the coronation holographs, a row of red, lolling tongues. Nnis CVI, in the green brocade cloth of state, looked as if he were attending a funeral.

The Moths' smiles were, in the event, short-lived. Emperors are restricted in many areas of their lives, but Nnis concluded that he could arrange his family life, at least, to suit himself. The City of Seven Bright Rings subsequently announced that the Dowager Mother would be built a new palace on Gosat, where she would become Custodian-Pensioner of the Imperial Entomological Collection. The Duke of Moth returned to Mothholm minus the cost of a lot of expensive coronation presents.

Nnis must have concluded that there was some point to being Emperor after all.

Nnis subsequently married about a dozen times. His harem was small—there was a certain resentment over that, particularly on the part of the Moths' hereditary enemies, who had been looking to get their own back—but what really got the traditionalists wailing was the fact that Nnis declined to sire any offspring.

There had never been an Empress; tradition decreed that the crown go to a male. The tradition had been founded before the days of widespread genetic technology, when a male heir could sire many more offspring than could any Empress. Gene technology made this requirement obsolete, but the necessity of a male Emperor was continued simply because it was tradition, and tradition was something a Khosalikh could never question.

Nnis, however, wanted to postpone the intrigue over the heir for as long as he could. As he liked his insects best when they were pinned to a mat, he liked his household quiet, quiet and unexciting. Predictable, calm, scholarly. His first inquiry, on being proposed a new wife, was whether or not she had a soft voice; the second was whether or not she had published.

Quiet he got. Forty years worth. And when excitement came at last, it more than made up for the previous two score years.

It has been a matter of historical debate concerning whether effective and spirited leadership from the Imperial City would have prevented, or altered the course of, the Human Rebellion. Probably not—prior to Nnis's accession the course of Imperial policy had been set, the ministers were in place, the humans already agitating. If Nnis had looked up from his collection long enough to notice there were problems, he might have brought them to his ministers' attention and they might have been compelled to look more closely . . . but it was not the Emperor's job to consider the inconceivable, and a successful revolt was simply that.

Nnis was the first Khosali Emperor to lose a war. *Ever.* Imagine that.

Had he suicided, no one would have blamed him, and most would have applauded. At least it would have shown an appreciation of his position. But his presence was necessary to maintain both the Emperor Principle and the peace. And, of course, there was no one to follow—he had seen to that.

But the shock was too much. His health collapsed and he went into his cold coffin. From there he kept a tenuous grip on affairs and on ritual. Kept soldiering on for two generations as the medical procedures used to keep the final darkness at bay grew ever more elaborate and extreme, and his hands upon the reins of Empire grew ever weaker, ever colder.

He never had an heir. His ministers had, years before, impressed upon him to contribute the royal seed to cryonic storage. Three containers were prepared—the donation was eventually made. But the war wrecked it all. Two containers were destroyed, another was missing and presumed lost. By the end of the war, his fertility had declined to the point where future contributions were pointless. Nontraditional means of succession, such as cloning, were denied the tradition-bound Emperor.

And there he sat for years, dreaming in his box, awaiting release, the last comforting silence. Wondering where things went wrong, what he could have done differently.

Wondering if they will ever let him die.

Lieutenant Navarre swung from side to side in his hammock and frowned into his receiver. While searching the house for further sign of theft, he had found the hammock in his uncle's storage closet and promptly strung it between two trees on the lawn. His telephone he always carried with him, on his belt. The Pompey High Seas Scouts are always prepared. On proper communications often depend lives.

He'd had a two hour nap, interrupted when a pair of plum-colored birds decided to play follow-the-leader through the leaves overhead. Then he decided to call Amalia Jensen and tell her about the theft at his uncle's place; and incidentally repay her dinner last night with an offer of one of his own. But there was no answer, and that was odd. Not even a robot or an answering device. And Jensen had told him she would be in all day.

It was as if communications had simply gone down.

He put his receiver down, swung his legs out of the hammock and reached for his uniform jacket and mourning cloak. He would deliver the message in person. He smiled as he thought of Amalia Jensen amid her scented bower.

So intent was he on this vision that, as he strode across the lawn adjusting his jacket and calling for the robot to lace him up, he forgot that he left his telephone sitting on the hammock. It glittered silver in the sun, rocking two and fro with the wind.

One of the plum-colored birds fluttered down onto the hammock. The telephone winked at her. She picked it up in her forepaws and flew into the sky.

The press found out that Maijstral had been expected at Nichole's hotel late last evening—a rumor Nichole had agreed with Roman to plant, a false trail laid by Roman for the benefit of his shadow. The media globes hadn't seen Maijstral enter, but then again he was known to be elusive. Nichole had declined to discuss the matter further, which only enhanced speculation.

Nichole knew how to prime the pump of rumor. It was her profession, after all.

And now came the phone call.

"Drake Maijstral, ma'am."

Nichole had programmed her bedroom with a deep masculine Khosali voice, deferent and respectful. This was in deliberate contrast to the brassier, female tones of her dermatology robot, which was carefully applying her cosmetics. She ordered the dermatologist to withdraw its apparatus and told the room to accept the call. Maijstral's life-size holographic head appeared on a level with her eyes. His hair was escaping the knot into which he'd tied it. He seemed not to have slept well.

"Hello, Maijstral. Did you have a profitable evening?"

"It was . . . an interesting night, Nichole." Something in his voice made her sit up.

"Are you all right, Drake?"

He hesitated. "Yes. But I must beg off luncheon today. You know I wouldn't leave you without escort were there not compelling reasons."

A challenge? she wondered. Arrest? Some kind of trap? She hadn't heard Maijstral's name on the vid save in connection with her own. Whatever the problem was, it wasn't public.

"Can I help?"

Maijstral's smile was strained. "It's very kind of you to ask, but no."

"Anything you need, Maijstral. We're friends. You know that."

He paused a moment before answering, then shook his head. "Your offer is very kind, but I think not. You should stay clear of this."

She rested her chin on her hand. "It's serious, then."

"Yes, milady. It is."

"Is Roman looking after you?"

He smiled. "Very well. Thank you."

"Take good care of yourself, Drake. Don't do anything foolish."

"I won't." He raised a glass of champagne into the holo field. "Thank you for understanding. I'll make it up to you when next we meet."

Nichole smiled. Maijstral always did have ten points for style. "I'll hold you to that," she said. She watched him sip from his glass, and she realized there was something about his manner that still bothered her. He was, she realized suddenly, shaken. Truly shaken. The champagne was a careful attempt at regaining *savoir faire.* She had never seen him in this state before, and if she hadn't known him very well for a brief interval she would never have noticed it. "Drake," she said suddenly, "call me tomorrow. I want to know how you are."

He moved the glass out of the holo field. His look was neutral. "Thank you," he said. "I'm flattered by your concern."

It was a typical Maijstral remark, but he'd spoken High Khosali, in the conjugation relating to the state of the universe. Ten points for style again, but there was still something seriously wrong.

Not the least of which was, Nichole now had no escort for a public luncheon. After Maijstral's head vanished from her room, she thought for a minute and told the room to dial the residence of Lieutenant Navarre.

He wasn't home. Navarre's telephone asked for a message, but Nichole declined to leave one. Members of the Diadem spoke face-to-face or not at all.

She thought for a moment, then decided to plead fatigue and beg off the lunch. The press, she knew, would assume Maijstral was still with her.

Good. Whatever was going on, Maijstral wouldn't be hurt if everyone assumed he was someplace he wasn't.

The plum-colored bird had flown her nest in alarm from the chirping sound made by Lieutenant Navarre's telephone. But the phone fell silent, and after a moment of contemplation the bird decided to make a cautious recce. She perched on a limb just out of reach and looked down at its home, one forepaw scratching her beak in puzzlement.

The telephone sat among the bird's treasures, bits of tinsel, a shiny candy wrapper, a fountain pen, several bright-colored rocks, a child's ring. The bird hated to concede its trove to the interloper. The damn thing had only been playing at being inanimate.

When the phone chirped again the bird raised her wings in alarm, but only retreated a few paces along the branch. The chirping sound continued. The bird's alarm decreased and she moved closer, a slow sense of delight beginning to trickle into her mind.

The thing talked! The bird had never had a treasure that talked before. The bird ruffled its feathers and said "Coo!"

The phone chirped on. The bird answered. Finally, in Peleng City, the insurance investigator hung up, and the phone was silent.

The plum-colored bird returned to its nest, happy in her new friend.

The materialist approach to life, as the plum-colored bird will attest, is not always compelled by the philistinism its detractors often allege. Consider the joys of surrounding oneself with the objects that bring comfort and pleasure—the good wines, the fine art, the leather-covered volume, the well-made conveyance—and one may very well bid the rest of the world go hang. There are worse ways to arrange one's life, and it is only when the materialist impulse moves from comfort to compulsion that it becomes obnoxious. No one needs more than one colander per residence, and when one makes a point of collecting platinum colanders with diamond-studded rims and allegorical reliefs on the base, and all for the purpose of showing up one's neighbors, then the observer can safely assume the materialist impulse has got out of hand.

Allowed thievery is based on materialism, but without philistinism. One searches for the perfect object, the best of its class, the rarest, the most astonishing—and then, through one's own efforts, one ventures to possess it. What might be a vulgar case of breaking-and-taking becomes instead a venture in aesthetic romanticism. A century ago Ralph Adverse saw the Eltdown Shard and knew he had to have it, that he could not rest until he held it in the palm of his hand and watched its dark splendors dance in the light of his homefire. No wonder he spent half his life trying to steal it—not to sell it, but to possess it for himself, for its own glorious sake—and in the end, having spent all the money he'd made over a lifetime of thievery in its pursuit, having at last clasped his hands and known it was gloriously his, he committed suicide with the Shard clutched to his bosom rather than have it auctioned by the Imperial Revenue Authority for back taxes. Who can blame him? He was a romantic first, a materialist second.

But one can be a materialist without having to go overboard. Consider the philosophy of the plum-colored bird: find something nice, take it home, sit on it and make friends.

The homely comforts are always the best.

Lieutenant Navarre gazed at the wreckage in Amalia Jensen's house. He had called the police as soon as he found Howard scattered over the roof. I'm being *persecuted,* he thought. Someone's following me around and *doing* this to me.

He followed Officer Pankat through the litter in the living room. Mortally wounded blossoms gave off their dying fragrance.

"I had dinner. We talked. I flew home." What else could he say? "No, I didn't see anyone. I barely knew the woman."

Officer Pankat looked at him through level almond eyes. "Do you think, sir, in view of the other incident last night, that someone might be persecuting you?"

Navarre started. He was just thinking that. But all he could think of saying was, "But why?"

Paavo Kuusinen stepped out of his flier and examined the yellow grass. Leaves rustled overhead in the gentle breeze. Amalia Jensen's pastel house stood half a mile away. Here, Kuusinen found, was where the two Khosali had waited out the night; he easily found the marks of the flier on the ground and two sets of prints, one small, one large, both identified, from the shape of the boot, as Khosali.

He had followed Sergeant Tvi for a while, from Navarre's manse to an estate which, on inquiry, he discovered was rented by the Imperialist Countess Anastasia. From there he followed Tvi to Amalia Jensen's, whence he had heard smashing noises and witnessed Tvi and her big associate carry out a limp body, which they transported to the Countess's. Kuusinen had then gone to Maijstral's place, but no one seemed to be home. He had checked the early reports on his scanner, heard there had been a robbery at Navarre's, and returned there in time to see Navarre take off in the direction of town. Kuusinen had followed, to discover Navarre lighting on Jensen's roof.

Kuusinen scoured the ground carefully and found a pair of empty hi-sticks that had probably been used by the big Khosalikh while the smaller one scouted Jensen's house. There was nothing else of interest.

He returned to his flier and told his scanner to seek the robbery report for Navarre's house. The report had added a description of the one object missing, a silver cryonic container. To the official description was added the description from the auctioneer's catalog: "with power source, Imperial seal, functional, c9, wt 16sm, 18x17ng." To this was appended: "value approx 18n."

Odd, Kuusinen thought. The container scarcely seemed valuable enough to justify all this fuss. He wondered what was in it, and considered for a moment all the activity he'd witnessed, the two Khosali consorting with the Imperialist Countess and a baron from the Imperium, and he wondered what all of this had to do with the silver container, Amalia Jensen, and the copper-skinned lieutenant from Pompey.

He had no idea at all. But he was fairly certain this puzzle had to do, in some inexplicable way, with Maijstral.

Kuusinen observed Lieutenant Navarre's flier rising from Amalia Jensen's roof and decided, for lack of any further ideas, to follow it. As he rose into the sky, he decided to hang on to Navarre for another few hours, then return to the Countess's place. Maybe one of them would lead him to Maijstral.

This was the most interesting diversion he'd had in a long time.

The silver container still sat on Maijstral's table, refusing to go away. Maijstral returned from his conversation with Nichole to find that, like a magnetic object, the Emperor's sperm receptacle had drawn the other three nearer to it. Gregor and Pietro had hitched their seats closer and were bent forward, barely glancing at each other even though they were in conversation. Roman, still standing, still trembling with some unspoken emotion, hovered over Gregor's shoulder, rising to tiptoe from time to time to gain a better view. It was a living demonstration of Imperial Presence.

"If the situation in the Empire remains unchanged," Pietro Quijano was saying, "Nnis may drag on for another few generations. When he finally shuffles off, the Blood Royal will have to assemble to choose another Emperor. It will take years for the family to make up its mind, and by the end of their deliberations we in the Constellation should have a good idea of who will come to power. The Human Constellation will have a long breathing space, and if the new Emperor's supporters are committed to reconquest, we'll have time to prepare."

"For the correct price, sir," said Maijstral as he slid into his chair, "the future of the Constellation may be yours to command." He leaned back, resisting the magnetism of the silver reliquary.

Pietro looked up at him, trying in vain to gaze through Maijstral's hooded eyes. "We only have sixty in the treasury, and we only got that because Miss Jensen took out a personal loan."

"Perhaps you should take out a loan yourself, Mr. Quijano."

"I'm a student. I'm doing postgraduate work in mathematics, and I'm not worth any money. But I'll give you the sixty right now."

"You are not Miss Jensen. My contract was with her."

Pietro's eyes showed desperation. "The Fate of the Constellation is at stake," he said. "Surely you can—"

"Mr. Quijano," said Maijstral, "perhaps in your enthusiasm something has slipped your mind."

"Sir? What is that?"

"I am, by profession, a thief. It is not my *job* to care about the Fate of the Constellation."

Gregor snickered, but Pietro was undeterred. "Surely there must be some human decency to which I can appeal."

"Human decency?" Maijstral appeared to consider the words. He shook his head. "I'm afraid not, Mr. Quijano. Such decency as I possess is almost certainly Khosali." He gave Pietro a thin smile. "The incident part, however, is entirely human."

Pietro Quijano looked at him for a long, cold moment. "Then, since Miss Jensen's the only person you'll deal with, let's find her."

Maijstral was about to point out that neither was it his job to rescue maidens in distress, but Gregor cleared his throat.

"Boss," he said, "it's bad form to let people go around stealing your clients. It lets them think they can push you around."

Maijstral frowned. "I'm not in the habit of exerting myself for nothing," he said.

"You want your client back, right, boss? Only too you do. There's a way to do it. Find her and get her loose."

"May I speak with you privately, sir?" The voice was Roman's, speaking in Khosali. Maijstral nodded.

He let Roman take him aside into Maijstral's bedroom. When Roman spoke, it was in High Khosali, and his voice trembled with suppressed emotion.

"Your client was stolen, sir," he said. "And with your business unconcluded. The kidnappers knew of your interest, but have not acted to preserve that interest or consult you. That is insult given, and considering their likely identity, an offense to honor. The insult must be answered."

Surprise rose in Maijstral as the High Khosali sentences followed one another in perfect form and rhythm, like the elements of some complex mathematics. Given Khosali premises, the conclusions were absolute. Maijstral tried to find a gap in the reasoning and failed.

So that's what Roman had been seething about. If Maijstral hadn't been so distracted by events, he would have realized it long since. He gave a reassuring nod.

"I give you thanks for your concern," he said, answering in High Khosali. "Your interest does you credit, Roman." Roman's eyes gleamed at the compliment. "I need no reminders to know that honor was offended," Maijstral went on, "but first I must decide with whom the offense lies, and how best to act, and I must also find out how much Mr. Quijano knows. An outright challenge might give these people more credit than they deserve."

Roman's ears pricked forward. "That is true, sir."

Maijstral raised a hand to Roman's shoulder. He dropped to standard Khosali. "I think we should return to Mr. Quijano."

"Yes, sir. Very good."

Maijstral gestured for Roman to precede him. He took his hand back from Roman's shoulder and observed that it trembled lightly. He clenched the hand into a fist and followed Roman into the living room. By a conscious effort of will, he did not grind his teeth.

"Very well," he said. "We should, at least, investigate the possibility of rescuing Miss Jensen. But where would they be holding her?"

Gregor frowned. "A safe house, maybe. Possibly."

"Perhaps not. The kidnapping showed every sign of being arranged in haste, within a few hours of my acquisition of the jug. They may not have had time to arrange for a safe house, though they may be arranging for one now. We should run a check for consular personnel, then for any residences they may possess outside the consulate."

"There is also the Countess," Roman said.

"Right," Gregor said. "I should cross-check the references for rented security. They may have laid on some extra."

Maijstral smiled. That was a good thought.

"Fine. If we get any cross-references, we'll go for aerial reconnaissance and perhaps check further by darksuit. Get about it, then."

Roman and Gregor glided away to their tasks. Maijstral settled back into his chair with a piece of fleth. Pietro Quijano was, he realized, looking at him in an expectant way.

"Yes, Mr. Quijano?"

"You're going to find Miss Jensen and then rescue her?"

"I said we would *investigate the possibility,* Mr. Quijano. Not quite the same thing."

"But you'll at least call the police?"

"No. I think not. The whole purpose of the kidnapping would have to come out. The law protects me after a few hours, but that doesn't apply to any of my patrons. I presume you would not wish it established that Miss Jensen hired me with criminal intent?"

Pietro looked a little pale. "No. I guess not." Maijstral nibbled his fleth. Gregor, from the hallway, spoke up.

"Perhaps we could get Lieutenant Navarre to help us."

Pietro scowled at the idea. Maijstral answered. "I scarcely think so. He would discover that Miss Jensen only entertained him last night for the purpose of getting him away from his house so that I could rob him."

"Oh."

Pietro brightened, then frowned again. "What if we can't rescue her, sir?"

Maijstral looked at the piece of fleth in his fingers. The hand no longer trembled. "In that event, Mr. Quijano," he said, "I shall have to challenge her kidnappers one by one. And kill them, one hopes. Family honor, alas, won't have it any other way—and challenging them is preferable, in my mind at least, to committing suicide and hoping it shames them into letting Miss Jensen go." He looked at Pietro with his lazy green eyes. "Unless, of course, you'd like to issue the challenges yourself?"

Pietro grew paler. "No, sir. I don't—it's not my province, you see."

"I understand. One can scarcely hope to vanquish an enemy in single combat through the use of higher mathematics alone." He finished his fleth and dusted his fingers, then stood. "Luncheon, Mr. Quijano?" he asked. "I think we're stocked with food."

"I'm not hungry." Pietro was staring into nowhere. "Thank you."

"I'll find myself a snack, then," Maijstral said. He stood and moved toward the kitchen.

What he really intended to do was get on the phone and rent another safe house. This one was hopelessly compromised. Pietro Quijano was on Maijstral's side for the present, but when and if Amalia Jensen was rescued that was likely to change.

Successful criminal masterminds, one notes, always look ahead.

Nichole was lunching on cold chicken, bean salad, and pickles; a humble meal she could eat only in private, but which she much preferred to the elaborate, often eccentric cuisine demanded by her role as a member of the Diadem. Even here, the meal was not entirely her own; since she was supposed to be hiding Maijstral here in her love nest, she'd had to order for two. The sight of the second plate made the meal more lonely than it should have been. Lightly downcast, she sipped her iced tea with lemon and wondered again what Maijstral was involved with.

The phone rang. Nichole sipped again and waited for the room to tell her who it was.

"The Countess Anastasia, ma'am," the room said finally. "Asking for Mr. Maijstral." Nichole turned around in surprise.

Well, she thought. Developments.

She ordered the room to create a holographic mirror image of her by way of making certain she was fit to show herself on the phone, patted her hair, then moved to another chair so that her meal would be out of sight and that her backdrop would suit her complexion. "By all means connect the Countess," she said.

Countess Anastasia was holographed from a point of view slightly below her chin, giving her a lofty elevation, allowing her to look at Nichole down her nose. Some people carried this to extremes, which made for an upsetting view if they neglected to clip all their nose hairs; but the Countess was more subtle and the effect was slight, but still observable.

"Nichole," she said coldly. She spoke in Khosali. "I asked for Drake Maijstral."

"I regret he's not here, my lady," Nichole said. "I would be happy to take a message, should I see him."

The Countess smiled thinly. "Ah. I must have been misinformed. The broadcast media, you understand."

"I regret to say, my lady, that the media are wont to report as fact all manner of speculation."

"Yes. That has been my experience as well. I would have given the reports no credence, you understand, save that I have been unable to reach Maijstral at home."

Nichole, looking at the Countess, wondered why Maijstral was so timorous around this woman. The Countess seemed, despite her breeding and apparent confidence, a pathetically insecure creature who had found salvation in the Imperialist Cause, quite the same way others found salvation in religion, or crank philosophy, or conspiracy theory—against one's own inner conviction of insignificance, a flailing, defiant, unfocused, but perfectly sincere protest. Nichole, thinking these thoughts, looked at the Countess and smiled helpfully.

"I will take a message, my lady," she said, "and relay it to Maijstral if I see him."

The Countess seemed cross. Nichole guessed that the Countess assumed Maijstral was hiding in Nichole's boudoir, listening in. "Very well," the Countess said. "Tell him this. He has something that I want, and I believe he will find the price to his liking."

"I will report the message faithfully, my lady."

"Thank you." The Countess smiled with a graciousness her hard eyes denied. "I regret having to bother you, ma'am."

"No bother at all, Countess. I enjoy doing things for my friends." Nichole was smiling back, a smile that betrayed a slight effort, the effect intending to show she knew the Countess's civility was a mask. Nuance, nuance. Nichole's specialty.

The Countess winked away.

Nichole let her smile relax. Maijstral, she thought, her alarm growing. What have you got yourself into?

SEVEN

"Relieving you," said Sergeant Tvi. She was carrying Amalia Jensen's food tray up the stairs. Khotvinn thankfully turned off his Ronnie Romper disguise and handed her the holo projector, gun, and manacle control.

"The prisoner has been quiet," he rumbled. Then he moved down the stairs, treading heavily, flexing his shoulders. Looking for something to hit.

Guarding prisoners. Pah. Breaking necks was more his style.

This was no work for a Khosalikh such as he. He stood 169ng, and his shoulders were 70ng across. His upper arms were 58ng around and his chest was wider around that the last tape measure he'd tried to measure it with. On his home planet—a frontier world, where Khosali power was tempered by scarce resources and the ferocity of native life-forms—he had been regarded with awe and fear. Awe and fear that were, so Khotvinn had always thought, perfectly justified.

Khotvinn stomped to his room, wanting to tread the lilies on his carpet. The room was furnished in the local milksop style: frilly things on the windows and bed, plush carpets, vases with flowers, an oversoft mattress on a bed that would alter its shape on command. It was the sort of thing Khotvinn had to guard against. If he wasn't careful, this kind of living could make him soft.

He had no intention of becoming soft. He was the imperious offspring of a superior brand of Khosali, the pioneers who had, by dint of their strength and will, driven back the frontiers of the Empire and subjugated entire planets full of alien inferiors. The effete Emperor back in his harem thought his victories had come at his own bidding. Bah! It was the people like Khotvinn who got the job done, and by the best and most effective way—smashing heads.

Khotvinn considered himself a bloody-handed reaver—titanic in his fury, awesome in his mirth, careless of the laws made to protect those weaker than himself. He recognized no custom save his own will, no motive save his own enrichment. He despised Allowed Burglars, taking advantage of loopholes in the law, sneaking into darkened houses at night. Better to proclaim yourself openly. And Sinn wasn't any better, using others to do his dirty work. The only one of this crowd he had any use for was the Countess, a woman who clearly worshipped strength, honor, and desperate deeds. Khotvinn was a born plunderer, and if his young career as an armed robber (and army deserter) hadn't been interrupted by a cowardly, puking little human weakling (who had dropped a brick on his head while hiding on a balcony), he would be plundering still.

Subsequently he had concluded that being a member of the Secret Dragoons could work to his advantage. He could study the stupid fools who surrounded him, learn their ways, and then, when the time was right, strike out on his own, leaving nothing but ruin and broken necks behind him.

Khotvinn reached under his bed and came up with his sword case. He drew out the long steel blade—no light alloys for him!—and raised it two-handed above his head. Carefully he pictured Baron Sinn in front of him, and then sliced the image from neck to crotch. The blade danced before him like a whirlwind, chopping Sinn to bits. His heart hammered. His blood raced. He was Khotvinn . . . *Khotvinn* . . . *KHOTVINN!* Glorious exemplar of his race! Furious brawler with sword of steel! Bloody ravager with a heart of careless majesty!

The antique vase splintered beneath Khotvinn's backswing and splattered the bedcovers with mangled roses. Khotvinn snarled and threw down his blade. It pierced the lily carpet and stuck in the floor, quivering.

Khotvinn spat. This was not a suitable room. This was not a suitable mission. His companions were not suitable.

With an easy gesture he yanked the sword from the floor. It hung in his hand like a tooth of omen. He considered his situation.

His companions—his so-called superiors—were holding the human, Jensen, for ransom. Holding a woman prisoner wasn't anything he couldn't do himself, or anything that required Tvi or Sinn.

His lips drew back, his tongue lolled. A glorious idea had entered his mind. Give Sinn the chop, he thought. Give the chop to Tvi. Then leave with Jensen over his shoulder, the Countess's ghastly milksop mansion burning behind him. A wonderful picture. What cared Khotvinn for the Fate of the Empire?

The smile began to fade. Who, exactly, was he supposed to sell Jensen *to?* He couldn't remember.

He'd have to keep his ears open and await his chance. His time, he knew, would come.

Khotvinn's grin broadened. Saliva dropped to the carpet. This was going to be great.

"I'm not advocating discrimination, you understand." Amalia Jensen's split lip had healed under the influence of a semilife patch, her swelling had likewise been reduced, and though the bruises still showed, the swelling and discomfort were down and she was speaking, and eating lunch, without difficulty.

Speaking and eating on the bed, from a tray, with her ankles held together. Tvi wasn't taking any chances.

"No, not discrimination. Just reasonable precautions. The Rebellion was successful because many of the rebels were highly placed in the Imperial bureaucracy and military, and were in a position to aid in the defection of entire Imperial squadrons. The Constellation should take precautions against just such an event. That's all I'm suggesting."

Tvi was still enjoying the role of a sophisticated mercenary, and she relaxed in her chair, a leg dangling over the chair arm, her stunner in one fist. "So nonhumans should never be put in positions of authority?" Tvi asked. "And this is what you call nondiscriminatory, Miss Jensen?"

Amalia frowned into her frappé. "It's a necessity. A regrettable one, I know. But humanity is simply too delicately placed to take a chance."

"It would seem to me, speaking strictly as an observer, that you're almost asking for betrayal. Why should anyone be loyal to a government that will never trust her?"

"Perhaps in a few generations, after the Imperial threat becomes less acute. . . ."

"And I must say, speaking again as an observer, that you seem rather naive about *human* nature."

A veil of steel seemed to move over Amalia Jensen's eyes. Tvi realized she may have offended by offering a judgment on Amalia's species. Oh well, she thought, what was the point of being a languid sophisticate if you couldn't offer sweeping judgments? Besides, this wasn't anything Amalia hadn't just done with respect to races other than her own. "Yes?" Amalia said. "How so?"

"Because you are underestimating the extent of human corruptibility, Miss Jensen. Why do you assume that an individual will be loyal simply because he is human? Are not humans as susceptible to greed, extortion, and treachery as any other? More so, if the stereotypes are to be believed." Seeing Amalia's dark glance, Tvi hastened to add, "Which I don't for a moment believe, by the way. But d'you see what I mean? If you waste all your resources averting treachery on the part of nonhumans who may not be traitors in the first place, you may be missing the humans who are."

"I'm not advocating for a minute spending *all* our resources doing any one thing," Amalia said. "But still, one may assume a certain species loyalty, yes? Why else would so many well-placed humans support the Rebellion, even though such support was largely against their own interests?"

"Greed and blackmail, for starters."

Amalia frowned and pushed her tray away. "That's not true."

"Probably not. Not in more than a few cases, anyway." Tvi threw her other leg over the chair arm and snuggled into the cushion. "I'm just offering a pair of motivations you seem not to have considered in the case of your own species, but are all too happy to attribute to others."

Amalia Jensen winced and turned her eyes away. "I understand the reasons for Ronnie Romper," she said, "but can't you get rid of the *smile,* somehow? It's just too distracting, having to debate that grin."

"I'm afraid not, Miss Jensen."

Amalia gave a sigh and put her chin on her hand. "I'll just have to bear up, then."

"Good advice, I'd say, for a woman in your situation."

Bingo, thought Gregor Norman. Point for me. He looked at the numbers shimmering on his computer screen and leaned back in his chair, lacing his hands behind his neck just above where the proximity wire in his collar interfaced his mind with the computer. A grin spread over his face. The champagne that still sparkled on the frontiers of his consciousness acted to widen the grin. He nodded in time to the Vivaldi he was playing on his Troxan sound deck, enjoyed his triumph for a few moments, then reached to the service plate on the wall and pressed the ideograph for "general announcement."

"Boss. I think I've found something."

"One moment."

If Gregor hadn't been anticipating, he never would have heard Maijstral enter. The man moved in such absolute silence that, in the early months of his apprenticeship, Gregor had wondered if there was something uncanny about it. Just good training, he finally decided, and began consciously to imitate him.

Gregor was a good thief, had always been. He'd been living by his wits for most of his life, but he knew he'd never make it to the top of the ratings as an Allowed Burglar.

The problem was those ten points for style. The people at the top of the charts—Alice Manderley, Geoff Fu George, Baron Drago—they fairly oozed style, and moved among their victims with such charm that it almost seemed as if no one in the company resented the way his valuables kept disappearing. Maijstral, for example, had all the advantages—gentle birth, schooling in the Empire, the right social connections. When the teenaged Gregor had heard about Maijstral and Nichole, he'd breathed fiery jealousy for weeks.

Gregor was Non-U, that was the trouble. Should he ever have occasion to meet Nichole, he wouldn't know how to make an approach, what to talk about. If he was to be a successful Allowed Burglar, he'd have to know how to move among these people, how they spoke, thought, interacted. He'd learned a lot just watching Maijstral. He was taking diction lessons. He'd learned that the hair style he'd favored on his home world would have got him challenges on half the planets in the Empire. He'd learned not to paint his face in the pastel colors he had favored in his youth, and to say "perhaps" instead of "maybe," and "vetch" instead of "clinker." But he still had a long way to go.

Anticipating, Gregor looked up just as Maijstral appeared, in his silence, behind Gregor's right shoulder. "I think I found it," he said. "I broke into the phone company's computers and got Countess Anastasia's numbers, including her address. I cross-checked the address with my security file and found out that Anastasia added multiple security to her residence just yesterday, which might mean she was anticipating having to put the snatch on Jensen."

"What sort of security?" Maijstral asked.

"Leapers, screamers, and flaxes."

"Go on."

"No hoppers. So it might not be individual objects she's guarding, but an area. Like an area holding a prisoner."

"Can you get a map of the building?"

"Maybe. Perhaps. I'll check the planning authority. That will give me a chance to use the peeler program Poston sold us."

"Can you find out whom the building belongs to?"

"Coming up."

Still leaning back in his chair, Gregor gave a mental command to his computer and supervised as it phoned the planning authority, then crashed through its defenses like an Imperial cruiser through an insect screen. Poston's peeler was brute force, no mistake, not a bit of elegance. No style points here. Gregor smiled as the data read across the visual centers of his brain.

"Woolvinn Leases, Ltd," he said. "Shall I look at the Countess's household computer, boss? If we can check her food shipments we might be able to find out how many people she has in there."

Maijstral considered this. "If you're certain it won't give us away. . . ."

"Not with Poston's peeler. I can always just ring off and say it was a mistake."

"Very well. Go ahead."

"Only too."

Gregor started the program on its merry way, his head bobbing to the sound of Vivaldi. He looked up at Maijstral, seeing the man withdrawn behind his hooded eyes. He thought about Maijstral's conversation with Pietro Quijano that morning, and a troubling thought entered his mind. He'd *assumed* that Maijstral had merely been playing with the man, but with Maijstral it was hard to tell.

"Boss?" he asked. "About the reliquary?"

Maijstral's expression was abstracted. "Yes, Gregor?"

"You were just pretending to consider selling the thing to the Imperials, correct? I mean, we really wouldn't do it, right?"

Maijstral's eyes turned to him. There was a hint of intensity behind the lidded eyes. "Would it bother you if we did?"

Gregor shifted uneasily in his chair. "Well, boss, I don't think much of the Constellation or the hacks that run it, but that doesn't mean I want to have aliens over us again. Let alone an Emperor. Not only that, but my granddad fought in the Rebellion, and he used to tell me a story about what it was like under the Empire. It wasn't good for a lot of people, boss."

Maijstral's smile was slight. Vivaldi was reaching a climax, and he seemed abstracted, his mind somewhere off in the music. "The possibility of the Empire returning," he said, "seems remote."

"Besides. Those people stole our client."

"That has not escaped my attention, Gregor."

Gregor frowned. He was not comforted.

Maijstral's hand reached for Gregor's sound deck, popped the trapdoor, removed Vivaldi. "What next?" he asked.

"The Snail."

Maijstral's hand flourished another recording. "Snail shall it be. I always like the D Minor." He dropped the recording into the trapdoor and pushed the play button. He turned to Gregor with a smile. "Anything from the Countess's?"

"Right." Gregor turned his attention to the data that had been winking in his mind for some moments. "Looks like the Countess had visitors last night. A lot of wine and dinner for four." He laughed. "The comp prepared breakfast for five this morning. Luncheon for five, too. Where'd number five come from?"

"I'm sure we can guess."

"And—let's see—she's ordered some tools, timber, plywood. . . ."

"It seems as if her ladyship might be nailing shut a window or two."

"It seems like. And she's also ordered a heavy-duty bolt, some tools for installation, and a Ronnie Romper disguise from a costume shop." He looked up at Maijstral. "Ronnie Romper?" he asked.

Music wafted into the room. Maijstral shrugged. "Perhaps Ronnie is her favorite. I always liked him when I was young."

"I never cared for him. It was the smile, I think. Never went away."

Maijstral nodded to the sound of violas. His eyes were dreamy. "The D Minor. I always liked those first four bars."

"Me, too, boss." Gregor looked at Maijstral, disquiet humming in his mind. He knew he'd been diverted from his question about the reliquary's ultimate fate—and expertly diverted, too—but his admiration for Maijstral's style had not obscured his disquiet. He had no objection to looking after profit, but neither did he enjoy the idea of the Imperium coming back.

All this, he concluded, was going to take some thinking about.

* * *

Woolvinn Leases had a small office in the center of Peleng City. Beside the door was a copper plate that was probably polished daily. The door was opaque from the outside but transparent from the inside, so that the functionary therein could observe the customer on his approach and decide on the proper attitude. Roman stepped through the door and gazed at the functionary through rose-colored spectacles. "Mr. Woolvinn, please."

"Mr. Woolvinn has been deceased for eighty years," the functionary reported. He was a Tanquer and looked up at Roman through slitted, supercilious nictitating membranes. "I will show you to Mr. Clive. Who may I tell him is calling?"

"My name is Castor. I am personal assistant to Lord Graves." Roman handed the Tanquer a card. The real Graves was a distant relation of Maijstral's who lived in the Imperium, a spare and miserly young gentleman who would have been mortally offended by the uses to which Roman put his name, but too parsimonious to send a message complaining about it.

"Sir." The Tanquer bowed, his striped tail swishing, and led Roman to an office paneled in light, varnished wood. "Please wait here, sir." The functionary indicated a chair, then a bar set into the wall. "May I offer you coffee, tea, rink, kif infusion? Wine, perhaps?"

"A kif infusion. Thank you."

Roman sipped his drink and felt a warm and secret joy. In addition to his ornamental spectacles he wore a soft grey jacket with a dark braided collar and black laces, an antique gorget of darkened Wilkinson steel, and handmade boots of brown leather. It was anything but what a servant should wear, and that was what gave Roman pleasure. He had always thought, in his heart of hearts, he would make a first-rate lord. He was secretly pleased that Woolvinn's had proven sufficiently old-fashioned not to have connected their computer files to the telephone, and that he'd have to do his reconnaissance the old-fashioned way.

Mr. Clive proved to be human, a middle-aged man of pleasant aspect and Empire-tailored coat. Roman sniffed ears and declined an offer of pastry.

"Is that a Jasper?" he asked, indicating a smooth silver-alloy construction rising gracefully in the corner. A lesser impersonator would have said "genuine Jasper."

"Indeed, yes," said Mr. Clive. "Our founder, Woolvinn the Elder, was a collector."

Roman sat, and Clive followed suit. "I congratulate Mr. Woolvinn on his tastes," Roman said. "My own taste runs more to Torfelks, but I understand that Jaspers are not easy to find nowadays. Lord Graves has a small collection to which he is always hoping to add, but alas, Jaspers are much harder to acquire these days than in the late Mr. Woolvinn's time."

"Indeed, yes," Mr. Clive murmured.

"Lord Graves wishes to make a tour of the Constellation," Roman said. "He hopes to spend a month on Peleng, beginning eighteen months from now. He wishes to have suitable accommodation."

"His lordship will doubtless want a house in town."

"In the country, methinks." The Countess Anastasia's residence had a rural address, and Maijstral had primed Roman with a description of her tastes. "A sizable place, suitable for entertaining his lordship's large acquaintance. Elegantly appointed, with an arbor for preference, perhaps a croquet court. Would this be possible?"

"Indeed, yes," Mr. Clive said, now for the third time. "We have several properties that might suit. In eighteen months, you say?"

"Indeed," said Roman. "Yes."

Roman viewed holographic representations of a number of residences, any of which might suit the given description. He knew that, in view of the amount of money they charged for a monthly rental, Woolvinn Ltd. would damn well *install* a croquet court if necessary. He looked at the address of each hologram, and when the fifth residence appeared, he leaned back and tilted his muzzle up to look through his spectacles at the neo-Georgian pile with its veined porcelain roof.

"Sink me," he said. "That's his lordship's taste, if ever I've seen it!"

Mr. Clive's ears pricked forward. A subtle light, far too tenuous to be called a gleam, crept into his eyes. "Let me show you the entry hall. Marble imported from Couscous."

Roman purred his joy over the Couscous marble, the furnishings, the exquisite taste and the care with which the house was assembled. Since Lord Graves traveled surrounded by numerous objets d'art, Roman inquired about security, and received a careful briefing concerning the mansion's protective systems. He asked for a copy of the company's hologram so that he could sent it to Lord Graves and his lordship could view the furnishings and appointments himself. This was happily provided. He asked if he could see the place. Mr. Clive said that the house was currently occupied by the Countess Anastasia and her suite, but that she had only rented the place for a month, and that he would call to see if a visit would be convenient for her. If he could have the number of Mr. Castor's telephone . . . ?

Roman gave him the number of the cottage where Maijstral was hiding and rose to give his conge. Mr. Clive showed him to the door and sniffed his ears.

Roman noticed that the functionary had completely unslitted his eyes (a compliment he assumed), and he gave the Tanquer a nod as he left. As he walked down the blue brick sidewalk, his private joy rekindled. For the brief moments of the two-hundred-yard walk between Woolvinn's and his flier, he abandoned himself entirely to the concept of Mr. Castor, associate of an Imperial lord, confidante of the aristocracy, dancing an elegant and graceful ballet amid the highest circles of Empire. . . .

Amazing, come to think of it, what a braided coat and a pair of rose-colored spectacles can do for a person. Here was Roman, the controlled and very muscular associate of a known thief, strolling down the street awarding benign and gracious nods to those he passed, a living embodiment of noblesse oblige and a glorious example of what a Khosalikh can be, given the removal of a few minor inhibitions. His secret joy seemed to communicate to those he met, and they went on their way with their hearts lightened, a spring growing in their step, smelling the fresher-seeming air, all pleased that the tall, dark Khosali lord seemed so happy merely to encounter them on the street. It was a small miracle, this two-hundred-yard stretch of shared bliss, but a miracle nonetheless.

Roman, still glowing with the inner conviction of being Mr. Castor, climbed graciously into his flier and took his miraculous way into the sky.

The Countess Anastasia heard Maijstral's household robot answer the telephone and dropped her phone into its cradle. Maijstral hadn't answered all day. He was probably in Nichole's suite, spending himself in some appalling sensual indulgence, when instead he could be here fighting for the Empire as his father and grandfather had done. . . .

It made the Countess want to spit.

"Maijstral is probably hiding out until the statue of limitations passes," said Baron Sinn. "We'll be able to get in touch with him tomorrow morning."

The Countess was still white about the nose. "This is frustrating.

I want the Imperial Artifact, and I want that Jensen creature out of my *house.*"

"There is no need to fear. There is no way she can know where she is being kept. She has not seen either of us."

The Countess frowned. "That isn't what I was worried about. Maijstral is . . . he's a lazy man. But he is not without his pride."

Sinn's ears turned thoughtfully downward. "You mean he may turn awkward."

"That is my fear. And he is very effective at what he actually puts his mind to. Perhaps we ought to increase the number of guards around the place." She put her hand on his arm, stroking the dense velvet. "There are two men I know. We've used them as security for Imperialist meetings, in case people try to disrupt us."

Sinn was thoughtful. "The fewer people who know, the better it will be for us."

"Oh, I wouldn't mention the real reason why they were here. Just that I had reason to suspect some trouble. We could give them rooms downstairs, that way they'd be within call but out of our way."

The Baron's diaphragm throbbed. "Very well, Countess," he said. "Make your call."

Smiling, Countess Anastasia reached again for the phone. She felt unaccountably buoyed. Even though the presence of the two men would probably not make any difference, it was still a comfort to be *doing* something.

"Perhaps later," she said, "you would join me for some croquet."

"Happily, my lady."

As she told the telephone whose number to call, the Countess pictured in her mind the smooth yellow sward, the click of mallets and balls, the brisk, fresh air. Baron Sinn searching for his ball amid a pile of kibble fruit. Lovely, lovely. And while she enjoyed herself, the plan would be moving forward. That was all she asked.

"I'm going to think for a while." Maijstral had just assembled his late luncheon, a pair of sandwiches on a tray. "Please don't disturb me unless you're positive it's very important."

Maijstral was good enough at being an aristocrat that neither Gregor nor Pietro Quijano thought to ask what he intended to think about, or how long it was going to take. Only Roman knew Maijstral well enough to detect a slight falsehood in his bearing, and Roman was off on an errand at Woolvinn Leases, Ltd.

The truth was that Maijstral had nothing better to do until Roman returned from his errand, and he didn't want to hang around gazing at the reliquary while Quijano continued his fretting. Maijstral, who actually planned to finish watching his Western while he ate his sandwiches, and afterward take a nap, knew that maintaining a certain level of mystery was an important factor in sustaining his position as leader, and that the admission of how he intended to spend the rest of the afternoon would not serve to enhance his mystique.

Maijstral sat cross-legged on his bed, while the Western played out to its cathartic end, Jesse and Priscilla dead, Bat wounded, the King alone . . . a lump rose in Maijstral's throat at the last lonely guitar chords from the man walking companionless into the bloody sunset. The tragedy was awesome and gorgeous, and Maijstral felt better instantly. He stifled his longing for a third sandwich—he would have longed for something different, but the kitchen was Roman's province and Maijstral didn't know how to fix anything else—and then Maijstral stretched out on his bed and tried to sleep.

Withal, this was perhaps an odd reaction for a man whose honor had just been mortally insulted. He should, perhaps, have been stamping and fuming and plotting bloody-handed deeds of revenge. No doubt that's what Robert the Butcher would have done. But Maijstral was more careless in these matters—in fact, he had no intention whatever of challenging Baron Sinn or anyone else, or indeed of risking his skin more than it had been risked already. He had just said that to impress Quijano, and because Roman expected it to be said. He knew how to play a part as well as anyone.

He knew that he was terribly deficient in his moral sense, but this knowledge seemed not to bother him. No doubt he was deficient in conscience as well.

Conscienceless, his nerves soothed by sandwiches and safe video tragedy, he slept well.

Roman changed into proper modest clothing before waking Maijstral, and bade a regretful farewell to Mr. Castor as he hung the braided jacket in his closet. Maijstral, used to being awakened at odd hours, snapped fully awake as soon as Roman scratched softly at the door.

Roman knew, as soon as he saw Maijstral stretched on the bed, that he had been secretly enjoying low entertainments again. Stifling a spasm of resignation, he reported his findings to Maijstral and watched as Maijstral ran through the hologram of Anastasia's residence. Maijstral ran through it twice, nervously twisting the diamond on his finger, then looked up.

"We shall have to make a plan," he said. "Do you think Mr. Quijano can handle a pistol?"

EIGHT

Paavo Kuusinen drowsed most of the afternoon away, stretched out full length beneath a yellow-leaved cricket tree. He was on a knoll about half a mile from Countess Anastasia's residence; by cracking open one eye he could look down across the back of the manse and the rear portico with its double row of pillars that overlooked the smooth expanse of the croquet court, a court surrounded by a grove of low, red-fruited kibble trees. Through the longfinders he carried, Kuusinen could see the back windows and occasional dim figures, usually robots, moving behind them. (From his comfortable position he couldn't see the boarded-up front window behind which Amalia Jensen languished in her well-fed exile, but then he was new at this sort of thing.) His flier was parked out of sight on the reverse slope of his knoll.

There hadn't been much to see since morning; only the Countess playing croquet with Baron Sinn. By putting his longfinders on maximum amplification, Kuusinen could see they both carried pistols as well as mallets. He watched long enough to note that the Countess was a furious and competitive player. She had given the Baron a ball of a peculiar shade of red, and when, with cracks that reverberated all the way to Kuusinen's knoll, she whacked Sinn's ball off beneath the kibble groves, Sinn was compelled to sort his ball out from fallen kibble fruit of an identical size and shade. Kuusinen concluded the color of the ball could not be anything other than deliberate psychological warfare on the part of the Countess. It worked. She won both games.

At siesta the games ended. Kuusinen drowsed. On waking he yawned, stretched, and searched the windows again with his longfinders. Nothing of interest. He went to the picnic basket he'd had a restaurant deliver, ate a cold salmon salad, and drank a bottle of rink. Perhaps, he thought, he should call Maijstral and tell him anonymously where Amalia Jensen was being held prisoner. He decided to wait until the morning before calling.

Stars appeared. A cool wind began to gust through the cricket tree. Kuusinen shivered and put on a cloak. In a moment, when the breeze fell silent, he heard the delicate whisper of a flier somewhere in the night sky. He trained his longfinders upward and saw the unmistakable silhouette of a Gustafson SC-700 moving against the Milky Way. He smiled. Maijstral's flier was a Gustafson.

The flier settled over a mile away, onto the far side of a tree-crowned ridge with a view of the front of the building. Kuusinen couldn't see them from his position; that didn't bother him. He got some system-assists from his flier and dry-swallowed them, intending to keep alert. Something was going to happen, and he was sure that when Maijstral made his move, he could get a view of it somehow.

Another flier whistled overhead, skimming Kuusinen's knoll. Kuusinen looked up and waved. Another Gustafson SC, close enough so that Kuusinen could see two people in it. It circled and landed by the first. In a few minutes, both fliers rose and sped off over the horizon.

Kuusinen frowned. Maijstral's behavior—if this *was* Maijstral—seemed odd. But then he realized that the fliers had probably been sent somewhere on autopilot, just in case anyone had seen them land.

Paavo Kuusinen smiled as the first wave of system-assists began to dance along his nerves. This was going to be fun.

"Hey. Do you know what you get when you cross a range-drover with a dithermoon? A baby who vetches in purple."

Amalia Jensen convulsed with laughter. She raised her bound ankles and kicked her legs as she cackled. Tvi grinned. It hadn't been a half-bad idea to leave Amalia efficiently tied up after siesta and slip downstairs for a bottle of wine. In order to avoid detection, she'd had to sneak down the circular stairs in the round library on the east side, but this was no problem for a practiced thief. She snuggled deeper into her overstuffed chair.

"My grandfather worked as a dithermoon for a season," Amalia said. "He had all sorts of stories. That was before the Rebellion. He commanded a cruiser at Khorn, but didn't meet Admiral Scholder till after the war." She sighed. "My father was in the Navy, too. I lived at sixteen bases before I was twelve. That's when my father died in the *Hotspur* accident and my mother came here. We lived with my grandfather till he died."

"My childhood was similar," Tvi said. "But my parents were both civil service." She supposed she wasn't giving too much away by that admission—Imperial civil servants numbered in the hundreds of millions.

"Most of the places were all right. The border's fairly close to Earth, so most of the bases were near or on planets that had been inhabited for a long time. It wasn't as if my dad was a member of the Pioneer Corps or anything."

"But it was still military. I can imagine."

"It was, well, disciplined. But that was all right. The part I didn't like was my father going away all the time."

"But you didn't join the Navy yourself."

Amalia Jensen shrugged. Her face was drained of expression. "I have got a mild form of epilepsy. It's controllable with medication, but it still disqualified me. It's not curable without great expense, and the Navy would prefer to spend the money training someone else."

"Sorry." Tvi wondered what epilepsy was. Something peculiar to humans, apparently.

"I could have got into Planetary Services. But for me it was the Navy or nothing." Tvi's stomachs rumbled. She looked at her watch and saw that Khotvinn would be bringing supper fairly soon. Better finish the bottle. "More wine?" she asked.

"Thank you. So I got into politics instead. It seemed the best way to serve. Outside the military, anyway." Tvi brought Amalia's wrists and ankles together, poured wine, stepped back across the room, and then sat in her chair again, all while Amalia went on talking.

"Your father would approve, you think?" Tvi asked.

"I think he would," Amalia said. "He and my grandfather were always strong prohumans."

Tvi lapped at her wine meditatively. "Mine doesn't approve of me at all," she said. "We were in constant combat when I was growing up. But I wonder. If my father had died when I was twelve, would I be in Imperial uniform, trying to be the best timeserver on fifty planets?"

Amalia Jensen seemed lost in thought. There was a knock on the door that made them jump, and then Khotvinn's voice.

"Relieving you."

Tvi lapped up the rest of her wine in a hurry, then hid the glass in a drawer. The little left in the bottle she poured into Amalia's cup.

"See you later," she said.

"Au revoir, Mr. Romper." With a drunken giggle.

Tvi was surprised to see a long sword strapped to Khotvinn's waist and a strange defiant gleam in his eye. Tvi wondered what notion had crossed the troglodyte's brain this time, then decided he'd probably spent the afternoon being fired up by a recording of *Ten Greatest Militarist Speeches* or something equally exciting. "The prisoner's in good spirits," she reported.

Khotvinn grunted. "What was the name of that person who was visiting her last night?"

Tvi was surprised by this evidence of interest. "Him? Lieutenant Navarre, I think."

"Hm. Good." Tvi could almost watch the slow tumblers of Khotvinn's mind clicking over. The fur on her shoulders rose slightly —the cave-dweller was perfectly eerie, with his sword and intent expression—then she consciously smoothed her fur and handed over the Ronnie Romper hologram. She was, on reflection, almost glad she didn't know what Khotvinn was thinking. It showed, she thought, that her ancestors, unlike his, had probably advanced somewhat in the last million or so years.

Tvi moved down the servants' stair, careful not to sway too drunkenly. Odd, she thought, that the captive was the only person in this place she could talk to. Amalia Jensen might be something of a political crank, but her opinions weren't vicious and at least she seemed a more balanced sort than the other cranks around here.

"There's some geezer on a knoll off to the northeast," Gregor said. He was in his darksuit, soft, loose crepe covering everything except the pale oval of his face, but hadn't yet turned on the camouflage holograms. "He's got a flier parked out of sight. He waved at us as we flew overhead. No effort made to conceal himself. There was nothing to hide behind but a tree that isn't even as thick around as he is."

"Do you think he's a lookout?" asked Pietro. He was wearing a spare darksuit, and weapons hung from his belt. He had proved a quick study at their use, but Maijstral and his assistants hadn't any idea of how he'd act when the real thing came, and decided to equip him only with nonlethal weapons against which their own darksuits had built-in protection.

"A lookout?" Maijstral asked. His voice came eerily from the cloudy blackness of a hologram. "Possibly, although I'd think it more likely he's police, or one of Miss Jensen's political contacts."

Pietro shook his head briefly. "No. Not one of us."

Maijstral went on. "He can't see half the approaches to the house from where he is—if he *is* a lookout he'd do better on the roof—but we may not be dealing with professionals here." He had just come down from a short flight above the trees, searching the front view of the house with longfinders. "There's a window boarded up on the second floor, near the southeast corner. Fairly obvious, but then the Countess was never subtle."

Gregor had a hologram projector in his hand. He touched a button and suddenly, glowing in the dark night air, the white expanse of the house appeared. Maijstral turned off his darksuit and pointed with a soft-gloved hand. "There."

Gregor altered the perspective of the hologram, moving through the second floor of the building.

The front of the building was shaped like a broad, shallow U, a covered veranda held within the U's gentle arms. On the southeast corner, second floor, was a drawing room that occupied the arm of the U on that story. Just to the north of the drawing room was a circular library, two stories in height, with an ornate, wrought-iron spiral stair and a large crystal chandelier. The western-facing windows of the drawing room looked out over the roof of the veranda, and in the drawing room's northwest corner was a door that led into the upper front hall. Moving down the hall, one door to the west, was the room with the boarded-up window.

Maijstral found the situation testing his temper.

"There's just too much access to the second floor," he muttered. "Look here. Inside the house, within a few paces of Miss Jensen's door, there's a servants' stairway, and just around the corner from that is the grand stairway to the ground floor. We've got the spiral staircase coming up the round library on the east side, and that stair has access to the southeast drawing room, and from the drawing room it's two paces to where they're keeping Miss Jensen. There are two stairs from the front porch to the balcony on the front portico, and they lead to Miss Jensen's window. And then elsewhere there are —let's see—four other stairways and two elevators."

"That gives us more ways out," Gregor offered.

"It also means that we can run into trouble on any route," Maijstral said. "We're going to have to assume that Miss Jensen is guarded, and we may not be able to deal with the guard in silence. Therefore we must plan against an alarm being given."

"A diversion, sir," suggested Pietro. "Some of us could try charging in the back way. . . ."

Maijstral turned his ears down in disapproval, and Pietro fell silent. "I think not," he said. "Splitting our forces invites chaos, and the diversion would accomplish little if they ignored you and instead concentrated on defending Miss Jensen." He frowned, twisting the ring on his finger. "What we need to do is seal off Miss Jensen's room for the time it takes to break her free. All we have to do is get an a-grav harness around her and a proximity wire around her neck. Then even if she's tied up, she can manage her own escape while we cover her withdrawal."

He gave his ring a final twist, as if in decision. "Very well. Roman, you and Mr. Quijano enter through the second story drawing room on the southeast corner. Roman, you will move to the hall door and stand by ready to deal with any guards in the corridor. Mr. Quijano, your particular job will be to block the door to the library staircase. Don't just lock it, put a piece of furniture in front of it, as heavy as you can carry. And then help Roman if he needs it. Gregor, you'll go in the unblocked window next to Miss Jensen's. Any guards in the corridor will be caught between you and Roman."

"And you, boss?"

"I will fly first to Miss Jensen's window. I want to make certain she's actually being held there before any of the rest of us make a move."

Pietro Quijano gave Maijstral an admiring look. The others accepted his plan without a word. Maijstral had his own reasons for wanting to go first, and wanting to be on the second floor balcony where there were no guards and a clear field for escape, and his reasons had nothing to do with a hope that Pietro might admire his bravery.

"We'll approach from the southeast to avoid detection from that fellow on the knoll, whatever he's doing there. Keep in cover till I give the signal—"

"Deus vult, sir?" offered Roman.

Maijstral smiled. Roman was ever prepared to trace Maijstral's ancestors far beyond the point that Maijstral found creditable. Jean Parisot de La Valette was, in any case, supposed to be a celibate, and furthermore would almost certainly not approve of his alleged descendant.

"Deus vult. Very well. Thank you, Roman."

Maijstral asked each of his companions to repeat his instructions aloud, making certain he knew what he was supposed to do, and then led them on a brisk hike along the bottom of the ridge, staying out of sight of the mansion, and then through the first tripwire alarm, the hemispheric cold-field that surrounded the building like an invisible bubble. Roman, controlling Pietro Quijano's darksuit through a proximity wire, showed the young man how to slip through the net.

A brightly lit flier appeared over the western horizon. Maijstral froze, snapping on his darksuit, his heart hammering in a perfectly absurd way. He was glad no one could see the way his hands had begun to tremble. Roman's darksuit was also turned on, but apparently he had raised his longfinders. "Dewayne Seven," he said.

An old model, not very fast. Visitors? Maijstral wondered. The flier circled, then landed out back. Not visitors, Maijstral concluded, if they were using the servants' entrance. Plumbers, cooks, maybe people installing new security gadgets. If the latter, it was time to move quickly.

"This may work to our advantage," he said. "They will be less likely to do violence if there are outsiders in the house."

Pietro Quijano looked dubious. He was still struggling with his darksuit, trying to get the night holograms on. Maijstral reached across the gap between them and pressed a stud on his belt.

"Thank you," Pietro said.

Maijstral did not reply. He was already flying toward the mansion, followed by one of his media globes, both of them keeping close to the ground.

Old General Gerald, breathing hard from the exertion of putting on his battle armor, crouched once again in the corner of his living room. During siesta his monitors had shown several overflights of his house, any one of which could have been Maijstral scouting his place in a flier. He couldn't be certain, of course, but he had what amounted to a moral certainty that Maijstral would come tonight.

He grinned a tight-lipped grin as he tracked over the data readouts from the various rooms of his house. He could track individual dust motes as they swirled above his bookshelves. Maijstral wouldn't have a chance.

This was going to be great.

Maijstral drifted across the thick, manicured lawn. The manse ahead of him blazed with floodlights; the planks that scarred the single upper window were an eyesore, an obvious sign of something out of place. Maijstral's sensors reached out, found and dissected the building's defenses. He reversed himself, oozed feet first through a network of flaxes, then reached the generator and silently disabled it. His surrounding hologramatic image—his darksuit was more advanced than Tvi's—began to take on the lighter tones of the spotlighted walls themselves.

He rose effortlessly to the second floor and neutralized a rank of leapers that Gregor's miniature beacons had pinpointed for him. He drifted to the window, carefully not touching the balcony with his feet, and peered between the cracks of the rough planks that had been nailed over the window. He could see nothing through the curtain beyond. Maijstral deployed his cutter and sliced a neat circle in one of the planks, then another circle in the window behind. He popped a micro media-globe through the hole, then guided it so that it peeked delicately beneath the lacy hem of the curtains. The globe's view was fed into Maijstral's brain.

Amalia Jensen lay on the curtained bed, eating supper from a tray. There was no one else in the room.

Relief eased through Maijstral's heart. This might be simple after all.

The matte-black media rolled along the bottom of the curtain, skated along the dark paneling of the room, slid up one of the bedposts, then finally drifted to a point within an inch or so of Amalia Jensen's left ear. Maijstral could see bruises on her cheek and felt a flash of anger. He spoke, subvocalizing into his throat mike, the globe whispering for him.

"Don't jump, Miss Jensen. This is Drake Maijstral."

She jumped anyway, but at least avoided tipping the tray. As her head spun toward the globe, Maijstral received a swift, distorted impression of wide eyes, parted lips, a swirling pattern of bruises, pores like meteor strikes.

"Please whisper, Miss Jensen. Are you being monitored in any way?"

The projection of her moving lips in Maijstral's mind made them seem as large as Fassbinder Gorge on Newton. "No," she said.

"There's a guard outside, and they warned me not to touch the window because there are alarms on it."

Maijstral reduced the scale of the unflattering close-up view and considered a moment. "I have fulfilled my half of the commission. I would like to discuss payment."

Her answering tone was puzzled. "But you came to get me out, didn't you? Once I'm free, we can complete the transfer."

"Miss Jensen, I merely came to make arrangements for the delivery of the artifact and the collection of my payment."

There was growing anger in Amalia's voice. "How can you expect me to pay you, Mr. Maijstral? I'm being held prisoner."

"Please lower your voice, Miss Jensen." Maijstral smiled behind his holographic screen. "I simply wished to confirm that your estimation of the situation is the same as mine."

"Of *course* it is! All you have to do is get me out of here, and then I'll pay you."

"I was about to mention, Miss Jensen, that I am not normally in the business of rescuing kidnapped persons."

"You could call the police."

"I'm afraid they would then discover that you had hired me to steal an invaluable object. I shouldn't like to get you in trouble, Miss Jensen. And in any case, I make a point of never dealing with the police."

There was a long silence. Maijstral turned his attention back to the image from his media globe; Amalia was scowling at it. Then, "What do you propose, Mr. Maijstral?"

"I suggest that we agree to cancel our earlier agreement, and reach a new one. For your liberty, I suggest a payment of sixty. After your safe delivery to your friends, we may negotiate for the sale of the Imperial Artifact."

"You aren't giving me much choice."

"On the contrary, the choice is entirely yours. You may accept my offer, or you may arrange for your own deliverance, or you may stay here until such time as your commission expires and I become a free agent."

"Where will I get the money?"

"You know your own finances best. But you are a member of a star-spanning political organization of considerable wealth, and whose interests might well be engaged. I suggest that you contact them."

"You're taking advantage."

Maijstral's answer was immediate. "Madam, you mistake me.

My nature and interest is but to perceive the situation and act upon it. I do not attempt the concealment of facts, for example the value that might attach to the contents of a silver object, or the drastic action some might take to acquire it."

Her decision, when it came, was quick, and there was steel in her voice. Maijstral suppressed a momentary surge of admiration.

"Done, then. Sixty to get me loose."

"And our earlier contract voided."

"Yes."

"Your obedient servant, ma'am. Please put the tray aside and be ready to move."

Maijstral made certain that the media globe had recorded the bargain, then shifted to his communications channel and whispered, "Deus vult."

Behind him, on the bare edge of his darksuit's perceptions, the rest of the party, clothed in night, began moving purposefully across the lawn. Things hadn't gone badly at all.

The Countess lit her cigarette by tapping it twice on the rear portico pillar and looked at her two henchmen, Chang and Bix. Both were brawny and well-muscled, each carrying a small suitcase and a larger satchel containing their gear. Both had removed their hats in her presence and, because their hands were carrying satchels, the hats ended up crushed in their armpits. "The robots haven't finished making up your rooms," she said. She spoke Khosali. "Let me show you to the library. You can wait there."

"Yes, my lady." Chang was the more vocal of the two, though neither were precisely fluent in any known language. "We're happy we could be of use."

"This way." She led them past the back study and the small ballroom, then through the billiard room to the library. Leather volumes gleamed in subdued light. She pivoted and gestured with the cigaret. Neuralgia crackled in her shoulders.

"Please feel free to go anywhere on the lower floors," she said. "You may order anything you like, and the house will bring it. On the upper floor there is a Very Important Guest"—she tried to inflect the capitals, and saw how their eyes flickered to the upper landing—"and it is urgent that our guest not be disturbed. If anything disturbing should occur, I'm confident you will know how to respond."

"Yes, my lady." Chang bowed stiffly, and Bix, after a pause, followed suit.

"I'll have the robot escort you to your room as soon as it's done readying it."

As the Countess left the room, neuralgia walked with needle toes along her arms and shoulders. She repressed an urge to stretch, move her arms. An Imperial aristocrat kept her shoulders back at all times.

She'd just have to schedule an extra session with her robot masseuse. The robot lacked the touch of her human one, but all the live servants had been shuttled to Peleng City as soon as she'd decided to go in for kidnapping.

Never mind. Service demanded the occasional sacrifice. This would, she concluded righteously, do her good in the end.

Baron Sinn wasn't certain he wanted to be recognized by the Countess's goons, so when their flier landed in the back he decided to take a stroll on the front porch. He stood silently by one of the Corinthian columns and pitched his cigaret onto the lawn. A robot would clean it up tomorrow.

A gust of wind ruffled his lace. He would have to shower tonight to get the smell of tobacco out of his fur. Another little price of diplomacy.

A few feet above Baron Sinn, Maijstral's beam cutter quietly sliced the planks blocking Amalia Jensen's window, then sliced the window itself. Planks and sheets of glass rose into the air above his head, held by a-grav. Gregor, nearly invisible in his chameleon darksuit, floated behind him and began moving the alarms on the next window.

Maijstral detected an alien scent, then froze. It was tobacco. Was someone smoking just under him? His nerves giving odd little leaps, Maijstral turned up his audio reception and, amid the amplified buzz of insects, distinctly heard Sinn's movements below. Maijstral gnawed his lip. He realized that all the person had to do was step off the porch and look up in order to notice the planks had been sliced from the window.

"Gregor," he said, subvocalizing, "there's someone just under us." The answer came back without pause.

"Khosali geezer. Gun under his jacket. Smokes Silvertips."

Maijstral blinked. Gregor quickly cut his window away and floated into the house.

Good idea, Maijstral decided. He drifted through the curtains.

Amalia Jensen looked at him coldly. "My hero," she said.

* * *

"Quite a place," said Bix.

"Only too, partner." Chang went to the wall service plate and touched the ideograph for "kitchen." "Send beer," he said.

"I've never seen so many books."

"My brother has a few."

Bix dropped his suitcase and satchel, then began moving up the stair, looking at titles as he went. *"Geographic Survey of Rose Territory, Peleng.* Twelve volumes. Who'd want to read that?"

"Phyllis Bertram's from Rose Territory."

"No, she's not. She's from Falkland."

"That's *in* Rose Territory."

"That's not true."

"Is so."

The pair's routine, developed over years of close association, was well-honed.

"Counter-Intuitive Approaches to Condensation Psychology. Complete Works of Bulwer-Lytton. Where did they *get* this stuff?"

Good question. Except for a few showpiece volumes, the books had been picked up as discards from local libraries, then bound in such a way as to look rare and valuable. Woolvinn Leases, Ltd. had a solid appreciation of the way books vanish into the pockets or luggage of tenants and subsequently migrate to places unknown, and so made certain that most of the books in their exquisitely appointed library were of incomparable dullness, the better to discourage theft.

"Who's Bulwer-Lytton?" Chang asked.

"No idea, partner."

Bix had advanced to the landing on the second floor. "There's more stuff here," he said. "Old videos. *King Lear."* He looked at Chang. "Who was that?"

"Tsanvinn Dynasty. He was the grandfather of the emperor that conquered Earth."

"That far back." He reached for the door to the southeast drawing room. "Wonder what's in here?" he asked.

"Don't. We're not supposed to . . ."

Pietro Quijano followed Roman's lead up the side of the house to the darkened windows of the southeast drawing room. He was beginning to get the hang of the darksuit, and flipped back and forth from his night image-intensifiers to infrared perception, enjoying, for its own sake, the contrast in viewpoints.

Roman worked deftly and quickly, and within a few seconds had a window cleared of alarms and sliced open. Pietro watched as the disconnected pane of glass floated gently skyward, then hung in midair, unaffected by the slight breeze. Then, with a start, he realized Roman had entered the building, and that he should follow.

Pietro's image-intensified view of the drawing room was devoid of texture—everything looked bright and without perspective. He dropped to the floor, soft carpeting absorbing his weight without a sound. Light was entering under both the door that led into the corridor and the other door that led to the circular library. He could hear voices from somewhere, but wasn't certain of their origin.

Roman was still floating, hovering by the door to the corridor. Quijano recollected he was supposed to block the library door and began looking for heavy furniture. There were two long couches, several chairs, a desk. He moved toward the desk and began to drag it over the deep pile carpet, tugging it toward the door. Roman's subvocal came in his ear.

"Don't. They might hear." Pietro froze in front of the library door.

"Wonder what's in here?" a voice said, from right on the other side of the door. Pietro turned toward the door, wondering what in heaven's name he could do. His heart boomed louder than the sound of the voice. This wasn't in the plan. He reached out with the idea of physically holding the door shut.

The door opened.

Bix's face gazed toward him in amiable curiosity. Pietro reacted instantly. He completely forgot the weapons at his belt, forgot that his darksuit made him difficult to see. He simply lashed out with a fist, his whole body behind it. The fist mashed Bix's nose and knocked him back against the landing's metal rail. Bix rebounded and Pietro lashed out again, catching him more by luck than design on the point of his jaw. Bix fell unconscious. Pietro stepped back into the drawing room and slammed the library door. He turned to Roman, who had drawn a weapon and would have used it if Pietro hadn't been in the way. Severe pain pulsed in Pietro's knuckles.

"We're in for it now," Pietro said. And then he clapped his hands over his mouth. He'd said it out loud.

Khotvinn's ears pricked at the sound of a voice. "We're in for it now." You certainly *are,* my lad, he thought; he spun, drew his sword with his left hand and his chugger with his right, and charged the door. He roared as he came.

Khotvinn the brave! Khotvinn the majestic!

He was going to carve the intruders like cheese.

* * *

Chang watched as Bix was knocked unconscious by a figure only dimly seen. He watched without surprise—Chang did not have enough imagination to possess much in the way of expectation, and therefore was never surprised when his expectations failed to come true.

The Very Important Personage, Chang decided, had a mean punch and a savage regard for his own privacy. He was *not* going to enjoy apologizing to the Countess for Bix's intrusion. Then he heard a bellow and the sound of firing, and decided something was wrong.

He went to the service plate and touched the ideograph for "General announcement."

"This is Chang in the library," he said. "There's a fight going on upstairs."

Then he went for his guns.

Roman heard Pietro's voice and felt at once the onset of dismay. He knew his action would have to be fast, and so he stifled the dismay swiftly and spun to the door that led into the corridor, wrenching it open, his gun ready. He observed a seven-foot-tall, red-haired puppet, a magic wand in his hand and a happy and slightly mischievous grin fixed to his face, leaping toward him, hanging in midair with one foot outthrust.

Roman stepped aside. The puppet was balanced to encounter a door and failed to hit one, and so flailed and came to a crash landing inside the drawing room. Pietro stared at the apparition. Roman fired his stunner and saw a coruscating energy pattern spatter bright colors across both the puppet and Pietro. Roman had known Pietro's screens could deal with the attack, but apparently the puppet's could as well. Hell. Roman slammed the door behind him and looked for something to hit the puppet with.

The puppet leaped to his feet, striking blindly in the unlighted room, unable to see his opponents in their darksuits. His grin was blinding. "Prepare to die, human scum!" he roared. He fired his own gun randomly. Explosive bullets blew furniture apart.

"Ronnie *Romper?*" said Pietro.

Maijstral got the a-grav harness around Amalia Jensen and put the proximity wire around her neck, and then his heart gave a lurch at the sound of Khotvinn's howl and the subsequent battle. "This way," he said, and arrowed straight for the window.

Standing on the porch outside, Baron Sinn glanced up in surprise at the ruckus, then drew his gun and sprinted for one of the outside stairways connecting the front porch with the balcony overhead, switching on his shields as he ran. He saw the cutaway boards that surrounded Amalia Jensen's window, then saw the visual quality of the window shift as Maijstral sliced through it in his darksuit. Sinn fired, his spitfire blowing flaming chunks out of the building.

Maijstral, completely by instinct, reversed himself and flew back through the window. Once inside he cursed himself for an idiot—he could have got clean away—then drew his own spitfire and blew more pieces out of the window, just by way of suggesting Baron Sinn not enter that way.

Amalia Jensen was floating in midroom, looking startled. Clearly without adequate protection, she could not leave via the window. "Beg pardon," Maijstral said. He opened the door. "*This* way," he said.

When the fighting started, Gregor was admiring—and mentally pricing—a Basil vase sitting atop an eight-hundred-year-old hand-carved bureau of Couscous marble. He was therefore a little late in wrenching open his door and sticking his nose and gun into the corridor, arriving just in time to see the door to the southeast drawing room slam shut. There was no one in the corridor. Then Baron Sinn's spitfire began blasting bits out of the wall behind him. Gregor concluded his stunner was a little inadequate to the occasion, put it away, and drew his disruptor.

The door to Amalia Jensen's room opened. "*This* way," said Maijstral's voice. A woman unfamiliar to Gregor floated out in an a-grav harness, followed by Maijstral, who was backing out, firing behind him.

"What's happening, boss?" Gregor asked.

Maijstral nearly jumped out of his skin.

Sergeant Tvi was eating dinner alone in the servants' kitchen when Chang's voice on the house intercom alerted her to fighting on the top floor.

Tvi to the rescue! she thought brightly. Her heart lifted at a mental picture of herself in the fight, charging to the last-minute salvation of the Imperium in a swell of dramatic music.

She switched on her darksuit, drew her gun, and flew at top speed up the servants' stair.

* * *

Savage joy filled Countess Anastasia as she heard Chang's announcement. She stepped to the nearest service plate and thumbed the ideograph for "general announcement."

"Kill them!" she shrieked, and then prepared to run for the sporting rifles in her private study. Then, as an afterthought, she touched the ideograph again.

"Be firm now," she added. Firmly.

The Countess's action may serve as an interesting comment on human nature. It is sometimes odd how, in times of stress, training takes hold. The Countess could have made her announcement simply by telling the house to do it for her, but in High Custom it is simply *not done* to turn and start yelling at inanimate objects, particularly when there are other sentients present. A graceful stroll to the nearest service plate, followed by a low-voiced command, is considered apropos for all but the most dire situations.

The Countess Anastasia, even when urging her friends to battle, remained a lady. Even if she found it necessary to involve herself personally in the slaughter, one may be certain she would somehow stay above it all, and do her best to avoid getting too much blood on her gown.

Noblesse is not inborn; it is learned, and it takes a long time. But once learned, it is hard to unlearn—it's fully as good as instinct. Thus does training triumph over circumstance.

Allowed Burglary furnishes another illustration. One steals—very well. But one steals with style and grace, and people forgive you, sometimes even hold the door for you as you step into the night with swag in hand. Training in politesse can hold up under the most amazing provocations, theft among them.

All one can hope for is that thief and victim will be playing by the same rules.

Things were well and truly afire in Amalia Jensen's former room. The closet door opened and a simpleton robot, whose usual job was to make certain clothing was hanging properly, extruded a long mechanical arm and began spraying fire retardant.

"Ronnie *Romper?*" Pietro asked, then clapped his hands over his mouth again as the giant red-haired pixie spun toward the sound of his voice and raised his magic wand. Pietro concluded the wand wasn't about to transport him to the Magic Planet of Adventure, where kindly Auntie June and crusty-but-softhearted Uncle Amos would offer him sage advice between bouts with prehistoric beasts or renegade aliens, but instead would probably cut him in half. He gave a yelp and dove at top speed behind the couch. The sword whistled as it sliced cushions.

Roman, standing behind Khotvinn, raised a metal chair and smashed it precisely into the side of Ronnie Romper's head. Ronnie yowled and spun, the magic wand scattering fairy dust in a glittering arc. A woman's voice on the household intercom promised death and firmness. Ronnie swung again, and Roman raised the chair to intercept. The sword cut halfway through the chair, then stuck, quivering. Roman gave the chair a wrench, tore the sword from Ronnie Romper's hand, and flung it into a corner.

"Flower lover!" Ronnie Romper roared. His fixed smile never moved.

Roman realized that Ronnie Romper was the one who had uprooted Amalia Jensen's flowers. Rage filled him.

"Barbarian," he said, and gave Ronnie Romper a solid punch in the nose. Ronnie swung wildly in retaliation, not coming close. Roman punched again, connected, kicked Ronnie in the midsection, then spun and kicked Ronnie square on the forehead. Khotvinn collapsed, stunned.

"Lout. That'll teach *you,*" said Roman firmly, and he dusted his hands and reached for the hallway door. (Politesse, politesse. Here's training again.) On opening the door, Roman saw Gregor, Maijstral, and Amalia Jensen in the hall.

"This way, sirs and madam," he said, and bowed with a flourish.

Tvi reached the top of the servants' stair. Through her sensory enhancements and the triumphant mental music she was playing as accompaniment to the video in her mind, she heard a strange Khosali voice, "This way, sirs and madam," and then the sound of people moving. There seemed to be a lot of them. She recollected suddenly that she had only a stunner and that real thieves disdain violence. She also realized that if she moved out of the door she would be unable to avoid any unfortunate consequences, just as she had when she had been halfway through Jensen's window.

She decided to wait awhile.

Baron Sinn realized his spitfire was running low on energy, that he had no reloads on him, and that he'd have to do something fast. He commended his soul to the Emperor and to the Sixteen Active and Twelve Passive Virtues, then sprinted forward and dove headfirst through the torn window into Amalia Jensen's room, hitting the floor and rolling, his gun ready.

The room was lit by flame, clouded by smoke. His eyes smarted. Vaguely, he saw a hand and a gun protruding from the closet, and with three wild shots of his spitfire he blew into fragments the simpleton robot that had been trying to put out the fire.

"Thagger," he said, realizing his error. And began to wheeze. The room was filling with smoke.

Pietro rose from his hiding place behind the cushions. Amalia Jensen was floating through the door after Maijstral. "Miss Jensen!" he said, delighted. He stepped out from his hiding place, tripped over Khotvinn's sword, which was still jammed halfway through an overturned chair, and crashed to the floor.

Amalia Jensen, hearing the crash, glanced in his direction. "Oh. Hullo, Pietro," she said.

Chang listened to the crashing and thumping from upstairs as he struggled into his shield belt and reached for his disruptor rifle. He looked up, frowned as he contemplated Bix's unconscious body, and decided that the direct approach, up the spiral staircase, was fraught with danger. He opened the French door onto the small east porch and glanced up at the windows of the southeast parlor. One of them seemed to have a neat hole in it. This was clearly the escape route for the wicked.

He smiled. He had them trapped, bigod!

He batted ferns out of his vision as he crouched behind a metal planter, then sighted in on the window. A more imaginative individual might have actually waited for the enemy to try to leave, then picked them off as they came out, one by one. Chang, as has already been observed, possessed no imagination.

The air sizzled as he fired.

Roman picked up Khotvinn's chugger, checked it for loads, and readied it for action. "This way," said Maijstral, pointing to the open window, and just as he was about to fling himself over the sill, warning lights began to blaze on his darksuit displays, indicating invisible disruptor bolts crackling through the window. Maijstral checked, glanced around, and saw the library door. He realized he was growing tired of being the first through an exit. He pointed.

"*That* way!" he said.

* * *

Tvi took a micro media-globe from her belt and let it look around the corner for her. She had to look carefully in order to see a single person, his presence marked only by the odd shimmery distortion of his darksuit. He stood in the drawing room door, apparently the rear guard. The rest had filed into the drawing room.

Tvi considered this. Dramatic music began welling in her mind. Tvi the Silent, Tvi the Thief, would creep up on this bunch from behind and bat them one by one! If she played this right, they wouldn't even know she was behind them.

Roman charged through the library door, saw motion below him, and, with three well-placed shots of Khotvinn's chugger, utterly demolished the robot that, per Chang's earlier request, had just arrived with a large selection of beer. Foam flooded the carpet. Roman felt a pang of regret.

"This way," he said, and flung himself over the railing, gliding to the first floor on a-grav. Maijstral, Amalia Jensen, and Pietro followed.

Tvi crouched, readied herself, then flung herself at top speed toward the shimmering figure in the door. Gregor's first bolt went wild and there wasn't time for a second. Tvi crashed into Gregor, driving him into the doorframe. The breath went out of him and he sagged to the ground. Tvi, seeing stars herself, groped for Gregor inside the darksuit screen, located his neck, reasoned there was a head above it somewhere, and lashed out with the butt of her stunner. The weapon connected and Gregor flopped to the floor.

Tvi grinned invisibly behind her holographic shroud. Things were looking up for the Fate of the Empire.

Khotvinn groped his way toward consciousness through a blaze of stars. A dozen puny humans hiding behind their darksuit screens must have set about him with clubs. But Khotvinn wasn't finished yet —he was sure he must have chopped five or six at least, and the rest couldn't have much fight in them. He climbed to his feet, groped for his sword, then dragged it out of the metal chair. He felt better immediately. Where were the stinking redbellies?

There was someone in a darksuit apparently engaged in a wrestling act in the corridor, and in the clear light of the library Khotvinn could see Amalia Jensen, her ankles still bound, beginning her descent to the first floor.

Light! Once he could *see* his foe, nothing could stop him! If the traitors hadn't turned out the lights, he would never have been overcome.

Roaring, Khotvinn raised his blade and charged.

Action at last! Death to traitors!

Warbling, Countess Anastasia raced down the corridor for the library, cradling her new Nana-Coulville custom mapper with the folding para-assault stock and Trotvinn XVII sights. Her little song was simple: "Kill, kill, kill . . . firmness, firmness, firmness . . ." But it was in High Khosali, in which each word made a comment on the word before, and it was heartfelt. She was singing with all her soul. Not even the great Sebastiana would have put more feeling into a lyric.

The simple pleasures, one is constantly reminded, are oft the best.

"Say," Pietro Quijano said, remembering to subvocalize for once, "shouldn't we wait for Gregor?" He was standing on the second-floor library landing to one side of the door, watching Amalia Jensen as she dropped down the center of the room toward the splatter of smoking robot and streaming beer that stained the costly carpet. And then Pietro heard a howl to freeze his blood. Ronnie Romper, he realized, was coming to chop Miss Jensen to bits!

Pietro's mind seemed to work, in that instant, with amazing clarity. He dropped to the landing and stuck his foot into the doorway.

Roaring, Ronnie Romper charged through the doorway, tripped over the foot (roaring), made an architecturally perfect arc (roaring) as he soared over Bix's unconscious form and the wrought-iron rail, and fell twenty feet (still roaring) to the library floor.

Ronnie landed and the mansion trembled. Beer fountained as high as the crystal chandelier. Amalia Jensen, who had been missed by inches, looked up in surprise.

Feeling a bit squeamish, Pietro gazed delicately over the rail. Ronnie was sprawled in an X below him, his never-altered grin beaming mischievously upward. Pietro felt his stomach turn over.

"Well. So much for *him!*" Amalia said. She looked from Pietro to Ronnie and back. "Thank you, Pietro," she said.

"You're welcome, Miss Jensen." In that bleak instant Pietro realized, sick at heart, that he would visit the Magic Planet of Adventure nevermore.

* * *

Tvi crouched in the doorway and watched in stunned amazement as the giant Ronnie Romper charged across the drawing room, a hoarse bellow issuing from behind the perpetual smile. There followed a crash, one that shook the entire house, but no shots, no sound of struggle.

It was time to do some more sneaking up, she decided.

Baron Sinn, commending his soul, etcetera, half overcome by smoke, charged into the corridor amid a gush of fire-generated camouflage. He could barely see, and he staggered as he lunged toward the southeast drawing room.

What he did see through his streaming eyes was a figure in a darksuit in the drawing room door. Obviously a miscreant. Sinn raised his spitfire and fired.

Tvi yelped as the spitfire blew away the wall just over her head. Her darksuit had given her a view of the corridor behind her, and she'd been thankful Sinn was there to back her up. Instead of offering to assist, her boss, without even a declaration of enmity, had gone and shot at her.

This, she concluded, was totally unfair. She did not think to wonder why the Baron had opened fire. The point uppermost in her mind was the doubt that her darksuit screens could handle spitfires.

Tvi flew like hell for the servants' stair. Another spitfire round blasted the wall as she ran.

Baron Sinn, gasping for breath, staggered in pursuit. Here was *one* he wasn't about to let get away.

Maijstral considered the French door onto the east terrace long enough to realize that whoever was firing disruptor bolts into the second story could as easily cover the east terrace from his position. He pointed at the door into the interior of the house.

"*That* way," he said. "Then north."

Roman flung open the door and lunged through it, colliding with the Countess Anastasia and knocking her sprawling. "Beg pardon, my lady," he said promptly, and, after relieving the Countess of her Nana-Coulville, gallantly offered to help her stand.

A deep X of anger marred Countess Anastasia's brow. "Die, redbellied wretch!" she barked, and batted Roman's hand aside.

Even well-trained politesse has its limits.

Roman stiffened. He bit back the comment that came to mind at this churlish display of unladylike behavior. "Good evening, my lady," he said in sepulchral, indignant tones, "Your obedient servant." He strode in high dudgeon toward the back of the house.

"Hey," said Pietro Quijano, "what about Gregor?"

He was still on the landing, listening to the spitfire bursts from the corridor where, so far as he knew, Gregor was standing alone against the Imperial hordes.

Maijstral did not, apparently, hear, since he was on his way into the corridor. The spitfire bursts came to an end.

"Gregor?" Pietro subvocalized, and heard a groan in reply.

He peered into the drawing room and saw Gregor's form sprawled in the doorway, a smoking spitfire hole in the wall over his head.

There seemed to be no enemies about. Pietro slipped back into the drawing room, got Gregor in a fireman's carry—easy, since Gregor on a-grav was virtually weightless—and hastened after the others.

Maijstral, on hearing Pietro's plaintive inquiries about Gregor, reflected on first thought that henchmen were, after all, expendable, and on second thought that Pietro was too. It wasn't as if they hadn't volunteered. Thus cheered, he floated near the ceiling to avoid the Countess—he was tempted to say something savage in passing, but decided to stay well to windward—and instead increased his speed, heading for the back of the house.

The party encountered nothing but a robot rushing for the servants' stair with a fire extinguisher, and then burst out of the back door and accelerated over the smooth croquet lawn. On the way they passed Tvi, who had jumped into Bix's flier and was trying to peel the lock and get it moving before the Baron drew another bead on her.

Maijstral called for his fliers to meet him at a rendezvous a mile ahead. Tvi got her Dewayne Seven started and raced away.

Baron Sinn burst out the back, waving his spitfire. Blinded by tears, he put a foot down on his kibble-colored croquet ball and crashed to the sward. Through his streaming eyes he could see nothing but a scatter of empty stars.

The first thing Bix smelled was beer. He put a hand to his wounded jaw and staggered to his feet. Stars flooded his vision. He swayed and clutched the wrought-iron rail. As his eyes focused, he saw Ronnie Romper sprawled amid a massive puddle below, surrounded by robot parts.

"Hey," he said. "Did I miss something?"

The Countess entered, back rigid, fists clenched. Furiously she kicked a robot part across the room.

"Swine!" she remarked.

Bix decided to keep out of sight. He had obviously done something wrong by opening the drawing room door.

In careful silence, he drew back into the drawing room and shut the door behind him.

NINE

Mr. Paavo Kuusinen was on the wrong side of the building to see much of what occurred at the Countess's mansion. He was resting under his tree, his arms pillowing his head, when suddenly he heard the sound of spitfires barking back and forth, accompanied by bright explosions from the front of the building. Kuusinen sprinted across the knoll to his flier and jumped in without bothering to open the door. He rolled back the canopy to get a better view and set the flier on a long banking curve to the south so that he could watch the building from a safe distance. He saw that the upper right front of the mansion was definitely on fire, but could see nothing else of interest. He continued to orbit, swinging wide around the back, and saw a figure leaving the back of the building. Kuusinen focused his longfinders and saw Amalia Jensen floating at great speed over the lawns and ornamental gardens behind the estate. If there was anyone with her, Kuusinen didn't spot him, but whatever the case, this looked like a clean getaway.

Kuusinen told his flier to circle and kept Amalia Jensen under observation. Presently two Gustafsons appeared over the horizon, Jensen floated into one of them, and darksuit screens appeared over each. Kuusinen swore. He tried to keep them on his detectors as they rose into the sky and sped off on two separate paths, but the disguise technology on each was too good, and they seemed to have special terrain-avoidance computers that kept them closer to the ground than Kuusinen dared fly.

Police and firefighters would soon be coming. It was time for Kuusinen to leave.

He decided to take up his surveillance again in the morning.

General Gerald snored gently in his battle armor, dreaming of glory. Maijstral had not come, would not be coming, but in his dreams the General fought a greater foe, the vast might of the Khosali Empire, the armada he had trained all his life to fight, now come at last.

"Next thing I knew," Gregor said, "Pietro was carrying me out."

There was an ever-darkening lump on his temple, which Roman now approached with a semilife patch. Gregor flinched from Roman's touch, took the patch himself, pulled his long hair out of the way, and gingerly applied the creature to his head. Happily released from suspended animation, the patch began to attach taproots to his skin and exchange healing drugs for nutrients.

Gregor could not recall being knocked out. The last thing he remembered was floating in the room next to Amalia's, admiring the Basil vase.

The others were in a much more ebullient mood. They hadn't ceased talking, laughing at their exploits, and exchanging stories since the fliers had parked at Maijstral's house.

Maijstral raised a glass of champagne. "Mr. Quijano," he said, "you have been a glorious asset to our cause. You disposed of two enemies, including the ferocious Romper, and rescued Gregor from the hostiles. I salute you, sir."

Pietro blushed and looked at his feet. "Wasn't much," he said.

"Quite the contrary," said Amalia. "Beating that Romper creature was more than I could accomplish, and I've been studying pom boxing for years." Pietro's blush deepened. Amalia was still hovering in midair until such time as Roman could locate a tool capable of getting the manacles off her ankles.

Roman refilled everyone's glass, then bowed and went in search of the appropriate cutter. Now that the rescue was over he had reverted to the role of impassive servant, changing from the one-piece darksuit to more formal apparel. Maijstral had changed clothing as well, into a lace-edged shirt and dark, embroidered housejacket—

meaning one he didn't have to be laced into—which was tailored not to show the pistol he still wore in a hidden pocket.

"By the way," Maijstral said, "I believe our hero is still wearing our screens and weapons."

"Oh. Right."

Pietro handed Maijstral a pistol, which vanished into another hidden pocket, and peeled himself out of the darksuit, which Maijstral dropped on a table. Gregor gave an unusually (for him) mellow smile as his healing patch fed him soothing chemicals.

"Do you think any of them were hurt?" Amalia asked. "Aside from Romper, I mean."

"I don't believe so," Maijstral said. "Were there any you particularly wanted injured?"

Amalia gnawed a lower lip. "No. Romper was the only one who went out of his way to be unpleasant. The rest were only doing their jobs. But you didn't see a small Khosalikh in any of the fighting?"

The others looked at each other. "I don't believe so," Maijstral said. "The only other Khosalikh I saw was the Baron." To Maijstral's surprise, Amalia seemed relieved. Maijstral decided not to offer comment.

Roman returned with the cutter and a microvision hood, which would enable him to perform the delicate task of removing the skin-thin manacles from Amalia's ankles. "Please come over to the sofa, miss," Roman said, "and put your feet up on the table." The others watched with bated breath, sipping champagne, as Roman pulled the hood over his head and carefully sliced the manacles away from her ankles and wrists.

Amalia stretched her legs. "That's much better. And not a scratch. Thank you, Roman."

"I'll bring another bottle," Roman said, and took his tools and the manacles away.

"Say," said Pietro, "why don't we show Miss Jensen the reliquary?" He reached into the rotating Bartlett Head. The hand groped, encountering nothing.

Maijstral sighed. It was unfortunate that a celebration as nice as this one was going to end so soon. Good thing, he thought, he'd just disarmed Pietro. He seemed pleasant enough, but with these impetuous young men of action one never really knew.

"Oh," Maijstral said as if he'd just remembered, "I moved the Imperial Artifact to another location. Just in case our enemies followed us back, or managed to capture one of us and gain the location of this place."

Pietro looked at him blankly. "When?"

"When we were flying toward the Countess's. You were in the other flier. I made just a short detour."

Pietro frowned. "Should we go fetch it? Then we can conclude the purchase."

Amalia Jensen put a hand on Pietro's arm. "Maijstral and I made other arrangements, Pietro," she said.

Pietro was bewildered. "When? You've been—"

"This reminds me . . . ," she said, standing and putting down her champagne. There was a growing coldness in her voice as she recalled facts which, in her joy at release, had been temporarily obscured. "We should leave, Pietro. We have many arrangements to make."

"We do? About what?"

Maijstral straightened his shoulders and put down his own glass. "Roman will take you where you wish to go," he said. High Custom smoothness had entered his voice.

"I thought the party was just starting," Pietro protested.

Roman entered with another bottle and perceived the change in atmosphere. He looked at Maijstral. "Sir?" he said.

"Please take our guests home."

Roman bowed. "Certainly, sir. Would you like a cloak, madam?"

"No. Thank you, Roman. I think we should just leave."

"As you wish, madam."

Towing Pietro by the arm, Amalia Jensen left through a door that Roman held for her. Maijstral picked up his glass again and sipped. The champagne tasted a little flat.

Gregor looked up at him in anesthetized joy. "Short party, boss," he said.

"Best we pack," Maijstral said. "We'll have to leave before Miss Jensen brings reinforcements."

"Say again, boss?"

"It is possible, Gregor, our friends may come back with guns and kill us," Maijstral explained.

Gregor absorbed this with a certain glassy-eyed effort. "Short party," he said again.

Maijstral decided that the situation was best summed up by recourse to Gregor's idiom. He put down his glass.

"Only too, Gregor. Time to pack."

* * *

It was still four hours before sunrise. The nightwind was up, scudding leaves along the yellowgrass borders of Amalia Jensen's lawn. She and Pietro watched from the roof as Roman's Gustafson soared out of sight. Amalia was poorer by sixty novae; her rescue having put her in debt for the next twelve years. Pietro turned to her in bafflement. "What's the problem, Miss Jensen?" he said.

She idly kicked at a piece of the dismembered Howard. It scuttered across the roof. "Come downstairs with me. I want to start cleaning up the mess, and I can explain while I do it."

Cleaning house is good therapy for anger, and though Amalia Jensen wasn't terribly good at it—Howard and his ilk normally handled this sort of thing—physical labor worked wonders for Amalia's mood as she explained how Maijstral had added conditions to her release. Pietro, who wasn't working as hard, found his anger growing as hers declined.

"Damn the man! If I'd known, I would have whacked him!"

"The point is, Pietro, I had no idea you were a member of the party," she said. "If I'd known you were present, I would have been able to refuse him, and then he couldn't just call off everything with you in his company—you would have known something was up."

"If he'd let me live," he said darkly.

"I could have handled it, though, if I'd thought it through. Just now I realized that I should have pointed out that his honor had been insulted when I was kidnapped, and if he didn't rescue me he'd have to start challenging people or else find another line of work."

"I'm tempted to challenge *him.*" Pietro pointed a finger at an imaginary Maijstral. "Bang. Send him off and take the artifact."

"If you challenged Maijstral you could be certain he wouldn't bring the artifact with him," Amalia said sensibly. "Besides, Pietro, you might lose." She put her hand on his arm. "You're going to be needed for other work, Pietro. We're going to have to locate the artifact and steal it, or if not steal it, destroy it."

Pietro felt a glorious confidence blazing in his soul. He *had* done rather well tonight, now that he thought about it, and he found himself longing for further action. His hands fairly ached to close around Maijstral's neck. He patted Amalia's hand.

"Right," he said. "I'll take care of it. We know where they're staying."

"We won't have guns," Amalia pointed out. "They do."

Pietro gave a bold smile. "We'll use strategy instead," he said.

"Good. Have you got one in mind?"

Beat. "No." Another beat. "Have you?"

"It's almost time for first breakfast. Let's have something to eat and give it a think, shall we?"

"Yes, Miss Jensen."

Her arm still in his, she steered Pietro toward the kitchen. "I think," she said, "in view of your rescuing me, you might call me Amalia."

"My pleasure," Pietro smiled. "Amalia." The name came to his lips like a lyric in a song.

A physician, assisted by numerous robots, was resetting Khotvinn's bones. The giant Khosalikh's howls echoed through the halls of the smoke-damaged manse.

Baron Sinn flicked fire-retardant foam from his sleeve. Ash rose in puffs from the velvet. Sinn's nose twitched. He smelled more like smoke than ever.

The firefighters and police had just left, puzzled by a wholly unconvincing tale of housebreaking and violence by persons unknown, and Sinn was going to have to brace the Countess for a session with the estate agents on the morrow. Chang and Bix had been sent home before the authorities arrived—Sinn distrusted their ability to remember any story that he and the Countess might concoct in order to explain their presence.

Another of Khotvinn's yells reverberated through the corridors. Sinn knocked on the door of the lower drawing room and heard the Countess's voice bid him enter.

"My lady."

The Countess was dressed in black silk lounging pajamas and a cheerful brocade dressing gown, the effect of which was somewhat marred by the addition of a pistol belt. She'd told the police that she was awakened from a sound sleep by the sudden flurry of shots, and she'd had to dress the part. Despite her clothes and the hour, the Countess didn't look at all sleepy; she sniffed the Baron's ears, lit a cigaret, and resumed her pacing, her shoulders square, her back unmoving.

"Tvi has still not reported in," the Baron said. "I hope she's following Maijstral."

"You're assuming she wasn't *working* for Maijstral," the Countess said.

"I don't see how she could have been corrupted. She doesn't know a soul on this planet—she came here with me when the consulate discovered the existence of the Imperial Relic."

Countess Anastasia turned toward him, pivoting her entire torso like a Khosalikh, her spine unbent. "Maijstral got to her somehow, I'm sure. Or that Jensen woman did."

"She might be a prisoner."

"She *might* be gathering mushrooms in the forest, my dear Baron. Or visiting an all-night boutique for some new apparel. We're going to have to face realities."

Sinn seated himself in a chair and watched the Countess pace. He was at low ebb, the situation had run clean out of his control, and he didn't like it. "Realities? Which realities do you mean, my lady?"

The Countess pivoted toward him again, her posture alternately more and less strained as she remained facing him while she paced back and forth. "Your Secret Dragoons have failed you, Baron," she said. "Tvi's missing, and Khotvinn's out of action for at least the next few days. We're going to have to mobilize my people for this, my lord."

Sinn shifted uncomfortably.

"Are you certain, my lady? Carrying out appropriate covert action, with its necessity of discretion, is an art form. The fewer people who know . . ."

The Countess stabbed the air with her cigaret. "We don't have to *tell* them anything. Just have everyone on the lookout for Maijstral, and have some here at the house, people like Chang and Bix, who can handle the rough stuff if—when—it's necessary."

Sinn rose from his chair. There was no choice anymore; the situation was dictating events. "No one must know the reason for this. Not your people, not mine."

The Countess took this rightly, as assent. She bowed toward him. "No one shall know. We shall invent a story that will satisfy inquiries. Perhaps over first breakfast." She walked to the service plate and touched the ideograph for "kitchen." "Will you join me, my lord?"

"With pleasure, Countess. But give me leave to wash first. I fear I'm a bit smoky."

"Thank you, sir."

"Only too, boss."

Gregor raised his cash counter to his mouth and bit it for luck. The gold ideograph for "money" gleamed against an eyetooth. The semilife patch on his temple looked like a strawberry birthmark.

Maijstral put his own cash counter in a pocket. He had just transferred to his henchmen their share of Amalia Jensen's sixty novae. The household robot finished clearing the breakfast plates from the table.

He had moved into a rented safe house in Peleng City after deciding that the city was where he was least likely to be looked for. The country house, in the meantime, had been programmed to look lively, keep window shades moving up and down, lights switching on and off.

The new town place was about forty years old and had been built during the period of architectural adventurism that followed the success of the Rebellion, when all the old boundaries were down and human horizons seemed unlimited. The house looked rather like a blue matte flying saucer crashed at a forty-degree angle into the corn-colored sward of a small ridge. At night its rim coruscated to alternating strobe lights and colored beams of coherent light. Gravity stabilizers kept everyone comfortably vertical with regard to the floors, though looking out the window and seeing the horizon tilted on edge could be unsettling until one got used to it.

The style seemed a bit quaint now, particularly the household fixtures, which were designed to look too much like what they were. Sinks and toilets featured gleaming pipes and spigots that wove in intricate, elaborate patterns above the taps. Service plates had metal studs, buttons, and flashing lights rather than simple ideographs. The household robots were designed to actually *look* mechanical—their arms and legs were driven by gears and hydraulic pistons and small electric motors, and they made rattling, clattering, and hissing noises when they were in action, as if they were somehow powered by steam. Their voices were obviously artificial and their cogitation was accompanied by blinking lights. Maijstral, who hated the very *idea* of cute robots, realized early on that if he stayed here very long he was going to have to take a heavy wrench to everything mechanical before the clattering and buzzing drove him mad.

Maijstral stood up from the breakfast table, stretched, and yawned. "Later today," he said, "we'll contact Miss Jensen and the Countess." He patted the pocket where his cash-piece rested. "A bidding war between them will serve us well, I think."

Gregor, Maijstral noticed, seemed not to be as cheered by the thought of money as was his usual wont. Maijstral wondered if the semilife patch had exhausted its resources of painkillers so quickly, then remembered Gregor's professed concern for the Fate of the Constellation. He nodded toward Gregor.

"Don't despair," he said. "I believe the result will be to your satisfaction." Gregor seemed to take cheer immediately. The robot, still clearing dishes, rattled the silverware in a calculated, programmed way. It did this every few seconds.

"I'm going to get some rest," Maijstral continued. "Wake me by thirteen if I'm not up. And have second breakfast ready by then."

Roman rose from the table. "Sir. A word."

"Of course, Roman. Come with me."

The dishes rattled again. Maijstral clenched his teeth.

He led Roman toward the saucer's living quarters. He put his gun on his bedside table and tossed his jacket over a chair. He looked up and noticed that Roman had one ear cocked toward the door, as if concerned about being overheard.

"Close the door if you like, Roman."

Roman's ear flickered, but stayed trained toward the door. "No need, sir," he said. His voice was low. Maijstral sat on the bed and began unlacing his cuffs. Roman moved toward him and automatically assumed the task. "I wonder if I may inquire," Roman said, "what you plan as the ultimate fate of the Imperial Artifact?"

Maijstral didn't even look up. "Sell it, of course," he said. "As soon as possible. It will only bring us trouble if we keep it."

Roman's shoulder fur rose under his clothes, a few strands escaping his collar. Silently he put Maijstral's cuffs in a drawer. "I think we may safely say," he said, "that honor was satisfied by Miss Jensen's rescue."

Maijstral tossed his shirt on top of his jacket and rotated his arm in its socket, wincing at a slight pain. He must have strained his shoulder at some point during the night's adventure. He spoke offhandedly. "Truly. I thank you, both for the observation and for your participation on my behalf."

"It would be a shame," Roman said, "to penalize the Imperial line in order to punish the rudeness of some of their adherents. But I suppose the Empire can command greater financial resources than Miss Jensen and her friends."

"Possibly." Maijstral had considered this. "But we must judge our demands carefully. At some point it would be cheaper simply to have us eliminated."

"Would they risk that?"

"Countess Anastasia would. Perhaps Baron Sinn would not."

"Still," said Roman, "I would not like to see a dynasty destroyed as a result of anyone's actions on Peleng."

Maijstral looked up at him. His smile was casual. "In that case, Roman, we must take care."

"As you say, sir."

"Was that all?"

"Yes, sir. Thank you."

"Close the door behind you, please."

As the door swung shut, Maijstral kicked his legs out and settled onto the bed, his mind humming. Any impulse to sleep had vanished. Roman, he had always known, was a traditionalist—insofar as Roman thought it proper to possess opinions, he probably regretted the existence of the Constellation and had a sentimental regard for the Empire in which he had never lived. Gregor, contrariwise, hated any aristrocracy and wished death to the Empire. Maijstral had it in his power to serve one of these ends, but not both.

The problem was that Maijstral counted on both his assistants for much. Gregor wanted money and instruction in *ton,* and could be kept content so long as he was paid in both. Roman was loyal to the Maijstral family—Maijstral knew Roman would never do anything underhanded, or betray any trust—but still Maijstral's future depended not simply on cooperation, but on *willing* cooperation. Their jobs were too critical—their hearts had to be in it, or mistakes could be made. If an alarm was overlooked, a tool left on a windowsill, a trap remained unsprung—who could say that it was an honest oversight, or the unconscious sabotage that could spring from a troubled mind?

He had to keep both his henchmen happy, and willing to continue insulating him from the menace represented by Humanity Prime and the Anastasia mob.

Maijstral nestled back against the pillows and closed his eyes. This was going to take some thought.

TEN

Nichole, stretched comfortably on a couch, contemplated her feet and thought about how ugly they had become. Her profession required her to spend hours on her feet, and though she'd had them reshaped five years before, they had already splayed a good deal and it was time for another rebuild. She'd have to arrange for a week or ten days away from people so that she could have the job done and get used to the results before she'd have to appear in public again.

She could see her minute reflection in each of her toenails. By way of good-morning she waved at her reflection, then wriggled her toes in answer. There was a chiming at her door.

"Second breakfast, madam."

"Bring it in, room."

A robot table floated in on a silent a-grav field, lowered its legs, planted itself. Room furniture readjusted to the new arrangement. A chair rolled to the table, then pulled back invitingly.

"Your breakfast, madam." An Emanuel Bach woodwind concerto sprang into existence around her.

"Thank you, room." She moved to the chair and seated herself. Covers rose from the plate, releasing steam. Second breakfast in Peleng was a lot heavier than first. She wasn't certain if Maijstral still wanted her to keep up the pretense he was staying with her, but she'd ordered only one breakfast, not being able to face two. She declined the table's offer and poured her own coffee.

There was another gentle chime. "Drake Maijstral, madam."

"Oh." She put down the cream jug. "Put him on directly."

Maijstral seemed in much better spirits. The old assurance gleamed in his green eyes, and Nichole's heart lifted to see it. Otherwise he was difficult to recognize—his face had been sprayed a pastel blue color, he was wearing ghastly earrings that winked on and off like mechanical toys, and behind him was a view of a game arcade.

Nichole, having got used to these little dodges four years ago, concluded that since he was using disguises and a public phone, he wasn't yet out of danger.

Nichole raised her cup and smiled. "Delighted to see you, Maijstral. You seem in good spirits."

"You look lovely. As ever, Nichole."

"I see your alarming taste in disguises hasn't altered."

He bowed toward the holo camera. "I plead the necessities of the service, madam." His eyes flickered to the boundaries of the holo image, as if trying to glance out of it. He touched a tentative finger to one of his earrings. "Pardon my boldness, but might I inquire whether you are breakfasting alone?"

"That depends, I daresay, on whether or not you're still supposed to be living here."

He smiled. "Unfortunately for our deception, its intended victims are all too well aware of where I was last night."

"I thought your address seemed buoyed by success. Did it go well, whatever it was?"

"Well enough. Villainy was thwarted, at any rate."

"Had the villainy in question anything to do with the Countess Anastasia?" Nichole smiled as she saw his eyelids twitch. "She called here yesterday and asked me to give a message to you. But the message may well be out of date by now."

Maijstral gave a lazy shrug. "Tell me. It might amuse."

"She said you had something she wanted, and that she was willing to pay for it. Sounds like a proper villain's message, I'd say."

He grinned. "That's indeed what it was. I'm pleased to hear she's willing to pay for my object. That's precisely what I had in mind."

Nichole laughed. "You seem to have things fairly well in hand."

"For the present." He glanced over his shoulder in a conspiratorial way.

"You are about to ask me for another favor," Nichole said.

Maijstral seemed a trifle embarrassed. "You're right, of course."

"I know you too well, Drake. Out with it."

"I observed that in your announced schedule, you have no appearances planned after meeting the methane creatures at the zoo, which interview should end at noon."

"That's true. It's my afternoon and evening off." Nichole wiggled her toes in the carpet in joyful anticipation of time to herself. She propped her chin on her hands and gave the Maijstral-image her girlish, ingenuous look. "You're not planning on interrupting my beauty rest, are you?"

"Only in a pleasant way, I hope. I was hoping you might invite the Maijstral of your choice to dinner."

Nichole laughed. "With your permission, Drake, I'll eat my breakfast while you explain what you meant by that."

"Please go ahead. I've eaten."

Merriment bubbled to the surface of her mind as Nichole listened to his scheme. She laughed.

"Very well, Maijstral, I'll do it. I've got a holo of you somewhere." She took a bite, then thoughtfully waved her fork at him. "Truth to tell, Drake, I'm grateful for this diversion of yours. Life in the Diadem has been uncommon tedious of late."

"My sympathies, lady."

She cocked an eyebrow at him. "I don't need facetious commiseration, Maijstral. Not from old friends."

"Apologies, Nichole." Promptly.

"Accepted." She took another bite, chewed thoughtfully, swallowed. "Do you not find, Drake, that your occupation, however well suited, begins to tire?"

Maijstral's expression was hooded. "It contents me well enough, my lady. Travel, new sights, new acquaintances, adventures when I wish them, relaxation when I need it . . . My celebrity is not sufficient to be obnoxious, but it is great enough that I am treated well where I go. I am rarely bored, my lady. If one has to have an occupation at all, mine seems a good sort to have."

"Your profession grants you more freedom than mine does me, Drake."

"That is true. You know why I—"

"I am beginning to wonder, Drake, whether or not you were right, four years ago."

Comprehension entered his eyes. "Ah."

"I travel more than you, but the new sights are always hidden behind a screen of hangers-on and gushing interviewers and a swarm of people eager to make an acquaintance . . . it's all the same, and it's all become unreal in quite the same way. My celebrity gets in the way of my work—it has *become* my work."

"You knew that, Nichole. You knew what the Diadem was about when you became a member."

"It's not the same as living it. I'm *supposed* to be an actress—my god, I haven't acted in two years!"

"Find a new play."

"There are only certain roles suitable for members of the Diadem. And they're unreal in the same way my life is unreal. And worse—they're *dull,* Drake. Impossibly dull."

Maijstral absorbed this. "Are you considering leaving the Diadem?"

"Considering. I haven't decided." Nichole wiggled her toes again. Maybe she wouldn't need to have her feet done after all.

Maijstral was looking at her intently. "Would you be happy, Nichole? Once you were outside?"

She shrugged. "I have a hard time remembering what it was like."

"I think you would not. I know you, Nichole."

Nichole stirred the food on her plate. "I'm two points down," she said.

"Ah."

"That's what this tour is about. I'm supposed to introduce my audience to new marvels. My writers are giving me mots for each of eight planets. Each guaranteed spontaneous, witty, and quotable."

"I think, if you don't mind my observation, that Nichole ushering tours of the Peleng City Zoo is not what your ratings need, no matter how glorious the collection."

She glanced up. "I know that. What else do you suggest?"

"Find a new play, Nichole. Something outside of what they've been giving you. Stretch the concept of a Diadem play. Stretch yourself."

Nichole's lips twisted in a wry smile. "And that's what I need? Just a new play? And . . . stretching?"

"Perhaps something else, my lady."

"Yes?"

There was amusement in his glance. "A new passion?" he suggested.

Nichole barked a laugh and flung a teaspoon through Maijstral's image. The coffee in her cup trembled in alarm. "Damn you, Maijstral. You know me too well. Won't you let me get away with anything?" Her laugh turned rueful. "All right. I'll tell my people to look for something."

"My lady, if you want a thing badly, you should look for it yourself."

Nichole sat for a moment, then slowly nodded. "Yes, Drake, I will. Thank you."

"It's the least I can do, considering how much you have helped me. We make light of it, but your assistance may yet save my life. These people I'm involved with . . . they're serious people, Nichole."

"I must take care to preserve your health, Maijstral. Your advice may prove invaluable to my career."

Maijstral glanced over his shoulder again. "I should end this, my lady. We have gone on too long for this line to be secure."

"Well. As usual, it's been refreshing. Give my love to Roman."

"I will."

"I hope I will see you in person before I leave."

Maijstral smiled. "You forget. I am seeing you tonight."

"Yes. Of course. *Au revoir,* then."

"Your most obedient, Nichole."

His blue-faced image vanished. Nichole thought for a moment, looking down at her toes, and tried to think of who she should call to have her feet done.

Khotvinn felt charged with energy. The semilife carapace that supported his crushed back and ribs had fed him enough drugs to obliterate the pain and infuse him with vigor. When the doctor added some patches to his legs that would make him relax and go to sleep, he waited till the human creature left, peeled off the disappointed creatures before they could take effect, and dropped them in the trash.

He hoisted himself out of his bed, reeled, then steadied. He bared his teeth and growled. The puny human redbellies were going to get what was coming to them.

His mind brooded darkly on revenge. He got his weapons out of the closet and donned them.

Khotvinn the Avenger! He needed to demolish something, and fast. He opened the window and got one leg over, then hesitated.

He realized he didn't know where he was going.

Khotvinn pulled the leg back in and thought for a long moment. He knew where Amalia Jensen lived—but the house was a wreck, the

Jensen creature probably wouldn't be living there, and the place might well be monitored by police. Tvi could have got him in, but she had disappeared. He could try Maijstral's residence, but he had no idea where Maijstral was.

The sound of voices filtered over the morning breezes. Khotvinn's ears cocked in their direction.

Time, he decided, to do a bit of skulking.

He slid over the windowsill, overbalanced, and grabbed a climbing vine to keep himself steady. The morning air still smelled of burning. Chuckling to himself, Khotvinn loped along the back porch until he stood beside the open window of the dining nook.

". . . and another to Lieutenant Navarre," Sinn's voice was saying. "Miss Jensen may stay with him." Khotvinn's ears pricked. This was the second time he'd heard the name of Navarre.

"And that odious Nichole woman." Countess Anastasia's voice.

A clatter of tableware obscured the Baron's next observation. "Far better to let the media do that for us," he then remarked. "The security around the Diadem is strict. Anyone lacking proper credentials and observed in Nichole's vicinity would be jailed, at least for inquiry."

"Perhaps you, yourself, Baron, might—"

"I'll do what I can, my lady." The next part of the conversation was dull, and consisted mainly of the Countess proposing names for various tasks, and Baron Sinn asking about their capabilities and credentials.

Khotvinn grinned. Navarre it would be, then! He smelled food and his stomachs growled.

He turned and began to lope toward the back kitchen door. He'd steal enough food for several days, find Jensen through her pal Navarre, and hold her for ransom to *both* sides. And while he was at it, he'd carve her companions like kidneys.

It was great to be alive.

The police left at last, unhappy with a tale of Ronnie Romper-garbed abductors who had held Amalia Jensen inexplicably for a day, neither asked for ransom nor committed any assault, then let her go. There was more to it, or so they clearly thought, but Amalia Jensen wasn't giving it to them. It was *her* kidnapping, she thought, and she could say what she liked.

Pietro was back in his own apartment—Amalia had decided there was no point in involving him in any police business. New household robots were moving silently about the place, wiping dust from corners, gorging themselves on debris she had missed on her first sweep. Amalia badly needed a rest, but duty demanded she supervise Pietro's mobilization of the local members of Humanity Prime, who were to be sent out to look for Maijstral and to keep an eye on Baron Sinn, the Countess, and the Khosali consulate. She sucked on a hi-stick and walked to her communications control plate. It had been replaced in the last few hours by technicians working overtime. Time to call Pietro.

The telephone chimed before she could touch the service plate. "Receive," she said, and looked at the holo image in surprise.

"Captain Tartaglia. This is a—"

"Surprise. I know." The captain was a short, broad-shouldered man, going bald in front. He had resigned from the military in order to devote himself to the good work of Humanity Prime, and prided himself on his "human" mannerisms—bluntness and belligerence to name two. Through dint of hard work and devotion to the cause, Tartaglia had worked his way up to Local Deputy Director—Amalia Jensen's immediate superior, in fact. Amalia had only met the man twice, and hid her instinctive dislike behind a screen of brisk politesse.

It had been Tartaglia who, in a coded message, had alerted her to the existence of the Imperial icon—apparently Humanity Prime discovered its existence from a double agent within the Imperial ranks. When she saw the thing in the auction catalog, she'd sent a message to him with a note of her intention to bid for it. She'd expected a congratulatory message in reply. Apparently, by return mail, she'd got Tartaglia himself.

Tartaglia looked at Amalia Jensen with small, dark, intelligent eyes. "What's the status of Artifact One?" he asked.

Amalia had never heard this term used before, but had no doubt what it meant.

"Not good, sir. It's been stolen by Drake Maijstral."

Tartaglia's expression barely changed. "Imperialist family."

"I don't think Maijstral himself is an Imperialist, sir. I think he intends to set up a bidding war between the Imperialists and ourselves."

The captain's eyes flashed contempt. "Rogue. Immoral. We'll deal with it."

"They're playing rough. The Imperialists, I mean. I was kidnapped, and Maijstral, with one of our people here, Pietro Quijano, set me at liberty."

"Oho." Tartaglia's eyebrows rose. "Why did Maijstral involve himself? Is there an attachment between the two of you?"

Amalia flushed. "Indeed not, sir. I think he set me free because he needed someone to conduct the bidding from our side."

"Good. I've brought a line of credit with me, and some of our best people. We'll get the thing from Maijstral one way or another."

Fear brushed lightly along Amalia Jensen's nerves. It occurred to her that Captain Tartaglia was not a nice person. She looked at his grim, amused countenance. "I'm sure we will," she said.

Lieutenant Navarre had intended to replace his missing portable telephone but hadn't got around to it, so it was largely a matter of luck that the call from Nichole came when he happened to be in his house. He thought he handled his end badly—he hemmed and hawed, flushed, yammered like a schoolboy—but then, after all, he was taken unawares, and one didn't receive a call from a member of the Human Diadem every day. Yes, he understood perfectly why he would have to be chauffeured. No, he didn't mind the element of intrigue—it would be amusing, haw haw.

He hung up and felt a rare sensation of surprise and anticipation. Nichole had always been one of his favorites. Though his vanity was not such as to think he would make an instant conquest, still he was pleased that out of all the men Nichole had met on Peleng, she had chosen to spend her few free hours with him. And the element of intrigue added, frankly, a touch of the bizarre. At the very least this was going to make an interesting story back home.

He decided to ask his vid to check its memory for the broadcasts it had received about Nichole's visit to Peleng. Maybe he'd be able to remember some of the best lines and compliment her on them.

Someone was home. The cold-field around the Scholder/Navarre place was down and this allowed Khotvinn to sneak right up to the windows without setting off alarms. A copper-skinned human stood in his atrium, trying on a series of shirts and jackets with the help of a robot, preening himself in the mirror while keeping one eye on the vid, which featured a blond woman talking about methane life-forms. Khotvinn couldn't be certain, but he thought the human was alone. No Jensen. Well—he'd get the information somehow.

Khotvinn opened a door—it wasn't locked—and slipped into the house. He padded down the short hallway that led to the atrium. "Unfortunately," the blond woman was saying, "few people *speak* methanite."

Khotvinn flicked on his Ronnie Romper hologram, drew his sword, then charged into the room, roaring. A single sweep of the sword sliced the robot in half. Lieutenant Navarre turned, only to be picked up by the neck and slammed against the wall.

"Where's Amalia Jensen?" Khotvinn roared. Navarre's eyes popped. He gave no answer. Khotvinn drove him into the wall again. *"Where's Amalia Jensen?"* There was only silence, except from the vid, which was going on about admirable communications at near absolute-zero temperatures. Navarre was turning purple. Khotvinn smashed him into the vid, which went silent.

"Where?" Slam. *"Where?"* Slam. *"Where?"* Slam.

Lieutenant Navarre, who was giving no answer for the very good reason that Khotvinn was strangling him, made a gurgling noise and passed out. Khotvinn growled his annoyance, held the dangling lieutenant for a moment, then dropped him. Lieutenant Navarre crumpled to the floor.

Not one to waste an opportunity, Khotvinn began ransacking the room. There had to be a clue in here somewhere.

Captain Tartaglia had taken charge so fast that Amalia Jensen had no clear recollection of how it had all come about. It seemed that an instant after Tartaglia had called her, she and Pietro were here, outside Maijstral's country cottage, with seven armed men that Tartaglia had brought with him from Pompey.

"This is Wade. In position."

Tartaglia smiled. "Acknowledge your transmission."

Amalia Jensen looked at him. "What about alarms, sir?"

"Fast in, fast out. That's the trick."

"What if the object isn't there?"

"Maijstral or his crew will be. Once we get them, we can make 'em talk." He shaded his small eyes. "Got plenty of experience at *that.* You don't maintain an empire without learning how to be persuasive."

Amalia was startled. "I thought," she said, "that *we* weren't the Empire."

Tartaglia was abrupt. "Call it what you will. Point is, we've got a lot of alien races that have to be kept in line. Otherwise we won't stay on top very long. Let 'em know who's boss, that's the ticket. Once they know that, we won't have any trouble."

Amalia glanced at Pietro and saw a queasy look on his face, which mirrored the sensation in her own heart. Maijstral had not used her well, but she wasn't altogether certain that he deserved what Tartaglia seemed ready to do to him.

"This is Royo. In position."

"Right. That's the last. Prepare to move."

Tartaglia turned to Amalia and Pietro. "Just stay out of the line of fire and you'll be all right. Leave everything up to us."

She nodded, secretly thankful. "Fine, sir."

"You've done your job just bringing us here. I'll see you get a commendation."

"Thank you, sir."

Hologram camouflage blossomed around Tartaglia's face. "Ready?" He was speaking to his troops. "Let's move out."

Then there was nothing but silent flickering in the air as Tartaglia and his people charged the house, then crashing noises as doors and windows went down before the assault. Amalia watched in silence, chewing her lip.

"Amalia," said Pietro, "I don't *like* these people."

She looked stolidly toward Maijstral's house. "I understand," she said, trying to be strong. This was a necessity. The Constellation's fate depended on this.

"We could have *bought* the damn thing back." He was silent for a moment. Then, "You know, I kind of liked Maijstral."

She gave him a look, and he flushed and looked at his feet. But she knew how he felt.

Whooping and smashing noises were coming from Maijstral's house. Amalia heard a robot protest, followed by a final-sounding crash. There weren't any sounds of battle. She wondered if Maijstral and his friends had been caught with their defenses down.

Gradually the noises died away. Then there was swift flickering across the grounds, followed by Tartaglia and his party appearing in front of Amalia, disappointment on their faces.

"No one there," Tartaglia said. "Artifact One is still at large."

Amalia Jensen tried very hard to control her feeling of relief. "They anticipated this," she said.

"We'll find 'em."

"They'll find us." Pietro surprised everyone by speaking up. "They want to sell us the artifact."

"Artifact One, you mean. Right." Tartaglia nodded. "We'll find 'em. That's what I said." He spoke to his troops. "Better get in our fliers. The police will be coming soon."

* * *

"Where?" Thud. *"Where?"* Thud. *"Where?"* Thud.

The man's name was Calvin. He was very good at his job and took pride in it. Silent, anonymous, efficient, discreet. What else was a security man for the Diadem to be?

"Where?" Thud. *"Where?"* Thud. *"Where?"* Thud.

Calvin was here to prep Lieutenant Navarre for his visit to Nichole—this visit in particular, with its unusual elements, seemed in need of advance work. But no sooner had he landed on the roof than he heard hoarse Khosali shouting and smashing noises.

It didn't sound like the sort of thing the Diadem wanted their members getting mixed up in. Calvin got quietly out of his flier, took his emergency kit out of the back, put on his shield and gun. He stepped through an upper door, gazed down off the atrium balcony, and saw Lieutenant Navarre below in the hands of a giant Ronnie Romper, the lieutenant being slammed doll-like into walls and furniture while the puppet snarled his question over and over.

"Where's Amalia Jensen?" Slam.

Calvin didn't hesitate. He'd seen stranger things in his career. Nor did he waste time wondering who Amalia Jensen might be. The important fact was that if this continued, Nichole's dinner date was liable to be ruined.

The security man glanced left and right, saw a dwarf zen tree in a heavy lead planter, and moved to pick it up. He looked over the balcony again, saw Ronnie Romper directly below him, aimed with care, and let the planter fall.

There was a horrid squelching noise. Ronnie Romper dropped to the carpet. Lieutenant Navarre fell onto a cushion, made a gasping sound, and grabbed his throat.

"Calvin, sir. Diadem security. Are you injured?"

Lieutenant Navarre looked with bulging eyes at the sprawled puppet. "Ronnie *Romper?*" he asked.

The security man drew his gun, reached carefully into the hologram, and snapped off the disguise. Khotvinn gazed lifelessly at the ceiling.

"Who's he?" Navarre demanded.

"Don't you know, sir?"

"Never seen him before. He was asking after Am—after someone I know. But I don't know where she is, and I couldn't tell him because he kept grabbing me by the throat. And who *he* is I have no idea."

Calvin examined Khotvinn with care. "He's dead now. We won't be able to question him."

Lieutenant Navarre's breathing was returning to normal. He stood and looked down at Khotvinn's body, then at Calvin. He smoothed his ruffled silks. "Thank you, sir," he said. "I'm grateful for your intervention."

"Just part of the job, sir."

"I am in your debt." An idea came to him. "I'm beginning to wonder," he said. "Strange things have been happening to me. A robbery, a friend of mine abducted . . . now this. I wonder if this is the person that's been doing it." He shrugged. "Best call the police, I suppose." He reached for the wall service plate.

Calvin put out a hand. "Sir," he said, "if you deal with the police now, you'll be late for your meeting with Nichole."

Lieutenant Navarre looked blank. "Yes, I daresay. But it can't be helped, can it?"

Calvin was smooth. "Sir, if I might recommend . . . ?"

"By all means."

"The Diadem has an understanding with the local police. I'm certain that, should Nichole ask, the police would be happy to forgo any interviews till a more convenient time."

Lieutenant Navarre seemed startled. "You can *do* that?"

"I'm positive, sir."

Navarre rubbed his back. "I seem to be pretty well bruised."

"Fortunately not on the face, sir. I can take you to a doctor and a masseur on the way if you like, sir. But we'd have to leave now."

Navarre looked at the sprawled body and hesitated. "Should we leave this behind?"

"No one will disturb it, I'm sure."

The lieutenant seemed to make his mind up. "Very well," he said, "I'll do as you advise."

Calvin gave a graceful, assenting bow. "Very good, sir."

Lieutenant Navarre removed his torn shirt and donned another. He looked at the selection of jackets he'd placed on his couch and paused.

Calvin spoke up. "If I may suggest, sir?"

"By all means."

"The white mourning jacket. Very suitable."

"Thank you, Calvin." Lieutenant Navarre drew on the jacket. Calvin helped lace him in, checking the jacket for weapons or hidden cameras as he did so.

"Shall we leave then, Calvin?"

"As you like, sir."

Lieutenant Navarre picked up his mourning cloak and carried it up the stair. Calvin followed on silent cat feet. Navarre activated the house security systems as he left and stepped out onto the roof.

"Thank you, Calvin. For everything."

Calvin opened the door of the heavy Jefferson-Singh limo. "It was nothing, sir. All in a day's work."

ELEVEN

Countess Anastasia watched on vid as Drake Maijstral stepped out of the Jefferson-Singh flier and into Nichole's arms. She noticed he was carrying a small bag. "Damn!" Her fist thudded into the arm of her stiff-backed wooden chair. The cigaret she was holding flung ashes onto a six-hundred-year-old carpet. A robot hastened to clean them up.

"We'll never get him out of there!" Her High Khosali parsing indicated near-apocalyptic frustration. "He's probably carrying the Imperial Relic in that bag."

Baron Sinn nodded philosophically. "The next move seems to be Maijstral's, my lady."

The Countess ground her teeth. "I like it not, Baron."

Baron Sinn liked it less. This meant he was going to be trapped in this house with an angry, restless Countess for a very long time. Perhaps he should give her a chance to work off her anger.

"Croquet, my lady?" he suggested, dooming himself to a day of chasing his ball beneath the kibble trees.

Her answer, tongue lolling, seemed the smile of a fiend.

* * *

Safely in Nichole's suite with Calvin and his associates on guard, Lieutenant Navarre toggled off the hologram of Drake Maijstral. Nichole laughed and offered her hand. Navarre gallantly sniffed her wrist, ignoring a persistent twinge of his bruised back.

"You looked very like Maijstral, dressed in mourning," she said. "I'm pleased to see you, Lieutenant."

"The pleasure," said Navarre, "is all mine." He was speaking the truth. He was thoroughly gratified to discover that he felt very safe here.

Maijstral turned off the vid and relaxed in his chair, happy. Nichole knew how to carry off a deception, and her foil, whoever he was, had played his part well, even to the duplicate of the diamond Maijstral wore on his finger.

A robot rattled past on an errand, making its usual bleeping noises. Maijstral clenched his teeth, then calmed himself. He was learning to hate the robots, but now was not the time for irritation. It was time to put forward his plan.

Tvi watched the vid with interest. She turned to the robot. "Bring up another bottle of the cabernet. The forty-four, if you please."

"Yes, madam."

Since her flight from the Anastasia residence she'd done fairly well. The first thing was to dump the Dewayne Seven and steal a new Jefferson-Singh Hi-Sport. Since she'd arrived on Peleng, she'd got used to them.

Then she'd found a place to hide out. It was a comfortable house of twelve rooms, apparently inhabited by a family whose interests took them to Nana for half the year. The household security was ancient and it had been child's play to reprogram it to treat her as a member of the family.

Now she'd have to find a way to earn a living. She sipped cabernet and thought about it.

Stealing seemed like a good idea.

She smiled. Life on Peleng was looking up.

"My name is Roman, my lord. At your service."

"Count Quik. Yours. Please sit."

Roman settled on a padded bench next to the Troxan. "I see you have returned to the methane environment exhibit."

"Not got look before properly. Nichole in way with globes. Many many crowdings."

"To be sure."

"I methane speak," said the Count.

Roman was inclined to wonder if he spoke methane in as singular a manner as he seemed to speak everything else, but the Count proceeded to demonstrate, leaning his pumpkin-sized head toward a microphone that remained as a relic of Nichole's visit. As the Count's voice pulsed through the supercool environment, the methane creatures blushed a delicate violet and began to cluster gelatinously toward the speakers. At their current rate it would take them about half an hour.

"Congratulations, my lord," Roman said. "You seem to have stimulated them admirably."

An answering communication moaned from hidden speakers. The Count listened and made his reply.

"I told them you are with. Interested they were." His head lolled in a peculiar Troxan manner. "Badly these speakers do. Troxans better makes speakers."

"Undoubtedly the best, sir," Roman said. The Troxan head was such a superb conductor of sound that they tended as a species to be very particular about audio equipment.

"Tell yourself," Count Quik suggested. "I tell will then the methane critters."

"I am a member of Drake Maijstral's entourage."

"Interesting. Translation problems many indeed. No word for 'thief' in methane world."

"Perhaps a better world than ours, my lord."

"But boring-er."

"Duller. Yes, my lord. No doubt."

The Count chatted with the methane creatures. They groaned in reply. Roman waited for a lapse in the conversation.

"Mr. Maijstral," he interjected, "asked me to find you."

Count Quik's deep goggle eyes swiveled to Roman. "Yes? Wherefore, Mr. Roman?"

"He hopes, sir, that you will consent to do him a service. He realizes this is an unusual request, but he hopes that once you understand the circumstances, you will do him the honor of acting for him in a matter of importance, in brief a matter concerning the Fate of the Empire. He hopes that the matter may be resolved quickly and satisfactorily, and in fine to your, and the Empire's, advantage."

Count Quik's expression did not—in fact could not—change, but it seemed to Roman that his gaze seemed to intensify.

"You intrigue, Mr. Roman. Please speak on. I am all ears."

Roman, as he prepared to unfold Maijstral's plot, reflected that, of all the times he had heard that last turn of phrase, this was the only time it might be, quite literally, true.

General Gerald gazed blearily at the young man on his doorstep. Since waking from his inutterably pleasant, thoroughly violent dreams at the first touch of dawn, he had climbed out of his armor and gone to bed, swearing to get enough sleep *this* time so that he wouldn't be caught nodding if Maijstral appeared tonight. The young man's appearance caught him by surprise. He didn't have visitors very often. Sometimes he wondered if he intimidated people.

The General could see the young man through the door without being observed himself. The visitor was dressed formally, but in a bright radical style that pushed at once the bounds of convention and the General's sense of the harmonic possibilities of color. Cheeky, the General thought, looking at him. Impudent. Needs discipline. Just look at the way his hands are stuck in his pockets, the hi-stick just hanging in his mouth. A tour in the service would do him good.

A tour in the service was the General's automatic prescription for many social ills. He opened the door.

"General Gerald?"

"Marines." Automatically. "Retired."

"My name is Gregor Norman. I am an associate of Drake Maijstral."

Surprise boiled in General Gerald's sleepy mind. "What's that to me?" he barked, his voice still on automatic pilot while he wondered what hell Maijstral was playing at. Some attempt to get him out of his house so that it could be rifled?

"Mr. Maijstral," Gregor said, "has come across something which may interest you. Something relating, believe it or don't, to nothing less than the Fate of the Constellation."

If this was a ploy, the General thought, it was a bold one.

General Gerald admired boldness.

He stepped back into his hallway. "Come in, youngster," he said.

"Thank you, General."

"Leave the damned hi-stick outside. Don't you know they're bad for you?"

Gregor hesitated a moment, then snapped the offending stimulant in half and put it in his pocket.

At least, the General thought with satisfaction, Maijstral had an assistant who knew how to obey orders.

* * *

The robot wove silently through the kibble arbor on its way toward Baron Sinn. Sinn was using his mallet to knock bits of fruit about, looking for his croquet ball. Thus far he hadn't achieved success.

The robot proffered a telephone. "My lord. A call from His Excellency Count Quik."

The Baron straightened. "He knows I'm here?" The robot, not possessing a sense of irony, offered no answer.

Sinn glanced out onto the croquet lawn and saw Countess Anastasia smoking a cigaret and gazing with malevolent satisfaction at him—and at the scatter of red beneath the kibble trees. "Very well," he said. "I'll take it."

The Baron, still kicking idly at fruit, took the telephone from the robot's manipulator. The robot hovered over fallen kibbles. Baron Sinn hesitated for a moment, glancing at the Countess and then at the robot, and then an idea struck him. His tongue lolled in a smile.

"Robot," he ordered, "pick up all the fruit and put it into piles." He held out a hand. "About this high. If you find a croquet ball, let it lie."

"Yes, my lord."

Sinn's grin broadened as the robot went on its way, then he touched the answer ideograph and the phone promptly projected a miniature hologram of Count Quik's round head before Sinn's snout.

"Good afternoon, Baron. Your most obedient."

"Your ever faithful, my lord. It is a pleasant surprise to hear from you."

"Is day for surprisings. Am myself surprised earlier."

"Pleasantly, I hope."

"I with friend spoke of Mr. Maijstral."

A rush of frantic energy sped through the Baron's nerves at the sound of Maijstral's name, but it was a few seconds before he was able to decipher the Count's syntax and make a guess at what Count Quik had actually intended.

"You spoke with a friend of Maijstral's, my lord?" Wanting to be absolutely certain.

"Correct is. Requested assistance mine as neutral third party, yet citizen of Empire. I gave."

Maijstral's insulating himself well, Baron Sinn thought with a certain amount of admiration. And he moves fast.

He kept his expression amiable. "That was very generous of you, my lord," he said.

"Offered compensation. Twenty percent. Declined."

"Of course, my lord."

"Disinteresting seemed best."

The robot was piling fruit into a small pyramid. No croquet ball yet.

Sinn, as if on cue, affected disinterest as he gazed at Count Quik. "What manner of assistance did Maijstral believe he needed from Your Excellency?"

"I bids transmit, my Baron."

"I understand." Sinn considered this for a moment. "Is there a place where you can be reached?"

"Yes. At Peleng Hotel now."

Behind his facade, Sinn cursed heartily. That was where Etienne, Nichole, and (presumably) Maijstral were staying, covered by Diadem security.

Delay, Baron Sinn thought. The longer the delay, the better chance of catching Maijstral outside of his paramour's protection. He peered benignly into the hologram.

"I have no bid at present, Excellency. But I have no doubt that I shall receive instructions from my consulate to offer one."

"Understandings, my lord. But dealings must be concluded in one local day. Thirty-eight hours."

Sinn cursed again. Maijstral seemed to have thought of everything. "I have no concrete assurance of what His Majesty's government will or will not offer," he said, "but I am certain they are willing to offer a fair price for return of the Imperial Artifact." Baron Sinn's ears pricked forward intently. "However, should the Imperial Artifact not be returned at the end of this adventure, I trust that your principal will take care to understand the consequences of such an unfriendly act. When great empires play for great stakes, the counters are oft at hazard."

"Understandings, Baron Sinn. Your servant, sir."

"Yours." Nuance, the Baron thought, nuance.

The Count's hologram faded. Baron Sinn noticed that the robot seemed to have left a single round, red object alone during the course of its pile-making. The Baron walked over to it and prodded it with his mallet. It was definitely his croquet ball.

He lit a cigaret and addressed the robot. "Continue piling the fruit."

"Yes, sir."

Baron Sinn drove his ball back into play and strolled back onto the lawn. The Countess tossed her cigaret off the playing field and walked to her ball.

"I set the robot to clearing the kibbles away. I hope you don't mind."

The Countess betrayed no sign of chagrin. "Not at all, Baron." She stood above her ball and readied her mallet. "I should have thought of that myself, when I handed you my special ball. Please forgive my lack of foresight."

"Of course, my lady."

Countess Anastasia squinted as she took aim. "Was the call anything of importance, Baron?" she asked.

The Baron timed his comment perfectly. "Maijstral's agent, my lady."

The stroke hit off-center and the ball spun off on a tangent. "Bad luck, Countess," said Baron Sinn, and prepared to roquet and drive the Countess's ball off the court, beneath her kibble trees.

He was beginning to enjoy the game.

"Of *course* I'll take the twenty percent, youngster! D'you take me for a fool?"

Paavo Kuusinen watched the game of croquet in mounting frustration. Nothing had developed at Amalia Jensen's place since the Humanity Prime goon squad had returned to its roost. Drake Maijstral was, it appeared, safely under Nichole's protection. Kuusinen had flown to the Countess's place in hope of seeing something dramatic, and found only a game of croquet and a robot piling kibble fruit.

Kuusinen sighed. He decided to fly to Lieutenant Navarre's in hope of viewing some new developments.

Since he'd been in on the beginning, he'd hate to miss the finish.

Amalia Jensen had spent the afternoon getting acquainted with the discouraging fact of her house being used as a barracks for a host of armed and belligerent men, and her response had finally been to throw up her hands in despair and retreat to her room. There she had been watching the video news, hoping to discover some news of Maijstral's current whereabouts, and listened instead to a report about the current wave of odd crimes affecting Peleng City and vicinity: one theft from Lieutenant Navarre's house that involved an object of small value taken by highly expensive means; one violent kidnapping followed a short time later by inexplicable release; one equally inexplicable armed attack on Countess Anastasia's mansion; a violent intrusion at a country house, where robots were shot and the house torn apart; and now—a late development—a violent attack on Lieutenant Navarre by a Khosalikh in a Ronnie Romper disguise.

Amalia Jensen straightened in her chair. The newscaster, a supercilious Khosalikh, pointed out that Ronnie Romper disguises had been used by the perpetrators of the Jensen kidnapping. Facts seemed scanty at the moment, but this didn't stop the news writers from speculating.

Cold fingers touched Amalia Jensen's neck at the report that Ronnie Romper had been killed during the attempt, apparently by a visitor who happened onto the scene. The newscast hadn't identified the Khosalikh even as to sex, and she couldn't be certain that it wasn't Tvi. In fact it very likely was, since the tall Khosalikh had probably been too badly injured in the attack on the Countess's mansion to participate in further devilment.

The door opened. Pietro burst in. "Have you seen the vid?" he asked.

"Yes."

"Why Navarre?"

She thought for a moment. "Good question," she said. "Perhaps they thought to find me there."

"And who was it that killed Ronnie? There's no identification at all."

"Something's going on."

"Damn right there is." This last was a comment from Captain Tartaglia, who had appeared in the doorway. Amalia quickly composed her features and tried to hide her reactive distaste at the sight of the man. Tartaglia scratched his chin and looked at the vid. "Maybe we should pick up this Navarre. Ask him some questions."

Amalia's heart thumped in alarm. "He seems to be well protected," she said.

"Take a look at his place, anyway."

"Police will be everywhere."

Tartaglia shrugged. "That's worth considering. Let me think about it."

The vid unit chimed. "Telephone call from General Gerald, madam. Marines. Retired."

Amalia felt a slow wave of surprise. She barely knew the man. "*Now* what?" she said. She turned to Tartaglia. "If you'll excuse me, Captain?"

Tartaglia shrugged again and turned to leave. Amalia accepted the call. Gerald's red face appeared on the vid. Amalia tried to seem politely interested.

"General Gerald. This is a surprise."

The General was grinning. "Drake Maijstral asked me to call you."

Behind her, Amalia heard Pietro's gasp of surprise, followed instantly by the sound of Captain Tartaglia's abrupt about-face in the hall and return to the room.

Amalia Jensen controlled her astonishment, and was mildly surprised at the coolness of her reply. Perhaps she was becoming accustomed to intrigue. "You are welcome to call at any time, General. I am surprised that Mr. Maijstral did not call with his own message."

"Perhaps he didn't want to get killed."

"Whatever our disagreements, we have not equipped every telephone on Peleng with an explosive device just on the chance that Maijstral might use it."

"Perhaps he wants to be careful. I am given to understand that some of your people broke into his house this morning."

There was an annoyed grunt from Tartaglia.

"Let's get to cases, shall we?" The General appeared to be enjoying himself. "You haven't exactly covered yourself with glory in this business so far, and I think Maijstral's being quite reasonable in offering you a chance to buy your way out of this situation." The General's smile broadened, conveying pure, malevolent joy. "Maijstral wishes the bidding concluded in the next thirty-eight hours—one day. I'm getting twenty percent as middleman. Do I hear any bids?"

Tartaglia pushed Amalia Jensen aside and squatted in front of the vid, inside range of the holo pickup. Amalia prickled.

"General. I'm Captain Tartaglia."

The General appeared to consult his memory. "I don't recall any captain by that name. An ex-captain, yes. Someone who left the service of the Constellation in order to join a crank paramilitary organization with delusions of grandeur."

Tartaglia's mouth was a grim line. "I'm surprised to see you involved in this, General. The Fate of the Constellation is at stake. Seems like all you seem to care about is your twenty percent."

The General turned red. Amalia winced at the volume of his reply. "I *cared* enough about the Constellation to have served six hitches in the marines, puppy! Marines, I will remind you, who are ready to fight against the Empire whether or not they've got an Emperor *or* his blasted jism! I *care* enough about the Constellation to have made this call! If I hadn't agreed to act as middleman here, you might have been left out of the deal altogether. I suggest, therefore, you *care* enough to come up with a reasonable bid!"

"If that's the way you want it, General."

"That's the way *Maijstral* wants it, puppy! If I had any resources to call on I'd bid for the thing myself, but I know how long it takes for the military to process an unorthodox requisition for funds. So it seems as if the Fate of the Constellation is in your hands, Heaven and the Virtues help us."

"Amateurs have their uses, then."

The General raised an admonishing finger. "Money speaks louder than sarcasm, puppy."

Amalia could see Tartaglia's hands trembling with suppressed rage. "Very well. A hundred and fifty. But tell Maijstral this. If he favors the Empire, he'd better get ready to spend the rest of his life across the border. And even then the Empire might not be healthy for him."

General Gerald was visibly unimpressed. "I'll transmit that message, puppy, but were I you, I wouldn't make threats you're not competent enough to carry out."

Tartaglia's answer was short. "A hundred and fifty. Tell Maijstral."

"I'll do it and be back in touch. I expect the bidding will go higher." His eyes seemed to search out of the holo projection, looking for Amalia. "Miss Jensen," he said, "I'm very disappointed at the company you keep."

The General's image faded, Tartaglia began to curse, and Amalia Jensen was left with a growing admiration for Maijstral's technique. He had chosen the perfect foil—someone whose sympathies would lie with the Constellation, but who was nevertheless perfectly honorable, and who would consider any interference with Maijstral a breach of that honor.

"We'll pick up the General!" Tartaglia was saying. "We'll get Maijstral's location out of him! And then—then—"

"He probably doesn't have that information," Amalia snapped. "Give Maijstral the credit for knowing his job. He's obviously running this through cutouts, and he wouldn't tell the cutouts his hiding place." She stood up and gazed into Captain Tartaglia's surprised eyes. "General Gerald has won any number of duels in the past, and I think if you sent your people after him, they'd come back damaged, you'd end up with a challenge you probably wouldn't win, and the Empire would get the artifact."

Tartaglia sneered. "Perhaps you think you should be running things."

"Perhaps Amalia *should,*" Pietro said. His voice caught them both by surprise. "She seems to have a better idea of how to deal with this situation."

"Damn that Maijstral!" Tartaglia beat the wall in fury. Amalia could hear the surprised reactions of his followers to the violence and noise. "Damn the man!"

"Damn him, indeed," Amalia said. She was, as before, surprised at her coolness. "Damn him all you like. But stop threatening him, or we'll lose it all."

Tartaglia fell silent, red-faced and baffled.

"Exactly," Pietro said. "Let *us* deal with it from now on."

He stepped across the room to link arms with Amalia. They had been through too much together for Tartaglia to throw it all away.

The sounds of the *Eroica,* perfectly rendered by Gregor's Troxan speakers, boomed from Maijstral's walls. A robot, bumbling about some task, gave a low whistle followed by a series of bleeps.

The last straw. Maijstral turned in his chair and shot the robot with his disruptor. The robot froze.

Maijstral knew he would probably have to pay damages, but decided that hearing the *Eroica* unhindered was worth the cost. Maijstral called up Peleng City's Personal Notices bulletin board, where General Gerald had posted Humanity Prime's bid. A smile crossed his face. A hundred and fifty. That wasn't bad, for a start. The Imperials hadn't tendered an offer yet.

Both sides had, however, made threats—the codes transmitted by both General Gerald and Count Quik made that clear.

This required thinking about. He told the vid to turn off, and the unit answered him with bleeping noises and flashing lights. Maijstral suppressed a spasm of irritation.

Both factions promised violence unless he sold the artifact to their side. If worse came to worst, the Empire could probably guard Maijstral better, but he preferred not to spend the rest of his life in hiding. And he didn't want to spend it in the Empire, either.

He thought about the situation for a moment, particularly in reference to his thoughts last evening, when Roman had mentioned his own bias toward the Empire. Then Maijstral smiled and nodded to himself. This called for a conspiracy.

Roman, who never trusted others to select Maijstral's food, was off on a provisioning errand. His absence provided a fine opportunity to inaugurate a small Romanless plot. Maijstral followed the crashing *Eroica* to Gregor's door and knocked softly.

"Gregor? May I speak with you?"

"Sure boss. Come in."

Gregor had taken one of the household robots apart and was examining its contents.

Two down! Maijstral thought cheerily.

Gregor put his tools on his desk and turned down the fourth movement with a sharp command directed at his audio deck.

Maijstral padded to a chair and coiled in it. "Feeling well?" he asked.

"Sure, boss." There was the merest trace of a bruise on Gregor's temple, but otherwise the semilife patch had done its work: reduced swelling, promoted healing, drawn up most of the bruise, and then expired in ultimate semilife bliss and dropped off.

"Gregor, both sides are making threats. I'm anticipating a certain level of danger here."

Gregor shrugged. "What else is new?"

"I'm afraid that neither of our clients may be happy without possession of the artifact."

"I'll be careful. Don't worry, boss, I want to keep my skin as well as anyone."

"It's not that. It's that . . ." Maijstral feigned hesitation. "I would prefer our Imperial friends to suffer disappointment."

Gregor grinned. He leaned forward. "So would I. How do we want to work it?"

There was a smile somewhere deep behind Maijstral's lazy eyes. This was going to be easier than he expected. "It occurred to me that the artifact must have survived some serious fighting. It would be a great shame if the Empire, on obtaining the artifact, discovered that it had been hit by a disruptor bolt or two."

"And sterilized?"

Maijstral raised his hands, palms-up. "They could hardly blame *us.*"

Gregor cackled with laughter. "That's pretty good, boss."

"Roman can't know, of course. It isn't that he's pro-Imperial, just that he would so disapprove of cheating a client."

Gregor gave a conspiratorial wink. "No problem. My eyes are sealed."

"But if we were to sell the Empire any of His Majesty's sperm, presumably our Constellation friends would want assurances that it was sterilized."

Gregor frowned. "I follow. Somehow we'd have to let Jensen and her friends see the sample's been sterilized before passing it to the Imperials." He shook his head in bafflement. "That's a tough one, boss."

Maijstral raised a hand. "I have an idea, Gregor," he said. "I believe it will work. Let's see if you agree."

"Baron Sinn. Your servant, sir."

"Count Quik. Ever yours."

"My consulate has authorized a bid of two hundred." This was a lie. Sinn was using his own line of credit—he, like General Gerald, understood this would take too long for the request to go through official channels.

"Will transmit, my Baron. My thanks."

Baron Sinn returned the phone to the robot and glanced from beneath the shade of the kibble trees toward where Countess Anastasia waited on the croquet court. She did not appear happy.

Unfortunate for her, Sinn thought as he returned to the game, swinging his mallet in a jaunty way. For some reason her play was off. The Baron was well on his way toward winning his second game.

"And then this giant creature jumped out of ambush. Wearing a puppet disguise, no less. He must have been insane. He seized me, threw me about the place, and kept asking after Miss Jensen."

"That must have been terrible."

"He kept strangling me. He wouldn't let me talk. Even if he took his hands off my throat, there was nothing I could have told him. I barely knew the woman. Until you told me, I had no idea she'd been released. If it wasn't for your man, I don't doubt I'd be lying dead in my uncle's house."

"Do you think it was the same person who broke into your uncle's house?"

"It's occurred to me. But that would mean the burglary is connected with the attack on Miss Jensen, and I can't think how that could be."

Nichole smiled, her mind bubbling with her own inward speculation. "Yes," she said. "Totally baffling."

Lieutenant Navarre propped his chin on his hand. He spoke thoughtfully. "Reminds me of a play I saw on Pompey. A strange complicated piece, written by one of our local playwrights. Drama, comedy, even a song or two. It had a glorious part for one of my favorite actresses." Pause. "She rather reminds me of you, my lady."

"Does she indeed?" Nichole put her hand on his arm. Her voice was a quiet purr. "Tell me all about it, Lieutenant. I'd love to hear everything you can remember."

It was almost time for siesta. Gregor was off on a brief errand to the nearest public phone in order to transmit the Imperial counterbid to General Gerald, leaving Roman to fix Maijstral's presiesta luncheon with equipment he had brought to the table on a cart. The hot dressing flamed in Roman's pan. Maijstral watched Roman's expert movements with admiration.

Time, obviously enough, for a conspiracy.

"Your salad, sir."

"Thank you, Roman. Is that kava-kivi I taste?"

"It is, sir. A small conceit of mine."

"A splendid idea, Roman. Let it occur to you in future, by all means."

"Thank you, sir."

Maijstral tasted the salad again. Roman busied himself with putting away his cooking implements. Maijstral put his fork down and tapped his fake diamond against a front tooth.

"Roman," he said. "May I ask your advice?"

Roman put down his spatula. "Sir. I would be honored."

Maijstral spoke in Khosali. The logic seemed to express itself better. "We have it in our power to effect the course of history."

"Sir."

"It is not a responsibility I have ever desired. My lifelong interests, I'm afraid, have been rather more pedestrian. These elements of galactic intrigue have caught me entirely by surprise."

"The circumstances of life do not ask permission, but compel as they will."

Maijstral smiled. This was Khosali proverb, and Roman to the bone.

"Very true," Maijstral assented. "Circumstance compelled me into this situation, and I *could,* if I desired, let circumstance compel me out of it."

Roman's interest was obviously piqued. "By allowing the bidding to proceed as it will, and delivering the reliquary to the highest bidder?"

Maijstral put down his fork. "Just so."

Roman's ears pricked forward. "You wish not to be compelled in such a way, sir?"

Maijstral drew his ear back into a pose of cautious reflection. He contemplated his cooling salad and wondered exactly how he was going to bring this off. He could tell Roman that Sinn and Amalia Jensen had threatened him, but that would just drive Roman into a righteous fury and before long Roman would start prodding Maijstral into challenging everyone in sight. Maijstral would have to find another way. "Roman," he said, "I have no desire to be responsible for the destruction of the Imperial line. It is the symbol of a civilization older than humanity. Regardless of politics, I do not feel that I have a right to say whether the Pendjalli should live or die."

"But honor compels you to maintain the honesty of the bidding."

"Yes." Maijstral picked up his fork and poked aimlessly at his salad. "You see me caught up in a dilemma, Roman."

"Sir, I hardly feel myself qualified to advise—"

Maijstral threw up his hands. "If not you, Roman, who?"

Roman's nostrils flickered in agitation. Maijstral was pleased with his own performance, but he knew that the cry of desperation was not entirely feigned. If he couldn't persuade Roman to a certain course of action, Peleng—and, for that matter, everywhere else—would become a far more dangerous place for all of them.

"Sir," Roman said, "pray allow me to think for a moment."

"Of course." Maijstral feigned a renewed interest in his salad and watched Roman through hooded eyes. The Khosalikh's nose twitched; his ears inclined back, left, right; his hands played over the cooking gear. Roman was clearly fighting something out in his mind.

"Sir," Roman said, "could it not be said that some duties transcend honor, and that the preservation of life is one of them? Could it not furthermore be said that the preservation of innocent life is in itself an honorable duty?"

Relief and joy bubbled into Maijstral. Carefully he suppressed all signs of it. "Well . . . ," he said.

"The Imperials, of course, consider the royal family itself the expression of a transcendent ideal, whatever the opinion on this side of the political boundary."

"Roman," Maijstral said, "it would mean deceiving our clients."

"That it would, sir."

"It would mean deceiving *Gregor.* Someone with his background would never understand our appreciation of the Pendjalli ideal."

Roman thought for a moment. "That would be difficult, sir."

Maijstral raised his napkin to his lips. "That is why we should plan now. While Gregor is away."

* * *

"Three hundred."

"Four-fifty."

"Seven hundred."

"A thousand."

"I didn't expect to see you until the swap, youngster. It might be dangerous for you if you're seen here."

"I took precautions. My boss has sent me with a proposition, General."

"Yes? You interest me."

"Mr. Maijstral isn't totally without sympathies in this job, General. He would prefer that one side—the human side—comes out on top."

The General's eyes twinkled. "He does? Tell me."

"Only too."

"Fifteen hundred."

"He wants it *how?*"

"Cash, Captain."

"Cash? Not a credit counter?" Pause. "There may not be that much cash on the planet."

"I am assured there is. There is always a demand for untraceable funds in even the most ordered society."

"Mr. Romans. Am pleased."

"You're too kind, my lord."

"Please share brandy."

"Your servant."

"Surprised you to see. After threatenings I thought you would stay close."

"Mr. Maijstral has sent me with a proposition. He is not entirely without conviction in this matter. He has a sentimental affection for the Imperial household, and wishes them long life and success."

"Very interesting. Please say more and continue."

"Wait a minute, youngster."

"Sir?"

"This sounds more complicated than necessary. How do I know you're not going to pull a switch?"

"The cryo container will be in plain sight the entire time. You'll be able to observe it, and Mr. Maijstral won't touch it. If we pull a switch, you'll know."

"But Mr. Romans, forgive me. How certains can we be of Imperial spunk?"

"Large areas of the Imperial genetics have been mapped, my lord. Certainly a comparison can be run just before the exchange."

"Gregor."

"Yes, boss."

"I shall have to run an errand tonight. Please don't mention my absence to Roman."

A smirk. "Right, boss. Like you say."

"Twenty-one hundred."

"Roman?"

"Sir?"

"I shall be away from the house tonight. I'm sure you can guess why."

Pause. "Yes, sir. Will you need my assistance?"

"I suspect the Peleng City sperm bank has only rudimentary security."

"As you like, sir."

"Please do not mention to Gregor that anything out of the ordinary has occurred."

"Indeed not, sir."

"Twenty-five."

"Twenty-eight fifty."

The Imperial Artifact sat gleaming on Maijstral's desk. He had just returned from his raid on the sperm bank and was still dressed in his darksuit. His bound hair was piled on the top of his head. He was wearing image-intensifiers over his eyes; his hands were sheathed in gloves that detected the flow of energy. The house was silent save for a bleeping robot—the last—bumbling about in the outside hallway.

Before him was equipment for the storage and preservation of

Khosali sperm. He had stolen no sperm himself—he had to use the Emperor's genuine article with the mapped Pendjalli genes, otherwise the deals he'd made would fall through.

Carefully he traced the patterns of the reliquary's design. The pulse of electrons beat against his temples.

He thought about his plan, and part of his mind quailed. He was needlessly complicating things. He was adding appreciably to his own danger.

Patterns formed in Maijstral's mind. Tools moved efficiently in his hands.

There was a click. A part of the artifact rotated, then slid aside. Frost formed in delicate patterns along the engraving as cryogenic chill touched the air.

The artifact was open, and at his mercy.

TWELVE

Confident in their dreams, the methane creatures in the Peleng City Zoo pursued their slow life as they slid through their frozen ammonia sea. Though they surely possessed language and limited understanding, their watchers were not certain whether or not to credit them with genuine intelligence. Insulated from an outside that would have vaporized them in an instant, the creatures crawled at glacial speed through their habitat, absorbing nutrition and each other, casting off waste and new individuals. Their perception limited to sound and touch, they were happy in their enclosure, safe from overly disturbing contact with the amusing delusions outside.

Those watching through the zoo monitors would have been surprised to discover that the methane creatures did not credit the watchers' reality. Instead the methanites were convinced that the odd pulsings directed toward them from the speakers were a form of consensual hallucination, an unintended by-product of their own vibrant fantasies. The methanites, for much of their history, had been constructing a long dramatic work—an elevated, intricate mosaic, abstract as an opera, torrid as a romance, filled with gods and devils, humor and philosophy, wonder and strangeness, the whole of which commented upon and criticized itself as it went. The endless work had taken on a complex life of its own, novel plot twists appearing unforeseen out of what had seemed to be simple dramatic devices, new insights into character blossoming with astonishing regularity even in characters so old their birth was coterminous with that of the species that had created them.

Attempts to communicate with the methanites had seemed, in the ammonia sea, to take on aspects of these spontaneously generated insights. This was, the creatures concluded, a new, intense form of hallucination, and they began a long discussion into the nature of their own subconscious, wondering whence such thoughts derived, a debate that (to date) has not been resolved. Count Quik's explanation of Maijstral's mode of living had sent a shock wave through the small methanite community; perhaps the concept of "thief" could be integrated with the Great Work, perhaps not. The concept presupposed material possessions, which the methanites did not have, and which they could not manipulate if they had. The notion of possession seemed, at the very least, a radical exercise in speculative philosophy. The methanite subconscious, the creatures concluded, was proving more inventive than had previously been suspected.

We should not feel too superior. The methanites' physical horizons may be limited, but their mental life is lively. Consider also how the methanite experience may be taken as a paradigm of our own. We, like the near-zero creatures, live bounded by conceptual walls of our own making, and they go by many names: religion skepticism, ideology, propriety, High Custom—indeed, High Custom is a deliberate exclusion of some modes of experience in favor of those considered more elevated or worthwhile. High Custom at least admits to its limitations. The totality of experience, the agon of corporal existence and the universe . . . no cultural or ideological construct seems to deal with the macrocosm at all well. The methanites have chosen their illusions, and seem happy with them. That is more than many of us can claim.

Paavo Kuusinen was feeling very much like a creature surrounded by walls not of his own making and was beginning to wonder if the events of the last few days might not, in fact, be some odd product of his fevered mind. He was frustrated with a day of watching people go about what seemed to be very ordinary lives—how could, after the last few days, everyone behave so normally? Kuusinen finally gave up his watch and went to his hotel for the evening. At least it would give him a chance to bathe and change clothes. His room seemed faintly surprised to see him—he hadn't been home for almost two days.

On rising, he ordered first breakfast and scanned the room's computers for any recent developments. The police remained baffled, Maijstral remained in Nichole's suite, and—Kuusinen's ears pricked forward—Nichole had announced Maijstral as her escort for this evening's farewell ball in honor of the Diadem's departure.

He paged through his messages, found his invitation waiting in computer storage, and ordered it (and the magnetic code strip that would get him past Diadem security) printed out.

At least tonight he'd be able to get a look at everybody. Maybe their behavior would tell him something.

"You'll excuse us, Lieutenant, I hope."

"Certainly, madam."

Lieutenant Navarre bowed, sniffed Nichole's ears and Maijstral's, and stepped from Nichole's parlor into her withdrawing room. The door slid shut behind him. Nichole looked at Maijstral with bright eyes. He smiled.

"A new passion, my lady?"

Nichole made a face. "I said, did I not, that you knew me too well?"

"He *has* been here two nights. There was no need for him to stay—he could have left wearing his own face. And now I find the two of you finishing breakfast."

She took his arm and sighed. "He is a startling man. He has a trick memory—can't forget anything. It's astonishing, the clarity of his recollections. And he's *done* things, Drake. Saved lives, risked his own. He's been doing all this while I've been taking tours in front of the cameras. With him, it's all been real."

"I wish you joy, Nichole."

She laughed. "Thank you, Drake. You know, I'm very glad to see you in one piece."

He smiled and kissed her. "Happy to *be* in one piece, my lady."

"Shall I order second breakfast?"

"Thank you, no. I've already eaten."

"Here. Sit beside me."

Maijstral removed some fax from his place and idly scanned the lines as he handed them to a robot. "A play, Nichole?"

She gave him a covert smile. "Indeed. Lieutenant Navarre suggested I would be good in it."

He looked at her. "Is he correct?"

"It's a marvelous part. The character is a manipulator and she plays half a dozen strong roles just in maneuvering the other characters into behaving as she wishes."

"Will you do it?"

"The character isn't exactly young. Once one starts doing mature parts, one can't exactly go back to playing ingenues."

"But you will do it, yes?"

"I think so." She bit her lower lip. "I wonder if I'm up to it. It calls for such range."

Maijstral took her hand and squeezed it. "Courage."

She smiled wanly. "Yes. I'll do it. I *know* I'll do it. But I'd just as soon agonize a little more over the decision if it's all the same to you. I'd hate to think I was taking it lightly."

"While you are agonizing, my lady, allow me to show you something." Maijstral pulled the lace back from his wrist, reached into a pocket, and raised his hand to show two small cryogenic vials in his palm. He rotated his wrist, showed Nichole the back of his hand, then rotated his wrist again. There was only one vial in his hand. Nichole nodded approvingly.

"Very good," she said. Maijstral made the motions again, and both vials appeared in his palm.

"Do you think, my lady," he asked, "that you can possibly learn to do this by tonight?"

Nichole looked stern. "I am not participating in any conspiracy, Maijstral, not without knowing what it's all about. Not even for you, Drake."

He bowed to her while the vials appeared and vanished between his fingers. "Naturally you must know, my lady," he said. "But I must caution you not to repeat anything I tell you to Lieutenant Navarre. If he found any of this out, he'd have to challenge half the people at the ball tonight." He looked at her and smiled, anticipating her reaction, the vials dancing in his fingers. "Nothing less," he said, "than the Fate of Civilization is at stake."

The ideographs for "happy journey" and "sad leave taking" floated solemnly through the air of the ballroom, oblivious to the dancing media globes. The orchestra, on an a-grav balcony near the ceiling, played music suitable for strolling about and being seen. Below the orchestra two Elvis impersonators cut each other dead. Etienne stood in solemn scarlet, fingered the hilt of his rapier (a reminder of his duel), and yawned politely into the faces of his admirers. Nichole was dressed in a slightly old-fashioned black gown that revealed her glorious pale shoulders and which featured panniers. She fended off questions about Drake Maijstral with practiced ease. Politicians and local celebrities baked in the strong light; the self-conscious sought alcoves and hovered by the punch bowl; others clustered in knots, their faces to the wall—an Imperialist knot at one end of the room, for example, or a Constellation knot at the other. Each knot frowned, scowled, shuffled its collective feet.

In between, another knot. Maijstral, Gregor, and Roman, facing outward, open to influence. Each smiling, each for reasons entirely his own.

"Yes. I don't need the glass anymore, thank the Virtues. The bruising's all gone." Covering a yawn.

"I notice you are armed this evening. Are you compelled to another encounter?"

Scowling. "I'm afraid I can't stay. I don't talk about that sort of thing."

"Drake."

"Nichole." He sniffed her gently, then kissed her wrist. Globes jostled for the best view. Nichole, smiling, spoke in an undertone. Her lips, to the complete frustration of video lip-readers, barely moved.

"I've asked the orchestra to play the Pilgrimage to the Cinnamon Temple for twice the usual number of measures. I trust that will suffice."

"Thank you, madam. I believe it will suit very well." He turned to the others in his entourage. "Nichole, may I present my associate, Roman?"

"Happy to see you again, my dear." For the benefit of the cameras. "We are old friends, of course."

Resonant sniffs. "I am honored, madam. You are most lovely tonight."

"Thank you, Roman. You look well."

"Very kind of you to notice, madam."

"Nichole," said Maijstral, "this is my junior associate, Mr. Gregor Norman."

"Mr. Norman."

"Ah. Charmed. Madam." Gregor, confronted far too suddenly by the appearance of a woman who personified years of adolescent yearning, lunged forth and seized Nichole's hand in his own damp palm. Nichole, with an assured turn of her arm, carefully avoided the dislocation of her elbow. Her smile remained tranquil. She turned to Roman. Gregor blinked sweat from his eyes and silently cursed himself.

"I hope you will come see me, before I leave. Perhaps tomorrow morning."

Roman's tongue lolled. "I would be delighted, should Mr. Maijstral not be needing me."

Maijstral gave an indulgent smile. He had never ceased to be a little bemused by the mutual attraction between Nichole and his servant. "Of course you may go, Roman," he said. "That is, assuming that any of us are still alive by morning."

"The Jensen woman is here."

"I have seen her, Countess."

"I don't like this last stratagem, Baron. It seems overly complicated to me."

"Maijstral wished to continue his life here in the Constellation. The Empire has no preference either way."

"But you trust him."

"Yes and no." A hesitation. "He knows what will happen if he disappoints us."

"Yes." The Countess's voice growled with satisfaction. "That is true. If he is afraid, he is our servant. Nothing else matters."

"The Imperials are here, Amalia."

"Yes, Pietro." She smiled. "Imperials doomed to disappointment. My favorite sort."

"You seem in good spirits."

"Why should I not be? We've won. And according to the broadcasts, the Imperial who died turned out to be the one I would have preferred dead." A moment's reflection. "Not that I would have wanted anyone dead, of course."

"Of course. I understood what you meant."

"And the one who was really . . . sort of nice . . . is still alive." She smiled, and took his hand. "Besides. After this is all over, we have our own plans."

"Lieutenant Navarre?"

"Yes, Mr.—I'm afraid my memory, sir . . . ?"

"Kuusinen. Your most obedient servant."

"Of course. You must forgive me."

"But certainly. The last few days must have been a strain."

Navarre looked about uneasily. He was still glancing over his shoulder every so often, looking for threats—mad puppets waving magic wands, that sort of thing.

"Yes," he said. "True."

"I wonder if there has been any news of your attacker's identity?"

"It appears he was a deserter from the Imperial Army. No one seems to have any idea how he got here, or what he thought he was doing. I suspect the creature must have been mad."

"No doubt. There is no word on his accomplice?"

"Accomplice, sir?"

"If your deserter was one of the Rompers involved in Miss Jensen's kidnapping, then he had a partner."

Navarre glanced over his shoulder again. He saw Nichole and smiled, his blood warming. She smiled back. "I have wondered about that," he said. "Of course, the security here is first-rate."

"Of course."

"Still. I'm glad I'm only on this planet for a short while."

"Your obedience, gentlemens."

"Count Quik. Your servant."

"Miss Nicholes. Most pleasant is my beseeing you."

"Thank you, my lord. If you will excuse me?"

"Certainlies." Turning to Roman and Maijstral. "Should we be about things?"

Nichole reached into her pannier with her right hand, felt the touch of the cryogenic vial. She practiced the switch, once, twice. Nodded to Etienne in passing, and practiced the switch again. Her heart was beating a little faster than usual—she wondered if her nervousness showed. This wasn't the type of performance she was used to. Lives depended on this.

She cast a glance across the room to Lieutenant Navarre. He was clearly visible: tall, copper-skinned, cloaked in mourning. She had the feeling that he would do far better in this kind of intrigue than she; he was, after all, a man of action. He was speaking to a man in an Imperial-cut coat who looked slightly familiar. Navarre glanced over his shoulder, saw Nichole, and nodded. At once her heart lifted.

Nichole performed the switch, flawlessly, the best she'd ever done.

She returned Navarre's smile and moved on, surrounded by the floating silver globes.

* * *

General Gerald loomed above the throng, his massive chest crowded with medals. He looked sternly down at Maijstral and briskly sniffed his neck. Maijstral sniffed back, his ears pinned back, his manner just as crisp. The General turned to Gregor.

"Are we ready, youngster?" Gregor bowed, his lace cuffs swishing the floor.

"At your service, General." General Gerald frowned. Try as he might to behave otherwise, there was something about Gregor that was definitely Non-U.

"Let's get about it, then," he growled.

Countess Anastasia stood motionless as a statue and watched Roman with eyes of ammonia ice. Baron Sinn's tongue lolled with satisfaction. "Definitely of the Imperial line."

Count Quik's melodious voice piped up in the small room. "Satisfaction, then?"

"Yes, my lord." Baron Sinn gave the vial to Roman, who drew a pocket disruptor.

"Please step back, My Lord Baron," he said, and quickly sterilized the analyzer, killing anything of Nnis CVI that remained in the machine. He bowed to the Baron. "Your servant," he said.

Baron Sinn hefted his small leather bag of cash. "Yours ever," he said.

Roman made his conge. "We shall meet again, my lord, as pilgrims to the Cinnamon Temple."

Roman and Count Quik took their leave. The Countess took the Baron's arm. "It's too complicated," she said.

"We have little choice. Our other options could have endangered the Imperial Relic."

"Nevertheless," the Countess said, "I find it difficult to believe in this miraculous switch."

"It seems well thought out."

"Simplest plans," the Countess said in her best High Khosali, "are easiest undertaken."

"How true," said the Baron piously, wrinkling his nose in distaste at this exchange of profundities. "But the best stew requires many ingredients." He felt the Countess's hand stiffen on his arm. Truly, he thought, he was learning how to deal with this woman.

"Paavo Kuusinen, madam. Your servant."

"Mr. Kuusinen. I believe we have met?"

"Very kind of you to remember, madam."

"Please walk by me. We shall converse."

"Delighted, Miss Nichole." She put her left arm through his right. He cleared his throat. "I wonder, madam, if I might have the honor of the Pilgrimage?"

"I'm afraid that dance is taken, Mr. Kuusinen. Perhaps the Crystal Leaf?"

"Enraptured, madam." Beat. "Madam, may I inquire if you are a bit nervous? Is there a way I can assist you?"

Nichole stiffened. "Why do you ask, Mr. Kuusinen?"

"Your right hand, madam. If you'll pardon the observation, you appear to be clutching something in your pannier."

Nichole's hand jerked from her pannier as if stung. She shot a look at Kuusinen, then calmed herself. "A gift, Mr. Kuusinen. It was presented to me just before my arrival, and I haven't had time to open it. I am in some suspense; I must be showing it."

"I understand, madam. I hope my impertinence is forgiven."

She gave him another look. His face was entirely too composed for her liking. "Naturally, sir," she said. And wondered.

"Mr. Maijstral?" The question came from a hovering media globe. It was a male Khosali voice.

"Sir?"

"May I inquire, with all delicacy, about your relationship with Miss Nichole?"

"We are old friends, sir."

"Perhaps more than that. You have spent three nights in her company."

"Have I?"

"Are you saying that you have not?"

"I suggest—'with all delicacy,' to use your own idiom—that your questions imply far more than ever my answers shall." He cocked an eye at Lieutenant Navarre. "But now, if you will excuse me, I must abandon this banquet of delicacy. I see another old friend across the room."

Captain Tartaglia, his rangers by his side, watched the vid with fury. What was the interviewer yammering about? Why didn't he ask him a meaningful question, such as where the hell was the Emperor's jism? If Tartaglia had been there, you could bet Maijstral would have to answer a sharp question or two.

Gnawing his lips in anger, Tartaglia searched the background for sight of Amalia Jensen and Pietro and saw only the erect, massive figure of the traitor General Gerald marching toward the back of the room. The invitations to the ball had been in their name, and neither of them had been willing to surrender their invitations to him. Damn them for insubordination!

Tasting blood, Captain Tartaglia growled at the video. Someone would pay for this if Maijstral's scheme was only a trick.

"Yes." Amalia Jensen smiled. "Definitely the Imperial culture."

"With your permission, madam."

Gregor drew his disruptor and, taking careful aim, fired three shots into the analyzer. The machine fizzled and died. General Gerald, looming behind Gregor, gave a massive chuckle.

Smiles spread across the features of Pietro and Amalia. "Sterilized," Pietro breathed. He hefted his bag of cash.

Gregor removed the vial from the machine. "The Imperials will receive this sterile vial. You, in return for your cash, will receive the remaining live culture. Until the dance starts you can keep me under observation to confirm that all will be as planned."

"Fear not, sir," Amalia said. "We shall."

"Mr. Maijstral," Gregor said, "will be on the side of the dance set away from any transfers. The vials won't go near him." He cleared his throat. "I suggested that. I thought you might like it better that way."

Maijstral and Lieutenant Navarre walked arm-in-arm down the length of the ballroom. "Please don't underestimate the pressures under which you will both live," Maijstral said. "Being watched all the time. Endless security arrangements. Intrusive questions."

Navarre cocked his ears in the direction of the hovering media globes. "I could get used to it," he said. And managed, for once, to stifle the impulse to glance over his shoulder.

"I could not, Lieutenant, and I had a certain amount of practice before I ever met Nichole. But I wish you more success than I."

"I thank you, sir. You have been more than generous, considering the circumstances."

The orchestra fell silent, and the audience tapped their feet in appreciation. Trumpets rang out. Lines for the Cinnamon Temple began to form.

* * *

Maijstral took Nichole's arm and sensed her nervousness. He squeezed her hand. "Courage, madam," he said. "I have every confidence."

"I'm afraid, Maijstral."

"You will do very well. Your stage fright, I seem to remember, always ends as the orchestra calls the overture."

"The overture just ended, and I am still trembling."

Green fires winked in Maijstral's lazy eyes. "The dance begins, madam. And with the dance, the comedy. For that is what this is, nothing more. We should laugh at this circumstance, not feel reproach." He kissed her hand and led her to her place.

"Count Quik. Your servants."

"Sallie Elrond, my lord. I saw you at the zoo yesterday."

"You seemed in familiarity."

"I spend a lot of time there. I speak methanite."

Pause. "Do you, indeed?"

"Paavo Kuusinen, madam. Will you do me the honor?"

"Amalia Jensen, sir. With pleasure."

"Your very obedient."

"Yours."

Kuusinen made a caper. "Allow me to remark, madam, that you seem quite recovered in spirits after your misadventure."

"Recovered, yes. Thank you."

"It cannot have been enjoyable, first being held prisoner and then becoming the object of public curiosity."

"I am the sensation of the moment, Mr. Kuusinen. Other sensations will follow, and I will return to thankful obscurity."

"You seem to be enjoying your brief encounter with celebrity."

"I am enjoying myself, sir. But perhaps not for that reason."

"Baron Sinn."

"Honored, my lord. Althegn Wohl."

"Mr. Wohl, I just recovered a bag belonging to Mr. Maijstral. Would you mind passing it along in his direction?"

"Ah. Oh. Certainly, my lord."

"I am obliged to you, sir."

"Pleased to see you, Etienne."

"Your servant, Maijstral. As always."

"You have not found Peleng to your taste. My condolences."

Etienne jigged about dutifully, one hand restraining his sword from lashing the people to either side. "Thank you for your sympathy, Maijstral. Though you might keep some in reserve. I'm scheduled to do Nana after this." He blinked. "Oh," he said. "Sorry, Maijstral. I forgot you were born there."

Maijstral cocked his head to one side and frowned. "You know," he said, "perhaps the glass suits you after all."

Etienne twirled one of his mustachios. "Do you really think so?"

"Your servant, Miss Jensen."

"Would you mind doing me a small service, sir?"

"Not at all, madam."

"I have found a bag belonging to Mr. Drake Maijstral. Would you mind passing it along the line toward him? I am certain he is anxious without it."

"Count Quik."

"Elvis Presley. Of Graceland."

"Honored, sir. I hope seeing Memphis soon."

Sergeant Tvi watched the dance as she lounged on her borrowed couch before the vid. The warm, buttery smell of leaf crumpets filled the room; she dusted yellow pigment from her finger as she ate. This life, so far, wasn't bad at all. She was wearing stolen jewels, and later that night (and before the ball ended) would probably go out and harvest some more.

Her only current problem was that she couldn't get off the planet—she didn't dare use her Imperial passport and she didn't know anyone on planet who could get her some new identification. Her training, unfortunately, hadn't encompassed forgery—as long as she was with the Secret Dragoons, Imperial consulates could give her perfectly authentic documents at any time.

Tvi saw Baron Sinn moving down the set with Countess Anastasia as his partner, and her ears flattened. She pointed an imaginary spitfire at them both. "Boom," she said. Right between the Countess's stiffened shoulders.

The media globe panned down the set past where Nichole and Maijstral were dancing more or less in the center, and then Tvi noticed Amalia Jensen moving up the set, partnered with a slight man in an Imperial-cut coat.

Her ears ticked forward. Perhaps, she thought, there was a solution here.

* * *

"I am told this bag belongs to Mr. Maijstral. Could you please send it along toward him?"

"I am Mr. Maijstral's associate, madam. Let me make certain it is the bag he lost."

Roman opened the bag and saw a substantial bundle of cash. He closed the bag.

"This is indeed what we missed, madam. Our thanks for its return."

He looked down the set and caught Maijstral's eye.

"General Gerald."

"Countess Anastasia."

A frigid silence prevailed.

"Gregor Norman, madam."

"Your servant, sir. I say—I have just received this bag, which I am told belongs to Mr. Maijstral. Would you mind propelling it in his direction?"

"Why not? Give it here."

Gregor's temporary partner was appalled as Gregor ferreted through the bag and swiftly determined that it did, indeed, contain something approximating the correct amount of cash. He looked down the set, caught Maijstral's eye, and waved.

The ears of Gregor's partner went back, and she bared her teeth. This was more than Non-U. It was sordid.

Paavo Kuusinen received a bag and felt of it before passing it on. A smile began to cross his features.

"They certainly have very active imaginations."

"To be sure."

"I have a theory. Perhaps it is the sort only an aristocratic dilettante could arrive at, but let me give you an idea. . . ."

"Your servant, Mr. Quijano."

"I thank you, General. Yours."

"Things should be over soon, youngster."

"Yes. Miss Jensen will be relieved when Captain Tartaglia moves out of her house."

"She should have thrown him out."

"It was easier for her to seek shelter at my house."

The General raised an eyebrow. "Yes?"

Pietro's face flushed. "We've been planning our future."

General Gerald smiled. His face was not accustomed to it and the result was somewhat more horrific than if he had turned red and yelled. "I hope it is a happy one, youngster. I think you're very well suited."

Pietro, mildly paralyzed by the General's appearance, took some time to react to what the General had actually said.

"Oh. Thank you, sir. I'm sure we'll be very happy."

"Sir. I have come upon this . . . object . . . which I believe fell from the pocket of Baron Sinn yonder. Would you mind terribly passing it up the set toward him?"

"They won't believe that we *exist?*"

"We are figments, if you will, of their subconscious. That is what I suspect."

"I can't . . . think . . . of anything that would contradict that interpretation."

"If true, it would prove a most illuminating view into their psychology."

Maijstral, preoccupied with dancing about Nichole and watching sidelong as the bags and vials progressed in the dance, had been listening to the high, resonant voice for some time before its familiarity caused him to glance toward the short, globe-headed figure on his left. Count Quik.

Count Quik, speaking Human Standard with absolute coherence. The Count's usual manner of speech, Maijstral realized, was purely an aristocratic affectation.

A bit startled, Maijstral almost missed a step. He recovered and danced on.

Tartaglia was in a rage. "Can you see it? What the hell is going on?"

"Maybe we should change the channel, Captain."

"Mind your own damned business."

"Sir. I believe you reverse here."

"Oh. Thank you, ah, madam."

Gregor clenched his teeth, jammed the leather bag in his armpit, and ducked beneath his partner's arm to his correct place. His line took two steps back without him, and just as he caught up they surged forward again. Gregor wiped sweat away and smeared cosmetic on his sleeve.

Damn this dance, anyway. He hadn't had enough time to learn it.

Now, at last, it was his turn to stay still while the third couples made a passage. Mentally counting out eight measures, Gregor reached into a pocket arm and came up with the sterile vial. He turned right on the eighth measure and did a back-to-back with his new temporary partner, a Tanquer in a pince-nez with smoked lenses. This uncovered a view of the pretty girl who would be his temporary partner in about forty-eight measures, and Gregor winked at her. She seemed surprised. Gregor and the Tanquer finished their back-to-back and commenced eight measures of siding.

"Sir," he said, producing the vial, "I have just picked up something belonging to Miss Amalia Jensen. Maybe we should give it back. Would you do me the favor of passing it down the line?"

The Tanquer's nictitating membranes slid shut, which, together with the smoked glass, produced an odd effect. "Very well, strange young person," he said, and took the vial.

Gregor capered back to his permanent partner and blinked sweat from his eyes. Thank God that was over.

Paavo Kuusinen looked down the set, saw something moving toward him. Looked up, saw something coming that way.

He thought a few figures ahead, made a rapid calculation. He hooked his arm through the arm of the Khosalikh next to him, swung the man around.

"Wait. Sir. This is next figure."

"No, sir. Now."

"Sir." The voice was pained. Kuusinen had just altered their progression. He and Kuusinen had just changed partners.

Amalia Jensen gave him a surprised look as the dance swept her away.

"Baron Sinn."

"General Gerald."

Gloating. "Try denying *now* that you're a spy."

The Baron was imperturbable. "I am a private nobleman, trying to do my Empire a service."

Hah, thought the General. You *think* we're going to get the real artifact, and that you're deceiving us by letting us think yours is going to be sterilized when it's not. But I *saw* your spunk get sterilized, and *know* all you're getting is small meaningless coils of dead protein. So there. Hah.

The plot made the General's head hurt, but one thing he knew. This was better than whipping the Imperial fleet. More *personally* satisfying.

"Navarre will be finishing his business here. The estate auction is in five days."

"I see."

"I've got one more stop on my tour, and then I'm going off to have my feet done. We'll meet on Fantome, and start making arrangements for the play."

"Perhaps"—dancing about her—"I'll manage to attend the premiere."

"The pickings would be good, Drake, but can you do a good imitation of a broken heart? You'd have to, you know."

Thoughtfully. "I suppose I could summon a tear or two."

"It would have to be more than that. After all, you're supposed to have engaged in a passionate and desperate romance with me here, all while I was falling in love with the handsome lieutenant. Going to the premiere might be more than your heart could bear."

Maijstral considered this while Nichole circled him. "Perhaps you are right. A mere display of manly grief wouldn't be enough."

"Pity we can't tell the truth. The public would be *enraged* to discover that you and I were faking a romance in order to pursue our various intrigues—the Diadem's followers insist on the authenticity of their illusions, and they'd want to pay us back for fooling them."

Maijstral reflected on his decision, four years ago, not to seek membership in the Diadem. He had no reason, he concluded, to regret it.

"I shall have to console myself with a recording," he said.

"I will send you one, but only if my performance is good. If I'm awful, I will burn every copy."

Maijstral smiled. "I shall consider the recording's arrival inevitable, madam." He turned left, Nichole faced the other way. He and Nichole would be separated for a while. This was the marching bit.

"Mr. Kuusinen, we meet again."

"Nichole, ever your servant."

Kuusinen was her new temporary partner. She didn't trust the man at all. And there was something about his smile she didn't like.

* * *

"Your servant, Miss Jensen."

"General Gerald."

"Your Mr. Quijano tells me you are going to join the Pioneers together. May I offer you my congratulations? Not many people are willing to do the hard work of colonization these days."

"Thank you, General."

"Your father would have been proud of you, miss."

A slow smile spread across Amalia's features. "General," she said, "I do believe you're right."

Maijstral was anticipating another attack of his residual childhood terror, but was pleasantly surprised to discover that his heart no longer quaked at the appearance of the Countess Anastasia. Instead it was the Countess who looked uncomfortable, standing stiffly, her shoulders thrown back unyielding as a yoke.

She looked at him with diamond-chip eyes. "How *could* you?" she asked.

How could I what? Maijstral wondered. Wreck her house, shoot at her servants, free her victim, deceive everyone in sight?

"Sorry, Mother," he said. "Force of circumstance, you know."

The accident wasn't Nichole's fault. Maijstral's plan called for three vials, as he was unwilling to trust to the coincidence of Nichole receiving both vials at the same time. He was being cautious, but he was also wrong.

The live culture, moving down the set toward Amalia Jensen, arrived first. Nichole smiled, accepted it with her left hand. Her right hand touched her pannier, where the other culture waited, for luck; but this wasn't the switch yet—she had to reach out with her right hand for Kuusinen, touch fingers, and walk around him. Then caper, then repeat.

At the end of the repetition, she turned to her right, ready to ask her new temporary partner to pass the vial on. But the new partner, a bewildered, elderly Khosalikh with more than his share of muzzle rings, had just received the sterile culture, and was holding it out to her.

Hands swung together. The vials clattered. The Khosalikh bumbled and banged them together again. Terror clutched Nichole as the vials clattered to the floor.

* * *

Paavo Kuusinen watched carefully at the objects tumbling from Nichole's fingers, perceived the look of horror on her face. Time seemed to stop.

Maijstral caught the movement out of the corner of his eye and froze in midmovement. The Countess thudded into him and drove her heel onto his instep. He didn't feel the pain.

Pietro Quijano stared in surprise as he danced across the set. He could have sworn he'd seen a vial clatter across the floor.

Baron Sinn saw the accident clearly and bared his teeth. His partner was frightened and took a step back.

Up and down the line, a sense of catastrophe began to spread. Few knew precisely what had gone wrong, but everyone realized that something had gone awry, and the rhythm of the dance was lost as heads began to crane left and right. Media globes swooped left and right, looking for the source of the turbulence.

The elderly Khosalikh murmured an apology, bowed, and picked up a vial. He looked at it in puzzlement. It *looked* identical to the one he'd just held. But was it?

Maijstral stood stock-still, picturing the Countess with a gun, Amalia Jensen with a gun, Imperial Marines and Constellation Death Commandos, all with guns. The Countess breathed insults at him, calling him an ungrateful wretch, a scoundrel, an incompetent, and no son of hers.

He wished the latter, at least, was true.

Paavo Kuusinen stepped forward. "Pardon me, madam," he said, and bent to pick up a vial at Nichole's feet. "*This,* sir, was yours," he said.

The elderly Khosalikh looked from one to the other. "It was?"

Nichole looked from one vial to the other and realized that her call had come. She made her decision; her hand dipped into her pannier and came up with the hidden vial. She took the vial from Kuusinen, made the switch flawlessly, and passed the switched vial to her left. "For Baron Sinn," she said.

The Imperial Marines started to fade from Maijstral's mind.

* * *

Nichole looked at the old gentleman, who was still gazing at his outstretched vial. She took his hand in hers, helped him turn around. "That is Miss Jensen's," she said. "Please send it down the set."

The Death Commandos began to turn transparent.

People began to remember their part in the dance. Gradually the lines sorted themselves out.

"I believe, sir," said Gregor, "that this is where you reverse."

"Oh. I don't doubt you are correct. Thank you, sir."

Gregor smiled in satisfaction. At least he remembered this part.

Pietro gnawed his lip as he operated his second scanner. He could hear the murmur of the crowd as, following the dance, they crowded toward the refreshment buffet.

His scanner rang. Relief flooded his mind. He looked at Amalia and grinned.

"It's the live culture. Now we know for certain the sterilized culture went the other way."

"Too complicated. I knew this wasn't going to work."

Lights flickered on the scanner. Baron Sinn rotated the display so that Countess Anastasia could see it.

"It's the Imperial Artifact, my lady. Unquestionably."

A certain dismay clamored in the Countess's mind. "Maijstral pulled off his switch, then."

"Apparently."

She conceded defeat. She squared her shoulders. "Long live the Pendjalli," she said. Her voice was like a trumpet call. Muted, perhaps, but sincere.

Baron Sinn echoed her. "Long live the Imperial line." In reverent tones.

He put the vial in his pocket and offered the Countess his arm. "Perhaps, my lady, it is time for us to depart."

Because, Maijstral thought, he found he could not act any other way. Somewhat to his surprise, there had proven more scruples in his makeup than ever he suspected. Even though he did not want to live in the Empire, or desire an Emperor over him, he could not coldly condemn the Imperial line to death, not when it meant so much to so many billions. If a threat to the Human Constellation resulted—and that was by no means certain—then that threat would have to be dealt with when it occurred. Maijstral could not assume the right to disrupt a millennia-old civilization on the half-chance there might be a conflict years down the line.

Besides. It was the Emperor's to begin with.

Baron Sinn had assured him the matter would be handled delicately. Concubines of good family would be found in the farther reaches. None would be impregnated for several years. None of the heirs would be revealed for decades. When they were placed before the public, rumors would be started; one of the other two artifacts had been discovered, or the Pendjalli had simply cloned poor Nnis in secrecy, against all tradition, and refused to admit it.

The resolution would be satisfyingly like an old romance. The unknown heir, raised as a foster child far away, would become the next Pendjalli, to his own surprise and the surprise of everyone else. And all because of an odd scruple in a thief. It warmed Maijstral's heart to think about it.

Was he being sentimental? he wondered. He could not tell.

"Sir?"

Maijstral turned to the globe hovering at chest height. It offered a human voice.

"Madam?" he replied.

"There seemed to be some manner of intrigue going on during the Pilgrimage, involving people passing things back and forth. Are you aware of the nature of these events?"

Maijstral shrugged. "No one passed anything to *me,*" he said. "Perhaps you should ask someone else."

"Are you going to be accompanying Nichole for the rest of her tour?"

Maijstral recollected that he should be suffering intimations of a broken heart by now.

"That has not been decided," he said. "Events have rather taken us by surprise."

And on that ambiguous note, Maijstral ended the interview.

Paavo Kuusinen, unnoticed, slipped from the hall. His face bore a smile.

His stay on Peleng, he decided, had been quite satisfactory.

He would have a lot to tell his employer.

He knew he would see Maijstral again.

THIRTEEN

Captain Tartaglia took careful aim with his disruptor. "Ready," he called. "Aim. Fire."

Fingers tightened on triggers. Silent, invisible energies flooded the darkness of Amalia Jensen's backyard.

Somewhere in the darkness, a nightbird called.

"Cease fire," said Tartaglia, and looked at the small vial propped on a chair.

It seemed unchanged. Tartaglia felt vaguely disappointed. I have destroyed you, inhuman scum, he thought, but the thought failed to comfort him.

Amalia Jensen put her pistol in its holster. She patted the pocket where Tartaglia's credit counter rested. She'd be able to pay her debts tomorrow. "There's a shuttle heading to the launching station in two hours," she said. "You and your people have ample time to book passage."

"Two hours?"

"Time enough, don't you think?" Amalia took the vial from the chair and held it up to the starlight. "I think I'll keep this. A souvenir." She put it in her pocket, then saw his frown and laughed. "I've earned it," she pointed out. "I was the one who was kidnapped."

Tartaglia conceded. "If you insist." He reflected that he'd still be able to make a terrific report to his superiors, and expect commendations and a promotion. The Strong Hand, he thought, would be nearer the top.

Amalia produced an envelope and handed it to Tartaglia. "My resignation from Humanity Prime," she said. "And Mr. Quijano's."

"Hm. What I might have expected from the fainthearts."

"Fainthearted? We're joining the Pioneer Corps, Captain. It's what we should have done in the first place."

Tartaglia told himself he didn't much care, and to concentrate instead on the commendations and promotions he could expect. For some reason he couldn't get excited about either.

He began giving orders for his troops to pack and head toward the shuttle.

The strains of "Farewell, Comrades, Farewell" floated over the terrace. Maijstral took a breath of cool air and contemplated his profits. Lord Giddon would be satisfied, the diamond ring would be redeemed, there would be enough left for some long-term investments. Always assuming, of course, that no new Lord Giddons showed up.

"Have you seen Gregor, Roman?"

"I believe he made a friend. One of Countess Tank's young ladies."

"That's the last we'll see of him tonight, I suppose."

Maijstral looked at his servant with cheerful regard. Everything had come out all right.

"Roman, I think we have done very well this evening."

"Yes, sir."

"I suppose that for our ultimate success we should thank Mr. Kuu—Kuusinen, was it?"

"I believe so, sir."

Maijstral frowned. "I'd like to thank him personally, but I suppose I should continue to stay out of it. There's no reason he should connect me with this."

"None whatever, sir."

Maijstral turned at the sound of footsteps behind him. Etienne stepped out onto the terrace with a young lady on his arm. Gold winked around one eye. Maijstral bowed.

"I see you have restored the glass, sir."

"I have, Maijstral. I think it suits me well."

"So it does."

Etienne turned to his lady. "The glass came about as a result of the Pearl Woman business. I suppose you've heard about it?"

"Yes, sir. I must have watched the record a dozen times. My heart was in my throat the whole time. I was so afraid for you I thought I would die."

Etienne smiled. Maijstral stepped forward.

"You will excuse us, I hope?"

"Certainly, Maijstral. Wish me luck on Nana."

Maijstral sniffed Etienne's cheek and received a poke from his starboard mustachio. Roman followed as he stepped back into the ballroom, seeing a few last dancers whirling to the last song, the rest slowly filing out. Maijstral observed Nichole walking arm-in-arm with Lieutenant Navarre and remembered to sigh.

It was time for him to work on his broken heart.

"Who is it?" Amalia called from the kitchen, where she was supervising the new robot as it stowed away the guest dishes and crystal that Tartaglia's rangers had used during their stay.

Pietro asked the room to give a holoview of the person on the roof. He squinted at the brightness of the daytime image. "I don't recognize her. A small Khosalikh in a Jefferson-Singh. Wearing a lot of jewelry."

"You don't say!" said Amalia. Pietro was surprised at the delight in her voice. She stuck her head out of the kitchen and looked at the holo. She frowned as she studied the image, then nodded. "I'll go meet her," she decided.

"Is it someone I should know?"

"I'll tell you later. It's a long story."

Amalia stepped onto the a-grav and rose to the roof. She shaded her eyes in the bright morning sun. She couldn't be entirely certain. "May I help you?" she asked.

"Perhaps." The Khosalikh also seemed uncertain. "Possibly you don't recognize me. My name is Tvi." Joy filled Amalia's heart.

"I recognize the voice perfectly well."

Tvi's tongue lolled as Amalia gave her a hug.

"I was uncertain of my reception."

"I think we can put politics aside for the nonce. May I offer you first breakfast?"

"Delighted, Miss Jensen." She held up a paper bag. "I brought some leaf crumpets."

"After all we've been through, I should think you could call me Amalia."

* * *

The smell of harness webbing and lubricant rose in General Gerald's nostrils. Mild regret filled his mind. He had disassembled his battle armor and was now crating it for storage.

Maijstral wouldn't come now, he was certain. The glorious battle he had anticipated would never take place.

He had no reason to feel disappointed, he thought. He had performed a singular service to the Constellation, and though his role would never become public, he could take satisfaction in a job well done, a long career crowned by one last glorious intrigue.

It was just a pity there wasn't more violence.

Pietro had just realized who, precisely, Tvi was. "This is one of your kidnappers?"

"Yes." Amalia grinned. "The nice one."

"The nice one!" Pietro's hands turned to fists. "She held you hostage!"

"Just doing my job, Mr. Quijano." Tvi licked jam from her fingers. "Normally I disdain violence, but it so happened I needed the work."

"Needed the work." Pietro repeated the words without seeming to grasp their meaning. He shook his head. "And now"—he pointed a breakfast fork at Tvi—"and now you propose to make Miss Jensen"—the fork swung toward Amalia—"Miss Jensen, *your former victim,* your agent for further crimes."

Tvi considered this summation. "That is correct, Mr. Quijano."

"And her former victim"—Amalia smiled—"proposes to accept."

"Amalia!"

"Well, why not? Tvi is going to be an Allowed Burglar whether we say so or not. Since she's going to steal, why not act as an agent in negotiating with the insurance companies and collect ten percent when she sells the stuff back? Particularly since I seem to have had some recent experience at these sorts of negotiations."

"Why not?" Pietro's mind floundered. *"Why not?"* His fingers began to crumble a leaf crumpet. "As I recall, your former position was that Allowed Burglary was a shameful remnant of a decadent Imperial culture, and that theft ought not to be allowed under any circumstances, and punished with imprisonment when it occurred."

Amalia looked at Tvi. "Perhaps," she said, "I found being held hostage a broadening experience. In any case, I'll only be working for Tvi until she can steal some appropriate identification and leave

Peleng. Besides," she added sensibly, "it isn't as if I'm *making* her steal."

"Sophistry, Amalia."

"Plus, if I'm to join the Pioneers I'll have to have my epilepsy dealt with, and Tvi's theft might as well pay for that as anything."

"I don't suppose," Pietro said, "the word of a fiancé stands for much in all of this."

Amalia put her hand on his. "I'm afraid not, love. My friendship with Tvi predates our latest, ah, arrangement."

Pietro sighed. "Friendship," he said, resigned. "Arrangements." He concluded there was little more to say on the subject. Domestic bliss, he thought, was largely a matter of compromise.

Sensibly, he reached for another crumpet and ate it.

It dissolved on his tongue like the taste of a new world.

Maijstral kissed Nichole's hand. "This, I take it, is where my heart gets broken for good and all."

Nichole smiled. "I'm afraid so, Maijstral." She patted the settee. "Come sit by me."

Maijstral glanced in the direction of her parlor as he sat. Morning light was flooding in the windows. "Lieutenant Navarre?" he asked.

"Giving his first press conference."

Maijstral raised his eyebrows. "Isn't that flinging him to the ravens a little early, my lady?"

She gave him a look. "He may as well get used to it. If he's going to get frightened off, it's best to know now rather than later."

He sighed. "That's true. Paying court to a member of the Diadem is not for the faint of heart."

She looked at him and put her hand on his. "I didn't aim that remark at you, Maijstral. I understood your decision entirely, much as I regretted your making it."

"I did not take offense."

There was a moment's silence. "So what will you do, Drake, to assuage your broken heart?"

There was a quiet glow deep within his lazy eyes. "Loot Peleng of everything I can carry off. It's the least this planet can do considering the trouble I've had here. Some of my targets are days overdue."

"Sounds as if you'll compensate for romantic disappointment well enough."

"I'll manage, my lady."

She smiled, squeezed his hand. "Are you pleased, then, Drake? With your part in this?"

"I cannot say I welcomed this, or am thankful I was involved. But it seems to have come out well enough, especially considering the potential for mayhem. I may even say that, for most of us anyway, I have achieved something of a happy ending."

Nichole's laughter rang in the room. "I suppose you have! Tell me—was it the ending you intended?"

His eyes were completely hidden. "Near enough, my lady," he said. And with that she had to be content.

HOUSE OF SHARDS

To Françoise Auclaire le Vison
"the Chef"
and Baron le Vison of Milwaukee
"the Waiter"
l'appétit vient en mangeant

. . . One false move and we could have a farce on our hands.

—Tom Stoppard,
On the Razzle

ONE

When one star gobbles another, the universe may be forgiven if it pauses to take breath. Imagine the sight: the smaller star a bright-haloed emptiness, a nullity that draws into itself vast ruddy flares of stellar matter until it consumes the very heart of its companion. People might well stop and stare. Some may even pay for the privilege.

Thus Silverside Station, a small asteroid held within view of the phenomenon by mighty anchors of self-generated gravitational energy. Small, hence exclusive. With exclusive rights to the view.

And about to have its grand opening.

A private media globe hung inconspicuously over the control console. Recording every word.

"Imagine it. Everyone on both sides of the border wanting to have a ticket. Salivating for one. Offering *anything* to get one. And the two of us, flying into Silverside on our own private racing yacht."

A doubtful frown. "I'm not certain of this rule banning the media. It seems extreme." A glance at the private globe. "I can't record myself. That's a little absurd."

"The ban only applies to *most* of the media, Pearl. Some will be there. Kyoko Asperson, for one."

"That," the Pearl said, her ears flattening, "will guarantee catastrophe."

Pearl Woman was tall and dark-haired. Her shoulders and arms bulged with transplanted muscle: in her youth she hunted daffles from proughback, and that takes upper-body strength. Her hair shagged from her head like the mane of a lion. She wore a single pearl hanging from the left ear, an object balanced artfully by a duelling scar on her right cheek. Both were her trademarks within the Diadem, never duplicated by others of that exclusive organization, though they were often imitated by her admirers across the Constellation.

The enthusiasm of Pearl Woman's companion was undimmed. "Only three of the Diadem were invited. Three of the Three Hundred. You and the Marquess Kotani and Zoot. Imagine that."

Pearl Woman gave her a look. "Advert. I need to dock the ship."

Sulkily. "You *could* put it on auto."

"Not my way, Advert."

Advert, with a self-conscious glance at the media globe, fell silent. She was young and pale and willowy, with wavy brown hair that fell halfway down her back. She had dropped her second name, hoping the Human Diadem might notice and consider her for the next vacancy. She wore silver rings on every finger, including the thumbs, and fondly hoped they (and perhaps the hair) might one day become her own trademark. Pearl Woman knew better, but had not as yet disillusioned her.

Advert was new to his sort of existence and still felt a little uncertain. Her remaining illusions, Pearl Woman thought, made her charming, though in an unformed sort of way. One day Advert's particular brand of charm would cease to hold its attraction; but that day had not as yet arrived.

Throughout their conversation, the awesome sight of one star consuming another had been splayed across the ship's viewscreens. Neither paid it the slightest attention.

The entry concourse was a long, low room, carpeted in dark green. Darker tapestries flashed winks of silver thread from the walls. The lighting was subdued, and a small orchestra played brisk tunes in the corner. People in uniforms stood behind desks; robots carried bags in efficient silence. Disembarking passengers took their time strolling toward the desks. It was not done to seem in a hurry.

"Pearl Woman. You are looking very dashing."

"Maijstral. It's been years."

"The matched swords are very elegant. What are they, small sabers?"

"Cutlasses. I thought they'd add a swashbuckling touch." Pearl Woman snicked one sword from its scabbard, performed a figure, returned it. Like the claws of a kitten, a touch of fear moved along Maijstral's nerves. Someone had tried to hack him to bits with a sword just recently, and the presence of edged weapons made him more than usually nervous.

He and Pearl Woman clasped hands (three fingers each) and sniffed one another's ears as, around them, the entry concourse bustled on. Maijstral was slightly taller than average, but he had to raise his head to reach the Pearl's neck.

Drake Maijstral's dark hair waved to his shoulders. He was dressed in grey. Lace floated casually at neck and wrists. He wore a large diamond on one finger, and leather buskins on his feet. His eyes were green and heavy-lidded; they gave an impression of laziness, or at least languor. He seemed to be in his mid-twenties.

Maijstral turned and indicated a restless young man dressed in violet plush. "My associate, Mr. Gregor Norman."

"Charmed, Mr. Norman," said Pearl Woman, "This is Advert, my companion."

Hands were clasped all around, but High Custom sniffing was avoided—the entry concourse was a little too common for High Custom unless rank and previous acquaintance demanded it. Maijstral and Advert offered one another two fingers, indicating a certain presumed intimacy through their common acquaintance with Pearl Woman. Pearl Woman and Advert gave one finger each to Gregor. Gregor gave two to Pearl Woman and three to Advert, the latter indicating a degree of hopefulness far above his station.

Advert sniffed and drew herself up. Gregor, who had spoken his greetings in a provincial accent that could only be described as cheeky, declined to be properly abashed and instead grinned.

The custom of hand-clasping, after an interval of several thousand years, was now a rage. It had been rediscovered by the Constellation Practices Authority, who recommended it a "natural, human gesture," and suggested it replace the elegant ear-sniffing of Khosali High Custom.

Traditionalists and Imperialists denounced the revival as vulgar. Pro-Constellation partisans adopted it eagerly. Saying hello had suddenly become a gesture fraught with political import.

That, and the issue of how many fingers to offer, had all society dizzy with new possibilities.

Pearl Woman took Maijstral's arm. They strolled lazily toward the customs desks.

Behind them, Gregor offered Advert his arm. She ignored it and followed the Pearl, her head high. Gregor gave another cheeky grin and then put a hi-stick in his mouth.

"Do you like the way Laurence is playing you in the vids?" Pearl Woman asked. "I didn't like him at first, but I think he's growing into the part."

"I've not seen him," Maijstral said. Pearl Woman gave a disbelieving grin. "People never believe me," Maijstral said equably, "but it's true."

"Is Roman with you?" Pearl Woman asked.

"Yes. Taking care of the baggage."

"Please give him my compliments."

Maijstral nodded. "I will. He will be pleased that you remembered him."

"You are out of mourning, I see."

"It's been over a year."

"That long? I had no idea."

"Thank you, by the way, for your condolences. That was kind of you."

"Are you His Grace of Dornier now? Should I be milording you?"

Amusement sparked in Maijstral's lazy eyes. "Heavens no," he said. "I'd feel foolish being the Duke of This and the Viscount of That, considering the family's lost almost all the estates during the Rebellion and there's nothing to be his grace the Duke *of.*"

Pearl Woman smiled. "I understand."

"The most ridiculous title, of course, is Hereditary Prince-Bishop of Nana. My father prevailed upon me to preach a sermon at my investiture, and I felt damned silly standing up in front of a packed cathedral. I'd just taken out my burglar's ticket, so I preached on tolerance." He cocked his head in remembrance. "It was well received, at least," he said. "And it entitled me to a small stipend. So it's not all bad."

The way ahead was clear, and they stepped to the customs counter. A Khosali female looked at them from behind the clean ebon surface. Eyes glittered from beneath the polished brim of a narrow cap tailored with notches to allow her pointed ears full movement.

"Mr. Maijstral," she said, pointing. "Your desk is over *there.*"

Disembarking from second class, a nondescript, portly man named Dolfuss picked up two heavy suitcases from the robot baggage carrier and began moving toward customs.

"Excuse me, sir," the robot said. "I will be happy to carry those."

Dolfuss ignored the robot and moved on.

The room glowed blue. Mr. Sun, sitting in his padded chair behind a U-shaped console, found it a soothing color.

He looked with satisfied eyes at his security monitors. Individual media globes had tagged everyone who had just disembarked, and images of each decked the walls. A hologram projector set into Mr. Sun's desk showed a file labelled *Known Associates.*

Gregor Norman, it said. *Human male, age 20 yrs.* The picture was an old one and showed Gregor wearing vulgar earrings and a grossly offensive hairstyle. A short arrest record was appended.

Next to Gregor floated the hologram of a Khosalikh wearing a subdued dark suit with a fashionable braided collar. *Roman,* it said. *Khosali male, age 46 yrs. Bodyservant. No arrests or convictions.*

Mr. Sun touched an ideogram on his console. Two of the video monitors flashed. *Match,* the console reported, and made a pleasant chirring sound.

Mr. Sun smiled. He touched another ideogram to transmit the pictures to Khamiss at the entry concourse.

Acknowledged, flashed the response.

Mr. Sun looked down at his uniform, brushed away a speck of lint. A simple touch, he thought. A simple gesture like *this,* he thought, and like the lint, the thieves are brushed away.

In his view, this set of burglars had a lot to atone for, and he intended the atonement start now.

"Mr. Norman," said Khamiss. "Your line is over there."

"I'd count those rings if I were you," Pearl Woman said.

Advert glanced in surprise at her fingers, and Pearl Woman smiled. Advert was so *easy.*

"Sometimes they'll take the jewelry right off you, right in public," Pearl Woman said. "It's vulgar, but sometimes Allowed Burglars like to show off."

"That Gregor person was vulgar enough, heaven knows." Advert looked dubiously at the trademark that dangled from the other woman's ear. "Aren't you worried, Pearl?"

Pearl Woman touched the matched silver hilts of her swords. "Not at all, Advert," she said. "It's for other people to worry, not me." She looked at Advert. "If Maijstral ever bothers you, there's something you can do to get rid of him."

"Yes?"

"Ask him if his mother is well."

"That's all?"

"It's always worked for me."

Dolfuss waited in a queue with the other second-class passengers. (Second-class passengers weren't expected to mind waiting in line.) The others were either servants of the first-class passengers or people who actually worked at Silverside, late arrivals come to take up their new jobs. Dolfuss was the only guest.

Dolfuss didn't care. He was enjoying himself.

Annoyance flickered across Maijstral's face. A tall, thin, grimly satisfied sort of person was looting his luggage. Gregor, a step back, gazed on in astonished dismay.

"Darksuit," said the man, a human named Kingston. His ears fluttered in disapproval. He lifted the object from Maijstral's trunk, and handed it to a robot. "Illegal onstation. It will be returned to you on your departure."

"The point of a darksuit," said Maijstral's servant, Roman, "is to blend in with the darkness. There is no darkness on this station. The suit would be useless."

Roman was a tall Khosalikh, erect, dignified, his ears folded in an expression of cold fury. He spoke Human Standard without accent and, considering the circumstances, with admirable restraint.

"You may complain to Mr. Sun if you wish," Kingston said. "He's head of security. I only enforce the regulations."

Roman's nostrils palpitated in anger. Maijstral gazed in cool annoyance at the sight of his belongings strewn over the concourse. He frowned..

"I see no need to appeal to underlings," he said. "I will complain to Baron Silverside in person."

"Nothing, sir, would give me greater pleasure," Kingston said, radiating grim happiness. He looked down at Gregor's trunk, then reached into it. He picked up a small gadget and held it up to the light.

"An electronic device of the sort referred to as a 'black box,' " he said. The quotes were clear in his voice. "Commonly used to interrupt alarm systems." He wagged a solemn finger at Gregor. "Very naughty, Mr. Norman," he said. "You'll get it back when you leave."

Gregor turned red. Maijstral folded his arms. "Must we be subjected to this amateur stand-up routine while you search our baggage?" he asked. "Let's get it over with, shall we?"

"Certainly, your worship," said Kingston. He handed the black box to his robot with an elaborate gesture. "Now let's see what Mr. Norman has in his gadget box, shall we?"

There seemed to be a delay in disembarking the second-class passengers. Dolfuss waited patiently, glancing over the concourse. There were supposed to be members of the Diadem here, and Dolfuss had always been a big Nichole fan.

The lounge bar, called the Shadow Room, was dark, quiet, scarcely inhabited. A woodwind quartet readied their equipment in a corner.

"Marquess."

"Your grace."

"I enjoyed the recordings of your last play. I only wish I'd had the chance to see it live."

"Thank you, your grace. The play did wonders for my share. I believe I saw you in that race on—Hrinn, was it?" The Diadem's researchers had given the Marquess Kotani current facts on every prominent person scheduled to be at Silverside, the better to be ready for informed conversation. The Marquess always did his homework.

"Yes. I did fairly well in the Hrinn race."

"Second only to Khottan."

The Duchess smiled. "Khottan," she said, "was lucky."

Kotani returned the smile. He was a spare, cultivated, brown-skinned human with a brief mustache, greying temples, and a distinguished profile. He had been born in the Empire and had made his reputation with the naturalness of his languor. He was one of the older members of the Diadem—their first lord—and his share had always remained in the top twenty.

The Marquess cast a careful glance over the lounge bar, seeing no one he cared to talk to other than the Duchess. "Will you join me at my table?" he asked.

"Alas," said the Duchess, "I am here to meet someone."

"Some other time, your grace." He sniffed her and withdrew.

Her grace Roberta Altunin, the Duchess of Benn, was nineteen and a gifted amateur athlete. Her hair was dark red and cut short, her eyes were deep violet, and she moved with grace and confidence. She had first-rate advisors, and they had suggested Silverside as a perfect location for her debut.

She stepped to the bar and ordered a cold rink. She nodded to the man standing next to her.

"Mr. Kuusinen."

"Your grace."

They clasped hands (one finger apiece) and lightly sniffed one another's ears. Mr. Paavo Kuusinen was a slight man with an unexceptional appearance. He wore a gree coat laced up the sides and back.

"The coat suits you, Kuusinen."

"Thank you. I discovered that my wardrobe marked me too easily as an Imperial citizen, so I had a new one made. Your gown is quite becoming, by the way."

Roberta smiled lightly. Her drink arrived, and she put her thumbprint on the chit.

"The *Count Boston* has arrived," Kuusinen said. His forefinger circled the rim of his glass. "I understand that Zoot is aboard. And Drake Maijstral, the burglar."

"Have you seen them?"

"I have seen Maijstral. He seemed to be having difficulty at customs."

Lines appeared between Roberta's brows. "Will that be a problem for him?"

"He seems a man of considerable resource. I'm sure he will rise above the difficulty."

She raised her glass, put it down again. "I don't want this to go wrong, Kuusinen."

"Geoff Fu George is already on station. Perhaps he would be more suitable. He has more resources to draw on."

"I want Maijstral." Firmly.

Kuusinen assented. The woman's mind was made up. "Your grace," he said.

Roberta glanced behind her, seeing Kotani in conversation with a short woman in bright clothes and a funny hat. "We shouldn't be seen together for very long, Kuusinen. Perhaps you should make your congé."

"As you wish, your grace."

They clasped hands, still one finger apiece, and sniffed. Kuusinen passed the woodwind quartet on his way to the door. Roberta took her drink and drifted in Kotani's direction. She noticed silver media globes hovering over Kotani's conversation.

". . . I'm still looking for something suitable," he was saying.

"I understand," the short woman agreed. She spoke a broad provincial accent that seemed less comically non-U than, somehow, a deliberate provocation. "It must be difficult finding a part nowadays that features the sort of old-fashioned character you favor."

Kotani stiffened slightly. "Not old-fashioned, my dear," he said. "Classical, I should think." He turned to Roberta. "Your grace, may I present Kyoko Asperson. Miss Asperson is a *personality journalist.*" He gave the words an unnecessary emphasis that indicated his distaste. "Miss Asperson, may I introduce her grace the Duchess of Benn."

Roberta offered the journalist a cautious finger during the handclasp, receiving two in exchange. Kyoko Asperson was a head shorter than Roberta, with straight black hair and a round face. She dressed in bright reds and yellows, and wore a odd mushroom-shaped hat. A loupe stuck over one eye allowed her to see through the lenses of her hovering media globes.

"Congratulations on your Hrinn race," Kyoko said. "You gave Khottan a run for his money."

"Metaphorical money, of course. An amateur event."

"Will you be turning professional anytime soon?"

Roberta sipped her drink. "Probably not. Though I haven't quite decided."

"You don't need the money, of course, but on the professional level the competition is more intense. Do you find yourself intimidated by the prospect?"

Roberta, having never considered this question, was mildly surprised. Amateur contests, in her circle anyway, were far more fashionable than professional competition. "Not at all," she said, truthfully, and then wondered if she'd said it convincingly enough. But Kyoko had already moved to the next question.

"Do you feel any pressure to turn professional simply in order to have people take you more seriously? Do you think that people take amateur sports *seriously* enough?"

The quartet began to play, starting with a high-pitched screech from the ristor. Roberta glanced at Kotani in dismay. He smiled at her and nodded, happy to be out of it.

Roberta resigned herself to a very long afternoon.

"Mr. Drake Maijstral?" Maijstral's interrogator was a slight man in a brown jacket.

"Yes. May I be of assistance?"

"Mencken, sir. VPL."

Mencken held out Maijstral's Very Private Letter. Throughout Maijstral's life, the appearance of a VPL courier would have been an occasion for dismay. Maijstral's father had used VPL almost exclusively, and his letters were either long lectures concerning Maijstral's faults, or requests for money in order to honor an old debt. Maijstral restrained his reflexive annoyance, signed for the letter, glanced at the seal, then broke it.

"Will there be a reply, sir?"

"Not now. Thank you."

"Your servent." Mencken bowed and withdrew. Maijstral looked at the card, then handed it to Roman. "We're invited to a wedding. Pietro Quijano and Amalia Jensen will be getting married on Earth in six months' time."

Roman read the card. "Will we be attending, sir?"

"Possibly. We're heading in that direction. I've never seen Earth."

"Nor have I."

"Perhaps it's about time we did. But I'll need some thought before I decide."

"Very well, sir."

The orchestra was packing up and heading for the main lounge. Dolfuss had finally arrived at the customs desk. "I feel so lucky," Dolfuss declared. "I won my ticket in a lottery. Otherwise I'd never have a chance to visit a place like this." He glanced around the room. "I'm impressed already!" he said.

The uniformed Tanquer closed her nictitating membranes, as if to deny what she was seeing. "Yes, sir," she said. "I understand just how lucky you feel."

"And I was able to schedule my ships so as to work in a business trip. Stop at Ranc on the way home. That's why I'm carrying my sample case."

The Tanquer's bushy tail twitched. "The exit is that way, sir. Your room is programmed to receive you."

"Thanks. I'm going to have fun here, I know it!"

Dolfuss laughed as he picked up his suitcases and walked for the exit. He was the only person carrying his own luggage. As he moved into the corridor, he saw Maijstral asking directions of a robot.

"Mr. Maijstral," he said.

"Mr. Dolfuss. I hope your journey was pleasant."

"It was. Very. I even made some sales."

"How fortunate."

"See you later."

Dolfuss bustled away. His head swivelled left and right. He was enjoying the scenery.

The robot was a latest-model Cygnus, a dark, polished ovoid that hovered a precise sixteen inches from the floor and did all its work with grappler beams. Its dark carapace bore an ideogram meaning "Advanced Object."

"As I was saying, sir," it said. "Take the second left, through the arcade, then your first right."

"Thank you," Maijstral said. "I don't know how I could have got lost so easily." A frown crossed his face. "I believe your carapace has something on it. Let me see."

As he leaned over the robot, he made a brushing gesture over the carapace with his hand. A programming spike was inserted into the robot's input connector. Maijstral brushed again. The spike was removed and palmed.

"There," he said. "Much better."

"Thank you, sir."

Stepping lightly, Maijstral began to stroll in the opposite direction from that which the robot had indicated.

The orchestra had moved from the entry concourse to the main lounge, appropriately called the White Room. The music was muffled by dazzling white couches, chairs, and carpeting, but the music was also echoed pleasantly by a sixteen-foot length of natural impact diamond that hung overhead. The stone had been discovered during the excavation; it wasn't gem quality, but it resonated well, and added a lustre to the room.

Overhead was a window, its view fixed at the sight of one star devouring another. The shutters were resolutely closed, awaiting the grand unveiling.

"Pearl Woman."

"My lord."

Kotani and the Pearl stood on the white soft carpet, sniffed, and gave each other three fingers—Diadem members were *de facto* intimates.

"Have you met Advert?"

"I don't believe so." (Sniff. Three fingers. Sniff.) "Charmed."

"Pleased to meet you, my lord."

Kotani cast a glance over his shoulder. "I just made my escape from Miss Asperson."

The Pearl gave a sniff. "I understood she was to be here."

"She is currently fashionable. Fashions pass, thankfully."

"One may hope her vogue will be of short duration."

"Have you seen Zoot?"

Pearl Woman shook her head. "Perhaps he's waiting to make a grand entrance."

"Perhaps," archly, "he's hiding from Asperson."

The orchestra came to the end of its piece. Those in the lounge tapped their feet in approval. The carpet absorbed the sound entirely.

Above, the diamond still rang.

"Shall we sit down, my lord?"

"Certainly." They found a settee and settled in. "Her grace Roberta is here," Kotani offered. "The Duchess of Benn."

"Ah. The racer."

"There will be a race tomorrow. Before the Duchess's coming-out ball."

"Perhaps I'll enter the race."

"She's very good."

"Perhaps I'll cheat." Smiling, a little too whitely.

"In that case," said Kotani, "I'll have to be very careful of my wager."

". . . then take the first right."

"Pardon me, but I think there's something on your carapace."

Mr. Sun looked with satisfaction at the piles of burglar equipment that had been confiscated from Maijstral's party. "That should serve to slow him down."

Kingston, his tall assistant, gave him a look. "You don't think it will stop him entirely?"

"I think he will have to steal *something*. After all, Geoff Fu George is here. Neither of them can afford to be shown up by the other."

"I suppose not."

"And there's another factor." Sun gave his assistant a significant look. "The Shard is here."

"Virtues!"

"We may *hope* the Virtues will prevail. And no swearing, Kingston."

"Sorry." He looked thoughtful. "Perhaps the rivalry will make them careless."

Sun's face split in a thin smile. "Yes. That's precisely what I'm counting on."

"Excuse me."

Kotani looked at the rotund figure, then blinked at the eye-scorching pattern of the man's jacket. "Yes? Mr.—"

"Dolfuss. I'm a big fan of yours. I was wondering . . ." Holding out a notebook and pen.

"Oh. Certainly." Kotani took the objects and turned to give Dolfuss the benefit of his noble profile.

"Do you suppose Nichole will be here?" Dolfuss asked. "I'm a particular fan of hers."

"I believe Nichole is touring with her new play." Kotani scrawled his signature, then looked at Dolfuss over the pen. "Mr. Dolfuss, I don't think I've seen you before. How came you here?"

"I won a raffle."

"I thought it must have been something like that."

"The first right, you say? Oh. I believe you have something on your carapace."

The woodwinds chortled away, laughing in their lower registers. Roberta passed them on her way out of the lounge. Behind her, Kyoko Asperson was interviewing one of the waiters.

"Your grace."

"Mr. Fu George." Roberta's lips turned up in an amused smile. "I have always expected to meet you sooner or later. I'm relieved the suspense is over at last."

Geoff Fu George offered her two fingers and delicately sniffed her ears. He received two fingers in return. A certain object of mutual interest assured them a degree of intimacy before they had ever met.

"I suppose—" he smiled "—it would be pointless to ask whether you have the Shard with you."

Her violet eyes sparkled. "I suppose it would," she said.

He bowed easily, conceding the point. Geoff Fu George was a compact, assured man of forty. His long blond hair (some of it, by now, implanted) was held with diamond pins and trailed down his back. He had been on top of the burglars' ratings for six years, since the Affaire of the Mirrorglass BellBox had put him solidly on top. His hairstyle was almost trademarked. He had once been asked to join the Diadem, and he had declined. The resulting sensation had assured him more celebrity than he would have received had he accepted.

"Will you take my arm?" he asked. "I was about to head for the Casino."

"With pleasure."

"I noticed that the station network ran a history of the Eltdown Shard earlier this afternoon. I suppose that could be a coincidence."

"I daresay." Smiling.

Through his jacket, Roberta could feel the outline of his gun against her arm. The corridor to the Casino was covered in a deep carpet woven of Kharolton moth wings. The wallpaper was patterned on the Cerulean Corridor in the City of Seven Bright Rings. The molding was blanchtree from Andover. Clearly Baron Silverside had spared no expense.

"I understand the customs people are unusually strict here on station," Roberta said. "I hope you haven't been inconvenienced."

"Only slightly. Still, I thought they were more officious than necessary. I shall speak to Baron Silverside when I see him."

A Cygnus robot passed them on its silent repellers. Its carapace gleamed in the subdued light.

"I understand you're racing tomorrow. I hope to watch, if circumstances permit."

Roberta gave him a sidelong look. "You don't want to take advantage of my being busy?"

He seemed offended. "Your grace," he said. "I wouldn't dream of interfering with your debut."

"Thank you." Surprised. "That's a kind thought."

"Just because I steal," said Fu George stiffly. "doesn't mean I'm a cad."

"Robot," said Gregor Norman. "I wonder if you could direct me to the Casino."

"Certainly, sir. Follow this corridor to the main lounge. Take the third arch on the right. It's marked with the ideogram for 'luck.' "

"Thank you. Excuse me, but I think you have something on your carapace."

"Thank you, sir."

"Only too." Meaning, only too happy.

Gregor deftly inserted the programming needle, gave the carapace a pat, then slipped the needle out. He and the robot parted company. At the first turning, he met a man in a loud jacket. The man was holding a notebook and looking at something therein with apparent delight.

"Mr. Dolfuss," Gregor said, and nodded.

"Mr. Norman." Nodding back.

Both went on their way, smiling.

Zoot paced back and forth in his room, then stopped and looked at himself in the mirror. His ears twitched uncomfortably. His diaphragm throbbed in resignation, and he resumed his pacing.

What the hell should he wear? That was the difficulty.

All the Diadem's advance people were humans, that was the problem. They didn't understand.

The advance people wanted him to wear his exploring togs. In the *lounge!* Before *dinner!*

His conservative Khosali soul was appaled by the idea. Wearing the environment suit seemed like an insult to Silverside and all it stood for: restraint, elegance, High Custom. But yet the Diadem people had seemed so certain that the suit was what his public expected from him.

A leaden distress settled in his soul. He looked at himself in the mirror again, seeing the trademark dark-grey environment suit with its pockets, its analyzers, its force-field repellers. His nostrils flared; his ears turned back.

"Room," he said. "What time is it?"

"Twenty-five thirteen Imperial Standard," said the room.

Zoot growled happily. Dinner would begin in just over an hour: there wasn't time to be seen in the lounge before he'd have to come back to the room to change. His hesitation had saved him.

"Room," he said. "Send a robot to help me dress."

He could have asked for one of the Diadem people, but they'd do nothing but set his nerves on edge.

The Casino featured the cool, respectful sound of money being lost. Not much money yet: the night was young and many guests had not yet arrived.

"Your grace," said Geoff Fu George, "may I present Pearl Woman and Mr. Drake Maijstral. Sir and madam, the Duchess of Benn."

"Your very obedient, your grace," said Maijstral. Roberta thought she could see a gleam of interest in Maijstral's hooded eyes before he sniffed her ears.

"Another man I've always expected to meet. My pleasure, sir."

"Your grace." Another set of sniffs. "May I present my companion, Advert."

"Miss Advert."

"Your very obedient, your grace."

Pearl Woman gave Roberta a calculated look. "I understand you will be racing tomorrow."

"Yes. A small amateur field."

"Perhaps I will enter."

Roberta smiled inwardly. A Diadem member would attract more attention to the race, hence to herself. The whole point of being here, after all, was to be noticed.

"I hope you shall. The company will be all the more distinguished by your presence."

"Perhaps you might be interested in a small side wager?"

"If it wouldn't compromise my amateur standing."

"I'm sure it would not."

"In that case, yes. Five novae?"

"Let's make it twenty."

"If you like."

Pearl Woman showed delicate incisors that matched her earring. "Done," she said.

Maijstral and Geoff Fu George exchanged handclasps while Pearl Woman spoke with Roberta. Maijstral offered two fingers and got one in return. It was, he reflected, nothing more than what he had expected.

Both men smiled. Their smiles lacked warmth.

"Maijstral," said Fu George, "have you heard the rumors coming out of the Constellation Practices Authority?"

"Referring to Allowed Burglary."

"Yes. They're considering an outright condemnation."

"That," said Maijstral, "could be unfortunate."

"They could put us in prison. Just for practicing our profession. We'd all have to move to the Empire. And I don't know about *you,*

Maijstral—" smiling, a bit more warmly "—but I *like* being a member of the majority species. Call me parochial if you like."

"The Constellation suits my temperament as well, Fu George."

"Then you'll join in the Burglar's Association? We're going to try to head this off before it gets out of committee."

Maijstral sighed. "I suppose I must."

"This is no time to be a maverick, Maijstral. Personal style is one thing; survival is quite another. Aldiss is holding the treasury. I hope we can count on a generous contribution." A thin smile. "The Sporting Commission has agreed to count it for points."

Another sigh, this one purely internal. "A generous contribution. Yes."

Geoff Fu George smiled again. Maijstral fancied he could feel its warmth on his skin. "I knew you would understand, once this was put to you in person. Aldiss told me he had the damndest time getting ahold of you by post. Even Very Private Letters seemed not to get through."

"My life has been irregular, of late."

Fu George glanced at Roberta. "I wonder if the Shard is on station?"

"I've no idea."

"I am very interested in the answer to that question, Maijstral. Very."

Maijstral gave him a look. His green eyes seemed less lazy than before. "Does that mean I am supposed to be uninterested?"

Fu George shook his head. "Not at all, old man. I was just talking to myself." He stood on tiptoe and craned his head across the Casino. "Ah. I believe I see Miss Runciter. Have you met her? Oh. I forget. Sorry, Maijstral. Tactless of me."

"No need to apologize."

"I should join her. You will excuse me?"

"Certainly." He offered Fu George his hand. One finger, as was no doubt proper.

Mr. Sun sat quietly in his blue heaven, awaiting information. He pictured himself as a spider in its lair, his fingers dancing on threads, each thread a monitor, a functionary.

The spider would never leave its home. Information would flow in, the spider would weigh it, judge it, define a response. Mr. Sun felt himself centered, ready, alive.

"Third ship's arriving, sir. *Viscount Cheng.*"

Khamiss's sharp Khosali face hovered holographically to one

side of Mr. Sun's monitors. Mr. Sun turned to face his assistant. There was a congregation of thieves in the Casino, and he was reluctant to face away.

"The Drawmiikh is aboard this one, sir," Khamiss said.

"I am aware of that, Miss Khamiss," Sun snapped. His irritaion was feigned: he really didn't mind her reminding him of things he hadn't actually forgotten, since this gave him a chance to impress listeners with the acuity of his memory.

"I want you to take charge of the Qlp party personally," he said. "I don't know what the creature is doing here, but I don't want incidents."

"Yes, sir."

"Take particular care, Khamiss."

"Very well, sir."

Her head vanished. Sun, with a happy sigh, returned to his monitors.

The burglars were talking as if they were old friends. Sun felt a grim satisfaction. If he had anything to say about it, talking was all they'd ever do.

Sun was on a mission, he considered, from God. Since the Rebellion, humanity had been asserting itself in the reaches, and had also been rediscovering its own suppressed heritage. Along with other rediscoveries—Shakespeare, Congo Veiling, Sherlock Holmes, and so on—ancient philosophies had been recovered. Mr. Sun had absorbed two of these. Besides becoming an ardent Holmes fan—the Manichean duality of Holmes and Moriarity appealed to him—Sun had become an adherent of a recently excavated creed called the New Puritanism.

Refined to its essence, the New Puritanism believed that every act had its cost, that everything had to be paid for. Sin was the occasion of a cosmic imbalance, and if the sinner didn't commit some act to compensate, the Almighty would do it for him; and the Almighty didn't care who got hurt in the process—God, according to the New Puritanism, didn't much care who got squashed when the Sin Balance was sufficiently out of alignment: He'd flatten anybody, sinner and nonsinner alike.

Mr. Sun hoped, in the small matter of Allowed Burglary, to be the Almighty's instrument in the business of flattening the wicked. Fu George and Maijstral had been sinning far too long; it was time, Sun was certain, they paid for it before some innocent party did the paying for them.

* * *

Khamiss watched her superior's face fade away, replaced by a holographic ideogram meaning "may I be of assistance?" She told the machine that it couldn't, and the ideogram disappeared.

Behind her, a woodwind quartet was setting up for the arrival of the next ship. Tuning, a bassoon bubbled away.

Khamiss straightened her uniform and squared her cap, awaiting the next ship and its cargo. She was young for the amount of responsibility she bore—she had just grown her first nose-rings, which proclaimed her age as twenty-five—and she was acutely aware of the burden of Sun's trust. She was second-in-command of security at the most exclusive resort in the known universe, and she fully intended to prove worthy of the task.

She glanced down at her medal and brushed it lightly with her fingers. The Qwarism Order of Public Service (Second Class), awarded her when she had stopped a fleeing burglar and held her prisoner for the authorities.

Khamiss had been a student at the time, studying to follow her parents' footsteps as an insurance broker for the three-century-old firm of Lewis, Khotvinn, & Co. How could she have known, when she was strolling home from school and happened to notice a small hologram-shrouded figure ghosting over the wall of the Reed Jewelry building, that it was an incident that would change her life forever?

It *was* luck that she happened to be carrying a briefcase heavy with insurance forms. It *was* luck that her first swing caught the camouflaged burglar square on the head and knocked her unconscious. But still, it wasn't the capture of just *any* thief that awarded her the Order of Public Service (Second Class).

Khamiss had caught (complete with a satchel full of gemstones that included the famous Zenith Blue) none other than Alice Manderley, renowned Allowed Burglar listed third in the ratings, a burglar whom the security services of fifty worlds had been unable to apprehend. Khamiss suddenly found herself a civilization-wide celebrity. Offers of employment appeared, and some of them were too good to pass up.

The most interesting had come from Mr. Sun, who was assembling a top-notch crew of security people which would offer its combined expertise to the elite throughout the civilized stars. Sun promised quick advancement, that and commissions for some of the most exotic and influential people in the Human Constellation.

Khamiss had done well in Sun's employment, though she hadn't caught any more top-ranked Allowed Burglars. But now, on Silverside Station, she had a very good chance.

Silverside Station had been designed partly as a deterrent to Allowed Burglary. Sun, who viewed Allowed Burglars with a particularly thoroughgoing aversion, had convinced Baron Silverside that Allowed Burglary ought to be abolished, and Silverside had given Mr. Sun a free hand in designing the station's security systems.

Sun was going after the burglars with all his cunning, all his intelligence, all the techniques he had created and savored over the years. Khamiss was going to help him.

But still, Khamiss couldn't find it in her soul to pursue the matter with quite as much alacrity as her employer. Had she known it was Alice Manderley in the darksuit and not some local thug, she might, in fact, have passed the woman by. She bore the institution of Allowed Burglary no grudge, nor any of its members.

But still, duty called. And tracking the burglars, she admitted, *might* just be fun.

Holograms announced the *Viscount Cheng's* successful docking. The woodwind quartet began to play. Khamiss nodded in time to the beat, and waited for the first wave of passengers.

"You'll excuse me, ladies, I hope." Geoff Fu George gave his formal congé to Advert, the Duchess, and lastly to Pearl Woman. As he sniffed her left ear, his lips closed delicately over the dangling pearl and the sonic cutters in his white implanted incisors neatly severed the dangling link. He slipped the pearl under his tongue, smiled, and stepped across the Casino toward Miss Vanessa Runciter.

Vanessa looked up at him and gave a near-imperceptible nod. Fu George knew that she'd caught everything on the micromedia globe she was wearing in her hair.

Satisfaction welled in him like warm water from a volcanic spring. He had practiced the stunt for months, ever since he had conceived the idea of separating Pearl Woman from her trademark, in public, without her knowledge. He had been a bit clumsy at first: Vanessa had lost a part of her earlobe, and even after surgery restored her appearance Fu George had a difficult time persuading her to resume practice. But return she did, and now he could perform the trick flawlessly.

The most satisfying part of his maneuver was that, since both he and Maijstral were present at the time, Pearl Woman wouldn't know which had done it. Her temper was famous, but he doubted she'd challenge without proof.

Fu George would sell it back to her, of course, through the most discreet agent he could find, assuming of course that she bid higher than any of her fans. But he wouldn't sell the trinket before everyone in the Constellation had taken note that the Pearl had lost her trademark, and the speculation concerning who had done it reached its height. At that point the video would be released, and it would be obvious to whom should belong the credit, and the points.

The Ratings Authority gave a full ten points for style. Geoff Fu George had it in abundance.

He wasn't on top by accident. He was very good at his work.

"Maijstral. I fancy a round or two of tiles. Will you join me?"

"Certainly, your grace." Mildly surprised at her suggestion, Maijstral offered Roberta his arm. Perhaps, he thought, she was just sizing up the opposition.

"I understand the customs people here are very rigorous," Roberta said. "I hope you are not entirely inconvenienced."

"I'm on station simply for the company."

Roberta shot him a look under her lashes. "Yes? How unfortunate. I hoped we might discuss . . . business matters."

Maijstral absorbed this. His lazy green eyes glowed. "I am entirely at your disposal, madam," he said, and sat her at the tiles table.

"Five a point?"

His voice betrayed a slight hesitation. "Very well," he said.

Lord Qlp *oozed* onto a concourse that echoed to the sound of a woodwind quartet.

Oozed, Khamiss thought. There was no other possible word. She tried very hard not to shudder.

Lord Qlp was one of the Drawmii, a particularly enigmatic species living almost entirely on Zynzlyp. Though the Drawmii were undoubtedly intelligent and (in their own opaque fashion) cultured, it had never been entirely established whether the Drawmii had ever *noticed* their conquest by the Khosali, or understood entirely what it meant. Very few of the Drawmii travelled off their native planet, and when they did their travels were obscure, their motives doubly so.

The Drawmii looked like glistening, eight-foot-long sea slugs. This one was green below and bright orange above, with mottled off-white warts scattered about its body. Five eyestalks sprouted along its back. It left a trail of slime as it moved.

Accompanying it was a female Khosalikh, about thirty, in the uniform of a Colonial Service diplomat. She wore a translation stud in one ear.

Khamiss stepped forward to offer her assistance and was

promptly staggered by Lord Qlp's appalling odor. Her nostrils slammed shut, and she only opened them by an act of will.

This, she realized, was the down side of working with the public.

"Khamiss, ma'am," she said in Human Standard, her voice a bit denasal. "Silverside security. I have been put entirely at your service. If you could give me its lordship's documents, I will process them directly."

A cigar, she thought. If I smoke a cigar, perhaps I won't have to smell this.

"I am Lady Dosvidern," the Khosalikh said. She spoke Khosali Standard. With polite restraint, she sniffed Khamiss's ears. "I am Lord Qlp's translator and assistant."

Lord Qlp raised its front end and made a series of blurting sounds. Lady Dosvidern listened, then translated. The voice she used when translating was different: deeper, more polished but less expressive, as if she felt it wasn't her place to interpret its lordship's remarks by means of locution. Her formality verged on High Khosali without quite losing the communicative ease of Standard.

"The temporal affinities have been propitiated. They are sound," she said.

Khamiss glanced from his lordship to Lady Dosvidern and back. "I am gratified to hear it, my lord," she said. A cigar, she thought. No. Wrong. *Lots* of cigars.

Lord Qlp spoke again. Its breath made its normal odor seem pleasant. "Silverside is an appropriate contextual mode," Lady Dosvidern said. "The requirements of the continuum are clear. The Protocol of Mission demands the location of the Duchess of Benn."

Khamiss's mind swam, but she understood the last sentence well enough. "I will see if I can locate her grace, my lord. If you will excuse me?" She turned on her heel and marched back to one of the desks. Never had station air tasted so sweet.

She shouldered aside the customs agent at the second-class counter—the second-class passengers would have to wait—and touched the ideogram for "security central." Sun's holographic profile appeared above the desk. His eyes were fixed ahead of him, presumably on his monitors.

"Mr. Sun," she said. "Lord Qlp wishes to meet the Duchess of Benn. Can you locate her for me, please?"

The answer was immediate. "She's in the Casino, playing tiles with Maijstral." Mr. Sun's tone made it clear that he had no respect whatever for Roberta's scale of values.

"Thank you, sir. Would you have a robot meet me there, and bring me a box of cigars?"

"I didn't know you smoked, Khamiss."

"I have started, sir."

Sun's expression was indifferent, yet resolute. Khamiss thought that Sun made a point of being indifferent to anything unusual, presumably in the hope this would demonstrate his own omnipotence. "As you like, Khamiss," he said. The hologram vanished.

Khamiss turned back to the Qlp party and saw Lady Dosvidern approaching on silent feet. While Khamiss waited she inclined her torso slightly to the left in order to peer around her ladyship and make certain that Lord Qlp wasn't up to any mischief. Apparently it was not: it was undulating slightly, perhaps with respiration, but not moving anywhere.

"Miss Khamiss," said her ladyship.

"Yes, my lady?"

Lady Dosvidern's voice was tactful. "Have you been provided as, ah, a full-time escort for Lord Qlp and myself?"

Khamiss was cautious. "If necessary, ma'am."

"I don't believe any such necessity exists," said her ladyship. "I have been travelling with Lord Qlp for some time. It is inactive most of the time, and although its, ah, olfactory presence can be overwhelming, it has never acted in such a way as to prove a hazard to other beings."

Relief bubbled in Khamiss's mind. "As your ladyship suggests," she said.

"And now," said Lady Dosvidern, "if I might trouble you to escort us to the Casino?"

Cigars, thought Khamiss.

"Certainly, my lady," she said.

Lord Qlp burbled a greeting as the two Khosali stepped toward him. Khamiss's nostrils clamped shut. She couldn't get them to open.

Afterward, she was denasal for hours.

"Drexler and Chalice will have everything ready by tonight," said Vanessa Runciter. She dressed in cool colors that emphasized her clear, pale skin; her hair was the color of smoke and piled on top of her head in an old-fashioned way, and she smoked a cigaret from a silver-banded obsidian holder. Her father had cornered the dither market on Khorn and left her the entire pile when he died: to others it seemed perfectly unfair that she was lovely as well as implausibly wealthy.

While waiting for Fu George to make his move, she had lost a cool four hundred novae at the markers table. Even the croupier had been impressed.

Vanessa put her arm through Fu George's. They began strolling toward an exit. "I've been making lists. We've got a lot to choose from. Kotani's diamond studs, Baroness Silverside's famous art collection, the Baron's cape, Madame la Riviere's antique necklace, jewelry of one sort or another from Lord and Lady Tvax, Colonel Thom, the Waltz twins, the Marchioness Bastwick, Adriaen, Commodore and Lady Andric . . ."

Fu George delicately raised his handkerchief to his lips, folded the pearl within it, put the handkerchief in his inside breast pocket. "And Advert," he said. "She's got a minor fortune and likes to display it."

Vanessa looked dubious. "It might be a bit dangerous, going to that quarter again."

"Ten points for style, my dear."

"True." Dubiously. She frowned as she concentrated on her list. "There's an antique store—expensive, some nice items, but nothing truly exciting. A rare book store. Drexler will have to look at that: I'm not enough of an expert. A jeweler's, but it would have considerable security. The main hotel safe."

"The Eltdown Shard," Fu George said.

Vanessa stopped in her tracks. "You're sure?'

"No. But the new Duchess is here, and this is her debut."

Vanessa took a languid puff on her cigaret as she glanced over the room. One of the many holographic ideograms for "good fortune" paraded over her head. "They had a history of the Shard on the station feed, did you notice? But perhaps that's just publicity. It's a long journey from the Empire. Providing security for that entire distance . . ."

"She can afford it."

Vanessa's eyes narrowed as she focused on the tiles table. "She's playing tiles with Maijstral. I don't like the looks of that."

"It means nothing. She is young, a social being. She conversed as pleasantly with me."

"I *still* don't like it, Geoff."

Vanessa and Maijstral had a history. Fu George, knowing this, discounted her objection and began moving in the direction of the exit once more. A Cygnus moved by on silent repellers, holding a tray of drinks in its invisible force field.

"We'll know for certain tomorrow night," Fu George said. "If she has the Shard, she'll wear it then."

"And until tomorrow?"

He thought for a moment. "The Waltz twins, I think," he said. "Both at once should be good for a few style points."

"Pardon me. I believe you have something on your carapace."

"Yes. He's got all the family titles now; he had his father declared dead a little over a year ago." Pearl Woman gave Advert a knowing look. "That was just before the new inheritance law came into effect. Maijstral saved himself a lot in taxes by getting the job done when he did."

Advert glanced over her shoulder. She could see Maijstral chatting to the Duchess as they bid their tiles. "Horrible," she said. "One hears of such things, but one never knows the people involved. It gives me a chill to look at him."

"No more a chill than Maijstral's dad got." Pearl Woman grinned and tossed her hair. Advert looked at her in horror.

"Pearl," she said. Pearl Woman looked at her, then frowned.

"What's wrong?"

Panic wailed in Advert's veins. "Pearl," she whispered desperately. *"Something's missing!"*

Mr. Paavo Kuusinen walked out of the Casino, the tip of his walking stick making a casual touch upon the mothwing carpet at every second step. He was keeping Vanessa Runciter and Geoff Fu George in sight. They seemed to be heading toward the main lounge.

A happy awareness tingled in his nerves, and he allowed himself a satisfied smile. He was pleased to discover that, of all the people in the Constellation, Fu George and Miss Runciter shared a secret with him alone.

Kuusinen knew where Pearl Woman's trademark was. He had been watching the party from the cashier's table, and had, by a stroke of fate, looked up just at the instant of the theft. Elegantly done, he had to admit.

The observation, lucky as it was, hadn't been made purely by chance. Kuusinen had a permanent, professional interest in Drake Maijstral and Geoff Fu George, and he had been watching them closely.

Unlike Roberta, he sensed something potentially catastrophic in the situation here. Silverside Station was a small place, two first-rank thieves like Maijstral and Fu George were unlikely to coexist happily, and the presence of other inflammatory characters like Pearl Woman and Kyoko Asperson wouldn't help.

For the present, however, Kuusinen was happy to possess his secret.

For a long, pleasant moment, he wondered what to do with it.

"Pardon me. I believe there's something on your carapace."

"Oh, no." Pearl Woman was appalled by the sight of the approaching mushroom-shaped hat surrounded by eight bright, bobbing media globes. The Pearl raked her fingers through her hair, drawing strands down over her left ear in hopes of concealing the empty chain. Advert clutched her other arm.

"Miss Asperson," Pearl Woman said, and bowed. She turned her head slightly, offering the globes a three-quarter profile.

Kyoko Asperson grinned up at her. "Pearl Woman," she said. The Pearl offered token sniffs; Pearl Woman tried to keep her head turned casually away. "So pleased to see you again. I believe this is Miss Advert?"

"Yes. Advert, allow me to introduce Kyoko Asperson."

"Your servant, miss."

"Yours."

"I'd be delighted to stay and chat, Miss Asperson," Pearl Woman said, "but I'm late for an appointment."

Kyoko's bright birdlike eyes flicked from one to the other.

"I understand entirely, Pearl. It was, however, Miss Advert whom I was hoping to interview."

Advert cast a cool glance at the Pearl and received a nod in return. She would cover Pearl Woman's retreat.

She took a breath and gazed into the awful loupe over Kyoko's eye. Terror touched her nerves with its delicate sable brush. "My pleasure, Miss Asperson. Shall we walk toward the lounge?"

"As you like."

Never, Advert thought, had a provincial accent sounded so ominous.

"Zoot! I hardly recognized you."

A surprised reply. "Sir?"

"Without your jacket, I mean."

"Oh. It's not really suitable for this lounge, I thought."

"I suppose. But I really expected to see you in it. My name's Dolfuss, by the way. Your obedient."

"Yours."

"Could I have your autograph?"

"Honored, sir."

"I was very disappointed Nichole isn't going to be here. She's one of my biggest fans. I mean—well, you know what I mean."

"I liked her last play very much."

"Saw that. Didn't care for it myself. Didn't seem to be the real *Nichole.*"

A short beat's pause. "Rather thought that was the point."

"Well. Shouldn't keep you. Thanks so much."

Zoot watched the man bustling away. His ears were down, and his diaphragm spasmed twice in resignation. Were his public *all* like this?

Perhaps, he thought guiltily, his advance people were right, and he should have worn the jacket.

Too late now. He adjusted the laces on his (perfectly conventional) dinner jacket and strolled toward the lounge.

"Don't alter your arrangements in any way," Maijstral said. "Just keep me informed of what they are."

"At present," said Roberta Altunin, the Duchess of Benn, "my arrangements consist of six very large Khosali with guns."

"Presumably they will not be on duty tomorrow night."

"No. They won't." She looked at him with a smile and clicked a pair of tiles together. "This is fun, you know."

Maijstral's expression was opaque. "Sixteen, your grace," he said, and placed a tile.

Roberta's smile broadened. "I was waiting for that." She turned over tiles. "There's thirty-two, and forty-eight, and sixty-four. And here's the Pierrot, so that's doubled to a hudred twenty-eight."

Maijstral surveyed the table and let out a long breath. "I'm afraid that's consummation." He turned over his remaining tiles. Resigned to his loss, he picked up a polychip from its rack, then touched to its smooth black surface a stylus that permanently rearranged its molecules. He wrote the amount, an ideogram that stood for "I.O.U.," then pressed his thumbprint to the back.

"Your grace," he said, offering it.

She accepted it. "I'm very good at things I care about," she said. "One of them is winning."

"I am beginning to understand that."

"Another game?"

Maijstral smiled thinly. "I think not, your grace. People in my profession shouldn't use up thier quota of luck in games of chance."

She laughed. "I suppose not. Good lord. What's that smell?"

People in the Casino began exclaiming and pointing. Maijstral leaned back in surprise at what he saw over Roberta's right shoulder. Roberta turned around to observe the astonishing sight of Lord Qlp oozing toward her, accompanied by two Khosali, a tall, expressionless female with a translation stud and a small female in the uniform of station security. The smaller of the pair was craning her head, turning left and right. An expression of relief entered her face. "Robot!" she called, and waved a hand.

Lord Qlp undulated to Roberta's side and made a squelching noise. She tried not to shrink back from the appalling smell.

"Your grace," said the tall Khosalikh, "allow me to present Lord Qlp." She was speaking High Khosali.

"Your servant," returned Roberta, denasal. She looked for ears to sniff and found none. She made an approximation and dipped her head twice. To inhale at all required a steely act of will that excited Maijstral's admiration.

The tall Khosalikh spoke. "I am Lady Dosvidern, Lord Qlp's translator and companion."

"My lady."

Lord Qlp lifted its forward half and burbled briefly. Lady Dosvidern folded her hands and translated. "The Protocols are in accord. Movement is propitious. The time of delivery has arrived."

Roberta looked at Maijstral for help. His ears flicked back and forth, indicating his own bafflement. "How nice," Roberta finally said.

Lord Qlp lowered its end to the floor and made loud, moist noises. Roberta felt warm breath on her ankles and drew them back. The Khosalikh in the security uniform, thankfully standing away, was lighting a cigar with a relieved expression.

Something thudded onto the carpet. "Oh," said Roberta.

Lord Qlp had just disgorged a hard, moist, glistening lump, about the size of two fists placed side-by-side.

Roberta stared at it. Lord Qlp reared up again and made a loud bellowing noise which Lady Dosvidern declined to translate.

There was a long pause. Maijstral observed a general movement toward the Casino's exits. He longed to join the crowd, but knew it would seem impolite to leave Roberta in the lurch.

It apparently occurred to Roberta that Lord Qlp was waiting for something. She looked up at it.

"Thank you," she said.

Without saying anything further, Lord Qlp turned and began to move toward the exit. It was followed by Lady Dosvidern and the security guard, puffing smoke.

Roberta called to a robot. "Please have this . . . object . . . delivered to my room," she said. The robot lifted the thing in its beams and moved toward an exit.

Maijstral stood and offered an arm. "Perhaps," he said, "we might look for some fresh air."

Roberta rose. "Thank you," she said.

"You handled that very well, your grace."

Roberta was surprised. "You think so? I just . . . reacted."

"Your instincts, if you don't mind my saying so, were impeccable."

"Well," she said, putting her arm through his, "let's hope this sort of thing doesn't go on all the rest of my stay."

The Cygnus delivered its burden into the reluctant hands of Roberta's lady's maid, and then began its return to the Casino.

On the way, it suddenly stopped, turned toward the wall, and used its beams to manipulate several hidden catches. The wall swung open, revealing a passage. The robot entered.

Alarms called urgently from Mr. Sun's console. He scanned his board and noticed that both Maijstral and Geoff Fu George had left the areas covered by his monitors. A tight smile moved across Mr. Sun's countenance. He pressed the ideogram for "general announcement." It was time for the Almighty to get a little of His own back.

"Strawberry Section, Access Tunnel Twelve." His voice was triumphant. "Watsons," he said, "the game's afoot!"

TWO

Khosali High Custom allows people, within certain well-defined limits, to steal for a living; and the societies of the Human Constellation, for lack of anything better after several thousand years of Khosali rule, follow High Custom. The Constellation Practices Authority exists for the purpose of altering High Custom in the image of redefined humanity, and the reason the Authority is necessary is that the Human Constellation lacks the self-generating regulatory apparatus possessed by Khosali custom.

The Empire's regulatory apparatus is, in fact, the Imperial family. Whatever is done by the Pendjalli, and in particular by the Pendjalli Emperor, exists *de jure* and exclusively within the context of High Custom. The Emperor himself can do no other: his behavior *dictates* High Custom.

The accepted reason for Allowed Burglary is that High Custom, besides reflecting the Khosali reverence for tradition, high-mindedness, and idealism, should also reflect another, more occult aspect of Khosali character, namely their (largely unacknowledged) admiration for individuals of low repute: thieves, charlatans, murderers, adulterers, self-slaughterers, drunks. Social xenologists have noted that High Custom not only allows these individuals to exist within the context of accepted society, but regulates their behavior, thus minimizing its negative effect upon society at large. Thus is a killer transformed into a duellist, a depressive into an idealistic suicide, an adulterer into an adventurer, a charlatan into an entertainer, and a burglar into a sportsman.

The regrettable truth is that these acknowledged reasons for Allowed Burglary are either window dressing or *post facto* rationalization. The real reason for this one particular aspect of High Custom is that Differs XXIII, the last Montiyy Emperor, was a kleptomaniac, driven by some inner compulsion to lift small, valuable objects from the apartments of his friends and ministers. Once this was observed, kleptomania and the Imperial ideal had to somehow be reconciled in the minds of his subjects: somehow Montiyy honor had to be preserved. The result was Allowed Burglary, permitted and regulated through the Imperial Sporting Commission under the benevolent sponsorship of His Imperial Majesty. Differs graciously withdrew his name from consideration in the rankings; and after knowledge of his thievery became semipublic (though never officially acknowledged), the negative effects of a breach of Imperial honor were buffered. In another victory for High Custom and the Imperial bureaucracy, and Imperial embarrassment had become, instead, a new fashion, and in time an industry.

One wonders if Differs' functionaries could have anticipated the results of their little effort at damage control: burglars recording their crimes so as to sell the recordings to the media; thieves making endorsements of alarm systems, shoes, jewelry, and nightwear; the rise of theft as a popular entertainment comparable to portball or hand volleys.

But that is a fact of existence: minor actions can have major consequences. An offhand remark at a party can end in two people facing each other with pistols, Imperial idiosyncracy can result in the expansion of bureaucracy and the rise of a minor industry, the abstraction of a bit of nacre dangling from a chain can change the lives of everyone involved.

Just watch.

"Mr. Maijstral."

"Mr. Dolfuss."

Dolfuss straightened, adjusted his appalling jacket. In spite of the jacket he now seemed dignified, poised, almost elegant. He even gave an impression of being thinner. "Thus far it's been a delight, sir," he said. "I've no idea when I've enjoyed myself more. Oh." He reached into a pocket. "My room key," he said. "The doorplate's keyed to my prints, but I suppose you won't want it to register your own."

"No. I rather suppose not." Maijstral pocketed the key. "Thank you, sir."

"See you later, Mr. Maijstral."

"Mr. Dolfuss."

Maijstral walked to Dolfuss's room, picked up the sample case that waited in the closet, then continued down the corridor to his own room. He declined to thumbprint open the lock—such things could be used by station security to keep track of people—and instead used his own key.

Maijstral's four-room suite was decorated in shades of brown. A holographic waterfall, silver and gold and bright diamond, cascaded down the center of the front room. Gregor Norman sat behind it, his feet on a small table, a hi-stick in his mouth. His hands beat a complex rhythm on his thighs. He straightened as Maijstral came in, looked at the case in Maijstral's hand, and grinned.

Maijstral put the case on the table. "I hope you won't mind opening this," he said.

"Only too." Meaning, only too pleased. Gregor touched the locks, then opened the case. He began unloading black boxes, alarm disruptors, dark suits, communication equipment, holographic projectors.

Gregor told the room to play a Vivaldi woodwind concerto adapted for Khosali instruments. Though baroque music was a passion with him, and he listened to it whenever possible, the concerto now had another function: Gregor wanted a lot of background noise in case Maijstral wanted to talk business. Sometimes, he had discovered, people were crude enough to put listening devices in their rooms.

Roman, Maijstral's Khosali servant, appeared on silent feet. He was tall for a Khosali—had he been human, he would have been a giant. He was forty-six years old, and his family had served Maijstral's for generations.

Maijstral looked happily at Roman. Roman was the only constant in his inconstant life. Roman combined the benevolent functions of parent, cook, valet, and (when necessary) leg breaker. In short, Roman was home. Life without Roman was unthinkable.

Roman took Maijstral's guns and knife, then unlaced his jacket and trousers. High Custom insisted on clothing that was difficult of access: it demonstrated the need for servants, or at least for cleverly programmed robots. Roman took the jacket and placed it on a hanger. Maijstral flexed his arms, rotated them, then stripped off his empty shoulder holster, sat down on a chair, and held up his feet. Roman drew off his buskins and trousers.

"We shall have to alter our schedule, gentlemen," Maijstral said. He planted his feet on the floor, dug his toes into the carpet. "Tonight's plan may proceed, but we should postpone our plans for tomorrow."

Gregor had strapped on goggles that allowed him to perceive energy field formations. He looked up at Maijstral with silver insect eyes. "Something has come up, sir?" The hi-stick bobbled in his mouth as he spoke.

Maijstral paused, enjoying the suspense. "The Eltdown Shard is onstation," he said. "Tomorrow night we're going to steal it."

There was a moment of silence, filled only by the whisper of air through the vents.

Roman folded Maijstral's trousers, the creases sharp as a knife. He put the trousers on a hanger.

"Very good, sir," he said. Which was Roman all over.

"With both of them in this small a place, what do you think of the possibility of a duel?"

"Miss Asperson, I hope they blow their brains out."

Paavo Kuusinen, pursuing the scent of mystery, followed Geoff Fu George and Vanessa Runciter to their suite. He walked past their door, stepped down a side corridor, and paused a moment, frowning. His cane tapped in time to his thoughts.

The period immediately following a theft by a registered burglar was the most dangerous for the thief: if he could hang onto his loot past midnight of the second day, it became his legal property; but in the interim he could be arrested for stealing. Furthermore, he had to keep the take in his possession, at his residence or on his person.

What would Fu George do with the pearl? Kuusinen wondered. Keep it in his room, or on his body?

A Cygnus Advanced Object, its black carapace reflecting each overhead spotlight as it glided down the hallway, lowered a covered tray before Fu George's door, politely knocked with its force fields, then moved on down the hall. Kuusinen ducked down his side corridor and sensed, rather than saw, the robot cross the corridor behind him. He heard Fu George's door open, then close.

Kuusinen hesitated, tapping his cane on the carpet. The robot had gone into a dead-end corridor, and he wondered why. Then he turned and retraced his steps.

He couldn't help himself. He was in the grip of a compulsion.

Paavo Kuusinen was the sort of man who was nagged at by irregularities. It wasn't that he disapproved of them, precisely: he didn't care whether or not things were irregular; he just wanted to know why. In this regard he was unlike, for example, Mr. Sun, who would in the same circumstances have done his best to make things regular again. But making discoveries was a compulsion for Kuusinen. Sometimes his compulsion aided him in his work; sometimes—as now—it was purely an interference.

He looked around the corner. An access panel was open in the wall of the dead-end corridor. The robot had obviously gone inside on some errand. Perhaps the access tunnel connected to another corridor somewhere.

Mystery solved. Kuusinen shrugged and began walking toward his own room. It was time to change for dinner.

It wasn't until he saw three uniformed security guards rushing up the corridor, each with hand on gun, that Kuusinen began to wonder.

Robot, he thought. Guards. Secret doors in the walls. Fu George and a covered tray.

Kuusinen sighed. He was beginning to get that nagging feeling again.

The soft sounds of a Snail concerto hung suspended from soft aural bands, filling the room. Another yellow light blinked on one of Gregor's boxes. He smirked. "Another Advanced Object in the walls," he said. This was the third light blinking on the box, the third in a row of twelve.

Roman was lacing Maijstral into a pair of trousers. The trousers were soft black; the laces were yellow. Roman's fingers moved deftly.

"I spoke briefly with Dolfuss," Maijstral said. He spoke Khosali Standard. "He's enjoying himself."

"I spent the voyage with him, in second class," Roman said, "and he never broke character once."

"I only hope no one recognizes him."

"It's been years since *Fin de Siecle.* He was a young man then; he's changed a great deal since. And the play toured only in the Empire."

"Until it was banned." Gregor, still bent over his equipment, spoke without looking up.

"Dolfuss shouldn't have been quite so ambiguous about the Emperor Principle. If the Empire had won the Rebellion, the play might have been taken as constructive social criticism. But the Empire was touchy about the defeat, and the play merely rubbed salt in the wound." Maijstral stretched a leg, tried a tentative dance step. "A little tight over the left hip, Roman," he said.

"Yes, sir." Roman began to rethread.

"Dolfuss has learned to make his points more subtly since, but still no one performs his work. A pity. I think this venture will enable him to mount his own production."

Maijstral looked up at the holographic waterfall. The liquid was unwaterlike, a quicksilver thing, falling like a slow, magic fantasy. "I wonder what Fu George is planning," he said.

Gregor, still wearing his goggles, seemed a particularly disreputable insect as he looked up. "He'll *have* to go for the Shard, won't he?" he said. "I mean, Ralph Adverse *died* for it years ago, and so did Sinn Junior, and that made it priceless. And no one's stolen it for forty years. Fu George's name would live forever if he got it."

"And survived," said Roman.

Maijstral watched insubstantial liquid tumbling over an insubstantial rim. "If it were me, I'd try for it," he said.

Gregor grinned. "It *is* you, boss."

Maijstral's head tilted as he considered this. The waterfall spilled in slow accompaniment to the Snail. "So it is," he decided. He tested his trousers again. "Good. Thank you, Roman."

Roman brought a jacket out. Maijstral put his arms in it. Roman began working with laces again.

Maijstral reached into the jacket pocket, took out a deck of cards with his right hand. He fanned them one-handed. The deuce of crowns jumped from the fan to his left hand. Then the throne of bells. Duchess of hearts.

"Vanessa Runciter is here," he said.

"So I understand, sir."

"It's a small world."

"Could you raise your left arm, please? I'm having trouble fitting the holster."

Maijstral lifted his arm. Cards spilled upward from right hand to left, defying gravity.

"I wonder," he said, "if Zoot's jacket would be worth a try?"

"I think not, sir. Our own darksuits are doubtless more advanced."

Maijstral sighed. "I suppose you're right. He'll probably be wearing it, anyway."

Another display lit on Gregor's machine. Two blinked off. "Two burrowers," he reported, "still in their holes."

"It was *awful,* Pearl. Just awful."

Pearl Woman gazed at a rotating hologram of herself. She had one of Advert's cloche hats pulled down over her ears, and the effect was hideous. She pulled the hat off and snarled.

"She asked me about the Diadem." Advert rattling on. "I don't know what I said. I just babbled on. I know I'm going to embarrass everyone."

"I'll have to plead illness for tonight," Pearl Woman said. "It's going to cause comment, but I'll have to do it."

"She asked me about your duel with Etienne. I didn't even *know* you then. But I did say I thought his eyeglass looked silly. And that the Diadem already had a duel that year, and that his timing lacked finesse." Advert laughed. "And *then* I said that Nichole's new play was unsuitable for her, that a Diadem role should have more grandeur. So maybe Asperson will quote me there. That would be lucky."

"I'll need you to go to the jewelry shops on Red Level," Pearl Woman said. "Find a substitute stone. It might fool them for a while. If I'm cornered, I can say the real one has been hidden, so it won't be stolen." She pounded a fist into her palm. "But then it would seem as if I were *afraid* of them."

"But I know I said something embarrassing about Rip and his friend—what's her name? Something about the way she laughs all the time."

"Are you listening, Advert?"

"Oh. Yes. I'm sorry. What did you want?"

Pearl Woman's eyes narrowed. "You should learn not to ask that sort of question, Advert. The answer might not be to your taste."

Another light glowed on Mr. Sun's console. Sun's nerves tautened. His blue heaven was beginning to smell of sweat and annoyance.

Sun touched an ideogram. "My lord," he said.

"Mr. Sun." Baron Silverside's anger translated very well to hologram. He was a compact, broad-shouldered man, a former amateur wrestler. Burnsides flared on either side of his face, a pale brown halo. One hand was visible, stroking the whiskers.

"What," the Baron demanded, "is the meaning of all these alerts? Have your people gone mad?"

Sun feigned surprise. "Sir?" he asked.

"They are running about the halls carrying guns while my guests are walking to dinner. I have been receiving complaints."

Both hands were stroking the whiskers now. Sun calmed his nerves. He was still the spider in its lair, ready to pounce. There had been a few problems: nothing he could not deal with. "Beg pardon, your lordship," Sun said. "We seem to have been receiving false alarms from the utility tunnels."

"You assured me," the Baron said, "the security system was infallible. And that your guards would be inconspicuous."

Sun could feel sweat prickling his forehead. "Sir," he said. "Begging your pardon, but I said *almost* . . ."

The Baron froze him with a look. He was twisting little lovelocks around his forefingers. "Sun," he said, "I will have no more of this. You have caught no burglars, and you have terrified my guests."

"My people are eager, of course," Sun said. "We have been drilling for a very long time. But I shall order them to be more . . . relaxed."

"Kyoko Asperson is here, Sun," the Baron said. "She would dearly love to report that I have a fool for head of security." His eyes turned to fire. *"Do not give her that opportunity, Sun."*

"Yes, my lord."

"That's all."

"Yes, my lord."

The ideogram for "may I be of assistance?" replaced the Baron's features. Sun snarled and told his console to turn it off.

Another alarm cried out. Sun's finger hovered over the ideogram for "general announcement," hesitated, then stabbed down.

"Another alarm," he said. "Watsons, let's *walk* to this one, shall we?"

"Ah. Zoot. We were wondering if you were indisposed."

"Marquess. Marchioness."

The Marchioness Kotani was a young, dark-haired woman with wide, tilted eyes, a full, pouting lower lip, and a distictive expression that was quite sullen yet in some inexpressible way attractive. Before her marriage, she'd been Lady Janetha Gorman, the daughter of an old and quite penniless Imperialist family; she had earned a living as a model and made periodic, if unsuccessful, forays into acting. Now that she was married, she had given up both modeling and acting. Even Kotani knew better than to use her in one of his plays.

"I expected to see you in your jacket," she said as she sniffed Zoot's ears. A choker of matched glowstones shone at her throat.

"Not for dinner, I think," Zoot said. He smiled, tongue lolling from his muzzle.

"One would have thought the Diadem would have insisted," said the Marchioness.

"There are still a few things," Zoot said stiffly, "in which I have a say."

"Bravo, Zoot," said the Marquess. His foot tapped the white carpet in brief applause. "Don't let 'em push you around. I speak from experience."

"I'm still disappointed," the Marchioness said. "You shall have to model the jacket for me."

Zoot inclined his head. "I should be most happy, milady."

Kotani cocked an eye in the direction of one of the entrances. "Here is Fu George. Take care with that necklace, my dear. I should hate to have to shoot the man over it. And I'd hate even more to have him shoot *me.*"

Geoff Fu George gave everyone a bow, sniffs, two fingers. From Kotani and Zoot he received one finger apiece; from the Marchioness, three.

"My compliments, my lady," he said, concealing his surprise. "The glowstones suit your eyes perfectly."

"Thank you, sir. The compliment means all the more coming from someone of your undoubted expertise."

"Perhaps, sir," said Zoot, "you might enlighten us as to the alarms that seem to have sent the security people into an uproar."

Fu George's ears twitched in bafflement. "I am as surprised as you are, sir," he said. "It's nothing to do with me. Ah," he said, addressing a Cygnus. "Bring me a cold rink, please."

"Yes, sir."

"Possibly it's Miajstral tripping a few alarms," Fu George said. His voice turned dubious. "But even *he's* not quite *that* clumsy, surely." He smiled at the Marchioness.

"D'you know there's a Drawmiikh onstation?" Kotani said. "A Drawmii lord, no less."

"I believe," Zoot said, "that any Drawmii sufficiently adventurous to leave its planet of origin and participate in the life of the Empire is almost always ennobled. It's a way of encouraging the others."

Kotani smiled. "Unsuccessful, I suppose."

"I believe so, Marquess. There are only a handful at any time."

The Marchioness turned her bored eyes on Zoot. "I wonder if we'll see the creature at dinner."

"I hope not, dearest," said Kotani. "It created quite a sensation in the Casino a few hours ago. Its lordship was quite noisy and, I am given to understand, it stank."

"The Drawmii have a very distinctive odor, or so I'm told," Zoot said. "I gather it takes getting used to."

"Media alert," Kotani said, seeing a pointed cap surrounded by floating silver balls. "I've been through it already; I beg your leave. Dearest," offering his arm.

"Milord."

Kyoko Asperson had changed for dinner: she wore baggy yellow trousers, a white shirt, a scarlet jacket, soft boots with gold tassels. If she weren't so short she could have been used as a beacon.

"Zoot. Mr. Fu George." Zoot, who like all Khosali had a very rigid spine, had to bend an uncomfortable distance to sniff her ears. "I reckoned you would be wearing your jacket."

Zoot's diaphragm pounded in annoyance. How often was he going to have to go through this? "Madam," he said, "surely not for dinner."

"Meals, in some restaurants," said Fu George, "may be considered unexplored territory. In that case, Zoot's jacket would be perfectly appropriate."

Media globes rotated, pointed in Fu George's direction. "I wonder," Kyoko said, "if you were surprised to hear that Drake Maijstral would be here?"

Geoff Fu George smiled. "I don't believe I've given it much thought."

"You're both in the first rank of your profession."

Fu George's head tipped; his eyes sparkled. The message was clear, though unvoiced: *If you say so.*

"Do you anticipate a duel between the two of you?"

A laugh. "We are speaking of a metaphorical duel, I take it?"

"Whatever kind of duel you like."

The famous Fu George smile became a little forced. "I am here only for the view, and to see my friends. What Maijstral's plans may be, I cannot say."

"So you concede any contest to Maijstral."

The smile was back, and genuine. "My dear Miss Asperson," he said, "I concede nothing at all." He sniffed her. "Your servant."

Reasonably pleased with himself, Fu George moved away. A

man in a green coat approached him. The man had a hand over one eye, and was blinking furiously with the other.

"Beg pardon, sir," the man said, "but may I borrow your handkerchief for a moment? I have something in my eye."

Fu George touched his breast pocket, felt the pearl still secure in the handkerchief, and hesitated. "My apologies, sir, I neglected to bring one."

"Sorry to bother you. I think the thing may be out, anyway." He stumbled away.

So, Paavo Kuusinen thought as he removed the hand from his eye. Fu George still has the pearl.

Interesting.

Maijstral could feel his deck of cards riding comfortably above his right hip in a pocket tailored just for them. The feeling was a pleasant one, far more pleasant than the gun under one arm, the knife up his sleeve, the other gun up the other sleeve. The cards were a reminder of pleasure; the hardware, of necessity.

A Cygnus approached. "Pardon me, robot," Maijstral said. "Can you direct me to the main lounge?"

The robot's voice was unusually resonant. Troxan engineering, Maijstral assumed as he reached into his pocket and palmed the programming needle.

"Pardon me," he said. "I think there is something on your carapace."

"Hullo, Maijstral." A familiar voice. "Nice of you to dust the robots."

Maijstral almost lost his grip on the needle. He straightened and returned it to his pocket.

"Hello, Vanessa."

Miss Runciter sniffed him, offered him three fingers. He gave her two in return. Her eyebrows rose.

"I thought we were old friends, Maijstral."

"I confess that I don't know what we are, Vanessa. I haven't seen you in almost three years. You left a bit suddenly, as I recall." He offered his arm, and then wondered how reluctant the offer was. "Going to dinner?"

"Yes. Thank you."

She was wearing a jet gown covered with dark red brocade that was shot with silver thread. She wore emerald earrings, a gold chain on one wrist. She looked very well indeed. "I keep thinking, Maijstral," she said, "we left some things unsaid."

"I doubt, Vanessa, that any of them need saying now."

She looked at him. "It's that way, is it?"

Smoothly. "I don't know what you mean."

"As you like." Her voice became reflective. "I don't like the way Laurence is playing you in the vids, Drake. Anaya was far smoother."

"I don't watch them."

"Still?"

"Still."

A brief silence, broken by Vanessa. "I lost a small fortune at markers this afternoon. I hope to win it back tonight."

"I lost at tiles."

"More than you could afford? Or is that still a problem?"

"It's not a problem," Maijstral said. "I've come into money recently. But it was more than I planned to lose."

"You should only play cards. If you lose you can start to cheat."

Maijstral smiled. "I could have cheated with the tiles. It's not as easy, but it can be done."

Her eyes were knowing. "But you wanted the Duchess to win. Do you think you can get closer to the Shard that way?"

"Perhaps," he said, "I merely wanted to get closer to the Duchess."

Vanessa was silent for a moment. Maijstral wondered at her peculiar vanity, that she was offended when men she had discarded were not faithful to her.

Ideograms announced the White Room. The orchestra was playing the same Snail concerto that Gregor had played in Maijstral's suite.

"I see Fu George. I'll see you later, Maijstral."

"Your servant."

They clasped hands, two fingers each. Maijstral repressed a shudder. He reflected that in a lifetime of dealing with thieves, fences, and other people little to be admired, Vanessa Runciter was the first and only sociopath he had ever met.

He watched her move away, then scanned the room and saw a man in a green coat walking toward him. He looked at the man in surprised recognition.

"Mr. Maijstral."

"Mr. Kuu—"

"Kuusinen, sir." Exchanging sniffs. "We met only briefly. I'm flattered you remember me."

"I have been meaning to thank you, sir," Maijstral said. "You were of some assistance, back on Peleng, to certain friends of mine."

Kuusinen smiled pleasantly. "That sir? I was simply on hand at the right time. Think nothing of it."

"Nevertheless, sir, you are a keen observer."

"Yes, I confess that," Kuusinen said. "I have a . . . facility. My eyes are always detecting little puzzles for my brain to solve."

"That is a lucky talent."

"There seem to be puzzles here," Kuusinen said. "In this room."

"Has your mind solved them?"

Kuusinen's tone was light. "Possibly. We will know for certain if Pearl Woman fails to appear for dinner."

Maijstral looked at the other man.

"Have you heard that she won't?"

"No. But if she were not to appear, that would be a puzzle, would it not?"

Maijstral's heavy-lidded eyes narrowed. "Yes," he said softly. "It would."

"Mr. Fu George seems very conscious of something in his breast pocket. A small something, I think. He keeps putting his hand there, then withdrawing it. Another mystery. Perhaps the two are connected."

There was a tingling in Maijstral's nerves. He was not certain whether this was a warning or the voice of opportunity. "Have you observed any other puzzles, Mr. Kuusinen?" he asked.

Kuusinen was ordering a drink from a robot. When he turned back to Maijstral, he smiled and said, "Something odd about the robots. I haven't decided what, just yet."

Maijstral's tingling turned cold. "No doubt the solution will come to you, sir."

"Or to my brain."

"Your brain. Yes." Maijstral's eyes, as if on cue, scanned the room again, fastened on Kotani and his wife. "I hope you will excuse me, Mr. Kuusinen," he said. "I see some old friends."

"Certainly, Mr. Maijstral."

"Your servant."

"Your very obedient."

Maijstral was very glad to get away. He felt Kuusinen's abnormally observant eyes on him all the way across the room.

"What do you think of the duel between Drake Maijstral and Geoff Fu George?"

Zoot gazed fixedly into the silver loupe over Kyoko Asperson's eye. "I don't think of it at all, I'm afraid."

"You don't follow the burglar standings?"

"It is not my preferred sport."

He was hoping, a bit wistfully, to lead the discussion toward portball; then he could lay down a smoke screen of chatter about portfires, snookerbacks, ridge plays, and the like. Kyoko Asperson refused to be distracted.

"Would you support the rumored action of the Constellation Practices Authority in trying to do away with Allowed Burglary altogether?"

"I am not familiar with that body's deliberations."

The journalist frowned for a moment. Zoot, for lack of anything else to do, continued gazing into her loupe.

"You are the only Khosali member of the Human Diadem," she said. Zoot readied himself: this was the prelude to the sorts of questions he got asked all the time. "Do you have any consciousness of being something of an experiment?"

"None," he said. "I am conscious primarily of the honor."

"Doesn't it handicap you? Don't you find your behavior constrained by your knowing that you are the only representative of your species in the Three Hundred?"

A palpable hit, but Zoot managed to avoid wincing. "Members of the Diadem excel at being themselves," he said. "Being myself is all I ever intended to do from the start."

"An admirable goal," Kyoko said. "If you can pull it off."

The Marquess Kotani cast a sympathetic glance in Zoot's direction. "Asperson will have to work damn hard to make that interview interesting," he said. "Zoot's share is slipping badly."

"I confess *I* don't find him interesting," said the Marchioness.

Kotani touched his mustache, then lifted his chin, gazing toward a nonexistent horizon and giving the Marchioness the benefit of his profile. "Men of action are so often dull in person, don't you think?" he said. "It's the ability to deal with things in a straightforward way. Admirable in its fashion, but hardly suitable for the Diadem."

"Here's Drake Maijstral." Her tilted eyes betrayed a glimmer of interest.

"My lord."

"Maijstral. Have you met my wife?"

"Honored, madam." Maijstral offered a finger in the handclasp and got three in return. He covered his surprise and smiled at Kotani.

"Mr. Maijstral," the Marchioness said. "We were just discussing men of action."

"I hope I am not included in their number," Maijstral said. "Being in essence a lazy man, I try to avoid action whenever possible."

"There," Kotani said. "My point exactly. And Maijstral's not dull."

"Surely not." The Marchioness looked at him through tilted eyes. "I'm pleased to find you taller than I thought, from seeing you only in video. I don't think Laurence's impersonation of you on vid does you justice, by the way."

"Is it an impersonation? Or is it just Laurence? I've never seen him, so I can't tell."

"Maijstral looks shorter because he's so compact," Kotani said. "He's very coordinated, moves well." He smiled at Maijstral. "It's a quality we share. People often think I appear shorter than my true height."

The Marchioness looked at Maijstral, then at her husband. "I don't think Maijstral's like you at all, Kotani."

"In that respect, dearest, he is."

"Not at all."

Kotani frowned minutely. "I think Asperson is heading this way. That woman is relentless." He held out his arm. "Shall we stroll toward the dining room?"

"If you like."

"Maijstral, we'll talk another time. When a certain person isn't eavesdropping."

"Sir. Madam."

Maijstral's heart sank. He was alone with Asperson, her next victim.

Zoot took three careful breaths and felt his tension begin to ebb. Asperson, apparently disappointed by his noncommittal answers, had gone in search of someone more obliging, or at any rate scandal-ridden or controversial.

Zoot reached in a pocket, took out a cigaret, licked the filter with his long, red tongue, and stuck the cigaret in his muzzle. He didn't smoke often in public—he fancied himself an example to others, and didn't want to encourage bad habits—but Asperson had him rattled.

Being himself, he had told Asperson, was all he ever intended to do. That was all the Diadem had ever asked of him. What he had never realized was that he would have to do it in public, in a grand, theatrical fashion, and to make it all seem natural and spontaneous and, worse, *interesting.*

Back when Zoot was leading his team in the Pioneer Corps, he hadn't had to worry about being interesting. The perils he faced were all the interest he, or anyone else, needed.

Zoot patted his pockets, looking for a cigaret lighter. He'd left it in his other jacket, the famous one. He stepped toward the nearest robot, intending to ask it for a light, but saw a tall female Khosalikh standing beneath the giant diamond, smoking a cigaret. He approached.

"Beg pardon, ma'am, but do you have a light?"

"Certainly." Her voice was clipped in a somewhat old-fashioned way. She produced a lighter. "You are Zoot, are you not?"

"Yes, madam."

"I am Lady Dosvidern."

They sniffed one another. Lady Dosvidern smelled of soap and a strong perfume. There was no hand-clasping, either, ridiculous unsanitary habit that it was.

"I am pleased," Lady Dosvidern said, "to see how you look in proper clothes."

Zoot kept his mouth from dropping open only by a sheer act of will. He looked at her.

"You *are?*" he asked.

"Were you surprised to find Geoff Fu George onstation?"

Maijstral gazed down at Kyoko Asperson's malevolent silver loupe. "On reflection," he said, "no."

"So you were surprised at first, then?"

Maijstral considered this. "No," he said, "I don't believe I was."

"Fu George is rated in first place by the Imperial Sporting Commission. You are rated seventh—"

"Sixth. Marquess Hottinn has been slipping since his incarceration."

"Sixth." Her remaining eye was bright. "Then my question is even more relevant. With the two of you here onstation, do you anticipate a duel between the two of you?"

Maijstral gave a brief laugh. "I am here only for the view, and the company."

"Fu George said the same thing. In almost the same words."

Maijstral smiled thinly. "I don't believe I'm surprised at that, either."

"So you concede any contest to Fu George."

"I am not in Fu George's class, Miss Asperson. A contest, to be any fun at all, must be between equals." He looked over the heads of the crowd, saw the back of Fu George's unmistakable blond mane, and next to him, fullface, Vanessa Runciter. She was laughing and gesturing with a cigaret holder. Her emerald earrings winked at him across the room. His ears went back.

"It's been a mixed year for you, hasn't it, Maijstral?"

The question drew him back to the interview. "How so?" he asked.

"Professionally, you've done well. Though the videos haven't yet been released, the Sporting Commission has advanced your rating. Your book on card manipulation has been well reviewed. Yet you've had a tragedy in the family, and your personal life has suffered a certain well-publicized disappointment."

She fell silent. Maijstral gazed at her with noncommital green eyes. "Pardon me, Miss Asperson," he said. "Was that a question?"

A grim smile settled into her lips. "If you like, I'll ask a proper one. Nichole left you for a Lieutenant Navarre, and he is now her personal manager. Have you any comment on her subsequent career?"

"I wish Nichole every success," said Maijstral. "She deserves it."

"Have you seen her new play?"

"I have seen recordings. I think she's magnificent."

"That's very generous of you. Yet here on Silverside, you have encountered another old flame. With Miss Runciter here in the company of Fu George, and Nichole's success on everyone's lips, aren't there a few too many sad reminders present?"

"Nichole is a dear friend. And Miss Runciter is from a long time ago."

As he spoke he heard, from across the room, a woman's laugh. He looked up, saw Vanessa looking at him. Their eyes met, and she lifted her glass to him. He nodded to her, and reached a mental resolution.

Damn Kuusinen's eyes, he thought. And his other parts, too.

He'd do it.

"Lord Qlp is inactive now," Lady Dosvidern said. "The Drawmii have five brains, you know, each with one eye and one ear. They spend a lot of time not moving, just talking to themselves. Crosstalk, we call it."

"I believe I'd heard something of the sort. That their interior life was somewhat complex."

"It makes being Lord Qlp's companion a little easier. I should have dinnertime to myself, and most of the evening, before Lord Qlp grows restless again."

"I should be honored, my lady, to take you in to dinner."

She smiled, her tongue lolling. "Thank you, sir. It would be my pleasure."

People talked without sound. The orchestra sawed away without any aural effect. Clear privacy screens, Maijstral reflected, are a wonderful device for creating inadvertent comedy.

"Gregor."

"Yes, boss?"

"Is Roman there? I want you both in the White Room as soon as possible."

"Something's up?"

"I'm going to do an unassisted crosstouch, and I want it recorded from two angles." Maijstral held the telephone with both hands, one cupped in front of his mouth, so as to inhibit lipreading.

The delight was palpable in Gregor's voice. "Unassisted? Right there in front of everybody? Terrific, boss. Ten points, for sure."

"Hurry. I expect the trumpets at any moment."

"Only too." Meaning, only too ready.

Maijstral put the phone down and told the privacy field to disperse. The sound of conversation returned, nearly drowning the orchestra. Maijstral glanced about and saw Advert huddling against the bar in an orange shell gown that clashed badly with her background, which was of bright closewood and mirrors. Deciding that Advert had failed to notice the clash and was therefore obviously very distraught, Maijstral concluded to rescue her. As he walked toward her, he saw something glitter against the hollow of her throat. Seeing him, she turned away and watched his approach through the mirrored Khanji relief behind the bar. Only when his arrival seemed inevitable did she turn to him. They exchanged two fingers and sniffed.

"My compliments on your choker, madam," Maijstral said. "The sapphire is wonderfully set off by the diamonds."

Advert raised a hand swiftly to her throat, as if to prevent him from snatching the choker then and there. Then she hesitated.

"Thank you." Through clenched teeth.

Maijstral glanced casually about the room. "Is not Pearl Woman here?" he asked. "There was something I particularly wanted to say to her."

"She isn't feeling well."

"I trust she will recover soon. Before the ball, I hope."

Sullenly. "I can't say."

"Perhaps my news will cheer her. I believe that she may have lost something, and I believe I know where it is."

Advert's eyes blazed. "So it *was* you."

Maijstral's lazy eyes widened in feigned surprise. "I said I knew where it was, Miss Advert. I did *not* say that I had it. I believe it was recovered by someone else, and I can probably get it."

Advert looked at him with suspicion. "What do you want?" she asked.

"May I escort you to your table? I think we may have a number of things to talk about."

She put her arm through his. Rings glittered against the dark material of his suit. "I'm not certain whether I should listen to this."

"You can always walk away."

She bit her lip. Maijstral guided her away from the clashing backdrop. She harmonized much better with white than with closewood and mirrors.

"I'll listen," she decided. "For now."

"Will you do me another favor, Miss Advert. Will you order a new deck of cards from one of the robots?"

Standing up amid the orchestra, trumpeters raised their instruments to their lips.

Trumpet calls rang from the giant diamond. A pair of leather-covered doors swung open. Couples began moving toward the dining room.

"The Waltz twins, definitely," Geoff Fu George said, wrapping Vanessa's arm in his. "Have you seen what they're wearing?"

"I've seen it," Vanessa said. They were barely moving their lips, wary of lip-readers hiding behind invisible cameras.

"They can't possibly wear those heavy pieces at the ball later."

"They may go in the hotel safe."

"In that case, we'll take them off the robot."

"Not as many points that way."

Fu George shrugged. "Risks of the game, Vanessa."

"I suppose. Look. There's Roman."

"Yes." Noncommittally.

"I always liked him. Perhaps I should say hello."

"Perhaps."

"He never approved of me, I always thought. He probably thought me a nouveau riche adventuress." She thought about this judgment for a brief moment. "He was perfectly right, of course."

"Oh." (A brush . . .)

"Ah." (. . . not a thud.)

Maijstral offered an excusatory smile. "My apologies. I must not have been looking where I was going."

Fu George looked at him and nodded. "Quite all right, Maijstral." He nodded. "Miss Advert."

"Mr. Fu George. Miss Runciter."

Maijstral stepped back. "Pray go on ahead of us."

Fu George was pleased. "Thank you, Maijstral."

The trumpets were still calling. In his formal dinner clothes, Roman watched, imperturbable, from his corner of the room. The trumpets were not, after all, calling for him.

"Another alert, Khamiss. Violet Corridor, Level Eight, Panel F22."

Sun's voice grated through Khamiss's skull. She drew her lips back in a snarl. She was getting tired of that particular voice and the inevitability of its announcements—Sun was fond of bone-conduction receivers, and this one was surgically implanted in the top of Khamiss's skull, where she couldn't get rid of it.

Khamiss turned back to her troopers. Her three uniformed subordinates were as weary as she, and she could see their stricken expressions, recognizing them as reflections of her own.

"Another one, ma'am?" asked one.

"Yes. Violet Corridor, Level Eight."

"We're not going to run all that distance, are we?"

Time, Khamiss realized, for a command decision. She knew, and her troops knew, that the alarm was false. Everyone but the guards were at dinner, and no one would be stealing now: their presence would be missed.

"We'll walk," Khamiss said. "At our own pace."

"Very good, ma'am."

Her upper stomach growled. Things were bad enough that she had to spend her day chasing up and down corridors; now she and her squad had to go without meals. She touched the microphone on her lapel.

"Mr. Sun," she said, "could you order a robot with some sandwiches to meet us in Violet Corridor? We're getting hungry."

"Certainly. I shall also send some bottles of rink."

Well, Khamiss thought. Things were looking up at least a bit. She began to feel a little more buoyant.

Her buoyancy fell considerably as she was informed that two more alarms had gone off before she and her weary troopers could quite respond to the first. She opened her bottle of rink with a move that could only be called desperate.

It was going to be a long night.

"If you will watch, madam." Maijstral fanned the cards on the perfect white of the tablecloth. This wasn't the deck Maijstral carried in his hidden pocket: this was a deck that Advert had just had delivered by one of the Cygnus robots.

"I'm watching, Maijstral." Advert, sitting in the dining room below the massive kaleidoscoping steel doors, was in a much better temper. She actually smiled at him.

He squared the deck. "Take you table knife and cut the deck at any point. Lift your card, look at the corner, then drop it."

"Very well." She did as he had asked. He squared the deck again (using a little finger break), shifted the deck from left hand to right (thumb holding the break), drank casually from his glass with the left. . . .

"Is this one in your book, Maijstral?"

"Actually, no." He put the glass down and moved the pack back to his left hand. (Maintaining the break, stepping the cards.) "My book is on advanced manipulations. This one's very elementary. I'm just doing it to warm up." (Glimpsing the card under the heel of the left hand: eight of crowns.) He squared the deck with his right hand, then offered it to Advert.

"Shuffle it, cut it. However many times you like." Riffling.

"I think the Pearl's going to be pleased."

"I daresay she'll be proud of you."

The lights of the dining room were darkening. Pale tablecloths glowed dimly. "Best hurry," said Maijstral.

"How do I know," casually, handing the pack to him, "you haven't hidden my card up your sleeve before you gave me the deck?"

He smiled. That was just the fear he intended to ease. "Let me run slowly through the deck. Take note that your card is there. Don't tell me when you see it, and I won't look at your face." (Spotting the eight of crowns, counting five cards above it. Breaking the deck there.)

"Did you see it?"

"Yes. It was in the deck." (A quick cut at the break.)

Maijstral put the deck down on the tabletop. "How many letters in your name?"

"Six."

"Turn over six cards."

The lights were almost entirely down. Advert had to squint at the deck. There was another trumpet cry.

"A-D-V-E-R-T. Oh." She laughed and held up the eight of crowns. Maijstral took it, took a pen from his pocket, signed the card, handed it back to her.

"Why don't you keep the deck as a souvenir?" Maijstral put the deck back in its box, wrapped it in a handkerchief, and signalled for a robot. "Have the robot take it to your room."

Advert smiled in admiration. "Yes," she said. "I believe I will."

"A great crosstouch. Better than any I've seen him do in practice."

"I believe," Roman said, "that the knowledge of his being on camera affects his performance for the better." He touched the micromedia globe in his pocket as a superstitious person would his Twalle amulet. "Mr. Maijstral always seems to work best under pressure." He looked up sharply. "Hush, now. Someone we know."

"Mr. Roman. Mr. Norman."

"Mr. Drexler. Mr. Chalice."

Roman and Gregor, walking toward the servants' dining room, sniffed and offered two comradely fingers to each of Geoff Fu George's principal assistants.

"Larmon and Hrang are not with you?" Roman inquired.

"No," Drexler said. "They would have loved to come, of course, but space is limited on this station, and Mr. Fu George won only two invitations in his card game with Lord Swann."

"Yes, I understand. I hope Miss Runciter's suite was not likewise restricted."

"She has her woman with her. Cooper."

"Miss Cooper isn't here?"

"She's getting Miss Runciter's ball gown ready. It's got a lot of special effects."

Roman gazed down his nose at Drexler. "Miss Cooper has my sympathy."

Drexler was a young male Khosalikh, not yet having reached first molt; he was a little shorter than average height but built broadly, as if for durability. He wore a gaudy stud in one ear, and

Roman suspected it contained a small camera. He was Geoff Fu George's technician.

Mr. Chalice was another one of Fu George's associates: he was human, thirtyish, and rail-thin. His hair was red, and his gangly movements seemed strangely disconnected, like those of a puppet. Roman had always thought Chalice had missed his true avocation, which was that of clown.

Roman had considerably more respect for clowns than for thieves. Maijstral's life's work, alas, had not been chosen with Roman's consultation.

Roman was forty-six and had begun to despair of ever living a regular life.

"Shall we dine together, gentlemen?" Chalice asked.

"Certainly."

"Why not?"

A robot guided them to a table for four. (The servants' restaurant had only nonliving maitre d's.) When the next robot came by, they ordered a bottle of wine for the table.

Drexler looked at his guests, tongue lolling in a smile. His ears pricked forward. "I hope you weren't overly inconvenienced by the customs people here."

"They confiscated a case of equipment." Gregor said. "But I expect we'll survive."

"That's good." Chalice seemed buoyant. "We'd hate to be the only thieves operating on this rock. If they don't know which of us did what job, we'll be able to use the confusion to our advantage."

"There's one job I'm really interested in," said Drexler. He tapped his wine glass meditatively. "The Shard."

Roman carefully avoided exchanging a glance with Gregor. "It may not be here," he said.

"Personally," Drexler said, "I think it is. Why else would the station vid run a documentary of its history? It's too much to expect that sort of thing to be a coincidence."

"If it's here," Roman said, "her grace the Duchess will wear it. She won't have brought it all this way *not* to wear it."

"Her grace the Duchess," Drexler said, "has a very large staff. Including six people of no apparent function, who have not been seen since their arrival." He glanced around the room. "And who are not here."

"Perhaps they are readying her gown."

"All six of them?"

Chalice laughed. "Some gown."

"Perhaps," Drexler said, "a wager is in order." Roman's ears perked forward.

"How so?"

"Perhaps we should make a wager concerning who will hold the Shard in his hands first. Someone on your side of the table, or someone on ours."

"It's a bet." Gregor's reply was instant.

"It may not," Roman insisted, "be here."

"If it's not," Drexler said, "or if no one gets it at all—which I doubt—then the wager will be void."

Roman considered this. Gregor nudged him under the table. Roman's diaphragm throbbed. "Very well," he said. "Five novae?"

"Let's make it ten," offered Drexler.

"Five is sufficient."

"Ten," said Gregor quickly. "We'll bet ten."

Roman's ears went back. "Ten," he sighed, feigning reluctance. "Very well." Drexler grinned and raised his glass.

"Gentlemen," he said, "I give you success."

"Success," Roman echoed, and lapped his wine.

Next to him, Roman could hear Gregor's fingers tap, tap, tapping on his knees. *Success,* they seemed to be tapping. *Success, success.*

Baron Silverside, good will welling in his broad frame, entered the dining room with the Duchess of Benn on one arm and the Baroness on the other. Roberta was taller than both by several inches. The Baron showed Roberta to his table, then turned to his guests. The lights dimmed, the trumpets called. A few tables away, Maijstral finished his card trick and called for a robot. Baron Silverside, beneficence waxing in his veins, caressed his burnsides and waited for his moment. He could see a red light that meant he was being projected, in hologram form, into the servants' and the employees' dining rooms.

A bright light came on to his right, a back light behind him (which illuminated his whiskers splendidly), a fill light to his left—he was going to do this properly. A trumpet called again. The room burst into applause.

"My lords, ladies, and gentlemen," began the Baron. His words were buried beneath the torrent of applause. The Baron was surprised. He hadn't even unleashed the good stuff yet.

He shuffled. He turned crimson. He yanked on his whiskers. He was having the time of his life.

* * *

Geoff Fu George sipped his wine and enjoyed seeing, without really looking at him, the Baron go through his agonies of pleasure. His eyes were not directed toward the Baron, but beside him, toward where Roberta was illuminated in stray light from the Baron's spots. She was not wearing the Shard—in fact her jewelry was modest, possibly to contrast, later, with the Shard when she finally chose to wear it—but he watched her nonetheless.

He wasn't certain why he watched. Perhaps he was looking for clues. Perhaps he just wanted some idea of her character. Perhaps he was hoping for an indication why she would have a game of tiles with Maijstral—something like a covert glance, a secret signal. (He saw none.) Perhaps he simply enjoyed looking at her—with her deep green gown complementing her strong, pale shoulders and dark red hair, she was worth looking at.

The applause finally died away. The Baron essayed again. "My lords, ladies, and gentlemen," he said. "I am flattered by your reception. When I first conceived the idea of this resort, I knew that, if it were to be a success, every detail would have to be accounted for. . . ."

The Baron droned on, his burnsides flaring against the darkness. Behind him, fidgeting with her tableware, was his Baroness, a short, driven woman who Fu George knew was a middling-successful painter and owner of one of the most prestigious small collections in the Constellation. The Baroness was painfully shy, and almost never appeared in public—when seen, she usually wore an elaborate, pleated skirt of a type she'd introduced a decade ago, and which everyone else had long since ceased to wear. Roberta watched with apparent interest as the Baron wandered into minutiae concerning the process of selecting the absolutely *right* asteroid. Fu George watched Roberta and wondered why she had played tiles with Maijstral.

"Milords, ladies, gentlemen, I shall digress no longer . . ."

The pearl. Fu George smiled. His hand strayed to his breast pocket.

". . . may I present the *raison d'être* of Silverside Station . . ."

Fu George's smile froze on his face. His hand plunged into his pocket. There was nothing there.

". . . one of Creation's own wonders . . ."

Fu George remembered the brush with Maijstral, the man's uncommon civility. Vanessa perceived his agitation. She put a hand on his arm. "What's wrong, Geoff?"

"Rathbon's Star and its companion!"

Soundlessly, the steel doors irised back. The room was bathed in the light of one star devouring another.

There was no applause. The sight was too awesome.

Fu George glared across the room at Maijstral. He was sitting next to Advert, and both were smiling as they tilted their heads back to watch Rathbon's Star being eaten.

Maijstral, Fu George thought. *This means war.*

THREE

The ball got under way two hours after dinner. The ballroom had no artificial light: the pulses and flares of Rathbon's Star provided both spectacle and illumination for the vast oval room. Maijstral shared the first dance with her grace the Duchess of Benn. Roberta's ball gown was blazing orange: eyes fixed on her as if she were a magnet. Baron Silverside and his lady, dancing just up the set, were eclipsed entirely.

Geoff Fu George, dancing a short distance away with Vanessa, couldn't keep his eyes off them. By those who make it their business to notice and remark upon such things, Fu George's intent gaze was noticed and remarked on.

Paavo Kuusinen had arrived late for the first dance, and so stood on the fringes of the ballroom, tapping his cane to the rhythm of the music, and watched the multitude. Because there was nothing to do, and because (being compulsive) he couldn't help himself, he glanced upward and numbered the media globes on the scene. There were eight, each controlled by Kyoko Asperson through her loupe.

At a Diadem event one could normally expect a great many

more, but Baron Silverside had been firm in the number of globes he would allow onstation to harass his guests.

Kuusinen, his compulsion unsated, began to count the number of instruments in the orchestra.

Mr. Chalice attached the portable power source to his coat and smiled. He donned the coat, turned the collar up, and *thought* himself invisible.

He glanced at his reflection in the triple mirror placed in Fu George's suite and saw in place of himself a distorted smear of color. He knew that smear for himself, that his body was obscured by holographic camouflage tuned to the color scheme of his background.

Geoff Fu George had known that Silverside was going to feature unprecedented security measures, and even before he'd won his invitations at cards, he prepared for dealing with same. He'd thought his usual trunk of equipment would be confiscated, and he had been right. He and his assistants had solved the problem by having miniaturized versions of their equipment built into their evening clothes.

The advanced and unobtrusive design was expensive, but then Fu George could afford the best. The proximity wire in the collar enabled the suit to be given mental commands: it was powered by a micro-source available for a modest price in the station's Electronic Boutique and Gadget Faire; and the darksuit could be used as an evening jacket, permitting instant changes from social to burgling mode.

Chalice's jacket was the last readied: he'd prepared Fu George's first, then Drexler's. All three of them had assignments this evening.

He grinned, Maijstral wasn't going to know what hit him.

Gregor looked up from his watch and glanced carefully into the unique view afforded him by his smoked spectacles. As with Kyoko Asperson's loupe, one lens was arranged to show the view transmitted by media globes, in Gregor's case the superimposed view of two corridors, each broadcast by one of a pair of micromedia globes, which were acting as lookout. Taking a final glance to make sure he wouldn't be observed, Gregor took a tool from his pocket, inserted it in the wall, and swung an access panel out on its hinges. He stepped into the utility space, strolled as far as the door to the next suite, and then strolled back. He checked his spectacles again—no one present—and stepped out. He pushed the wall back into its place.

He walked twenty paces to an elevator and pressed the button.

While he waited he took a hi-stick from his pocket and put it in his mouth.

He was going to the ball.

"Pearl Woman!" Delight shone from Kotani's features. He sniffed her ears and offered her three fingers.

"Marquess," said the Pearl.

"You look wonderful. I was given to understand you were ill."

"A brief indisposition. I am entirely recovered." Pearl Woman was flushed and laughing, dressed in an embroidered silk gown. A bandanna was wrapped around her leonine hair, its loose ends dangling above the trademark earring. She was truly radiant, the source of her radiance being relief. Her clothing had been thrown on at the last minute, but fortunately she had the sort of looks which were improved by a slight dishevelment. She'd been standing over a jeweler for most of the last two hours, badgering him while he reassembled the earring. It was now one link shorter, but no one could be expected to detect such an insignificant change.

Pearl Woman glanced over the ballroom. "Is Advert here?"

"Speaking to Janetha. There."

"Ah. You'll excuse me, Marquess?"

"Of course, Pearl."

"Your servant."

"Yours."

Drake Maijstral stepped into one of the private salons off the main ballroom. Gregor, a few moments later, followed, the hi-stick still in his mouth. An opaque privacy screen flickered into existence behind them.

A minute or so later, Gregor and his hi-stick were observed to leave.

Roman stepped around a corner and saw a group of tired, dispirited security guards led by the gangling figure of Kingston. Kingston, he saw, seemed to have forsaken his jester mode. Roman stepped back out of sight, waited until they'd gone on their way, then stepped into the corridor again.

A Cygnus robot passed by, carrying a tray with an empty wine bottle and empty glasses.

Roman glanced right and left, saw no one, took a tool from his pocket, and opened the wall. He closed the wall behind him, took a short stroll, opened the wall at another access point, and stepped into the corridor.

There was no one to see him.

Paavo Kuusinen, who had just noticed Gregor leave the ballroom, looked to his right and observed Fu George sliding out by another door. Smiling, he drifted toward the buffet and picked up a glass of rink.

Sipping, he perceived Kyoko Asperson, dressed in green and purple and with her loupe missing from over her eye, leaving by the same door as had Gregor. He looked up and saw her media globes still circling the assembly. Carefully, he counted them. There were six.

He frowned. Then he began to smile.

"Advert. Marchioness." Sniffing.

"Pearl Woman."

"Pearl!" Advert was delighted. "You look *splendid!*"

"Thank you, Advert. Enthusiasm becomes you, as always." She glanced at the Marchioness. "My lady, if you would excuse us? There was a small confusion regarding our bags, and I need to speak with Advert and sort things out."

"Certainly." Sniffs. "Your very obedient."

"And yours."

Pearl Woman took Advert's arm and pulled her aside, facing the wall. Advert wasn't practiced at speaking without moving her lips, and some important things needed to be said.

"Where were you when I got back from dinner?" Advert asked. "I dressed and you weren't there at all."

"I was hunting a jeweler."

"I wanted to tell you *everything.*"

"You know, then, how it is that my pearl came to my room inside a deck of cards signed by Drake Maijstral, wrapped in a handkerchief with Fu George's monogram on it, and delivered by robot."

"Yes." Advert was laughing. "I arranged it. You see, Fu George was the one who stole your pearl. He had it wrapped in his handkerchief, and was carrying it in his pocket. And Maijstral agreed to take the pearl back for us. Wasn't that lucky?"

Pearl Woman gave her a look. "And the deck of cards?"

"Maijstral was doing a card trick, and he had to put the pearl *somewhere* so that he could send it to you. You know, I think Maijstral is quite a nice man. He's very entertaining."

"How much did you agree to pay him?"

Advert bit her lip. Pearl Woman's eyes narrowed.

"How much, Advert?"

"Sixty."

Pearl Woman looked at the wall for a long moment. Her expression was calculating. "Not as bad as it could have been."

"Pearl, I've never done anything like this before. I didn't know how much to offer. And there wasn't any time to think. We only had a few minutes before Fu George went in to dinner."

"What did that have to do with it?"

Pause. "Oh." Another pause. "It seemed important at the time." Advert's voice grew forlorn. "I *did* talk him down from eighty."

Pearl Woman tossed her head. The pearl danced at the end of its chain. "Well. At least it's done."

Advert's fingers fidgeted with her rings. "You're not going to challenge Fu George, are you?"

Pearl Woman glanced over her shoulder at the other guests. "I think not."

Advert let out a breath. "Good. I'm so relieved."

Pearl Woman tossed her head again. It was becoming a habitual gesture, allowing her to assure herself the pearl was still there by the weight of it dancing against her neck.

Her voice was calculating. "I *had* an encounter a little over a year ago, and I couldn't count on my points rising by that much if I had another. They might even go down." She frowned. "And I still can't prove that Fu George did it."

Advert's eyes widened. "Whatever do you mean?"

"Maijstral might have had the pearl all along. He may have put it in one of Fu George's handkerchiefs to make you *think* Fu George had it."

Advert considered this for a moment. "Ah," she said.

"All this may have been an elaborate scheme to get me to challenge Fu George so that Maijstral could have the thieving here to himself."

Advert twisted her rings again and said nothing.

"That would be very like Maijstral," Pearl Woman went on. "He's always been more subtle than was good for . . . well, for anyone around him."

"Oh." There was a long pause. "Pearl." Advert's voice was tentative. "You know, I've already paid Maijstral the money. He sent for one of those chips from the Casino."

Pearl Woman sighed. "I'm inclined to think he had the pearl all along. He certainly took advantage of the situation quickly enough." She turned and began walking toward the other dancers. Advert followed. "Where *is* Fu George, anyway?" Pearl Woman wondered. "I'd like to see the look on his face when I dangle the pearl in front of his eyes. If he *did* take it, he might not know I've got it back."

"The point is, Pearl," Advert said, "that sixty set me back a lot. When we consider how much it cost just to *stay* here . . ."

Pearl Woman gave her a casual glance. "You know I don't have that kind of money, Advert. After what I paid for the yacht, I'm completely skinned."

"But Pearl. You must have—"

"I'll get some royalties in a few months, of course. And if I win some races, well, things will get better." She gave Advert a sidelong look. "You know, Advert, one shouldn't become so dependent on the material aspects of existence."

"You're about to sign a contract with—"

"Until then"—Pearl Woman smiled at Advert—"I'm entirely dependent on the goodwill of my friends." She put her arm in Advert's.

Advert let herself be drawn toward the ballroom floor. Her face was growing pale.

Pearl Woman glanced over the room, looking for Fu George. Inwardly, she was entirely satisfied.

If one was to have protegés, she thought, one ought at least to get some use out of them.

Roman, walking slowly down the corridor, observed an acquaintance walking in the opposite direction.

"Mr. Chalice." He nodded.

"Mr. Roman."

Ten novae, Roman thought, and smiled.

"Lady Dosvidern."

"Your grace."

"I wonder if you might walk with me."

"Happily, your grace." She took Roberta's arm and began to promenade.

"I'm afraid, my lady, that I have to confess to you my ignorance," Roberta said.

Lady Dosvidern's ears pricked toward her. "Is that so, your grace? I can't imagine your grace's ignorance including anything of importance."

"You're very kind. But no, I'm afraid I have a most embarrassing confession." She gave Lady Dosvidern a warm smile. "I must confess ignorance, my lady, as to the precise meaning of the honor, and the object, which Lord Qlp bestowed upon me this afternoon."

"Ah. That." Lady Dosvidern seemed bemused. "I'm afraid, your grace, my ignorance but only equals yours."

Roberta stopped. Her ears flattened in disbelief. "Truly?" she said.

"I know only that Lord Qlp insisted that it and your grace had to meet. I had no idea it was going to make you a gift, or what that gift was going to be."

"You have no notion of the significance of the object?"

"Not only have I no knowledge of its significance, your grace, I'm afraid I must confess I have never seen an object of that nature before."

Roberta frowned. "Drawmii do not . . . disgorge such objects regularly?"

"Not to my knowledge, your grace. And I have lived on Zynzlyp and in Lord Qlp's company for almost four years."

"How strange."

"Strange. That is Zynzlyp and the Drawmii in sum."

"My lady." Zoot bowed toward them. "Your grace."

"Zoot." Lady Dosvidern was smiling. "Such a pleasure to see you again. Please join us."

The two sniffed the newcomer, and linked arms, one on either side him.

"I was hoping, Lady Dosvidern, to ask for the honor of the next dance."

"Certainly, sir."

Roberta looked at the adventurer. "I enjoyed your last play, Zoot," she said.

"Thank you, your grace."

"I thought the critics were most unfair. The play didn't quite have the exotic appeal of the earlier series, but it seemed solidly done."

Zoot's nostrils flickered. "That seems to be the general opinion, your grace."

"I suspect the writers did not have as thorough a grasp of the material as on the earlier plays."

"I confess that's true, your grace. I have had some discussions with them on that matter. But it's difficult to find people who are at once writers and xenobiologists."

"I can imagine."

"I offered to advise them on Pioneer Corps procedure, but they were not receptive. They kept referring to their dramatic license. Unfortunately," he huffed, "I suspect their licenses had long expired."

A trumpet spoke, calling with perfect synchronicity at the precise moment of a particularly bright solar flare. Lady Dosvidern's eyes gleamed, briefly, red.

"Your grace," she said. "I hope you will excuse us. Our dance beckons."

"Certainly. My lady. Zoot."

"Your grace."

Roberta turned, looking for a partner, and smiled. Paavo Kuusinen was approaching.

"Marchioness Kotani?"

The Marchioness blinked. "Yes?"

"My name is Dolfuss, ma'am. I've always been an admirer of your husband. May I have the honor of this dance?"

The Marchioness looked left and right, seeking aid. There was none. She turned her eyes to Dolfuss and forced a smile.

"Certainly sir."

Grinning, Dolfuss offered an arm.

Consider the magic inherent even in modern life. One is at a resort hotel. One but touches ideograms on a service plate, and lights come on, breakfast is delivered, music floats on the air as if played by an invisible orchestra. Fresh water gushes from taps, robots appear to help you dress, the room is warmed or cooled at your command.

One might well picture a horde of bustling spirits dancing attendance, Ariels sweating manfully in service to their Prosperos. A first-class resort will strive to maintain this image: the omnipotence of their guests is a happy illusion shared, ideally, both by guests and management.

The reality, of course, is more prosaic, but the element of magic is not entirely absent. To demonstrate:

An artificial environment such as an asteroid resort inevitably poses unique problems in architecture. Water, power, air, and gravity must be created and delivered to where they are needed, and conduits for these resources, like the conduits for people, needs must be drilled through solid rock. And, should anything go wrong with the necessary deliveries, the conduits must be easy of access to persons charged with their repair.

One could create separate utility tunnels, but why bother? The utility tunnels would only be delivering their necessities to the same places to which the personnel tunnels would be delivering people. The creators of Silverside Station built their tunnels in parallel—one set for people, appropriately panelled and carpeted and papered in the finest taste. Marching alongside is another, secret set, built to carry the utility mains, and of immediate access behind false walls. Utilities can thus be maintained and repaired by people moving behind the walls, who can work without the distracting necessity of having to rip up floors or ceilings, disturbing people moving in the main tunnels, or (even worse) interfering with the residents' illusion that a host of Ariels is really at work, delivering all conveniences without human effort.

The utility tunnels are tall, narrow, and cramped. Movement is necessarily restricted.

But movement there is. Water, power, gravity, sewage . . . and other things.

Not Ariel or Caliban, not exactly. But something a bit more magical than anything the designers intended.

Drake Maijstral reached for a control on his belt and turned off the hologram that made him look like Gregor Norman. He took the hi-stick from his mouth and put it in his pocket—a nice touch, he'd thought, a magician's touch, insisting Gregor have a stick in his mouth when he entered the private salon. It made the illusion of the false Gregor all that much more convincing.

A micromedia globe hovered overhead, recording everything for posterity and Maijstral's eventual enrichment. Maijstral paused outside the Waltz twins' suite, took a tool from his pocket, and opened the wall. He donned a pair of goggles that would allow him to detect energy sources and see in the dark.

The utility tunnel smelled of fresh paint. Fingers moving nimbly, Maijstral disconnected the lock on the Waltz twins' door and then stepped out of the tunnel.

He had probably tripped at least one alarm in the tunnel, but it would be indistinguishable from the other alarms his reprogrammed robots were creating everywhere onstation. He could safely assume that the alarm would be ignored, or if answered, answered far too late.

Back in the main corridor, Maijstral stepped to the Waltz twins' door. It was already open.

Frowning, soundless, Maijstral pushed the door open. Moments before, he'd seen the elderly Waltz twins step onto the dance floor and engage in a dance far more vigorous than would seem safe for ladies of their age.

A pattern of energy displayed itself across Maijstral's goggles. The pattern of energy appeared to be dumping heavy, old-fashioned jewelry into a flat case.

"Sorry, Maijstral," said Geoff Fu George. "You're a little late."

"Didn't mean to interrupt," Maijstral said, and closed the door.

He glanced at his chronometer. Time, he thought, for Plan Two.

He retrieved his gear from the tunnel and, looking fore and aft to make certain he was unobserved, began to run. His low-heeled buskins made no sound.

Paavo Kuusinen turned the Duchess of Benn under his right arm. She spun to her place and smiled.

"You're a smooth dancer, Kuusinen," she said.

"I thank your grace." Properly.

Roberta looked at Kuusinen thoughtfully. "You have that secret look, Kuusinen."

"Do I?" His face disclosed a quiet smile as he danced a brief jig about her.

"What are you involved with?"

"I have engaged in a slight intrigue, my lady," he said. "Raising Maijstral's stock, as against that of Geoff Fu George."

"Very good, Kuusinen."

Kuusinen gave her a pensive look. "I'm having second thoughts, I'm afraid." Roberta danced in place, her heels flashing. "I'm afraid I've just heightened the rivalry."

"The better for us, then."

"Possibly, your grace. If it doesn't get out of control."

They touched hands, moved three vigorous, hopping steps to the right. Down the set, one of the Waltz twins gave a whoop.

Roberta retired a pace. Kuusinen made a flourishing bow. She smiled at him as they passed right, then left. "There's another mystery to which you might address your talents, if you're not feeling overstrained."

"Your grace?"

"The object that Lord Qlp gave me this afternoon."

"Ah. I heard about that."

"It looked at first like a wet lump. But now it's dried off, and it's looking more . . . interesting."

"How so, your grace?"

"There are . . . colors in it. Patterns. And the patterns change. It seems to have some form of internal life. I asked Lady Dosvidern about it, but she affects to be as baffled as I."

"Perhaps you ought to have it checked, your grace. It might be unhealthy in some way."

Roberta laughed. "The least of my worries, sir. But still, I'd like you to see the thing."

"Happily, your grace."

She regarded him carefully. "You still have that secret look, Kuusinen."

"Have I, your grace?" Touching hands again, and hopping to the left. Still holding hands (his left, her right), they turned up the set and began to perform an intricate series of steps while maintaining forward motion. Roberta sighed.

"Very well, Kuusinen. I won't insist. But I hope you'll let me know when something is about to happen."

"I will, your grace." He caught her eye and smiled. "You may depend on it."

Mr. Sun sat fidgeting in his cool blue heaven, possessed of a growing conviction that Lucifer had somehow got in amongst the angels and all PanDaemonium was going to break loose at any instant.

Alarms were still going off with dismal regularity. There were thirty lights on his board, and more appearing every minute. His people were an hour late in answering them.

Perhaps, he thought, something in the unique character of Silverside's Star had wildly increased the local rate of entropic decay. The security system on which Sun had labored for the better part of two years was falling apart at the first crisis, and Sun found himself helpless to cope with the shock.

He knew he had to deal with the situation somehow, take command. He had no idea how.

A light winked into existence on his console. He pressed an ideogram, said, "Yes."

"Khamiss, sir." Which Sun could see perfectly well, as a hologram of Khamiss's head had just appeared in the control room. Khamiss was looking weary about the eyes.

"Yes, Khamiss?"

"We've finished on Azure Corridor. No sign of anything out of the ordinary."

"Very well," said Mr. Sun. He reset the alarm on Azure Corridor. "Peach Division next, eighth deep."

"Sir." Speaking very carefully. "I think it's time for a command decision. My people are growing tired, and we haven't found a single intrusion."

Sun frowned. Entropic decay, it appeared, was beginning to spread to his minions. The Sin Balance was tilting in an ominous way. Sun needed to restore order to the universe, and do it immediately. "We cannot concede the battlefield to the enemy," he said. "If we do, we'll be allowing all manner of mischief to take place."

"With all respect, sir, we're not halting mischief now. We're doing precisely what our opponents want us to do—running ourselves ragged chasing false alarms."

Sun drew himself up. "Do you have any concrete suggestions, Khamiss?" he demanded. "Or are you just asking to be taken off the detail?"

"Perhaps we can have our computer experts review the alarm systems. Perhaps the programming has been interfered with."

"I've done that. They haven't found anything yet."

"In that case, sir, may I suggest that we make some attempt to categorize these alarms and respond only to those with high priority. I think we can safely ignore all alarms in remote parts of the station, or alarms that go off when our principal burglars are known to be somewhere else, and concentrate our forces on recent alarms that go off in the dead of night, or other prime thieving times."

Sun glared stonily at Khamiss's hologram. Khamiss's suggestions made perfect sense, but still it seemed to Sun that this constituted a challenge to his authority.

"I will consider the suggestion, Khamiss," he said. "In the meantime, you're due in Peach Division."

The weariness around Khamiss's eyes became more apparent. "Very well, sir."

Good, Sun thought. The incipient mutiny was quelled. Time for a bit of encouragement from the generalissimo. He would raise the level of morale and return to his troops their sharp combative edge.

"Keep fighting the good fight," Sun said. He broke into a rare smile. "You and your men are to be congratulated. You're doing very well."

"Thank you, sir."

"Lord bless you."

The hologram vanished.

The blue command center hummed on. Three more alarms went off in swift succession.

Very well, Sun thought. Prioritize. Everything fits into a category, and some of these alarms must seem more suspicious than others.

If this weren't someone else's idea, he'd implement it immediately.

Khamiss leaned wearily against the wall. Her crew echoed her posture. "Right," she said. "I hereby declare that the burglars have won."

One of her troopers, a young human, looked at her with an insubordinate grin. "Does this mean we fall on our swords, ma'am?"

"No. It means we go to the employees' lounge and get something to eat."

"Yes, ma'am."

"Ma'am." Another human, a blonde named Gretchen. "I have a bottle of hross in my room. It's only a few corridors down."

"By all means fetch it."

Khamiss smiled. For the first time in hours, her security division was moving with alacrity.

Leadership, she thought. There was nothing like it.

Geoff Fu George stepped back from the closet door and admired his handiwork. His blind looked exactly like the top of the closet, and no one could see the jewelry concealed above the false ceiling.

Moving in confident silence, Fu George let himself out of the Waltz twins' room and locked the door behind him. Mentally, using the proximity wire in his collar, he checked his darksuit's chronometers, turned off the holographic camouflage, and retrieved his hovering media globe, which he put in his pocket. He began moving briskly toward the ballroom.

Allowed Burglars are most vulnerable during the period immediately following their crime: the rules of their profession demand that they keep the swag in their residence, or on their person, until midnight following the day of the crime. Usually they accomplish this by renting another residence under a false name, simply hiding out for the day following the theft.

On Silverside Station, hiding out was impossible. Fu George knew for a certainty that his room would be searched if a theft was committed, and that his person would be at least scrutinized. He had therefore decided *not* to steal the Waltz twins' jewelry, at least not for the present—he merely made it appear that the jewels *had* been stolen, by hiding them above the false ceiling in the closet. He'd enter the room later and perform a genuine theft, but by that time the authorities would assume the one-day deadline had passed, and he'd be safe with the stuff in his rooms.

Idly, he wondered how Maijstral was coping with the problem.

Strains of music wafted up the corridor. It was the same dance he'd just ducked out of; his work was adhering to schedule.

Scheduling was important tonight: he planned to strike at least once more.

"The Colonial Service cannot be as dull as you say, madam," Zoot said. "After all, how dull can it be to engage in important Imperial business? Interact with subject species? Conduct important treaty negotiations?" He and Lady Dosvidern were walking to the buffet following the conclusion of the last dance.

Lady Dosvidern smiled, her tongue lolling. "On *Zynzlyp?* With the *Drawmii?*"

Zoot considered this. "Well, my lady," he said, "perhaps Zynzlyp is an exceptional case."

"The Drawmii are a bit more entertaining than the average subject, to be sure. Entertaining," she qualified, "by virtue of their unpredictability. But even that can grow tedious—and as for my posts previous to Zynzlp, the most exciting treaty negotiation I can recall had to do with a last will and testament that divided an estate contrary to local custom, and which had taken two centuries to move through the Imperial courts to the point where someone in the Service had to deal with it."

"The details," stoutly, "must have been fascinating."

"*I* somehow avoided fascination. Thank you. The champagne, if you please." She lapped daintily in the wide glass, then looked up. "And while I was thus avoiding fascination, *you,* sir, were off making a hero of yourself in the Pioneer Corps, and have now gone on to greater celebrity in the Diadem. Your health, sir." She raised her glass.

"Life in the Diadem is not as you suppose," Zoot said.

"Please," she said, taking his arm again, "do not disillusion me. On a place as barren as Zynzlyp, I found the Diadem my only solace and recreation. Tell me, if you please, only the exciting parts."

"If you like, my lady."

Zoot was, after all, used to this by now.

* * *

"Fu George." Grinning. "Perhaps you'll give me this dance."

"Honored, Pearl Woman." Careful not to look at what dangled from her ear. "You look very stylish this evening."

"Thank you." Her grin broadened. "You look a bit out of sorts, yourself."

"Really? I can't think why."

He sniffed her carefully and offered her two fingers. She gave him three in return. No doubt his theft of her property had made them, in Pearl's estimation at least, intimates.

Fu George noticed that she tossed her head after the sniff, to know whether the pearl was still present. Intrigued, he stepped onto the dance floor.

Perhaps, he thought, he could hold a substitute pearl under his tongue. Make the bite, and somehow switch pearls on her. She might not notice the absence of the real one for hours, even days. And he'd arrange for his own, substitute pearl to dissolve after a day or so, just so she'd know it was gone.

But how to make the switch? And how to fuse the new pearl to the old chain? And would this all require new dentistry?

Perhaps the long months he'd spent practicing this stunt weren't lost, after all.

Fu George began the dance, his mind abuzz with speculation.

Pearl Woman, for her part, was disappointed in his lack of reaction to the reappearance of her trademark. She'd hoped for at least a little jolt of surprise, perhaps even a double take. Instead, the only difference in his usual manner was that he seemed a little abstracted.

Oh well, at least she had her coup planned for the morrow.

That *was* going to be fun.

A cheeping noise began to sound somewhere in Lady Dosvidern's pocket. Her nostrils flickered, and she halted her dance in midcaper.

"You will excuse me, I hope," she said. "Lord Qlp has come out of his crosstalk, and my attendance is required."

Zoot offered his arm. "Will you allow me to take you to your suite?"

"That won't be necessary, but I thank you. You'd best keep our place in the set, otherwise our neighbors will be put out."

"I hope I shall see you again."

"I will be looking forward, sir. Your servant." She sniffed him and walked quickly toward the exit.

There was nothing to do but continue the dance. Zoot, feeling foolish, raised his arm and tried very hard to pretend Lady Dosvidern was turning under it. He was surprised when a hand took his, and he looked down to see a woman dressed in a patchwork motley of green and purple.

"I hope you don't mind," said Kyoko Asperson. "But I'm tired of standing on the sidelines and waiting for someone to do something exciting."

"The night is young, Miss Asperson. Excitement may yet manifest." He looked down at her. The loupe was off her eye: apparently she had put her media globes on autopilot.

"Only too." Meaning, only too right. She glanced at him and brightened. "I hope you and Lady Dosvidern haven't quarreled. She left in a hurry." She and Zoot circled the couple on their right in stately fashion.

"Not at all, Miss Asperson," Zoot said. "Her attendance was required on Lord Qlp."

"Odd, don't you think?"

"How so? It is her duty."

"Not that, Zoot. Just that a Drawmiikh is here at all."

"The Drawmii are not given to explaining themselves. I'm sure its lordship has a reason."

"I'm sure it does. I'd just like to know what it is."

"I suppose that will become clear later."

"Maybe."

He gave her a sharp glance. The word *maybe* was bad ton. *Perhaps* was far more suitable.

These humans, he thought. One never knew what they'd say next.

The orchestra was finishing the dance when Gregor Norman, hi-stick in his mouth, was observed to return to the ballroom. He stepped behind the screen that cut off the private salon from the main room and gave a cheery wave to the figure of Drake Maijstral that waited for him on a severe, straight-backed Louis Quinze chair.

The hologram of Maijstral dissolved and became Gregor. "You're late, boss," he said. "Run into any trouble?"

The hologram of Gregor dissolved and became Maijstral. "Geoff Fu George was already in the Waltz twins' room when I arrived," he said. "I went on to the next target."

Gregor looked dubious. "That was a risk. Roman wasn't covering you in that direction. You should have got at least one of us to help you carry the swag. There must have been a lot of it."

"There was. But I wanted to get to it before Fu George showed up, and I was able to hustle it down the corridor on a-grav."

"You've been gone for two dances. You'll have been missed."

"I'll stay for the rest of the ball and make up for it."

Maijstral pressed the proper ideograph on the service plate and asked the room to give him a holograph-mirror, and a perfect three-dimensional image of himself appeared in the middle of the salon. He removed the silver pins that held back his hair, let it fall to his shoulders, and straightened his jacket. Gregor rose from his chair and looked in his pocket for a hi-stick.

"So now we just have fun, eh, boss?"

Maijstral smiled. "We have good reason to feel pleased with ourselves." He told the room to remove the opaque screen. Sights and sounds of the dance filled the doorway. Maijstral noticed one figure standing apart from the others and frowned.

"D'you see that man, Gregor?"

"You mean Kuusinen? He helped us out on Peleng."

"He spoke to me earlier. I found his converse alarming, in a quiet sort of way. I think he's some kind of policeman."

"Really?" Gregor looked interested. "Are you sure?"

"No, but let's not take chances. Be careful around him. Don't give anything away."

"Right, boss." Gregor peered past Maijstral toward the dancers. "I'll keep an eye out."

There was a moment of mutual embarrassment as Khamiss and her squad entered the employees' kitchen and encountered Kingston and his squad returning from the buffet with laden trays. But then grins and bottles broke out, and beneath the spectacle of one sun devouring another a spontaneous party began. Sore feet were elevated on cushions, groaning bellies were silenced by first-rate food, palates soothed by drink.

Every so often, Khamiss and Kingston would leave the party and report that they'd just scouted another corridor and found nothing out of the ordinary. Each time they did this, the false report seemed more and more hilarious. Sun, as was his wont, seemed not to notice anything amiss.

Khamiss raised her glass. "To leadership," she said.

"Leadership," Kingston echoed, and touched his rim to hers.

Another few hours and their shift would be over.

* * *

"My lord Silverside."

"Fu George. I hope you are finding your accommodations to your taste."

"The rooms and much else, my lord. I have been inconvenienced by one thing only."

Baron Silverside raised his brows. "Yes? Pray tell me, sir."

"Your security service, my lord. They seem . . . excessively zealous."

"They are zealous on my express instructions."

Fu George feigned shock. "I am dismayed, sir."

Silverside fluffed his burnsides. "This is *my* station, sir. I intend that it be run by *my* custom."

"No one disputes your right, my lord."

"I intend that my guests should be entirely at their ease, and the prospect of one's property vanishing can make one uneasy. I feel it my duty as host to relieve any source of perturbation."

"But, with all respect, my lord, my profession is sanctioned by High Custom and by both Imperial and Constellation law."

"They can sanction it all they wish, sir. There is nothing in law or custom, however, that says your profession must be made easy."

"Sir!"

"There are many professions difficult to practice on Silverside. Range-drover, say, or quellsider. Yours is simply among them."

"Come, sir. Can you compare a quellsider with a profession sanctioned by High Custom?"

Fu George, truth to tell, was enjoying this. He knew one fatuous nobleman who was going to pay for this, and soon.

Silverside fluffed his whiskers again and gazed self-importantly at the orchestra. "Merely an instance, Fu George. If you will pardon me for a moment . . . ?"

"Your servant, sir."

As Fu George stepped toward the buffet, Vanessa Runciter took his arm. "I've been watching Maijstral," he said. "I think he and Gregor pulled a Lugar switch."

"Yes, so I discovered. I encountered him a short while ago, in the Waltz twins' room. I got there first."

A pleased smile drifted across Vanessa's features. "Very good, Geoff."

"The least I can do to him, considering his behavior this afternoon."

She gave him a look. Vanessa had not been at all happy when Fu George informed her that she'd lost an earlobe for nothing.

"I've been thinking about that, Geoff. Where do you suppose he's going to hide his take?"

"I don't suppose he could have hit upon the same device we're using, do you?"

"It might be worthy of investigation. If we could preempt him everywhere . . ."

Geoff Fu George began to smile. "It would only be what he deserved."

She patted his arm. "My thoughts exactly."

"Hello. You're Gregor Norman, aren't you?"

"Yes. Your servant, Miss Asperson."

"Likewise. Had a good and profitable evening?"

Gregor grinned. "Had a nice dinner. I'm not much good at dancing, though."

"I think the next is a slow one. Silent Equations, according to my card. Will you join me?"

"Only too." Meaning, only too happy. "I hope you don't mind me stepping all over you."

"I'll look out for your feet, you look out for mine. Right?"

"Right." Gregor looked down at her. "Aren't you supposed to be on the job?"

"I've got all the globes dispersed and on autopilot. Nothing much exciting happens at grand balls, anyway."

Gregor, who could recall at least one hair-raising grand ball on Peleng, jauntily agreed.

"By the way," he said, looking at her costume. "I think green and purple suit you very well."

"Maijstral."

"Marchioness." Sniffs. "Will you join me for the Silent Equations?"

"Happily, my lady."

They clasped hands, faced one another, then turned their heads toward the orchestra, awaiting the first throb of music. They observed, standing by the orchestra, the Marquess speaking with Baron and Baroness Silverside. They seemed quite intent on their conversation.

"Kotani," said the Marchioness, "has a plan. He wants to do his next play here, and set its action on Silverside Station. He conceives that this will enhance the station's reputation as a place for society to meet, and will provide a perfect backdrop for his own work."

"The Silversides seem interested."

She glanced at Maijstral from the corners of her slanted eyes. "I think it will be a difficult sale. We've heard that Silverside has had other offers."

"Not from anyone of his lordship's stature, I'm sure."

"Very likely. But no doubt Silverside has been approached by people offering him a greater share of the profits. Kotani keeps his money close. I've always thought it his greatest failing as a lord."

Maijstral glanced at her ladyship's matched bracelets and choker: blue corundum, silver, and diamond, with tiny implanted glowstones hidden in the settings to make them gleam with a subtle inner light. She caught his look, and her sullen mouth turned upward in a smile.

"He is generous, yes, with some things, particularly if it might touch on his own reputation. He is not generous with his time, however. I daresay he'll be in conference with the Silversides all week."

"I hope your ladyship will not be too much alone."

She looked into his lidded eyes. "I share your hope, sir," she said, and then laughed. "But speaking of profits, I hope this evening has been profitable for *you.*"

Maijstral gave a lazy shrug. "I thought talk of business bored you, my lady."

"Most business, yes."

The orchestra began to play. The couples, holding hands and still maintaining their strict line fore-and-aft, began to revolve around mutual centers of gravity, moving in an unconscious imitation of the singularity above their heads, which, in its predatory orbit, circled the equator of its hapless primary every twelve minutes.

The dancers below, their appetites somewhat less all-embracing than that of the singularity, continued moving in their orbits.

All save one.

Geoff Fu George met with Drexler and Chalice in the corridor leading to Baron Silverside's private residence. Drexler's eyes were closed; he was communicating with the proximity wire in his collar and making mystic passes in the air with his hands. (His sleeves contained detectors.) "A rank of flaxes under the carpet," he concluded. "There are leapers set the door. Pulse alarms inside, and tremblors on the floor, ceiling, and walls. More leapers on the picture frames."

"Right," said Fu George. One could learn a lot by using the right detectors, and also by burglarizing the offices of Silverside's contractors. He buttoned his jacket tight and pulsed a mental command to his flight harness, which raised him several inches from the floor. With practiced ease, Fu George threaded his way through the net of flaxes, then paused by the door, scouting it carefully with his energy detectors before stopping to neutralize the leapers. His assistants followed him, as did a pair of micromedia globes. By the rules of Allowed Burglary, assistants were permitted only as far as the door: Fu George had to do the rest himself. Fu George opened the door and coasted inside.

He glanced over Baroness Silverside's famous art gallery, seeing barren picture frames and pedestals that held only empty air.

Maijstral, he thought. *You're going to pay for this.*

When the police made their unmistakable arrival, Maijstral was sitting cross-legged on his bed, massaging his feet and watching a video Western. *Rendezvous at Coffeyville* was one of his favorites. The Western featured Marcus Ruthven as Grat Dalton, and had been directed by the great Fastinn, whose training with the Imperial Theatre had, no doubt, contributed to the tangible, forbidding sense of inevitability that engulfed the main characters as they assembled, plotted, and began the raid that would result in their destruction.

The Daltons, wearing identical grey dusters and moving in line abreast on matched black chargers, trotted toward the twin banks that represented the summit of their criminal ambitions. The town was ominously quiet. Somewhere a dog was barking. Crouching in attics, citizens sighted over buffalo guns. Maijstral gnawed a thumbnail, his nerves humming with suspense.

Someone knocked on Maijstral's door. It was an authoritative knock: one could not mistake it, and Maijstral had heard it on many worlds, in many rented rooms. The police.

The knock brought Maijstral reluctantly back to the present. He uncrossed his legs and told the room to hold the Coffeyville massacre till later.

Roman entered. His ears turned back in disapproval as he observed the frozen figures of men wearing Stetsons: he was ever dismayed by Maijstral's low taste in entertainment. "Beg pardon, sir," he said, "but the police are here. Mr. Kingston is with them."

"Ah. Our comic." He rose from the bed, smoothed his dressing gown, and pushed his long hair back from his face. "Very well," he said. "I shall speak to the gentlemen."

Maijstral found Kingston in the front room, his troopers arrayed in a flying wedge behind him. Gregor surveyed them, his mien hostile.

"Just making sure they won't take anything, boss," he said.

"Beg pardon," Kingston said. His face was set in a fuddled smile. "Regrettably, sir, I must search your room. Some objects of value have been missed."

"Really?" Maijstral said. "Why search my room, of all rooms on the station?"

Kingston gave an elaborate bow. "Sir, your worship can guess why, I'm sure."

"It is my humor to hear you say it."

"Very well then, sir. I search your room because there has been stealing going on, and because you have been known to steal."

"This seems like persecution, Mr. Kingston. Has any witness connected me with the missing objects? I spent my entire evening in public. When were these nameless crimes committed?"

"I know nothing of your evening, sir, but searched you and yours shall surely be." Kingston swayed as he spoke.

The man is drunk, Maijstral thought in surprise. "I take it, then," he said, "you have no confidence in your own handiwork. You took care—*very personal* care—to make certain I had no way to practice my profession on Silverside Station. If you really think I've been taking things I've no right to, it would seem you confess yourself incompetent."

Kingston's good humor snapped like a twig. "Search 'em," he growled, and his troopers spread out over the suite, deploying their detectors.

And found, of course, nothing.

Maijstral returned to his room and participated, while dressing, in the vicarious catharsis of the Coffeyville massacre. He then left his room and, after making certain he was not being followed, walked down deserted corridors to the room of Mr. Dolfuss, where he gave a knock.

Dolfuss opened in a few seconds. He was carrying an overnight bag. "Mr. Maijstral. I've been waiting up."

"The police took a little longer than expected. Perhaps they were a little behind in making their calls."

"Very good, sir. Sleep well."

"And you."

Dolfuss took himself and his bag down the corridor, where he would spend the night on Maijstral's mattress.

Maijstral, for his part, undressed and happily reposed himself on Dolfuss's bed, beneath which were elements of one of the finest private collections in the Human Constellation, that of the Baroness Silverside.

FOUR

Silver media globes orbited Baron Silverside like Indians in one of Maijstral's Westerns circling a beleagured wagon train. The Baron looked at the globes through red-rimmed, weary eyes.

"Miss Asperson," he said.

"Baron," said Kyoko. This morning she was dressed in yellow with a silver-wire pattern. It stood out against the subdued decor of the White Room like an explosion in a paint factory. "My condolences on your loss."

"There is yet time. We may see the objects recovered."

"That's not likely, is it?" Kyoko Asperson's question appeared all innocence. "You haven't found the loot after the first few hours, and I wonder how you can expect to find it now that you've exhausted all the likely places to look. After all, an entire art collection can't be hidden very easily. You *built* this station, Baron—where is left to look? Where would you suggest the police go?"

The Baron looked away, found himself looking straight into a media globe, then looked up. He scowled. "I leave that to Mr. Sun, my head of security."

"Understandable, sir. It is his area of expertise." Kyoko smiled. "Would it be possible for me to speak to Mr. Sun?"

"He is very busy. You understand, I'm sure."

"Still, sir, it would be fascinating for my viewers to see such a man at his craft. His job must be an intricate one, and he is charged with considerable responsibility. After all, you must have spent a small fortune altering the design of the station so as to accommodate his security schemes. I'm sure my audience would like to discover whether it is well spent."

Baron Silverside began to stroke his burnsides. "Matters of finance are of little importance beside the comfort of my guests, madam," he said. "But if you wish to see Mr. Sun at work, I will try to arrange it. I only trust you will not reveal any of his secrets to your public."

"I will be discreet, my lord. Thank you."

The media globes ceased their rotation and arranged themselves in formation above Kyoko's head. Bidding the Baron adieu, she felt entirely satisfied with the interview.

Kyoko wanted to see this policeman, this Mr. Sun. Events were beginning to form a pattern in her mind, and Mr. Sun was part of the pattern, an important one. She had begun to see him as one element of a triptych, Maijstral and Fu George and Sun, each orbiting Silverside Station as Rathbon's Star was being orbited by its devouring companion, each held in place by the tension of mutual antagonism.

Kyoko Asperson was not just an interviewer: she fancied herself a dramatist, a dramatist who worked with living, unknowing subjects. Seeing a patten in life, and making it come to the fore fully realized, flowing before the enraptured eyes of her audience.

There were dramatic possibilities here. One had only to make certain the possibilities were realized.

A Cygnus robot hummed past Gregor as he reached for the lock with his left hand and performed a quick snap-off. Pleased with having done the job one-handed, Gregor opened the door and stepped into the ballroom.

The huge oval room was empty of people. Robots polished the floor, unimpressed by the awesome light of Rathbon's Star. Gregor smiled.

Reviewing wiring diagrams in his head, Gregor turned on his harness repellers and rose toward the ceiling. He'd spent the morning assembling devices patched together from harmless objects purchased in the Electronic Boutique and Gadget Faire, and now he intended to give them a field test.

* * *

"Pearl Woman. You're looking dashing."

"Kotani." She sniffed Kotani's ears and offered three fingers. "How are your schemes prospering?"

Kotani drew himself up. "Schemes?" He put a hand to his heart. "I, my dear? Schemes?"

She took his arm. "I observed you in consultation with Baron Silverside last night, Kotani. I know you wouldn't be devoting so much time to a self-important dullard unless you had something in mind."

Kotani gave a graceful smile. "Oh, very well," he said, "I have *projects,* certainly. But I would never *scheme.*" He sniffed. "I'm not Drake Maijstral, after all."

Pearl Woman smiled. "How do your . . . projects . . . fare, then?"

"Things are going forward. Some details remain." He looked at her. "I missed you at luncheon."

"I had some fruit in my room. I'm racing this afternoon, remember."

"The Baron's oddsmakers are giving you five to three against."

"And the odds on the Duchess?"

"Even."

"Perhaps I should effect a limp. That would change the odds a bit." Pearl Woman stretched one leg behind her and massaged her thigh thoughtfully.

"You're planning on winning, then?"

"Of course. You know me, Kotani. I don't toss competitions. Besides," she gave a private smile, "I've just come back from the racetrack. I was doing a little practicing while everyone else was having lunch. I know a few tricks that her grace has probably not encountered in her amateur league." She started to walk again, limping slightly, then frowned. She adjusted the limp, making it a bit more subtle.

Kotani smiled at her performance. "My bets will be on you, of course."

"Thank you, Kotani. Your confidence bolsters me. You always had a good head for money."

"Baron Silverside."

The Baron's color rose at the sound of Maijstral's voice, and his burnsides seemed to prickle aloft like the nape hair of a growling animal. Maijstral did not offer him a handclasp, nor (so far as Maijstral could discern) did Baron Silverside take note of that fact.

"Maijstral," said the Baron.

"Baron, I really must complain about your police. I know they have their duty to perform, but their activities amount to nothing short of harassment."

"Maijstral," said the Baron again. His eyes were red, his voice rasping. Perhaps, Maijstral thought, he has been forsaking sleep in order to yell at subordinates.

"They rummaged through my bags and confiscated a large amount of my personal property on my arrival—"

"Maijstral." The Baron's color was rising through the purple end of the spectrum.

"—and last night a gang of them appeared in my rooms and disturbed me and my associates at our rest. As the officious Mr. Kingston had already deprived me of any means of practicing my profession, I consider their visit both a badgering and an impertinence. I'm certain this is not the reputation that Silverside Station wishes to acquire in relation to its guests. I wanted to bring this to your personal attention, Baron. Your reputation is such that I know you will want to see to the matter personally."

"If it was you, Maijstral . . ."

Maijstral looked surprised. "It can't be me, Baron, not unless your police are incompetent or somehow corruptible, and I'm sure they're not. They're merely officious and heavy-handed." He smiled. "In any case, I'm sure your agents will be approached quite soon by someone who will offer a most reasonable price for your lady's collection. And you will have gained sensational publicity for your station that may, in the end, prove priceless. Good day to you, my lord."

The Baron said nothing in reply. His voice appeared to have failed him. Maijstral sniffed his ears and went on his way.

Silverside wasn't feeling conversational today, anyway.

Roman sat in his room and busied himself with sewing. He normally depended on tailors and robots for this sort of thing, but he didn't wish to explain to a tailor just exactly what he would need this precise object *for.* Therefore Roman plied the needle, stitching the hem of a drawstring bag.

Before him, on a table, was another project. Roman was charting Drake Maijstral's genealogy.

Roman had always been bothered by the fact that he could trace his own lineage back over ten thousand years, connecting it to outposts of the Empire, conquests from the Khosali's very first leap into space, whereas Maijstral's ancestry could barely be traced past Earth's conquest.

Roman's sense of fitness was disturbed by this. It had not seemed *right,* somehow, that the servant should have a longer ancestry than the master.

Therefore he had commenced genealogical researches. Long ago he'd come across a dubious connection to Jean Parisot de la Valette; but that connection, via the wrong side of the blanket, seemed unsatisfactory for any number of reasons, less because of the element of bastardy than because Roman couldn't prove it. Roman dug deeper. He discovered, in another branch of Maijstral's family tree entirely, the name of Altan Khan, who if not as admirable a character as Valette seemed at least a bit more solidly within the family tree.

Roman kept persevering, but after years of searching, the Maijstral family tree proved barren of fruit. To Roman's unvoiced dismay, his employer looked to be merely the descendant of a ruthless, opportunistic Maltese nobody who managed, by dint of oppression of his own species, to worm himself into the Imperial favor and get himself a patent of nobility.

But now, it seemed, Roman's perseverence might have paid off. Was the Matilda, born in Karlskrona as the daughter of Rudolf von Steinberg, the same Matilda, daughter of Rudolphus the Dane, who after a brief visit to England contracted a morganatic marriage to the elderly fourth son of Edmund Beaufort I, Earl and Marquess of Dorset? Matilda daughter-of-Rudolf was a proven descendant of Henry the Lion, and was thus crossed with the Welfs, Frederick Barbarossa, and the Plantagenets. The Beauforts crossed both the Plantagenets and the Tudors, and through them to the ruling houses of all Europe.

Through all those ruling families, Roman could make use of their own family trees that traced their ancestry back any number of directions, usually ending up at either Noah or Wotan. Neither of these two figures were as old as Roman's own confirmed ancestors, but Roman supposed they would have to do—it would be hard to trace genealogy back past the alleged creation of the Earth.

But still there was no confirmation. Were the two Matildas the same?

Roman had queried genealogical libraries on Earth. An answer had not yet come. He was in a fever of anticipation. He expected it at the arrival of each transmission of mail.

For the moment, however, he had naught to do but sew his drawstring bag.

A subtle shadow seemed to cross his perceptions. Roman's ears pricked forward. He suspected, without knowing how, that something was amiss in the front room. He rose from his seat, made certain his gun was loose in its holster, and glided silently forward.

In the front room the holographic waterfall splashed silently into its basin. Roman saw nothing else. He reached into a pocket, drew out a pair of goggles, pulled them over his eyes. Even with enhanced vision, he could see nothing.

His nose twitched. He could *smell* something wrong. Someone had been here, perceived Roman's presence, and left again.

The police, he thought, might be trying to gather intelligence. Or the intruder might be a rival.

He returned to his room, collected his sewing, and returned to the front room, where he settled on the couch with his gun in his lap. If anyone tried to break in, he'd be ready for them.

Behind him, the waterfall continued its silent descent.

"Roman was there, boss," Drexler said. "I barely got out in time."

"No sign of the art collection, I suppose?"

"Afraid not, boss."

Geoff Fu George shrugged. "I really didn't think Maijstral would stow the stuff in his suite, but it seemed worth a look."

"He's got to be living in a blind."

Fu George sighed. "I daresay. It'll be hard to find."

"Shall I follow him tonight?"

"We've got other things to do this evening. The Duchess's ball will prove perfect cover for any number of activities."

"In my spare time, I mean."

"If you can find any spare time, Drexler, you may use it to pursue Maijstral all you like."

"Only too."

Meaning, only too ready. Fu George gave a cold smile.

"I'm going to pursue him myself, Drexler," he said. "At the race, this afternoon. I know a few things about the Pearl, and I think tomorrow may find Maijstral a humbler man." His smile broadened. "Very much humbler, I suspect."

"Mr. Sun." At the sound of Baron Silverside's voice, Sun hastily buttoned up his tunic, brushed his hair out of his eyes, and leaned forward over his humming console. At least a dozen alarm lights winked at him.

The day, he concluded sadly, wasn't going to get any better.

After breakfast the Baron Silverside had finished his raving, and Mr. Sun entrusted the command center to a subordinate in order to collect a few hours' sleep, but now the pressure of his responsibilities had driven him back to the job. He had been appalled at the wholesale thievery that had gone on last night. All indulgence and license had, in the end, to be paid for, if not by the indulgees then by someone else. And now his security systems had failed utterly, his promises to the Baron were all naught, and for this his body and mind should atone.

He was not alone in his atonement. As of noon, all his crews were now working double shifts.

"Sir," he said, and touched an ideogram.

The Baron's burnsides were showing evidence of hard handling. "Sun," he said. "I trust you have made progress?"

"I am trying to prioritize the alarms, my lord," Sun said. "We will be responding only to—"

The Baron turned red. *"I meant progress in finding my wife's collection!"* he barked. His fists closed on his burnsides and made tearing movements.

Mr. Sun felt his scalp prickle with sweat. "Sir. We're hoping for clues."

The Baron's glare was that of a demon. Sun could almost see the flames of perdition behind the dark pupils, lapping from the Baron's mouth. "You designed the gallery, Sun, and it security system. You gave me certain guarantees . . ."

"No system is foolproof, sir. But—"

"This was not," acidly, "what you said at the time."

"Sir." Sun could feel hopeless despair welling up in him. Last night the Baron had shouted at him for *hours*—Sun's ears were still ringing. Now Silverside showed every sign of beginning again. "This is the first test of new equipment under field conditions. I think certain allowances should be made—"

"No allowances where my wife's collection is concerned! None!"

"No, sir. Of course not. But—"

"Find it, Sun." The Baron's lips drew back in a snarl. "Find it, or you'll have the pleasure of explaining to Kyoko Asperson and billions of her interested viewers exactly what went wrong."

Horror crept coldly along the back of Sun's neck. "My lord!" he protested.

"Find it, Sun. Or else."

"Sir."

"And another thing, Sun." Abruptly. "Maijstral just came by to speak to me. He was gloating."

"I'm most sorry to hear that, sir."

"He as much said that he's bought someone in my police service. Is it *you* he's bought, Sun?"

Indignation gave Sun's chin an assertive tug upward. "Sir. He was lying, trying to lead us astray. I'll stake my reputation on it."

The Baron's look was cold. "That's precisely what you *are* doing, Sun."

The hologram disappeared, replaced by the service ideogram. Sun banished it and mopped sweat from his forehead.

Slowly, as he sat alone in his blue heaven, resolve began to fill him. Very well, he thought. If the Baron insists on *results.*

He touched the ideogram for general announcement. "Watsons," he said. "We are now at Degree Absolute!"

"Marchioness. Perhaps you would oblige me."

"Only too happily, Maijstral."

"Please sit on my left." Smiling, the Marchioness joined him on the white settee. He scooped up cards from the surface of the low table before him and squared the deck, then offered it to her. "Please glance through the deck and remove all the rovers."

Music and conversation vibrated from the diamond above their heads. The Marchioness was dressed in a light grey that complemented her coloring wonderfully. She took the pack and gave him a glance. "Your metaphors are appropriate, Maijstral."

"How so?"

Her fingers sorted nimbly through the deck. "The rovers are elusive cards, elusive as conjurers when they perform their tricks. Rovers are therefore my favorite. I suppose they are about to make me jump through hoops."

"Not unwillingly, I hope."

She laughed. "I have always found rovers irresistible, sir. Now what must I do?"

"Put the rovers on top, my lady."

"That will please them." Archly.

Maijstral took the deck from her hand and dealt the four top cards facedown onto the table.

"Now the rovers are on the table. Correct, my lady?"

"If you insist, Maijstral."

He dropped the deck to the table again. "Prove it if you like. Turn them over."

The Marchioness did so. "So. The rovers have been exposed." She looked at him. "Is that the trick, sir? I expected something a little more . . . intricate."

"The rovers have a few surprises left, my lady." The rovers were placed atop the deck again. Careful of his sight lines, Maijstral picked up the pack with his right hand. He dealt the top four cards down in one pile, turning the last over to assure her it was still a rover, then put the four cards on top and handed her the deck. He put his hand on hers. Her hand was warm.

"If you will allow me to guide you, my lady," he said. "Put the top rover here, then the others so." Making four cards arranged in a neat rectangle. "Now deal three cards on top of each."

"The rovers shall be resurrected, I hope."

"They shall roam, as is their nature." He guided her hand as she created four piles. He took the deck from her hand. "Indicate two of the piles, if you please." She pointed to two of the piles, the second and third, and he took them from the table and put them atop the deck. "Point to another pile." She pointed to the first. "That pile shall be spared," Maijstral said; he took the fourth and added it to the deck. He took her hand again, placed it on the remaining pile.

"Will you cover the rover, my lady?"

"It would give me nothing but satisfaction to do so, Maijstral."

He took his hand away. "We now have one rover buried under three other cards, all held prisoner beneath your hand."

"That seems to be the case."

"Firstly, I would like to remove the three other cards, *so* . . ." He made a swift movement of his left hand, which held the deck. With the sound of riffling, three cards appeared inside the crook of the Marchioness's elbow, held in Maijstral's right hand. She gave a laugh of surprise.

"A minor effect," Maijstral said. "I couldn't resist. But now, something a little more interesting. I intend to transfer the three rovers in the deck to the pile beneath your ladyship's hand."

Her pouting lips drew into a smile. "Rovers beneath my hand. My hand shall be envied."

Maijstral drew the deck down the inside of her forearm, moving gently but quite deliberately along the ulnar nerve. The Marchioness shivered.

"Look in the pile, madam," he said. She turned the cards over one by one, revealing the four rovers.

"Your rovers are thieves, Maijstral," she said. "They have stolen into my hand."

"You must be wary of rovers, my lady. They are liable to steal into any number of private places."

She looked at him. "Few but rovers are so bold."

There was an amused light in his hidden eyes as he drew the deck along her forearm again. "Not so. Look in your left sleeve pocket, and there you will find the three cards that were formerly under your hand."

The Marchioness looked, found them, and looked at him sternly. "Your commoner cards have been a little free with my person, Maijstral."

"Apologies, my lady. I seek only to amuse."

She laughed. "Fortunately your cards have a light touch." She tapped her foot on the floor in the pattern meant to applaud something surprising, yet delightful. A robot moved by, and the Marchioness signalled it and asked it to bring drinks. She leaned back in her chair.

"Another trick, my lady?"

"I think not." Feigning pique, she took the pack from his hands. "I'm confiscating the deck for its impertinence."

"The cards only strayed in sport, my lady."

She tilted her head, looked at him sidelong. "Perhaps you and your cards can stray later, Maijstral. But not now."

"I am at your service, madam."

"So one may hope."

The Marchioness looked up sharply at the shadow of media globes and saw Kyoko Asperson advancing toward them. Kyoko made a token bob toward them in lieu of bending over the table to sniff ears.

"Up to your old tricks, Maijstral?" she asked.

"Only exercising my hands, Miss Asperson."

"So I perceived. Will you do a trick for me?"

"I'm afraid my lady has forbidden me any further sleights." He glanced up at the hovering globes. "Besides, you'd record them and expose my manipulations."

"I'll turn the globes off if you like." Kyoko dropped into a seat near them. "Or record them from one angle only. Whichever you prefer. I like magic tricks, and I don't think it's clever to spoil them."

Maijstral bowed to her. "Thank you, madam. I wish all audiences preferred the delights of wonder to the inevitable disenchantment that comes with disclosure."

"That being your attitude, I don't suppose you'd like to disclose who took the Waltz twins' jewels, or the choicest objects in the Baroness's collection, or Madame la Riviere's necklace."

Maijstral's heavy-lidded eyes glowed with hidden amusement. "I'm afraid, once again, I prefer wonderment to disclosure," he said.

"I figured that." Kyoko leaned across the table, forcing an intimacy that compelled Maijstral to tilt back in his chair. She pursued her advantage. "How do you suppose the duel will end? Between Geoff Fu George and another thief who shall remain nameless?"

Maijstral smiled. "I would say, madam, that it's far too early to venture a guess."

"Would you give me your thoughts on another contest? The race this afternoon."

He steepled his fingers. "Difficult. I have not studied the field."

"Be a sport, Maijstral. No one's going to shoot you for being wrong."

Maijstral gave the matter some thought, then conceded. "Very well. I would venture to guess that the Duchess of Benn will be the victor."

"Why so?"

"I don't believe there is anyone present who matches her in expertise or training."

"Not Pearl Woman? She's raced professionally."

"Her last race was a few years ago, I believe. Though of course she is a master tactician."

The Marchioness fidgeted with the deck of cards. She made an impatient swipe at her hair, brushing it behind her ear, then stood. Maijstral, perceiving the movement, rose with her. "I ordered drinks a while ago," she said. "I'm going to go look for them."

"Marchioness. Your servant."

"Maijstral." She offered him three fingers as they parted. "Perhaps we shall meet again. At one or another sporting event, perhaps."

"Looking forward, my lady."

Maijstral returned to his seat. Kyoko was glancing left and right.

"Do you know where Gregor is?" she asked.

Maijstral was surprised. "I'm afraid not," he said. "He's off on his own somewhere."

Kyoko gave a shrug. "In that case, can you do a card trick?"

"Happily. We should signal a robot for a deck."

Kyoko did so. When the pack arrived, her eight media globes

paused in their orbits, then dropped one by one to the white carpet. She took the cards from their pack.

"Right," she said, grinning. "What am I supposed to do?"

Khamiss was a mass of pain, from her head (too much hross in the lounge) to her feet (chasing down too many corridors). Her blistered feet had by now been cared for, decorated with semilife patches that promoted anaesthesia and healing; but regardless of what she did for the headache, it pounded on. The headache, in fact, had seemed to multiply its force the instant she was informed she'd be working a double shift, and multiply again since she'd been told about Degree Absolute.

At least on her current assignment she'd get to wear her own footwear. She replaced the uniform boots with comfortable sneedskin pumps, threw off the uniform trousers and jacket, and called for a robot to lace her into correct lounging attire.

She called for a holograph-mirror and looked at it anxiously. Her dress was correct, but was it sublime enough to pass in this company? Khamiss turned left and right, patted the coat, the pockets. There was something *not right* about it, but she couldn't say what. Perhaps it was not a current cut. To make matters worse, there was an unsightly bulge over her gun, and no matter how she tugged the jacket, the bulge would not disappear. Perhaps she should go to Essenden's Armory on Level Nine and buy a smaller pistol.

The hell with it. If Sun wanted her to look more inconspicuous, let *him* buy the damn gun.

Her duties under Degree Absolute were to follow Drake Maijstral and never let him out of her sight. She was not optimistic about the outcome. Maijstral was intelligent—wouldn't he *notice* a strange Khosali female following him around the lonely corridors with a bulky service pistol jammed in her armpit?

Well. Hers was not to reason why. She dismissed the robot and stepped out of her quarters. She'd look for Maijstral in the Shadow Room and the main lounge.

As she approached the White Room, she heard music, the sounds projected along the carpeted corridors by the peculiar resonance of the giant diamond. A Khosalikh taller than she, wearing a peculiar jacket, appeared from a side corridor and almost walked into her. She looked at him in surprise and, just as she was about to step aside to let him pass, remembered that she was now a guest and not a functionary. She drew her ears back in assumed hauteur.

"Oh," said Zoot. "I beg your pardon."

"I beg yours."

"I am Zoot, madam."

"I am Khamiss." They exchanged sniffs.

Zoot was, she observed, wearing his famous jacket. She realized, a bit despondently, that it was very likely cut so as to hold any number of weapons.

Zoot offered his arm. "If I may escort you, madam."

Surprise washed over her. "Ah. Certainly, sir."

She took his arm and they began walking in the direction of the music. Pleasure warmed Khamiss at the thought of entering the White Room on the arm of the celebrated pioneer.

Undercover work, she realized, had a lot to recommend it.

"Maijstral." Kotani's ears pricked forward. "Fortuitous to meet you."

Maijstral sniffed him. "A pleasure to see you, sir, at any time. But why fortuitous?"

"I am seeking a wager."

"For the race, you mean? The house is accepting bets, is it not?"

Maijstral stepped onto the conveyer that was moving toward the station's racetrack. Kotani followed him and waved a languid hand.

"The house is accepting bets, yes. But there's no sport in that."

"Or good odds for your favorite?"

Kotani smiled and acknowledged the hit. "I don't think the house knows that Pearl Woman has pulled a muscle in her thigh. It would be foolish to back her at house odds."

Green amusement flickered in Maijstral's shuttered eyes. "Indeed? Why not bet on someone else, then?"

"Because I can't resist good odds, Maijstral. Offer me some!"

"Five to three, then. In favor of her grace the Duchess."

Kotani scowled. "Those are the odds the house has been offering. Give me three to one, at least."

"*I* don't know that the Pearl has injured herself."

"Look at her yourself, when you get the chance. It's plain to see, she's favoring one leg."

Maijstral gave a casual glance over his shoulder and observed, thirty feet behind, a female Khosalikh in a mass-produced lounge jacket. A bulky pistol was crammed in her armpit, straining the laces. He recognized her from the customs dock, turned back to Kotani, and smiled.

"The question is," he said, "has she really injured herself? Or is it sham? A sham injury would be quite like her, you know." Kotani rolled his eyes with impatience. Maijstral shrugged. "Very well, Kotani," he said. "I'll give you two to one, if you like."

"Damnation," said Kotani. He gnawed his lip. "Very well. Twenty novae?"

"To my forty, you mean?"

"Yes."

"Let's say my twenty, your ten."

Kotani looked at him. "You ain't as poverty-stricken as you pretend, Maijstral. You can afford a real wager."

"You're not as strapped as you pretend, either. But I've already made some bets: this one is just to oblige you."

Kotani gave a jerk of his head, indicating reluctant consent. "Very well, Maijstral. If it's all you can afford."

Laughter bubbled silently in Maijstral's mind. Kotani was subtle about everything but money—where cash was concerned, Kotani was a blunt instrument. His boyhood home had been noble, like Maijstral's own, but notoriously poor, also like Maijstral's. Through boyhood circumstance, Maijstral had learned fecklessness; but Kotani had learned parsimony.

He glanced ahead down the panelled corridor and thought about what Kotani's insistence on a bet might mean. Kotani thought Pearl Woman a certainty; and that meant the injury was feigned; and probably also meant that Pearl thought she was certain to win.

Maijstral stepped out of the conveyer and glanced over the gallery. The racecourse, looking like a simple hedgemaze tilted on edge, waited behind a glass wall. Spectator tables were stacked steeply before the course, some of them occupied. At the far end of the gallery, near the entrance that led to the starting gate, Maijstral saw Roberta standing amid a crowd of well-wishers. She was dressed in burnt-orange silks, and her helmet dangled from her hand.

"Maijstral. Pleased to see you."

Maijstral turned abruptly at the sound of Fu George's voice. "Fu George," he said, and exchanged sniffs. "Miss Runciter."

"Drake."

Vanessa was dressed in a chitin-gown studded with pearls. A matching cigaret holder, all complicated filters and laminated layers, was propped in her hand. In her other hand was a tote ticket. Maijstral observed she'd put a hundred on the Pearl to win.

"You're just the person I wanted to see," Fu George said.

Maijstral's green eyes seemed unusually intense. "You aren't by any chance looking for someone to give you odds on the Pearl?"

Vanessa cast Fu George a quick, disturbed glance, which was all Maijstral needed to know that, somehow, the fix was in.

"The Pearl's injured, you know," Fu George said. "She was trying to hide it earlier, but she couldn't conceal it entirely. Still," he sighed heavily. "I feel I ought to support her."

"That's kind of you, Fu George. It's the least I can do to oblige such a devoted friend." Maijstral frowned as he considered. "Two to one, Fu George? A quiller on her grace?"

Fu George seemed surprised. "Uncommonly generous of you, Maijstral." Then he smiled. "Still, after last night, I suppose you can afford it. I accept. Half a quiller on the Pearl against a quiller on the Duchess." They clasped hands, two fingers each. Maijstral was not surprised at the sudden elevation in his status: suckers are ever the friends of those who bilk them. Maijstral glanced over his shoulder at the Duchess.

"I should offer my best wishes to the woman on whose shoulders my quiller is riding," he said. "I hope you will excuse me."

"Certainly, Maijstral." They sniffed each other's ears. Maijstral turned to Vanessa.

"Congratulations on your performance last night, by the way," she said. "That was fast work."

"Thank you, Vanessa. Very kind."

Maijstral sniffed her and moved away. As he passed in front of the gallery he saw Kingston, the policeman, sitting alone at one of the tables, his glance fixed unhappily on Geoff Fu George. Kingston was dressed in mufti and appeared to have something bulky under his left arm. Maijstral smiled and walked on.

The knot around the Duchess had thinned. Maijstral stepped toward her. He noticed that she was wearing the traditional stripes of bright paint on her cheeks: they were burnt orange, to match her silks. She looked up and saw him; she smiled.

"Maijstral. I'm pleased to see you here."

"Your grace, I wouldn't have missed it. I was surprised not to see you earlier."

Roberta waved a hand. "All the preparations for the debut tonight. There's still so much to be seen to."

"I wouldn't be too concerned. These things have a habit of looking after themselves."

Roberta's answer was tart. "Not around me, they don't. I see to them myself, or they don't get done."

"Perhaps it's best you've been keeping busy, then."

She began strapping on her helmet. "Wish me luck, Maijstral."

"With all my heart, your grace. And my pocketbook."

Roberta seemed pleasantly surprised. "You can't have got good odds. All the betting seems to be on second or third place. Have you heard that Pearl Woman's been hurt?"

Maijstral looked at her. "I wouldn't have too much confidence in that, your grace. I seem to be finding a lot of takers for my bets."

She frowned and gazed at him for the space of half a moment. "Do you truly? Who, may I ask?"

"Kotani. Fu George. And Miss Runciter held a tote ticket for the Pearl."

Roberta's violet eyes glittered. "Interesting." She reached out a hand. "Thank you, Maijstral."

"Your obedient servant."

He kissed the hand and stepped away, and behind him there was a sudden loud murmuring, as of a crowd experiencing surprise. Maijstral turned and saw Lord Qlp undulating along the gallery toward him, its five eyes peering in his direction. Lady Dosvidern, demurely avoiding the slime trail, followed the Drawmiikh. Maijstral braced himself for the odor. When it arrived the smell almost knocked him down. The volume of conversation from the audience increased radically as a wave of the Drawmiikh's scent rolled over them. Khosali, with noses more sensitive than those of humans, seemed particularly affected.

Maijstral bowed, summoned his resolve, and made approximate sniffs toward Lord Qlp's head. To inhale at all required considerable willpower. The Drawmiikh ignored Maijstral and continued its motion, forcing Maijstral to move fast to keep from being knocked aside.

Lord Qlp halted in front of Roberta. "Lord Qlp," she said, and sniffed it. It reared back, its foremost eye looking directly in her face, and made a series of sucking sounds.

"Are not the Protocols correct?" Lady Dosvidern translated. "Is it not the Time of Exchange? Is not the Exchange correct in its commodity?"

Roberta gazed at the Drawmiikh for a long moment. It seemed to be expecting an answer. She looked at Lady Dosvidern for help. Lady Dosvidern's ears flicked back and forth, signalling her own bewilderment.

Roberta turned her eyes back to Lord Qlp. "I cannot say, my lord," she said.

Lord Qlp's reply was loud and violent. Its whole body trembled with the force of its ejaculation. "Interference!" Lady Dosvidern said. Her expression was bewildered, but her voice was calm and firm. "Your grace must guard the Protocols!"

Roberta considered this for half a second. "I have every intention," she said firmly, "of doing just that."

The answer seemed to please Lord Qlp. It bent its head and began to make gagging sounds. Many in the audience turned away or covered their eyes.

There was a thump. Lord Qlp had disgorged another object. There was a moment of silence.

"Thank you, my lord," said Roberta. Lord Qlp, after reversing its rearmost eye, began to undulate the way it had come without bothering to turn around.

"Allow me, your grace." Maijstral moved quickly. He unfolded his handkerchief and bent to retrieve the object. He wrapped the thing neatly in his handkerchief and rose. It was wet and implastic. Roberta had already signalled a robot.

Lord Qlp moved quickly to the exit and disappeared. Relieved, the audience began to chatter and wave handkerchiefs to disperse the stench.

"Thank you, Maijstral," Roberta said. Maijstral gave the object to the robot, and Roberta gave instructions for the thing to be delivered to her rooms.

"I wonder," Maijstral said, "how Lady Dosvidern deals with its lordship's odor."

"She's probably had surgery on her nasal centers."

"I should have thought of that." He looked at her. "Do you suppose that Lady Dosvidern could offer enlightenment on this . . . excrescence, your grace?"

"I've already asked. She's as puzzled as I." She looked over Maijstral's shoulder, and her face turned cold. "Here's that Asperson person," she said. "I suppose her media globes got an eyeful of what just happened."

"My condolences, your grace. I'm sure you'll handle any awkward questions."

"How can I answer questions when I don't know what just happened?" Her ears turned down in annoyance, and then she shrugged. "Well, I'll just have to pretend omniscience." She brightened a bit. "That could be fun, I suppose."

"Enjoy, your grace."

"Thanks for your assistance, Maijstral. I'll have the handkerchief returned." She began strapping on her helmet.

Maijstral turned, bowed toward Kyoko Asperson as the journalist advanced toward Roberta, and wondered where to sit. Kotani, the Marchioness, Fu George, and Vanessa were standing in a knot, and appeared to be taking care not to look in his direction. Maijstral saw Zoot talking to the armed female Khosalikh who had been his tail, and he considered for a moment the temptation to drop by Zoot's table and see how she handled it.

Pearl Woman, dressed in white silks, was poised by one entrance. An expression of annoynance was visible through the white stripes on her face, and Maijstral guessed she had made her grand entrance only to be upstaged by the arrival of Lord Qlp. Advert, looking uncertain, was fluttering by her elbow. Maijstral strolled toward them.

"Luck, Pearl," he offered, and sniffed her. "Good afternoon, Advert." He couldn't help but notice that if Pearl Woman was still wearing her pearl, it was hidden under her helmet strap.

"Thanks, Maijstral. I daresay I'll need it." She flexed one leg carefully. "I should warm up for a few moments. Pardon me."

"Certainly." She moved off. Maijstral admired the subtlety of her limp for a brief moment, then he turned to Advert.

"Will you join me at my table?"

"Yes. Thank you, Mr. Maijstral."

"My pleasure." He escorted her into the gallery. Advert bit her lip and clutched at something in her pocket.

"Are you anxious for Pearl Woman?" Maijstral asked. "She'll be all right, you know. That leg injury won't incapacitate her."

"She asked me to bet." She raised her hand from her pocket and mutely displayed two credit chips. Maijstral could clearly see the imprints of her nails on her palm.

"She gave you money to bet on her?"

She swallowed and gave a quick nod. "Fifty novae. I don't know where she got it. She hasn't any money herself. Borrowed it from someone, I suppose."

"She wants you to bet her to win."

"Yes."

"And you don't think she'll come in first."

Advert shook her head, not trusting herself to speak.

"I see," said Maijstral. He signalled a waiter for drinks and considered the situation. He had known Pearl Woman long enough to be perfectly certain that the money was the Pearl's and that Pearl Woman's poverty was a pose. He knew that Advert had ransomed the Pearl's trademark with her own money, and that Pearl Woman had probably not covered the expense.

Maijstral also knew that he could not say so, particularly to Advert, without running a risk of Pearl Woman jamming one of her cutlasses between his ribs.

He wondered briefly why Pearl Woman hadn't let Advert know about her injury being feigned. Probably, he decided, the Pearl was afraid Advert would somehow give the trick away.

"I wanted to make a bet on my own," Advert said miserably. "Bet on her grace, but making a bet on someone else feels so . . . *disloyal.*"

Maijstral looked at her. "Miss Advert, I've had a bit more experience in these matters. Will you follow my advice?"

Advert thought for a moment, then gave a hesitant nod.

"Very well. You must bet Pearl Woman's money as she asked you. You are not the custodian of her pocketbook, and she may have had reasons for making the bet of which you are unaware."

Advert heaved a sigh. "I suppose so."

"But make your own bet," Maijstral went on, "according to your own judgement. It's not disloyal of you to think that the Duchess may win: she is clearly the favorite. Money has no loyalty, and neither have wagers. Money is far too serious a thing to owe sentimental allegiance to one person's friendship or another's."

Advert did not seem comforted. "Very well," she said. She looked over the company. "Who shall I bet with, I wonder?"

"Very little time remains. You'll have to bet on the tote, I'm afraid, and you won't get as good odds as you might on a private bet. I'll make the bets for you, if you like."

"Yes. Thank you, Mr. Maijstral."

Maijstral took the money and stepped to the tote, made Advert's bets, made a bet on the Duchess for himself, and returned to the table. The drinks had arrived in the meantime, and Advert had finished half of her own. Maijstral handed her the coded betting tokens and sipped his drink.

Advert was looking at Roberta, who was going through a careful warm-up after having finished her interview with Kyoko Asperson. "I envy her," she said. "She's had so many advantages."

Maijstral gazed at the Duchess. "You find her an object of envy? I do not."

Advert was surprised. "Why? She's got money, talent, looks, intelligence. A title. She's even got the Eltdown Shard, for heaven's sake." She sighed. "And assurance, too."

Maijstral smiled. "And assurance. All that, yes." Maijstral steepled his fingertips and contemplated the Duchess. "She is the head of an old and very regal Imperial family, and they raise their heirs very carefully. From her earliest days her grace has been strictly schooled in what was expected of her. The training is severe and uncompromising, begun before she was even aware of being trained, not entirely ending until the day of her death. She has been allowed no distractions and very few pleasures—the family will have seen to that. The training is intended to do one of three things: make her a duchess, break her, or force her into rebellion. She's too strong to be broken, and too responsible to rebel. She probably has a half-dozen brothers and sisters, and it was Roberta who was chosen as heir, not the others. Her grace is a successful product of a very difficult school, but that doesn't make her an object of envy." Maijstral twisted the diamond on his finger. "I'm sorry for her, I'm afraid."

Advert gazed at him in cool fascination. "You've got an old title, too, don't you?" she asked.

He nodded. "Yes, I do. But I escaped my fate. There was no money left, you see, and no property to speak of. Nothing to be responsible *to.*" He gave a lazy shrug and smiled. "There are still restrictions, even in the Constellation. Certain occupations I cannot put my hand to, not if I expect to retain the regard of my peers. It's lucky I'm allowed to steal: otherwise I'd have to be a drunkard or a fortune hunter, and those alternatives would be," offering a slight smile, "tedious, as well as unsuited to my temperament. Any of those alternatives, however—" he nodded toward Roberta "—is preferable to what her grace will be compelled to undergo fairly shortly."

Advert's glance trailed toward Roberta. "How so?"

"I expect she'll be made to give up the racing. It's allowed here because it puts her name forward and makes for a splashier debut, but after this the racing will have no more practical use." He frowned, settling into his chair and his lecture. "The point of a debut, you see, is to advertise the fact that you're ready for marriage. In a year or two the family will arrange a husband for her, and then she'll spend the next ten years or so giving birth to a series of minor nobles, one of whom will, after going through the conditioning, doubtless make a suitable heir to the title and the fortune and the Shard and all the rest of it. Hers will be real pregnancies, too—artificial wombs aren't customary in the old families. So then she'll spend years supervising the children's education and such, and after they're all safely grown she can relax a bit. She'll be allowed to be a cynical old lady and make cutting remarks at parties. By then she'll be a family character, and her remarks won't matter. Some people in her situation drink or tyrannize their children, but I think her grace is probably too honest for that."

Advert, gazing soberly at the Duchess, raised a hand to her throat. Light glittered from her many rings. "You make it seem so sad," she said.

"I suppose it is. She'll never know what it is to choose her own course. She's not Pearl Woman, who runs her life exactly as she wants it."

"But she's a duchess. She's got the money and so on in her own right. Can't she just break away from it all?"

"The path of rebellion. That's possible, of course," Maijstral conceded. "That's where the training comes in, though. The chorus of Duty, Duty, Duty that she's been hearing since before she could remember. It's hard not to listen to that song, not when she's never listened to anything else. She *could* break away, I suppose. It takes a certain strength of will, and her grace has will in abundance." He gave Roberta a careful look. "I don't think it's likely, though. The tendencies would have been visible before now."

Advert looked at her lap. "I'd no idea," she said.

"Why should you? You're lucky enough not to have been born to it. You're allowed to make choices."

"Yes." She gave a brave grin. "Like the bet, yes?"

"Yes. The bet. No matter how the race turns out, you have reason to rejoice. On your own behalf, or the Pearl's."

Trumpets began to sound. The Priests of the Game appeared in their brocaded robes, incense rising from jewelled censers. The six racers, standing in their bright colors, assumed the Posture of Respect and Submission. Thankfully, the incense drowned Lord Qlp's remaining stench.

Maijstral leaned forward across the table, chin on his fist. The race was going to be very interesting: he wanted very much to know whether his judgement in this matter was sound.

His judgement of Roberta in particular.

FIVE

The scent of incense still stung Maijstral's nostrils. The Priests, having invoked the Active and Passive Virtues, finished their High Khosali chant and took their positions as referees. The race, its religious character now established, was ready to begin.

Three pairs of racers, each in their bright silks, crouched in the chute leading to the racecourse. Pearl Woman and Roberta, the favorites, formed the last pair of the three. Crowd sounds died away as the five-second gong sounded. The first pair of racers flexed their feet and ankles, making sure of their traction.

Floating holograms counted the seconds. Three. Two. One. Begin.

The first tone sounded. The first pair of racers flung themselves into the racecourse as the Priests moaned.

"Hello, Kyoko. Can I join you?"

"Gregor! Please sit down."

"I'm not interrupting your work, am I?"

"Not at all. I'm recording the race for later. I haven't seen you today."

Gregor touched his stomach. "A touch of the steggo—I think it was the roast fleth."

"Sorry to hear that. You're all right now, aren't you?"

"Right as Robbler." Grinning. "So who's going to win, then?"

Gravity channels had been cut off in the racecourse, and the racers flew like mapper charges on the first straight. Each tucked, rolled, came out feetfirst as they hit the initial turn.

The second tone sounded. The next pair of racers hurled themselves into weightlessness.

"Dear. Who's the one in red?"

Consulting the tote board. "Allekh."

"He's got a good turn. He won at least half a second on that first corner." Kotani leaned forward and smiled. "Pearl Woman will catch him, though, I'm certain."

"I've bet the Pearl for second. Her grace for first."

"You should follow my advice on betting matters, dear. I happen to know Pearl Woman will win."

"Think you so?" The Marchioness was amused. "I disagree."

A sharp look. "Have you heard something?"

"No." A smile played about her sullen mouth. "Just an intuition that there's a wild card somewhere in this deck. A rover, perhaps."

"You're growing cryptic, my dear."

"Intuitions aren't supposed to be orderly, Kotani."

Marquess Kotani raised an eyebrow. "*Mine* are. And mine are betting on Pearl Woman."

Roberta's face was expressionless beneath the rim of her helmet, but there was something very intense about her eyes. Maijstral was reassured. Perhaps he had guessed correctly.

Roberta hadn't even spared Pearl Woman a glance as they waited in the chute; but Maijstral believed her concentration was such that she was perfectly aware of Pearl Woman's posture, the precise degree of tension in her legs, her back. . . . Maijstral suspected Roberta knew to the fraction of an inch where Pearl Woman was placed.

The third tone sounded. Roberta and Pearl Woman sprang from the chute to the sound of groaning Priests.

"There seems to be something in front of your face. Like a heat shimmer."

"Yes. My jacket. I built a magnifying field into it. Does it annoy you?"

"Not at all." Pause. "So you can watch the race close up."

"So I can see clearly at a distance, yes."

"Very handy."

"It seemed a sensible thing to have. I never realized how people would make a fuss."

"You sound as if you haven't enjoyed the attention you've been getting."

"Not exactly." Zoot's diaphragm throbbed in resignation. "It's just that—I don't know quite how to say this—the *quality* of it leaves something to be desired."

"Pearl's got ahead of her!" Excitedly.

"She's good on the long straights. Her grace is known to excel in the tight corners."

"She's ahead! She's ahead!"

Maijstral noticed that Advert's hands had become fists. Her nails were probably doing more damage to her palms.

He glanced about, saw his female Khosali shadow talking to Zoot, then saw, above them and almost in the last row, Mr. Paavo Kuusinen. Mr. Kuusinen, he realized, was in a position from which he could watch the entire company. At this precise moment, however, Kuusinen was watching Maijstral.

Maijstral nodded, raised his drink in salute.

Kuusinen did likewise.

Maijstral turned back to the race and scowled. Something was wrong about that man.

There were barking noises from the Priests.

"A penalty. Who's in green?"

"Charusiri."

"She used her upper arms. The slut."

"It *is* an amateur event, Vanessa."

"A two-second penalty. They should disqualify her entirely."

Smiling. "Perhaps they should just dismember her and have it over."

"Maybe they should, Geoff." Vanessa's eyes blazed. "I *hate* that sort of thing."

The lead racer flung herself down a short straight, tucked, tumbled in air, touched on her lower back, and bounced to cut a corner on a forty-five-degree angle. Her body straightened as she kicked out, feet driving into the wall as she hurled herself on a new trajectory.

Just behind, Allekh caught his elbow on another's knee. The two tangled and thrashed, bouncing off walls. Penalty lights flashed.

"Are you expecting a crime at this event, ma'am?"

"Sir!" Khamiss looked at Zoot in astonishment. "What do you mean?"

"I first saw you in uniform at the entry port. Now I see you in civilian clothes with a pistol under your arm. I assume that since you're so conspicuously armed, you are therefore working. Am I not correct, ma'am?"

"Oh." Khamiss licked her nose disconsolately. "I'm supposed to be watching Drake Maijstral. And Kingston over there is following Geoff Fu George."

"Isn't that a little . . . unsubtle?" A less tactful person would have said *obvious.* Khamiss appreciated the courtesy.

"I daresay. But Baroness Silverside's collection has been stolen, and the Baron's a bit upset."

"I understand. Still, were I Maijstral, I'd complain. And if the complaints weren't listened to, I imagine Maijstral and Fu George between them could greatly reduce Silverside Station's popularity. Were I a prominent member of society, I would not want to attend a resort where guests were followed by armed employees."

"My superiors doubtless feel that exceptions can be made in the case of known thieves. Besides," grinning, "you are one, aren't you?"

Zoot was startled. "Are what, ma'am?"

"A prominent member of society."

"Oh. I suppose I am."

"And an observant one. We didn't exchange a single word at the entry port, and you still remembered my face."

"I've trained myself to remember things."

"I envy you the talent. In my line of work, it would be very handy."

"I've got a system for recalling faces. I'll teach it to you, if you like."

"Would you? That's very kind."

"Not at all. My pleasure."

The racecourse was only slightly wider than two of the racers travelling shoulder-to-shoulder. It was possible to physically block someone trying to pass, and the rules allowed it, but blocking only invited a collision that could wreck both racers' times and might end in penalty assessment.

Pearl Woman, maintaining her half-second lead over Roberta, had approached the racer immediately ahead of her, a Tanquer dressed in violet. Pearl Woman hung back through a series of short straights, then gathered her powerful legs beneath her and launched herself on a diverging pass. She squeezed between the Tanquer and the wall, touched the wall lightly, a graze on her stomach, and then rebounded gently into the other racer's path. The violet racer flailed in an attempt to avoid fouling her, but Pearl Woman had already tucked into a ball and was ready for the next corner.

The Pearl cast a glance over her shoulder. The flailing racer was squarely in Roberta's path.

Well, she thought. *That should hold her for a while.*

"Well done, Pearl Woman!" Vanessa tapped her foot in a congratulatory rhythm.

"Yes. Quite." Fu George's drink was covered in frost. He removed his numbed fingers and frowned. "Drexler and Chalice are mapping the route from the ballroom to the Duchess's suite."

"Good. You'll do the pick-off after the ball, then?"

"Yes. I don't want to give Maijstral too much time. He's already too friendly with her grace."

"What if her guards are with her?"

"We'll use dazzlers and smoke. Once we're inside, they won't be able to shoot without risking her grace. And we'll have the advantage of surprise." He chipped frost from his drink with his fingernail. "Once we have the Shard, we'll hide it in her grace's suite. Then remove it after the time has passed."

"The plan seems a little . . ."

"Over-direct? Violent?"

"Yes."

"I know." Frowning. "No points for style. Maijstral hasn't given me any time."

"This may sound a little odd, Fu George," hesitantly, "but have you considered simply approaching the Duchess?"

Pause. "I . . . *assumed* . . . she wouldn't make an arrangement about something as notorious as the Shard."

"Think about it, Fu George."

Fu George said nothing. He was already thinking very hard indeed.

* * *

Roberta passed the violet Tanquer on the next long straight. Concluding her first lap, Pearl Woman increased her lead over Roberta during the long, straight outer passages; but once she got into the twisting, shorter, inner passage, she lost time. Her massive upper body lacked flexibility: forbidden by the rules from using the power of her arms and shoulders, caught in a part of the course that demanded quick reverses and compact athleticism, Pearl Woman's rebounds were slow and slightly off-course. Roberta, who was surprisingly limber for a woman her height, began to shorten Pearl Woman's lead. By the time they reached the next long straight, she was only a fraction of a second behind.

Maijstral leaned forward. Now, he thought, he'd see it. The fix or whatever it was.

"Oh, yeah. I've been on my own since I was twelve."

"In this current line of business?"

"Or something like it. I mean, they won't give you a burglar's ticket till you're sixteen, right?"

"Right."

"So I got interested in the technical end of the business. That way it wasn't me the police came looking for." There had been a few arrests to help him decide on that course, but Gregor saw no point in mentioning them.

"Hey." Kyoko's voice broke with excitement. "Hey. Did you see *that?*"

"Damnation!"

Smiling. "I told you, dear."

"Oh, *no!*" Biting a knuckle. "How did it *happen?*"

"Take comfort." Admiration rose in Maijstral's mind. "You've won your bet."

Pearl Woman's coup, Maijstral thought, had been perfectly timed and beautifully executed. Entering the first of the long back straights, her kickoff had seemed to go wrong. The pulled muscle had, to all appearances, taken its revenge. Pearl Woman had been propelled on a slightly wrong angle, drifting toward one of the walls. She tucked and prepared to carom off.

Roberta saw her chance and leaped for it. Her kickoff was flawless, her trajectory down the middle of the course perfectly timed to pass Pearl Woman just as the Pearl grazed the wall.

Roberta, in her tuck, had to reverse herself, touch the far wall with her feet, kick out and alter trajectory to fly down the next straight. She came out of her tuck, her legs cocked and ready.

Pearl Woman grazed on her helmet, came out of her tuck, prepared for her own change of course. She looked above her, left, and right, trying to find Roberta. She searched everywhere but where Roberta actually was, behind and below her. Pearl Woman was trying, Maijstral thought, to establish in the minds of the audience and Priests that she didn't know where Roberta was, and show that a foul was the last thing on her mind.

Roberta touched and kicked. Pearl Woman came down on top of her, her own legs lashing out.

Maijstral deduced that Pearl Woman intended to kick the Duchess on her thigh or knee as Roberta passed below her, crippling her for the rest of the race. But somehow Pearl Woman's driving feet passed through Roberta's legs without connecting—Roberta had twisted slightly in her trajectory change, and Pearl Woman flailed, bouncing into the corridor wall and missing her course alteration.

The proof of Pearl Woman's intent, Maijstral later concluded, was that loss of control. Had Pearl Woman *intended* to kick the wall, her course change should have gone off without a hitch. But since she *intended* to connect with Roberta, her timing was thrown off by her miss and she bounced hopelessly into the corner.

Maijstral settled back into his chair and smiled.

"What bad luck!" Advert cried.

"Yes," Maijstral said. "One might call it that."

Roberta passed the other racers to come in first, not simply in time-corrected listings but actually ahead of the others, even those who had started before her. She left the course to the enthusiastic, foot-tapping applause of the spectators, and the Priests of the Game, pouring incense, set up a hymn. Pearl Woman finished fifth.

"I think," Maijstral said, rising, "you should avoid mentioning your bets to the Pearl."

Advert nodded. "Yes. I'd already thought that."

"Please give her my condolences. It was a brave attempt."

"I'll do that. Thank you, Mr. Maijstral."

"Your servant, ma'am."

* * *

Khamiss sighed as she saw Maijstral rise from his place. "Duty calls, I'm afraid."

Zoot rose with her. The nebulous magnification field in front of his face vanished. "Please contact me when you're free. I'll tell you about my identification method."

"I'm working double shifts. But by midnight the Baroness's art collection will either be recovered or belong to the burglar forever, so perhaps I'll have more freedom tomorrow."

"Madam. Your very obedient."

"And yours."

"I'd never have got this far on my own. I'm learning a lot from him."

"Such as?"

"Ton and things. How to behave around people who are rich enough to have stuff I want to steal."

Kyoko laughed. "Ton and things," she repeated.

"I've got a bit to learn yet." With wounded dignity. "The point is, High Custom folk behave in different ways from the people I grew up with. I've got to learn how to use that, see?"

Kyoko looked at him. "Learning how to make use of the way people behave is different from turning yourself into an imitation aristocrat."

Gregor's ears flicked dismissal. "I didn't make the rules. It's their game. I've got to play it the way they want, or I don't play it at all."

"That isn't my point. My point is that you should make use of who you *are.*"

"Of *course* I—"

Kyoko held up a hand. "How long have you been with Maijstral?"

"Four years."

"Yes. Four years to integrate yourself with High Custom. While everyone else here has been working at it their entire lives."

Gregor scowled. "I'm bright. I can learn."

Kyoko tipped her head to one side. "I'm sure you can, and have. My point is that you can't succeed *entirely.* The people on Silverside Station have had the same education, the same training, and moved in the same circles for years. They can spot a phony by his dress, his manners, his language—or just by the set of his ears."

Gregor threw up his hands. "So what am I supposed to do? Just resign myself to living as a servant for the rest of my life?"

"Of course not." Kyoko looked at him coolly. "I'm here, aren't I? Moving in the highest circles and behaving just the way I like. And I was brought up on the frontier, more than fifty light-years from the nearest noble house."

"You're a performer. That's different."

"Tell me how."

"You—you need to present a personality for your viewers. It doesn't matter as much what sort of personality that is."

"It's *access* that matters, Gregor," Kyoko said. "Once you're accepted in this crowd, you can do anything you want. Ask embarrassing questions, expose secrets, or steal. The trick is that first acceptance."

"So how did you get accepted, then?"

"I conducted Saxony Weil's first interview in twenty years. The first since the scandal."

"And how'd you manage that?"

Kyoko smiled thinly. "I was very young, and I pretended more naiveté than I possessed. She wanted to get her version of events on the record, and thought she could use me. She assumed I'd be so awed that I wouldn't ask hard questions, and sufficiently inexperienced that I wouldn't check the record about what actually happened all those years ago. She spun a web of lies, and I called her down on each one."

"I sort of remember hearing about that. Never saw the interview, though. Didn't know anything about Saxony What's-'er-name."

"One critic called it 'the definitive demolition.' I liked that." She frowned and sipped her drink. "She wanted to use me, and I used her instead, and now I'm famous and she's still in exile. All I did was know my job, and my audience, and be myself." She stood and put her loupe in her eye. "I've got to talk to Pearl Woman before she leaves. If she thinks she can race in front of *me* and get away with an attempt to break the Duchess's knees, she'd better think again. See you later, I hope."

Gregor grinned at her. "Only too."

"Bye." Gregor watched, his mind buzzing, as Kyoko's marshalled media globes began to arrow toward Pearl Woman like a squadron of warships stooping on a target.

The Marquess Kotani was strolling rather rapidly from the arena when Maijstral intercepted him. Kotani wasn't precisely running away: he was merely giving the Fates a chance to intervene between himself and his debt. Once caught, Kotani handed over the money with a flourish and congratulations, then made a much more leisurely exit. Maijstral collected his half-quiller from Fu George, who wrote his marker in an offhand way while conducting a conversation with the Marchioness Kotani and Vanessa Runciter, and who then offered Maijstral a single finger in his handclasp. Smiling for his own reasons, Maijstral put his winnings in his pocket and strolled toward the knot of well-wishers that surrounded Roberta.

"Great race," Mr. Dolfuss was remarking. "Never seen a better."

"Thank you, sir," Roberta said. She pulled off her helmet and shook her bobbed hair.

"But what were the Priests singing afterward?" Dolfuss asked. "I couldn't make it out." He was using his actor's voice that boomed loud in the enclosed space. Those nearby were falling silent, partly because they'd been outshouted and partly out of embarrassment for the man.

"They were thanking the Virtues and the Emperor for a race well run," Roberta said. Her voice was softer than usual: perhaps she was trying to lead by example.

"What's the Emperor got to do with it?" Dolfuss demanded. "We don't even *have* an Emperor any more. It doesn't make any sense."

"If you'll forgive my interruption, sir, it has never been a requirement of religion to make sense," Maijstral said.

"Of *course* it's supposed to make sense!" Dolfuss barked. "What's the point of a religion that don't explain things?" But Maijstral had turned to Roberta and offered her two fingers.

"Congratulations, your grace," he said. "You came close to mishap, but you avoided it splendidly."

There was a secret gleam in Maijstral's eyes, one answered in the eyes of the Duchess. "I had warning, sir. Perhaps I'm intuitive that way."

"That would explain it. It's lucky *I* was intuitive enough to bet on your success."

"I'm pleased to be the author of your good fortune."

Dolfuss, in the meantime, had spotted someone over the heads of the crowd. With roaring apologies, to which no one listened, he made his way toward Pearl Woman. Maijstral, pleased by his confederate's performance, smiled as he watched the actor leave, a smile entirely misunderstood by those present.

"You'll pardon me, I hope," Roberta said. "I have to make preparations for the ball."

"Your grace." Maijstral sniffed her and watched her leave. From somewhere he could hear Dolfuss's voice on high, offering his sympathy to Pearl Woman on her damned bad luck. Maijstral remembered he had a bet on the tote and walked toward the stair. Climbing, he passed by Khamiss, who, cursing under her breath, was compelled to jump aside to make way for him. Maijstral bowed and brushed past, nudging Khamiss's gun with his elbow. Khamiss's ears drew down in mortification, and she wearily reversed course and trudged up the stairs after Maijstral.

Standing by the cashier were the Marchioness and Mr. Paavo Kuusinen. The Marchioness smiled and waved. "Collecting your winnings, Maijstral?" she asked.

"I was lucky."

"My husband was not. Despite his other splendid qualities, he is simply not the sort of man who should gamble."

"How unfortunate."

She gave an easy laugh and brandished her winnings. "I always win by betting contrary to his instructions. I'm afraid it puts him in a temper."

Maijstral turned to Kuusinen. "Did you win yourself, sir?"

Kuusinen smiled politely. "I did indeed. I've seen her grace race before, and I was confident there was no one in this field she couldn't cope with."

"An astute observation," Maijstral said, wondering. *Cope,* he thought, was an odd word to choose. *Win against* might have been more obvious.

Kuusinen, therefore, had seen Pearl Woman's stratagem and recognized it for what it was. The man was disturbingly acute.

"Cash your marker, Maijstral," the Marchioness said gaily. "Then we can stroll to the White Room."

"I'd be honored, my lady," Maijstral said, and stepped to the cashier's desk.

As he deposited his winnings into his hotel account, he could feel Kuusinen's unsettling gaze on the back of his neck. The man sees too much, he thought, and whether he's police or not, this bodes ill.

"A moment, your grace, if you please."

Roberta cast a look over her shoulder at Geoff Fu George. "If you don't mind walking with me. I'm in something of a hurry."

"You're walking in my direction anyway." Smoothly. Fu George matched his stride to hers and offered his congratulations.

"It was noble of you," Roberta said, "to bet on Pearl Woman, despite her injury."

Fu George stiffened in surprise. "I wonder," he asked, "how your grace knew of my wager?"

Roberta shrugged. "Drake Maijstral mentioned you and he had made a wager."

"Indeed." His face darkened. Now he knew how he'd lost: Maijstral had put her on her guard somehow. Drake Maijstral, he thought, has a lot to answer for.

"Your debut tonight," he said, "is certain to be a success."

"Thank you. Success is something I'm counting on."

"Success becomes you well," Fu George said. "But I wonder if you have ever considered your debut being marked not only by success, but by sensation?"

She gave him a look. "Sensation? How so, sir?"

Fu George gave a deprecating laugh. "I don't mean anything vulgar. No arguments, no duels, no scandalous fashion . . ."

"Ah. I perceive your intent."

Fu George smiled. "Your grace is quick."

Roberta laughed. "I'm afraid the family would not approve of such a major sensation, Mr. Fu George. But perhaps a minor one could be arranged afterward. Why don't you speak to me after the ball?"

"I would be most happy."

"Here's my door. Your servant, sir."

"Yours, madam."

Geoff Fu George stood outside the door for a moment and gnawed his lip. Was Roberta just putting him off, or was she serious about the minor sensation? Should he proceed with the lift tonight, or not?

He'd go ahead, he decided. With Maijstral on station, he had no choice; he couldn't afford to give Maijstral a chance at the Shard.

Confident in his assessment, Fu George turned and stepped toward his room. He and his assistants would have to choreograph their movements perfectly, and that would require careful preparation and rehearsal.

He wasn't going to let Maijstral show him up again.

"Pleased to see you again. May I join you?"

Khamiss looked up and smiled. "Of course. You're very welcome."

Zoot drew the next chair closer, then dropped into it. "I see you're still keeping Maijstral in sight."

"And vice versa." Dourly. "He knows I'm here."

Zoot's magnifier appeared briefly in the air as he gazed across the White Room toward where Maijstral was seated with the Marchioness. The magnifier disappeared, and Zoot turned to Khamiss. "I thought you might be interested in a physiognomy lesson. I've nothing else planned for the afternoon."

Khamiss brightened. "I'd like nothing better."

"The theory is based on using geometry to divide the body and the head into zones, and then finding something in one of the zones that is unique and can compel recall. For instance, the human head can be divided evenly along a lateral line running left to right across the eyes. . . ."

Khamiss was surprised. "The eyes are in the horizontal centerline of the human head? I thought they were . . . rather lower down."

"That's an optical illusion. Because we're taller. Let me show you." Zoot took a notebook from his pocket and drew an oval on it with a pen. He bisected it, added eyes, a button nose, a mouth, and hair. A recognizable human, withal.

"I see."

"The upper attachment of the human's ears to the head are also on a line with the eyes. So . . ." Still drawing.

"Right. So if the ears are placed higher or lower than the corners of the eyes, then that's a distinguishing mark."

Zoot's tongue lolled in approval. "Quite. That's not a common one, however." He sketched idly. "I use a human head as an illustration because their ovoid shape makes for a simpler geometry. Khosali heads are formed along the lines of an oblate hexagon, the upper half larger than the lower."

Zoot continued adding lines to his pad. Khamiss watched and made comments, but her observations dwindled off after a few moments. Zoot's head, she noticed, was quite an admirable hexagon in its way.

"Damn!" Khamiss jumped up. Zoot glanced at her in alarm.

"Something wrong, miss?"

"Maijstral's leaving. I've got to run. Thank you."

"We can continue later."

"Thanks. Bye."

Heart pounding, Khamiss sped across the White Room as Maijstral sniffed the Marchioness's ears and moved toward an exit. She was aware of people looking at her.

She slowed, her ears turning down in embarrassment. Maijstral was waiting for her anyway, arms folded, standing in the doorway.

SIX

Some objects have a way of becoming magic. They need not be the biggest or even the best of their type; yet somehow they gather romance unto themselves, and become legend. The Felkhorvinn Tapestry is one such object; and a sect of ascetic carpetmarkers on Pessch has even gone so far as to deify its architect, Pers the Younger. The Felkhorvinn is a little unusual to fit into the category of Magic Objects, in that it's very large: in fact it's so big that it's only been stolen once, by that romantic collector of objects-not-his-own, Ralph Adverse.

For usually it's theft that deifies an object, imbues it with the proper aura of romance. Would La Giaconda's smile seem quite so intriguing had it not been coveted, stolen, and cherished by so many? Would the Hope Diamond have shone quite so brilliantly had its origins not been so mysterious, and had all its owners, beginning with Louis XVI and Antoinette, died in such fateful, inexorable ways? Would Prince Orloff have paid quite so much for his blue-white stone had it not been pried from the eye of an Indian idol? Would the Zoot Torque have become the most celebrated piece of Imperial regalia had not Ralph Adverse managed to worm his way into the City of Seven Bright Rings and get his hands on it?

Most of the Magic Objects moving about the universe are, in fact, gems of one sort or another. The fact is that gems are portable and therefore more easily stolen; and when stolen in the right circumstance, by the right people, an object can be invested with the necessary aura of enchantment. Nothing could make it more romantic than the right theft, lest it be the right death. Blood, it seems, is more effective in creating romance than mere larceny.

Of the glowstones, those rare and lambent objects hurled at relativistic velocities from the cores of dying stars, none is more famous than the Eltdown Shard, which has seen more than its share of death and peculation. When the Countess Ankh was informed by her lover, the financier Collinen, that they must part, she saw no alternative but to disembowel the man and place his organs in cryogenic containers intended originally for selected parts of his pet Farq shepherds. She committed this crime not because she was sorry at losing Collinen, but rather because Collinen owned the Shard, and upon losing her lover she lost her access to its glorious fires, its cool and subtle majesty. (But perhaps she cared for Collinen after all: when the police finally blasted their way into Castle Sumador, they found the Shard in the same cryogenic container as the dead man's heart. Moved by this evidence of sentiment, the Emperor permitted his cousin her choice of deaths.)

Two Allowed Burglars later tried for the Shard and died; Ralph Adverse tried and succeeded, then later, when his lifestrand frayed at last, killed himself with the Shard clutched to his bosom, thus confirming his own legend and the Shard's. Other glowstones are larger, and others display the light of long-dead stars more beautifully; but none has as much romance as the Shard, none has its magic.

And none has its fatal attraction. Its relativistic flames have attracted many a moth, and few have escaped without burning. That's the problem with magic: it can exalt, or destroy, or do both at once; and few can honestly claim to predict which course a Magic Object will take once it has admirers in its spell.

The spell of the Shard had clearly been cast on the Silverside Ballroom. The air of expectancy was tangible: beneath the flares of Rathbon's Star the atmosphere was hushed, almost reverent. Costumes glittered; crystal goblets rang; people conversed; but still all this small world waited, knowing *something* was going to happen.

Drake Maijstral was perfectly recognizable through his domino mask. He was costumed as Grat Dalton, a six-gun on one hip and an elegant rapier on the other. Maijstral's brown hair had been darkened for the occasion, drawn back to a knot behind; glittering gemstones dangled from his ears. The red light of Rathbon's Star, reflecting from his white ruff, darkened his complexion to that of an outdoorsman gunslinger—the effect had been carefully calculated. He spun his six-shooter on his fingers as he padded through the ballroom.

People were talking about him. He gave no sign of knowing.

Baron Silverside's expression was stony. "You have instructed your people, Mr. Sun?"

"I have, my lord." Dutifully.

"Everyone is on alert?"

"Yes, my lord." Another alarm blinked on Sun's control board. He ignored it.

"Maijstral and Fu George will be followed wherever they go?"

"They will, my lord." Another alarm blinked. Against his will, a muscle in Sun's cheek twitched.

"Because they're sure to try something tonight, and if we can find out where they've been concealing the loot, we'll be able to find my lady's collection."

Sun chose his words carefully. "We have every reason to hope, my lord."

The Baron's reaction was icy. "*You* have every reason to *hope,* Sun. *Hope* that you find the collection, and *hope* that you toss these thieves in the calabozo. Because Kyoko Asperson is *hoping* to crucify you in an interview, and if we don't find the collection, I *hope* to hand her the nails and hammer."

More alarms winked. Sun swallowed hard. "I understand, my lord."

"I *hope* so, Mr. Sun. I *hope* so."

Khamiss was dressed as a waiter, in severe black with yellow collar tabs and cuffs. The waiter's uniform had been drawn from central supply and was not tailored for the service pistol that was still jammed in her armpit.

In something close to despair, she followed Maijstral through the crowd. People kept asking her for drinks, and she kept having to turn slightly away from them, concealing the bulge in her armpit, and then apologize for not being able to bring refreshments.

The night could only get worse.

* * *

"Mr. Maijstral?"

Kyoko Asperson was dressed as Ronnie Romper, a popular red-haired puppet whose visits to the Magic Planet of Adventure had entranced generations of children.

The last individual Maijstral encountered who dressed as Ronnie Romper had been a seven-foot-tall homicidal maniac who had tried to dissect Maijstral with a broadsword. The experience had been a particularly unhappy one, since the maniac, like a creature out of nightmare, had to be killed repeatedly before he finally snuffed the candle at last. The memory unsettled Maijstral's nerves.

Getting a grip on himself, he doffed his Stetson and sniffed this shorter Ronnie's ears, an act that took a certain effort. "Miss Asperson," he said.

"A fine costume, sir. Very appropriate."

"Thank you." The gleaming six-shooter spun as it marched down Maijstral's fingers. "Yours seems appropriately magical."

Kyoko sighed, a sound that seemed odd in a puppet. She gestured with her wand, scattering holographic fairy dust. "Tonight's magic belongs to the Shard, alas."

"If it's here."

The puppet cocked its head. "Do you really believe it isn't?"

Maijstral regarded the crowd. "If it isn't, there's been a criminal waste of anticipation."

"And preparation?"

Maijstral smiled. "On the part of *some* people, perhaps."

"Not yourself."

"Of course not." He glanced over his shoulder at Khamiss. "I'm being followed by armed police. I'd have to be mad to attempt anything here."

"So in the matter of your duel with Fu George . . ."

Maijstral's nerves, which he had been making a deliberate effort to soothe, promptly unstrung once again at the word *duel,* which reminded him of yet another unhappy experience in his past. He stiffened.

"I'm not in his class, as I believe I've said," Maijstral said. "To challenge Mr. Fu George to a duel, or to anything else, would be an act of presumption."

Kyoko lowered her voice. "I'll presume for you," she said confidentially. "I'm betting on you, Maijstral. The odds on the tote were too great to resist."

Maijstral wasn't entirely surprised by this. "They've posted odds in the Casino, then?"

"Yes. Two and a half to one in favor of Fu George."

Maijstral's eyes glittered in amusement. "Perhaps I'll lay a wager myself. The odds *do* seem a little excessive." He bowed and doffed the Stetson again. "Your servant, madam."

"The Casino odds are encouraging. They have every confidence in you. And," hand tightening on his arm, "so do I."

"Thank you, Vanessa dearest. But this situation *is* a bit unfair, you'll admit. If I outpoint Maijstral, it's only what's expected of me. If Maijstral's luck is in and he outpoints *me,* it's an upset and everyone starts speculating whether or not I'm slipping."

"This should put you on your mettle."

"My dear." An offended tone. "I'm never *off* it."

Vanessa's eyes glittered. "Personally, I'm quite excited by the competition."

"Should I believe the Duchess or not? That's the question."

"You were going to try for the Shard sooner or later anyway. You've always told me."

"Yes. But on grounds of my own choosing. *This* business . . . I'll be getting no points for style, that's certain."

"I think the costume will add points in that department, don't you?"

"I hope so." Approaching the door to the ballroom. "Well, here we go."

Geoff Fu George presented his pair of invitations. Seeing his name and coupling it with the costume, the majordomo's jaw dropped in a perfect attitude of astonishment.

Vanessa, who was dressed spectacularly in feathery orange, resigned herself to letting Fu George outshine her.

Roman strolled into the ballroom on the heels of Vanessa and Fu George. His invitation proclaimed him to be Lord Graves, who was, as it happens, a real person—a human in fact, a distant relative of Maijstral's who lived in the Empire. The door security, still goggling after Fu George's costume, passed him without a glance.

Roman was dressed as a Montiyy noble in the distinctive flounced overcoat and tall tapering hat. He carried a walking stick and wore a signet ring on one finger. From his considerable height, he peered down the length of his muzzle at the other guests and graciously inclined his head toward anyone who looked at him.

He *was* Lord Graves. No one who saw Roman doubted it for an instant. Even Maijstral, who had been looking for him, had to look twice to make sure.

Roman, Maijstral had to admit, was magnificent. His large, heavily muscled frame had somehow become suffused with nobility, elegance, courtesy. Noblesse oblige dripped like honey from his fingertips. People were warmed by his very presence.

If there were any justice, Maijstral thought, Roman would have been born a lord, and Maijstral something else. Roman was so *good* at it—he embodied the noble virtues and graces, and did so with an elegance that Maijstral knew perfectly well he himself did not possess. Maijstral knew how to act a lord; Roman knew how to *be* one.

Maijstral, standing across the room from the false Lord Graves, spared a few moments for the pure enjoyment of watching Roman live the life he deserved.

"A splendid costume. Countess Riefers, is it not?"

"Thank you, Zoot." Lady Dosvidern smiled. "Will you take my arm?"

"Gladly, my lady. Its lordship is in crosstalk?"

"Yes. It's been in a trance with itself since the, ah, incident this afternoon, and will be for many hours yet. I know the signs. The eyestalks have almost entirely withdrawn."

"Have you derived any notion of why its lordship is behaving this way?"

"Not yet, no. *Protocols? Time of Exchange?* The terms and context are new to me."

"But you have a clue?"

"No, not really. It's all very hard to sort out." Her diaphragm pulsed in despair. "Each of the Drawmiikh's brains has a different social function and personality, and when Drawmii meet one another each brain has its own say, and each has a different relationship with each of the *other* Drawmiikh's brains."

"A simple conversation must take a long time."

"There *is* no such thing as a simple conversation on Zynzlyp. The brains have their own quirks, and even with Qlp I have a hard time knowing who's talking at any one time. Sometimes I think even the Drawmii don't keep things straight. I know I can't." She looked up at Zoot and patted his arm. "Well," she said, "at least *now* I know whom I'm talking to."

"Pardon me, but can you bring us a pair of rink and sodas?"

"I'm afraid not, sir. I'm on an errand already."

* * *

"You'll forgive me, dear. I should speak to Silverside."

"He seems in something of a temper. Perhaps you shouldn't."

"Darling, you misunderstand my intention. I will catch him at a disadvantage. He may be inclined to make concessions."

Languidly. "If you insist, dearest." The Marchioness's eyes widened. "Good grief! Look at Fu George!"

Kotani gave a glance. His languor vanished at once. "Sink me! *That* should put the fat in the fire!"

Excitedly. "Is the Duchess here? Has she seen him?" Pause. "I can't believe he actually altered his hairstyle."

Spinning, winking silver . . .

"Casino? I was wondering what odds are offered on the score between Maijstral and Geoff Fu George."

"Three to one, sir. On Fu George. Three-point spread."

"The odds have changed."

"Yes. Have you seen Fu George's costume for the ball?"

"I understand." Spinning. "I would like to place a bet. Four quillers on Maijstral. Bill it to the Coronet Suite."

"Yes, sir."

The six-gun spun again, and dropped into its holster. Maijstral turned off the privacy screen, adjusted his hat, and returned to the ball.

"Perhaps," said Vanessa Runciter, *"I* should speak to her."

"We don't have time to arrange anything. Our plans are set."

"But still, Fu George . . ."

"I've got to beat Maijstral to this one. You know that."

"Yes."

"And here I am dressed as Ralph Adverse. I'm as good as shouting my intention to go after the Shard."

"Yes." Petulant by now. "Do what you wish, Geoff. I'm just trying to *help."*

"Imagine, Pearl. We may be witnesses to the crime of the century!"

"I am agog with anticipation," Pearl Woman said, her voice without enthusiasm. She was dressed as an Earth pirate in tall boots, headscarf, and eyepatch; her matched cutlasses gleamed. She had made an attempt to look authentic, not that anyone here would notice.

Advert was dressed as a dithermoon in bright silks, her swept-brim hat pinned at a jaunty angle. "Have you seen Fu George's costume?" she asked.

"Ralph Adverse. Yes. I've seen it." Pearl Woman winced at the pain in her thigh. Life had, unfortunately, imitated art: she had genuinely strained a leg muscle in a futile but heroic attempt to catch the Duchess in the last stages of the race.

"Fu George may steal the Shard right in front of our eyes!"

Pearl Woman winced again at the sight of someone approaching. "Just what I need. Kyoko Asperson."

"Who? Oh. The Ronnie Romper?"

"Yes. The Ronnie Romper with the media globes. Who else might he be?"

"I *love* Ronnie Romper. Being here is just like being on the Magic Planet of Adventure."

Pearl Woman smiled for the cameras. "You and Ronnie Romper have so much in common," she said, just in time for Kyoko to hear. "Empty heads, for one."

"My lady."

"Maijstral!" Happily. "I hope you have some diversion planned. Kotani has abandoned me again."

"That was callous of him." Sniffing her. "But do not despair. The evening promises excitement."

"I hope that means you're going to kidnap the Shard."

Maijstral smiled. "Ah. That, too."

Paavo Kuusinen, dressed as a red rover in hat, ruffles, and boots, walked observant among the crowd and counted media globes.

He couldn't help himself. He also was beginning to think it was important.

He counted, nodded, stepped to a telephone. Activating the privacy screen, he bet fifty novae on Drake Maijstral. He then made another bet on someone else.

"Yes, Kyoko. Advert's costume is lovely, isn't it? The dithermoon was my idea. The finger rings, of course, are Advert's own unmistakable contribution."

"Bring me some more brandy, will you?"

"I'm afraid I can't, ma'am."

"Why not?" Belligerently.

"I am already on an errand, ma'am."

"You're just *standing* there, staring at the cowboy. You're a waiter, aren't you?"

"Brandy. Right. Coming up."

"Get *on* with it."

Khamiss's mortification knew no bounds.

"You have no idea how relieved I am to be here, Zoot." Her fingers dug into his arm. "It's been so long since I was able to talk to anyone who wasn't—"

"Lord Qlp?"

"Lord Qlp. Yes. All five of it."

"Yes. The dithermoon *is* appropriate, isn't it. Dear Advert is in such a dither most of the time."

"Yes, Maijstral. I can give you the first dance. I can give you the last, as well. I only hope it's a slow one."

The entrance was timed perfectly, just as anticipation had built as far as possible. Right at the moment when people were about to forget they were in suspense and get on with enjoying themselves, the cymbals crashed, trumpets blared, and the Duchess of Benn made her entrance.

With the Eltdown Shard gleaming at her throat.

SEVEN

The Eltdown Shard was still in the two-century-old Orkhor setting, which made the Shard the centerpiece of an elaborate necklace first worn by the Fourteenth Duchess. The setting featured twenty smaller glowstones. The dark Shard was teardrop-shaped, the narrow end downward, elaborately cut and faceted. Gleaming in the heart of the Shard, multiplied by the facets, a dying star was captured.

Her grace was dressed as the Countess Ankh, with a black-furred artificial Khosali head encompassing her own. Its brown eyes, made of dark glowstones, gleamed with a diabolical inner light. Her clothing was a dull red that, in the light of Rathbon's Star, brightened to the color of fresh blood. A thousand gemstones were sewn into the blouse and long coat; at her every gesture they flashed fire. Her loose trousers were tucked into ruby-heeled boots made of diresnake skin. At her waist she carried a curved sword identical to that with which the luckless Collinen had met his end.

Roberta stalked into the ballroom, her false ears cocked forward in defiance, the artificial muzzle set in a snarl of scorn. The costume was fully as sensational as the gem that pulsed in the dark hollow of her throat, and Roberta knew it.

Ralph Adverse walked toward her and bowed. "Your grace," he said. "My fervent congratulations on your debut, and on your sensational costume. I'm sure the Countess Ankh herself never looked better."

"Thank you, Fu George." Roberta had to give the man credit—he was keeping his eyes on her face and off the Eltdown Shard. The gem's dark fires, however, shone in his eyes.

"Will you take my arm, milady?"

"Certainly, sir." They sniffed hello and began walking down the length of the ballroom. Guests parted before them, some with awe, but most because there was a general movement toward the telephones—people were placing bets.

"Now I can understand your disinclination to accept my offer of this afternoon," Fu George said. "Any sensation planned by me would pale beside your own."

"You do yourself injury, sir. Anyone arriving at a ball of mine dressed as Ralph Adverse cannot claim to be a stranger to sensation."

"I wonder, your grace, if you have given my idea any further thought."

"I have scarcely had time to think at all." Her costume head cocked an ear toward him. "But I will give your offer my best reflection, once I have a free moment. Tomorrow I should have several free moments—at least three or four."

"You do me honor to consider the proposal. I wonder if you would also give me the honor of a dance."

"The first I must give to Baron Silverside. The second I've already promised. Would the third suit? I believe it's the Pilgrimage."

"Appropriate, your grace. For a pilgrim I surely am, come to worship at your shrine."

Maijstral, hoping not to think of the figure from his past as an omen, was trying not to notice Ronnie Romper. He was about to commit the crime of the century, and he preferred not to have to think of anything at all.

He danced the first dance with the Marchioness Kotani, the second, as promised, with the Duchess. Roberta moved superbly in the heavy costume, her assured athlete's balance coping well with the weight of the jewels and head. Maijstral found himself admiring her, her self-reliance, her intelligence, her determination. Birth had given her advantages; but Roberta had made careful use of them—a calculated use, but Maijstral couldn't fault her there. In Roberta's social stratum, one either calculated or one drowned. There was no other choice.

The dance was a slow one, and the measured rhythms served to calm Maijstral's nerves. As the dance ended and Maijstral escorted Roberta to the buffet, he felt ready, his limbs tingling with anticipation, his touch sure. "I hope your grace will give me another dance," Maijstral said.

"I'm afraid not. As official hostess, I should circulate."

"I'm desolated, madam. Will your grace take champagne?"

"Just fruit juice, I think. The brightcrisp."

Maijstral handed the Duchess her drink, then took champagne for himself. He glanced over his shoulder to make sure that Roman was in position, standing near Baroness Silverside. He noticed Geoff Fu George moving through the crowd, heading toward Roberta.

The moment seemed ripe. The crime of the century, he thought. Readiness warmed his veins. He was faintly surprised that he didn't feel the least nervous.

"You will excuse me, your grace. I must congratulate Miss Advert on her costume."

"Certainly, Maijstral." She raised her glass. "We'll speak later."

Maijstral sniffed her, turned, and took four careful, measured paces. The champagne glass was three-quarters full in his left hand. The orchestra was tuning; the crowd was milling; the volume of conversation rose.

Maijstral's empty right hand dropped to his pocket and palmed two micromedia globes. Balancing the champagne glass carefully, Maijstral raised his left hand casually to his lapel and hooked the little finger over the loop of a drawstring bag that was folded carefully in an inner pocket of his coat. He seized mental control of the micromedia globes with the proximity wire in his Stetson, then his right hand emerged from his pocket, reached across his body to his rapier, and pressed a button on the hilt.

With a sudden crash of metal the room was plunged into total darkness. Someone screamed. Thanks to Gregor's tinkering in the ballroom that afternoon, Maijstral had been able to override the command circuits on the steel crash shutters, which were supposed to slam shut overhead in the event that Silverside Station was in danger of colliding with a runaway yacht or a careless meteor.

In one smooth gesture, Maijstral dropped the palmed micromedia globes, turned, and drew the hilt of his rapier—the hilt came away in his hand, revealing sonic cutters hidden in the sword-blade.

The Eltdown Shard was the only source of light in the room, marking Maijstral's target. Countess Ankh's ghostly head, back to Maijstral, loomed above the precious glow. The micromedia globes rose to hover overhead, recording everything with ultrasensitive scanners. Maijstral took four measured steps toward the Duchess, cut the chain of the necklace, snagged it between his fingers, and dropped it into the drawstring bag that he had pulled from his jacket with the little finger of his left hand.

The orchestra, seeking to assuage panic, began a shaky rendition of "When the Moonlight is Mellow."

Maijstral turned again and took four measured paces to his starting point. Behind him he was aware of a disturbance. He pulled taut the drawstrings and flung the bag and the Shard high into the air. One micromedia globe followed it; the other dropped into his pocket. He slipped the sonic cutters back into the false blade of his rapier, an act that automatically sent out a signal that cancelled Gregor's interrupt signal on the emergency lighting.

When light first returned to the ballroom, Maijstral was observed standing where he had been when the lights went out, a puzzled expression on his face, a fizzing glass of champagne undisturbed in his hand. . . .

Four paces behind him, Geoff Fu George lay sprawled on the floor, rubbing his eye. The Duchess of Benn, reacting belatedly to the theft of her gem, had struck out blindly into the darkness and flattened him with a single punch.

"Seal the doors!" Baron Silverside's voice rose above the sudden turmoil. "Security to the doors!" And then, his finger pointing toward Fu George like the Hand of Doom, *"Seize that man!"*

The Shard, meanwhile, was closer to Baron Silverside than the latter suspected. The drawstring bag, containing an a-grav homing device and attracted by a transmitter planted in Roman's signet ring, had flown straight across the room and thunked solidly into Roman's hand. The micromedia globe following had been taken under command by the proximity wire in Roman's collar and dropped down the front of his carrick, whence it peeked out from beneath one of the capes and witnessed the next maneuver.

While the Baron shouted, Roman quietly approached the Baroness from behind. The drawstring bag, weightless with its a-grav repellers, was quickly attached by a small adhesive to the inside of one of the Baroness Silverside's elaborate, pleated skirts.

Smiling, Roman ordered the micromedia globe to roll into his pocket. Humming "When the Moonlight turns Mellow," Lord Graves quietly walked away into the crowd, his walking stick touching the floor at every third step, clearly someone too refined to have anything to do with thieves.

There was a palpable air of excitement in Sun's blue heaven. "Right. Watsons!" Sun barked. "Take Fu George behind a privacy screen and search him. Search any of his associates who may be present. Then search Maijstral and any of *his* assistants. And meanwhile *don't let anybody out of the ballroom!"*

"It looks as if Fu George may have beaten you to it," Kyoko Asperson remarked. Her media globes were circling the opaque privacy screen within which Fu George was being searched.

The privacy screen dropped and Fu George stepped into the crowd. His confident grin seemed a little strained. His eye was beginning to swell and turn purple.

Maijstral smiled. "It looks to me as if Fu George is the one that got beat," he said, and drained the last of his champagne.

"Search Vanessa Runciter!" Sun barked. "Then get Maijstral in there!"

"My condolences, your grace," Zoot offered. "I trust the stone will be recovered."

"One way or another," Roberta said. She was worried. She didn't know *who* had her necklace.

"I'm sure they'll get it back," Pearl Woman said. Unconsciously, she tilted her head to feel the reassuring weight of her pearl against her neck.

"I hope this won't delay the ball fatally," Roberta said. She managed a brave grin. "I realize they have to search people, but can't the rest of us go on dancing?"

Zoot's foot tapped the floor in an admiring pattern of applause. "Well said, your grace," he offered.

"Well, let's!" Roberta declared. She tried to signal the orchestra leader, but failed. "You'll pardon me," she said, and began to walk toward the floating gallery where the orchestra perched.

"May I have the honor of this dance, madam?" Zoot asked, turning to Pearl Woman.

"Certainly." Taking his arm.

"My compliments on your pirate costume, by the way. It looks very authentic."

Pearl Woman was surprised. "I didn't think anyone would notice."

"Old Earth costume is a hobby of mine. There's such a variety, you know."

"No, I didn't."

"Oh, yes. Why, in the age of piracy alone there was quite an amazing diversity of costume. Between the Barbary Corsairs and the Ladronese of Ms. Ching Yih there was a prodigious difference."

"Really? Tell me about it."

She could use this, Pearl Woman thought as Zoot launched into a lecture concerning Pierre le Grand and the dread Bartholemew Roberts. She'd have someone write her a play about Earth pirates—this Ms. Ching Yih sounded promising—with lots of costumes, action, sword fights, armed ships zooming about the atmosphere on scalloped wings . . .

It was time she appeared in a romance. It had been a few years.

"No luck, sir."

"Damnation." Sun scowled. Blinking alarm lights filled his console. "Very well. We'll search *everybody* as they leave the ball."

Khamiss looked startled. "Can we *do* that, sir?"

"Ask the Baron his permission, but I'm sure he'll give it. This is the Eltdown Shard we're talking about, not some damned chunk of asteroid."

"Mr. Sun!" The Baron's scowling visage appeared over Sun's console. Alarm lights shone through his holographic image. "Have you found the Shard?"

Sun touched an ideogram and ended the conversation with Khamiss. "I was just about to speak with you, my lord," he said. "We haven't turned up the Shard yet, but it's probably in the ballroom somewhere. If I could have your permission to search each guest upon leaving . . . ?"

The Baron seemed a little taken aback, but once he got used to the idea, he seemed to grow more cheerful. "Ye-es," he said, stroking his burnsides thoughtfully. "Yes, I believe that would be justified under the circumstances."

"And if by some mischance we fail to recover the stone, then my people can continue following the suspects. They may lead us to their treasure troves."

Baron Silverside brightened again at the thought of recovering his wife's collection. "Yes," he said again. "Good man, Sun. That's the ticket."

"Thank you, sir."

"Remember what's at stake, Sun." Somehow, with Baron Silverside looking pleased, the threat seemed all the worse. Sun commended his soul to the Eternal.

"I remember, sir."

"See that you do, Sun."

Another alarm blinked on.

"Yes, sir. I know very well."

The Baron disappeared. Sun looked sullenly at the control board and its winking lights. Finally his temper snapped.

"Cancel all alarms!" he roared.

The console obeyed. For a few minutes anyway, there was peace.

"Roman? Is that *you?"*

"Yes, Miss Runciter."

Vanessa looked at him in astonishment. She had just danced three figures with the Khosalikh in the carrick and tall hat, thinking only there was something familiar about him, and only now realized she had known him for years.

"Roman," she said, "you are an absolute treasure. You make a wonderful good Montiyy."

"Thank you, madam."

"Surprisingly good," she said, her eyes narrowing.

Roman could read her like a book.

The Pilgrimage to the Cinnamon Temple was under way by the time Maijstral stepped from the privacy screen. He had been searched by a female Khosalikh in a waiter's uniform, the same who had been following him the last two days, and she had clearly been embarrassed by having to face him again: she wouldn't even look at his face. Were it not for the fact that a number of her confederates were watching, he could probably have kept the Shard on his person the entire time, moving it from pocket to pocket while she turned her eyes away and patted at him.

Maijstral decided not to join the dance. The urge to glibber and gambol, he reflected, might get the better of him. He refreshed his champagne glass and noticed a figure in layered silks standing by one of the barred doors. He approached her.

"Miss Advert."

Turning away. "Maijstral." He saw that she was weeping, her

mouth rammed into a clenched fist. He reached into a pocket for a handkerchief.

"May I be of assistance?"

She took the handkerchief and said no. Maijstral waited for her to finish dabbing her eyes, then proffered his champagne. Advert returned his handkerchief, took the glass, gulped, returned the glass, took the handkerchief again.

"It's the Pearl, of course," Advert said.

"I thought so."

Her words were spaced by sobs and gasps for breath, but Maijstral was able to follow it. "She insulted me. (Gasp.) In front of Kyoko Asperson. (Gasp.) Several (gasp) times. Called me brainless (gasp). With Kyoko and her globes hearing (gasp) everything. She was so *cutting!* (Gasp.) Making witty jokes at my expense. *And I couldn't think of anything to do! I just stood there!*"

"I'm sorry," Maijstral said, as she exchanged handkerchief for champagne again.

"Why did she *do* it? I thought we were *friends!*" Advert tossed off the champagne and handed Maijstral the empty glass. He gave her his handkerchief again and Advert began wringing it.

"Pearl Woman is a member of the Diadem," Maijstral said. "There's that to consider."

"It puts her under pressure, of course, and perhaps she needs—"

"The Diadem do nothing in public without reason," Maijstral said. "That is another consideration."

Advert paused in surprise, handkerchief halfway to her eyes. "You think so? You think it was calculated?"

"Pearl Woman has had many protegés, Advert. She is very sophisticated and very talented, and because of who she is, she can trust very few people. Among the Three Hundred, people use other people, and often use them badly."

Advert looked at him. "You were offered Diadem membership, weren't you?"

"Not formally. But yes, I knew I'd be accepted."

"With Nichole sponsoring you. And you turned it down."

"Yes."

"Was it because you'd have to be . . . cruel?"

"No. I simply didn't want to live in the public eye for the rest of my life."

"Have you regretted your decision?"

"From time to time. But, to be honest, my regret is halfhearted, and never very serious. When I remember what it was like living with Nichole, with billions of people interested in my every move, I'm quite thankful I don't have to deal with those pressures." He gave a brief smile. "Made it hard to earn my living, for one thing."

Advert looked at her rings. Her voice was subdued. "I thought Pearl Woman and I were special friends. I suppose that was silly of me."

"I can't say. But I know that Pearl Woman doesn't adopt just anybody. She did see *something* in you, Advert."

Advert swallowed hard. She gave a brave smile and handed Maijstral his handkerchief. "She used me. Spent my money, let me support her. And I ransomed her pearl."

"But she gave you access to the Diadem in return, let you live the kind of life you thought you wanted. Perhaps she considers this a fair exchange."

"It's not." Her expression hardened. "Not at all."

"Perhaps this is her way of educating you. The Three Hundred use people, and in return are used by the institution of the Diadem. Not everyone is cut out for a life like that. It may be better that you know what it's really like."

"Still." Advert's look was cold. "She ought not to be allowed to get away with it entirely. Not in front of Kyoko and everybody."

Maijstral thought about this for a moment. "You don't want to call her out, of course."

"No!" Advert seemed shocked. Her expression, after consideration, turned calculating. "No," she repeated. "For a start, she'd win, and even though she'd be upset by being made to fight twice in a year, it wouldn't be worth it to me. I just think—maybe she should have a taste of her own medicine, that's all."

"There's her pearl." Tentatively. "She could . . . lose it again."

Advert seemed surprised, then she thought for a moment. "And people could find out, this time," she said slowly. There was a certain enthusiasm in her look, but she frowned and shook her head. "I'll have to think about that, Mr. Maijstral."

"Call me Drake. And let me know what you decide."

"Certainly." Advert gave a tentative smile. "Thank you."

He sniffed her ears. The Pilgrimage was coming to an end, and he headed back to the buffet to refill his champagne glass before the dancers began to crowd around.

"Fu George." Slipping her arm through his.

"Yes?"

"You'll never guess who I just danced with."

"A big Khosalikh built like a pom boxer and wearing a funny overcoat."

Laughing. "Yes. He *is* a pom boxer, too. But the pom boxer is Roman."

Fu George's eyes widened. "Roman? Here?"

"He may well have the Shard on him."

Fu George looked at Roman and frowned. "I think this is worth a recce."

"I'd say so."

"If you'll excuse me, my dear . . . ?"

"Of course. But get some semilife patches on that eye soon, won't you? It's really starting to look ugly."

The Duchess of Benn stalked through the room, breathing fire. Maijstral was on his third glass of champagne, and in a sunny mood. "A setback, your grace?" Maijstral asked.

Beneath the Khosali head, Roberta's violet eyes flashed anger. "Those fools are going to search everyone on leaving. *My guests!*"

Maijstral held his glass to the light, admiring the golden rise of bubbles. "Shocking."

She glared at him. "Treating my guests as if they were . . ."

"Thieves, my lady?"

Roberta froze for a moment, then laughed. "Thieves, yes." She looked at him. "I take it you are pleased with the results of the evening."

"I have no reason to be unhappy."

"And you've anticipated the searches, I suppose?"

Maijstral's heavy lids rose to reveal amused green eyes. "I have laid my plans."

Suddenly cheered, Roberta gave another laugh. "So all my guests are going to be searched for nothing."

"That seems likely. If the guards find any secrets, none will be mine."

She shook her head. "I didn't have time to think when the lights went out. I just reacted. Lucky I hit Fu George and not you."

"You wouldn't have caught me."

Roberta looked at him. "You're very sure of yourself."

"In some things. As sure as you are on a racecourse."

She thought about this, then turned to look at Baron Silverside. Anger entered her voice again. "That pompous idiot. I hope you get to *keep* his damned collection."

"I hope so, too."

She gave a laugh. "That *was* you? Interesting."

Maijstral's lazy eyes turned cautious. "Perhaps we should not speak any longer. You're supposed to be the one who's just lost your greatest treasure, and I'm supposed to be the one who may have taken it. People may hope for at least a small display of bad temper."

She nodded. "You're right. I forgot for a moment."

"Your grace." He sniffed her farewell. She stiffened, as if offended.

Both turned at the sound of a smack, and neither could help laughing once they did.

Roman had just felt Fu George's fingers in his pocket, and without thought had driven his elbow into Fu George's uninjured eye and knocked him to the floor.

EIGHT

Drexler's ears were cocked at an indignant angle. His lips drew back from his muzzle in a snarl. "Roman *struck* you, sir?"

Geoff Fu George had changed from his Ralph Adverse costume into his evening jacket with the built-in darksuit. He applied a semilife patch to one of his blackened eyes. The little creature, happy in its purpose, awoke from its stasis and began to set its taproots into the swollen tissue.

"It was involuntary, I suspect," Fu George said. "He's a trained fighter, and I must have been more careless than usual. I triggered his reflexes." He sighed. "Anyway, he didn't have the Shard."

"With all respect, sir, Roman is also good enough to know when to use his reflexes and when not to. Perhaps," flexing his muscles, "I should have a chat with our Mr. Roman concerning this promiscuous use of 'reflexes.' "

Fu George looked at him sharply. "None of *that,* Drexler. Ten points for style, remember. Grudge matches aren't good ton."

Drexler snarled again, but didn't insist.

"What I need you to do, Drexler," Fu George said, "is follow him. Pick Roman up outside the ballroom and don't let him go. If we can find Maijstral's blind, we find the Eltdown Shard."

"And then what?"

Fu George looked at him in surprise. "I steal it, of course. If he can steal the Pearl's trinket from me, I can do it back to him."

"What about Gregor?"

"I've got Chalice waiting outside Maijstral's suite. If Gregor appears, Chalice will follow him."

"And Maijstral himself?"

Fu George trimmed a dormant semilife patch with a pair of pocket scissors. "Vanessa will do the shadowing there."

"And you, sir?"

"I'll be working. Have you noticed that the Marchioness changed her jewelry since this afternoon? I doubt she bothered to send her afternoon jewels to the hotel safe, do you?"

Drexler grinned. "I doubt it, sir."

The phone chimed once for attention. "Mr. Gregor Norman," it reported, "wishes to speak to Mr. Chalice or Mr. Drexler."

Interest flared in Fu George's wounded eyes. "Answer," he told Drexler. "Examine the background in the holo figure. Try and work out where he is."

Gregor's location was clear enough once his hologram appeared, obvious from the resonant quality of his voice, a quality that could only have arisen from his standing in the White Room, near the giant impact diamond.

"Mr. Drexler?" he said, grinning. "I think it's time you and Chalice began raising your ten novae."

"That's a little premature, don't you think?"

"The bet concerned who had his hands on it first, and that's already been decided. I won't show you the vids till tomorrow, of course, but I thought I'd give you a day's notice so you could start raising the money."

Drexler bit back the impluse to make a further bet concerning who would get to *keep* the stone—but that would give things away.

"Thank you, Gregor," he said. "I appreciate the consideration."

"Only too." Meaning, only too *very, very* pleased.

Fu George was on his feet the instant the hologram was replaced by the "at your service" ideogram. "Get to Chalice," Fu George said. "Tell him Gregor's in the White Room. I'll head to the White Room directly."

"Sir!"

Fu George took two fast steps toward the door, then hesitated. He returned, seized his box of semilife patches, and then ran like hell.

He met no one in the halls save a pair of robots and the security man Kingston, who had been following him all day. The both of them had been engaged in a daylong pretence that Fu George didn't know he was being followed, a pretence that was strained to the limits as Kingston was forced to sprint after his suspect. Fu George slowed as he entered the White Room, hearing as he walked the peculiar, resonant quality of the diamond as it reflected the orchestra and Kingston's hurried footsteps behind.

He straightened his jacket, shot his lace, and entered the room. Save for the bartender and a pair of serving robots, the orchestra was playing to an empty room.

Fu George turned and left frowning, passing Kingston once again, much to the latter's exasperation. Since the pearl business, all Fu George had done was to react to Maijstral—he had let Maijstral panic him into advancing his attempt to steal the Shard, and now all Fu George could do was follow Maijstral and his people in hopes of finding out something useful. Somehow Fu George had lost all initiative to Maijstral, and that was bad. He had to *do* something, he decided, something that might serve to define the situation and compel events to start moving his way once again.

He'd give Kingston the slip, he decided, then go out and steal something. At least it would make him feel better.

His tread was lighter as he stepped down the hallway. Pity he hadn't been able to intercept Gregor in the White Room.

The White Room. The place hung humming in his memory, resonating like the giant diamond. He realized that it hadn't occurred to him to wonder what Maijstral's chief technician was *doing* in the White Room.

He hesitated, then began to retrace his steps. As he crossed paths with Kingston again, he heard his tail mutter something about why didn't he make up his mind, for heaven's sake? Fu George walked to the bartender and ordered a brightcrisp.

"What time," he asked casually, "do you close tonight?"

The bartender told him. And there was his answer.

Mortification, it seemed, knew no end. Not only was Khamiss, still dressed as a waiter, following Maijstral again, it now appeared that someone was following *her.* She *thought* her tail was Vanessa Runciter, but the woman was still wearing her feathery orange ball costume and Khamiss couldn't be certain.

Maijstral, having been searched once more on leaving the Duchess's ball, was now walking, apparently at random, through the residential quarters of the station, twirling his gun as he moved. Maijstral was obviously up to *something,* but Khamiss couldn't believe the man didn't know he was being shadowed. She hadn't been able to believe in her role for some time, and she couldn't put any feeling into her skulking at all.

She craned around a corner, not bothering to just peek with one eye or try to hide, instead resignedly leaning out in plain view as she watched Maijstral walking up the soft carpet. Maijstral came to a four-way intersection, looked both ways, stepped to his right, hesitated, then abruptly jumped to his left.

Excitement burned in Khamiss. She swept around the corner and accelerated, moving at a run down the corridor, then stopped to peek around the next corner. Maijstral's figure dashed past another intersection, running flat out. Khamiss followed at a dead run.

The collision came too quickly for Khamiss to react. Without warning, a brilliantly costumed figure appeared in her path. The collision flung them to the floor in a tangle of flailing arms and thrashing legs. Khamiss's pistol spilled out of its holster and flew across the carpet.

Khamiss sat up, her head ringing, and looked up into the blazing eyes of Vanessa Runciter. "Idiot!" Vanessa spat. There was a bright scarlet abrasion on her pale cheek. "Can't you do a simple tail job right?"

Rage flared in Khamiss. *"I'm* not the one who's tailing someone while dressed like a big orange bird." Maijstral had *intended* this to happen, Khamiss realized: he'd seen his shadows from the start and doubled back to force them to collide. Khamiss and Vanessa had fallen into a trap.

Khamiss floundered after her pistol. "Didn't your nannybot ever tell you to look both ways?"

"I had a *live* nanny, you imbecile." Vanessa rose to her feet and flung her cape back over her shoulder. She hobbled after one of her shoes, which was lying near Khamiss's pistol.

"Even more reason to listen to her." Khamiss's hand closed on the pistol, and she rammed the bulky object back into her armpit. She picked up Vanessa's shoe and handed it to her.

"Thank you." Said without thought. Vanessa put a tentative hand to her cheek, came away with blood. "I could *kill* you for this," she said, enraged again.

"Just try it." Khamiss stood and drew herself to her full height, a head taller than the human. "Just try it," she repeated, rather liking the sound of the words.

Vanessa glared at her but said nothing. Did these High Custom people fight duels with waiters? Khamiss wondered. She decided to keep the initiative now that she seemed to have it.

"Why were you following Maijstral, anyway?" she said. And then, "Or was it *me* you were following?"

Vanessa decided on a belligerent response. "Who says I was following Maijstral? And who the hell would follow you?"

"You would. It was obvious. You were clumsy enough."

It was *wonderful,* Khamiss was finding, being belligerent to a guest. She should abuse her station more often.

Something caught Khamiss's attention, a movement out of the corner of her eye. She turned and saw a tiny black marble rolling along the ceiling, a little sphere that stayed in the shadows and tried to be inconspicuous.

With a practiced movement, Khamiss drew her service pistol. Vanessa gave a gasp and, assuming she was about to be turned to toasted cheese, clawed for the tiny chugger she carried under her cape. Khamiss lined up the micromedia globe over the sights and squeezed the trigger. Flame burst from the ceiling. The globe ran for cover. More fire leaped out, and the globe fell, rolled, and died.

Fire alarms wailed. Robot arms appeared from the service corridor and began spraying foam. Khamiss rather enjoyed the spectacle.

Being aggressive was so *satisfying,* she thought.

Vanessa finally got her gun out. She pointed it in at least three directions before she realized she was in no danger.

Khamiss ignored the foam that spattered her waiter's costume. She holstered her spitfire, and walked to the charred micromedia globe. She picked up the globe and let it roll in her hand. She turned to Vanessa.

"Yours?"

Vanessa, clutching her pistol, shook her head. Foam speckled her hair. She put her pistol back in its holster. She reached for her cigaret holder and a pack of Silvertips.

"Who was the operator trying to follow?" Khamiss wondered. "Maijstral? You? Me?"

"Who cares? *We've* lost him, that's the main point." Vanessa lit a Silvertip.

A robot fire fighter promptly covered her face with foam.

Five . . . Four . . . Three . . .

Baroness Silverside was growing larger in the view of Gregor's skulking micromedia marble.

Two . . . One . . . Now.

Gregor stepped briskly around the corner and walked deliberately into the Baroness.

"Beg pardon, madam."

The Baroness looked at him with irritation. "Be careful, young man," she said.

As Gregor walked away, he whistled his micromedia globe from the ceiling. He ordered it into his inside coat pocket, next to the glory that was the Eltdown Shard.

"It's after midnight, Sun."

"Yes, my lord."

"You have not recovered my wife's collection."

Sun gazed bleakly into a future that held no place for him. A sinner, he thought, in the hands of an angry god. Dangling over the candle flame like a spider, all for his own unperceived fault.

"Alas, my lord," he said.

Baron Silverside looked upon him with the face of the Angel of Judgement. "You will pay for this, Sun."

Sun acceded to the inevitable. "I know, my lord," he said. He suspected he would never cease paying.

The Duchess of Benn exchanged condolences with Baron Silverside, then let Kotani drag the Baron away for another conference. The orchestra members, instruments dangling from their hands, were making their way out by another entrance. Roberta looked at her last remaining guest, Paavo Kuusinen. He bowed over her hand as he clasped it: one finger, as was proper.

"Congratulations, your grace," he said. "You've achieved your object. A sensational debut."

"Thank you, Mr. Kuusinen. I couldn't have done it without your help."

"You are far too gracious." He glanced at the last of the musicians as they filed out to the waiting security watsons, who were frisking them in a final hope of locating the Shard. "I wonder how he got it out?" he asked.

"We'll have to wait for the videos to come out. Six months or so."

"Yes, your grace. I suppose we'll have to contain our curiosity till then." He frowned as he glanced up at Rathbon's Star, its astonishing display revealed once again now that Silverside personnel had removed Gregor's overrides.

"I hope the second part of your grace's plan goes as smoothly as the first," he said.

"Do you think it might not?"

"I suspect complications. There are . . . undercurrents."

Countess Ankh's artificial ears tilted forward in curiosity. "Do you think Geoff Fu George might interfere?"

"He might, particularly if he thought his position as top-ranked thief was in danger. He lost a number of style points when your grace knocked him down; that might even put his rating in danger." He glanced over the empty ballroom. "But I think there's something else going on. I don't know whether it concerns us or not; but it would be well to be cautious."

"You pique my curiosity, Kuusinen."

"I would prefer not to speculate until I have further information." He glanced over the ballroom. "Shall I escort you to your room?"

"That would be pleasant. Please take my arm."

"Ever your servant, your grace."

Drake Maijstral, still clothed as a bank robber, folded the Marchioness Kotani in his arms and kissed her. His pulse sped; his knees grew weak. His mind was racing.

Maijstral was trying to calculate his chances of getting killed. The Marquess, he knew, was a very good shot. But the Marchioness had assured him Kotani would be spending the night harassing Baron Silverside; in any case the two had separate rooms, and the chance of discovery was therefore slight.

It wasn't as if he hadn't earned this, after all. How often did one commit the crime of the century right in the middle of a public function and get away with it? Maybe, for a single night at least, one could get away with anything.

He decided to take the risk.

Still, it was not passion for the Marchioness that made his heart throb and turned his knees watery—rather, the thought of a pistol with Kotani at one end of it and himself at the other.

The kiss ended. The Marchioness gazed up at him with glowing eyes. "I'll call a robot for you," she said, and brushed his cheek with the back of her hand. She touched the service plate and cast a look over her shoulder. "My rover," she said, and stepped into her dressing room. The dressing room door closed. The robot bustled out of a closet and unlaced Maijstral's jacket and trousers.

Maijstral dismissed the robot, sat on the bed, and pulled off his boots. "Fu George," he said, "I think this is your moment to leave."

An annoyed grunt came from beneath the bed.

"And kindly replace anything you stole," Maijstral went on. "Otherwise her ladyship will think I took it."

"Damn it, Maijstral," Fu George said as he rolled out of hiding. "You owe me something for this."

"Something, agreed," Maijstral said. "Not the Shard. The Shard is more than just something."

"Did I *ask* for the blasted Shard?"

Fu George's darksuit made his outlines uncertain, but the Marchioness's jewels, falling from the vagueness of Fu George's hand into the open jewel case, were clear. Maijstral rose from the bed to let Fu George out. Fu George turned.

"You're going to stay here for the night, are you?" he asked. "I wouldn't want to run into you again."

"I'm not planning on breaking into any rooms tonight, if that's what you want to know." Which was true to the letter, Maijstral reflected, if not quite to the spirit of Fu George's question.

"Your servant."

"Thank you, Fu George. You've been very decent. I hope you get style points out of this, at least."

"Your very obedient. And hasty." The shape rose on a-grav repellers and fled down the corridor.

Maijstral closed the door and stepped into the bedroom again just as the Marchioness entered from her dressing room. She wore a mothwing nightgown. Dark gemstones dangled from her ears and brushed against her neck. Her pouting mouth was drawn in a smile.

"Was someone here?" she asked.

"No one of consequence," Maijstral said, and dismissed Fu George, like her husband, from his mind.

"Thank you, Zoot. It's been the most delightful evening I've spent since . . ." Her ears fluttered helplessly. "Since I was condemned to Zynzlyp." She and Zoot stopped at her door.

"It has been entirely my pleasure, my lady. It's the greatest pity the evening must come to an end."

Lady Dosvidern looked at him with burning eyes. "It need not, you know," she said.

Zoot's heart boomed like a gong.

"Oh," he said. "Do you think so?"

"Yes. I think so," she confirmed, and lovingly closed her canines on one of his ears.

Eight silver media globes circled in a perfect halo over Kyoko Asperson's bed. Gregor kissed her and reached for his trousers.

"Time for bed check, lover," he said.

Kyoko sat up. "I didn't realize Maijstral ran such a tight ship."

"Sorry. Burglar's hours and all that. The boss might need me for something or other." Pulling on his pants.

"Can you come by later?"

"It would have to be *very* later."

She cocked her head. "I'll be here all morning. I can't sleep *too* late, because Baron Silverside gave me an interview with the head of security here—" She laughed at Gregor's sudden tigerish grin. "An interview about all the chaos you've been causing."

"What time is the interview?"

"Noonish. Why do you ask?"

A knowing smile. "Nothing."

"Come on." Coaxing.

"Forget I said anything."

"You can tell *me.*"

"Not yet I can't. I'd like to see the man sweat, though."

"Speaking of *sweating* . . ." She reached to the bedside table for her loupe and stuck it in her eye. One of the media globes detached itself from its circuit and hovered in front of Gregor.

"Tell me, Mr. Norman," she said, "what's a noted burglar like yourself doing in this shocking state of undress, here in someone else's room?"

Gregor looked wide-eyed at the media globe and gasped in feigned surprise. "I'm afraid I've been the victim of a crime, Miss Asperson. A terrible crime."

"Yes?" Kyoko leaned forward intently. "And what might that be?"

Gregor leaned forward himself till their noses were almost touching. "Someone robbed me of my affections, that's what."

Kyoko grinned and kissed him. "G'night, sad victim that you are."

"Goodnight, thief."

He reached for his boots.

The White Room burned red in the nighttime, illuminated only by Rathbon's Star. Stark black shadows lay with precise knife edges on the soft blood-red carpet. Above, the impact diamond rang faintly with echoes of distant life.

Ghosts moved in the ruddy light. Nearly invisible, their shadows danced on the carpet, flickered on the walls, played tag with the rainbows cast by the giant diamond.

The ghost dance was witnessed by two people, each viewing the action via separate media globes set high in a place of vantage.

At the sight of the ghosts and their purposeful dance, the onlookers smiled.

Advert looked at the treasure in her hand and her fingers trembled as a wave of terror passed through her. Panic churned in her mind. Her fingers clamped shut. Moving as silently as she could, she stepped from Pearl Woman's bedroom into the front room of their suite.

Once in the front room she whispered for a spotlight and opened her hand. Her treasure seemed insignificant in her pink palm: a pearl, a length of minute chain, an ear-clasp.

She looked at the thing and experienced a wave of giddiness. She felt as she had when she was ten years old, and successfully evaded her nannybot to meet with her friends at midnight in the Haunted Pavilion.

She realized she was enjoying herself. She closed her fist around the treasure and performed a brief, giddy dance.

Serve her *right,* she thought.

"Did you really get the Eltdown Shard?"

"Perhaps." Maijstral reached for the bottle of champagne that a Cygnus robot had just delivered to the room.

"I'd like to see it."

"That might be possible. After tomorrow midnight, of course."

Her fingers lazily brushed the skin of her throat. Her tilted eyes challenged him. "I'd like to *wear* it."

He smiled as he poured the champagne. "I think it could be arranged. Assuming I've got it, of course."

"Of course." Crystal rang as the glasses touched. Maijstral raised his glass to his lips. A knock thundered on the door.

There was a practiced blur of motion. Moving swiftly and in perfect silence, Maijstral left the bed, scooped up his clothes, flung them through the open closet door, picked up his riding boots, sword, and gunbelt, and then loped for the closet, the champagne glass still in his hand. The Marchioness watched him through laughing eyes.

"Darling?" Kotani's voice, speaking Khosali Standard. "Why is your door locked?"

Maijstral turned in the closet, surveyed the room for signs of his presence, found none, and sotto voce told the closet door to shut as he glided backward, obscuring himself behind the Marchioness's clothing.

"I cannot close the door," the closet said, speaking Human Standard, as Maijstral had. "My sensors inform me there is a person inside."

The Marchioness glanced in apprehension at the closet, then at the door that was keeping her husband at bay. "What time is it, dear?" she called.

"I *am* the person inside," Maijstral explained, trying to keep his voice to a whisper. "Shut the door, please." His heart crashed in his ears as the closet's idiot brain considered the problem. Blackness ringed his vision, narrowing it. He appeared to be gazing at the world through the barrel of a gun. I am *not* going to faint, he told himself. He downed the champagne as a restorative.

"Five," said Kotani, "or thereabouts. Did I wake you?"

"I was dozing," said the Marchioness. She was looking more and more alarmed as she perceived the closet's stubbornness. She rose from the bed and donned her mothwing gown.

"Great news!" called Kotani. "Open the door. I want to tell you."

"Just a moment," said the Marchioness. She stepped into her changing room. Maijstral seized the closet door and tried to haul it shut.

"Do not attempt to close the doors manually," the closet said. "Damage to the mechanism may result."

"Then *shut the door,*" Maijstral whispered. If he had his burglar's tools with him, this wouldn't have been a problem.

"There is a person inside the closet." Happy to get back on track again. "I cannot shut the door with a person inside. Please leave the closet."

Maijstral could feel beads of sweat gathering on his scalp. Terror yowled blindly in his brain. He gave the closet door a final despairing yank. The closet door yanked back. He thought about letting himself out the other door into the corridor, the exit used by Fu George, but decided against it. A man standing unclothed in the hallway might become subject to unfortunate amounts of attention. Not to mention derision.

"Do not close the door manually," the closet said again. "Damage to the mechanism may result."

"Why have you locked the door?" Kotani asked. His tone was growing suspicious.

The Marchioness reappeared, looking desperate. She had a spray bottle of scent in her hand, and she perfumed herself wildly as she searched her mind for an answer.

"I'm afraid of burglars," she said. "I have my jewelry here."

The door rattled from within as Kotani tried the knob. "I *told* you," condescendingly, "to keep your jewels in the station safe."

"I'm sorry, dear." Her eyes implored Maijstral to *do* something. Maijstral, in the last seconds before his vision faded away entirely, glanced desperately for another hiding place, recalled where he had found Fu George, and dived for the bed. As he rolled beneath it he heard the closet door slide triumphantly shut. The air was drenched with perfume. The Marchioness unlocked the door.

"Would you like some champagne?" she said, a bit breathlessly.

Kotani stepped in. "A nightcap would be pleasant," he said. "I've just struck a deal with Silverside."

"Congratulations, dearest. Would you fetch a glass from the other room?"

"A better deal than I expected, my only," Kotani crowed as Maijstral heard his footsteps leave the room. "In view of his problems with security here, the fact they'll be highly publicized, and the damage to his custom that could result, he conceded any percentage of gross revenues in hopes my play will contribute to restoring any of the station's lost ton. He's got a profit percentage only. I think the poor fellow was so down he was prepared to concede anything."

"Splendid, dear." Kotani's footsteps returned. Maijstral, over the demon pulse of his heart, heard champagne being poured, then the sound of a sneeze.

"Allergic to champagne, my dear?"

"Not at all, Janetha-my-dove. Your scent is exquisite, but you seem to have applied it a little generously this evening."

"I wanted to smell good for you."

"A charming and considerate thought, dearest. But it is a bit . . . overwhelming." He sneezed again.

"Shall we step into the other room? Perhaps a little fresh air might help."

"An excellent suggestion, my heart."

Good grief, thought Maijstral. Kotani's conversation in private was just like those in his plays. No wonder the Marchioness was getting restless. Who wants to live with someone who's a paragon of courtesy and sophistication even when sneezing?

The door closed behind them. Maijstral let a long breath out. Moving in trained silence, he rolled from under the bed and, in as low a voice as possible, asked the closet door to open. The moronic mechanism was happy to oblige. Maijstral drew his belongings into his arms and decided that he wasn't about to take a chance of Kotani walking in on him half-dressed. Therefore he rolled under the bed again and began dragging on his clothes. On his way to Dolfuss's room he'd be walking unlaced—no trained bots-of-the-wardrobe available in the corridor—but that would be far less conspicuous than wearing nothing at all.

There wasn't much clearance under the bed, but Maijstral was agile: he was performing the last operation, shrugging into his jacket, when the door to the front room opened again. Maijstral's heart leaped into his throat. He froze.

The door closed. Lady Janetha's plump, pretty feet appeared beside the bed. "Maijstral?" A whisper. "Are you still there?"

"My lady." He worked his way to the edge of the bed and stuck his head out.

"I wanted to say goodnight to you properly." She knelt and kissed him. Maijstral, almost smothered by her perfume, managed to give a convincing imitation of passion while keeping one eye cocked on the inner door.

"Don't forget," she said. "I'd like to feel the Shard against my skin."

"Tomorrow night," Maijstral promised. He could use Dolfuss's room for the assignation: no sense in taking ridiculous chances again.

"I wager you've done this sort of thing before. Your leap into the closet was a thing of beauty. You were hiding before I even had the chance to blink."

He appraised her. "I suspect you're not new to this, either. The trick with the perfume was a good one."

He rolled out from beneath the bed and hitched his trousers up. The Marchioness brushed her lips against his, took the champagne bottle, and stepped through the door with a careless laugh.

Maijstral knotted his trouser-laces, tugged his jacket close around him, and stepped out the other exit into the hallway. He yawned. There was one more thing he must do, and then sleep.

* * *

"Ah. He's making his move. You see?"

"Just like we thought, boss."

"Brilliant, my dear." The sound of a kiss. "We've got him where we want him."

Geoff Fu George smiled, brushed his lips over Vanessa Runciter's knuckles, and turned back to the video. The picture was blurred. It looked like a double exposure.

In the center was the giant impact diamond, picked out in the darkened White Room by spotlights. But right next to it was another, identical diamond, with straps around it and a blurring about its rim. The second diamond was moving, dropping downward.

"Follow that, Drexler," Fu George said.

"Yes, sir."

"Prepare to send the globe on its way. Don't get too close, now."

"Sir."

Fu George gave a cold, deliberate laugh. His eyes glowed as he looked at the screen. "A lovely decoy that Maijstral's made. With a holographic image of the diamond hanging there, no one will even know it's missing."

The diamond sailed to the floor in its a-grav harness, then disappeared into a laundry cart. Sheets and blankets moved to cover it.

"He'll snap off the hologram at some suitably dramatic moment," Vanessa said. "With hundreds of people in the room, no doubt, to be fooled into thinking he somehow made the diamond vanish in front of their eyes."

"More style points that way."

"He thinks like a conjurer, boss," said Chalice.

"I'm moving the globe, sir," Drexler said. The point of view began to shift as the globe followed the cart, which was rolling, apparently under its own power, out of the room.

"Leading us right to the Shard," Chalice said. He gave a barking laugh. "This is great, boss. Almost worth losing ten novae for."

"Ten novae?" Fu George asked, distracted.

Vanessa's eyes glittered. She put her hands on Fu George's shoulders. "When will you take Maijstral's loot, dear?"

"Ah." Forgetting the ten novae. "That will depend, lover. We'll have to see if the room is guarded. It would be best to wait till the place is vacant."

"Pity you can't just turn Maijstral and his friends into stripped electrons."

Fu George patted her hand. "Now, now. No style points for violence."

Vanessa's mouth tightened. She touched the semilife patch on her cheek and eye, where Khamiss's elbow had bruised her. "More's the pity, Fu George," she said. "More's the pity."

As Maijstral, a mere blur in his darksuit, pushed the laundry cart down the corridor, Drexler's media globe followed cautiously behind. Drexler knew that Maijstral's darksuit contained detectors that might spot the motion of his globe: he kept his distance, and crept around corners with caution. He had no need to keep close, fortunately; the laundry cart was a large target. Drexler was entirely pleased with himself.

He might have been less pleased had he known that he, himself, was being followed.

Behind Drexler's globe came another, one that moved cautiously, keeping Drexler's dark sphere just in sight . . . following Drexler's globe, which was following Maijstral, who was moving at all deliberate speed to his hideout.

The second globe's operator was *very* pleased. And happily making plans for the morrow.

Dolfuss held open the door of his room as Maijstral pushed the laundry cart inside. As Dolfuss closed the door behind him, Maijstral turned off his holographic camouflage, stripped the darksuit's hood from his head, and shook out his long hair.

"Things went well, sir?" Dolfuss inquired.

"Very well indeed." Maijstral picked up the sixteen-foot impact diamond—in its harness, it was weightless. He frowned for a moment, then moved toward the closet.

"Full of art, I'm afraid," Dolfuss said.

"Well." Maijstral set the diamond down. "I suppose it will have to stand in the corner."

"Best not take any more bulky loot, sir."

Maijstral took off his signature ring, which he wore over his suit gloves, and began to peel off the darksuit. "I intend to take no more loot at all," he said. "A wise thief quits while he's ahead."

"I'd say you have reason enough to be pleased." Dolfuss reached for the Eltdown Shard, which had been tossed rather carelessly on the bureau top. The dark stone glowed softly in his hand.

"Pity I couldn't have watched you take it," he said. "But boors—even phony boors—don't get invited to the more exclusive parties. I spent the evening watching an old vid. *Prince of Tyre,* by Shaxberd. What a piece of rubbish."

"I like much of his other work." Maijstral cocked an eye at the actor. "The *Llyr* might suit you. You're old enough for the part."

"Too depressing. Satire's more my style."

"It dates rather more quickly than other sorts of comedy, however."

"True, sir. But while it lasts, it has more bite."

"I've subscribed to Aristide's translations. *Comedy of Errors* is the next."

"Farce. Even worse. It's so low."

"Taking the last few days into account, it does seem more true to life."

"Precisely my point, sir. If you take my meaning."

Maijstral reached for his dressing gown. "Literary debates later, I think. For now, I want only bath and bed."

"I'll get out of your way, then," said Dolfuss.

"Would you mind taking the cart with you, Mr. Dolfuss? Just leave it somewhere."

"As you like, sir." But he hesitated, frowning at the Shard in his hand. "Do you think, Mr. Maijstral, that the Shard is worth all the fuss? All the lives?"

Maijstral gave a self-satisfied laugh. "It's not worth *my* life, at any rate."

Dolfuss smiled. "As you say." He put the stone on the bureau and stepped toward the door. "Have a pleasant night, sir."

"I'm sure I will. And you."

"Your servant."

Dolfuss pushed the cart out of the room. Maijstral told the room lights to grow dimmer, and then told the room to ready his bath. The sound of running water came from the bathroom.

Maijstral looked at his Grat Dalton costume, now tossed on a chair, and smiled. Even the Dalton Brothers had never pulled off a string of robberies as glorious as this one.

Like Drexler, like Fu George, like the operator of the second globe, he was very pleased with himself.

Elsewhere in the night, unobserved by anyone, magic was happening. Wrapped in dark cloth, discarded in a corner of a room, a pair of objects were transforming themselves. Cold fire ran over their surfaces: burning red, cold violet, electric green . . . shimmering, iridescent, and wonderful.

Silent. Unseen. Entirely unanticipated.

NINE

"Miss Asperson? Kyoko?" Gregor rapped on the door. There was no answer. Must be a sound sleeper, he thought. He reached into his pocket for a touchwire, snapped off the lock, then entered Kyoko's room.

"Kyoko?"

The room was empty. Six abandoned media globes circled the bed like moons bereft of their primary. The vidset was on.

The vidset was repeating, over and over, all known biographical data on Mr. Sun, Silverside's head of security. Gregor watched for a few minutes, learned nothing of any significance, and shrugged and left the room. Kyoko must have been studying for her interview. Poor Mr. Sun, Gregor thought, and grinned.

Too bad he'd lost his affections to such an early riser.

Sex and death have an unfortunate association in the Khosali mind. Every child of the Empire is brought up on tales of the disgraced Madame Phone and the spectacular suicide of her lover Baron Khale, whose internal organs were, as specified in his will, preserved and set up in a monument as a warning to future generations.

Studies by curious anthropologists have shown that the Khosali sex drive is at least as strong as the human; yet it remains a fact that adultery among Khosali is fairly rare, and though many Khosali do not marry till late in life, they manage to remain fairly chaste during bachelorhood. Adultery and fornication are often accompanied by elaborate displays of anguish and torment that must, in the words of Mad Julius (a human wit and debauchee), be at least as much fun as the act itself. (After making this remark poor Julius was banned from the City of Seven Bright Rings by an emperor who was himself a bit prickly on the subject of adultery, having been tormented throughout his life by a vain and perfectly chaste devotion to the wife of one of his ministers. Khosali emperors are only rarely known for appreciating jokes they suspect might be aimed at them.)

Human sexual attitudes and behaviors have continually proven a scandal (and a fascination) to the Khosali, and have contributed unfortunately to the frivolous stereotype with which the Khosali view humanity. If the humans can't be serious about sex, the Khosali wonder, what *can* they be serious about?

The fact remains, however, that only rarely does a human caught in adultery have the decency to slaughter himself in rightful atonement. For a Khosalikh caught in the wrong bed, a last regretful note (to be published afterward), a pistol, and a final cry of long life to the Emperor are often the only proper recourse. Retreating to the cloister, devoting a fortune to charity, or spontaneous enlistment in the Emperor's service are also popular. The point is that atonement should be seen to happen. One is not permitted the social luxury of private regret.

Flouting conventional Khosali taste is the Human Diadem, whose affaires are often broadcast before their audience of billions. That many of these billions consist of fascinated Khosali is, no doubt, a manifestation of Khosali, as well as human, perversity.

A Khosali in love is often a Khosali in torment, anguished and tortured, with High Custom gazing balefully over one shoulder and the Grim Reaper over the other. This is only decent. One cannot help but contrast the unfortunate behavior of Maijstral, who not only enjoyed himself with another's spouse but declined to feel sorry afterward; and who, if caught, wouldn't have slain himself, but would if possible have avoided death altogether (or at least made Kotani do it for him); and who (conclusive evidence of his froward nature) had the unmitigated gall to sleep soundly upon returning to his own room. His conscience should at least have made him thrash the mattress a little.

No wonder humanity proved ungovernable. One only wonders how they govern themselves.

A Cygnus robot scuttled into the hallway, its dignity upset by a kick that almost knocked it off its repellers. *"Where is it?"* Pearl Woman's tone mingled rage with incredulity. There were soft thuds as pillows and bedding hit the wall. Advert, her heart thumping, stepped from her dressing room and, with effort, gave Pearl Woman a soothing smile.

"Perhaps you left it in another room."

"I remember very distinctly where I left it." Pearl Woman's voice was edged with menace. She limped across the room—booting the robot had re-strained her leg muscle—and reached for one of her matched cutlasses. She drew it and the cutlass sliced air in accompaniment to her thoughts. "I can't *believe* Fu George or Maijstral went after it *again,"* she said. Slice. "That would be so . . ." Slice. "Redundant."

"Perhaps it was a different one, this time. I mean the *other* one, the one who didn't take it last time. Possibly he did it to show up the other one. Whichever that was."

The Pearl's trademark was in one of Advert's inner pockets. She fancied she could feel it against her skin, a burning weight. Her excitement made her giggle.

Pearl Woman fixed her with a look. "What's so funny?"

Advert laughed again. "I was just thinking. Maybe I could hire the other one to get it back. Like last time."

The Pearl snarled. "I'll do it myself, thank you." The cutlass whirled over her head, cut air as it diced an imaginary enemy. "I'll do it *my* way." The cutlass flew through the air, sliced an innocent korni bloom above a rare matched Basil vase, and buried its point in the wall.

"But Pearl." Advert, to her rising pleasure, was finding this deception easier by the minute. "You can't leave the room, not without your trademark. Kyoko Asperson might notice it's gone."

A growl came from Pearl Woman's throat. The other cutlass snicked from the scabbard and flashed through the air like silver lightning. Pearl Woman lunged, then grimaced and clutched her thigh. The muscle had betrayed her again. She flung the cutlass across the room, and another innocent korni bud died. The second vase trembled but did not fall.

"Very well, Advert," she growled. "You're right, I can't risk it.

Just go out and make yourself visible. Perhaps someone will approach you."

Advert's heart leaped. "You'll get your pearl back," she said, "if I have anything to say about it."

She turned and left the room, her feet so light she felt as if she were dancing.

Vanessa Runciter put her feet into her semilife boots and felt them roll up her ankles, calves, and thighs. She bent down, smoothed the dark proughskin with her hands, and asked the Cygnus for her matching jacket.

"Geoff," she said, "shall we find breakfast? We haven't tried Lebaron's yet."

Fu George appeared from the bathroom, still in his dressing gown. Gorged semilife patches surrounded his eyes. "I really don't feel like appearing in public, Vanessa," he said. "Let's have Lebaron's bring our breakfast here."

The robot began lacing Vanessa into her jacket. She reached for her cigaret holder—ebony with a matching proughskin band—and inserted a Silvertip. "If we're going to steal Maijstral's treasure trove," she said, "we shouldn't do it on an empty stomach."

Over the years Fu George had grown used to the gratuitous *we*. "There's no hurry. Maijstral won't be rising early. I doubt he'll make an appearance before sixteen."

Vanessa flicked her proughskin lighter. "Why sixteen, Geoff?"

"According to the station bulletin, that's when he's doing his magic act in the White Room."

The light hesitated halfway to the Silvertip. "Ah," she said.

"Quite so. His friends won't miss his performance, so his loot probably won't be guarded. That's when we do the job." He peered at her from between the swollen patches. "I'd like you to be in the lounge for the show. Advance lookout, if you like. I'm sure Maijstral's laid traps protecting his stash, so I'll need both Chalice and Drexler."

"Sixteen. So that's when we do the job?"

Nodding. "That's when we do it." That *we,* it appears, was catching.

Drake Maijstral, drowsing, rolled over and bunched the pillow under his head. His hand touched the alarmed box wherein he'd hidden the Eltdown Shard. Still half asleep, he smiled, and fell into a dream in which, a mysterious masked figure in black, he appeared before the

Dalton Brothers as they rode into Coffeyville, and warned them away, telling them of a fabulous gem in the next town, ready for the picking.

"Miss Asperson. You're up early."

"I'm an early riser, Miss Advert. And I have an interview in a few minutes." Smiling. "You seem in high spirits. You're practically skipping down the hall."

"I'm on a secret mission."

"You don't say." The media globes performed a subtle change of position. "May I inquire as to its nature?"

"I doubt I can trust you with secrets." Advert's rings glittered as she wrung her hands in make-believe indecision. "Besides, it's not my secret. It's Pearl Woman's."

"Surely it can't be all that bad."

"But it is!" Glee bubbled in Advert like fine champagne. *Let* everyone think her scatterbrained—*she* knew better.

"Pearl Woman had her pearl stolen last night," Advert said. "She doesn't dare go out in public without it. I'm supposed to ransom it quietly and get it back before anyone notices."

Kyoko gave her a surprised look. "If this is such a secret, Miss Advert, why are you telling me?"

"Well, really, Kyoko—why should Pearl *care?* It's just an earring, after all."

Advert was beginning to realize how much fun people like Geoff Fu George and Drake Maijstral must have had, what with their opportunities to masquerade so often as someone they weren't.

"It's her Diadem trademark," Kyoko said. "She's never seen without it."

"I've seen her without it. Most of her friends have, I imagine. I think it's silly to invest so much meaning in a little trinket, don't you? Just because the public expects it?" She smiled. "That sort of thing can become a trap, can't it?"

"I suppose so."

"A trap," Advert repeated happily. A trap into which she'd just dropped Pearl Woman, and serve her right.

"One shouldn't become so dependent on the material aspect of existence," Advert said. "That's what Pearl Woman's always told *me."*

"Thanks for the chat, Miss Advert. I wish you luck on your mission."

"Thanks, Kyoko. I'm sure it'll go all right." *Right as Robbler,* she thought, and went skipping toward the White Room, wondering in whom else to confide.

Paavo Kuusinen had risen early. He hadn't slept much, as his mind, like a tongue unable to leave off prodding the site of a missing tooth, had been unable to cease working on a problem. He ate breakfast in his room and then set off on a private quest of his own. When last observed, he thought, she'd gone *this* way.

It took him some time, but he knew approximately what he was looking for, and with persistence he found it. A hammock, a cache, a disabled alarm.

Good, he thought as he stepped toward his quarters. Now maybe he could stop *worrying* about it.

Mr. Sun had neither eaten nor slept. He felt completely numb: he had been unable to summon the energy even to leave his control room, the azure, murmuring scene of his martyrdom. Transfixed by the awesome spectacle of his own downfall, he was unable even to rouse himself to Kyoko Asperson's first knock. He opened his door to her second rap.

"Mr. Sun. I hope you are well this morning." There was a brilliant smile on Kyoko Asperson's round face. Sun couldn't stop staring at it. She looked, he thought, like a daffle gazing at a prough, preparing herself to spring and rend it limb from limb. He couldn't remember having seen a more sinister expression in his life.

"Miss Asperson. Please come in."

He retreated deeper into his whispering blue heaven. Silver globes pursued him, diving gaily into the room's corners, swooping irreverently over the console like a flock of frivolous birds. Kyoko, her horrible smile still brightening her features, stepped into the control room and perched on the edge of the console.

The room was very quiet. Sun had disconnected the alarms: nothing would interrupt this inquisition.

He had been judged and found wanting.

His time of atonement was nigh.

Diamond studs winked at collar and jacket front. "I hope you can amuse yourself while I nail down my agreement with the Baron."

"I expect I'll visit the White Room and watch Maijstral's performance."

A sniff. "Trickery and illusion. One can do anything with holograms these days." Kotani's ears went back. "Still, dearest, one may attend such an event simply to be seen."

"I don't know, my love. From time to time, a little trickery can add spice to life."

Kotani gave her a look. "You really are turning cryptic, dearest."

"I assure you," putting her arm through his, "that in future I'll be very, very careful."

Zoot, pulling his costume about him, stepped from hiding in Lady Dosvidern's bathroom only after the Cygnus had left. He didn't want even the robot to know he'd spent the night here. Lady Dosvidern smiled at him from over a stack of waffles. "Honey?" she asked. "Or renbroke?"

"Renbroke. Thank you." He took his pistol from the table, put it in its holster, and seated himself at the breakfast table. The tablecloth was dark red, setting off the silver jugs filled with coffee, tea, and hot rink. His splendid breakfast lay on Brightring tableware. ("By appt. to His Serenity," etc.) He was eating as well as the Emperor, he reflected—or at least as well as the Emperor *had* eaten, before he'd lost the Rebellion, molted, and retired to his cold box. In which case, Zoot concluded, he was eating *better* than the Emperor—and in better company.

Lady Dosvidern reached across the table and took his hand. Adorably she licked honey from her nose. He cocked his ears forward and smiled at her. Sunshine filled his heart.

"Will you marry me?" he asked.

Her ears flickered in surprise. She stared at him. "Didn't you know, dearest?"

"Know what?"

"I'm already married." She licked a bit of waffle from her fork. "To Lord Qlp, in fact."

Zoot gazed at her blankly.

"It's not *much* of a marriage," Lady Dosvidern said, offhand. "Lord Qlp only has a masculine title for sake of convenience, since it's married to a female. I'm not sure what sex it is, truth to tell, and I doubt it realized what marriage is, anyway. So I'm *almost* free. And the title comes with the arrangement, and a nice pension, so I don't mind, really."

Zoot reached for a cup of coffee, missed, tried again, and spilled half of it lifting the cup to his muzzle. Interspecies marriages were very rare, almost universally frowned upon, and generally based on motives either mercenary or . . . the last, Zoot decided firmly, did not bear thinking about.

"I'm . . . surprised," Zoot managed to say. Hot coffee burned his tongue.

"Travelling with *one* Drawmiikh, believe me, is far better than being stuck on a planet absolutely *teeming* with the creatures." She smiled. Her fingers caressed his arm. "Its lordship is usually very quiet, you know. It travels wherever I suggest. Perhaps you and I can arrange a mutual agenda."

"Perhaps." Zoot felt a bit feverish. He put down the coffee cup. Lady Dosvidern laughed.

"You look so *shocked,*" she said. "And you a member of the Diadem!"

Zoot was seeking a reply to this when the inner door burst open. Zoot leaped to his feet. His nostrils were assaulted by an appalling stench as Lord Qlp entered. Its body convulsed in agitation. Lady Dosvidern ran for her translation stud.

"Alarm!" its lordship said, bubbling in barely understandable Khosali. "Astonishment!"

Zoot's soul wailed. "I believe I can explain, my lord," he said quickly. "It's all my fault."

Lord Qlp thrashed about as if in pain. Its eyestalks whipped in all directions, glaring. "Interference!" it howled.

"I see that you have reason to be upset, my lord," Zoot said. "But appearances can be deceiving, and I . . ."

Lord Qlp reared on its hindquarters, boomed loudly in its own language, then lowered itself to the floor and skated away with remarkable speed. Zoot took a hesitant step after it.

"My lord," he said. "I, ah . . ."

Lady Dosvidern gripped his wrist. "I've never seen it this upset. I've got to be with it."

An agony of distress clawed at Zoot's mind. He'd destroyed Lady Dosvidern's reputation, her marriage, her hopes of happiness. "I understand," he said. Lady Dosvidern ran for the closet and her clothes, shouting at the service plate to send her a wardrobe-bot.

Horrible, Zoot thought, horrible. However could he atone?

Khamiss slumbered on. Her feet, semilife patches decorating the blisters, were propped on pillows. Her gun hung from a peg in a closet.

Her waiter's jacket, the left armpit torn, lay on the floor. Degree

Absolute had been cancelled. Khamiss was taking full advantage of it.

Maijstral, as the robot tightened his laces, watched with one eye a play on the station vid. An old-fashioned farce, the current scene featured milord's mistress, dressed as a maid, hiding behind the Montiyy screen in the corner, while milord's daughter and her suitor were beneath under the bed. Milady's current lover was in the closet, and the Marine captain who hoped to be her next was smothering in a trunk. A private detective swung madly in the chandelier, taking notes.

In a firm voice, Maijstral told the vid to turn itself off. It was one thing for one's life to threaten to turn into farce, he thought; it was quite another for an impertinent video play to remind one of the fact.

His head swimming, Zoot allowed Lady Dosvidern's robot to lace up his suit. He was feeling slightly ill. *Apprehended!* he thought. *Doomed!* Lord Qlp had rushed out without paying attention to his protestations, and Lady Dosvidern, as soon as she was decently clothed, had followed. Zoot had not only compromised a lady; he'd compromised a diplomatic mission. The consequences could be nothing short of hideous.

He lurched into the corridor. Something glanced off his forehead and he stumbled forward, almost knocking Kyoko Asperson to the floor. He reached out a hand to steady her while another careless media globe banged off his skull.

"I'm terribly sorry, Miss Asperson," he said. "I wasn't looking where I was going. Please forgive me."

Kyoko looked up at him while her media globes moved into assault formation. Her ears cocked forward. "You seem distracted, sir," she said.

"I'm truly sorry. An unforgivable lapse."

"Ah." Her silver loupe gazed at him like the blank eye of doom. "I forgive your lack of attention, Zoot. Lady Dosvidern is, no doubt, a distracting individual."

Zoot started, guilty memories flooding his brain. He drew himself up. "Lady Dosvidern?" he said. The words came out a yelp, and he cleared his throat and lowered his voice. "Whatever do you mean?"

Kyoko gave a disbelieving grin. "You're leaving her suite after noon, there's a breakfast cart set for two here in the corridor, and you're still dressed for last night's ball. Forgive me for making the assumption that she's been entertaining you for the last ten or twelve hours."

Horror crystallized in Zoot's mind. Everything was becoming *public.* He had to retrieve the situation somehow; he owed Lady Dosvidern that, at least. "Yes," he said, and forced a grin. "Lady Dosvidern's company, and that of her husband, was most stim—most *entertaining.* I confess I entirely lost track of the time."

"Lady Dosvidern's husband?" Kyoko's eyes barely concealed their rapture.

"Yes." He flicked his ears to indicate puzzlement. "You didn't know?" His facial muscles, he realized, were betraying him, producing odd tics and quiverings that he was finding impossible to squelch on command.

"I'm afraid that information escaped my researchers. She's married to Lord Qlp, then?"

"Happily. A devoted couple, so unusual and yet so . . ." He flailed for the next word. "Unusual," he repeated, and then he gave a frantic smile. "You must forgive me, Miss Asperson." He sniffed her. "I've got to be about my, ah, my breakfast. I mean business."

"Certainly, Zoot. It's been most . . . illuminating. I hope we can meet later, and then you can tell me what you and the Drawmiikh talked about till noon."

"Yes, yes." Zoot felt the fur between his ears rise in an involuntary attack posture. He swiped at it with the back of his hand. "Delightful. Later. Yes. Charmed."

Somehow he managed not to run. The effort cost him dearly, though; he kept lurching like Quasimodo at every other step.

One way out, he thought. He felt feverishly for his pistol. One way out.

The Duchess of Benn sat in her room, savoring her coffee and her triumph. A few minutes after midnight tonight, she thought, and she'd ransom the Shard. She wouldn't tell anybody, would keep it secret for months before she wore it again, and then the occasion would be a special event—Special Event, rather. She had begun thinking of it that way.

Roberta smiled and took another sip of coffee. The Special Event was going to be a surprise, perhaps even more sensational than this last.

There was a pounding at the front door of her suite, followed by a turmoil among her household staff. Annoyed at the interruption, she cocked an ear in that direction and continued sipping coffee. The commotion increased. Roberta frowned, and then her door burst open and Lord Qlp flung itself in. Roberta stood, wondering whether to be alarmed or affronted. Lord Qlp's ghastly odor, in the event, prevented either stance from gaining much ground. She raised a hand to her face, intending to cover her mouth and nose, and then remembered her manners and forced the hand to her side.

"Sorry, your grace." Her butler, Kovinn, hovering in the door, wrung her hands. "Its lordship just . . . insisted."

"Interference!" Lord Qlp thrashed in distress. "Alarms!"

Roberta steeled herself. "Very well, Kovinn. You may go." She looked at Lord Qlp. "Coffee, my lord?" she asked, denasal.

"Ah . . ." said Kovinn, but then another figure pushed past her. It was Lady Dosvidern, disheveled, tugging at the laces of her jacket.

"Beg pardon, your grace," she said breathlessly. "But I thought—"

"You and its lordship are welcome at any time," Roberta said, as if these things happened every day. The stench was making her glassy-eyed. "But have you any notion—?"

"Afraid not, your grace."

Lord Qlp continued thrashing. It belched out something in its own tongue. Roberta took a step back from the violence of its speech.

"Humiliation!" Lady Dosvidern said. Her tone was bewildered. "Has not the Time of Exchange passed?" More belching noises. "Has not the Commodity been sufficient?" The sluglike body convulsed. Something flung itself across the room, thudded into a chair. It was, Roberta saw, another oval exudate similar to those which Lord Qlp had already spit up in her presence.

Lord Qlp roared in its bubbling tongue. Its eyes whipped wildly at the ends of their stalks. "The Commodity is thrice-offered! Discontinuation of existence is necessary if humiliation is increased! May one not be vouchsafed a glimpse of the Preciosity, the Eye at the Center of Existence, the Perfected Tear?"

"Tear?" Roberta said. Her own eyes were growing tearful at the continued olfactory onslaught. Lord Qlp's phrases gathered in her mind, and in a glorious wave of prescience she realized what Lord Qlp had been going on about all this time.

"The Eltdown Shard?" she said. "You wish to trade for it?"

"Yes! Yes! Yes!" Lord Qlp bounced high in eagerness. Its High Khosali was not quite grammatical—the sentences did not comment on one another in the preferred contextual mode—but its meaning was clear.

"I'd be happy to show you the Shard, your lordship," Roberta said, "but I'm afraid the Shard has been stolen."

Lord Qlp's response filled Roberta with alarm. It moaned as if in pain. It fell heavily on its side and thrashed, knocking a chair halfway across the room. It boomed painfully, and Roberta held her hands over her ears.

"Woe, woe!" Lady Dosvidern translated. "Your Existenceship promised to guarantee the Exchange!"

"I did?" Roberta searched her memory. "I suppose I did, then," she said, recalling her conversation with its lordship just prior to the race.

"The Condition is altered. Discontinuation of existence is necessary for assuagement."

A chill crept into Roberta's heart as she thought she understood what Lord Qlp meant. "No!" Roberta said. "You don't have to kill yourself. It's not your fault!" She thought frantically. "Can't you just take the . . . objects . . . back?"

Lady Dosvidern's expression was frantic as she translated the bubbling sounds. "Exchange has already commenced. Blamings are impertinent. Zynzlyp awaits the Object of Desire. All meaning is now invested in the Perfected Creation. Pointlessness of existence is alternative! Planetary discontinuation will soon be necessary!"

Alarms clattered in Roberta's mind. Was Lord Qlp talking about the suicide of his entire *species?* She shook her head frantically, tried to think. She had to *do* something.

"I will locate the Shard!" Roberta declared. "I will bring it to you!"

Lord Qlp wrenched itself upright and began undulating out of the room. "Crosstalk necessary before further action. Must consider method of regaining Center of Meaning."

Roberta's mind swam with relief. It didn't sound as if Lord Qlp was planning on murdering itself anytime soon. She'd have a while, at least, to get the Eltdown Shard from Maijstral and bring it to its lordship.

Lady Dosvidern was following Lord Qlp from the chamber. She looked terrified. Roberta snatched at her sleeve. Wild-eyed, Lady Dosvidern spun, her arm trembling in Roberta's grasp.

"Wait!" Roberta said. "I'll try to get the Shard from—from whoever has it. Don't let its lordship do anything hasty in the meantime."

"Yes, your grace." Lady Dosvidern ran after Lord Qlp. Roberta stepped to the service plate and touched the ideogram for "telephone."

"This is the Duchess of Benn," she said. "Call Drake Maijstral's room. Inform him this is an emergency."

Just below the service plate, Roberta saw the two objects that Lord Qlp had previously offered her, each wrapped in a dinner napkin. While the phone rang endlessly, Roberta bent to unwrap them. She gasped in surprise.

Enchantment dazzled her eyes. The objects of exchange had transformed, become something magic and beautiful.

Colors spun bright webs at Roberta's feet. Iridescence shimmered, altered, became substantial. The telephone rang on and on.

TEN

"Miss Asperson."

"Miss Runciter. Are you here for the magic show?"

"I'm here by chance, but if Maijstral's putting on a show, I daresay I'll sit through it. Even though I know his tricks."

"Perhaps he's learned some new ones." A beat's pause. "You seem to have met with some injury. I hope you are well."

Vanessa touched her cheek. The semilife patches had happily sopped up most of the swelling before expiring in gorged bliss, but faint bruising was still visible even through her cosmetic. "An accident, unfortunately."

"A pity. Bad luck seems to be making the rounds. First Mr. Fu George, then yourself."

"Luck has a way of turning."

"Looking at the both of you, one might almost think Fu George and yourself had been in a brawl."

"Neither of us would ever condescend to brawl, Miss Asperson." A cold smile. "Good afternoon."

"Your servant."

* * *

"Miss Advert."

"Marchioness. Will you sit by me?"

"Gladly. It's very kind of you to share." Settling into her seat. "You've got a very good view of the stage."

"From here I can watch Maijstral. It's very important that I do so. I'm on a secret mission for Pearl Woman."

"Really?"

"Yes. I'm afraid she's just too desolate to appear in public right now." Smiling. "She's lost something very important to her."

Roberta's holographic head and shoulders floated in Lady Dosvidern's video display. Lady Dosvidern observed that the Duchess had changed into a one-piece racing suit, probably in case she had to get somewhere in a hurry.

"I haven't been able to find Mai—to find the person who took the Shard. I've told his suite to give him my message when he arrives, and I've sent my household staff looking."

Lady Dosvidern tried to conceal her nervousness. She ceased her pacing and faced the holo cameras. "I looked in on its lordship a few minutes ago. It was still in deep crosstalk. Eyes and ears totally withdrawn."

Roberta gave a relieved sigh. "So Lord Qlp isn't likely to kill itself in the next few minutes."

"I'm not sure what it would kill itself *with.* Neither of us carries guns. It doesn't have wrists to slice. There isn't anyplace high to throw itself from."

"There are airlocks."

Lady Dosvidern's ears turned down. "Oh. I hadn't thought about that."

Roberta's violet eyes glittered as she considered possibilities. "Unfortunately there's no way to stop someone from killing itself. The right to self-annihilation is supported by High Custom. I assume we can't prove it's insane?"

"By what standards?" she asked. "Its lordship is perfectly mad by the standards of the Khosali or humanity, but it's entirely normal for a Drawmiikh, I think." Helplessness filled Lady Dosvidern. Was she responsible for this? What if Lord Qlp really *was* angry about Zoot? Standards, Lady Dosvidern wondered. Did Drawmii standards include sexual jealousy? She hadn't thought so.

"Its lordship is normal," Roberta repeated, "except that it travels."

"Yes. Of course."

Roberta gazed into the holo camera. "*Why,* Lady Dosvidern, does it travel?"

"Your grace?" Surprised.

"Why does it travel, and how long has it done so?"

A moment's thought. "Four years now. It approached the Imperial Protector and requested permission to leave Zynzlyp. The Lady Protector promptly gave it a pension, a title, and . . . ah . . . made other arrangements."

"Did it say *why* it wanted to travel?"

"It didn't need to. The Lady Protector was so delighted to have one of the Drawmii take an interest in anything outside of Zynzlyp that she didn't inquire."

"Didn't *you* ask its lordship? You've been travelling with Lord Qlp for . . . how long now?"

"Since the beginning. And no, I never asked—one doesn't ask a Drawmiikh *why* it does anything. If one gets any response at all, one gets an incomprehensible recitation of the latest debate between its five brains, with annotations and second thoughts by each of the brains in turn. Anything a Drawmiikh does is by consensus." She thought a moment further. "But its lordship never decided the schedule. It always let me choose the itinerary."

"Silverside Station was your idea, my lady?"

"Of course, your grace. I didn't want to miss the opening of such an exclusive resort, not when I had the means to attend."

"So its lordship didn't come here on purpose to trade for the Eltdown Shard?"

"No. I didn't even realize it *knew* about the Shard."

"There was a history of the Shard on the station vid. Did its lordship by any chance catch sight of it?"

Lady Dosvidern froze. "Yes. It did. I was watching it off the station feed while waiting for the *Viscount Cheng* to dock. We were sharing quarters at the time and . . ." She frowned. "I remember its lordship was very restless. I assumed it just wanted to leave the ship."

"So that was when its lordship conceived the notion that the Eltdown Shard was the foundation of reality."

Lady Dosvidern's ears flickered. "Is that what it did? I didn't understand that part."

"That's what it seemed to imply. That the Shard was Perfected Creation, that the alternative to its possession was the pointlessness of existence and planetary . . . was *discontinuation* the word, my lady?"

"Good grief." Private relief rose in Lady Dosvidern. She and Zoot hadn't anything to do with this after all.

"Lord Qlp came here on a search for meaning, and apparently it found what it was looking for. Unfortunately someone stole the Perfected Creation, and now it's upset." Roberta considered this notion for a moment. "For which I can't blame its lordship, I suppose. If someone stole *my* species' meaning, I daresay I'd be annoyed."

"Yes." Abstractedly.

"My lady, if I may make a suggestion, perhaps you should speak to Lord Qlp again and assure it that meaning shall be restored within a few minutes if we're lucky, and at the very latest a few minutes after midnight."

"It's hard to talk to when it's in crosstalk."

"Perhaps you should try, my lady."

Lady Dosvidern's diaphragm throbbed. "Yes," she said. "I suppose you're right. Thank you for the suggestion, your grace."

"I'll wait."

In case Lord Qlp attempted something drastic, Lady Dosvidern had left ajar the door between Lord Qlp's room and the front room of the suite. She stepped to the door and saw, through the crack, that the vidset was on, set to a schematic of Silverside Station's power system. Curious, Lady Dosvidern thought, but at least its lordship is at home.

But its lordship wasn't. When she pushed open the door, she saw that the door between the private room and the hallway was ajar, and that Lord Qlp was gone.

"Miss Runciter, is it?"

"Yes." Lighting a Silvertip, looking at him with one eyebrow raised. "Who're you?"

"My name's Dolfuss. I'd just like to say that I've seen you on vid often, and I admire your sense of style. All that leather, now—that's the way I think a woman of your type should dress." He gave a booming laugh. "You're my favorite, next to Nichole. I can see why Geoff Fu George keeps you around."

Vanessa smiled. "Thank you, Mr. Dolfuss." To Dolfuss's surprise, she put her arm through his. "Would you join me for Maijstral's program? I have some seats reserved, right up close."

Astonished laughter boomed out. "If my friends could see me now! They'd be jealous as anything."

"Your friends have taste, I see. Like yourself. Good afternoon, Mr. Kuusinen."

"Your servant, madam. Mr. Dolfuss."

"I saw that orange number you wore last night," Dolfuss said. "Made you look like a big pismire bird. You ever seen one of those?"

"I'm afraid not. You'll have to tell me all about it."

"I think the woodwinds were a little *off* just now, don't you?"

"Not now, dear. Maijstral's started."

"They just didn't sound as *full* as they did yesterday."

Paavo Kuusinen listened to his neighbors' conversation with only a fragment of his attention. He was concentrating on working out how Drake Maijstral did the Disappearing Bartender. Here the bartender was, plainly the Khosalikh on duty and not a plant, tugged from behind the bar and asked to mix a road agent while standing inside a roomy felt-covered box. To the sound of the shaking mixer, the box was closed, knocked to pieces with hammers wielded by Roman and Gregor, reassembled twenty feet away, and opened. To enthusiastic foot-tapping applause, the bartender appeared and a road agent was poured from the mixer into a glass held by Drake Maijstral. Maijstral smiled, tossed off the drink, and pronounced it excellent. The bartender was sent back to his duty.

Kuusinen frowned. How the hell was it done? The White Room had no stage, therefore no trapdoors. The box had been literally taken apart. The sound of the shaker had continued throughout.

Damnation. Kuusinen had been up all night working on one puzzle, and now here was another, come to torment him.

The shaker was the key. There had to be a *reason* why the sound had continued. But what was it?

But now another illusion commenced. Kuusinen soon figured out how it was done—that wasn't Maijstral's hand holding up the screen by its corner; that hand was a clever fake, complete with trademark diamond ring. Maijstral's real hand was elsewhere, manipulating things. And when Roman walked onstage to give Maijstral a prop that could have been on Maijstral's table all along, Kuusinen realized that Roman had passed Maijstral something he had concealed beneath his coat.

Having lost interest for the present, Kuusinen glanced over the audience. Why, he wondered, had Vanessa Runciter claimed that insufferable oaf Dolfuss? Normally she ate such people for breakfast. Doubtless, Kuusinen considered, this was part of a scheme. Kuusinen craned his neck, looked for Geoff Fu George or his assistants, and failed to see any of them. It seemed likely that Dolfuss was getting his room ransacked right now, with Miss Runciter on hand to alert the thieves should Dolfuss tire of the magic act and decide to stroll back to his suite.

Pleased with his feat of deduction, Kuusinen turned back to the program.

One of Kyoko Asperson's media globes hovered closer, taking a first-row seat for the climax of the illusion. Kuusinen looked approvingly at the arrangement of media globes—in order that the tricks wouldn't be given away unfairly, the globes had been arranged with careful regard for Maijstral's sight lines.

The trick, the one Kuusinen had figured out, was building to a satisfactory conclusion. Kuusinen, because he couldn't help himself, started counting the media globes again, and received a mild surprise.

Khamiss, her feet up, watched the magic show on station vid, broadcast live by Kyoko Asperson's globes. Not having noticed the phony hand, she wriggled her toes in silent, delighted applause at the production of the live clacklo, wondering how it was done.

Her phone rang. Feeling too lazy to reach the service plate, she told the room to record the performance and put the caller on vid.

Appearing on her vid unit was an elderly Tanquer that Khamiss recognized as a female who worked at the front desk. The Tanquer's eyes bulged and her whiskers trembled; she looked on the verge of hysteria.

Tanquers, Khamiss knew, suffered from an unfortunate fact of evolution. In their early history they were prey to a large carnivore that would stalk and kill anything that moved, but which would leave a motionless victim alone. Tanquers, in a crisis, were therefore subject to a Darwinian tendency to wring their hands, dither, and become subject to the vapors. As compensation they were masters of orderly procedure; but they tended to unravel in an emergency.

"You're with security, aren't you? I need your help!"

Khamiss smiled: she was off-duty. "Call security central," she said. "I can't—"

"I've tried!" Desperately. "I've been trying to reach Mr. Sun, but I can't get an answer!" The Tanquer made a strangled noise.

"That's strange. Perhaps someone's interfering with communications." Khamiss perked her ears forward. "What's the problem, then, ma'am?"

The Tanquer's tall, bushy tail swished frantically behind her head. "Someone's just stolen the hotel safe!"

"Oh." Khamiss sat bolt upright. "The *entire* safe?" she asked.

"Ye-es!" A wail of perfect despair.

"Continue your attempts to contact Mr. Sun. I'll be there as soon as I can."

While she flung on her uniform, Khamiss told her phone to contact as many members of her security detail as possible. She sent some to lurk outside Fu George's room—she assumed Maijstral, whatever his talents as a magician, hadn't been doing a live performance and robbing the safe simultaneously—and Khamiss told others to meet her at the location of the hotel safe. Once dressed, she ran flat out for Sun's headquarters.

The scent of smoke and the sight of flying robots told Khamiss what had happened before she saw the headquarters door. She was forced to slow to a walk—firefighting robots crowded the hallways, and there was retardant foam on the mothwing carpets. Mr. Sun, purple of feature, lay propped against the wall, wheezing into a handkerchief as bright red smoke poured from the door that led into his blue heaven.

Moving carefully so as not to slide on foam, Khamiss approached her boss.

"Are you all right, sir?"

Sun waved his hand feebly. Bronchial spasms reduced him to monosyllables. "Smoke bombs. In the console. Planted." He rallied enough to make a furious Holmesian declaration. *"Game's afoot!"*

"Someone's stolen the entire hotel safe."

Mr. Sun's purple tones darkened. His eyes popped. He clutched at his throat, unable to speak.

"Shall I handle it, sir?" Tactfully.

Sun gave a frantic nod. Khamiss raced away.

"And now—" removing the ring from his hand "—the Disappearing Diamond."

"Your grace. Have you heard from your people?"

"I'm afraid not, my lady. I don't know when I'll be able to retrieve the Shard. Have you located its lordship?"

"Its mucous trail led to one of the central elevators, but I lost it there. It had been looking at plans for the station power plant, so I ran there, but its lordship never appeared."

"Grief."

"I don't know what to do. Do you suppose I should alert station security?"

"I've been trying that, my lady. They don't answer."

* * *

Heavy beam cutters, Khamiss recognized at once. The thief had started in a storage locker, cut a hole in the wall, then cut the entire safe from its cradle. At least a dozen alarms must have been triggered, but Mr. Sun's headquarters had been filled with smoke and the alarms had been ignored. She picked up a telephone.

"Contact Mr. Kingston," she said. "Tell him to search Geoff Fu George's room at once."

The diamond ring, placed in an envelope sealed with red wax, rose slowly in the air, swooping upward in slow, graceful arcs in response to gentle waves of Maijstral's hand. The envelope, flaring redly in the light of Rathbon's Star, rose higher, higher, hovering at last in front of the giant impact diamond.

There was a startling bang, a gush of red smoke, and bits of the envelope fell in slow charred droplets toward the floor. There were shouts from Maijstral's audience as they began to realize it wasn't just the diamond ring that had disappeared.

Overtaken by sensation at the vanished giant diamond, few of the audience observed the ring that glittered on Maijstral's finger as he took his bow. Overshadowed by the large effect, Maijstral thought, the reappearance of the smaller diamond proved somewhat anticlimactic. He wouldn't use it as a finale again.

Kuusinen realized, as he stood and tapped his foot in the applause-pattern for "joyous surprise," why the woodwinds' sound had been off. The resonance provided by the diamond was missing, which meant of course the diamond had been missing for quite some time, and replaced by an illusion. Maijstral hadn't stolen it just now: it had been gone at least since morning.

Pleased with his acuity, Kuusinen turned from the performance to see Roberta's butler Kovinn walk into the room and do a perfect double take at the sight of Maijstral speaking to a gathering of his admirers. Kovinn fairly leaped for one of the telephones and slammed down an opaque privacy screen.

Kuusinen's nerves began to tingle. His walking stick tapping the floor, he moved so as to place himself between Kovinn and Maijstral. Another mystery, he thought resignedly, was clearly at hand. And here he'd planned to have luncheon undisturbed.

Khamiss appropriated the station's central switchboard as a poor substitute for Sun's console, but her hunt hadn't got very far. The hulk of the safe had been found in a service elevator, neatly peeled, all its contents gone. Fu George's room had been searched, but nothing had been found, and neither Fu George nor his assistants had been seen.

What now? Khamiss, marshalling her watsons, was beginning to appreciate what Sun had been going through the last few days. The desk Tanquer's whiskers were becoming sadly disordered as a result of the unexpected interruption in her routine, and her tail, following its evolutionary imperative, kept wrapping itself around her neck and tightening. Khamiss was beginning to be irritated by the constant sounds of strangulation.

"Don't you have a guest to take care of?" she asked.

More choking noises. "No. I'm just here in case someone needs to send a message offstation. What's that?"

"What's what?"

The Tanquer pointed to a light that had just started blinking. "That. An incoming radio transmission from somewhere in the system. We're not expecting any ships for three more days."

"Let's listen."

Khamiss turned on the audio. Incomprehensible bellowing filled the air.

"Yes, your grace. Maijstral was in public all this time."

"You mean all any of us had to do was look at the station bulletin board and see that his performance was listed all along?"

"I'm afraid so, your grace."

"Hold him there. I'm on my way."

"My rover."

"Lady Janetha." Maijstral took her hand and sniffed her ears, observing to his satisfaction that she wore the emerald earrings he'd saved from Fu George the previous night. "I hope you slept well."

"I found the ball and its aftermath so stimulating that I collapsed straightaway into the land of dreams. Yourself?"

"I slept very well. In fact I haven't had breakfast yet."

"Poor rover, creating a sensation on an empty stomach."

"I thought to try Lebaron's. Would you join me?"

"Gladly." She took his arm. "Though breakfasting *à deux* in your rooms might prove an interesting alternative."

"Unfortunately the local watsons are due to sack my suite at any moment. I'm afraid intimate meals might be fraught with inconvenience."

Her ears flickered in disappointment. "Lebaron's, then."

"Perhaps we can arrange a dinner later. After the security people have found someone else to harass."

"I hope so, Maijstral." She brightened. "I've just heard the most interesting news about Pearl Woman. Perhaps you had something to do with it."

Vanessa Runciter finished her polite applause and reached for a cigaret. Dolfuss looked at her. "I thought I'd take a look at the Casino," he said. "I haven't been there yet. Would you like to join me?"

Vanessa smiled smoothly. "Of course, Mr. Dolfuss. I was heading there myself."

Alarms clanged vaguely in Dolfuss's nerves. Why was Vanessa Runciter being so friendly?

"Great!" he said. "I'm happy as anything."

She lit the Silvertip in its ebony holder. "You *do* play tiles, don't you?" It might be fun, she realized, to pauperize this geck in retaliation for having to sit next to him through Maijstral's performance.

Dolfuss frowned. "Tiles? I'm afraid not."

"Or pasters?"

Dolfuss shrugged hopelessly. "Sorry. I play cheeseup from time to time, but I always lose."

Vanessa brightened. She put her arm through Dolfuss's. "Cheeseup, then. We'll have a jolly time."

"I'm not certain I can afford the stakes."

Vanessa looked at him in mock-indignation. "Mr. Dolfuss, I'm surprised! I thought *everyone* could afford a nova a point."

"A nova a point?" Dolfuss strove to master his shock. "Well, I suppose . . ."

"Settled then," Vanessa said, and smiled.

Ah, Dolfuss thought, and cancelled his internal alarm. She just wanted to fleece him. Reason enough to be friendly.

Bellowing still echoed from the receiver. The Tanquer's fingers danced over her keyboard. "Wait a minute. That signal's coming from the *Viscount Cheng.*"

"I thought she was waiting in the dock."

"She is. I think."

"Then why doesn't whoever's making that awful noise use the telephone? *Cheng*'s got communication through the station coupling."

"Oh, no." The Tanquer's tail began to make self-throttling gestures again.

"Stop strangling yourself," Khamiss said edgily, her patience frayed entirely, "and tell me what just happened."

The voice was a burbling whisper. *"Viscount Cheng.* It isn't in dock."

Khamiss looked at the Tanquer in shock. "You mean someone's just stolen a *passenger liner?"*

The Tanquer's eyes were bulging with self-inflicted oxygen deprivation. Still she managed to give an affirmative blink.

Khamiss looked at the Tanquer, then at the board. There had to be a proper response to this.

If only she knew what it was.

Paavo Kuusinen was poised and ready when Kovinn finished her phone call and dropped her privacy screen. She goggled when she saw that Maijstral was gone. Kuusinen approached.

"May I be of service, Kovinn?"

"Yes. Have you seen Drake Maijstral?"

"I believe he and the Marchioness Kotani were walking in that direction. Please allow me to accompany you."

"Thank you, Mr. Kuusinen. If I lost Maijstral again, I don't know what kind of trouble might result."

"Perhaps," lightly, "if I knew the nature of the crisis, I might be able to assist."

"I'm afraid I don't really know, except that it has to do with Lord Qlp. It burst in on her grace this morning, and—there's Maijstral. Sir! Sir!"

Kuusinen watched as Kovinn broke into a run. The mystery, it seemed, was deepening.

Cheng's captain was a short Khosali female who was clearly annoyed at being roused out of bed. Khamiss suspected, from the way she kept looking over her shoulder, that she was not alone. Khamiss also couldn't help but notice that the captain's annoyance increased a chance resemblance to the crusty-but-loyal Cap'n Bob, one of the fixtures on the Ronnie Romper program.

"Well, no," the captain said as she fingered the collar of her dressing gown. "There was no one aboard *Cheng* except the maintenance robots. We all have four days' station leave."

"So anyone could have got onto the ship."

"The airlock was sealed, and only the ship's officers had the codes, but I suppose the lock could have been broken . . ." The captain's ears suddenly pricked forward in alarm. "What's happened aboard my *Cheng?*"

"It appears someone's stolen your ship."

"The whole thing?"

Given time and thought, Khamiss might have found the captain's response curious and asked if the captain were more accustomed to having her ship stolen one piece at a time. Under the pressure of the emergency, however, Khamiss could only reply in the affirmative.

"The whole thing, ma'am. Sorry."

The captain sat down suddenly. The phone camera, with a jolt, tracked her collapse. The resemblance to Cap'n Bob became even more pronounced.

"I don't suppose," she said, "there's any way this could be kept quiet."

"Advert. What news?" Pearl Woman's holographic face, broadcast against the opalescence of one of the White Room's privacy screens, showed taut signs of strain. Her fingers twined in her leonine hair, drawing it down over her ear. The duelling scar gave her anxiety a sinister cast.

Advert, trying to remember not to giggle with joy, nodded and gave what she hoped was an encouraging smile. "I know who's got the pearl," she said.

Pearl Woman's eyes gleamed with a tigerish light. "Good. Give me the name."

"The name was given me in confidence. I'm sorry, but in return for the information I had to promise not to tell."

"Come now, Advert. You can tell me. After all, I—"

"The price is ninety." Firmly.

Baffled rage entered Pearl Woman's face. "That's outrageous! Last time he only asked sixty."

"Apparently the stakes in the contest between Fu George and Maijstral have risen. The price is firm, but at least it includes media rights. No one will ever know the pearl was taken."

"Drat." Pearl Woman chewed her lower lip. "Very well," she said. "If you'd be so kind as to advance me the money, I'll—"

"Pearl!" Advert widened her eyes in feigned surprise. "I don't have anything *like* ninety novae. I spent everything paying for the pearl last time. Now that you've gone and lost it again, I'm afraid you'll have to raise the money yourself."

With visible care, Pearl Woman mastered her indignation. "Are you certain you can't give me ten or twenty? Perhaps you can get an advance on your allowance."

"Sorry, Pearl." Advert struggled to contain her inward delight and simulate proper regret. "I'm really broke. Possibly you can get a loan from the Marquess Kotani. Or an advance from the Diadem."

Pearl Woman's eyes narrowed. "I don't know if it's worth ninety, Advert. Can't you negotiate?"

"I wouldn't know how. Besides, as I said, the price is really firm."

"Let me think about it."

"I don't know how much longer the offer will hold. The price may go up."

"I said I'll think about it." The Pearl's face was hard.

"Very well. But one shouldn't become so dependent on the material aspects of existence. You've told me that often enough."

Pearl Woman's face vanished before Advert had quite finished, replaced by the "at your service" ideogram. Advert gave a short, delighted laugh, then composed her features carefully and dropped the privacy screen. The White Room leaped into existence around her. Kotani was passing by, walking stick dangling form his fingers. It was time, Advert thought, to increase the pressure.

"Ah," she said. "Marquess Kotani. I'm afraid the Pearl is in an unpleasant situation, and I was wondering if I might ask your advice."

"Thank you so much for waiting. I know her grace will be eternally thankful."

"If it is, as you say, an emergency, then how could I refuse? It's cost me nothing but a late breakfast."

"No doubt," observed the Marchioness tautly, as the others moved away, "her grace has her own reasons for interrupting Maijstral's breakfast. Whatever they may be." The sullen quality of her beauty had increased.

Paavo Kuusinen followed Maijstral's party in companionable silence. He was thinking about the Disappearing Bartender.

Kyoko Asperson told her telephone to record, then rang Pearl Woman's suite. She smiled as she saw that Pearl Woman only answered on audio.

"I apologize, Miss Asperson, but I just stepped out of bed and I'm not presentable."

"I understand. I'm sure you must be prostrate."

"Oh?" Badly disguised suspicion.

"I gather you've lost some property."

Pearl Woman's voice turned cool. "Might I ask where you obtained this information?"

"Sorry, Pearl Woman, but you know that I can't say. I have to protect the confidentiality of my sources."

"It was just that I wondered who might be spreading this story about me. It's quite inaccurate, you know."

"Really? I'll have to question my source further."

There was a moment's suspicious pause. "I'll see you later this afternoon," she said, "and we'll straighten out the entire misunderstanding."

"I'll be looking forward. Thank you."

"At your service, Miss Asperson."

Kyoko rang off. Smiling, she sent one of her media globes to hover outside Singh's Jewelers on the main commercial level, just in case Pearl Woman decided to purchase a substitute.

"You know, I keep thinking I've heard that voice somewhere before."

"That bellowing sound?" The Tanquer shrugged delicately. "How dreadful. It sounds like a large and very wild beast."

"Wait a moment." Recollection rose in Khamiss, then clarified. Her nostrils slammed shut at the memory. She touched an ideogram on the console.

"Get me Lord Qlp's suite," she said, denasal. "I'd like to speak to Lady Dosvidern."

"An interspecies emergency?" Maijstral gave the situation a moment of thought. "Do you truly think Lord Qlp might do away with itself?"

Roberta gave an exasperated wave of her hands. "I think Lord Qlp's *species* might do away with itself." She glanced above and made certain no hovering media globes were recording their conversation. "I'll pay you the amount we agreed upon, and I'll pay it right now. You won't be involved any further in the matter of Lord Qlp."

Maijstral frowned and twisted his diamond ring. Roberta's appeal *might,* of course, be part of an elaborate trap, an attempt to catch him red-handed with the Eltdown Shard before it was legally his. On the other hand, the situation seeemd too implausibly bizarre to constitute a trap—if Roberta were involved in an attempt to snare him, Maijstral suspected the excuse offered him might be more conventional: a family crisis, say, that required her instant departure from Silverside and the immediate ransoming of the Shard.

"Give me a moment," he said. "I must offer my apologies to the Marchioness."

"Of course."

Maijstral stepped toward where the Marchioness waited out of earshot and leaned toward her, speaking in her ear. "I'm afraid this is a matter of some urgency, my lady."

The Marchioness drew herself up. "If it's quite *that* important, Maijstral . . ."

"There may be lives at stake. I still trust we may sup together, perhaps tonight."

She looked at him suspiciously, then relaxed her famous pout. "Perhaps," she said. "I'll have to see what Kotani has planned."

"Till later, then." He sniffed her and turned, seeing Roman and Gregor moving some of his equipment to their suite. He caught Roman's eye. Roman nodded, then glided across the room toward him.

"I require a tail track to Dolfuss's room," Maijstral said. "I need to run a very important errand, and her grace and I may be followed."

Roman's eyes glittered. "Shall I tell Gregor, sir?"

"Yes. The more eyes and detectors, the better. Have robots take the stage equipment back to the Coronet Suite."

"At once, sir."

Roberta was speaking with Paavo Kuusinen. Suspicion awakened in Maijstral, and he gave the man a cautious nod. "Shall we go, your grace?"

"Yes." She hesitated. "May Mr. Kuusinen accompany us?"

"With respect, I'd rather he didn't. My apologies, Mr. Kuusinen, but this is private business."

Kuusinen bowed stiffly. "No offence taken, sir."

"Your grace?"

"Yes." Roberta moved at once for the exit. "Let's hurry, if we may."

"Yes," Lady Dosvidern said. "That's its lordship's voice. You've found Lord Qlp, then?"

"In a manner of speaking, my lady," Khamiss said. "It appears that its lordship has stolen the *Viscount Cheng.*"

Lady Dosvidern's muzzle gaped in surprise.

"My lady," Khamiss went on, "could you come to our communications room? I think we may need a translator."

* * *

"Excuse me, Vanessa," Dolfuss said. He looked at his cards with a puzzled expression. "Could you remind me of the sequence from secundus onward?"

Vanessa looked at him from over her cards and smiled. "Of course, Mr. Dolfuss. Secundus, response, octet, and cheeseup."

"Ah." Dolfuss frowned over his cards for another moment, his brows knit, then he put his hand on the table.

"That's octet," he said. "Isn't it?"

"Yes," she said. "Congratulations, Mr. Dolfuss." She folded her hand and dropped her cards atop the discard pile.

"And with the Emperor in Elevation, isn't that something else?"

"Camembert." Stonily.

Dolfuss grinned. "So that gives me forty-one, right? My luck is in this afternoon."

"It seems so."

Dolfuss's laugh boomed across the Casino. Heads turned. "I *thought* that's what it was!" he roared. *"Camembert!"* Heads turned away.

Vanessa reached for the cards and began to shuffle. "I hope you will consent to another game, Mr. Dolfuss," she said.

"For you, lady," Dolfuss said, "anything. Anything at all."

Zoot gazed at the contents of his closet in bleak despair. How to dress for one's suicide? he wondered. Did this count as a formal event, or was he allowed to dress casually?

Formal, he decided. Go with dignity.

He reached for his evening clothes, then hesitated. The jacket he'd invented might be more appropriate: it was his trademark, after all. If the back of his head was blown off, he thought morbidly, at least he'd be recognizable.

He stood away from the closet. Perhaps he should just write the note first. Traditionally this was done in High Khosali, in which the parsing of each sentence commented on the sentence before, the whole unrolling, ideally anyway, in as precise and rigorous terms as a mathematical statement. Zoot spoke High Khosali fairly well, but minor mistakes were easy to make; and he had to be careful as possible. Nobody wanted to be known for bungling his last words, and Zoot would need to produce two sets of them. A public apology, suitably phrased, to be found in his breast pocket, along with a private note to Lady Dosvidern to be hand delivered by a discreet member of the Very Private Letter service, apologizing for destroying her reputation. There were certain delicacies to be observed as well: in the public statement, he had to make his reasons for killing himself clear, publicly exonerate the lady of all suspicion, and yet in so doing never mention her by name.

It was ironic, Zoot thought, that the cause of all this was just the sort of thing that members of the Diadem were *supposed* to do. He was *expected* to have affaires and scrapes and then have them broadcast throughout the Constellation and Empire by the Diadem's own exclusive news service. But Diadem members weren't supposed to botch things, weren't supposed to babble and stare when subjected to pointed interviews, to blurt out obvious untruths and cause potential Colonial Service incidents between opaque aliens and their wives.

There was only one way for a gentleman to behave once he'd wrecked things to *that* degree.

Zoot stepped to the closet again, hesitated once more.

It was a practical issue that finally decided him. After he'd blown his brains out, the famous jacket would be a lot easier to clean than would formal evening clothes.

He still had to write his note.

Suicides, he realized in growing despair, were much more complicated than they seemed.

Maijstral hastened down the corridor with her grace of Benn at his side. Roman and Gregor followed behind, hovering at the edge of Maijstral's awareness, their detectors deployed. Roberta had a stylus and one of the credit chips from the Casino: carefully she rearranged molecules as she walked, wrote an amount, signed and thumbprinted it. She handed it to Maijstral.

"There. Your losses at tiles multiplied by a large factor."

Maijstral came to Dolfuss's door. He reached for the lock, hesitated, drew his hand back. Electricity crackled through his nerves.

"What's wrong?" asked Roberta.

Maijstral did not quite trust himself to speak; instead his hand went to the small of his back and drew out a pistol. His other hand took Roberta's shoulder; he gently guided her away from the line of fire. Turning toward Roman and Gregor, he gestured significantly with the pistol. Weapons drawn, detectors screening their eyes, the pair moved silently down the corridor. Roman reached into a pocket and handed Maijstral a pair of detector goggles: he drew them on with his free hand. A pair of media globes rose out of Roman's pocket and hovered in the air.

Maijstral paused for a moment of consideration. Roman and Gregor waited.

Roberta, violet eyes alight, bent and drew a small, elegant Nana-Coulville Elite spitfire from an ankle holster. Roman and Gregor observed this with a certain amount of admiration.

Maijstral, with careful consideration for the state of his nerves, concluded that he was not going to be the first person into the room. With gestures, Maijstral told Roman to dive through the door: he and Gregor would provide cover fire and support.

Roman bowed; he flexed his muscles, set his pistol to "lethal," opened the door lock with a touch of his hand, and charged.

Through the haze of his fear, Maijstral experienced a moment of admiration for the absolute grace of Roman's movement, for the elegance of Roman's execution, his total silence.

Roman entered low and dove to his right out of the line of fire. A media globe swooped over his head. Maijstral and Gregor followed, guns thrust forward.

The giant impact diamond was propped in a corner. No person was visible. The bed was unmade—Maijstral hadn't permitted maid service since he'd begun stowing his loot in the room.

Roman, Gregor, and Maijstral fanned over the room. Maijstral's heart thundered in his breast. He dropped by the bed—into convenient cover—and kept his arms locked rigid in a firing position, thereby feigning an inspection of anything beneath the mattress. There was, he discovered, nothing—none of the rolled paintings or compact sculptures that had once belonged to the Baroness Silverside and that, as of midnight, had become his personal property. Anger growled in his nerves. He stood, flipped over his pillow. The box with the Eltdown Shard was gone.

Roberta glided into the room, pistol ready in her hand, her eyes questioning.

Maijstral stepped to the closet and pointed his pistol at the closed door. "Fu George," he said, "come out, please."

There was a moment's pause, then the closet door came open. Geoff Fu George, elegantly attired in an evening jacket that made an unfortunate contrast to the bruising around his eyes, smiled ruefully. A pair of media globes orbited his head as he stepped into the room. Apparently, with his equipment, he'd managed to overcome the closet's reluctance to close.

"Gentlemen," he said, and bowed. "Your grace."

Fu George, Maijstral realized, had four pistols pointed at him.

Maijstral's nervousness eased; he seemed to be in control of the situation.

"The Shard, if you please," Maijstral said.

Fu George spread in hands in a helpless gesture.

"Sorry, Maijstral," he said. "I'd be perfectly happy to oblige you, but as it happens I don't have it."

"Its lordship is threatening the station?" Khamiss stared at Lady Dosvidern in surprise.

Lord Qlp's voice boomed from the speakers. "It says," Lady Dosvidern said, her voice trembling, "that if it doesn't get the Perfected Tear, it's going to ram the *Viscount Cheng* into the antimatter bottle in the surface power plant and blow everything up."

Khamiss ignored strangling sounds from the Tanquer and considered the situation, wondering primarily if it was still possible to throw up her hands and turn the situation over to Mr. Sun.

Mr. Sun's choked, purple face rose in her mind. Probably not, she decided.

"Can its lordship *do* that?" Lady Dosvidern said. "Is there really antimatter onstation?" Her eyes were hopeless. "Isn't that old-fashioned? I thought everyone used sidestep systems these days."

"Silverside Station's in an unstable orbit around an unstable star system," Khamiss said. "There's tremendous gravitational stress, and we need to adjust our position and gravity from one second to the next. Energy expenditure is enormous, and a matter-antimatter reaction was the most efficient way to provide it. The power plant got put on the surface so that if there was a problem with the magnetic containment bottle, the anitmatter would boil off into space instead of blowing up Silverside." Her ears flicked uncertainly. "That was the hope, at any rate."

"There's nothing protecting the bottle?"

"Cold fields to keep out the odd meteor strike. But I doubt they're strong enough to keep out anything with the size and mass of the *Viscount Cheng.*"

There was a thud. Khamiss glanced over her shoulder and observed that the Tanquer had passed out from lack of oxygen.

"Good," she said. "She was making me nervous."

Advert smiled as she entered Pearl Woman's suite. "I'm so glad you changed your mind," she said. "I really think it's for the best."

Pearl Woman looked at her without joy. "I really wish you'd tell me," she said.

"Pearl! You know I promised."

"I'm not entirely happy about the way the price went up."

"I'm sorry, Pearl, but you really shouldn't have delayed."

Pearl Woman handed Advert a credit chip. "Here," she said. "A hundred."

Advert looked at the chip and smiled. "I'll be right back. Wait here." She paused in the doorway. "You're doing the right thing. I'm sure of it."

"I'm afraid the place was gutted before I arrived," Geoff Fu George said. "The only thing of value remaining was the big diamond—I suppose it was too awkward to transport." His ears fluttered in an offhand way. "Sorry, Maijstral. Say, can I lower my hands?"

Maijstral stared at Fu George over the sights of his pistol. Anger tugged at his nerves, his mind, his trigger finger.

"I can't accept that, Fu George," he said. "My swag's stolen, and you're in my closet. These are facts difficult to ignore."

"About my hands, Maijstral."

"I need the Eltdown Shard. I need it *now.*"

"The boss is telling the truth."

Startled, Maijstral swung his pistol to cover the new voice, his heart hammering anew. Chalice had appeared in the doorway—also, strangely, in evening dress. Observing that Roberta and Gregor had Chalice covered, Maijstral swung back to Fu George.

"Shut the door, Roman," he said. "Let's keep this gathering private, shall we?"

"It took us a long time to get through your traps and alarms." Chalice stepped into the room while Roman stepped behind him to close the door. "Once we got through, Mr. Fu George entered and found your room plundered. I was running black boxes outside. I heard you coming and hid around the corner. It was too late for the boss to get away."

Maijstral kept his pistol aimed four inches below Fu George's famous hairline. Probably Fu George's evening jacket/darksuit contained defenses; but since his encounters with the Ronnie Romper creature on Peleng, Maijstral had been carrying the most powerful Trilby 8 spitfire available, and he was reasonably certain of blasting through Fu George's shields. This certainty served to elevate his confidence.

"I might point out," he said, "that we've caught you red-handed in an act of burglary. We've got *recordings.* I don't know what Baron Silverside intends for anyone caught stealing on his station, but he's a sovereign lord here and he's got a very simple and very medieval court system in which he plays both judge and advocate; and I assume that there would be little problem for him in sentencing you to ten or twelve years of breaking rocks on Gosat. I suggest therefore that returning my property would seem by far the most convenient alternative."

"Love to oblige, old man," Fu George said. "Unfortunately, it ain't in the cards. Look, can I put my hands down?"

"You may *not,*" Maijstral snarled at him, happy to vent his anger. "I *like* you with your hands in the air. I think it suits you. Perhaps you'll be *buried* that way."

"I prefer cremation, old man. Incidentally, I wouldn't put too much trust in those recordings. They also record the presence of this big diamond, which I suspect is not yet your legal property."

Maijstral hesitated, then smiled. "This isn't my room. The diamond has nothing to do with me."

"If this isn't your room, then what are you doing in it?"

"Making an arrest, looks like."

"Mr. Fu George," Roberta said. "There are lives at stake here."

Fu George offered her a graceful inclination of his head. "No one regrets that more than I, your grace. Except possibly for Chalice."

"That isn't what I meant." Quickly, her pistol trained unerringly on Chalice's right ear, Roberta explained Lord Qlp's behavior and its threat of planetary discontinuation.

"Very strange, your grace," Fu George said. "Were the Shard in my possession, I'd be happy to arrange its ransom. However, as I have no idea where the Shard might be—"

Maijstral's exasperation boiled over. "Oh, shut up," he said. "I don't believe you."

Fu George raised an eyebrow. "Are you calling me a liar, Maijstral?"

"Damn right I am," Maijstral snarled. *"Old man."* He glanced over his shoulder at the Duchess. "I'm going to have Roman and Gregor hold Fu George here while I take a look in his suite. The Shard may be there."

While Maijstral spoke, Fu George glided forward with absolute, professional silence; Maijstral turned back at the motion and saw a slight smile on Fu George's face in the instant before the man's right fist filled the vision of his left eye.

The fist drove full-force into the detector goggles, which in turn drove into Maijstral's eye. Caught by surprise, Maijstral sat down on the bed. In purest reflex, he jabbed his pistol into Fu George's midsection: Fu George folded backward into the closet, cracking his head on the back wall. One of Dolfuss's loud jackets dropped silently on his head.

"Are you injured, sir?" the closet said. "I can summon medical assistance if necessary."

"I will ask the Marquess Kotani to act for me," Fu George said, his voice muffled. "And thanks anyway, closet, but I don't need your help."

Horror glibbered in Maijstral's mind at the realization of his own invidious carelessness. He had called Fu George a liar, which was a killing offence, and he'd done it in front of witnesses; he could have got away with an apology save that Fu George had then gone and hit him, which was *another* killing offence, and this meant he couldn't possibly escape the inevitable violence. Maijstral was possessed by a desperate need to shriek and dive under the bed, but his body seemed paralyzed, so instead he simply sat where he was, pistol braced, while he gazed at Fu George's plaid-draped form and contemplated his own speechless terror.

Training, in the end, loosened his voice. The Nnoivarl Academy had drilled its students well, or at any rate well enough to be able to speak formulae while terrified witless.

"Your grace," Maijstral said while his mind cringed at what his mouth actually had the audacity to say, "will you do me the inestimable favor of acting for me in this matter?"

"I would be honored, Maijstral." She paused for a moment's thought. "So what do we do now? Are you still going to search Fu George's suite?" Maijstral felt the Trilby begin to quake in his hands, and he lowered the pistol while he contemplated his situation. His stolen loot, the Eltdown Shard, and even planetary discontinuation had begun to assume an air of insignificance.

"There wouldn't be a lot of point," Chalice interrupted. "Drexler was with us, helping with the black boxes. He's run back to guard the suite."

"Fu George," Maijstral said. "Take that stupid thing off your head and leave."

"Your servant," replied Fu George's muffled voice. "Old man." Fu George removed Dolfuss's jacket, rose from the closet, and brushed at his clothing. "Come, Chalice."

"Good work, sir," Chalice said.

"Mr. Chalice," Roman said, as he showed the others the door. "I believe you still owe Gregor and me ten novae."

Fu George looked at his assistant. "Ten novae?"

Maijstral stared down at the pistol in his hands and wondered if it was too late to shoot the pair of them. Perhaps he could arrive at a plausible reason for it later.

No. There were too many witnesses.

The words took up a dull refrain in his head. Too many witnesses. Too many witnesses. Too many witnesses.

The door closed shut behind Chalice and Fu George. Maijstral put his gun on the bed and stretched out with his head on the pillow. He looked up at Dolfuss's empty ceiling. There was a moment's silence.

"I don't see what else we could have done," Roberta said.

"I'm sorry, sir," Roman said. "It's my fault. Once I closed the door, I should have returned to help you cover Fu George."

"If it's *your* fault," Maijstral almost said, *"you* fight the man," but he bit the words back. No purpose would be served by getting his servant and chief henchman angry at him.

"Don't blame yourself," he said. He felt mild surprise at how well he was articulating. "I let things get out of control."

"You handled that real cool, boss." Gregor's tones were admiring. Another savage comment came to Maijstral's mind, and again Maijstral squelched it.

Roberta bent to return her pistol to its holster. When she straightened, there was a serious light in her eyes. "What weapons?" she asked.

Maijstral's mind curdled as it raced through the appalling possibilities. The inventory of classical Khosali duelling weapons, developed over millennia, was impressive. There were weapons for cutting, weapons for hacking, weapons that shot flame or explosive bolts. There were strangling cords and bludgeons and sophisticated devices for picking apart the opponent's mind and leaving him a pain-riven vegetable all the rest of his days. The weapons had one thing in common: Maijstral had no confidence in his ability to damage Fu George with any of them.

Why, he asked the ceiling, had he been born in a society that countenanced mutual slaughter, but only so long as the slaughter was done on what purported to be a fair basis? Why was *fairness* the criterion? Why not *cleverness?* If one could cleverly arrange matters so that one's opponent had no chance whatever of survival, and oneself had every possible chance, why should any reasonable individual object? Why *shouldn't* the clever survive over the stupid? Wouldn't it improve the breed in the long run?

Maijstral waved an airy hand.

"Chugger," he said. "And let's not use explosive bullets or automatic fire. Far too vulgar." The point of a chugger duel was that each side got only one shot. He wasn't going to give Fu George more than one try at him.

"Very well."

"Anything you *won't* use?"

Everything! his mind squalled, but instead his voice was calm. "Axes. Clubs. Pole weapons. That sort of thing. Too . . ." *Brutal,* he almost said, but corrected himself at the last second. ". . . common."

"How about psych-scanners?"

Maijstral thought for a long moment. A psych-scanner in the hands of an expert could turn an opponent's brain into a mass of toasted cheese. Against a stupid or slow man, Maijstral would have had every confidence in using a scanner. Unfortunately Fu George was neither stupid nor slow.

He thought about the long nightmare that might result, with Fu George slamming at his brain for hours while he gibbered in terror and tried to evade the relentless psychic blast. No, he decided. Pistols were a lot quicker.

"I'd rather not," he said. "Scanners are an honorable weapon, but too often they leave both combatants brain-dead. I'd prefer one of us survive this."

"Bravo, boss. Only too." Gregor gave a laugh as he beat out a quick pattern on the bureau.

Maijstral looked at him bleakly. Gregor had been impressed by his chivalry, but Maijstral, to himself at least, meant only that he intended himself to be the survivor, and to hell with anything else. He'd rigged a chugger duel in his youth, when he'd been driven into an encounter during his last year at the Nnoivarl Academy; he wasn't sure he could work the same trick with a scanner.

"Any feelings about swords?" Roberta asked.

Wrong phrasing, Maijstral thought. He had very clear feelings about swords, though none of them capable of articulation in this company.

"I would prefer smallswords," he said. "Or rapier and targe." Keep the damage to a minimum, he thought, with a light weapon. Perhaps he could manage to get himself scratched on the arm and pronounce honor satisfied.

"I would also prefer," Maijstral said, "that the meeting be postponed for a few days. I'd like to get to the bottom of this Shard business first."

"Thank you, Maijstral," Roberta said. "I appreciate that."

"I am at your service, your grace." Delay the thing as long as possible, he thought, which would give him a greater chance to fix the outcome. Perhaps, he thought cheerlessly, he could just poison Fu George in the night. Or get him arrested.

"What shall we do about the Shard?"

"If I were you, I'd try to buy it from Fu George. If you approach him privately, he may act differently than when he had my gun pointed at his head."

She looked at him with a frown. "I suppose I should see him as soon as possible."

"Right now, if you like."

"Yes. Thank you, Maijstral. I'll see Kotani as soon as the present crisis is over."

"Don't hurry on my account," Maijstral almost said. Instead he said merely, "Your servant."

"Yours."

Roberta bowed and left. Maijstral stared at Dolfuss's ceiling and asked it a long series of questions. There was no reply.

Viscount Cheng's captain, whom Khamiss was beginning to think of as Cap'n Bob, gazed in surprise at the unconscious body of the Tanquer.

"Er," she began, "is this somehow related to our problem?"

"Not really," Khamiss said. She turned to the console. "Ring the Duchess of Benn's suite," she said. "Then ring the White Room, the other lounges, each restaurant, the Casino, and all the shops on the commercial level. Give them the following message: should anyone see her grace the Duchess of Benn, Drake Maijstral, or Geoff Fu George, please have them call Khamiss at the central switchboard. Inform them that this is a serious emergency. End of message."

"At your service," said the console.

Kovinn answered the Duchess's phone. "Is her grace in?" Khamiss asked.

"I'm afraid not, ma'am."

"I need to speak with her right away. This is an emergency."

Kovinn's ears twitched. "Very well, madam. I shall inform her grace when she arrives."

"My name is Khamiss. I'm at the central communications switchboard. Please beg her grace to call me as soon as she arrives."

"I will give her your message."

"Thank you." Khamiss rang off, then frowned and looked at the console. What next?

Cap'n Bob provided the answer. "Does Baron Silverside know?"

"No." She turned to the console, an order poised on her lips, and then she hesitated, a clear picture rising in her mind of Baron Silverside having a fit of hysterics and tearing out hunks of whisker.

"Let's not," she decided.

"Cheeseup!" called Dolfuss at the top of his lungs. By this point spectators' heads had ceased to turn at the sound of his roars, but instead had begun ducking between shoulders as if caught in an exploding hailstorm of bad taste. Dolfuss laid down his cards. "And I've got the Emperor in what-d'you-call-it, and that's . . ."

"Cheddar," said Vanessa.

"Right. How many points?"

Vanessa laid down her cards. "Sixty-four."

"Right again." He beamed. "I'm glad you suggested this game. Winning this one hand I've earned more cash than I get in sales commissions for a whole year."

Vanessa rose from her seat. "It's been a . . . *unique* experience, Mr. Dolfuss," she said. "I regret I must leave you."

"Too bad." Smirking. "Sorry to see you go. If you could, ah . . . ?" He took one of the betting chips and handed it to her. He looked at the score. "That's a total of two hundred and forty-four."

"Yes." She wrote the amount and signed it, then handed the chip back. *Choke on it,* she thought.

Dolfuss grinned and twitched the lapels of his green-on-yellow jacket. "Maybe I ought to travel to these sorts of places more often. I figured I wouldn't be able to afford them, but maybe I can after all." He gave Vanessa a speculative look. "Where are you travelling next? Maybe we can meet for another game, ha ha."

"I'm afraid my plans are unsettled; I really can't say where I'll be. Good afternoon, Mr. Dolfuss."

"Afternoon."

Seething, her whole being shrieking for bloody vengeance, Vanessa began moving toward the exit, then checked when she saw Fu George walking toward her. She approached him and took his arm.

"I damn well hope you got the Shard," she said. "Somebody ought to be rewarded for my spending an hour with the most repulsive individual I've ever met."

"Maijstral caught me." Simply.

Vanessa bared her teeth. "I could kill him."

Fu George raised a contemplative eyebrow. "You may not have to, my dear. I may do it for you."

Roberta found only Drexler in Fu George's suite. The Khosalikh agreed to have Fu George call her as soon as he returned, and Roberta began her return to her rooms. While waiting she could call the Marquess Kotani and agree upon a time to meet and arrange the encounter between Maijstral and Fu George. As she entered her corridor, she saw Paavo Kuusinen ahead of her, holding his walking stick meditatively behind him with both hands. Her pace increased.

"Mr. Kuusinen!"

He turned, saw her, and waited while she hastened to him. "I hope things have been arranged satisfactorily, your grace," he said. With some difficulty he matched her long-legged stride.

"Things are wretched. Maijstral lost the Shard and Fu George was caught red-handed in the room. Fu George denied stealing the Shard, and now he and Maijstral are going to fight a duel. I'm Maijstral's second. I just tried to speak to Fu George privately to see if we could reach an arrangement about the Shard, but he's not home."

Kuusinen stopped dead, his eyes opaque. Roberta, knowing him, paused. "Yes, Kuusinen? What is it?"

"A moment, your grace." Lost in thought, he paused, touched his chin with the head of his cane. He looked at her.

"Where is Maijstral now? I need to give him some information."

"I believe he's in a room on the Green Level. I don't quite remember the number."

"Would you do me the kindness of showing me where it is?"

"Certainly." She began striding down the corridor again. Kuusinen, after a skip or two, matched her pace. Roberta looked at him. He was frowning at the carpet.

"Are you going to tell me what's on your mind, Mr. Kuusinen?"

Kuusinen was startled. "I beg your pardon, your grace. I was . . . lost in thought." He cleared his throat. "It's rather complicated. Let me begin at the ball, that first night."

They arrived at the door of an elevator, and Roberta touched the service ideogram.

Kuusinen spoke on.

"What other ships are in dock?"

Cap'n Bob called up the manifests. "*Count Boston* will arrive in three days. Other than that, there are only private yachts belonging to Miss Vanessa Runciter, Baron Silverside, and Pearl Woman." She frowned. "The Baron's yacht is down for maintenance."

"Runciter's probably vanished along with Fu George," Khamiss mused. She turned to the console. "Contact Pearl Woman's suite."

Maijstral was not pleased to see Mr. Kuusinen, with or without the Duchess. He had just got a handle on his nerves, and the presence of his second reminded him of things he preferred to keep safely buried in the back of his mind. After Roman let the pair in, Maijstral remained prone on Dolfuss's bed, asking rhetorical questions of the ceiling while Kuusinen prosed on.

"The press is restricted here, you see. No one reporter is allowed to control more than eight media globes at any one time. So when I noticed that there were only six at the ball, and then six at your performance this afternoon, it became clear that they were being used elsewhere."

A flash of insight struck Maijstral. Quite suddenly he realized where this was going. He sat up abruptly. Hope floundered to the surface of his mind like an escaped convict pursuing daylight at the end of a long tunnel.

"Tell me more," he said.

Bells of doom tolling in his mind, pistol firmly snugged in a harness built into his jacket, Zoot walked with a cold, sepulchral tread toward the docks. A series of practical decisions had brought him here. He had been intending to kill himself in the bath, where it would be easy to clean up; but then he realized that the charge might go through his head into the room adjacent and do someone damage. He's decided therefore to kill himself in an isolated airlock, where the station crew would find it easier to clean up the mess and where no one else could get hurt.

Lord Qlp boomed on. Lady Dosvidern's expression alternated between despair and bafflement.

Pearl Woman, smiling triumphantly, seemed a bit surprised when she saw that it was Khamiss who called her.

"How may I help you, madam?" she asked.

"We have an emergency situation on the station," Khamiss said. "Lives are at stake. I wonder if we might meet you at the docks and perhaps ask for the codes to your yacht."

Pearl Woman tilted her head, permitting a view of the trademark that dangled from her ear. "Of course," she said. Her powerful shoulder muscles flexed. "I can be there in a few minutes." Her expression turned puzzled. "By the way," she added, "what's that *noise?*"

Khamiss hesitated. "Could I possibly explain later? It's part of our problem."

"Very well." She looked out of the camera's range. "Fetch the cutlasses, Advert. And some of our media globes."

Her hologram vanished. Lord Qlp's voice continued to roar from its speaker.

"Oh, no." Khamiss looked up sharply at Lady Dosvidern's tone.

"What's wrong?"

Lady Dosvidern's expression was stricken.

"Its lordship just imposed a deadline. We have one hour before it transmits its final message to Zynzlyp and blows up the station."

Khamiss rose from her chair, her hand resting on her holster. "Then I'll have to hurry," she said.

Once out the door she began to run.

Though she ran as fast as she could, she was possessed the while by a certain sense of futility. Once she got to the docks, she had no clear idea what she was going to do.

"Drake Maijstral's on the phone." Vanessa Runciter's eyes glittered coldly. "Trying to wriggle out of the encounter, no doubt."

Mild surprise overtook Fu George's features. "Odd. I wonder what he intends?" He and Vanessa had, just that moment, returned to their suite to find emergency lights blinking all over the telephone equipment—Drexler, crouched behind the sofa with detectors strapped over his eyes and a pistol in his hand, had steadfastly been refusing all communication. Vanessa had reached for the phone to check for messages just as a holographic Maijstral popped into view.

Fu George stepped to before the telephone. "Maijstral," he said, "are you certain this is quite regular?"

Maijstral's lazy green eyes, despite the bruising around the left, glowed with silent delight. "I'll confess to irregularity," he said, "but I think we find ourselves in an irregular situation."

Fu George raised an eyebrow. *"We?"* he asked. He'd take this gratuitous plural from Vanessa, but hardly from the man he expected to blast out of his boots in a day or two.

"I know this is an extremely odd request, Fu George," Maijstral said, "but would you do me the irregular favor of meeting me down on Mauve Level, outside room sixteen?"

Ignoring Vanessa's mime of outrage, Fu George gazed deliberately at Maijstral and assumed a look of gravity. "This had better be good," he said.

Pearl Woman was dashingly dressed in boots, pantaloons, a short-sleeved, quilted Quivira jacket, and her matched cutlasses. The butt of a Fantod Exquisite mapper protruded discreetly from the open jacket. Her private media globes, technically illegal onstation, orbited silently overhead. She listened to Khamiss's hasty story, then nodded.

"So you want to use my yacht to get some of your people across to the liner?"

"Right. Or, if necessary, ram the *Cheng* and disable it."

"Qlp will see you coming. He can't miss something the size of a yacht heading for him."

Khamiss's nostrils fluttered hopelessly. "I don't know what else to do."

Pearl Woman considered the question. "Maybe we could cross unobserved from an airlock to the liner."

Khamiss was in no mood to question the sudden gratuitous *we* in Pearl Woman's conversation, nor for that matter the illegal media globes that recorded the debate.

"*Cheng*'s got exterior cameras as well as detectors. If they're in use, its lordship will see us." Khamiss's diaphragm pulsed. "I may as well use the yacht. It will give me more options."

Pearl Woman frowned. "Do you by any chance have access to darksuits?"

Khamiss looked at her in slow surprise. "We confiscated darksuits from Maijstral and Fu George when they came on station."

"Excellent. They'll have antidetection mechanisms built in."

"The suits are in impoundment. Just over there."

Pearl Woman smiled. She drew her Fantod and spun it in her hand.

"Let's get them," she said, and her smile broadened. "You know, Miss Khamiss, I was planning on being bored today. It's nice to know I'll be disappointed."

Gregor and Roman, hopping and clashing elbows in their haste, were changing into their darksuits in the bathroom. Maijstral had adopted a more leisurely pace; he was letting the closet robot unlace his jacket and the sideseams of his trousers.

"Mr. Kuusinen, I thank you," he said. "I don't think you need be present at the finale unless you wish to be."

"I prefer to remain in the background, sir." Kuusinen bowed. "I wish you success."

Maijstral tore off his jacket, falling bands, and holster. "Your grace," he said as he unstrapped his knife from his forearm, "I thank you for bringing this to my attention."

"Pleased to be of help, Maijstral. Do you still want me to see Kotani?"

"Not until this business is resolved."

Roberta drew back her ears. "You wouldn't have a spare dark-suit, would you?"

"Not here. My spares are impounded at customs."

"Too bad, Maijstral. I'd like to be in on the finish, but I'm afraid I can't be seen in your company—I can't afford the appearance of colluding with you in the theft of my own treasure."

"I'll give you first view of the recordings, your grace."

"It's not the same as being there."

"Alas, not."

The door opened. Roman and Gregor stepped out, darksuit hoods drawn over their heads.

"We're ready, boss," Gregor said.

"If you'll excuse me, your grace."

"Maijstral." She stepped toward him and gently sniffed his ears. "Good luck." Surprise stirred in Maijstral. In the parting handclasp, the Duchess had offered him three fingers.

Vanessa Runciter, fashionably ornate detector goggles over her eyes, reached into the closet for her Nana-Coulville rifle. "Nana-Coulville," as the advertisements read, "gunmaker by appointment to His Imperial Majesty Nnis CVI," never mentioning that the Emperor had been frozen stiff for two generations and that even when he was alive he preferred stalking insects with nets to shooting live animals for sport. Vanessa's lightweight mapper was not precisely a sporting weapon, being intended for driving large-caliber slugs through force fields and into the bodies of sentient beings, whence the victims' nervous systems would be mapped within seconds and permanently short-circuited by the single-minded, homicidal, miniature intelligence concealed in the hard casing of the bullet.

Vanessa, pleased at the heft of the weapon in her hands, formed in her mind the happy image of little jagged lightning bolts running along the network of Drake Maijstral's nerves, turning them black as charcoal. Cheered by the graphic quality of the picture, Vanessa paused and smiled. It was a pity that Maijstral was going to get his comeuppance at Fu George's hands, not her own.

But maybe not. Perhaps Maijstral had lured Fu George and Drexler off to Mauve Level in order to loot his suite; in which case he would find Vanessa, Chalice, and a magazine full of nasty homicidal bullets waiting for him.

Dwelling on this cheerful thought, Vanessa glanced up, her detector goggles showing her the pulses of energy from the alarms set in the false closet ceiling atop which Fu George had stowed his loot. Vanessa's smile vanished. There was something wrong here.

She leaned the gun against the wall, reached up on tiptoe, and disengaged the false ceiling. Alarms failed to clang. The ceiling was suspiciously light.

The loot had gone. Vanessa flung the false ceiling across the room and sent crystal glasses hopping from the portable bar to the floor. Unsatisfactorily, none broke.

Maijstral! she thought.

"Chalice!" she shouted, and reached again for her gun. "To arms!"

"Boss," said Gregor. "I think I should tell you something."

"Later, Gregor."

"It's sort of important."

Maijstral looked at him in irritation. *"Later,"* he said more firmly.

Gregor shrugged and gave up. "Right," he said. "Like you say."

Maijstral, Roman, and Gregor stepped from Dolfuss's room, then rose on a-grav harnesses and sped down the corridor. Camouflage holograms blossomed around them. Dodging the occasional startled pedestrian, they soared straight to a communications main, entered, dropped three storeys to the Mauve Level, then raced onward. Mauve Level was devoted largely to storage of food, water, furniture, and other bulky items: the party encountered no employees or guests as they flew to their destination.

Geoff Fu George, his countenance displaying suspicion, waited with Drexler. Chalice and Vanessa, Maijstral assumed, were guarding Fu George's suite.

As Maijstral settled to the floor, Fu George folded his arms and gave him a cool look. "I hope you have an explanation for this, Maijstral."

"Yes. One moment." He gestured to his two assistants. They

deployed media globes, stepped to one of the false walls, inserted passkeys, and swung the false wall up on its hinges.

A startled Kyoko Asperson hung in a hammock stretched inside the utility corridor. Media globes circled over her head. Loot was piled high around her. There was clearly no room left for the impact diamond. The Eltdown Shard glowed at her throat. She raised a hand.

"Hi there." Tentatively.

"Boss," Gregor said. "This was what I wanted to talk to you about."

The airlock door closed silently behind him, a gateway from the world Zoot had known to the world awaiting him.

He glanced over the empty airlock and gave a long sigh as he ran over a mental checklist, assuring himself that there was nothing left to do with his life but finish himself off. Apparently, he concluded, there wasn't. His diaphragm pulsed reflectively.

His farewell text, sealed in an envelope, made a crinkling noise in his breast pocket as drew his disruptor and set the selector to "lethal." He licked his nose and pressed the barrel of the gun to his temple just below the left ear. His heart beat a slow dirge in his chest.

His eyes shut tight, he commended himself ritually to the Sixteen Active and Twelve Passive Virtues, then conjured in his mind's eye the image of Lady Dosvidern, in whose name he committed this act. The image, he discovered, was maddeningly indistinct. The situation was too distracting for proper meditation. Zoot growled and concentrated harder. The image hardened. Better.

Goodbye, cruel world, he thought, and prepared to squeeze the trigger.

The door behind him opened.

Zoot yowled in surprise and jumped three feet, his pulse hammering harder than it had when he was about to kill himself. He whirled and saw Khamiss and Pearl Woman standing in the airlock door, pistols in their hands.

Pearl Woman grinned at him. "Thought you were going to get away with it, eh?"

Zoot stared. "Your pardon?" he asked.

Pearl Woman stepped into the airlock. "You're not doing this alone, you know."

"I'm not?" He wondered briefly if he should ask them why they were doing away with themselves; then decided the question was in bad taste.

Pearl Woman laughed. "Thought you'd get sole credit, didn't you?"

Through his fog of bewilderment, Zoot became aware that his features were, once again, running through a long repertoire of ticks and palpitations. He drew himself up and summoned indignation.

"Ladies," he demanded, "what in heaven's name are you doing here?"

Pearl Woman touched the ideograms that controlled the airlock. "We're here for the same reason as you," she said. "Don't be naive."

Zoot looked at her as the door cycled shut. There must be some perspective on this, he thought desperately, in which all will make sense.

Khamiss stepped close to him. She put her hand on his arm and softly sniffed his ear. "Thank you, Zoot," she said. "I'm glad you're with us."

Zoot looked at her. His diaphragm gave a final, resigned spasm. "You're welcome," he said.

Hello, cruel world.

"Air's getting ready to cycle out," Pearl Woman said. "Turn on your fields."

For the first time Zoot noticed that the Pearl and Khamiss were both dressed in one-piece garments, Pearl Woman with her swords belted on over her clothes. The two intruders blurred slightly as they turned on the force fields that would capture and preserve the air around them.

Zoot had built a similar field into his jacket, mainly to aid in river crossings or diving into predator-filled waters. With a push of his mind, he turned it on.

He was long past the point of trying to figure things out. He'd follow the others and hope, eventually, everything made sense.

He was too confused to feel relief.

"Good work, Kuusinen. I am in your debt."

"All in a day's work, your grace." The door to Roberta's suite swung open. She stepped in and glanced in surprise at her telephone.

"Look at all the emergency lights," she said. "I wonder what's going on *now?*"

"A common thief," Fu George said. "I'm surprised at you, Miss Asperson."

Kyoko reached into a pocket. "Hardly common," she said. "Here's my burglar's ticket. Read it and weep."

Fu George looked at it, then handed it to Maijstral, who saw that it had been issued three years before to a Michi K. Asperson by the Imperial Sporting Commission representative on Khovenburg. He handed the ticket back and turned to Fu George.

"Do you recall this name on the listings?" he asked.

"I'm ranked third from the bottom." Kyoko smiled. "Most of my jobs haven't received any publicity."

"I see," Fu George said. "You were going to release all the recordings to the Commission at once, then leap to the top of the ratings all in one go."

"Something like that. I figured that would be worth a lot of style points."

"And in the meantime you would be able to use your job as interviewer to get close to people and plan your jobs. Very neat, Miss Asperson. I congratulate you." Fu George had, while speaking, reached into the hiding place, removed bundles and boxes, and begun to sort through them.

"I don't have the advantage of gentle birth," Kyoko said. "I've got to make up for it somehow."

"Wait a moment," said Fu George. He looked up in surprise. "These are mine!" He brandished a handful of the Waltz twins' jewels. "When did you take these?"

Kyoko shrugged modestly. "About an hour ago."

"While I was in Maijstral's blind, being held at gunpoint."

She looked from Fu George to Maijstral, rising delight on her round face. "At gunpoint? Really?"

"At gunpoint," Maijstral said, narrowing his eyes over his pistol's sights. "Really." This woman, he realized, had almost got him killed. He stepped closer to her and, manfully resisting the impulse to strangle her, delicately removed the Eltdown Shard from her neck. She watched with regret as the Shard dropped into Maijstral's darksuit pocket. Regret changed to indignation as Maijstral's hand moved to one of her boxes, snagged Madame la Riviere's diamond necklace, and dropped it into the same pocket.

"Hey, that was mine! I didn't take it from either of you!"

Maijstral smiled delicately and opened another box. Emerald brilliants dangled from his fingers, then disappeared into the cargo compartment built into the darksuit's back. "You may object if you wish, Miss Asperson," he said. "You can even call for help if that is your preference. But if you summon the authorities, you will doubtless be apprehended for theft of the Shard and for what also appear to be numerous other items discovered missing in the last day or so, including personal property belonging to Mr. Fu George and myself. Fu George and I, of course, have the recordings that *prove* that the items were stolen, legally, by us, and are now our property." Dusky pearls glowed magically in air as Maijstral tossed a necklace to Roman, who caught it deftly and stowed it in a pocket.

Kyoko sighed. "Easy come, easy go," she said.

"Besides, Miss Asperson," Fu George said cheerfully, "Maijstral and I can steal from you if we feel like it. It's what we do for a *living.*" Lady Tvax's glowstone bracelets disappeared into a pocket. He frowned at Kyoko. "Not only that, you've been going about asking provocative questions about our *duel,* as you put it, and I don't care for that. Theft is one thing, provoking antagonism quite another." He stripped the cover from an elastic box and tipped it to show the contents to Maijstral. "Quite a lot here, wouldn't you say?"

Kyoko gave a laugh. "I robbed the hotel safe." Smugly. "It was easy once I sabotaged the central security console during an interview."

"My congratulations. I'm sure Maijstral and I are duly grateful." Fu George handed the box to Drexler.

"Careful, Fu George," Maijstral said. "We should divide this evenly."

Fu George gave Maijstral a look. "You owe me one, I believe. For last night."

"Ah. How discourteous of me to forget. My apologies."

"Think nothing of it, old boy."

Kyoko's hoard gradually resolved itself into two piles. Maijstral's was the larger, mainly because of the considerable bulk of the Baroness Silverside's art collection. Pockets bulged with small items of sculpture and jewelry. "Gregor," Maijstral said. "Ask the station to send us a large robot. We'll take my collection to our room."

"I saw a cargobot around the corner. I'll do a snap-off on it."

"Very well."

Fu George holstered his weapon. "I believe Drexler and I will take our leave. It was clever of you to have worked out what happened."

Maijstral gave him a careless smile. "It was easy," lying cheerfully, "once I realized the significance of the media globes."

"Still, a very impressive piece of deduction."

"Thank you, Fu George."

Fu George raised a hand to pat his famous hair into place. "As far as our encounter goes, Maijstral . . ."

"Yes?" Glee danced wickedly in Maijstral's heart.

"Do you think at this point a meeting is strictly necessary?"

Maijstral stroked his chin and feigned consideration. "I shouldn't think so," he said, putting a touch of reluctance into his voice. "I'll speak to the Duchess and ask her not to see Kotani after all."

"Very well." Fu George grinned whitely. "Your servant, Maijstral."

"Yours."

Fu George and Drexler made their congé and departed. Maijstral waited by his pile, his gun still trained deliberately on Kyoko Asperson—he wasn't about to be caught again. Kyoko, he observed, seemed a bit depressed.

"Don't be too cast down, Miss Asperson," Maijstral said. "You'll still get quite a few style points out of this adventure."

"I suppose I shall."

"I imagine your recordings will go for a very high price. Of course, the Silverside material will have to be spliced with mine and Fu George's to make any sense, but I suppose we'll all three get a sizeable advance, considering the, ah, sensational nature of the material."

"Got the bot, boss." Gregor sailed into sight standing on the platform of a transport robot. The robot came to a stop and Gregor stepped off. "Robot," he instructed, "put this pile on board. Be gentle, since some of it's fragile."

"Yes, sir." Invisible tractors and repellers began lifting the precious objects and placing them on the robot's bed. Gregor stood by, his fingers tapping a hesitant rhythm on the robot's skull.

"Boss," he said. "I'd like to make it clear that I didn't have anything to do with this."

Maijstral looked at him in surprise, then remembered himself and returned his attention to Kyoko and his firearm. "I never thought you had, Gregor," he said.

"See, Miss Asperson and I have got sort of involved. But I never told her anything about our jobs."

Maijstral concealed his surprise.

"That's true, Maijstral." Kyoko's face was earnest. "He never told me anything, though I did try to worm a *little* information out of him. I got most of my information by following you around with micromedia globes. I was careful, and you didn't detect them."

"Ah." Maijstral contemplated Kyoko's round face over his gunsight and, mentally, squeezed his trigger repeatedly. "A word of advice, Gregor," he said. "Never get involved with the media."

"Right, boss. I'll keep that in mind."

The robot loaded the last of the loot. "Robot," Maijstral ordered, "take these to the elevator. At walking speed."

"Yes, sir."

Maijstral and Roman walked backward down the corridor after the robot, their guns still drawn in hopes of discouraging Kyoko from an act of desperation. They rounded a corner and slowly headed for the nearest elevator.

"Well done, sir," Roman said.

"Thank you, Roman."

"Should I holster my gun?"

"Let's get in the elevator first." They continued their slow walk, arrived at a bank of three elevators, and stopped before the middle one. Doors opened before Gregor could touch the ideogram.

"Hello," Gregor said, surprised. "Good afternoon, your grace. Mr. Kuusinen."

Maijstral, still walking backward, snapped on his detectors. The pickups in the rear of his darksuit gave him a clear image of Roberta and Kuusinen, who had just appeared as the leftmost elevator opened. Both appeared a bit breathless.

"Your grace," Maijstral said.

"The emergency's turned very serious," Roberta said. "I'll need the Shard."

"Certainly." He plucked it from his pocket and held it out to her. She took it.

The doors of the elevator on the far right opened.

"Have you seen Fu George?" Roberta asked.

Maijstral smiled. "Taken care of."

"A-*ha!*" Maijstral turned in surprise at the sound of Vanessa Runciter's voice. She and Chalice had just leaped from the elevator, guns in their hands. Vanessa's mapper was pointed at Maijstral. Her face was torn by loathing.

"Assassin," she said. "I'll take care of *you.*" And then, as Maijstral gaped at her in astonishment, she pulled the trigger.

The giant *Viscount Cheng* floated above, over the asteroid's close horizon. Khamiss's flesh prickled at the sight: three of them were going up against *that?* Followed by Pearl Woman and Zoot, she took cover behind a landing cradle and paused to consider the situation. The others clustered next to her, merging their force fields and creating a common atmosphere in which they could all speak.

"Zoot," she asked, "will your jacket hide you from detectors?"

"I'm afraid not. There isn't much call for that on unexplored planets. But I've got simple darksuit projectors, to confuse native predators."

Khamiss glanced at the vast liner once again and reminded herself that there was only one Drawmiikh aboard: even with five eyes he couldn't be watching everything. She pulsed a series of minor commands to her suit and found that it obeyed her with surprising speed and ease. It was easier to be a first-rank burglar than she'd thought.

"I'll try to provide a screen for all of us," she said. "Zoot, if you'll put your arms around my waist from behind, and Pearl Woman in turn holds onto you, I think we'll present a smaller profile."

"Very well."

Zoot maneuvered himself behind her, locking arms around her waist. His furry chin settled on her shoulder. The contact reassured her; she experienced a wave of thankfulness that she wasn't alone in this. Holographic camouflage appeared around them and they began moving.

Rathbon's Star rose blazing above the rock's horizon. Red light dazzled Khamiss's eyes. *Cheng* was getting larger and larger. Her darksuit informed her that the ship's scanners were active; but the suit also countered the scans automatically. The admiration Khamiss felt for the suit's builder increased. Her confidence grew. So did the *Viscount Cheng.*

Khamiss's half-blinded eyes perceived a dorsal airlock and she headed for it. As the ship grew nearer, her suit began to signal her, little abstruse symbols and numbers appearing in the visual centers of her brain. She tried to puzzle them out, but couldn't. The signals continued. An urgent audio tone made her jump. Rathbon's Star dazzled her vision.

"We're getting close," Zoot said, his tone a bit worried; and Khamiss's awareness rose from the darksuit's signals to observe the *Cheng* was very near indeed. Its size had confused her as to distance. She slammed on the repellers, but too late.

Khamiss went face first into the *Cheng*'s hull next to the airlock. There was another impact as Zoot slammed into her from behind, then a third as Pearl Woman entered the crush.

The repellers now reversed, the accordion rebounded, sailing backward into space. Cymbals crashed in Khamiss's skull. She tried to head for the airlock again, but symbols were still pulsing in her mind and she wasn't entirely used to the suit yet. The audio tone blatted in her aural centers, distracting her. The *Cheng* came up very fast.

Khamiss hit muzzle first again. Zoot knocked the wind out of her; Pearl Woman bent some ribs. The three bounded back.

Her mind thoroughly awash by now, Khamiss got one mental command confused with another and piled on the speed. The urgent audio tone startled her and she didn't notice the *Cheng* coming up until she went into it nose first.

Zoot slammed into her again.

Pearl Woman brought up the rear. The three rebounded once more.

"That was fun," Pearl Woman said. "Shall we do it again?"

"Madam, allow me," said Zoot, a bit breathless. Gratitude filled Khamiss's reeling brain as Zoot, using his own repellers, guided all three precisely to the airlock. Khamiss dabbed with her cuff at her bleeding nose.

"Sorry," she mumbled.

"How do we get in, precisely?" Pearl Woman said. "If we open the airlock, Qlp's going to see it on the control panel."

"I can get us in," Khamiss said, denasal. Her head was still spinning. "This suit has everything necessary to cut out the alarms. Just give me a moment."

Gradually Khamiss's spinning mind stabilized. The symbols and audio she'd been receiving, she realized dully, were meant to inform her of the swift approach of something solid.

"Live and learn," she muttered.

Pearl Woman looked at her. "Can we save the maxims for later?"

Khamiss opened Maijstral's belt pouches and surveyed the contents. Her job as a security officer allowed her to recognize most of the objects therein, but unfortunately she had never actually operated any of them before. Her ears twitched in puzzlement.

Pearl Woman stepped closer to her, merging air pockets. "I hate to impart a traumatizing sense of urgency," she said, "but if you don't open the door very quickly, we're all going to run out of air."

"A moment. I'm not entirely familiar with the equipment."

"I think that point has already been demonstrated," Pearl Woman said, "but thank you for the reminder."

Khamiss took a moment to smooth her rising hackles. Moving deliberately, she chose the detector she thought she needed, scanned the door, and perceived the energies operating in the door's lock. The lock was simple—this was a personnel hatch, not a security door, and its operation was as simple as possible for the convenience of the crew. She reached for what she recognized as a tossoff remote and placed it above the lock, cutting out the circuit that would report the lock's status to *Cheng*'s control room. Then, with an insouciant gesture, she triggered the circuit that would open the airlock door.

Pleasure trickled through her as the door began to open.

"Very professional, Miss Khamiss," Zoot said. He handed her a handkerchief, and Khamiss placed it to her nose.

Pearl Woman had already dropped into the airlock. Media globes recorded her movements. Her mouthed comments were fortunately inaudible through the vacuum of space.

Khamiss and Zoot followed. The door closed and air rushed in.

Pearl Woman drew her Fantod in one hand and a cutlass in the other. Her smile was cheerful.

"Now the fun starts," she said.

Vanessa Runciter had always suffered from an excess of passion. Her first slug therefore missed—she was so passionately angry that she fired her rifle from the hip, and the round went wide.

An electric shriek of fear crackled up Maijstral's spine. He forgot he had a pistol in his hand, forgot where he was and what he had around him—instead he slammed on his darksuit's shields, his camouflage, and his a-grav harness, and went skimming backward at full speed.

A blaze of Roman's spitfire charges fountained off Vanessa's shields. Out of the corner of his eye Maijstral saw Roman moving, Chalice charging, and then his vision went to hell as disaster struck. He had forgotten the robot and the pile of loot that were just behind him, and his lower body struck the robot with a numbing crunch. His velocity was such that, on impact, his feet were thrown skyward—his boots hit the ceiling and rebounded; and this impact, in turn, threw his head upward. Stars filled Maijstral's vision as his skull rang against porcelain-covered asteroid material. He hit the ceiling a second time. His gun clattered to the floor.

Maijstral threw his a-grav repellers into neutral. His velocity diminished. Through the galaxies that exploded behind his eyes, he dimly saw Gregor jump behind the robot while clawing desperately for his pistol, Roman flattening Chalice with an expert roundhouse kick to the head and then leaping vainly for Vanessa, and, most horribly, Vanessa shouldering her rifle and taking careful aim, pointing the barrel directly between Maijstral's eyes. . . .

A lunging form intervened. Roberta flung herself from the elevator in a perfect racer's pass, feet first, legs lashing out in a kick at the precise moment of impact. Vanessa's ribs caved in with an audible crack and she flew like a broken doll across the hallway. The mapper slug went into Baroness Silverside's collection and demolished a genuine Adrian bronze of Flashman Capone, the famous stage actor and swindler.

Roberta twisted in midair and landed, amazingly enough, on her feet. She reached for Vanessa's rifle, snatched it, and drove the stock of the Nana-Coulville quite deliberately into Vanessa's face. Vanessa fell to the floor unconscious.

"Hit her again," Maijstral wanted to say, "she might be faking." But he seemed unable to speak. Instead he floated near the ceiling and watched as Roman and Gregor relieved Vanessa and Chalice of their gear.

"Are you all right, sir?" The voice was Paavo Kuusinen's.

Maijstral willed off his camouflage and made an affirmative gesture with his ears. He looked down at Kuusinen.

"I believe so," he said, pleased to discover his voice working again.

He lowered himself to the floor. He found to his surprise that his legs would support him. He bent to pick up his pistol.

"If you don't mind an inquiry, sir," Kuusinen said, "what was that about?"

Maijstral looked at the two unconscious bodies and could only flutter his ears in bewilderment.

Chalice moaned. He stirred himself and opened his eyes to find himself staring into a circle of pistols. Gregor gave him a look.

"Isn't this a little overdone," he said, "just to escape a ten-novae debt?"

His mind aswim, Zoot stepped from the airlock into *Viscount Cheng*'s crew quarters. Khamiss and Pearl Woman, weapons in their hands, glanced fore and aft at the complex pattern of small rooms, then looked at each other. "Where's a service plate?" Pearl Woman asked. "We'll ask the ship for a path to the control room."

"That way," Zoot said, pointing aft. He wondered if he should draw his weapon, then decided to keep it holstered for the time being. He stepped out of the airlock and began moving toward the ship's stern. Pearl Woman looked at him suspiciously.

"How do you know?"

Zoot was offhand. "I'm familiar with the specifications of the Celebrated Noble class."

Pearl Woman's suspicion was undiminished. "How? Do you stay up at night studying ship architecture?"

"I travelled in the crew quarters of the *Baron Marbles* once, when I was on the Ottoman expedition."

"I see." Still unconvinced.

Zoot led them to an elevator and called for it. "The control room's a short distance from the elevator." He looked at his companions and a flood of doubt entered his mind. He still had no clear notion what he and the others were doing here. He gnawed his lip, then spoke cautiously.

"I wonder, ladies, how we're going to handle the, ah, problem."

Khamiss's tone was worried. "Lord Qlp's got five brains. It'll be hard to knock out."

Lord Qlp? Zoot wondered.

The elevator arrived and the party stepped into it. "If we can catch its lordship by surprise," Pearl Woman said, "we can put a volley into it. That should probably do the job. My mapper can burn its nerves in a few seconds."

Khamiss seemed undecided. "I'd hate to kill it. It's probably just crazy."

"It might well be Lord Qlp or us. Or even Lord Qlp and the station."

"I'd still prefer to give it a chance to surrender. Or stun it."

Danger to the station? Zoot thought. And then, Lord Qlp?

"That may not be possible," Pearl Woman said. "It may be armed. It may also have ordered the ship to dive into the antimatter bottle on oral command—it'd only need a second or two."

Antimatter bottle? Zoot thought. He drew his pistol and contemplated both the setting and the consequences of an accident with a large antimatter container. His diaphragm pulsed in resignation and he clicked the setting to "nonlethal."

"I would prefer to stun its lordship if possible," he said. "The three of us should be able to do that, certainly."

The elevator doors opened. Pearl Woman looked disgruntled, then holstered her pistol, which had no nonlethal setting. "Right," she said. "I've an idea." She stepped out of the elevator, glanced left and right, and stepped through an open office door labelled "Purser." When she returned it was with a small container.

"I'll tell it I've got the Shard," she said. "That should distract it for a few seconds."

Shard? thought Zoot.

"Good idea," Khamiss said. "Best speak in Khosali—its lordship may not understand Human Standard."

The hallway was far more sumptuous than the crew quarters: parquet flooring, hand-woven, sound-absorbent tapestries featuring scenes of festive aristocrats dining amidst exotic splendor. "The command center is just through those doors," Zoot said, pointing to a pair of doors made of mottled ceramic and decorated with reliefs featuring the high points of Viscount Cheng's colorful Colonial Service career.

"Let me check it." Khamiss stepped forward and deployed her detectors. She found the door locked and alarmed and, moving carefully, she deployed her unfamiliar equipment and took apart its defenses. "Ready," she said.

The Shard? Zoot thought. He looked at Pearl Woman and the box. An idea struck him.

"Here," he said. "Take one of my lights." He took a pencil flash from his inner jacket rig and gave it to the Pearl. "Turn it on and put it in the box. When you open it, the interior should glow. It may look as if the Shard is inside."

"Thank you, Zoot."

Pearl Woman brushed her leonine hair back from her eyes. One of her media globes circled to record her from a more favorable angle. "I'll go through the right door while you hide behind the left. I'll use the darksuit to fly across the room. When I've got its attention directed toward me, step into the doorway and open fire." She gave a devil-may-care grin for benefit of the recorder. "Let's go," she said.

Lord Qlp, Zoot mused, and the Eltdown Shard. Antimatter bottles, and a liner apparently stolen. Were things unusually confused right now, he wondered, or had life always been this way and Zoot not noticed?

"Very good," he said. Readiness coursed through him. At the worst, he reflected, he'd only kill himself in this adventure, and that was what he'd set out to do in the first place.

Zoot stepped behind the door and deployed his jacket's darksuit projectors. They were far less sophisticated than those built into the suits Khamiss and Pearl Woman were wearing, providing only a cloud of darkness that obscured his outline rather than causing it to blend in with the background, but he concluded that it might serve to confuse Lord Qlp even so.

Khamiss stepped behind him and triggered her own camouflage. She pressed close. Zoot could hear her heart thudding against his backbone.

"Good luck," she said.

"Same to you."

Pearl Woman took a breath, stationed her globes for best advantage, and flung herself through the door. Lord Qlp's sputtering, booming voice, formerly suppressed by the sound screens in the door, was suddenly very loud. Zoot could feel Khamiss jump in surprise at its lordship's volume.

"I've got the Shard!" Pearl Woman shouted, in Khosali Standard. "Put down the pistols! I've got the Shard!"

Pistols? thought Zoot, alarmed at the plural. For a frantic moment he considered changing his weapon's setting to "lethal," decided against it, then stepped into the doorway and braced his own pistol to fire.

The control room was very large and sumptuously appointed—travellers sometimes stopped by to chat with the captain, and expected the amenities. Pearl Woman floated against the far wall, shouting frantically, waving the bag under her chin. Ghostly light from the flash illuminated her face from below.

Lord Qlp had disdained the padded captain's chair and instead was reared up near the communications console at the front of the room. Two of its eyestalks had wrapped themselves around pistol butts and triggers, the eyes laid along the barrels in order to sight them. The guns were both directed toward Pearl Woman.

Zoot thought fast. Lord Qlp had a mouth at either end, and therefore both mouths should be stunned first in order to end any possibility of an oral command being given. That, unfortunately, would leave the pistols free to fire. Concern for Pearl Woman and Khamiss flashed into his mind. He overrode it with an act of will.

He fired for the upper end first. Lord Qlp gave a startled belch from its lower mouth and fell forward across the console. One of its pistols went off, and a chugger slug exploded off the wall near Pearl Woman. Khamiss's stunner crackled and Lord Qlp twitched. Pearl Woman flung the bag at Lord Qlp and commenced a zigzag path across the room while drawing her cutlasses. Explosive chugger rounds blew holes in the ceiling. Zoot fired for the lower mouth. Lord Qlp collapsed. One of its pistols trained toward Khamiss, and alarm flared in Zoot as his next shot missed.

Pearl Woman gave a shout and flung a cutlass. It sliced the eyestalk neatly and the pistol fell. Khamiss and Zoot fired four or five more times each. Lord Qlp thrashed and lay still.

Zoot stepped to the navigation console in three fast strides. "Display course plot," he said. The computer obliged, showing a trajectory plotted, sure enough, right into the magnetic bottle that held antimatter for the power station.

"Cancel plotted course," Zoot said, and the plot vanished.

Pearl Woman gave a triumphant laugh and performed a somersault in the air en route to the navigation console. "I did it!" she cackled. "That cutlass was right on target!" Her exuberance turned to shouts of joy. *"Yaaaaaah! Yaaaaaah!"* She touched the controls to the video unit and broadcast her image to Silverside Station. The hologram of a wide-eyed Tanquer appeared over the console, with the *Cheng*'s captain peering anxiously over her shoulder.

Pearl Woman smiled and turned her head slightly to display the pearl dangling from one ear. She brandished her remaining cutlass. "This is Pearl Woman," she said. "We have retrieved the situation. All's well."

The Tanquer's eyes rolled up into her nictitating membranes as she passed out. There was an audible thump as she hit the floor.

"Send a crew to bring us to dock," Pearl Woman said to the remaining figure of Cap'n Bob. She peered into the hologram. "And who *was* that, anyway?"

"I'm not sure," said the captain. "Whoever she is, she's rather odd."

Zoot put his pistol in his holster and looked at Khamiss. Khamiss held his gaze for a moment. Zoot felt a glorious moment of internal warmth. Khamiss looked away. Confusion roiled in Zoot's breast. He turned back to the course plotter and felt something awkward in his breast pocket. He was surprised to remember that it was his suicide note.

He took the envelope from his pocket and looked at it for a long moment. Then he tore it in half, then put it in the nearest disposal.

Lord Qlp gave a belch. Pearl Woman looked up, alarmed. Its lordship twitched, then spoke distinctly in Khosali.

"I'm bored," it said. "Bored, bored, bored."

Zoot and Khamiss weren't listening. They were gazing at one another in some surprise.

ELEVEN

Voices in the White Room were resonating perfectly once again. Five days after its disappearance, the giant impact diamond had been ransomed and restored to its place of honor.

"Yes. After all those shots, its lordship *was* a little scrambled. One of its brains began to babble uncontrollably."

"About the Drawmii's, ah, existential dilemma."

"Yes." Zoot gazed into Kyoko's hovering media globes. "It seems that the Drawmii's multiple brains provide sophisticated and subtle modes of converse unavailable to the rest of us. They consider us terribly unsophisticated by comparison."

"And their lack of interaction with the Empire was not the result of their alien thought patterns, but because they were, ah . . ."

"They found us incomparably tedious."

"Right." Kyoko gave a half-believing smile. "Who could find *us* dull? I ask you."

"The thought is a bit humbling, I must admit." Zoot frowned at Kyoko's loupe. "But be that as it may, the Drawmii concluded that if the Khosali and other member species of the Empire were the best the universe could offer them, they might as well destroy themselves before they were all bored to death. Lord Qlp was sent forth as an ambassador, hoping to find some token which might give his species hope."

"And he found the Eltdown Shard."

"It appears so. Perhaps we'll never understand its reasons for choosing the Shard; presumably we can all be thankful it found *something* worth living for. It intended to purchase the Shard with the unique . . . tokens . . . that it manufactured in its innards, but the Shard was stolen, and its lordship began to lose all hope. *That,"* emphatically, "was when Lady Dosvidern became alarmed and contacted me, as an expert in xenobiology. She and I tried for an entire night to make sense of Lord Qlp's cryptic remarks. Unfortunately I was unable to help her."

Kyoko smiled thinly. "That was why you spent the night in her suite."

"And why I couldn't tell you the truth concerning why I was there. Yes."

Zoot grinned at her, tongue lolling from a corner of his muzzle. He was pleased to discover that his facial muscles were obeying him this time, not betraying him with twitches and tics. Now that he had a plausible story, there was no reason to do away with himself. He was thankful for that, as by now he had other plans.

"Incidentally, Miss Asperson," Zoot said, "I have another pair of announcements. Firstly, I intend to retire from the Diadem."

Kyoko's visible eye widened. "After your greatest achievement? Your ratings are certain to take a leap."

Zoot allowed a touch of regret to enter his expression. "I've enjoyed my time in the Diadem, of course, but I'm afraid I've found that celebrity is interfering with my true business, which is xenobiology. I intend to join the next plotting expedition bound outward."

"Well." Kyoko appeared to be considering matters. "A vacancy among the Three Hundred."

"I'm certain it will be filled by someone worthy."

"Of course."

"Perhaps yourself. When Maijstral and Fu George revealed your covert activities two days ago, it created a sensation."

Kyoko gave him a look. "You said two announcements, I believe."

"Ah. Forgive me. And the most important announcement of all, too." Zoot grinned. "I intend marriage."

"Congratulations. Do I know the lady?"

"Miss Khamiss. She will be resigning her security job and joining me in the expedition."

Kyoko gave a laugh. "Interesting how the crises in Silverside Station have tended to resolve into romance."

"Has there been more than one?"

"Yes. But it would be inappropriate to speak of the other at this stage."

"Ah." Zoot grinned again. "In that case, let discretion reign. By all means."

Baron Silverside still frowned and flushed angrily at the provoking sight of Mr. Sun. Even the sight of Mr. Sun in a robe and cowl, eccentric dress even for a fashionable resort.

"My resignation, sir."

"Accepted."

So much for ceremony, thought Mr. Sun. Well. He must atone for his faults. Let the atonement begin now.

"I have taken second-class passage on the *Count Boston,*" said Sun. "I will enter a New Puritan monastery on Khorn."

The Baron smiled. "Very good, Mr. Sun. You may rest assured that in the ensuing years I will often be comforted by the thought of your cleaning latrines and flagellating yourself."

Sun only bowed. Things had come about this way, he was certain, because of some fault within his character. He knew not what the fault was, only that it was there, and that somehow it had put him in dutch with the Almighty.

Now he would have many years—decades, perhaps—to discover what it was.

"Miss Khamiss has given notice also," the Baron said, and frowned. "Despite my offers of a higher salary."

"Mr. Kingston is perfectly qualified," Sun said. "He is a little frivolous in his parts, but I think he is solid enough."

Baron Silverside gave him a suspicious look. He was not prepared to accept any of Sun's judgements at their face value.

"Very well, Sun," he said. "If you are finished . . . ?"

As he stepped from the Baron's office, Sun was surprised to feel a blossom of happiness opening in his soul. Atonement, he found, had left him oddly content.

"It bothers me that I've been contacted about the diamond but not about the other. I'll increase the offer by a quiller."

"Thank you, my lord, but I think not." Geoff Fu George smiled placatingly at the holographic image of Baron Silverside. "Maijstral and I seem to have arrived at a delicate arrangement on these matters. I would not care to disturb it."

"I wish you would reconsider, Fu George." Baron Silverside scowled in thought. "It is a very pretty piece of money."

"Your lordship's offer has been kind," said Fu George, "but I think not."

"If that's your final word." Gruffly.

"I'm afraid it is. Your obedient servant."

"Yours."

Fu George turned from the telephone and stepped to his suite, where Vanessa was supervising the packing of his loot. Vanessa gave him a look. The look was odd, but Fu George couldn't tell whether the oddness was intentional or rather a result of the fact that Vanessa's face, at the moment, simply *looked* odd. The bruising had been massive, the nose had been broken, and for the last several days Vanessa had been in seclusion with a mass of semilife forms attached to her face.

"I wish you had accepted the Baron's offer," she said, denasal. She rotated toward him stiffly: the ribs were healing fast under hormone infusions, but were still giving her trouble. "I'd like to see Maijstral lose that art collection."

Fu George placed bits of foam packing around the delicate settings of an antique necklace. "I'd rather not try for Maijstral's loot again. Our working against one another has been fraught with more than the usual amount of hazard. Kyoko used our rivalry for her own ends. I'd prefer not to be rendered so vulnerable again."

She lit a cigaret. "Still," she said, "one last coup seems such a tempting idea. What with the collection *and* the Shard *and* that display with the diamond, Maijstral may end up with a lot of points in the next rating. He's certain to receive a promotion. He may even take first place."

Fu George closed the jewel case. "It had to happen sooner or later, Vanessa."

"I don't like the idea of our not being on top."

Our? thought Fu George. He sighed and turned to her. "We've got all the money and fame we could desire," he said. "It's been fun. But sooner or later someone else was going to take first, or I was going to get careless or unlucky and end up in prison somewhere. And very soon the Constellation Practices Authority may well recommend Allowed Burglary be *dis*allowed throughout the Human Constellation, which would substantially decrease the amount of enjoyment to be had from this profession." He spread his hands. "Perhaps the time has come for a gracious retirement."

Smoke curled disdainfully from Vanessa's nostrils. "And do *what,* Fu George? Do you want me to spend our declining years on our back terrace, watching the robots trim the hedges while you write your memoirs?"

"Hardly that."

"I like spice in my life, Fu George. Excitement. *I'm* still young, you know."

Fu George ignored this reflection on his age. "I thought the Diadem might be persuaded to renew their offer. That would guarantee us travel and celebrity."

"Hm."

"In any case, I have no intention of retiring as long as I'm still in first place."

"*That* was why I wanted you to take the collection."

"That subject of conversation," Fu George said, turning back to his jewels, "has long ceased to be of interest to me."

"Hm," said Vanessa again, and breathed in smoke. This was going to take some thinking about.

"I think not, my lord," Maijstral said. Baron Silverside glared at him stonily.

"It's a good offer," he said.

"I prefer to decline. Fu George and I are professionals, after all. We don't pursue foolish rivalries."

"If that's your last word."

"It is. Thank you, however, for considering me."

The Baron broke the connection. Maijstral let the service hologram float in his bedroom and stepped into the front room of his suite. The Marquess and Marchioness Kotani were returning their drinks to Roman's tray.

"Another drink, my lady? My lord?"

"No, Roman," Kotani said, speaking for both. "Thank you."

"My apologies," Maijstral said. "A personal call."

Kotani lifted an eyebrow. "Not getting another bid, were you?"

"He doesn't know I have the collection. Not for certain, anyway. He keeps trying to hire me to steal it from Fu George."

"I'm afraid this last week has cost the Baron rather heavily."

"But not in custom, I daresay. After the last seven days, Silverside Station is certain to become established as one of the most fashionable resorts in the Constellation. Were I the Baron, I might well consider my losses justified."

"Quite." Kotani smiled thinly. "Lucky that I struck my arrangement with the Baron before that fact became obvious to him."

Maijstral bowed. "I congratulate you on your sense of timing, my lord."

"This means Kotani and I will revisit Silverside for the play," said the Marchioness. She looked at Maijstral from beneath her lashes. "The place has such fond memories for me, such . . . sympathetic resonance."

"I'm glad," said Maijstral, seating himself, "that your ladyship found your stay fulfilling."

"And," looking at him, "I shall be taking memories with me, in the form of the collection. I will delight in installing such a distinguished accumulation of artwork at home in Kotani Castle."

Kotani patted her arm. "This idea of yours was inspired, dearest," he said. "I barely had to make a single correction after all those negotiations with Maijstral."

"I think," she said, no longer daring to look at Maijstral, "the negotiations were my favorite part."

"And now, my lord . . .?" Maijstral held up a Casino betting chip and a molecular pencil.

"Certainly. My pleasure." Kotani wrote an amount, signed, printed. Maijstral took the chip and placed it in his pocket.

"I'll have one of my people deliver the collection this afternoon," Maijstral said. "In plenty of time for the departure of the *Boston.*"

Kotani stood. "I have arrangements to make, alas," he said. Maijstral stood and the two men sniffed ears. "Your servant."

"Your very obedient. Oh. Beg pardon, my lord. My shoe caught in the carpet."

"Think nothing of it, Maijstral."

"My lady." Maijstral helped the Marchioness to rise.

"It has been a great pleasure, Maijstral." She sniffed his ears and clasped his hand. Maijstral stiffened slightly in surprise.

"Yours ever, my lady," he said.

After Roman closed the door behind them, Maijstral looked at the object in his right palm. It was a small jewelled pin, fashioned of silver, rubies, and brilliants, in the shape of the Rover of Hearts. The ideogram for Singh's Jewelers was stamped on the back.

"How very thoughtful of her ladyship," Maijstral said. He opened his other hand, which held the two diamond studs Kotani had worn in his left cuff. He had taken the studs off the right cuff in greeting, and the two securing the jacket while giving him his drinks. Stealing the studs hadn't been difficult: replacing them had. The phony diamonds would dissolve in a matter of weeks. Maijstral dropped the pair of studs in his left jacket pocket, along with the other four.

The Rover of Hearts he pinned to his lapel.

Shifting chromatics blazed from the three objects on Roberta's table. "The colors appears to be the result of bacterial action," Roberta said. "They do not seem to feed on anything but light, and most of that they give off as phosphorescence. Another drink, Kuusinen?"

"Thank you, your grace." Roberta signalled Kovinn and Kuusinen returned his attention to the three objects. "I have looked into the xenobiological files on the Drawmii," he reported, "and so far as I can tell these three objects are absolutely unique. Nothing like them as been reported—if others exist at all they are a very close Drawmii secret."

"They are valuable, then, these alien hairballs."

"Your grace," solemnly, "they are priceless."

Roberta took a sip of roxburgh wine. "Oh, dear," she said. "I've had to employ six people just to guard the Eltdown Shard. How many guards will I need for these?"

"I would keep the objects in separate places, your grace. You don't want to lose all three at once."

"I'll do that. I have enough vaults in enough residences, gracious knows."

"Thank you, Kovinn." Kuusinen took his glass from Kovinn's tray.

"Kovinn," said Roberta. "You may take the objects away and pack them."

"Yes, your grace."

Kuusinen looked at Roberta from over the rim of his glass. "What now, your grace?"

"The Special Event, of course."

"Yes. Of course. The Event." He sighed. "The other candidates have been dropped, then? It's to be Maijstral?"

"Almost certainly. But just in case, I desire you continue your inquiries elsewhere."

"As you wish, your grace."

"Send the reports to me—you have my schedule—and then, if you don't hear from me otherwise, take ship for Nana."

"And speak to Maijstral's father?"

"Yes."

Kuusinen sighed. "I hate talking to the dead. They're so . . . faded."

"I gather old Dornier was pretty faded when he was alive."

"And Maijstral's mother?"

Roberta's expression was cold. "I've met her, and once was enough. We can leave that woman out of it."

"I'll be happy not to see her. I tried to stay out of her sight that one time, but still she may remember me."

"Yes. Her memories on that occasion would not be happy ones."

Resigned to another half-year of travel, Kuusinen raised his glass and drank.

"It's lordship will be returning to Zynzlyp," Lady Dosvidern said. "It has swallowed the Shard in order to keep it safe, and will regurgitate it on Zynzlyp. I think even Fu George would have trouble stealing the Shard from the Drawmiikh's insides."

"It sounds quite secure," Zoot said.

"I'm given to understand that the Imperial Sporting Commission, at the request of the Colonial Service, is considering the placing of a ban on future theft of the Eltdown Shard—they don't want a High Custom sporting event causing the suicide of an entire planetary population."

"Very wise," said Zoot. Despite the fact that he and Lady Dosvidern were having what to all appearances was an innocent conversation at a public table in the White Room, Zoot found himself jittery; he kept cocking his ears back as if to listen for people sneaking up behind him. He had difficulty keeping his eyes focused on Lady Dosvidern. Every time he looked at her, he kept imagining (with convincing realism) the pressure of a pistol barrel to his head.

"And of course"—Lady Dosvidern smiled—"Lord Qlp's return to its planet of origin will mean that I'll be free."

"You won't be taking up residence on its lordship's estate?"

Lady Dosvidern's ears turned down in disdain. "Its lordship's estate consists of three stone huts, two of which are filled with livestock. No, I had an arrangement with the Colonial Service. Now that my task is over, I'll be collecting my pension and leaving Zynzlyp forever. I won't be returning unless Lord Qlp leaves again, and I doubt it will be doing that." She smiled at him. "Perhaps we can meet somewhere."

The very idea conjured in Zoot an instinct to run from the room as fast as his legs could carry him. Zoot suppressed this and drew his face into a semblance of regret. "My lady, I am sorry to report that I'm really not cut out for adultery."

Lady Dosvidern seemed amused. "How odd. And this from a member of the Diadem. It's not as if my marriage to Lord Qlp were anything but a diplomatic fiction."

"Yet. Still."

"Zoot! May I speak with you?" Pearl Woman, hands on cutlass hilts, came swaggering to Zoot's chair. Relieved beyond all measure by the interruption, he stood and sniffed her.

"Pearl Woman."

"I wonder, Zoot, if Lady Dosvidern will let me borrow you for a few moments. I'd like to talk about my new project."

"Ah—with your permission, my lady?"

"Very well." Showing nettled regret.

Pearl Woman tugged on his arm, drawing him away. "I wanted to ask you about Old Earth pirates. Now that my stock's high, I'd like to make a good deal for my next feature, and I think a romance about pirates might be just the ticket."

Relief spread gratefully through Zoot. "Yes," he said. "I am entirely at your service."

"Deus vult."

Roman had made the security arrangements for Dolfuss's room, and Roman, as Maijstral had discovered over the years, was fond of passwords that reflected the life and career of Maijstral's alleged Crusader ancestor. "Deus vult" was his favorite, but "incarnatus" was high on his list, as was "crux mihi ancora." It was fully characteristic of Roman, Maijstral thought, to assign passwords based on a religion that he venerated for its part in the life of Maijstral's supposed forefather, but which, had Roman been left to himself, he would have found violent, simplistic, and distasteful—the ritual cannibalism aspect alone would have turned his ears back, had he given it any thought.

But Roman probably hadn't given it any thought. Because Maijstral's ancestors had taken sides in the Crusades, Roman, being loyal, would also take sides, even though Roman, knowing Maijstral, therefore knew to his sorrow that Maijstral never gave the Crusades or religion a single thought except when Roman reminded him about them. That, Maijstral concluded, was one of the comforting things about Roman. He was predictable in his loyalty to Maijstral and the family, no matter that Maijstral strained the loyalty from time to time.

The door opened. "Hi, boss," said Gregor.

Maijstral stepped inside Dolfuss's room. Dolfuss was nervously covering the door with a pistol. "The collection is packed?" Maijstral asked.

"Everything's ready, boss."

Maijstral cast a glance over the room. All had been packed save for some of Gregor's equipment for monitoring the Cygnus robots. No lights were glowing on Gregor's apparatus: the robots had all been instructed to stop their opening the utility passageways and setting off alarms. All the security people would know was that alarms would cease—the stratagem itself was secure till next time.

"A good thing it's nearly over," said Dolfuss. He holstered his gun and sat on the bed. "Firearms make me apprehensive. I'm happy not to have to stand guard much longer."

Maijstral smiled at Dolfuss. "I didn't really think anyone would make a try for our hoard, but I thought an attempt would be a lot less likely if we kept two armed men here around the clock. No sense in handing anyone an irresistible temptation." His smile broadened as he opened one of his cases and dropped Kotani's studs into it. "We're just keeping Fu George and Kyoko Asperson honest."

"Happy to provide such a reinforcement to public morality." Dolfuss took the gun from his holster again and put it on the bed; he found the thing uncomfortable. "I'll be even more happy," he added, "to tread the boards again."

"That may be sooner than you think. Our thefts have turned out to be far more sensational than I ever envisioned, and in addition to your advance you'll be getting sizeable royalties from the sale of the recordings to the media. Your name will be placed before the public again. If you announce the opening of a new theater, here in the Constellation where the Imperial bureaucracy won't ban your works, I should think you'd have no lack of backers."

"Thank you, sir," said Dolfuss. "Barring the element of gunplay, it's been a most enlightening stay."

Maijstral smiled privately. He could only agree.

He turned to Gregor. "I think I'll accompany you to Kotani's suite," he said. "For the sake of public morality, if nothing else."

"Great," said Gregor. He put a hi-stick in his mouth. "I sort of wanted to talk to you anyway."

Maijstral donned his shields while Gregor asked the service plate to send a porterbot. When it arrived Gregor carefully stacked

Baroness Silverside's collection on its luggage rack, then the two checked their pistols and left for Kotani's suite.

"The thing is, boss," Gregor said, "I don't think much of this polish is wearing off."

Maijstral looked at him. "Beg pardon?"

"You've taught me a lot, boss," Gregor said. "Don't think I'm not grateful. I've got a lot more finesse than I used to have, but I don't seem to be absorbing much in the way of ton, if you see my point."

"Such things take time, Gregor."

"More time than I've got, maybe. I mean perhaps." He threw up his hands. "See what I mean? I keep saying *maybe* after three years. It's a dead giveaway."

Maijstral looked at him sidelong. "I suppose Kyoko Asperson has something to do with this."

"Yes. What I mean is, she's started with a background like mine, poor smashed-up family on a hick planet, and she's made it in the larger world. Not by trying to turn herself into a noble, but just by being herself."

Maijstral frowned. "She is herself in a very studied way, Gregor. She works at it very hard, perhaps harder than I do at being a lord."

"You don't have to work at being a lord. You *are* a lord. Or at least you have the option of being a lord or not." Gregor sucked nervously on his hi-stick. "I'm not a lord, and I won't ever be mistaken for one. So what I've decided is that I shouldn't be working with a lord, but with someone who has the kind of style I can use." He gave a heavy sigh. "So I'll be leaving on the *Boston* with Miss Asperson, is what I'm saying. I'm sorry to leave you in the lurch, but you and Roman can do pretty well with all the stuff I've built for you until you can find a replacement. And that shouldn't be too hard—not with the way your rating's going to rocket after all this."

Maijstral considered this for a long moment. "You have style aplenty, Gregor. Not my kind, but it's there. I've known that all along."

"Oh." Gregor appeared surprised. "Thank you, boss."

"I don't think you need to work with Miss Asperson just to discover something you already know."

"Thanks anyway. But I've made up my mind. I'm still leaving with her."

"A delicate matter, Gregor." Maijstral pursed his lips. "Should you leave my employment, you leave with a knowledge of my techniques and apparatus. Miss Asperson has already demonstrated a regrettable tendency to take advantage of any inner knowledge. . . ."

"Boss!" Gregor was scandalized. "I wouldn't let her do anything like that!"

"I'm relieved to hear it."

"You should see the junk she's got. Ancient. I'm surprised she hasn't got pinched a dozen times over. And the maintenance!"

Maijstral sighed. He had enjoyed Gregor's company, the younger man's appalling lack of manners having struck him as thoroughly refreshing. Gregor, Maijstral knew, would be missed. He decided to surrender with grace.

"Very well. I wish you and Miss Asperson all possible happiness."

Gregor brightened. "Thanks. A lot. Really."

"You're welcome. Really."

"The return trip will be second class, unfortunately," said Zoot. "The Diadem paid for the trip out; I'll have to dip into my own funds for the journey back. Even then, we'll probably need help financing any expeditions. Fortunately," his ears flickering, "my ratings are up, and the media should pay well."

"I don't mind second class," said Khamiss. "That's how I got here." She turned from her closet and held up her uniform jacket. "Do you think I should take my uniform? As a souvenir?"

"If you like, dearest. Why not? You were wearing it when we met."

"Which reminds me that you still haven't finished the lesson in physiognomy."

His tongue hung amused from the corner of his mouth. "On the passage, then."

She folded the jacket, placed it in her suitcase. Her service pistol was already packed. She stood back. "There."

"Put your wedding clothes on top," Zoot said. "The first day out of port will be a busy one, and *Cheng*'s captain may only have a few minutes to marry us."

"And after all we went through for her and her ship. What an ingrate."

Zoot put his arms around her and tenderly took one of her ears between his canines. Khamiss stroked his fury neck.

"I still don't know her name," she said. "I hope I don't call her Cap'n Bobby by accident."

Zoot didn't understand that remark, but wasn't about to let go of her ear in order to ask. He was finding it quite pleasant here.

Goodbye, he thought, cruel world.

Advert stood on the customs dock. Her feet were unshod, and there were rings on her toes as well as her fingers. The idea had come to her only a few days ago: she'd used some of the Pearl's money to purchase the rings from Singh's.

Pearl Woman, having finished her interview with Kyoko Asperson, waved at her from across the room. Advert turned to the Marchioness Kotani, made her congé, and advanced toward the Pearl.

Pearl Woman grinned at her. "Have you said your farewells?"

Advert nodded.

"Good. Shall we take our leave? I don't feel like waiting for the *Cheng* and the *Boston* to leave first."

"As you like. It's not your style to wait, after all."

Pearl Woman took Advert's arm and began walking with her to the private dock nearby. She gave Advert a careful look.

"You know," she said, "there's something different about you, these last few days."

Advert smiled. "Is there?"

"Yes. You seem to carry yourself differently. I can't put my finger on it."

Advert put her hand in her pocket and felt the credit chip there, the one with Pearl Woman's money. "I can't think what it could be," she said.

"Still. It suits you, Advert. There's something much more . . . intriguing about you."

"I'm glad you think so."

"An air of mystery, almost." Pearl Woman gave a laugh. "You know, I'm considering skipping our next planned stop and heading straight for Kapodistrias. The plans for the pirate project are advancing, and I know I could line up some backing there."

"I've never been to Kapodistrias. Is there anything to see?"

"Not much besides a big ocean. I was amazed to discover that Earth pirates didn't have flight—they actually sailed from place to place on boats, powered by wind. But I expect you'll be too busy for sightseeing. I have plans for you, Advert. There's a part in the pirate project that's perfect for you, if you'll take it. An ingenue role." Pearl Woman grinned. "Perhaps I'll rescue you from a fate worse than death."

Advert looked at Pearl Woman and considered for a long moment. "I'd like a clearer idea of the nature of the part before I give a definite answer."

Pearl Woman laughed. She squeezed Advert's arm. "There *has* been a change, Advert. A very interesting one."

Advert's ears perked forward in a gesture meant to be modest. Pleasure welled into her. "I hope so," she said.

"It's been an interesting few days," said the Duchess of Benn. "I hope the rest of my journey will offer something to equal it."

"Personally," said Drake Maijstral, "I could do with a rest." He paused. "I thank you both again, your grace, Mr. Kuusinen, for your assistance here. I might not have survived without you."

"You're very welcome, Drake. I've had fun." Her violet eyes sparkled. "Perhaps I'll see you later. I'm taking the grand tour, after all, and we may encounter one another."

Maijstral inclined his head. "I desire nothing else, your grace." *Fun,* he thought.

Roberta turned to Roman. "I also hope I see you again, Roman. Take care of Maijstral, will you?"

Roman stifled his surprise. "I'll do my best, your grace." More surprise was stifled as she stood on tiptoe to sniff his ears. She turned to sniff Maijstral, giving him three fingers to his cautious two, and then headed for her berth on the *Count Boston.*

Paavo Kuusinen clasped Maijstral's hand—one finger each—and they sniffed farewell. Maijstral looked at him, his shuttered green eyes betraying a gleam of interest. "Mr. Kuusinen," he said. "You've rendered me considerable assistance on two separate occasions, and I regret that I know so little of you. For instance, I have no idea of your occupation."

"I am an attorney, sir. I work for her grace."

"Ah. Very interesting."

Kuusinen gave an offhand flick of his ears. "Not very, sir. I find the practice of law too predictable. The labyrinths of sentient nature are more of interest to me."

Maijstral paused a moment while wondering, precisely, how to reply to this strange remark. "As they are to us all," he said finally.

"Your servant."

"Your obedient."

Maijstral suppressed a minor tremor as he watched Paavo Kuusinen follow the Duchess across the concourse to the *Boston*'s dock. Despite the man's assistance, Maijstral was happy to be rid of him.

"Sir?" A diffident voice intruded upon Maijstral's meditations. He turned to see a tidy human in a nondescript brown jacket.

"Ah. Mr. Mencken."

"I am pleased you remember my name, sir. Your Very Private Letter."

Maijstral took the envelope and looked at the VPL seal. "Thank you."

"Your servant."

Mencken disappeared into the crowd. Maijstral glanced at the seal again, then broke it. The scented paper told him of its source before he unfolded the note. The message was curt, the calligraphy hastily-formed but recognizable. Maijstral had an image of her bent over a desk, Mencken or someone like him standing behind her, waiting for the letter.

> Drake,
>
> Troubled in spirit, alas. Navarre has blossomed, been offered Diadem membership. Myself have rediscovered the stage, find the whole D. business distracting. I'd like to go on, but a meeting would be better. Is possible?
>
> Sorry about this, Drake. Honest.
>
> N.

Maijstral read the message twice, first hastily, then not. He put it back in its envelope and handed both to Roman.

"Destroy, please."

"Yes, sir. I hope she is well."

Maijstral frowned. "Entering a depressed phase, I think."

"She recovers quickly, sir. I wouldn't be overly concerned."

"Still. I wish she had someone around her she could trust."

"So do I, sir."

"Someone like you, Roman."

Roman bowed. "Thank you, sir." Carrying the envelope, he headed toward the nearest disposal. Maijstral looked after him and considered how much better a place the universe would be if *everyone* had someone like Roman to look after them.

"Drake." Vanessa Runciter's voice, hovering just over one shoulder.

He turned toward her, brushing her gently with his arm. He stepped back, putting distance between them. A translucent veil,

Maijstral was pleased to note, was drawn across her face to hide the damage.

"Hello, Vanessa."

"I just wanted to say that I'm sorry I shot at you. I thought you'd just done in Fu George, you see."

"It's forgotten, Vanessa." Politely.

She cocked her head and looked at him. "You're going to do very well out of this last few days, you know."

"That seems likely."

Her voice was harsh. "Fu George is thinking about retirement. It all sounds pretty ghastly."

"He has earned his retirement, to be sure."

"I never said he hadn't. Just that it wasn't for me." She paused for a long moment, staring at him, then finally spoke. "Perhaps we ought to meet, Drake."

Maijstral was surprised at the cool firmness of his reply. "I think not, Vanessa."

She took a few seconds to absorb this, still looking at him, then nodded briskly. "If that's how you want it."

"I'm afraid it is." Even more firmly.

She turned abruptly and was gone. Maijstral let out a slow, relieved breath. A few years ago, he reflected, he might well have given a different answer.

He was suddenly aware of Roman's presence. He glanced at Roman, then back at Vanessa. "You know, Roman," he said, as he handed Roman her gun and bracelet—not being foolish, he'd taken the gun first. "I hadn't perceived until now the resemblance in character between Vanessa Runciter and my mother."

"Really, sir? It was the first thing I noted about her."

Maijstral looked at him in surprise as the gun and bracelet vanished. Roman's expression was carefully opaque. Maijstral sighed and turned away.

"We should escort our baggage to the *Cheng,*" he said. "I think we've said all our necessary goodbyes to anyone leaving on the *Boston.*" He turned and began to walk back to the residential quarters, where Dolfuss, with his pistol, was still standing over the baggage like Marshall Wild Bill Hickock guarding a gold shipment.

"Maijstral! A moment!"

Kyoko Asperson, dressed in yellow and violet motley, was leaping up and down, waving her arms, media globes dancing over her head. Maijstral patiently awaited her arrival. She gave him a wide grin and, while sniffing him, bussed him on both cheeks.

Maijstral's hand dipped into her pocket, returned with something small.

"Gregor told me how nice you were about his leaving," she said. "I'd like to thank you."

"We'll be sorry to lose him, but—" He dropped the stolen object in a pocket and threw up his hands. "I'd hate to stand in his way. Or in the way of true love, for that matter."

Kyoko colored prettily. One of her media globes moved closer to him. "Any final comments for the record, Mr. Maijstral?" she asked. "Any last thoughts on the subject of Silverside Station and what happened here?"

Maijstral considered this for a long moment. His lazy eyes glittered.

"I'd say that events came perilously close to farce," he said, "but that fortunately farce was averted."

Kyoko was surprised. "Thank you," she said.

"Your servant."

Maijstral stepped toward his room, Roman moving silently behind. He reached into his pocket and came up with the object he'd removed from Kyoko's pocket: a pearl dangling from a broken chain. He'd seen Kyoko's altered media globe, with its force cutters and grapplers, hovering near Pearl Woman's ear during the last interview, and guessed the rest. He handed the pearl to Roman. Roman cleared his throat.

"Yes, Roman?"

Roman's voice was carefully articulated. "Farce, sir?" he said.

A memory of terror gusted through Maijstral's mind, followed by that of an argumentative closet door, a dark, glowing gem, a vanishing diamond, a playing card glowing with brilliants. . . .

"For example, Roman," he said. "Had I said yes to Vanessa just now, that would have turned this comedy to farce. As I said no, farce was avoided."

Roman digested this for a moment. "I understand, sir," he said. "Quite perfectly."

ROCK
OF
AGES

For Rebecca, with thanks

"Tyrawley and I have been dead these
two years; but we don't choose to
have it known."
Boswell's *Johnson,* 3 April 1773

ONE

It was a strange way to treat an Object of Desire.

The third wife of Francesco di Bartolommeo di Zanobi del Giocondo was centuries old but had lost none of her appeal. Admirers still came to extol her fine forehead and delicate hands—to offer her worship, to pay court, to covet. With lombardy poplar stiffening her spine, she received them all with the same temperate brown gaze, the same equable expression, the same intriguing smile.

Perhaps the smile was difficult on occasion to maintain, as some of her admirers were more extreme than others. More than once she had been abducted from her home; more than once she'd been rescued or ransomed or snatched from oblivion at the last second.

Today maintaining the smile must have been a struggle. In a semicircle around her were a squad of policemen, all in battle gear, all, with unforgivable rudeness, facing outward, their backs to her. She was surrounded by the invisible globe of a cold-field. Layered defenses, arrays of screamers and leapers, studded the floor, ceiling, and the walls to either side of her throne.

Facing her were two men. One was tall, white-haired, and gaunt. The other was of medium height—though, even facing the squad of police in battle array, he seemed taller. He wore his hair long, had buskins on his feet, a large diamond ring on one finger, and looked on the world with heavy-lidded green eyes that gave his face an indolent expression. He was in his late twenties.

"How do you like our La Gioconda?" the white-haired man asked. His voice was loud. Perhaps it was rude of him to say it within her earshot, but that was his way—he affected to be hard of hearing, and had a tendency to shout.

"I would like her better, Lord Huyghe, if I could get a little closer."

"Perhaps, Maijstral, if you asked *politely.*"

The line of police stiffened. Gloved fingers edged closer to weapons.

Drake Maijstral moved forward on silent feet and raised his hands. The guardians' trigger fingers vibrated with tension . . . and then Maijstral made a simple gesture as if to part waters.

"If you please—?" he said.

Reluctantly the line of guards parted and shuffled aside. An official—the lady's chief attendant, a Tanquer named Horving—seemed about to strangle himself with his own tail. Maijstral's lazy eyes, glowing with amusement, looked La Gioconda up and down. His ears twitched forward.

"I like her *sfumato,*" he said. "And it's a pleasant face, that should wear well. One could have it on one's wall and not tire of it easily."

At this ominous news Horving's breath began to wheeze through a constricted windpipe. It was difficult to tell if his pop eyes were a result of outrage or strangulation. Lord Huyghe—he was an art historian—ambled forward and bent to peer at the lady's features.

"Mona Lisa is an old friend," he said. "We're on first-name terms."

"I congratulate you on the acquaintance. I know only her cousin—the *Lady with an Ermine.*"

"Ah. I don't believe I've had the pleasure."

Maijstral once had six days to make the acquaintance of *Lady with an Ermine,* the period between his theft of the painting and the time he sold it back to the owner's insurance company.

"In Prince Chan's collection, on Nana," he said. "The *Lady,* like Mona Lisa, is celebrated for the elusive quality of her smile. It makes one wonder if the artist had a way of amusing women."

"I believe history is silent on the matter," Huyghe said.

Horving, anoxic, collapsed to the floor with a hollow wooden boom. One of the policemen growled. Maijstral looked up.

"Don't look at *me,"* he said. *"I* didn't do it."

He gave La Gioconda a final, searching look, then withdrew. Huyghe followed and took his arm.

"Shall we go on to the Venetians, Maijstral?"

"Let's jump ahead to the Flemish. There's a Vermeer I have my eye on."

The two left the room and turned down the corridor. A squad of police anxiously trotted after. The guards had been expecting Maijstral to view the collection in order, Italians followed by Flemish. Maijstral's jumping about had destroyed their operational plan, and their officers were forced to improvise.

While flustered security men dashed from one place to another, Maijstral walked with perfect ease next to the historian. If one must view famous art treasures through a picket fence of policemen, he considered, the least one could do is tweak them from time to time.

"I heard from your father, incidentally," Huyghe said. His booming voice echoed in the corridor.

Maijstral frowned. "Recently?"

"Only a few days ago, through VPL. He asked me to look after you and make certain that you weren't associating with any—" He smiled. "Rude or unsuitable companions."

Maijstral sighed. No sooner had Gustav Maijstral been pronounced dead and laid to rest in his tomb on Nana than he took up a large correspondence, usually through the expensive Very Private Letter service—either complaints to his son about Maijstral's habits, demands for money to honor some old debt that he'd forgotten about for twenty years, notes to friends complaining about Maijstral's neglect, or suggestions to old creditors that they approach Maijstral and demand he pay up.

"Gustav said he hoped to see me soon," Huyghe boomed. "I don't suppose you permit him the funds to travel—?"

"He's quite safe in his tomb," Maijstral said. "He'd only get into trouble if he travelled." He looked at the older man. "I'm afraid his mind was wandering, Lord Huyghe. It happens so easily to the dead, you know."

"I quite understand," Huyghe said.

Maijstral found Vermeer's *Lacemaker* as splendid as advertisied, and he enjoyed the other Flemish works, although he wondered aloud why so many still lifes were the remnants of meals—dirty forks and smeared dishes hardly seemed the most cultivated subjects for fine art.

"If you were a starving artist," Huyghe asked, "would you let a meal stand for the amount of time it took to paint it?"

"Ah," Maijstral said. "I entirely take your point."

After viewing the collection, Huyghe and Maijstral strolled out of the Louvre toward where Huyghe's red Sportsman flyer waited on the old vintage concrete drive. Media globes, circling in a holding pattern over the car, spotted their quarry and zoomed in, jostling for the better shots, Maijstral framed by the Pei pyramid, the Khorkhinn carousel, the Floating Saucer of the Tuileries.

"May we expect a robbery at the Louvre anytime soon?" one asked.

"I'm here on vacation," Maijstral said. "I've never been to Earth before, and I have no intention of spoiling my pleasure here by indulging in my profession. I have too little time to properly appreciate my heritage: Paris, Edo, Tejas, Memphis . . ."

"Do you expect the recent recommendation of the Constellation Practices Authority, condemning burglary and urging that it be banned, to have any real effect on your occupation?"

Maijstral considered an answer. "Allowed Burglary is a custom that predates human civilization," he said. "One hopes that the various parliaments of the Constellation will have consideration for its antiquity."

"You think, then," a new voice, "that the Human Constellation should maintain inhuman customs even when they're contrary to traditional human civilization?"

Maijstral's green eyes glittered from behind heavy lids. The question was provocative, particularly the word *inhuman,* which had recently taken on a nasty edge. His own view was that the phrase "human civilization" had been something of a contradiction in terms until humanity had found itself annexed by an alien power; but he didn't want to make a reply as provocative as the question had been, so he temporized.

"I'm entirely in favor of human civilization," he said, "but there's nothing civilized in change for its own sake. Why alter an institution that works, and that has been providing sport and entertainment for millennia?"

"Do you think you'll hold the championship as long as Geoff Fu George?"

Maijstral smiled. "Fu George is incomparable," he said. "I was lucky at Silverside Station, and if he hadn't retired, I'm certain he'd still hold first place."

"Nichole is onplanet," another globe said. "Do you plan to see *her?"*

At that point one alarm after another began to sing from the Louvre. Guards—massed near the entrance to see Maijstral off—jostled one another in confusion. Maijstral smiled in amusement: someone had decided to pull a job when the guards had their attention elsewhere. He turned to Huyghe.

"Let's be on our way," he said, "before they try to pin this one on *me."*

The red Sportsman arrowed into the Parisian sky. Maijstral sighed as the media globes fell astern.

"How did Fu George put up with it all those years?" he asked.

"He had a more sizeable entourage than you," Huyghe said. "That time on Silverside Station, he was restricted in the number of people he could bring. Just two."

"Two and Vanessa Runciter," Maijstral said, "and she's worth an army." He shivered at a memory of staring down the barrel of Vanessa Runciter's rifle.

"Still, I'm afraid you'll need more people."

"I'm trying," Maijstral said, "but you'd be surprised at how hard it is to find promising young criminals these days."

A few minutes later the Sportsman set down on Huyghe's estate southwest of Krakow. Maijstral thanked his host for the tour of Earth's most renowned gallery, then made his way to his room to dress for dinner.

In his room Maijstral was met by his servant, Roman. Roman was tall even for a Khosalikh, and his family had been in the service of Maijstral's for more generations than Maijstral could, or for that matter cared, to count.

Maijstral handed Roman his pistols—he'd left his knife behind, as a courtesy to the museum's canvases—and then Roman began to unlace his jacket.

Roman's ears twitched forward. "I understand there was some difficulty at the museum, sir," he said.

"Not really. But just in case the police decide to doubt the evidence of their eyes and conclude it *was* me somehow, we might tidy things a bit—I don't know what the local regulations allow in the way of burglar gear."

"News flashes indicate the theft may have been successful, sir."

"Ah. In that case we may as well resign ourselves to a visit from the authorities."

A few weeks earlier, the Imperial Sporting Commission had, somewhat to Maijstral's dismay, rated him the top-ranked Allowed Burglar in all known space. Maijstral had never permitted himself to consider himself a serious candidate—during his entire professional career, Geoff Fu George had occupied the top spot, a position he'd secured during the Affaire of the Mirrorglass BellBox and in subsequent years made his own. But Fu George had just retired, two other leading candidates had the bad fortune to be sent to prison, and—Maijstral might as well admit it—he'd outdone himself on Silverside Station and come out of the business with a truly astounding array of swag. He'd managed to outscore the nearest rival by all of twenty points.

Roman finished unlacing Maijstral's jacket, and after picking off an offending piece of lint, carried the garment to the closet. Maijstral picked up a pair of binoculars and gazed out the window, trying to locate the detectives he knew were lurking on the fringes of the Huyghe estate.

Being first in the ratings, Maijstral had discovered, guaranteed the champion an unfortunate amount of attention from the local authorities.

There the police were, he discovered, behind some shrubs. The detectives were too dignified to actually crouch down behind the foliage, and were trying to act as if it were perfectly natural for some badly dressed, slightly seedy public servants to spend hours loitering behind the thorn bushes.

Maijstral couldn't help but hope they would fall into them.

Once Roman had finished dressing him, Maijstral glided silently into the study next door, where Drexler, a glass in his eye, was absorbed in the microscopic innards of a piece of burglar equipment, in this case a flax-jammer.

"The authorities should be here shortly," Maijstral said. "There's been a successful burglary at the Louvre."

Drexler turned in his chair and looked at Maijstral over his shoulder. He was a Khosalikh, having just reached maturity with his first molt. He was a little shorter than average—which made him about the size of a tall human—but was built very stoutly, as if for the long haul.

"Beg pardon, sir," he said, "but you shouldn't have done a job on a place like the Louvre without proper support."

"I didn't," Maijstral said. "Someone else timed a robbery to coincide with my visit."

Drexler's ears flattened. "I hope this doesn't turn into another Silverside Station situation," he said.

"I devoutly hope not," Maijstral said. "But if anything in your bag of tricks is illegal in Western Ukrania, or wherever it is we are, then please make it disappear for a bit."

"Absolutely," Drexler said. He put his work in a foam-lined case, put the case in a tough canvas drawstring bag, and tossed the bag in the air, where it stayed. At a (verbal) command, the window opened, and then at a (silent, electronic) command from the proximity wire in Drexler's collar, the drawstring bag flew out.

"I'll put it in a tree a few kilometers away, all right?" Drexler said, and his tongue lolled in a Khosalikh smile.

"Fine. Thank you."

"I didn't have anything actually illegal, but if the police confiscated it, it might be a while before it was returned, and then it might come back damaged."

"Very good."

"These things have been known to happen."

"Quite so. Thank you."

Maijstral returned to his dressing room, silently contemplating the problem of Drexler.

Drexler, like Maijstral, had experienced the madness of Silverside Station firsthand, but from an opposing vantage point. He'd furnished technical support for Geoff Fu George, and had been up to his muzzle in the mad contending scramble for loot that marked Silverside's social debut. Fu George's retirement had coincided with Maijstral's own tech leaving his employ, and Drexler had then offered his services to Maijstral. Maijstral hired him, albeit provisionally. Thus far the arrangement had worked well enough, though Maijstral hadn't precisely put Drexler's abilities to the test: he hadn't done any major jobs for the last few months.

But something, Maijstral thought, was missing. Maijstral had no complaints with Drexler's performance or abilities—Fu George wouldn't have hired anything but the best—but there was an intangible *something* that kept Maijstral from feeling entirely at home around Drexler.

It bothered him. It wasn't that he disliked Drexler, it was just that he never found himself at ease around the Khosalikh, and he didn't know why. The fact that Drexler was a Khosalikh was not at issue, either, since Maijstral was perfectly comfortable around Roman.

Chemistry, he supposed. Regrettable, but there you are.

Maijstral finished dressing. Roman silently offered him his weapons, and Maijstral stowed them away. Distantly, Maijstral heard the booming of the dinner gong.

"Will you be needing anything else, sir?" Roman asked.

The room darkened as if a mass of ravens had flown beneath the sun. Maijstral looked out the window to see a phalanx of shiny black police fliers settling onto Lord Huyghe's lawn. Irritation crabbed at his nerves.

"What did I tell you?" he demanded. "They're not going to leave me alone for a blasted second on this blasted planet!"

He really *was* on vacation. He had come to Earth to attend the wedding of two acquaintances and sometime employers, Amalia Jensen and Pietro Quijano, and he was staying on as a tourist. He didn't want to steal anything on this trip, but it seemed as if no one was willing to take his word for it.

"Perhaps their visit will be brief," Roman comforted.

Maijstral took a few deep breaths and tried to dispel his pique.

"Stay in the room, will you," Maijstral said, "and make sure the cops don't steal anything."

Roman, ever the perfect servant, bowed.

"Very good, sir," he said.

Dinner was not delayed, though it was disturbed somewhat by the sound of heavy police boots tramping up and down the halls. The local police commissaire, a bushy-whiskered old soul named Przemysl, was invited to join Maijstral and Lord and Lady Huyghe, and sat down just in time for the soup course.

"Sorry about this," he apologized, speaking precisely in Khosali Standard. "Were it up to me, I wouldn't interrupt you till after dinnertime; but orders come from on high, you know. When they unified the police forces, I knew this sort of thing would happen." He brandished his spoon. " 'Listen,' I told them, 'those bureaucrats in Beijing won't care a stick about the feelings of the local gentry. They'll have me interrupting people at mealtimes, or dragging them out of their beds when you might just as well wait till after they've had breakfast.' And see if it hasn't happened." He turned his eyes piously to Heaven. "The Virtues only know what will happen if the Security and Sedition Act is passed. Then none of us will be safe."

"What exactly was taken from the Louvre?" Lord Huyghe asked.

Przemysl cast a knowing glance at Maijstral. "A painting undergoing cleaning and restoration," he said. "Titian's *Man with a Glove.*"

"Ah yes," Huyghe said. "I'd marked its absence."

Bootheels clicked on the dining room floor as a tall, frowning police officer stalked into the room. She was human, with blondish hair tucked, somewhat unsuccessfully, into a gleaming black-visored helmet more suitable to the Dread Squad of the Constellation Death Commandos than to a public servant approaching a person of distinction at his dinner. Her face was chiselled. Her manner was correct, but curt. Her uniform was of black leather and had many gleaming buttons. The others rose as she marched to Lord Huyghe's elbow. She saluted.

"Sir," she said, speaking Human Standard, "I am Colonel-General Denise Vandergilt. I would like to request permission for police to inspect the paintings in your gallery in order to make certain that the stolen picture is not hidden beneath them."

Lord Huyghe frowned and spoke in his normal—booming—conversational tones. Maijstral had to offer reluctant congratulations to Vandergilt for the fact she didn't leap back, flinch, or assume she was about to be assaulted and draw her pistol.

"What means do you intend to use?" Huyghe roared.

"For the inspection? Passive broadband fluorocameras. No injury to your canvases is possible."

"Ah. Very well." Huyghe waved his napkin, a signal for the other diners to resume their seats. "As you like, then."

Vandergilt's expression grew abstract for a moment as she pulsed silent commands to her troops through her in-the-helmet scrambler.

Lady Huyghe lowered her spoon and pricked her ears forward. She was a quiet woman, perhaps as a result of her husband shouting at her all these years, and when she spoke it was generally to the point.

"Colonel-General?" she said. "I don't believe that is a rank in the local constabulary, is it?"

"I am a member of the Constellation Special Services Corps, ma'am," Vandergilt said.

"The Colonel-General came here specially from Beijing," Przemysl said. His expression invited sympathy from the diners.

"And what precisely," Lady Huyghe asked, "does the Special Services Corps *do?*"

Vandergilt noticed that a disobedient strand of hair had drooped out from under her helmet. "We maintain the political security of the Human Constellation against foreign and domestic threats, ma'am," she said, stuffing hair into her helmet with one efficient black-gloved hand, "and investigate those deemed worthy of special interest to the Administration."

"Gracious," Lady Huyghe blinked. She turned to her husband. "Do you suppose there might be anyone of that description at our table?"

Vandergilt frowned. "If you won't mind an observation, ma'am, I am surprised that the owners of a select art collection such as yourself and, ah, Mr. Huyghe, would have as your houseguest a person whose profession it is to steal."

"Ha!" Lord Huyghe said abruptly. Vandergilt gave a little start, as if a pistol had just gone off near her ear. A strand of blond hair fell in her eyes.

"Maijstral's father and I were at school together," Huyghe said. "It's natural to offer hospitality to the son of an old friend."

"And of course I wouldn't steal from my host," Maijstral said. "That would be rude."

"And the name's Behrens, by the way," Huyghe added. "Anthony Behrens. Huyghe's just the title."

"Thank you, Mr. Behrens," Vandergilt said. She tried, and failed, to stuff the strand of hair back in her helmet. "I appreciate your reminding me that the title is, in the Constellation, only a courtesy."

Lady Huyghe frowned gently. "I believe," she said, "that *courtesy* is the operative word."

Vandergilt flushed. Her eyes narrowed as she looked at Lord and Lady Huyghe, and, watching her, Maijstral suspected she would be opening a file on them the second she returned to Beijing. Maijstral's father had been a notorious Imperialist, and now it seemed likely that Gustav Maijstral's school chum and his wife were about to suffer a case of dossier-by-association.

"Flattered as I am by the attention," Maijstral said, "I wonder how I merit it. How does being an Allowed Burglar—an occupation perfectly legal under Constellation law—somehow merit this, ah, *special interest* of nothing less than a full Colonel-General?"

"We do not believe," Vandergilt said, "that an inhuman sport like Allowed Burglary will be legal for long. And even Allowed Burglary permits me to arrest you if I catch you in the act or shortly thereafter."

Maijstral's ears flattened. His green eyes glittered under his lazy eyelids. "I hope I shall be able to offer you and your people sufficient exercise," he said.

Przemysl beamed at him from across the table, and Maijstral sensed approval from Lord and Lady Huyghe. No doubt, he thought, they were anticipating Maijstral's leading this officious officer in a merry chase from vault to hideout and back again.

Maijstral knew he did not deserve the credit granted him by his fellow diners. He was damned if he was going to steal anything while a leather-clad fanatic like this was lurking about, just waiting to drag him off to Beijing and drop him in a lightless dungeon, no doubt one equipped with fetters, damp straw, rats, and other traditional paraphernalia. . . .

Vandergilt drew herself up. She knew a challenge when she heard one. "We have no intention, you see," she declaimed, "of allowing a notorious character such as yourself to plunder the heritage of the Human Constellation for his own aggrandizement." Her black-gloved hand rose, hesitated.

"Would you like a pin, dear?" Lady Huyghe asked.

"No. Thank you. If you'll excuse me, Mr. and Mrs. Behrens?"

She turned on her heel and stalked off. Lord Huyghe gave a sigh. "Thank the Virtues," he said, "she was only here for the soup course."

The police withdrew just as the meal got to its brandy-and-cigars stage, something that disappointed old Przemysl, who had only got halfway through his Monte Cristo before he had to leave.

"I like the fellow, you know," Huyghe said as he settled back into his chair, "but I'm rather glad he's gone. There are a few things I'd like to discuss with you, Drake, if you've no objection."

"None at all," Maijstral said. "By the way, is that a Jasper in the corner?"

Huyghe smiled. "It is indeed. An atypical piece—you have a good eye."

"I didn't know you collected moderns."

Lady Huyghe tapped ash from her Cohima and contemplated the brandy in her snifter. "My taste, actually," she said. "The piece struck my fancy years ago, and Tony bought it for my birthday."

"How thoughtful," Maijstral said.

"I was wondering, Drake," Huyghe said, "if you'd be interested in any commissions while you're here. There are some pieces in private collections that I'm itching to get a look at, but their owners are quite reclusive, and I'm afraid the only way I'll ever see them is if I arrange for them to . . ." He tapped cigar ash. "To appear in my own collection," he finished.

"I'd love to oblige," Maijstral said, "but my stay on Earth already suffers from an overfull programme. Perhaps I can give you an introduction to someone in the burglar line who will be able to accommodate you."

"I'd appreciate that very much." A light glowed in Huyghe's eyes. "I imagine you've got quite a few surprises planned for that Vandergilt character, eh?"

Maijstral smiled thinly. "Ye-es," he drawled. Not the least of which, he considered, was the fact he wouldn't be stealing anything at all while he was here.

Later that evening, Maijstral politely sniffed Lord Huyghe's ears and Lady Huyghe's wrist, then returned to his chambers determined to order Drexler and Roman to get rid of all the burglar equipment for the length of time they stayed on Earth. No point in getting arrested for carrying gear he had no intention of using, and which might be technically illegal in some jurisdiction or other.

Maijstral opened his door and told the room to turn on the lights. He looked up and his heart gave a leap of terror. He stared at his dresser and only managed to avoid gibbering because he was speechless with fear.

Atop his dresser, fresh from cleaning and restoration, was Titian's *Man with a Glove.*

TWO

Sweat prickled on Maijstral's scalp. He was being set up. He pictured Colonel-General Vandergilt kicking in the door with her heavy black boots, smiling an evil smile as she raised her mapper and squeezed the trigger. Caught red-handed, she'd say, too bad he tried to escape. . . .

Maijstral turned to the service plate, intending to summon Roman and have his servant somehow get the painting *away.*

"Hallo," said a voice. Maijstral spun around and winced as a brass doorknob punched his kidney. In an upper corner of the room, colors shifted as the holographic projectors of a darksuit turned themselves off to reveal a small woman, hand raised in a cheerful wave.

"Sorry if I startled you," she said. She floated to the floor a few feet in front of Maijstral. "I just wanted to show you my bag from the Louvre."

Maijstral made an effort to move his thrashing heart from his throat to a more conventional location. "You've shown it to me," Maijstral said. "Now please leave."

The woman held out her hand. "Conchita Sparrow," she said. "Pleased to meet you."

Her accent was uncouth and her hair was arranged in a kind of informal, outlandish dorsal fin on top of her head, perhaps in hope of making her seem taller. Her face was bright-eyed and pleasant, though not beautiful. Maijstral hesitantly reached out a hand, offered her a cautious one-fingered handclasp. She gave him two fingers in return, a presumption of a greater intimacy than Maijstral was willing, given the circumtances, to contemplate.

"Actually," she said, "I was looking for a tech designer job. I thought you might be more interested in looking at my recordings if I showed you how useful I could be."

Maijstral's eyes—wide open for once—moved to the Titian. "You may have proved far more useful to the police than to me," he said. "They were just here looking for that painting."

"I know," she grinned. "I saw them leave. Don't worry—they didn't see me. Especially not those two clots out in the thorn bushes—they couldn't skulk their way out of a dead people's convention. The only person who saw me was one of your people, the one in the darksuit, and he took off."

A cold finger touched Maijstral on the neck. "A darksuit?" he asked.

"Yeah. A good one—most detectors wouldn't have spotted it, but mine did. He flew in just after the cops left—he stopped at your window, looked in for a moment, then flew on. That's when he saw me and flew off."

"A moment, Miss Sparrow," Maijstral said. He reached to the wall by the door and touched the service plate. "Roman? Drexler? Were either of you just out on the grounds?"

The answers were negative. Maijstral turned to Conchita Sparrow.

"I'll look at your recordings if you like," he said, "but that person lurking around outside was probably a member of the Special Services Corps, and will be very happy to send me to prison for possession of that painting. So if you would oblige me by taking it *very far away,* I'll be in your debt."

"Only too," Conchita said, meaning *Only too happy.* Maijstral raised an eyebrow at this cheeky piece of cant. Conchita stepped toward the painting, took a bag out of her darksuit, and slipped it over the painting. Once bagged, the painting levitated as of its own free will, then followed Conchita to the window. Before she slipped through the drape she turned on the holo projectors of her darksuit, and blended almost indistinguishably with the background.

"The recordings are in your upper right drawer," she said. "Happy to've met you!"

The drapes parted, the window opened, and out she flew.

Maijstral went to his bureau drawer, saw a recording sphere lying there, and then marched to the service plate to summon Roman and Drexler.

They searched Maijstral's room for the next hour, but found no more surprises.

Next morning Maijstral bade farewell to Lord and Lady Huyghe and set off for North America. Once airborne, Maijstral put his car on autopilot and reviewed Conchita's recordings with Roman and Drexler. He understood why she was seeking employment as a tech. Though her equipment was first-rate—her black boxes always worked, and her darksuit's equipment wove an elegant path through a wide assortment of alarms—she was nevertheless a very poor thief. She was too nervous: she dropped things, or performed operations in the wrong order and had to start over, and once she forgot to tell her darksuit to neutralize a set of flaxes and had to fly in disarray when the alarms began to ring.

"She's a disaster," Drexler snickered, as he watched Conchita head for the horizon.

"Still," Roman said, "she would not be employed for her abilities as a thief. Her gear really is her strong point—it works flawlessly."

"When she remembers to use it," Drexler grinned, his tongue lolling. "She hasn't done anything I can't do. And besides, what happens if you need her to pinch something for you?"

"Quite," Maijstral said.

Drexler might lack a certain bonhomie, he reflected, but at least he didn't show up uninvited in one's bedroom with a stolen art treasure moments after irksomely fanatic police decided to search the place.

"Roman," he said, "put Sparrow in the file. We might hand her some contract work if Drexler is ever overburdened."

"I won't be overburdened at the rate we're going, Mr. Maijstral," Drexler said. "When are we going to steal something really big?"

"After vacation," Maijstral said, and was aware of Drexler's diaphragm pulsing in resignation.

Let it pulse, he thought. Drexler hadn't met Colonel-General Vandergilt.

* * *

"Maijstral," said Prince Joseph Bob, "I don't believe you've met my family."

"Haven't had the pleasure."

The young Lord Joseph Bob had been one of Maijstral's school friends at the Nnoivarl Academy. He hadn't changed much in the last twelve years—he was still tall and rangy and blond, and he still looked every bit the champion athlete he had been in school. The best pistol shot in the Academy, a top sabre man on the fencing team, a first-class swimmer, an excellent jumper and runner, first prize for debate . . . the list of accomplishments went on and on.

His huge house south of Fort Worth was situated on an estate that stretched as far as the hill country west of Austin. The drawing room, where Maijstral was meeting the Prince's family, seemed to range at least half that distance.

"This is my wife, Arlette," Joseph Bob said.

"Charmed."

The marriage was less than a year old, and it was clear to Maijstral that they would have beautiful children. Princess Arlette—the media called her "Lady Bob"—was almost as tall as her husband, with honey-colored hair and large dark eyes. Maijstral gave her two fingers in handclasp and sniffed her wrist and ears.

"Joe's told me a lot about you," Arlette said.

"Oh dear."

"He was *very* complimentary."

Maijstral smiled. "Of course, he never knew me well."

"And *this,*" said Joseph Bob, "is my brother Will."

"Ah," Maijstral said, "the Bubber."

Just as the brother of King Louis always assumed the title of Monsieur, the brother of the Prince of Tejas was always the Bubber (the *r,* with genteel courtesy, is almost silent). Maijstral, acquainted only through his brother, sniffed his ears, offered him a modest two fingers, and received three informal digits in return.

"Do you still do card tricks?" the Bubber asked. He was neither as tall nor as rangy nor as blond as his brother, though his expression was more genial. He had come into the Nnoivarl Academy the year Maijstral left, and Maijstral had never really known him.

"Of course," Maijstral said.

"Joe always said you were good."

"After supper, if you like."

"That would be delightful. Thank you."

Maijstral made a mental note to tell Roman to lay out the dinner jacket with the trick pockets. He turned to the Prince.

"I was wondering if I might ask a favor," he said.

"Of course."

"While I'm here, I'd like to learn to ride a horse."

"Really?" The Prince seemed faintly surprised. "Very well, if you like. Will can set you up—he's in charge of the stables."

"Sir." Joseph Bob's butler appeared in the doorway. "There is a slight disturbance at the front gate. Newton has apprehended a pair of interlopers who claim to be lost. They also claim to be police."

"Lost?" the Prince said. "On *my* property?"

Maijstral gave a sigh. "J.B.," he said, "I suppose I had better tell you about Colonel-General Vandergilt."

Later, as Maijstral went to his quarters to dress for supper, he turned a corner in the hallway and received a start. Coming toward him was a short, nondescript man in a green jacket.

"Mr. Kuusinen," Maijstral said, and offered two fingers.

"Your servant, sir. I'm pleased you remembered my name." Kuusinen gave two fingers in return and sniffed Maijstral's ears.

Maijstral was not likely to forget the name of Paavo Kuusinen anytime soon. The man had a habit of turning up. Twice now, on Peleng and again on Silverside Station, Kuusinen had been a part of adventures Maijstral would just as soon forget.

On those occasions Kuusinen had actually been of great assistance to Maijstral, but the very sight of the man made Maijstral uneasy. Call it ingratitude if you will.

"What brings you to Earth?" Maijstral asked.

"I'm still her grace's attorney, of course," Kuusinen said, "and she is here, as a guest."

"Roberta?" Maijstral said. "Here?"

"Indeed."

Roberta Altunin, the Duchess of Benn, was a famous amateur racer and the former owner of the Eltdown Shard, the fabulous gem which Maijstral had once had the pleasure and glory of stealing.

"Curious," Maijstral said, "that the Prince never mentioned she was here."

"You'll meet at supper at any case."

"Yes. I will. Your servant."

"And yours."

They sniffed ears again and parted, Maijstral frowning. He'd come to think of Kuusinen as a creature of omen—not necessarily *ill* omen, since after all the man had been of service—but at least a harbinger of unsettling times.

Once in his suite, Maijstral settled his unease by watching a Western till it was time to dress. This one, *The Long Night of Billy the Kid,* was an old-fashioned tragedy featuring the legendary rivalry between Billy and Elvis Presley for the affections of Katie Elder. Katie's heart belonged to Billy, but despite her tearful pleadings Billy rode the outlaw trail; and finally, brokenhearted Katie left Billy to go on tour with Elvis as a backup singer, while Billy rode on to his long-foreshadowed death at the hands of the greenhorn inventor-turned-lawman Nikola Tesla.

It was wonderful. Maijstral, transfixed by the ancient, fateful myth being brought to life, watched with an aching heart as the awesome story unfolded in its somber, tragic perfection.

And while he watched, he paid particular attention to the horses.

He was really looking forward to lessons.

Paavo Kuusinen, after leaving Maijstral in the hall, turned a corner and began counting doors. He counted the light fixtures and power outlets as well, but only because he was compulsive that way—counting the doors really had purpose.

When he came to the eighth door, he knocked. A servant opened the door and he entered.

"Your grace," he said.

The Duchess of Benn was a tall, graceful woman, eighteen years old, with short red hair and intense violet eyes. She held out a hand and Kuusinen took it, sniffed the wrist.

"Maijstral's arrived?" she asked.

"An hour ago or thereabouts."

"Good. And the, ah—the package?"

"It will be in place by tomorrow evening."

"Splendid. The Special Event goes forward." She smiled. "I will look forward to enjoying Maijstral's surprise."

Kuusinen bowed again. "As shall I, your grace. To be sure."

THREE

His heart still brimming with the glory and tragedy of his Western, Maijstral glided down the balcony to join the others in the drawing room. Before making his entrance, he absently patted one of the hidden pockets in his jacket to make certain the stacked deck of cards was in its nesting place.

He had also prepared his ground by having Roman bribe one of the footmen serving dinner tonight. It was nothing, he reflected, that Houdini hadn't done.

Maijstral stepped into the drawing room. The Prince's string quartet played Haydn in one corner—among them Maijstral recognized Will, the Bubber, who puffed out his cheeks as he sawed away on his cello and stared intently at the music. The regular cellist, he observed, was standing out, absently fingering his own instrument in a corner of the room.

Standing with her back toward Maijstral was Roberta, the Duchess of Benn. She was speaking to an elderly Khosalikh female who stood shorter than Maijstral, which made her a miniature by Khosalikh standards. Roberta's gown was cut quite low in back and Maijstral approached slowly, the better able to appreciate the curve of Roberta's supple spine, the play of shadows beneath her scapulae.

"Your grace," he said, speaking in Khosali Standard.

Roberta gave a start, a larger one than Maijstral's usual silent approaches generally warranted. Maijstral confirmed an old suspicion that her grace of Benn was a bit too tightly wound.

"You startled me," she gasped, which was, Maijstral reflected, not only a fairly redundant remark for someone who's just jumped half a foot, but was what people *always* said in these situations.

"My apologies," Maijstral said. "I'm light-footed by profession, and sometimes I forget that I should shuffle a bit or clear my throat." Which is, more or less, what *he* always said in these situations.

Maijstral offered three fingers in handclasp—having once stolen her jewelry permitted him a certain intimacy—and was given three in return. They approached one another and sniffed one another's ears, and then Maijstral sniffed Roberta's wrist. The odor of Roberta's perfume sent a shimmer of pleasure up Maijstral's spine, something that caused him to reflect that the custom of shaking hands—recently revived by the Constellation Practices Authority as a "natural, human custom" to replace the refined ear-sniffing of the Khosali Empire—had a long way to travel before it could replace the voluptuous pleasure of approaching a beautiful woman's pulsing throat and taking a glorious whiff.

"It's an unexpected pleasure to see you," Maijstral said. "I ran into your Mr. Kuusinen, who informed me you were here."

"Allow me to introduce my Aunt Bathsheba," Roberta said. "She's my favorite member of the family. We call her Batty."

"Your servant," Maijstral said. Aunt Batty's soft dark fur was thinned with age, and she'd perched a pair of spectacles on her muzzle. Some lace hung from her pointed ears.

Maijstral was too familiar with the genealogies of aristocratic Imperial families, with their sibs-by-adoption and cousins-german and morganatic marriages and fostering-patterns, to wonder how a human duchess managed to have a Khosali aunt. He sniffed Aunt Batty's ears and offered her two fingers in handclasp, and she returned him three.

"Forgive the intimacy," she said, "but I feel as if I know you quite well. I'm writing a multivolume work about you, you see."

Maijstral blinked. He didn't know whether to believe this remark, or, if believed, to take it seriously.

"Are you indeed?" he managed.

"Two volumes so far. The first was rather twee, I think in retrospect, but the style of the second settled down nicely, so I have hopes for the third."

Maijstral sighed. Any number of hack biographies had appeared since he'd been ranked first in the burglar standings, and most were filled with a glittering scintillation of errors, some of which he'd cheerfully supplied himself.

"I hardly think myself worthy of the attention," he said.

"On the contrary," Batty said. "I've found you quite an interesting character, well worth the study. Of course I've had to make a few guesses concerning things not on the public record. And now that I've met you, I'll be most interested to discover whether my surmises are anywhere near the mark."

Maijstral laughed uncomfortably. "I hope I won't disappoint you."

"I'm sure you won't, however it turns out. Unlike so many of my species, I'm almost never disappointed in humans—even when someone does something that I can't entirely approve of, it's always for the most *interesting* reasons."

Maijstral was at a loss for a response to this. He couldn't tell whether she disapproved of him already, or planned to disapprove in the future, or if the remark wasn't directed to him at all, but rather to the general run of her biographical victims. . . . So he said the only thing available to him, which was, "Ah."

"And there are so many people here who have known you," Batty went on. "Roberta, of course, and the Prince, who knew you at school. And Mr. Kuusinen—well, he's a first-class observer, and I've already spoken to him."

Maijstral felt a chill of alarm at the mention of Kuusinen's name. The man was far *too* first-class an observer. There were certain things he hoped Kuusinen never guessed at—there was a little service he'd done the Empire, for one, that could get him killed if certain parties in the Human Constellation ever discovered it.

"Perhaps I could answer some of your questions," he said, "and spare you the trouble of researching me through acquaintances."

"That's very kind," Batty said, "but it's not my method. I do all the research first, then speak to the subject last."

Speak to the subject, Maijstral thought. He wondered if *corner the victim* might be more appropriate.

The Haydn quartet drew to a close, the Bubber sawing away with evident enjoyment. There was scattered applause, and then the sound of the dinner gong. With relief, Maijstral bowed toward Roberta.

"May I take you in to dinner?"

"I believe Will is taking me in," Roberta smiled. "But you may take in Aunt Batty, if you like."

"A pleasure," Maijstral said, and felt rather like the condemned man taking a stroll with his executioner.

Loud hosannas began to sound as Maijstral and Batty entered the dining room. Startled, Maijstral looked up to discover a music loft above the door, with an entire choir singing away.

"I'd no idea we were going to be so honored," Maijstral said. "A chorus *and* a quartet."

"Oh," Batty said, a bit offhand, "we hear this every night. His highness supports a full complement of musicians and singers."

That, Maijstral reflected, was where adroit politics would get you. Joseph Bob's family had gained their initial wealth and title through energetic support of the Khosali Empire; and their riches and renown had only increased in the last few generations, since they'd been early and distinguished supporters of the Great Rebellion.

Once Maijstral's family had commanded wealth and station nearly equal to that of the Princes of Tejas. Unfortunately Maijstral's grandfather had been a far more fanatic supporter of the Khosali Empire even than most Khosali, and the family fortune waned with the fortunes of the Empire. Until a few years ago Maijstral had spent his life scurrying from one hideaway to another, the bill collectors just behind.

Fortunately burglary, once you reached Maijstral's level, paid well. And now that Maijstral had signed a number of endorsement contracts, it looked as if he'd never lack for funds again.

Maijstral helped Aunt Batty to her chair and sat in his own, between Batty and Roberta, half-expecting at any second to hear the crash of doors and the tramp of jackboots as Colonel-General Vandergilt marched in with a warrant for his arrest for some crime he had neither committed nor even heard of. But nothing happened, so he turned to the Bubber, seated on the other side of Roberta, and said, "Perhaps, in thanks for your music, I might offer a little amusement of my own. Perhaps you could send a footman for a deck of cards."

Card tricks alternated with supper courses. Maijstral thought he performed well, though the sight of Roberta's bare shoulders next to him was a constant, if perfectly agreeable, distraction.

Maijstral squared his cards and paused in his patter while the dessert course was brought in—Tuscan-style leaping clouds, light and frothy, with warm jugs of coffee liqueur sauce. The Bubber poured sauce on his dessert and picked up his spoon.

"If you'll pardon me, your grace," Maijstral said, rose in his chair, and reached across Roberta's plate to plunge his fingers into the Bubber's dessert. Princess Arlette gasped. The Bubber seemed at a loss for a response. "Would this be your card?" Maijstral asked, and raised the three of crowns from the Bubber's plate. Little dessert-cloudlets rained from the card, but it was perfectly recognizable.

"Yes!" the Bubber gasped.

"Another dessert, if you please," Maijstral told the footman. "And another deck of cards—this one is soiled." He showed the card to the others, and there was a round of applause, feet tapping the floor in the pattern for "surprise and appreciation."

Maijstral wiped his fingers and the card with his napkin and left the card faceup on the table, a reminder of his prowess. He always possessed a certain sense of wonder himself at how the simplest effects produced the greatest reaction—the others assumed he'd performed some master sleight right in front of the Bubber's nose, whereas in fact he'd merely had Roman bribe the footman to put a prearranged card in the Bubber's dessert. Any actual skill lay in getting the Bubber to choose the three of crowns in the first place, but that was a fairly elementary "force," as the jargon had it, and hardly a challenge.

He'd worked for *years* on much more sophisticated tricks that never made such an impression.

He turned to Roberta. "My apologies, once more, your grace, for reaching across you so rudely."

"You are entirely forgiven," Roberta said. There was a glow in her violet eyes.

"Still, by way of apology, I'd like to offer to perform a trick where you, not I, am in command. As soon as they clear away the last course."

She smiled. "One dessert on top of another, it would seem. I'll strive not to bolt the first so as to get to the other quicker."

"Let the first add savor to the second, your grace."

Roberta gave him a graceful nod. "You are a master *saucier,* Maijstral. I shall trust your taste in dessert courses."

After the last of the dishes were cleared away, Maijstral broke the seal on the new deck and shuffled it. It was a matter of little moment to switch the new deck for the deck of identical pattern that he'd been carrying in his pocket.

"Your grace," Maijstral said, "I would like, by way of example, to deal each of us a hand of court-imago."

"I thought you said *I* was to be in charge," Roberta said.

"But I want you to know *why* you shall be in charge, and to that end—six cards, so."

The cards sped across the table. Joseph Bob and Arlette leaned forward in their chairs to peer at the action. Kuusinen watched with an expressionless face and an intense narrowing of the eyes.

Roberta picked up her hand and sorted the cards.

"Is it a passable hand, your grace?"

"I would wager on it, were I playing court-imago."

"Please lay it down." It was a Little Prough. Maijstral turned his own cards over, showing a Big Prough.

"I win," he said. "But it was unfair, was it not?"

"Yes."

"Why?"

"Because you dealt the cards, and you are a card manipulator."

"True. Therefore, it would give you more of a chance if I were to shuffle, and you were to cut the cards, yes?"

Roberta considered this. "I suppose," she said.

Maijstral reinserted the used cards into the deck, seemingly at random (but not randomly at all), and shuffled the deck with a theatrical flourish that served artfully to disguise the fact that the order of the cards was not altered in any way whatever. He placed the cards on the table.

"Cut, if you please."

The Duchess obliged. Maijstral dealt her four tens and himself four princesses.

"Was that fair?" he asked.

"I think not."

"Why not?"

"Because . . ." Her eyes narrowed as she considered the possibilities, "you could have nullified the cut in some way. Or somehow forced me to cut where you wanted me to."

Maijstral smiled. "Very good, your grace. I could have done both, had I wanted." He swept up the cards and put them in his deck. "This time I will shuffle the cards, and then you will shuffle the cards. I will deal a hand to everyone here, and you may choose the best of them to go up against my hand."

The cards were shuffled and dealt. The others at the table compared hands, and Arlette's crown stairway was chosen as the best.

"I'm afraid that isn't good enough," Maijstral said, and turned over his own hand, six major powers in a row, a full council.

Roberta's ears flattened. "You promised that I would be in charge, Maijstral. All I have been doing is following your lead."

"That is true," Maijstral said. "I've been most unfair—because it was I who dealt the cards, and I'm a card manipulator and might have arranged somehow to have the best hand." He pushed the deck toward Roberta. "Therefore, this time, *you* shuffle, *you* deal a hand to everyone here, *you* choose which of the other hands to match against mine. And we shall see what occurs."

Roberta smiled at the challenge, and reached for the cards. She shuffled and dealt. This time a pair of princesses was the best anyone could manage. Roberta gave Maijstral an apologetic look.

"Not very good, I'm afraid."

"No. I'm afraid not." Maijstral turned over his own cards, a full court from the rover to the emperor of ships, the highest possible hand in court-imago.

The Bubber, baffled, looked through his cards, then took the deck and fingered his way through it.

"It seems," Roberta said, "that I haven't been in charge at all."

Maijstral fingered his diamond ring. "I'm afraid not," he said. "My character, alas, is fatally flawed—I'm a liar. And a cheat. And, of course," he added, with an apologetic smile, "I steal."

Roberta gave a smile. "I believe I am personally acquainted with that last facet of your character, somewhat to my cost."

The Bubber took Maijstral's cards and looked at them in hopes of finding some clue to the mystery. "Maijstral," he said, "how did you *do* it?"

Maijstral's eyes gleamed beneath their lazy lids. "With great skill and a mischievous if refined sense of *diablerie,*" he said. He reached for his glass of wine. "Perhaps we should let the servants clear the table."

The company adjourned for brandy, coffee, and tobacco to the Colt Drawing Room, named after the antique firearms that Joseph Bob collected, and which were displayed in artistic array on the wall. One weapon, however, was under glass in a display case. "The first Colt revolving chugger," Joseph Bob said.

"The wood pattern seems an odd design choice," Kuusinen observed.

"That isn't ornamentation," Joseph Bob said. "The pistol's actually made of wood. It's a model that Colt carved on a sea voyage.

Once he returned, he built a working chugger out of metal and patented his process."

"They built pistols out of *metal?*" Roberta said. "That seems as outlandish as a pistol of wood. Why would Mr. Colt use metal?"

"It wouldn't do to admit this in certain political circles," Joseph Bob said, "but here among friends, I believe I might observe that human technology was not always as advanced as it is at present."

Roberta briefly touched her tongue to the corner of her mouth, a simulacrum of Khosali mirth. Maijstral had noticed that the human residents of the Empire, where the Khosali were in the majority, more often used Khosali gestures than humans of the constellation.

"Here are a pair of chuggers you might recognize, Maijstral," Joseph Bob said, and indicated a matched pair of pistols on the wall.

Cold trickled up Maijstral's spine as he looked at the weapons. Years ago, when he was sixteen, he'd fought a duel with those pistols, and the horror he'd felt at the time had never left him.

"Oh yes," Maijstral said unenthusiastically. "I recognize them perfectly well."

"Back in our Academy days," Joseph Bob told the others, "Maijstral fought a duel with those pistols. I wasn't there—the seconds wouldn't allow witnesses—but everyone said Maijstral was the coolest fellow imaginable."

Maijstral looked at the assembled company and felt sweat gathering at his nape. What others mistook for coolness had been, in fact, a pure, horrified paralysis.

"I'm sure the others exaggerated," Maijstral said.

Joseph Bob put a hearty hand on Maijstral's shoulder. "Quite a feat, though, fighting a duel at that age—what were we? Sixteen? Seventeen?"

"Too young," Maijstral said.

"I've always envied you the experience. Here I am, a crack pistol shot and an exemplary swordsman, and I've never once had an encounter! I've always wanted a chance, but everyone's always been so *polite* to me."

Arlette looked a little nonplussed at this evidence of her husband's bloodthirstiness. Maijstral raised a thin smile. His ears pricked forward. "If I ever have another fight," he said, "you can substitute for me if you like."

Joseph Bob gave a hearty laugh. "Oh," he said, "I wish I could!"

"We youngsters were jealous of you," the Bubber offered. "And that girl of yours who was the cause of it all—we were jealous of her, too. Quite a pippin, that Zoe."

"Maijstral started quite a fad," Joseph Bob added. "There must have been a dozen challenges among the underclassmen before the term was out. We seniors had to suppress them all, of course."

Maijstral sincerely wished someone would act to suppress this topic of conversation. He didn't care for his youthful follies being the subject of quite this much speculation. He observed that Kuusinen was watching him with interest, and Maijstral liked neither the intrigued tilt to Aunt Batty's head nor the glitter in her eye. Probably she was planning on adding another note to her three-volume biography.

And Roberta, he noted, was looking at him with an admiration that made him thoroughly uneasy. On Silverside Station she had served as his second on a duel that, fortunately for him, had not actually come off. He didn't want to leave anyone with the impression he was a fire-eater happy to swashbuckle his way through life in search of deadly encounters. A reputation like that could attract more danger than it would keep away—just look at the career of Pearl Woman or Etienne, to name two among the Three Hundred who were constantly having to hack their way out of one lethal situation or another.

Perhaps, Maijstral considered, it was time for a bit of misdirection. "Say," he said, turning to an intriguing-looking shoulder weapon with Troxan markings, "what is *that* used for? Is that a *harpoon* of some sort?"

Annoyance flared in Maijstral as Joseph Bob clung to his reminiscence. "D'you know, Maijstral," he said, "after I got the pistols back, I couldn't hit a blessed thing with either one of 'em. Turned out the sights were out of true."

Maijstral suppressed a jolt of alarm, and instead said, "Perhaps the seconds were careless in handling them afterward. Asad and Zah were pretty excited by the whole business."

"I wonder—d'you suppose it was one of the masters bent on avoiding bloodshed?" Joseph Bob fingered his chin analytically. "Perhaps if word of the duel got out, one of our housemasters could have got into my room with his passkey and twitched the sights out of alignment."

It had been Maijstal, of course, far gone in the depths of terror, who had crept into Joseph Bob's room and tweaked the foresights with a handy pair of pliers. It had been his first successful breaking and entering, one of those painful, involuntary milestones on his path to the present. How many other people, one could well ask, have discovered their own utter cowardice and the silent joys of burglary at the same time?

Maijstral affected to consider Joseph Bob's theory. It occurred to him that the notion was far too close to the truth, and probably ought to be discredited altogether. "I think your theory probably gives the masters too much credit," he said. "It was never my impression that they knew anything we were doing, let alone anything we were *trying* to hide from them." His lazy lids closed over his eyes, leaving only slits. "I'm inclined to suspect it was just careless handling by the seconds. Julian and I held the pistols only for a moment or two, just long enough to shoot, but the seconds probably had them for hours."

"Mm," Joseph Bob conceded. "Very likely."

"Now what is this—*harpoon* sort of thing?" Maijstral asked, once more attempting his diversion.

As Joseph Bob went on to explain that the harpoon gun was intended to anchor the wandering, homicidal trees that lurched about one of the Troxan homeworlds, Maijstral viewed the other guests from beneath his slitted lids. Arlette, the Bubber, and Roberta seemed perfectly willing to be diverted by the harpoon gun. Kuusinen's polite expression, as ever, revealed little. But Aunt Batty's lace-covered ears were cocked forward, and her tongue lolled in a smug little smile—as if, Maijstral concluded, some pet theory of hers had just been confirmed.

He wondered if there were some way he could read this biography.

Perhaps, it occurred to him, he could *steal* it.

The string quartet's rendition of a Frayng piece echoed up the hall as the company made their way to their rooms.

"I say—Maijstral?"

"Yes, Bubber?"

"Oh, call me Will, won't you? I don't care much for meaningless titles, and I guess you don't, either, considering you don't use yours."

"Will. Yes. You may call me Drake, if you like. How may I help you?"

"I was wondering if we might do a trade. I'd be most happy to teach you to ride a horse tomorrow, and—well, what I want is—I, ah—could you teach me magic?"

A pause. "Well." Another pause. "I would be happy to teach you a few things, of course. But I won't be spending that much time here in Tejas, and I won't be able to give you anything but a few fundamentals."

"Oh, that would be fine. I understand your time is limited. But I'd like to find out if magic is something I could really master—you know, I've always lived with J.B., and he's a perfectly splendid person, but he's so *good* at everything. A better shot than me, a better fencer, a better rider . . . and probably a better lord, if it comes to that. And I can play the cello pretty well, but I'm not as good as the fellow who's normally got the job . . . so anyway, I thought if I could master something that J.B. isn't good at, then . . . well, I'd like to give it a try, anyway."

"I would be happy to teach you what I can."

"Thank you. Er—Drake?"

"Yes, Will?"

"Did I just say something—you know—pathetic?"

"Not at all, Will."

"Thank you." A sigh. "I'm relieved."

"Good night, Will."

"Good night. And thank you."

"Dear?" Strolling up the stairway a few moments later. "Did you really envy Maijstral his duel?"

"Oh, yes. Of course. It's a chance to find out what you're really made of, isn't it?"

"Don't you think you know what you're made of, Joe?"

"Well." A nervous laugh. "Not the way Maijstral does, I'm sure. I've done well, but then I started out with so many advantages that I would have had to work hard at doing badly in order to make a failure of myself. I certainly haven't been tested, not the way my grandfather was in the Great Rebellion, nor the way Maijstral was before he was twenty."

"You got *me* all on your own, Joe."

The sound of a kiss.

"Well," reflectively, "perhaps I haven't done so badly, after all."

The same stair. Another pair.

"Do things progress, Kuusinen?"

"Indeed, your grace. The mechanics of smuggling an object as large as a coffin into the house without Maijstral's knowledge presented some difficulties, but now that he's decided to go riding tomorrow, I believe we can use the window of opportunity afforded by his absence."

"And his servants?"

"His Highness's butler has been instructed to divert them. They, and your servants as well, will be taken on a special picnic tomorrow morning."

"Very good. Perhaps I will take exercise with Maijstral and make certain he'll be gone for a sufficient length of time."

"An admirable addition to the plan, your grace."

"I don't believe it will be any great sacrifice—it will be a perfectly pleasant morning, given good weather."

"Of course, your grace."

Another pause. "Is that Snail they're performing?"

"Frayng, your grace."

"Ah. I can never tell them apart."

"Hardly anyone ever can. I believe that's why they were provoked into their unfortunate duel—each thought the other was imitating him."

"They fought with bassoons, did they not?"

"Yes. Bassoons, your grace. Not the most graceful of weapons, but then they both died, so perhaps there is some hidden martial quality to the instrument of which we are unaware."

"Good grief!"

"Oh. Sorry, Mr. Maijstral. I really didn't mean to startle you."

Maijstral contemplated the jutting finlike pompadour sticking up above his rack of suits. "If you didn't mean to startle me," he said, "why did you hide in my closet?"

Conchita Sparrow's genial face worked its way out from between a pair of jackets. "One of your servants was in here a minute ago, and I didn't want him to see me, so I just nipped in for a second." She fondled a shoulder seam. "Nice suit, this green one. I like the cut."

"Thank you, Miss Sparrow. Would you care to step into the room now?"

"Only too." Conchita left the closet, took a breath, and grinned. "It was stuffy in there." She looked around the room. "Can you give me a drink or something?"

Maijstral, ignoring this last request, folded his arms and regarded the intruder. "The matter of your being in my closet is now explained, but we have yet to address the question of your being in my room in the first place. Have you dropped off another stolen art treasure?"

"Oh. No. I was just wondering if you'd had a chance to review my recordings."

"You needn't have come in person. You could have phoned. Or you could have knocked on the front door and asked for me."

"Well, yes," Conchita admitted. "But I wanted to show you how well I could neutralize the security in this place." Her eyes widened. "Oh. The closet. One moment."

She reached into the closet and removed the command override she'd placed on the closet's command systems. "Close the doors, please."

"I have been interfered with." The closet's tone was sulky.

"Close the doors, please."

The doors closed with a final grumble. Conchita turned to Maijstral and grinned.

"Your technical ability is without question," Maijstral said. "But I already employ a tech. The only work I could offer you is perhaps an occasional contract, and that only rarely."

Conchita's face fell. "Oh, come on, Mr. Maijstral," she said. "Your life would never be dull with me around!"

This, Maijstral considered, was becoming all too plain. "Perhaps that's so," he said, "but I can't fire a perfectly good employee just to relieve the tedium." At that point there was a knock at the door.

He and Conchita looked at each other for a moment, and then Conchita turned to the closet. "Open, please," she said.

"I won't," the closet said. "You interfered with my mechanisms."

"Open, closet," Maijstral said.

"Well," the closet said, "for *you.*"

The closet opened and Conchita ducked inside, jabbing her command override into the closet's systems as she did so. The doors shut smoothly, and Maijstral went to answer the knock.

Kuusinen's head was cocked slightly in an inquiring manner. "I hope I do not interrupt, sir," he said.

Maijstral unconsciously straightened his jacket. "Oh. Not at all. Would you come in?"

"Thank you, no. I had only a single question to ask you," Kuusinen said. "I hope you won't consider it impertinent, but I'm afraid I'm compulsive in certain ways, and I won't be able to sleep unless I know the answer."

"I will do my utmost to assume you rest, Mr. Kuusinen."

"What do you call the technique you used in the trick where the cards were hidden under the creamer? The one where you substituted one card on the very top of the deck for another?"

Maijstral blinked. "I must have performed the trick very poorly for you to have noticed."

"On the contrary," Kuusinen said, "your working of the trick was excellent, and I noticed nothing at the time. But, in thinking about the trick afterward, I realized how it had to be done, and—I apologize again—I was consumed with a desire for the information."

"I would be obliged if you refrained from sharing your line of reasoning with the others."

"I won't, I assure you. This is purely for my own satisfaction."

"The technique is called a top change."

Kuusinen closed his eyes and absorbed the bit of jargon with an expression akin to bliss. His eyes fluttered open. "Thank you, sir."

"I hope you sleep well."

"I'm sure I shall."

Maijstral closed the door and was on his way to the closet when he was interrupted by a gentle chime from the phone. He answered, and the visage of the Duchess of Benn appeared on the screen.

"If you're looking for Mr. Kuusinen," Maijstral said, "he just left."

"I wasn't, actually," Roberta said. "I was hoping that I might invite myself along on your riding trip tomorrow."

"You're most welcome," Maijstral said, "but I'm afraid I won't be a very challenging companion. I've never been on a horse in my life."

"Neither have I. We shall learn together."

"I shall look forward."

"Good night, Maijstral."

"Good night, your grace."

Maijstral turned from the phone to see the closet door gliding open. Conchita appeared. "Was that the Duchess of Benn?" she asked.

"It was."

"That's fingo all right!"

Maijstral raised his eyebrows at this piece of cant. "Sorry?" he said.

"I mean, I'm impressed. You stole the Eltdown Shard from her and she not only still speaks to you, she looks for ways to ride off into the sunset with you."

Maijstral blinked. There was a lot more to the Eltdown Shard story than ever reached the public, and he intended it stay that way. "I believe you were leaving," he said.

"Well." Conchita shrugged. "I suppose I was."

"Shall I open a window for you?"

"No thanks. I got in through the ventilation."

She popped a grill off the wall, floated up off the floor, entered feetfirst, and paused to give a wave before she disappeared into the ventilator shaft. Maijstral walked to the service plate and touched it.

"Roman. Would you come in here, if you please?"

It was Drexler's voice that answered. "Sorry, Mr. Maijstral. Roman left before dinner and hasn't returned. May I be of service?"

Maijstral paused. It was most unlike Roman to be absent at this hour, when he was usually required to unlace Maijstral from his jacket and trousers. Maijstral would have to summon a robot to do the job.

"Did Roman say where he was going?"

"No, sir. May I help you?"

First things first, Maijstral thought. "Yes," he said. "Miss Sparrow has returned. I don't know if she left anything behind, but if she did, I want it found."

"I'll take care of that right away, sir."

"Thank you, Drexler."

Another long search of his own quarters, Maijstral thought wearily.

He hoped he wouldn't have to get used to this.

FOUR

Maijstral arrived for his ride dressed in what he believed to be the correct costume: wide Stetson hat, large bandanna, leather vest, fringed chaps, high-heeled proughskin boots with pointed toes, silver rowel spurs that gleamed in the sunlight, a stunner in the shape of one of Mr. Colt's revolvers on one hip and a waspish rapier on the other.

Will, the Bubber, regarded Maijstral with an expression of genial surprise as he stalked into the stables on his tall heels. "Very authentic," he said.

"Am I . . . overdressed?" Maijstral said. The Bubber's costume complemented his own only in the matter of boots.

"I don't *think* we're going to be attacked by outlaws," the Bubber said, "but I'm sure that if we are, we'll be thankful for the hardware. And I wasn't planning on riding through heavy brush, either, though the chaps will be useful if we do."

Roberta arrived, dressed casually, and looked at Maijstral in surprise. "I've seen that costume before," she offered. "You wore it on the night of the Grand Ball on Silverside, when you stole my necklace."

"I hope the associations aren't too unpleasant."

Roberta offered an ambiguous smile. "Quite the contrary. It was an exhilarating evening."

"Perhaps," said the Bubber, "I should introduce you to your horses. And, ah, Drake—I'd take off those spurs if I were you. There might be an accident."

Maijstral had fantasized himself flying along on a midnight steed, a lean animal, all clean streamlined angles and flying mane and surging muscle, but his horse turned out to be a gentle, middle-aged grey mare named Morganna, who jogged along the path without any apparent need for direction on Maijstral's part. Even so Maijstral found the sensation a bit alarming. The large beast moving beneath him gave him the sensation of being harnessed to a slow-motion earthquake, a natural force of sufficient power to cause injury if he made the wrong move. Still, he and the horse managed to get along well enough, and he found himself enjoying the experience.

Roberta was less successful. It became obvious from the first that she and her mount were engaged in a furious contest of wills from which, very possibly, there would be but one survivor.

"I can't understand it," the Bubber remarked, after they'd been riding about ten minutes. "Ringo's been a perfectly tractable animal till now."

"If this beast doesn't soon learn to obey," Roberta said through clenched teeth, "I'm going to break every single one of its ribs."

Roberta was a world-class racer, with the powerful legs necessary to negotiate the turns and leaps of the zero-gravity maze, and she might well have been capable of carrying out her threat.

"Just try to relax," the Bubber suggested.

Ringo regarded the Duchess from a red, rolling eye, ears flattened. *"Relax?"* Roberta cried. *"How?* With this *wretched animal* confounding my every . . ."

Roberta urged it forward, and instead, out of contrariness, it backed. Roberta's ears drew back in anger. She kicked the horse to get it moving, those powerful racer's legs driving into the animal's ribs . . . and Ringo took off with a bound, almost flinging Roberta over its tail, and raced top speed across country. Roberta hung on gamely, crouched over the horse's neck, and hurled abuse into its ear as it carried her off.

Maijstral watched in alarm at this development right out of one of his Westerns. The heroine's animal had run off with her, and it was clearly up to the hero to do something about it. If Elvis had been here, or Jesse James, the course of action would have been clear. But Maijstral, an equestrian tyro, was helpless to intervene. If he'd only worn an a-grav harness, he could have flown after the Duchess and plucked her from the saddle with ease.

Fortunately the Bubber was up to the challenge and raced off in pursuit. Maijstral peered anxiously after, but all he could see were two swiftly moving clouds of dust aiming for a convergence on the horizon. After a certain amount of negotiation with his animal he managed to work it up to a trot; and he jounced along in pursuit, feeling as if life had just handed him the sidekick role.

Eventually, emerging from the heat shimmer on the horizon came the Bubber on his horse, with Roberta mounted behind and a lathered Ringo following on a lead. The Bubber was grinning, and even Roberta had a smile tugging at her lips.

"I trust you're not injured?" Maijstral asked.

"Not at all," Roberta said. "Will was the perfect rescuer. Snatched me right out of the saddle and set me on his horse behind as if I were a child." She patted the Bubber on the shoulder. "You're stronger than you look."

The Bubber seemed pleased. "There's a trick to it. You just have to know how."

"And how do you know these tricks? Do you go plucking ladies off runaway horses every day of the week?"

The Bubber flushed a little. "I used to do a little acrobatic riding, but I haven't done anything like that in years. Surprising how the reflexes come back." He shaded his eyes and looked toward the sprawl of the Prince's residence, still looming on the horizon, then turned to Maijstral. "I'm sorry to cut your lesson short, Drake, but we'd best return to the stables."

Roberta looked firm. "I think not," she said. "You and Maijstral go on with your plans." She kicked one leg up over the Bubber's head—her athleticism was so effortless that it did not surprise—and slid off the saddle to the ground. "I shall *walk* Ringo back to the stables," she said. "And if the beast gives me trouble, I shall simply break the animal's knees."

The Bubber looked dubious. "We'll take you back," he said. "I'm sure Drake doesn't mind."

"Not at all," Maijstral said.

Roberta's violet eyes flashed. *"Maijstral,"* she said. *"Go for your ride."*

Maijstral blinked. He had encountered Roberta's force of will before, and on consideration it amazed him that Ringo had managed to resist it for so long. "Your grace," he said, "if you insist."

"I do." She turned to the Bubber, and her face assumed a less

stern expression. "I'm perfectly capable of walking the couple of leagues to the stables. I'm a racer, after all."

"Well," frowning, "if you're sure . . ."

Roberta took her leave and began her walk, the exhausted, chastened horse following. Maijstral and the Bubber turned their horses and began a trot back to the road.

"Rather high-strung, ain't she?" the Bubber said.

"She has more reason for temperament than most," Maijstral said. "She is young, and has been to a strict school. No doubt she wishes to prove herself worthy of all the trust that has been placed in her. And of course she has to be constantly wary of people who want to take advantage of her—fortune hunters and so on."

The Bubber's ears reddened. "Well, yes," he said, "families can be a bother sometime. I find I'm glad I'm not the heir—I've much more freedom that way. I've got enough money to be comfortable, and J.B.'s kind enough to employ me at things I enjoy. Fortunately we get along."

"My titles came with no money or property," Maijstral said, "only debts. It was hard to think of them as an advantage."

They rode along pleasantly for a while, each with his own thoughts.

"Drake?" the Bubber said. "When do you think you might teach me a little magic?"

"Right now, if you like."

"Now?"

"A little theory, anyway."

"Oh. Well. To be sure."

"We have several varieties of effects to consider," Maijstral began. "All classic visual effects fall into one of a few categories—vanishing, production, transformation, transposition, restoration, penetration, and levitation."

"That seems rather a long list." Dubiously.

"Some effects are merely the reversal of another, vanishing and production for example. Allow me to give an example of each."

Discoursing thus, the two rode on companionably.

Behind them, out of sight of the two, a large transport craft descended onto the Prince's lawn to unload its cargo.

One large coffin.

After luncheon the Prince, his family, and his guests boarded a large flier and sped to the Grand Canyon, where, after a leisurely drift down the length of the Canyon at about medium altitude, with the

Colorado still far below and the canyon walls looming high on either side, the flier soared effortlessly upward to a landing at Cape Solitude. There everyone disembarked to observe the Colorado stretching on down the length of Marble Canyon, and marvelled at the side canyon's grand, if inaccurately named, magnificence.

As the others absorbed the Canyon's splendor, Maijstral carefully watched Joseph Bob from beneath his lazy eyelids. He wanted to do a card trick that would astound everyone, but it required knowing the subject well. In the cant, it required "taking dead aim" at Joseph Bob.

But he wasn't certain if he knew Joseph Bob well enough. Maijstral had, during their school years in the Empire, known the young princeling as well as anyone, but he hadn't seen the man since graduation.

But Joseph Bob seemed not to have changed at all. Matured a bit, certainly, but in essence he seemed the same young human Maijstral had known at the Academy.

Well, Maijstral thought, he might as well find out. If this didn't work, he'd cover it with another trick.

The others were starting to drift back to the flier in preparation to moving to another vantage point. Maijstral approached Joseph Bob.

"Would you mind assisting me in a card trick?" he asked.

"Here?" Joseph Bob seemed surprised. "If you like."

"Perhaps we could use the table near that, ah, tree-ish thing."

"That's a Jasperian Sprout Vine."

"It is? So that's what a sprout vine looks like."

The others followed as Maijstral and Joseph Bob approached the table. They sat on opposite sides of the table, and Maijstral produced a deck of cards. He spread them expertly, faceup, in front of the Prince.

"If you could point to a card?"

Joseph Bob pointed to the four of ships. Triumph flooded Maijstral's blood. He swept up the cards, shuffled, handed the deck to Joseph Bob.

"Find your card, if you please."

Joseph Bob looked through the deck for the four of ships but failed to find it.

"Count them, please."

Joseph Bob counted the cards. Glancing around the table, Maijstral noted the little bobs of the spectators' heads as they counted along with him.

"There are only sixty-three," Joseph Bob said. "The four of ships is missing."

Maijstral's eyes glinted green from behind his heavy lids. "Perhaps," he said, "you might find the missing card in the inside left breast pocket of your jacket."

Joseph Bob reached into his jacket experimentally, and then his eyes widened. He withdrew his hand and in it, the four of ships.

"You were on the other side of the table from me the entire time," he said. "How did you *do* that?"

Taking dead aim, Maijstral thought, and gathered up the cards. He rose from his seat and looked out over the Canyon.

"Perhaps we might seek another point of advantage."

"I don't see why we should bother," Joseph Bob muttered, his ears pricking back in puzzlement, "since the advantage is all yours."

The afternoon was spent flitting from one part of the Canyon to the next, and ended with cocktails and a light buffet in the Redwall Cavern. Then the flier returned to the Prince's estate, where Roman helped lace Maijstral into his formal dinner dress.

Roman was feeling a warm, mild burning sensation precisely in the middle of his broad back, where he couldn't scratch it. All day he had felt mild fevers alternate with light chills. Phantom itches moved from place to place over his body, and wherever he scratched, his fine black fur flew.

As he'd experienced this twenty-odd times before, he knew perfectly well what was going to happen. He was about to enter molt.

Roman *hated* molt. He was an exceptionally bad molter, and his molts put him out of sorts for weeks. And the fact that the molt meant he was a year older did not improve his humor.

Another year, he might have thought, in service to Maijstral. Another year of being an assistant thief, occasional leg-breaker, and general voice of responsibility in a most irregular world.

Roman *might* have thought that . . . but he didn't. He was far too disciplined, too Khosali, ever to criticize his employer, even mentally. The most he would ever allow himself was an occasional diaphragm pulse of resignation.

"Did you have a pleasant afternoon, sir?" he asked as he did up the side-laces of Maijstral's jacket.

"Very satisfactory," Maijstral said. He looked at Roman over his shoulder. "A little looser in the armpit, please."

"Very good, sir." Roman pried at the laces.

"You were out last night," Maijstral said.

"I regret I wasn't back in time to unlace you," Roman said. "I lost track of time."

Maijstral tugged experimentally at his lapel, worked his arm in its socket. "I hope you had a pleasant time, wherever you were."

"I was at the library, sir."

"Oh." Maistral was surprised. "Well, I hope your reading was pleasant."

"I was reading history, sir," Roman said. "It was very fulfilling."

Which was a statement calculated to end Maijstral's questions. Roman, as well as the Duchess, had his own Special Project, one he had been working on for years, a project that involved Maijstral.

Last night, in the library in Rome, Roman had found the crucial bit of evidence that had brought the project to its climax. He just didn't want Maijstral knowing about it yet.

Roman handed Maijstral his pistol, which was promptly stowed in the armpit holster, and then Maijstral made his way downstairs to dinner.

Relieved to be left alone, Roman went straight to the service plate and called for a robot to come to the room and scratch the fiery itch in the center of his back.

Dinner featured pleasant conversation and no card tricks—Maijstral understood that to be consistently amazing is, in the long run, to risk becoming consistently predictable, if not consistently dull. Besides, Maijstral was very pleased with the one trick he'd performed that day, and had no desire to perform other tricks that weren't as spectacular.

After dinner, Joseph Bob, the Bubber, and Arlette played a three-sided game of puff-sticks in the drawing room, while Maijstral browsed along the bookshelves. There were a lot of histories and biographies, many of which concerned members of the Prince's family. Maijstral browsed the pages of one of these—it concerned the great Flax-Seed Scandal that rocked the Empire in the decade before the Rebellion, and the then-Bubber's ambiguous role therein—and discovered that the margins had been annotated in pencil. Most of the annotations were in the human alphabet, and consisted of the letter "L" or the letters "DL," sometimes followed by an exclamation mark.

Maijstral waited for an auspicious moment to interrupt the puff-sticks game, then asked Joseph Bob what the letters meant. The Prince gave the book a glance.

"Oh, that's my grandfather's notes," he said. "He annotated all the histories that way. L stands for 'lie,' and DL for 'damned lie.' "

Maijstral smiled. "I am enlightened," he said. "Thank you." As he returned to the bookshelf the Duchess of Benn approached, rustling in a silk gown of imperial purple that admirably echoed her violet eyes.

"Maijstral," Roberta said, "I was wondering if you might join Kuusinen and me for a moment. There is something upstairs that might interest you."

"Of course, your grace." Maijstral closed the book and returned it to the shelves.

Feeling the sort of languid curiosity that is the best one can hope for after a large, well-prepared meal, Maijstral followed after Roberta. Little warning spikes of pain jumped along his thighs as he climbed up the stairs—the morning's riding, he thought. Roberta's gown plunged behind, and he found himself enjoying, once more, the supple play of muscle and shadow on the Duchess's back.

Roberta led Maijstral past her own suite, then opened a door into another room and stepped inside. Maijstral followed, saw what waited therein, and stopped dead. Kuusinen almost ran into him from behind.

Maijstral's first thought was that Conchita Sparrow had really outdone herself this time—not only stealing a huge cryocoffin from somewhere, but sneaking it past Joseph Bob's security and hiding it in the room—but then he began to recognize the coffin's sweeping bronze lines, turned into little classical scrolls on either end, and he frowned and stepped into the room, a song of warning keening in the back of his head.

Aunt Batty, he observed, had been keeping the coffin company: she was well established in a rocking chair in one corner, surrounded by a little thicket of manuscript on which she'd been working. Evidently the coffin's appearance was not a surprise to her, or to anyone in the Duchess's party.

Maijstral looked at the Imperial Arms and Lineage etched into the coffin lid, and it only confirmed his worst suspicions. His heart sank.

"Hello, Dad," he said. "How did you get here?"

A plaintive voice came from the coffin.

"Is it time for my cocoa yet?" it asked.

FIVE

Maijstral had believed that he had kept his late father without enough funds to travel, and as his father's legal guardian he'd forbade his father to borrow. Well, he thought, his dad had got the funds from *somewhere,* probably a little account he'd been hiding all these years, or maybe an old friend who'd been persuaded to make a loan; and Maijstral would have to get the lawyers to start searching for the source . . . *after,* Maijstral considered, the late Gustav Maijstral was shipped home to his tomb and safely reinstalled in the home of his ancestors.

"Drake?" the corpse inquired. "Is that you, Drake?"

"Yes, Dad," Maijstral sighed. "It's me."

"I came here for a very good reason," Gustav Maijstral said firmly. "I want my cocoa!" And then added, ". . . I *think.* I *think* that's why I'm here."

"Dad," Maijstral said patiently, "you can't have cocoa. You're dead."

Maijstral gave an apologetic look to the others while his father mulled this over.

"Oh yes," the corpse remarked. "You're right. I'm dead. I forgot."

It is impossible not to observe that the former Duke of Dornier, ex-Viscount Sing, onetime Prince-Bishop of Nana, and late Hereditary Captain-General of the Green Legion had not been a particularly astute man while alive, and that death had not improved him.

Kuusinen cleared his throat tactfully. Roberta took the hint and turned to Maijstral.

"Actually," she said, "it's my fault he's here."

"Oh yes!" the corpse added. "That's right!" He sighed, which came out of the coffin's speakers as a faint electronic sizzle. "I keep forgetting these things. . . ."

Maijstral turned his bewildered attention to Roberta. "He came to see *you?*" he asked.

"Not exactly," she said. "I arranged for him to be brought here to see you, but . . ."

"I remember! I remember!" the corpse cried triumphantly. "I remember why I'm here!" And then the voice trailed away. "I *thought* I remembered . . . just a moment . . . maybe it'll come back."

Roberta passed a hand over her brow. "This isn't working out the way I'd hoped," she said. "Kuusinen, can you help me?"

Kuusinen nodded and turned to Maijstral. "As you know, I am her grace's solicitor. Two years ago, her grace instructed me to undertake certain researches having to do with a Special Project she was undertaking in regard to her future. You and your family were among those to whom I devoted my efforts."

Maijstral's head was whirling, but he managed to put his finger on at least one important point. "That's why I keep running into you," he said. "On Peleng, and Silverside Station, and . . ."

"Just so," Kuusinen nodded.

"And what was the tenor of these researches?"

Kuusinen looked appropriately grave. "The contract of a matrimonial alliance," he said, "between Her Grace the Duchess of Benn and . . ."

Maijstral jumped as if stung. *"No!"* he said.

The others stared at him.

"Absolutely not," Maijstral said.

Roberta's eyes were wide. Her lower lip trembled. "But . . . why not?" she asked.

Maijstral folded his arms and looked stern. "I absolutely forbid you to marry my father. He's married already, for one thing, and for another he's dead, and I don't care what your demented relations told you would make a good dynastic alliance, you'd just be throwing your life away. . . ."

His words trickled away as Roberta's real intent slowly filtered its way into his mind.

"Oh," he said.

In Maijstral's defense it must be said that this really *was* a surprise. He'd been thrown off-balance by his father's arrival, and made slow by a good dinner, and wasn't operating at full speed.

All that said, he certainly proved a bit dense on this occasion. However, one should remember that this sort of thing happens to the best of us, and usually, alas, where personal matters are concerned.

"Well, yes," Roberta admitted. "It was you I was planning to marry, Drake."

Maijstral's head whirled, but even through all his inner confusion he couldn't help but admire Roberta's style . . . to have Kuusinen quietly case him for a year, to carry her valuable jewels to Silverside Station as a way of bringing herself together with Maijstral, and then to arrange for all the necessities of the formal betrothal as dictated by Khosali High Custom: a representative from each of the families (his father for the Maijstrals and, he presumed, Aunt Batty on the Duchess's side), a meeting on neutral ground (the estate of the Prince of Tejas), a neutral who had doubtless conspired with her to sneak Maijstral's father onto the premises while Maijstral was at the Grand Canyon or on his morning ride. He wouldn't be surprised if there was an Imperial Recorder stowed away in the next room, ready to transcribe all the niggling little details of noble lineage and so forth on a formal betrothal written with a jade pen on the tanned hide of a grookh, proper for transmission to the City of Seven Bright Rings, where the Khosali Emperor himself, Nnis CVI, would give his formal permission for the wedding. . . .

Permission in these cases was never denied, of course. Nnis CVI had retired to his cryocoffin long ago, and was probably in worse shape than Maijstral's father.

Roberta had acted brilliantly, and in so doing had displayed a surprising amount of subtlety for one so young. Maijstral was struck with awe.

He was also struck by the realization that he didn't know whether he wanted to marry Roberta or not. She was young, she was attractive, she was intelligent and interesting, she was staggeringly rich, and she was thoroughly worthy of admiration . . . but yet.

But yet. She was not, in his brief experience, an *easy* person. She was high-strung, she was quick-tempered, she was a fierce competitor who raced in the highest amateur league. Her force of will was prodigious. Maijstral admired her, but thus far he'd succeeded in admiring her only at a distance. Who knew what emotion might result from closer proximity?

Maijstral became aware that the others were watching him with their ears cocked forward in expectation. Clearly some manner of reply was required. He bowed toward the Duchess and placed a hand over his heart without quite knowing what he was going to say. Fortunately, his training came to the fore.

The Nnoivarl Academy, ridiculous though its curriculum might be in any practical respect, is at least good for seeing its graduates through a crisis of style.

"I am astounded by your consideration," Maijstral said. "I had never thought to look so high." As he rose from his bow, he regarded Roberta carefully through half-closed lazy-lidded eyes—was that a trace of disappointment he saw mirrored in her face? Had she expected, he wondered, for him to throw himself into her arms?

If so, he considered, she shouldn't have surrounded herself with all these intermediaries.

Delay, he thought. He still had no idea what his response would be—or, for that matter, *could* be.

"I should consult with my father to determine his wishes," Maijstral said, then gave the coffin a dubious glance. "Insofar as they *can* be determined," he added.

"Drake's going to marry the Duchess!" sang the corpse. *"That's* why I'm here! Wonderful girl! Imperial family! Good match! When the Emperor comes back, we'll all live like kings!"

Well, Maijstral thought, *that* sounded like consent.

The impulse to delay was still uppermost in his thoughts. He turned to Roberta, his ears flicking forward. "Your grace," he said, "may we speak to each other alone? Perhaps in the next room?"

Roberta bit her lip. "There's an Imperial Recorder in the next room," she said.

Knew it, Maijstral thought.

"But we can use my parlor," Roberta added. "It's only a few doors away."

"The parlor will suit perfectly well." Maijstral turned to Aunt Batty and bowed. "If you will excuse us."

He offered Roberta his arm and she took it. As he closed the door behind them, she looked at him and bit her lip.

"You're not angry, are you?"

"Of course not. I'm . . . stunned."

"You didn't have any idea? Really?"

"I thought Kuusinen had been scouting me out on account of your jewels. I'd no idea you had any . . . other interest."

She opened the door to her parlor and passed inside. Maijstral sat down on a small settee, and Roberta sat next to him. His big diamond flashed as he reached to take her hand.

"How exactly . . . did this come about?" he asked.

Roberta looked at him with her violet eyes. "Well, the family were pressuring me to marry. And you can't imagine the sort of candidates they came up with. . . ."

"Indeed I can," Maijstral said. "Elderly bishops, and gawky schoolboys who can barely walk without falling down, middle-aged sportsmen gone to seed, a widowed duke looking for his fourth wife, lots of hopeful cousins who want your money, and an adopted human son of a Fifth-Degree Imperial Khosali Prince who is very fat and at least a hundred."

Roberta smiled. "I can see you've met them."

"On the contrary. I've met their sisters."

Roberta gave him a knowing look. "I see. Well, you know the situation, then. All the candidates were so *hopeless* . . . and, of course, *safe,* in the purely dynastic sense, of course. So I decided that, if I had to marry, I would at least find a candidate who suited me better."

"And I was chosen? Out of all our busy galaxy?"

Her ears reddened a bit. "I had a short list of about a dozen," she confessed. "Paavo Kuusinen met all of them, over the course of a few years, and sent in his reports, and I arranged to meet some of the more promising candidates myself, and . . . well, I made my choice on Silverside Station, when I met you. Since then I had to travel back to the Empire to inform my family, and, well, to inform yours. Such as he is."

"You could have done far worse," Maijstral said. "You could have contacted my mother."

Roberta bit her lip. "We don't have to invite her to the wedding, do we?"

"Don't ask her for my sake. But if we don't invite her, she'll probably crash the reception anyway, with an escort of His Majesty's Secret Dragoons."

"We'll try to contain her somehow."

They looked at each other for a moment, then self-consciously looked away. "I still don't know how you fastened upon *me,"* Maijstral said. "You made your decision years ago, apparently, before I was very well-known to the public."

"I knew a few things about you," Roberta said. "I knew you would inherit an old title, which removed any objection on account of birth. I knew your parents were dedicated Imperialists, and your grandfather old Dornier was the most famous human Imperialist of all, so that removed any objections on account of politics and your citizenship in the Constellation. You were poor, of course, but I've got so much money that I certainly don't need to marry it, and anyway you've eliminated that objection yourself by earning a fortune in the last year. . . ."

"But why me? There must be a thousand poor, virtuous, titled Imperialists out there."

"Well." A little smile crept onto her face. "If you stand to inherit a fabulous gem like the Eltdown Shard, you spend a lot of your girlhood trying to imagine who's going to try to steal it from you. Trying to picture the romantic stranger who's going to fly in the window some night. And, of course, your family security people keep a list of all the top burglars, and you get dossiers . . . your face crossed my desk when you took out your burglar's license, and I remember thinking, Well, *there's* one I wouldn't mind meeting some dark night . . ."

"I took out my ticket ages ago. You must have been just a girl."

"Oh yes. Red hair and freckles and a school uniform that wouldn't fit. I'm glad you didn't know me then."

"I'm pleased to know you now."

"Are you?" Her eyes sparkled with interest. "Had you considered me a marriage candidate?"

"Frankly, no. I hadn't thought of myself as suitable." Maijstral touched his chin thoughtfully with a forefinger and regarded her, absorbing the creamy shoulders, the intriguing shadows about her clavicles, the gems that sparkled about her neck.

"I *had* thought about trying to get you into bed," he said, "but on Silverside we were both busy, and we had a business relationship besides, and since I've arrived here there hasn't been time."

She flushed becomingly. "Well," she said. "At least you noticed I was trying to make myself attractive."

"Your grace," Maijstral said, "I would have had to be as inhuman as a Drawmiikh *not* to notice."

Roberta smiled a little. "That inhuman, eh?"

There was a moment of silence as the two shared a memory. A

Drawmiikh, they had once discovered, was more unforgettable, and inhuman, than either anticipated.

"Your grace," Maijstral finally said, "this whole marriage situation seems impossibly complex. Couldn't you just be my mistress for a while?"

She gave a little smile. "I *could,*" she conceded, "but they'd probably make me marry someone else first."

"I suspected as much," Maijstral said. There was another little pause. "You saved my life," he added, apropos perhaps of nothing. "When that madwoman attacked me."

"Yes. I did, didn't I?"

He looked at her. "Have I ever thanked you properly?"

Kissing Roberta, Maijstral discovered, was very pleasant, and he prolonged this pleasure for some little while. When there was a pause, Roberta said, "What do we tell everyone?"

"Tell them," Maijstral said, "that negotiations are ongoing."

Negotiations onwent a while longer, and then Maijstral and Roberta returned to his father's room holding hands. Kuusinen and Aunt Batty looked up expectantly.

"We have more talking to do," Maijstral said.

"What's the problem?" Gustav Maijstral demanded. "Is the girl ugly or something?"

"No, Dad," Maijstral said. "Her grace is very beautiful."

"I order you to marry her whether she's ugly or not!" the corpse said. "Gad, son, the girl is rich! Think of all the money for the Cause!"

Maijstral offered the Duchess an apologetic glance. Money and the Cause were two of his father's favorite topics, and once the old man had broached either subject it was difficult to keep him from enlarging upon it. Maijstral spoke up quickly.

"Time for your cocoa, Dad," he said.

An hour or so later Maijstral returned to his own room and called for Roman to unlace him. The tall Khosalikh arrived with a thick leather tube under one arm.

Maijstral looked at the tube, then at Roman, and then at the bare patch of pink flesh on the underside of Roman's muzzle. He thought he recognized the dangerous red-rimmed look smouldering in Roman's eyes, and ventured a cautious question.

"Are you molting again, Roman?"

"It *has* been a year since the last molt, sir." Roman put the tube on a table and turned to attend Maijstral.

"That long, eh?"

Maijstral made a mental note not to overstress Roman in the next week or so, and not to send Roman on one of the errands that sometimes proved necessary in his line of work—breaking the odd leg, say—not, anyway, unless Maijstral wanted the leg well and truly broken. Roman was not a good molter, and during the height of molt his normally moderate temper tended to veer unpredictably toward the savage.

"Sorry," Maijstral said. "If you want to just take a week off, I can get along with Drexler and a few robots to handle the lacing and unlacing."

Roman's ears flattened. "I am perfectly capable of discharging my duties, sir," he said.

Maijstral recognized the finality in Roman's tone. "Of course," Maijstral said. "I never had any doubts on that score whatever, I merely wished to make you as comfortable as possible."

He raised his arms to give Roman access to the side-laces. Roman picked at the lace-points expertly. "Was the evening enjoyable, sir?" he said.

"It was eventful, at least," Maijstral said, and gave his servant a sly, sidelong look. "Her Grace the Duchess of Benn made me an offer of marriage."

Roman's ears stood straight up, as did the surprised hair on top of his head. "Indeed, sir?" he said.

Maijstral smiled. He hardly ever saw Roman nonplussed. "She even arranged for my father to come here to Tejas to put his blessing on the union."

"His late grace is here?"

"Yes. You should probably pay your respects tomorrow."

"I will not fail to do so, sir." Roman smoothed down his top-hair, and a swatch of it came away in his fingers. His father had served the late Duke with the same resigned, halfdespairing dedication with which Roman served Maijstral, and his grandfather had served Maijstral's grandfather, and so on back to the first Baron Drago, the Viceroy of Greater Italia in the early days of Imperial conquest.

Roman looked at the tuft of hair in his fingers with distaste and, rather than let it fall to the carpet, stowed it in his pocket. He returned to picking at Maijstral's laces.

"May I inquire as to the nature of the reply with which you favored her grace, sir?" he asked, his feigned casualness so studied that Maijstral was forced to turn away with a smile.

"Her grace and I," he said airily, "are still discussing the matter."

Well might Roman's diaphragm pulse in resignation at this answer. Despite the familiarity brought on by years of association, despite all the adventures shared and obstacles overcome, when all was said and done Maijstral was, quite simply, incomprehensible.

"Very good, sir," Roman said. Dutiful, as always.

Roman was all too familiar with the defects of Maijstral's situation. They could be summed up as follows:

Money. For most of his life, Maijstral had been desperately short of money. This situation was not, Roman knew, Maijstral's doing, but that of his father, who had spent such of the family money as survived the Rebellion in crackpot Imperialist political schemes and who on his death had left Maijstral with nothing but debt.

Maijstral's response to his fiscal dilemma was reflected in Defect Number Two, to wit:

Profession. What better way to get money than to steal it? Allowed Burglary was legal—though barely, in the Human Constellation—and it was, thanks to its regulation by the Imperial Sporting Commission, a profession that a gentleman could adopt without danger of losing his position in society.

But some respectable professions were still more respectable than others. Allowed Burglary was lumped in with various other wayward callings, like drunkenness, banking, and the composition of satires, that were permitted but not precisely overwhelmed by the honors and distinctions given more respectable characters like civil servants, courtiers, great actors, military officers, or Elvis impersonators.

If one was a burglar, one was compelled to associate with many of the wrong sort: fences, enforcers, people willing to sell their employers' secrets, the agents of insurance companies (parasites of parasites, in Roman's view). Allowed Burglary required an irregular life, and constant travel both to avoid the police and to find new objects to steal. Often burglary was dangerous. It was irregular. Sometimes it was sordid.

But, Roman was willing to concede, it was necessary in Maijstral's case. It was where his master's talents lay, and his master, alas, needed to earn a living. His attempts to do so, and to live in the social stratum to which he was born, involved Defect Number Three:

Position. Though he preferred not to use his title, Maijstral's theoretical social position was perfectly on a par with the Duchess of

Benn's, if not slightly better: he was descended from one of the oldest human families ennobled by the Imperium—which wasn't much compared with an old Khosali title that might go back tens of thousands of years, but it was pretty good as humans go.

But, due to the misfortunes of his recent ancestors, the titles were empty of anything save honor and debt. Someone of the exalted rank of the Duke of Dornier should move effortlessly in the highest society (without, needless to say, having to steal), should grace government ministries with his talents, should endow foundations and pioneer planets—and, if the political situation should call for his employment as the Hereditary Captain-General of the Green Legion, he should occasionally go out and conquer something.

But none of this was possible without money. It cost a lot to live in the highest reaches of society, and Maijstral had no sources of income not connected with burglary—even the Green Legion was mothballed, its existence memorialized only by a few ancient battle flags hung in a side chapel in the City of Seven Bright Rings. Thanks to a devoted attention to his profession and the fame this had brought him, Maijstral was only now beginning to enjoy the pleasant and civilized mode of life which should have been his from the beginning. But Allowed Burglary was a precarious existence at best, with arrest always a possibility, and though Maijstral's income was now a comfortable one, it wasn't anywhere near the state that would have permitted him to live as effortlessly and gloriously as the Duke of Dornier, in Roman's estimation, ought.

Marriage with the Duchess of Benn solved every single one of Maijstral's problems. He would have access to as much money as anyone would desire. He would no longer have to earn a living as a burglar. And he would be able to live fully up to his position.

It was, in Roman's view, nothing less than Maijstral's *duty* to marry the Duchess. Personalities and the complications of human character didn't enter into it—as far as Roman could tell, they were unintelligible anyway, even to humans.

Roman finished Maijstral's side-laces and deftly pulled off Maijstral's jacket and put it in the closet. Maijstral began working at the side-laces of his trousers.

"I would like, on this auspicious occasion, to make a small presentation," Roman said. He shifted his shoulders in his jacket. That itch between his shoulder blades was back.

Maijstral's ears pricked back in surprise. He looked at the leather tube, then back to Roman.

"Pray go ahead," he said.

Roman retrieved the tube, uncapped it, and drew forth a scroll. The scroll had been made of grookh hide of the finest quality, thinner than paper and more resilient than steel, suitable in fact for a Memorial to the Throne.

But whereas a Memorial would be written with a jade-tipped pen in large, florid handwriting—emperors and their advisors have to read a *lot* of documents, and they appreciate large print—the writing on Roman's scroll was quite literally microscopic. There was a device in the lid of the scroll case that enabled one to read it.

Roman felt his heart swelling with pride as he laid the scroll out on a table. "This is the culmination of years of research," he said. "A kind of hobby of mine."

This was Roman's Special Project. Many long hours in the composition, he hoped it would prove decisive in this business of marriage. Reminding of the awesome weight and majesty of his ancestors might inspire Maijstral to prove worthy of them.

The itch burned in the center of Roman's back. Inwardly he snarled in annoyance.

Maijstral looked at the endless lines of tiny print in bewilderment. His trousers were unlaced and he had to hold them up with one hand. "There's certainly a lot here," he said.

"I have taken the liberty of tracing the history of the Maijstral family," Roman said.

Maijstral's ears cocked forward. "Really? *My* family?"

"Indeed, sir. You will observe—"

"Why not your own family?" Maijstral asked.

Roman's ears flicked in annoyance. The itch brought a growl to his lips. "My family's history has already been very well documented, sir," he said. Like most Khosali, his ancestry could be traced many thousands of years past the Khosali conquest of Earth . . . though, also like most Khosali, he was too polite to mention it.

"If you will observe, sir," Roman began, and deployed the reading mechanism, "I have made some rather interesting discoveries. Your ancestors are far more distinguished than either of us had any reason to suspect."

"Yes? That Crusader fellow you always talk about—you confirmed him?"

"Jean Parisot de La Valette," Roman said. "Indisputably. My library researches took me, last night, to Rome, where I had the honor of personally inspecting the records of the Knights of St. John. I found undisputable confirmation, which you will observe . . ." He placed the reader. "Here."

"Most interesting." Maijstral manipulated the reader with one hand and hitched up his pants with the other. "The wrong side of the blanket, of course," he noted. "Typical of my family, I suppose."

Roman's diaphragm throbbed. He wished Maijstral wouldn't disparage his ancestors in that fashion.

One of Roman's hands crept around behind his back and covertly began to scratch. No good—Khosali spines are somewhat less flexible than those of humans, and he didn't come anywhere near the itch.

"You will also observe Edmund Beaufort I, Earl and Marquess of Dorset," Roman said. "His fourth son married a Matilda of Denmark, who was descended from Henry the Lion. You are thus a descendant not only of the Welfs, but Frederick Barbarossa, the Plantagenets, the Tudors, and all the ruling houses of Europe."

"You don't say," Maijstral murmured.

"And on the Asian side," scratching furiously, "there is Altan Khan and the Vietnamese emperor Gia-Long, not to mention—"

Maijstral was peering at the top of the list. "Who's this Wotan person?" he asked. "He seems to be right at the head of the list, but he doesn't have any dates."

"Ah." Roman's diaphragm pulsed again, and he gave up the scratching. "Allow me to explain, sir."

"Thank you, Roman," Maijstral said. "It is a wonderful treasure."

"Thank you, sir."

"It must have taken you many hours. I'm impressed, as always, by your dedication."

Roman's black fur rippled with pride. A few little tufts drifted toward the floor. "Thank you," he said. "It was a privilege to work on such a project."

"My trousers," Maijstral said, and handed over his pants. Roman hung them in the closet and retrieved Maijstral's dressing gown. Maijstral shrugged into the gown and sealed it.

"That will be all, Roman, I think," Maijstral said.

"Very good, sir. Shall I leave the genealogy on the table?"

"Please do. I may wish to look at it."

"Very good, sir."

"Thank you very much for the gift," Maijstral said.

"It was entirely my pleasure, sir."

Roman bowed and left the room. Maijstral walked to the table and sighed as he looked at the scroll.

As if he didn't have enough to do with ancestors today, he

thought. Not only was his father here to urge him to do the right thing, but now Roman had brought in the kinfolk all the way back to Wotan.

Maijstral had really done his best to ignore the fact that he was heir to a dynasty, and now the whole business had dropped right on his head like a sandbag flung from Heaven.

It wasn't that he disliked the Duchess. It wasn't that he disliked the thought of marriage. But somehow it was all too pat, all too . . . foreordained.

Oh well, he thought glumly, maybe it *was* time to marry and settle down and produce more Maijstrals. Though why the universe needed more Maijstrals was beyond his capacity to explain.

Idly, he glanced at the genealogy—there was a complicated bit of business involving a Prince Boris of Gleb, who apparently married his aunt, and Maijstral couldn't help but wonder what the family had said about *that.*

He very carefully rolled up the scroll and stowed it away in its tube. There was all too much to think about without worrying about Prince Boris's problems.

He took a casual stroll about the room, making certain that neither Conchita Sparrow nor Colonel-General Vandergilt was hiding in the closet or under the bed, and then climbed into bed and told the lights to extinguish themselves.

The situation revolved slowly in his mind. He would probably not sleep tonight.

There was a gentle knock at the door. *Now* what? Maijstral thought.

He put on his dressing gown and approached the door. Wary force of habit made him keep well to one side as he said, "Who is it?"

"Roberta. May I come in?"

Maijstral opened the door and revealed Roberta silhouetted in the hall light. She wore a dressing gown and a somewhat furtive expression. She stepped in, and Maijstral closed the door behind her.

"Well," she said.

Maijstral regarded her in the dim light. She was standing very close, and he could feel her body's warmth.

"Well," he echoed.

"I was just in my room thinking—" she began, and then stopped. "Look, Drake," she finally said, "would you mind kissing me again?"

"No. Not at all."

Maijstral put his arms around her and performed as requested. The kiss was a pleasantly lengthy one.

"Oh good," the Duchess murmured. "That helps."

"I am happy to oblige."

Her eyes, dark in the unlit room, looked up at his. "Do you remember earlier this evening," she said, "when we were alone, and you asked if I could just be your mistress for a while?"

Maijstral smiled. "I believe I recall that remark, yes."

"Well . . ." she drawled, and gave a little laugh. "Here's your chance."

Maijstral's ears flickered in surprise. "I see," he said.

"This one's free, you know," Roberta added. "It has nothing to do with whether you should to marry me or not."

"You are . . ." Maijstral searched for words, "remarkably direct, your grace."

"Roberta."

"Roberta."

"Bobbie, if you like," she said. "But only Aunt Batty calls me that anymore."

"I think I prefer Roberta."

"So do I."

Maijstral contemplated the woman in his arms. Roberta kissed his chin.

"Can we go to bed now?" she asked.

"Certainly."

Well, Maijstral thought, no doubt Prince Boris and Altan Khan would approve.

He drew her bedward. "I've had a very active life, you know," she remarked. "Going to school, and racing, and running all the planets I've inherited . . ."

"No doubt," Maijstral murmured. He kissed the juncture between clavicle and neck, and Roberta shivered.

"And of course I've been very thoroughly chaperoned," she went on.

"How frustrating."

"Yes. So what I'm trying to say is—*Wow!"* Maijstral's researches had encountered a particularly sensitive point. "What I'm trying to say," she repeated, "is that I'm not very practiced at this."

"I will bear that in mind."

"I'm not practiced at all, in fact."

"Oh." Maijstral halted in surprise and looked at Roberta.

"I have a very good imagination," she added. "I hope that will help to make up for any lack of genuine experience."

"No doubt," Maijstral said, half to himself. And then, "Your grace, are you absolutely certain you want to do this?"

"Oh good grief yes," Roberta said quickly. "It's about time, don't you think?" She laughed. "If we're to be married, it'll make the long engagement go more quickly. And if we're not, at least I'll have had the man of my dreams."

Maijstral nodded. A glittering midnight gleam entered his lazy eyes.

"Well," he said finally, "I hope I prove worthy of that imagination of yours."

Maijstral was awakened by an authoritative knock on his door. The situation—loud banging on door, girl next to him in the bed—awakened a long-standing reflex of many years' duration. He made a smooth vault from the bed, snatched dressing gown and pistol, and was halfway to the window before he was brought up short by a bolt of pain that seized his nether regions in a grip of iron.

Staggered, he leaned on a table for support and looked about him. Roberta was blinking at him lazily from her pillow, and the knocking continued.

He took a step toward the door and the pain clutched him again. What, he tried to remember, had he and Roberta *done* last night?

And then he realized that the pain probably had a lot more to do with his first horseback ride than anything he and Roberta had got up to in bed.

"Just a moment," Maijstral called, and put on his dressing gown. He found Roberta's gown and gallantly held it out for her. She rose gracefully from bed and slipped her arms into the silk-lined sleeves.

"This way," Maijstral said, and turned to the closet. "Closet," he said, "open."

The closet obliged. Maijstral escorted the Duchess inside, and observed that Conchita Sparrow's command override, which she had left behind, was still in place, a fortunate accident in that it would allow the closet door to close with someone inside. He kissed Roberta, who looked up at him with amusement glittering in her eyes, and then he told the closet to close.

The hammering on the door recommenced. Maijstral looked down at the gun in his hand and wondered how it had come there.

Perhaps, however, it was best to be cautious.

"Who is it?" he demanded.

"Joseph Bob," came the answer.

There was a knock on the inner door that led to his sitting room, and Drexler stepped in, his ears cocked grimly forward. "Trouble, boss," he said. "There's a fleet of police fliers dropping on the lawn."

"Ah," Maijstral said. "I see. Someone must have stolen something, somewhere, and the cops are trying to pin it on us."

"Roman's making sure the rooms are clean," Drexler said.

The hammering started again. Maijstral hobbled toward the door and opened it. Joseph Bob, Arlette, and the Bubber were outside, each looking hastily dressed, and each wearing a grim expression.

"What's the problem?" Maijstral asked.

"There's an item missing," Joseph Bob said. "And though we're quite sure you have nothing to do with its disappearance . . ." Words, or perhaps tact, failed him, and he looked around for support.

"We're sure you will want to demonstrate your innocence," Arlette filled in, "and won't mind if we search your rooms."

Behind Maijstral the window darkened as a pair of police in a-grav harness took up position. Maijstral turned to the window and cocked an eyebrow.

"Did you *have* to invite the cops?" he asked.

Joseph Bob frowned. "I didn't," he said. "One of the servants must have called them."

"Well," Maijstral said, "I'm sorry, but neither you nor they can search my rooms. I stand on my rights as a citizen of the Human Constellation. Good morning."

He shut the door in Joseph Bob's surprised face, then hobbled toward a chair and sat down. Pain shot through his thighs.

"Maijstral," came a muffled voice. "Be reasonable, now. Open the blasted door."

"Citizens of the Human Constellation can be unreasonable if they want," Maijstral said, and adjusted his position to an attitude that only caused pain if he happened to move or breathe. He turned to Drexler. "I don't suppose you can produce some coffee?" he asked.

Drexler look at him in surprise. "I'll see what I can do."

Drexler headed for the sitting room. There was a pounding on the door, followed by Joseph Bob's voice. "Maijstral!" he said. "Open the door! Damn it, I *own* this door!"

"I'd advise you not to dent it, then," Maijstral said.

He could hear the tramp of boots out in the corridor, and then a muffled conversation. "We're getting a warrant!" Joseph Bob called.

"I hardly think you've got grounds," Maijstral said. "Somebody stole something. You've got no reason to think it was me."

"We'll *find* grounds," promised another voice, and Maijstral was not surprised to recognize that of Colonel-General Vandergilt.

"If you can get a warrant on these grounds," Maijstral said, "it won't stand up in court, and you know it."

Pure bluff of course, but he *hoped* it was true.

Maijstral had dressed—a painful operation—moved to the sitting room, and finished half his coffee by the time the warrant arrived. Drexler and Roman had joined him. Roman wasn't looking his best, with patches of grey skin where his fur had fallen out and a dangerous red-rimmed look to his eyes.

Those in the corridor pushed the warrant under the door. Maijstral nodded to Roman, who picked the warrant up and looked at it. He looked at Maijstral and snarled.

Maijstral was not accustomed to seeing his servant snarl—Roman was fairly mild-mannered, and broke legs and arms only with reluctance. It took Maijstral a half second or so to overcome his surprise, and then he shrugged. He'd done his best to preserve decorum.

"May as well open the door," he said.

Joseph Bob and his family entered on a flood of uniformed constabulary. The Prince of Tejas looked apoplectic as he stalked toward Maijstral's chair. The police deployed weapons and detectors.

"Blast it, Maijstral!" he said.

"You might have given me time for coffee," Maijstral said. He put down his cup and managed to rise to his feet without more than a wince of pain crossing his features.

There was a crash as a policewoman knocked over a small table and dropped a six-hundred-year-old Pendjalli vase to the floor.

"I'll assume responsibility for the damage, sir," said Colonel-General Vandergilt as she marched into the room. "My department will pay."

"I didn't know your department had *that much money,*" Maijstral said. Vandergilt looked doubtful for a moment. Maijstral began to lurch toward the bedroom. He wished to be present when Roberta was discovered, and offer such moral support as was possible.

"Not so fast, Maijstral," said Colonel-General Vandergilt. She stepped forward in her black uniform, silver buttons shining. "You'll have to be searched." So eager was she to get about the searching that no less than three separate strands of hair had escaped her helmet and were dangling in her eyes.

"You can search me in the bedroom as well as anywhere," Maijstral said, and kept moving.

"Life-form in the closet!" called a policeman from the bedroom, and suddenly there was the businesslike clacking of weapons being readied, and the cops began to deploy into attack formations.

Alarm flashed through Maijstral. "Put the guns down!" he said hastily. He had arrived in the bedroom door and was acutely aware that anyone firing would probably have to shoot right through him. He gingerly stepped to one side.

"Closet," he said. "Open."

Roberta looked quite cool as she stepped into full view, wearing her dressing gown as if she were making her grand entrance at a ball, and if Maijstral hadn't been quite so concerned about all the guns levelled at his spleen, he might have spared a moment or two for admiration.

No guns crackled, and Maijstral breathed a fervent sigh of relief. "Ah," he said, and stepped into the bedroom. "Ladies and gentlemen, allow me to introduce my alibi, Her Grace the Duchess of Benn. Your grace, this is Colonel-General Denise Vandergilt, Constellation Special Services."

Colonel-General Vandergilt stuffed stray hair into her helmet and stalked into the center of the room, followed by Joseph Bob and his family. Vandergilt looked coldly at the Duchess while the Prince and his family looked in surprise at each other.

"What's your real name?" Vandergilt said. "I don't use titles."

"No titles?" Roberta said. Her eyebrows rose. "Fine with me—*Denise.* My name is Roberta Altunin."

Vandergilt looked as if she was adding the name to some mental dossier, which she probably was.

Maijstral turned to Joseph Bob, who was beginning to look abashed. "I would have let you in earlier," he said, "but there are certain things a gentleman—"

"Object in the ventilator!" called a policeman.

Maijstral threw up his hands. This was going to be a long morning.

"It's the right wave pattern," the policeman added, peering at his detectors.

The ventilator was pulled away, and Colonel-General Vandergilt produced a "fingerprint handkerchief," which, despite its name, was a handkerchief guaranteed not to remove fingerprints, and which could be used for holding and transporting evidence. She reached into the ventilator and took out the object therein. When she showed it to the assembled company, there was a triumphant glow in her eyes.

"Is this your property, sir?" she asked the Prince.

The room reeled about Maijstral. He wanted to clutch his heart, fall to his knees, and (were ashes only available) pour ashes on his head.

Displayed on the white handkerchief was the prototype wooden revolver of Colonel Samuel Colt.

"I didn't do it!" Maijstral said.

Colonel-General Vandergilt smiled thinly. "That's what they all say." She handed the pistol to an underling. "Have that checked for fingerprints," she said.

Had not Maijstral been preoccupied by visions of the fate that awaited him—red-robed judges, unfriendly prison wardens, overly friendly fellow inmates, fetters, thumbscrews, and so on—he would have noticed Joseph Bob turning a dangerous shade of red.

Vandergilt puffed her cheeks and blew a strand of hair out of her face—she didn't want to spoil her big moment—and then looked stern and dropped a black-gauntleted hand on Maijstral's shoulder.

"Drake Maijstral, you're under arrest!" she proclaimed, then turned to Roberta. "And so are your accomplices," she added, and smiled.

"Accomplices!" Roberta said, outraged.

"Accomplices," Vandergilt repeated, and then she turned to Joseph Bob. "Sir, if you will accompany us to the police station, you can make a formal identification of your property and sign a complaint."

"I didn't do it," Maijstral said again, but no one seemed to be listening to him.

"Complaint?" Joseph Bob muttered. He was bright scarlet. "Complaint? Damned if I'll sign a complaint! A guest in my home!"

Maijstral looked at Joseph Bob in sudden hope. Joseph Bob was going to save him! he thought. His old school chum! Good old J.B.!

The Colonel-General looked puzzled. "Sir," she said, "if you don't sign the complaint, I won't be able to arrest Maijstral and his gang."

"I'll be signing no complaints!" Joseph Bob said, and then he turned to Maijstral, and Maijstral's heart stopped at the fury in the Prince's eyes. Joseph Bob shook a finger in Maijstral's face. "A guest in my home, and you steal from me!"

"I didn't do it," Maijstral pointed out.

Joseph Bob socked him in the jaw. It was a clean, professional punch, one that would make any pom boxer proud, and it knocked Maijstral sprawling.

Joseph Bob had a number of intentions at this point, all of which were fated to go sadly awry. His first intention was to stand commandingly over Maijstral's prone body while denouncing him, a dramatic pose recommended by any number of precedents derived from the theater. Unfortunately Joseph Bob had just broken two knuckles on Maijstral's head and spoiled his intended effect by hopping around the room while clutching his wounded hand.

"Maijstral!" he yelped, turning white. "I'll have satisfaction on the field of honor! My brother will speak for me!"

Joseph Bob's second intention, likewise derived from the theater, was to stalk dramatically from the room and leave behind an awed silence, an intention that was frustrated, in the first instance, by the rather crabbed, hunched-over stance his wound was compelling him to adopt, and in the second, by the well-delivered power kick that Roman planted in his face.

Roman, as it happens, *was* a pom boxer, and in the course of avenging his employer against a dastardly surprise attack, he knew better than to risk fragile hand bones battering away at the solid bone of someone's skull, not when a better weapon was at hand—in this case, a foot encased in a sturdy boot.

Joseph Bob's nose exploded like an overripe kibble fruit, and the Prince de Tejas sailed backward into Maijstral's room and joined him on the carpet.

Arlette flung herself down on her husband, either to assure herself as to his well-being or to protect him against further assault.

His remaining fur bristling, Roman advanced, a huge, alarming, red-eyed menace, but was brought up short by the weapons of a dozen or so police that were suddenly thrust up under his muzzle.

"Roman," Roberta warned. *"Don't."*

Roman fell back, but the snarl remained on his face.

He really *was* a bad molter.

Maijstral, to this point, had been too stunned by Joseph Bob's punch to be able to react to any of the subsequent events. He tried to sit up, then decided that remaining prone might prove a course easier to sustain. Roberta dropped to his side and cradled his head in her hands. "Are you all right?" she asked.

"No," Maijstral said, and felt a certain pride at retaining his grip on both speech and reality.

"Shall I stand as your second?" Roberta asked. "I've had practice at it, after all."

Maijstral, who didn't at this point wish to attempt more syllables than absolutely necessary, nodded his answer. She turned to the Bubber.

"Will," she said, "I'll talk to you later." She looked at the others. "I believe the rest of you no longer have any business here."

Joseph Bob was unable to regain his feet, and he was carried from the room by the police. When Roman kicked someone, the someone stayed kicked.

Maijstral, the chimes in his head subsiding, realized that he'd been saved from the prison by virtue of the fact that he was about to die in a duel with the finest swordsman and pistol shot in the Principality of Tejas.

SIX

Roman, Drexler," Maijstral said, "I want Conchita Sparrow brought to me. I confess I do not care how this is accomplished. But as I intend that she confess to framing me, I would prefer her conscious, or at least capable of consciousness, by the time she actually arrives."

"Very good, sir," said Roman.

"Take any recordings you may find. When she stole the pistol, she may have recorded her mission to sell on the market."

"Yes, sir."

"Go at once."

"Very good, sir."

Drexler and Roman bowed and, after stuffing their clothing with weapons, made their exit, Roman trailing a fine cloud of black hair as he left. Maijstral fingered the large semilife patch that was extending its anaesthetic tendrils into his damaged flesh and considered that, if he were Conchita Sparrow and saw Roman in his current state coming toward her with evil intent, he'd confess on the spot.

He rose stiffly from his chair and lurched toward the service plate, where he summoned robots to carry his belongings to his rented flier. It was now impossible to stay at Joseph Bob's estate. He would be moving to the next place on his itinerary, the Underwater Palace of Quintana Roo, where he had been invited for a weekend. He would be arriving a few days early, but fortunately that was all right with Prince Hunac, his host, who already had many guests in residence.

There was a knock on the door, and Roberta stepped in without waiting for a reply. She kissed Maijstral's cheek, thoughtfully choosing the undamaged one. "I've been talking to the Bubber," she said. "I thought he and I had best establish a few protocols at the start."

"Very sensible," Maijstral said. He was all in favor of protocols and technicalities, anything that would delay or complicate the situation long enough so that Maijstral could either find the real culprit and get the duel called off, or alternatively somehow fix the encounter's outcome. Either way, as far as Maijstral was concerned, would prove satisfactory.

He hobbled to the sofa and sat down with a sigh of pain. Roberta joined him. The latest-model Windsong robots entered the room on silent repellers, and on Maijstral's instructions picked up his luggage in their invisible grapplers and carried it off.

"Will doesn't think you did it, either," Roberta said. "He ventured the opinion that you're a sufficiently good magician that, if you'd *known* the pistol was there, you could have kept anyone from finding it. So he's inclined to help Joseph Bob see reason."

"And Joseph Bob?"

"Disinclined to see any reason whatever, I'm afraid. And Roman's knocking him silly didn't help matters."

"Hmm."

"He insists that you're at fault for 'permitting your servant to attack him,' as I believe he phrased it."

Indignation flamed in Maijstral. "I don't know how I could have stopped Roman, since I'd just been floored by His Highness's sneaky punch," he said. And then he realized he was being indignant and made an effort to suppress it. People torn by indignation didn't wriggle out of duels, and *that,* he reminded himself, was what he was after.

"It occurred to me to point this out," Roberta said, "but I decided it wouldn't improve matters, so I didn't."

"Quite rightly," Maijstral said.

Roberta smiled. "Thank you," she said. "Now, I suppose, we ought to discuss weapons."

Oh, why bring *them* into it, Maijstral thought.

Still, best to get it clear. The array of duelling weapons permitted by Khosali High Custom was truly staggering, and there had to be *some* that would give Maijstral an advantage.

"Joseph Bob is an expert pistol shot, and a fine swordsman," he said. "I would prefer to leave those out of the picture entirely."

"Very well."

"I'd also like to delay the whole business," Maijstral said. "Give tempers a chance to cool, and give me a chance to find the real culprit and prove it was she who stole the pistol."

"She?" Roberta's eyebrows lifted. "Do you know who did it?"

"A licensed burglar named Conchita Sparrow. She's been trying to get herself hired as my tech, and I turned her down. By way of demonstrating her abilities, she broke in here two nights ago, interestingly enough by way of the same ventilator shaft in which Colonel Colt's pistol was found."

Roberta cocked her head to one side as she considered this. "It sounds plausible, at least. You don't have any other idea who might have been responsible?"

"So far as I know, I don't have an enemy in the world. Unless it's one of your beaux," he added, "mad with jealousy." He tried to smile, but pain stabbed his jaw, and he winced instead.

"Poor Drake." She patted his uninjured cheek again. "What, by the way, do we tell the family?"

"Tell them the whole thing's a misunderstanding."

"No." She smiled patiently. "I mean about *us.*"

"Oh." Maijstral blinked. Preoccupied with his own problem, he'd quite forgotten the whole matter of his betrothal.

"Well," he said, "it seems to me that it would be unfair of me to make you a widow before we're even engaged. Why don't we tell the family that we're postponing any announcement until my business with Joseph Bob is resolved?"

A shadow of disappointment crossed Roberta's face. "Very well," she said, and rose. "I'll go tell them now."

She walked toward the door. "Roberta?" he said.

She turned. "Yes?"

"Thank you."

She smiled. "You're very welcome."

"And will you do me another favor?"

"If I can."

"Will you ship my father down to Quintana Roo for me? I'll look after him from there."

"Of course," she said, and made her exit.

* * *

"I didn't do it!" Conchita Sparrow yelped.

Drexler advanced menacingly, a hi-stick dangling from his muzzle. "Pull the other one," he said, demonstrating a surprising grasp of Human Standard vernacular. (In Khosali it would have come out "Drag the remaining unity," which would have lacked the colloquial verve of the original.)

In any language it was purely a figure of speech, since Conchita Sparrow was in no position to pull anything. Roman, by contrast, was in a position to pull all the legs required, as he was holding her by one ankle over the edge of Kanab, one of the Grand Canyon's more impressive side canyons.

"Honest!" Conchita said. "I didn't do it!"

"I bet Roman is getting tired," Drexler said. "Aren't you, Roman?"

"I could lose my grip at any moment," Roman warned. He loosened his grasp slightly, just enough for Conchita to fall a few inches, and then caught her again. Conchita gave a strangled shriek.

Drexler took a languid draw on his hi-stick. "Careful, Roman," he said, relishing the opportunity once again to demonstrate his grasp of slang, "you might do the lady a mischief."

Maijstral contemplated this picture with pleasure. Roman, a menacing piebald giant big even for a Khosalikh, held Conchita, small even for a human, at arm's length, with rather more ease than Maijstral could hold a child. Media globes, controlled by the proximity wire in Maijstral's collar, circled the pair like orbiting satellites, ready to record any revelations that might drop from Conchita's lips.

"Give a moment to your surroundings, Miss Sparrow," Maijstral said. Walking bowlegged to minimize his pain, he approached the edge and regarded the deep canyon below. He took a deep, appreciative breath. "Consider the eons that must have gone into the creation of this magnificent sight into which, at any instant, you may take flight. Consider the work of millennia, as erosion, as vast landslides, as the uplift of the local geology all did their work. Consider its glory in comparison with the alteration in the local formation you will make when you strike the ground below. Which is to say—" He looked at her meaningfully. *"None at all."*

Maijstral threw out his arms to glory in the Canyon's vastness. "Consider the gorgeousness that will be your last living vision—will you appreciate it as you fall, I wonder?"

"I'll be too busy screaming my head off," Conchita said.

"Tell us what we want to hear," Maijstral said, "and there will be no need for screaming at all."

"I didn't do it!" she screamed. Which was followed by a somewhat less coherent scream, abruptly cut off, as Roman's grip relaxed, then firmed again.

"I can prove it!" she said. "I was out stealing last night! I recorded everything—it's in those spheres your goons captured!"

"His *what?"* Drexler growled, his bristling.

"Assistants! Associates! Whatever!"

Annoyance crackled along Maijstral's nerves. He really didn't want to credit the notion that Conchita actually had an alibi.

"Stealing where?" he asked. "And what?"

"In Australia. An entire consignment of rare pink and green Australian diamonds from the Nokh & Nokh depository. No style points, but I needed the cash."

Maijstral frowned. Conchita's story had the discouraging ring of truth.

It must be admitted that sometimes even Allowed Burglars—whose calling glorified, nay demanded, the search for and acquisition of the rare, the wonderful, and the celebrated—sometimes even Allowed Burglars demonstrated a regrettable lack of regard for the possibilities of their profession and merely stole things for the money. Usually, it must be said, in bulk, Conchita's vaultful of diamonds being a good example. Because these jobs were rarely granted anything like the full ten points awarded for style, many were never submitted to the Imperial Sporting Commission for rating, but merely went to support the burglar in maintaining the high style with which he floated from place to place, looking for rarer forms of plunder.

Maijstral, particularly in his early days as a burglar, had been known to plunder the odd diamond vault himself. And even Ralph Adverse, the most legendary burglar of all, Ralph Adverse of the Losey Portrait, the Manchester Apollo, and the Eltdown Shard itself, was said to have knocked over a bank or two when the opportunity presented.

"Drexler," Maijstral said, "go to the flier and check the news bulletins. Find out if Nokh & Nokh had a robbery in the last day or so."

Drexler snapped his hi-stick in two and tossed the broken bits into the Canyon. "Whether she's telling the truth or not," he said, "she still called me a goon. *I* think we should chuck her in just for that."

"Sir," Roman said, as Drexler walked toward the flier, "it would have been daylight in Australia when the pistol was stolen. Hardly an ideal time to break into a vault."

Maijstral brightened. "Daylight, eh?" he said cheerfully. He turned to Conchita. "What do you say to that, Miss Sparrow?"

"It was William Bligh Day," Conchita said. "A holiday. I had the whole day to plunder the vault."

Maijstral scowled. He was vexed with William Bligh, and he didn't even know who Bligh was.

This was unfortunate, for had Maijstral only known it, Bligh had much in common with Maijstral's family, specifically Maijstral's grandfather. Both Bligh and Governor His Grace Robert, Duke of Dornier, had the misfortune to suffer mutinies and handle them badly. Bligh suffered no less than two mutinies during his naval career, and then suffered the final martyrdom when the entire continent of Australia mutinied against his administration. Duke Robert had only one mutiny to deal with, but he mishandled it so spectacularly that his name, and that of his descendants, were blighted forevermore.

It is instructive to observe how the Khosali dealt with each of these unfortunate officers. With their passion for law, discipline, and regularity, the Khosali were sympathetic to Bligh, viewed him as a martyr to Order, and created a holiday for him. Statues were built to him throughout Oceania. Duke Robert, by contrast, had acquired such an infamous reputation that the Khosali preferred to treat him gingerly, when they treated him at all. No mention was made of him, no statues built, no holidays declared. No posthumous decorations were ordered. The Green Legion was mothballed, and any mentions in the official histories were as terse and uninformative as possible.

Even the Khosali quest for Order has its limits.

"Bad news, boss," Drexler said from the flier. "Nokh & Nokh got knocked over."

Maijstral took the bad news stoically. He turned to Roman. "You might as well let Miss Sparrow down, and she can show us her recordings of the happy event."

"Do I have to?" Conchita said, rising and dusting herself off. "I didn't exactly cover myself with glory on this one."

Which proved to be an understatement. The burglary had begun quite well, with Conchita's black boxes successfully overcoming the vault's alarm systems, defense robots, and locking mechanism. She walked into the vault looking very pleased with herself, and then carefully closed the vault door behind her so that no passing guard might see that the huge round door was open.

At this point Drexler's tongue flopped from his mouth in uncontrollable mirth. Maijstral turned away so that Conchita wouldn't see his smile. Only Roman managed to maintain his previous demeanor —which was not in his case difficult, considering that he was nearly psychotic with surging hormones, continual itching, and persistent shedding.

For Conchita had just locked herself in the vault. With all her vault-springing mechanisms left *outside.*

The video-Conchita, however, took some time to realize this. She emptied the vault of its contents, packed everything neatly into the levitating luggage she'd brought with her. She was looking quite relieved that she hadn't bungled anything for a change . . . and then she turned to leave.

She looked at the door. Frowned. Frowned some more. Drexler began massaging his diaphragm, which was cramping with pleasure. "I can't look," he moaned.

"All my black boxes worked," Conchita said defensively. "That's my specialty."

"How did you get out?" Maijstral asked.

"Vaults aren't constructed so as to prevent people from breaking *out,*" Conchita said. "I had to improvise some tools from bits of my luggage and some things I'd found in the vaults."

"And how long did this take you?" Maijstral asked.

"Nine hours," Conchita said in a small voice.

"I think," Maijstral said as he turned off the display, "that we may spare ourselves the next nine hours of video."

"Perhaps we could just skip to the end," Drexler suggested cheerfully.

Maijstral turned to Conchita. "I apologize for the hasty assumptions that led me to bring you here. My associates will return you to your home."

"Thank you." She gazed at the surrounding countryside through the flier's transparent top. "It was nice to get a chance to see the Grand Canyon. Even though I've lived on Earth all my life, I'd never come here."

"And you were favored with a unique perspective of the Canyon that few others will ever have experienced."

She giggled. "True." Her brow furrowed. "What is it all about, anyway? What exactly was I supposed to have done?"

"Well," Maijstral sighed, "I suppose after all this I might well owe you an explanation."

He told her, briefly, the facts of the case. She whistled.

"You're in the soup, all right. And that explains how you came to have a semilife patch on your face. But how did you figure it was me that did it?"

"I'd turned you down when you applied for a job."

"What—you don't have any worse enemies?"

Maijstral frowned thoughtfully. "It would appear that I do."

"Any idea who they are?"

Maijstral flattened his ears in perplexity. "No one really comes to mind," he said. "Colonel-General Vandergilt, of course, but I don't know whether she's fanatic enough to plant evidence, or for that matter whether she or her associates have the skill to do it. Putting the pistol in the ventilator of the room I was sleeping in would have taken no small ability."

"But Vandergilt's a member of the Special Services Corps, right?" Conchita said. "Then she's a spy, or at least knows spies. That pistol might have been planted by a government burglar, not one of us stylish amateurs."

Maijstral considered this and felt a nebulous, creeping sort of gloom float into his mind, like a low cloud casting cold shadows on his thoughts.

"Or possibly the burglar was one who'd been arrested, and was given special consideration if he agreed to set you up," Conchita added. "Maybe you should check to see which burglars have been arrested lately and then let loose. Drexler"—smiling over her shoulder—"can you spare a hi-stick?"

Drexler scowled as he forked over the intoxicant.

"Roman . . ." Maijstral began.

"Very good, sir. I'll check the arrest records as soon as I take the young lady home."

Conchita turned to Maijstral. Her eyes sparkled. "Maybe I could help," she said. "I have some contacts among Earth burglars. I'll make a few calls and see if I pick up any rumors."

"I would appreciate that," Maijstral said.

"I *told* you I could prove useful."

"So you did." Maijstral opened the flier and stepped out. "I thank you in advance for any information you may discover."

"I say we still chuck her in," Drexler growled. "She called me a goon."

Conchita stuck out her tongue at him, but Maijstral gave no sign that he had heard. He hadn't.

An image was repeating itself in his mind over and over again: Joseph Bob pointing a pistol at him, squeezing the trigger, and firing. The image recurred with minor variations, all of which involved the pistol's muzzle getting larger and larger.

Cold sweat trickled down Maijstral's neck.

He was going to have to think of something fast.

SEVEN

There were a lot of colorful stories about Prince Hunac, and for the most part he did a good job of living up to them. He was, for starters, the direct descendant of the Kings of Palenque, whose descent and lineage had been carefully hidden away during the Spanish and Ladino occupation, but which were nevertheless fully documented by records immaculately kept in their original Mayan script. When the Khosali had conquered the Ladinos, and for that matter everyone else, and when subsequently the black-furred conquerors had proved to be such thoroughgoing legitimists as to restore to at least some of their former glory various Habsburgs and Bourbons and Wittelsbachs and all the other smug, dreary royalty from which humanity had after bloody centuries finally unsaddled itself, the lords of Palenque had emerged from seclusion to present their credentials. The City of Seven Bright Rings had been pleased to recognize their legitimacy and made them Dukes of Palenque and later Princes of Quintana Roo.

During the Great Rebellion, Prince Hunac's family had sensibly taken both sides, some fighting with the Emperor, others with the rebellious humans. After the Rebellion's success, Prince Hunac's grandmother, a rebel leader, had been appointed heir, and the family thus retained its land and wealth after the establishment of the Human Constellation.

Though Maijstral had never met Prince Hunac, he'd naturally heard of him. Leaving behind a fine record as a dashing eccentric and sportsman, Hunac had graduated ten years ahead of Maijstral at the Nnoivarl Academy. (Just because Hunac's ancestor had fought for the Rebellion was no reason for the family to turn up its noses at the social advantages of a thoroughgoing Imperialist education.) Hunac had become something of a legend at the school because of his adoption of the stylish dress of the Khosali Al-Ashi Dynasty, which involved elaborate feathered cloaks and headdresses similar to what Hunac's royal ancestors might have worn on formal occasions. He had kept quetzal birds in his rooms, and was alleged to conduct elaborate religious rituals in secret, not only to maintain his own status among his subjects but, it was said, to maintain the integrity of the universe.

Since leaving the Academy, Hunac had sponsored hundreds of archaeological expeditions in his native Yucatan. He had donated tens of thousands of items to museums, kept thousands of others in his collection, and contributed greatly to the understanding of the native cultures of the area. He had also made a name for himself as an oceanographer, in which role he charted any number of obscure ocean depths, restored fish populations, and, of course, built the fabulous Underwater Palace on, or rather in, the reefs of Cozumel.

But Hunac was most famous as a host. His week-long theme parties rolled on for half the weeks of the year, and to those with anxieties over their status in the *ton,* it was a comforting confirmation of one's social arrival to receive one of Hunac's invitations.

Celebrated and renowned though the Prince was, Maijstral hadn't been prepared for one aspect—the Prince's size. Hunac was *short.* Shorter even than Conchita. Almost as short as a Troxan.

Short. Hunac was very, very short. Maijstral had not been prepared.

Maijstral advanced, clasped hands—two friendly fingers each—and then Maijstral bent a surprising distance to sniff the Prince's ears. Hunac smiled up at him and spoke in Khosali Standard. "The Show Business Party is still under way," he said. "The Glorious Achievers' Party, which was to be yours, won't be on for a few days, but I imagine you'll find people to talk to in the meantime. The fellow who plays you on video, for one."

Maijstral looked around at people drifting through the reception area. "Anaya's here?" he said.

"That's the *old* video Maijstral. Laurence is the new one. Don't you keep up with your own exploits?"

"I'm afraid I haven't seen either one."

Hunac cocked an eyebrow. "Really? How modest of you."

It wasn't modesty, Maijstral wanted to explain, but pure lack of interest. After living with Nichole for several years, he'd had all he needed of actors and their concerns. And he knew that though the thefts in the videos themselves were based on his own professional recordings, with his image electronically altered, the fictional dramas surrounding the thefts were so contrived and awful he didn't want to be caught watching them.

But it didn't seem the sort of thing to admit at a show business party. Where there were celebrities, there were reporters, and where there were reporters, there were usually hovering media globes recording conversations and replaying them for Empire-wide audiences.

Maijstral hadn't seen any so far, but that didn't mean they weren't there.

"Please have a drink," Hunac said hospitably, "and meet some people. If you want to go out and tour the reefs, we can equip you with a submarine or diving gear—whichever is to your taste."

Maijstral gazed out at the reefs surrounding him. "Thank you," he said. "I'd like that."

Celebrated though Prince Hunac was, the majesty of his person was somewhat overwhelmed by the aquatic glory of his surroundings. Cozumel's reefs—huge coral castles, honeycombed with tunnels and alive with blazing color—loomed on either side, visible through the reception room's transparent dome. Mayan steles from the Prince's collection stood in a circle around the reception area, looking like an underwater homage to Stonehenge. Ideograms for "ocean world" and "palace of the lord" floated holographically in the air.

Hunac took Maijstral's arm and began strolling toward the bar. "I was wondering if you might give me some advice regarding security matters," he said. "I have so many rare and valuable things, and it's only a matter of time before a real first-rate burglar takes a crack at them."

"Your palace is secure by its very nature," Maijstral said. "It's accessible only through the tunnel from the mainland or by submarine. I would hate to try to steal anything here—getting away would be a challenge."

"It's a complication, admittedly—have some of this Rhenish, it's splendid—but for someone as inventive as yourself, surely it's only a matter of false credentials or flummoxing an airlock. Child's play, I'm sure."

Maijstral sipped his wine. "Hardly that." He gave the matter thought. "A place like this would be a major operation. One would need many assistants, which multiplies the number of misunderstandings or mistakes that could occur. If one went in by submarine, one would have to take immense trouble to keep your underwater sensors from seeing it—I take it you *have* underwater sensors?"

"Oh yes."

"Well, the cost of preparing the submarine would be high, which would necessitate stealing a whole submarineful of artifacts in order to make a profit, and the sheer size of the operation would make it dangerous."

"Profit isn't always the motive for Allowed Burglary, is it?" Hunac said. "Sometimes you steal for the sheer glory of it, or to publicly surmount an obstacle, or because there's simply something you want to possess. Ralph Adverse, for example—he stole the most beautiful objects, but he died bankrupt, because he wanted them for their beauty alone, and not for the wealth they could bring him."

"You won't find many Ralph Adverses in the burglary business these days," Maijstral said.

"You disappoint me, Maijstral."

Maijstral thoughtfully sipped at his drink. "I would say," he said, "that your chief danger comes, as you say, from someone entering under false credentials, stealing something valuable but fairly portable, and then just riding the train to the surface through the tunnel."

"Or," Hunac smiled, "I could invite someone into my home who *is* a burglar, simply because I thought he would make an interesting guest. And he could take something, thinking that my hospitality would extend to such a thing. In this assumption, of course, he would be wrong."

He had shifted to High Khosali, unmatched for both difficulty of parsing and precision of communication, as each word commented on the word before it, thus adding cumulative impact to the entire statement.

A cold current wafted up Maijstral's spine at the whiteness of Hunac's smile.

"Naturally the burglar would be wrong," Maijstral said, responding after a moment's hesitation in the same difficult parsing. He added a commonplace aphorism of the sort that was frequently found in High Khosali, because it saved the trouble of constructing something original.

"Hospitality should at all points be respected," he said.

Hunac's smile whitened. "I have heard something of your problem with Joseph Bob."

Maijstral felt himself stiffening. "It is a misunderstanding," he said.

"I am pleased to hear it. I mention the matter only to make certain that no such misunderstandings ever plague our friendship."

"I am certain they will not."

Hunac shifted back to Khosali Standard. "Very good." He patted Maijstral's arm, then turned to an approaching guest. The guest looked remarkably like Elvis Presley, white suit, jeweled wrestler's belt, and all.

"Maijstral, have you met Major Ruth Song?"

"I have not had the pleasure. Charmed."

Maijstral offered Major Song two fingers in the handclasp—everyone knows Elvis, after all—and received a single formal finger in reply. She stiffened a bit as he sniffed her ears. Perhaps, he thought, she did not wish him to inspect her cosmetic job at such close range. No need to be so nervous, Maijstral thought: the work was very good, and had turned her into a remarkably successful facsimile Elvis.

"I hope to persuade Major Song to perform tonight," Hunac remarked.

"I will look forward with pleasure," Maijstral said.

"Thank you," Song said. "I need to stay in practice, with the Memphis Olympiad coming up."

She replied, oddly, in Human Standard, not Khosali, and Maijstral and Hunac obliged her by switching languages.

"Major Song is ranked very high by the cognoscenti," Hunac said. "She stands a very good chance of winning."

"I hope to attend the Olympiad myself," Maijstral said. "I wish you the very best of luck in the competition."

"Thank you. If you'll excuse me?"

Major Song made her congé, swirled her cape, and left. Hunac frowned. "How odd."

"Sir?" Maijstral said.

"She obviously intended to order a drink. But now she's left without one."

Maijstral flicked his ears. "Perhaps she forgot. Or remembered an errand."

"Perhaps."

"I see the riding lights of a new submarine arriving at the port—

red, white, green, I'm afraid I don't know it offhand. Still, whoever's inside, I should offer my greetings—Maijstral, I hope you will have a pleasant stay."

Hunac made his way toward the airlock. Maijstral resisted the impulse to gulp his drink—the reminder of his trouble with Joseph Bob had not been pleasant—and then drifted through the reception area, looking for someone he knew. A lot of the faces looked familiar, and he knew he'd seen them on video, but he couldn't remember precisely where, and he couldn't remember their names.

There was one young man, unfamiliar to Maijstral and dressed rather dramatically in black, who was looking at him as if he were undecided whether to approach and introduce himself. Maijstral assumed he was some sort of burglary fan, and, as he didn't feel like talking to fans at the moment, he turned away and wandered on, and then recognized someone and approached to sniff her ears.

"Hello, Alice. Congratulations on obtaining your freedom."

Each gave the other two fingers: they were professional acquaintances, but not intimates.

Alice Manderley was a woman of middle years, dark-haired and slender. She was also one of the best burglars in the galaxy, a consistent high performer who always outpointed Maijstral in the ratings. She had been rated third, and was a contender to succeed Geoff Fu George as first in the ratings, until she encountered ill luck while attempting to steal the famous Zenith Blue.

"I hope prison was not too bad," Maijstral said.

"It was *prison,*" Alice said. "Of *course* it was bad. Even the *nicest conceivable* prison is bad." Her brow furrowed and her voice grew harsh. "And to think I was put there by an *amateur.* She was on her way to school, saw the shimmer of my darksuit, and hit me with a briefcase full of study materials. Knocked me unconscious. I can't *believe* my luck." She scowled. "They gave her the Qwarism Order of Public Service (Second Class). *Second class!* What kind of insult was *that,* I ask you!"

Alice seemed likely to continue in this vein for some time, and Maijstral thought it a good idea to change the subject. "It is a surprise to see you here among the actors," he said, "though of course a delightful one."

"I'm with Kenny. There's a producer here he wants to talk to."

"Oh. Of course."

Kenny Chang was Alice's husband, a notably unsuccessful actor whose personal charm seemed unable to translate properly to video or the stage.

Maijstral was nearly as disinclined to talk about Kenny's career as he was to chat about the features of Alice's prison.

"Are you going to get your ticket renewed?" he asked.

Alice sighed. "I already have. I must admit that burglary has lost much of its appeal, but while I was in stir Kenny took a flier on Forthright bonds, and now I need to get us out of debt."

Maijstral had been offered the same bonds less than a year ago, and had walked away with a loathly shudder. The Forthright Company had been such an obvious swindle (the company's chairman, Xovalkh, was ranked near the top of the Imperial Sporting Commission's ratings for confidence men) that the only investors likely to actually turn over their funds were either the brain-damaged or those who purchased bonds solely for their entertainment value—Xovalkh was quite a performer, for those who appreciated that sort of thing.

Maijstral suspected that Kenny did not, however, belong to this latter category of investor.

"Well," he said, "if you have any plans for the near future, I could offer you logistical support. I'm on vacation, and I don't want my crew to get rusty."

Alice looked at him with a peculiar expression. "That's kind of you, Maijstral," she said.

"Drexler in particular has been complaining I don't give him enough to do."

"I have my people already picked out. But thank you."

"Ah well. If I can give help of that sort, let me know."

"Thanks." She looked over Maijstral's shoulder. "There's a young man who keeps staring at us."

"Dressed in black? I noticed him earlier."

"He looks familiar, but I can't place him."

"I hope he is not a connoisseur of burglary statistics."

Alice made a face. "I will make a point of avoiding him."

Maijstral glanced to his right, and was surprised to see Aunt Batty making her way toward him. He sniffed her lace-covered ears and touched his tongue to his lips in a subdued Khosali smile.

"That was your submarine that just arrived?"

"Yes, indeed."

"Is her grace with you?"

"No, I'm afraid she's still in negotiation with the Bubber. It's just me and your father."

"Your *father* is here?" Alice asked. "Didn't I hear he'd died?"

"Yes, on both counts," Maijstral said. "We're having a sort of a family conference. Alice Manderley, may I present—" He looked at Aunt Batty and blinked. "I'm afraid I only know you as Bathsheba."

Batty took Alice's hand and sniffed her ears. "I'm the Honorable Bathsheba sar Altunin," she said, indicating her adoptive family, "but you can call me Batty."

"How do you do?"

"I am sorry to have saddled you with my father," Maijstral said. "But I'm afraid my life has been more disorganized than usual—"

"No need to apologize. Gustav and I have been having a perfectly fine time, just chatting away."

Maijstral's ears pricked forward in surprise. "Indeed? And what do you chat about?"

"You, mostly."

"Ah. For your work."

Batty lapped daintily at her drink. "Yes. I think the third volume is shaping up in a most interesting fashion."

When all this was over, Maijstral thought, he *would* steal those manuscripts.

"I'm not certain I would trust this particular source overmuch," Maijstral said, "given the state of his memory. He keeps forgetting he's dead, for one thing."

Aunt Batty's tongue lolled in a smile. "I *have* noticed that, dear, yes. But I do try in my best historian's fashion to confirm everything with another source."

"Very good."

"For example, was your stuffed bear's name really Peter Pajamas?"

Maijstral blinked. "Do you know, I believe it was. This is the first time I've thought of that in—well, decades, I suppose."

Alice had been watching this dialogue with little indication of interest, but smiled at this last. "I perceive my own stuffed bear approaching," she said. "Batty, may I present my husband, Kenny."

"Hi," Kenny said.

He was a handsome man with long, fashionably careless hair. He had, to a discerning eye, rather overdone the fashionable carelessness, with his falling bands partially undone, his collar turned up, his day's growth of beard, *and* his hands in his pockets, but perhaps this was a matter of taste.

Maijstral, considering for a moment Kenny as stuffed bear, concluded that Peter Pajamas had a decided advantage in brains.

"I talked to Winky," Kenny informed Alice, "and he said I'd fit the part hand in glove, but it's not up to him. it's up to the people with the money, so who knows? He says he'll call."

"Perhaps he will," Alice said.

Probably, Maijstral thought, he wouldn't, even though Kenny seemed to be on nickname terms with him five minutes after acquaintance.

He really didn't know anyone who'd call Kenny voluntarily.

"There's such a lot of deal-making going on here," Kenny said. "I've really got to stay on the jump. Have you met that Elvis? Major Song?"

Alice's ears flattened. "Yes," she said shortly.

"Loathsome little weasel, but there's money there. Maybe if I just sing the praises of the Security and Sedition Act, and pretend to hate the rats long enough—"

Alice put a hand on his arm. "Stay away from her, dear. She's not an association that would do you any good. Not in the long run."

Kenny considered this, scratching his day's beard. "Well, if you say so. Plenty of other mammals in this terrarium." He grinned. "Hey, that was pretty good, wasn't it? 'Cause we're in a kind of a reverse fishbowl here, right? And it's the fish that are looking in. Get it?"

"Very good, Ken," Alice said.

"Well, I'm off to corner myself a—" He started to leave, then seemed to notice Maijstral for the first time. "Say, Drake," he said, "you know Nichole's going to be here?"

"So I understand," Maijstral said.

"You and she are still friends, right? I mean, no hard feelings or anything."

"No."

"Not after she took up with you on that what's-its-name planet, Peleng, and then dumped you for that fellow she's living with now."

"It didn't happen," Maijstral said.

"Hm?" Kenny looked surprised. "No, really. She's living with him. It was in the news and everything. He's her set designer or something."

"I mean," Maijstral said patiently, "that Nichole and I were not involved on Peleng, and, insofar as we weren't involved, she didn't jettison me when she took up with Lieutenant Navarre."

"Oh." Kenny took a moment to process this—the thought that something reported in the media might be a falsehood was obviously a difficult one for him—and then he brightened. "Well, good. You're still friends, then. You wouldn't mind introducing me to her, would you? I'd love a chance to work with Nichole if I could. Associating with the Diadem never hurts a fellow's career."

Poor Nichole, Maijstral thought. Still, celebrity was something she had chosen, along with all the little annoyances that went with it. Annoyances with names like Kenny or Winky or Vang-Thokk.

"Should the opportunity present itself," Maijstral said, "I will make the introduction, yes."

Kenny looked over Maijstral's shoulder and frowned. "There's a fellow in black keeps staring at me. He probably wants an autograph or something, the vermin. I'll just roll away, then, and keep out of his way."

"Bye," Maijstral said.

When he'd been living with Nicole, he'd had *many* conversations just like this one.

"I believe I'll accompany Kenny," Alice said, and made her congé.

Batty and Maijstral looked at one another.

"What a . . . *forceful* young man," Batty said.

"It could be worse," Maijstral said. "He could drink."

"Your father," said Batty, "has been put in my room."

"That's exceedingly good of you," Maijstral said. "We can move him to my suite later, and I can engage someone to look after him."

"As you like, dear, but that really won't be necessary. I'm growing accustomed to him, and as it was our family that brought him here in the first place, I have no objections to looking after him until you get over your trouble with Joseph Bob."

At the expense, Maijstral considered, of having Batty dig farther into his life history. Still and all, his father didn't really know anything likely to prove too embarrassing—since he'd reached the age of reason, Maijstral had kept his family strictly away from anything important—and so all the little gems Batty was likely to discover would be of the Peter Pajamas variety, domestic and perhaps even endearing.

Besides, sharing digs with a dead man, even a father, was hardly to his taste.

"If you truly don't mind," Maijstral said.

"That young man is still staring at us," Batty observed.

A silver sphere descended from somewhere near the ceiling and swooped closer to Maijstral. Following it, on foot, came a young woman with an unusually sculptured hair arrangement and a peculiar bell-shaped skirt.

"Mr. Maijstral?" she said, in Human Standard. "I'm Mangula Arish from the Talon News Service."

The appearance of such a person was inevitable, of course. Maijstral's lazy-lidded eyes half closed as they regarded the journalist.

"How do you do?" Replying in the same language.

A second media globe joined the first, recording the subject from another angle. "Has your journey to Earth been productive?" Mangula asked.

"No," Maijstral said, "but then I had not intended to produce anything while I was here."

"I meant," patiently, "will we see the disappearance of any of Earth's finer artworks or gemstones while you are on-planet?"

Maijstral sighed and once again told the truth, perfectly aware that no one would ever believe him. "I am here on vacation, and to attend the wedding of some acquaintances. If anything disappears, it won't be my fault."

"Is this restraint motivated by any regard for Earth's great history and its priceless collection of treasures?"

Maijstral's eyes narrowed to slits. "It is motivated by the fact I am on vacation."

"Do you intend to offer an apology to the people of Earth while you are here?"

Maijstral's eyes opened in surprise. "Apologize?" he said. "What have I to apologize for?"

"It was on Earth that your grandfather, the Imperial official better known as Robert the Butcher, committed the great majority of his crimes against his own people."

Maijstral's ears cocked forward as he feigned puzzlement. "And therefore?"

"And therefore," the journalist went on, "you, as his descendent, might be expected to apologize for his behavior."

"I was not even alive at the time, miss," Maijstral said, "and had nothing whatever to do with my grandfather's decisions, the actions that resulted from them, or any of the consequent suffering. But if anyone can receive comfort by an apology from someone who had nothing to do with the acts being apologized for, then I will happily offer mine, for whatever good they will do."

He was tempted to apologize as well for the acts of other bad eggs such as Jesse James and Mad Julius, considering that he had about equally to do with those, but some lingering sense of diplomacy kept his mouth shut.

As for Mangula, it took her a moment or two to disentangle the grammatical complexities of Maijstral's last statement. She blinked. "So you *do* apologize?" she asked.

"I thought I already had."

Mangula blinked again. The whole apology question had been one she'd raised herself on the assumption that, however Maijstral answered, she'd be able to turn it into something provocative, but it hadn't turned out quite the way she'd wished, and so she plunged ahead, hoping to be able to provoke a bit of sensation out of the jumble.

"Do you disavow the Cause for which your grandfather fought?"

Maijstral thoughtfully fingered the semilife patch along his jawline.

"Miss Arish, I believe history has disavowed my grandfather's Cause more than I ever could. I wish everyone well, and I desire peace for all, regardless of their politics, and really, what more can I say?"

It would require a fair degree of context removal—"editing," in the journalistic sense—to make anything remotely sensational out of this, and Mangula decided to end the interview and let her news director decide what to do with the results.

As a consequence, she completely forgot to inquire as to the significance of Maijstral's semilife patch, which by now had become rather prominent in view of the swelling its rooted tendrils were sopping up—and that inquiry would have given her a scoop indeed.

"Thank you, Mr. Maijstral," she said, and made her exit, silver globes swooping after her.

"Does that sort of thing happen *all the time?"* Batty asked.

"Oh yes," Maijstral said. "More now than ever."

"What a strange life you must lead, I'm sure."

"One must be sure to always make one's answers to the media as complex and laden of context as possible. They can never make a simple, sensational story out of it that way. Not without a good deal of effort, anyway."

Batty's eyes shifted over Maijstral's shoulder again. "That young man in black is approaching. And he's got a friend with him."

Maijstral sighed—the last two people who spoke to him had been rather a trial, and there was no guarantee that this one would be any different. Still, he turned to face the newcomers with as civil a face as possible.

The young man in black had long hair styled similarly to Maijstral's, and Maijstral observed he wore a large diamond on one finger —the same finger as Maijstral's own diamond, and a very similar diamond at that. The man's friend wore a bottle green coat and gold jewelry.

"Maijstral," the man in black said, offering Maijstral three fingers in the handclasp to Maijstral's one, "I'm Laurence."

Maijstral sniffed the actor's ears. "Pleased to meet you," he said. "I'm told you do me rather well."

The actor stepped back with a look of surprise. "It sounds as if you haven't seen me."

Maijstral probably should have assured the young man that he'd seen him scads of times, and thought him very good, not that his opinion really counted, but fortunately it was shared by all the very best critics, and Laurence must surely be pleased—after which Laurence would have gone off a happy man. But events had thrown off Maijstral's social timing, and he'd already had to deal with one actor today and his patience was probably shorter than usual, and so he did the worst thing possible, which was (once again) to tell the truth.

"I'm sorry to say I haven't," he said. "My life is rather pressing and I have little time for video. But I'm told that many people prefer you to that, ah, other fellow."

"Anaya."

"Quite so. My apologies, anyway, for not recognizing you." Laurence frowned, and his ears were pinned back, but he turned to his friend and made the introduction.

"This is Deco, my companion."

"Pleased to meet you," Maijstral said. He had discerned by this point that he'd made a gaffe, and in amends gave two fingers to Deco's one, then mentally sighed at how it did not seem possible to achieve social attunement this afternoon no matter how hard he tried.

Maijstral introduced Aunt Batty, and then the four stared at each other for a long, uncomfortable moment.

"It is a most-attractive dwelling, is it not?" Batty finally said. "Most underwater environments give one such a sense of confinement, but Prince Hunac has made everything here so spacious that one's sense of claustrophobia is quite underwhelmed."

"True," Deco said.

"Very," said Laurence.

Silence reigned once more. Aunt Batty concluded that she'd done her best.

Laurence, it should be observed, did not actually play Maijstral on video. He played a character superficially similar to Maijstral, or at least similar to who Maijstral might have been if he were the hero of a video series—brave, stalwart, chivalrous, handy with his fists, and staggeringly successful with women. The company that made the series had (after the Imperial Sporting Commission) first call on the videos Maijstral made while stealing, and mixed Maijstral's videos with their own, altering Maijstral's image to that of Laurence. It was *understood* that Laurence was playing Maijstral, even if the character had a different name, and it was suggested that all the video adventures, preposterous though they were, were in some sense true, that they all offered details of Maijstral's life that had not been made public. And since Maijstral could never commit as many burglaries as a character in a weekly series, the producers bought videos from other burglars who were unlucky enough not to have series characters designed after them, and likewise altered the image to that of Laurence—and in the end Maijstral got the credit for a lot of spectacular capers that he had never actually performed.

"I see you wear a diamond ring," Maijstral observed.

"Yes." Laurence brightened. "It's just like yours. I use it as a focus, when I'm acting—I look at the ring, and I say to myself, *I'm Drake Maijstral, I'm the greatest burglar ever.* And then I do my scene."

"But you wear the ring when you're not acting," Maijstral said. "Doesn't that cause confusion? When you look down at your plate at luncheon, for example, and see the ring, don't you say to yourself, *I'm a burglar,* and then have to fight away a crisis of identity along with an impulse to slip the silverware up your sleeve?"

"But Laurence *is* a terrific burglar," Deco said. "He's had lots of practice."

Maijstral looked at Laurence in surprise. "Do you actually steal?" he said.

Laurence flushed. "Well, no. My contract doesn't permit—it wouldn't do for the star of a series to end up in prison. But I've done everything *but* steal."

"He's got a very good darksuit," Deco said. "I made it myself—I've studied how all the tech is done. Sometimes he flies out at night, just *being a burglar,* you know."

"It's really helped my interpretation of the role," Laurence said.

Maijstral looked from one to the other and decided that, yes, he was intended to be impressed by this. He was trying to decide how to respond when one of Hunac's servants approached.

"Sir, a message for you. Miss Nichole. There is a privacy booth in the corner."

Maijstral manufactured an apologetic look. "My apologies, gentlemen," he said, and moved away.

"Umm," Laurence called after him. "You know—I really wanted to talk to you about Nichole. . . ."

Maijstral escaped to the privacy booth and activated the field that sealed him off from any eavesdroppers and lip-readers. At a command Nichole's face appeared before him.

She was a tall blond woman located ambiguously on the cusp between mid and late thirties, and she was one of the Three Hundred who were so famous they bore only a forename. She was, technically speaking, an actress, but her real profession was so far above a mere *actress,* above *celebrity,* even above *star,* that only a place in some fairly all-embracing pantheon could probably do justice to her standing.

When she spoke, entire planets hushed to hear her words. People she had never heard of, and never *would* hear of, committed suicide at the thought they were unworthy to share the universe with her. Obscure alien races knelt at her image and spit up, with appropriate ritual obeisance, offerings of the very best regurgitated fish-liver wine.

She was, so to speak, colossal. Even for a member of the Diadem she was big.

Maijstral had once turned down a chance to join the Human Diadem and live on the same plateau as Nichole. The refusal had made him, briefly, more famous than if he had accepted, but the industry that was Nichole rolled on without him, generating more fame, more glory, more worship, while the comparatively small enterprise that was Maijstral, denied the constant barrage of publicity and glory granted members of the Diadem, was compelled to sneak up on success and win it by strategem rather than bag it in one grand rush.

But when Nichole's image appeared before Maijstral, it was not that of a distant goddess, but rather that of an old friend. It did Maijstral's heart good to see her. In this crisis, it was good to know who one could trust, and Nichole was a true and tested comrade in adversity.

"Hello, Nichole," he said.

Nichole's superb eyes glittered with concern. "Drake," she said, "what's this I hear about a duel between you and the Prince of Tejas?"

"I see that I can spare you a certain degree of exposition," Maijstral said. "How did you hear about it?"

"Diadem security, of course," Nichole said. "Background checks on everyone at the party."

"Of course," Maijstral agreed.

Members of the Diadem floated through existence in their own perfect world, with no stray locks out of place, no buttons unfastened, and certainly no rude interlopers trying to crash the party. Diadem security, smooth, efficient, and all-embracing, was the envy of all people of prominence, including the Constellation's President. His own security problems were never dealt with in such a seamless way.

Of course, he didn't pay his own guards nearly as much. And for that matter he wasn't nearly as famous as Nichole, something he found just as galling as the difference in service.

"What in heaven's name provoked this?" Nichole asked.

Maijstral told her. Her look softened.

"Oh, Drake," she sighed, "and I thought, when we met, that I was going to unburden my problems on *you.*"

"This may be your last chance," Maijstral muttered darkly.

"Who's acting for you?" Nichole asked.

Maijstral told her. Nichole frowned. "Isn't she awfully young?"

"She's quite mature for her years."

"Still, it's your *life* that's at stake."

Maijstral winced. He did not need reminding.

"You have no idea who provoked this?" Nichole went on.

"No. I've been racking my brains, but I can't think of anyone who would really want to—"

"I will have Diadem security begin an in-depth survey of everyone you know."

Gratification sprang warmly to life in Maijstral's heart. "Thank you." A cold little icicle of suspicion touched his thoughts. "Your people keep track of burglars, yes?"

"More or less automatically, yes."

"You might have them concentrate on Alice Manderley. Check the status of her bank accounts."

Nichole nodded. "Right away. And I'll advance my schedule and arrive tomorrow morning, so that we can confer," Nichole said. "I'd come sooner, but there's a reception this evening I can't escape—the King of Libya." A frown crossed her face. "I *think* it's Libya. I haven't had my briefing yet."

"I'm sure he will be pleasant, whatever he's the king of," Maijstral said. "Kings have every reason to be pleased with their lot. And in the meantime, I will be very pleased to see you tomorrow."

Doubt entered Nichole's voice. "Drake?" she said. "What if they do it again?"

Maijstral stared, his blood running chill.

He would have thought of this himself if he'd not been so completely distracted.

"Why would they?" he asked in desperation.

Nichole's ears flickered. "Why did they do it *once?*"

"I will arrange for security."

"That would be advisable." She smiled. "Please give my best to Roman, by the way."

Maijstral fled to his chambers as soon as the conversation ended, striding past Laurence and his companion, who seemed to want to converse again.

When Maijstral arrived, the room was empty save for the reef fish under the room's bubble aquarium dome. Maijstral went to the service place and touched the ideogram for "service."

"Roman?"

"At once, sir."

When Roman arrived, Maijstral was shocked at the transformation. Roman was bald, grey-skinned, red-eyed, and he scratched continually, his hands moving, void of volition, from one bodily torment to the next. Maijstral had never seen Roman this bad.

"It has occurred to me," Maijstral said, "that whoever planted the pistol on us might well try again."

Roman growled, a long, ominous sound. Maijstral smoothed down the hairs that had just risen on his neck.

"I want maximum security on our rooms," Maijstral said. "Every alarm and detector we can acquire. Every nasty little surprise that we wouldn't want to encounter ourselves in the course of our business. Plant them *all.*"

A grim light of satisfaction entered Roman's agate eyes. "Very good, sir," he said.

Another cold suspicion lodged in Maijstral's breast. "You might check all the alarms personally," he added. "I'd rather you arranged things, rather than Drexler."

Roman stiffened. Another low growl rolled from his throat. "Am I to understand that we are no longer trusting Mr. Drexler, sir?"

"We are trusting no one, Roman. Drexler was working for Fu George on Silverside Station, remember, against our interests. It's possible, if unlikely, that he may have conceived an elaborate plan of revenge. Or someone may have conceived it for him."

"Vanessa Runciter, sir?"

Maijstral's brow darkened. Now *there* was someone for Nichole's people to look into. "I wouldn't put it past her," he said. "So when you have no other duties, you might simply make it your business to keep tabs on Drexler."

"Very good, sir."

"One other thing," Maijstral said. "Nichole sends her love."

Roman's ears flattened in pleasure. He and Nichole had always had a most sympathetic relationship.

"I hope we are still trusting Miss Nichole," he ventured.

"Of course we are."

Roman's tongue lolled in a smile. "Very *good,* sir."

Maijstral had just finished dressing for dinner when Roberta called. His insides quailed as he saw the grim expression in her violet eyes.

"What news?" he said, and hoped his voice didn't quaver.

"Joseph Bob continues to insist on the fight, and continues to insist that it be soon. There's no getting around it, and he's got the right. Unless you'd rather he called in the cops, of course."

Maijstral sat down and suppressed an instinct to swab away the sweat that had just appeared on his brow.

"How soon?" he asked.

"The day after tomorrow. The meeting is on an island in the Dry Tortugas. The Prince wanted pistols, then swords, and I said no to both."

"Very good."

"So we've settled on a weapon with which neither of you have any experience. It's called a *dire staff.*"

Maijstral quailed at the very name. He tugged at his throat lace. "I don't believe I'm familiar with that weapon. . . ." he managed.

Roberta's hands waved near the phone's service panel, and next to her image appeared the staff, a long steel pole with a complicated knot of interwoven steel blades on one end and a blunt protrusion on the other.

"It was used in ritual combat by the Hennese," Roberta said. "It has blades at one end and a low-level stunner at the other. The combatants are placed within reach of one another right at the start, so that anyone attempting to use the stunner exposes himself to a possible attack from the bladed end. And the stunner is, as I said, low-level, so it will only slow the target down, not actually drop them."

"So the point of combat with this weapon is to slow the enemy with the stunner, then butcher him with the other end once he can't defend himself."

"Apparently."

"How charming." Maijstral was appalled.

Roberta's eyes flashed. "Well, what could I *do,* Drake? We had to settle on *some* weapon or other. They'll all kill you very messily one way or another, but at least Joseph Bob hasn't ever had time to practice with one of these, so you'll have an even chance."

Maijstral took a deep breath. All was not lost. He could still try to fix this somehow, just as he fixed his last fight when he was at the Nnoivarl Academy.

"I'm sorry if I sounded upset," Maijstral said. "I *am* upset, of course, but not by you."

Her look softened. "I will have a staff sent to you tomorrow so that you can get the feel of the thing. We're borrowing some from a collector on Mars. He made it a condition that he witness the fight—he's always wanted to see the things used." She frowned. "The rules call for an objective witness anyway, so that seems all right."

Maijstral's mind raced. So, he thought, Joseph Bob would be practicing with his own dire staff as soon as it came down from Mars. Which meant that Maijstral could get to it and sabotage it somehow.

"Who did you say used these things?" he asked. "I didn't catch the name."

"The Hennese."

"And what are they? A religious sect of some sort?"

"No. A minor race. The Empire conquered them a few millennia ago, but they've subsequently become extinct."

Cold foreboding squatted heavily on Maijstral's breast. "And why did they all die off?" he asked.

"Well." Roberta reddened. "They kept fighting each other with dire staffs, for one thing."

"I thought as much. Thank you."

Cowards die many times before their deaths, as Shaxpur remarks in his newly translated play, *Tsar Iulius, "the valiant never taste of death but once."* After the conversation ended, Maijstral sat in silence for a long, endless moment, dying many times.

He could fix the stunner, he thought, but how could he fix a nest of glittering, sharp blades on the end of a *stick?*

This was going to take a lot of thought.

He rose and went to the service plate. "Roman," he said, "come and unlace me. I won't be going to dinner after all."

He seemed to have lost his appetite.

EIGHT

The glories of Palancar towered toward the distant sun, layer after layer of coral and sponge, anemone and fans and gorgonia, every form and color in the world piled atop one another and reaching toward the sky. Among all this richness swarmed the fish, as brightly colored as the corals: grouper and barracuda, squirrelfish and angels, trunkfish and parrot fish and triggerfish.

Nothing was visible that was not alive.

Turn 180 degrees and there was only one ocean, a clear and perfect Cherenkov blue, reaching straight down a thousand meters and going on all the way to the mainland. The color was so blue that, looking at it, you could feel *blueness* prickling all the way along your skin.

Nothing alive was visible in that blue, nothing at all.

Nichole and Maijstral floated along the wall, hovering in the interface between the lonely blue and the bright, bustling swarm that was the coral wall. They communicated with one another along a cyphered link.

It was the only way, given the circumstances, they could achieve any degree of privacy.

"I wonder if we will find a splendid toadfish," Nichole said. "It's supposed to be the best. Quite rare."

"You heard that in your briefing, yes?"

"Yes. Of course."

Members of the Human Diadem were briefed before every appearance in order to give them something to view and talk about. They learned about the best people, the best art, the best food, the best architecture, the best sights, and—apparently—the best toadfish.

At least they were the best in the opinion of the Diadem's research staff, who were, of course, the best researchers money could buy.

Maijstral had lived without these briefings for several years now, and found himself perfectly content to exist without his every opinion being scripted ahead of time.

"I am surprised that the Diadem's researchers didn't offer to find a toadfish and tag it so that you could locate it and appreciate it properly," Maijstral said.

"They did. But I thought we'd prefer privacy."

"Thank you."

The two floated along a narrow passageway between two giant coral ramparts. Bright swaying tendrils trailed above them in the strong current like old friends waving good-bye.

"I have narrowed somewhat your range of suspects," Nichole said. "Alice Manderley arrived on Earth only yesterday on a liner from Qwarism, where she was released from prison last month."

"I see."

"Her bank account *has* registered a substantial increase which our researchers weren't able to account for—five hundred novae—but she may have signed some endorsement deal, or been paid for a commission that hasn't become public. The researchers will continue their efforts."

"They may as well not, since Alice is no longer a suspect."

"Drake," severely, "that's what they're *for.*"

"Well then. If you like."

Nichole continued. "Vanessa Runciter is in the Empire with her new consort, Lord Pasco."

"The foundation garment fellow?"

"Yes."

"I wouldn't have thought Vanessa would *need* that as yet."

"She has expensive tastes. I doubt it's the underwear she needs."

"True."

"Being in the Empire, of course, doesn't rule out the possibility of Vanessa's hiring it done, but it puts her so far out of communication with any hireling that it would make it impossible to coordinate anything."

"True."

"And your mother is also in the Empire, a guest at Lord Moth's hunting lodge."

Maijstral's relations with his mother were such that he had no objection to her inclusion among the list of suspects.

His mother held many grudges. That she would hold a lethal grudge against her only son was not absolutely out of the question.

A flash of deep paranoia lit Maijstral's brain. "She's nowhere near Vanessa, is she?"

"No. Pasco and Vanessa were clean on the other side of the Empire from Mothholm, on Krpntsz."

"Krpntsz? I heard the fishing is good."

"According to our researchers," airily, "the place is passe."

The water brightened as they passed from the shadowed valley to a plateau of white coral sand. Nichole looked about, frowned, and commanded her repellers to move toward the nearest coral castle.

A grouper, long as Maijstral's arm, floated nearby and wondered whether or not to ask for a handout.

"Have you considered Joseph Bob's brother?" Nichole asked.

"The Bubber?" Maijstral blinked. "No, I haven't."

"I presume he is his brother's heir, since Joseph Bob has only recently married and hasn't yet fathered a child. If you kill the Prince, the Bubber gets the title and everything else. He'd be one of the richest people on Earth."

"And he might be under the impression that I'm quite the dashing blade," Maijstral said. "Joseph Bob spent the evening talking about that stupid encounter I had in school—he made me sound perfectly heroic. Will might think I could kill his brother with a snap of my fingers."

"Think about it, Drake. He's the only person I can think of who would actually benefit from this situation."

Maijstral did just that, coldly considering the Bubber in the role of blackhearted conspirator. He didn't quite think that the Will he'd met was entirely up to the role, but then . . . a true blackhearted conspirator would seem perfectly innocent, wouldn't he?

Perhaps it had been the Bubber who'd suggested the dire staff, the ghastly weapon that would give Maijstral a good crack at killing Joseph Bob. And probably the Bubber could have opened the display case and removed the revolver simply by giving the proper codes. The only question was whether he had the ability to silently place the revolver in the ventilation shaft, and Maijstral rather suspected the answer was yes.

And if Will was really behind the whole thing, how could Maijstral prove it?

Tempting though it was to hang the Bubber upside down over the Grand Canyon, he suspected that if Will were really blackhearted as all that, not only would the Bubber not confess, but he'd probably end up challenging Maijstral to a second duel following the first.

Of course, Maijstral thought, a bit cheered by the idea, he could always let him *fall.* . . .

Thinking these thoughts, Maijstral followed Nichole into a downward-slanting cave. A wall of bright silver fish flashed on and off ahead, turning to and fro in unison, as if they were a form of living heliograph sending a message.

"I also wonder about the Duchess of Benn, Drake," Nichole said. "You stole the Shard from her, after all. I wonder if there's any ill feeling."

Thoughts of the Bubber fled Maijstral's mind as paranoia closed in once again. Roberta—a force for evil! The *Black Widow*—luring a man into her embrace, then *destroying him!*

The *dire staff!* his brain yelped. It was all part of her plot!

But after a brief, giddy moment in which the ocean did backflips, rationality managed a cautious, delicate return.

"I think not," he said. "The circumstances of the theft of the Shard were not such as to create a grudge. And besides, her grace has favored me with an offer of marriage."

Nichole's perfect blue eyes, the exact shade of the great deep, widened in surprise.

"Congratulations," she said softly.

"Thank you."

"It's a brilliant match."

"I wish I knew whether my brilliance was sufficient to the occasion."

Her brows lifted in surprise. "You told her no?"

"I haven't given her an answer at all." When Nichole continued looking at him, he added, "The matter of the duel came up immediately afterward."

"I see." She looked away. "Perhaps someone in her family is opposed to the match."

Maijstral could hardly see Aunt Batty climbing about in ventilators, but then there was also Paavo Kuusinen, a fellow who seemed to have hidden resources.

"Paavo Kuusinen is here," he said. "You remember him from Peleng. He's the Duchess's attorney. And spy."

"He helped us on Peleng."

"He may have changed his mind."

"And the Duchess has a large family. There might be some thwarted suitor hanging about." She looked thoughtful. "I'll have the researchers get to work on them."

"Any other suspects?"

"The researchers have only had a few hours, Drake."

"*I* may have only a few hours."

"I will tell them to make haste."

The profound blue of the great deep beckoned ahead, surrounded by rust-colored coral fronds. Nichole and Maijstral floated from the dark cavern out onto the coral wall, into the light, the blaze of color.

"Perhaps," Nichole decided, "I shall tell them now. Shall we return to the palace?"

"As you like."

They floated back along the wall, each wrapped in thought. The ever-hopeful grouper followed, its own thoughts perfectly visible on its face. The magnificence of the reef, the clarity of the water, the warmth of the sun, made even Maijstral's predicament seem remote.

Strangely, Maijstral found himself wanting to get wet. Both he and Nichole were cloaked in their own private force fields, which kept air in while screening out both water and pressure. Air was provided through a little bottle and freshened through a rebreathing unit that clipped to the belt. Propulsion was provided by the same repeller units that powered personal fliers and Maijstral's darksuit.

This arrangement was convenient, and prevented both the bends and nitrogen narcosis, but it lacked intimacy. The coral castles and darting fish that surrounded them were inspiring Maijstral to attempt a closer acquaintance.

If he lived, he reminded himself. If he lived.

The lights of the Underwater Palace were in sight when two other divers floated toward them.

"Why, hello!" said Laurence.

"What a coincidence!" said Deco.

Maijstral, certain that no coincidence obtained, nevertheless put on a civil face and introduced the two to Nichole.

"We're just going out to view the reef," Laurence said. "Shall we join you?"

"Alas," Maijstral said, "we were just going in. Don't let us keep you."

The two could not keep their dismay from reflecting on their faces. Maijstral and Nichole smilingly said their adieux and made their way to the airlock.

"I say," Laurence called after. "Were you lucky enough to see a toadfish?"

After entering through the airlock and turning in their diving gear, Maijstral and Nichole strolled to her suite, and the invincible Diadem security closed softly, silently, and inscrutably behind them.

Maijstral felt a knot of tension ease within himself. It felt so wonderfully safe here.

"Wine?" Nichole asked. "Coffee? Rink?"

"Rink."

"Rink for two, Daphne," Nichole said, speaking to a servant so professionally unobtrusive that Maijstral hadn't even realized she was present. Daphne poured drinks, served them, and at Nichole's command vanished into the aether from which Diadem servants came.

The only problem with the discreet, efficient servants that came with the Diadem, Maijstral reflected, was that they were working for the Diadem, not for oneself. One couldn't have a private little fit of anger, a minor nervous breakdown, or a silent moment of drunken obliteration in the privacy of one's own salon without everything being reported to the media titans who controlled the Diadem, and whose job it was to exploit any of these perfectly understandable human vagaries for the entertainment of billions.

Maijstral and Nichole sipped and sat beside one another on a small sofa. Nichole kicked off her shoes and held out her feet.

"Do you like my feet, Drake?" she said. "I had them done on Cornish."

"They are fine feet, Nichole."

She frowned at them critically. "I loved them at first, but now . . . well, perhaps the nail area could be slightly reduced, don't you think?"

"They're *your* feet. I don't think it proper to express an opinion other than to say that in their present state they seem perfectly desirable feet to me."

She laughed. "You see what trivialities I concern myself with."

"Not entirely trivial, I suspect," Maijstral said. "Have I been selfish, talking only of my problems?"

Nichole sighed. "My problems are rather less urgent than yours."

"Nevertheless," Maijstral said, "you sent me a message when I was on Silverside."

"I was not happy then."

"Are you happy now?"

She bit her lip. "Navarre is going to accept Diadem membership. His designs are reaching a huge audience."

"Please give him my congratulations."

"And I have decided—I think—to leave the Diadem."

How many goddesses, Maijstral wondered, have chosen to abdicate?

"Are you certain?" he asked.

"I think so. It was that last play that did it, I think—I have discovered that I would rather be an actress than a celebrity."

"It has always been my impression that you were nothing less than superb at being both at once."

She smiled, touched his hand. "Thank you, Drake. But if one is a member of the Three Hundred, one is encouraged to take only those parts that enhance one's celebrity, that contribute to one's mystique and glamor. Any touch of the *real* is discouraged. And I find myself increasingly interested in the real." She looked thoughtful. "One is always attracted by what one does not possess, and whatever the many attractions of my current existence, reality isn't numbered among them."

"You were very fine in that play."

"The Diadem didn't like it. Neither did a lot of my fans."

"They will grow to adore it, given time. They just need to grow accustomed to your range."

Nichole sipped at her rink, tilted her head, looked at Maijstral. "You were offered Diadem membership," she said, "and turned it down. I'm afraid I was offended—at the time I interpreted it as a rejection of me . . . and so I rejected you."

"Things end," Maijstral said, "and it doesn't have to be anyone's fault."

"That's generous of you, Drake," Nichole said, "but it remains that the Diadem came between us. That barrier may soon be removed. And the Diadem may soon become a barrier between me and Navarre." She sighed. "The fact is, I'm a few days too late.

Because if your unforgivably young and attractive Duchess hadn't beaten me to it, I would have proposed marriage myself."

Maijstral's lazy-lidded eyes opened to their widest possible extent. Only through force of will did he manage to keep his jaw from dropping.

Nichole's divinely blue eyes moistened. "And damn it," she said, "now that girl could get you *killed.*"

Maijstral's social antennae might not have been functioning at their best in the last few days, but at least he knew when to take a woman into his arms and kiss her.

He was, he thought to his amazement, perfectly safe here. Not even Colonel-General Vandergilt would be likely to get through the perfect wall of Diadem security.

Only one thought clouded his mind. "Where," he asked through a haze of kisses, "is Navarre?"

"One of the moons of Jupiter. Designing someone's yacht."

At least this spared Maijstral from the possibility of another challenge.

Safe, he thought. *Safe, safe, safe.*

It made Nichole all the more desirable.

NINE

Some hours later Maijstral left Nichole's suite in order to dress for supper. There was to be some manner of spectacle beforehand, in the Shrine Room, with Prince Hunac and his assistants carrying out one of the rites he was permitted to perform in public.

Maijstral stepped into the central reception area and felt a cold hand touch his neck, the uneasy sensation that he was out of Diadem security and anything could happen to him now.

"Sir."

It was Paavo Kuusinen, wearing a green suit of the latest Constellation cut and looking, as usual, perfectly inscrutable.

"Mr. Kuusinen," sniffing his ears, "is her grace here?"

"No. She and the Bubber are still making preparations for the encounter tomorrow. It is a surprisingly complex business."

Maijstral's blood curdled at this reminder of the following dawn. He continued moving across the reception area toward his own apartments, and Kuusinen followed.

"I am charged," Kuusinen said, "along with the other reason for being here, with sending you her loving regards."

"And your other reason?"

"I have brought your dire staff, sir, along with a mock-up

weapon should you desire to practice. I would be honored to be your partner in that practice if you should so desire."

Maijstral could feel sweat popping out on his brow at the thought. "I suppose a little practice would not be amiss," he said. At least it might give him some idea how to sabotage Joseph Bob's weapon.

"Perhaps after supper," Kuusinen suggested.

"Perhaps."

"I had the weapons delivered to your rooms."

Where, no doubt, they would stand propped up in the corner like sentinels at the gate of the Beyond, grim reminders of the fate to come.

"Thank you," Maijstral managed. "I wonder, Mr. Kuusinen, if—"

"Maijstral! Oh, Maijstral!" Laurence approached, smiling, his diamond winking. "I was wondering if—"

"I beg your pardon," Maijstral said without breaking stride, "but I have no time at present. Perhaps later—?"

"Ah. Oh." Laurence blinked, left behind in the dust. "Very well."

"Mr. Kuusinen," Maijstral continued, "I wonder if you would apply your splendid mind to the matter of the Bubber."

"Yes?" Kuusinen was all attention.

As they walked down the corridor toward Maijstral's rooms, Maijstral outlined Nichole's notion that the whole business of the duel might be the result of a plot by the Bubber to inherit the Princedom of Tejas.

"A provoking theory, sir," Kuusinen said. "But if it is true, how may it be proved? And proved by tomorrow morning?"

"*Proving* is precisely the matter to which I hope you might turn your mind."

Kuusinen gave it a few seconds' thought. "Amateur thieves often make mistakes, I should imagine," he ventured. "Leaving fingerprints, say. But there would be no surprise should the Bubber's fingerprints appear on the stolen revolver. He may have handled it frequently."

A thought—a wonderful, glorious thought!—occurred to Maijstral. "There are other places to leave fingerprints," he said. "Inside the duct, for example."

"Ah." Kuusinen nodded. "But did the police examine the duct for fingerprints? Or gather any other kind of forensic evidence?"

"No. His Highness declined to sign a complaint against me, and they terminated their investigation. But—" Maijstral found himself growing cheerful. "But I could go into the duct, tonight, with methods of detecting fingerprints, to see if I could find any latent evidence."

Kuusinen gave this further thought as well. "I'm afraid that you're hardly an unbiased witness," he said. "One might do better at asking the Prince if he would be willing to hire a private firm to examine the duct."

"I'm scarcely in a position to do that."

"Perhaps her grace, however, is. In her capacity as your second."

Hope blossomed in Maijstral, and he found himself walking for a moment with buoyant tread, but further thought cast him down again.

"But, acting as my second, she'd have to ask through the Bubber," he pointed out. "And if he's guilty, he won't let it happen."

"Ah." Kuusinen frowned. "Well, perhaps it will work and perhaps it will not. I will communicate with her grace on the matter nonetheless."

"I would be very appreciative."

Maijstral went through the complex procedure necessary to enter his booby-trapped room without tripping every alarm within a hundred leagues, and then he and Kuusinen entered.

"I see the dire staff is here," Kuusinen said. "Would you like me to demonstrate?"

Panic throbbed in Maijstral's heart at the very thought.

"Oh," he said, "there's plenty of time for that."

Kuusinen seemed a bit surprised. "Very well," he said smoothly. "Perhaps I should take my leave and give you a chance to dress for supper."

"I thank you for your efforts. And when you speak to her grace, please give her my love."

"I will."

Did he love the Duchess? he wondered as he saw Kuusinen to the door. Did he love Nichole? The answer to the first question, he suspected, ranged from *quite possibly* to *very likely,* and to the second *yes, probably,* but that provided no solution to the question of whether he wanted to marry either of them.

It was legally possible to marry *both,* of course, but he suspected the women in question would not be open to the suggestion, and in any case the solution was more likely to double, rather than answer, his dilemma.

He glanced over his shoulder at the dire staffs and shuddered.

The staffs, he realized, *did* offer a solution to the question of marriage, but one he would rather not consider.

In a mood to break bones and bang heads, Roman entered Maijstral's room. His naked skin was a shedding, flaking, burning torment, and he felt as if molten metal were coursing along his nerves. His muzzle, where the new age-ring was growing, was on fire.

Annihilation seemed a worthwhile alternative. Lacking that, he would have happily settled for the cheerful oblivion of psychopathic violence.

Unfortunately neither seemed likely. Instead Roman found Maijstral in a contemplative mood, studying the genealogy that Roman had prepared.

"You called, sir?" Roman said.

Normal words for a servant to address to his employer, but there must have been something odd in the inflection, because Maijstral gave a start and looked wildly at Roman for a moment, as if a threatening stranger had just entered and growled out a threat. But Maijstral's heavy-lidded eyes shuttered again, and he looked again at the long scroll.

"I observe you have left room for my descendants," he said.

"Yes," Roman said. Normally he would have said something more polished, along the lines of, *Indeed, I hope to be able to inscribe each happy event, and soon,* appropriate sentiment mixed with a decided hint that it was high time Maijstral got betrothed to his duchess. But in his current crazed condition, complex sentences were rather beyond him, and simple declaratives were more the thing.

Maijstral continued gazing at the scroll.

"I have spent the day with Miss Nichole," Maijstral said.

I trust the sojourn was pleasant would have been something along Roman's normal lines at this point, but the thought of Nichole—he had always been passionately fond of Nichole—sent his thought-impulses veering off into any number of unexpected byways, and he managed no reply at all.

Maijstral, who had raised one eyebrow in anticipation of a reply, waited for a moment and then lowered it. He pursed his lips and gazed at the scroll again.

"She tells me that she is considering leaving the Diadem," he said. "And she has also favored me with a proposal of marriage."

Roman's ears flattened in amazement and his tongue flopped from his muzzle. His thought-impulses scattered, re-formed, scattered again. *Nichole!* Always his favorite—the only human to cause him to forget his usual prejudice against actresses and celebrities. But . . . but . . . *duty!* It was Maijstral's *duty* to marry the Duchess.

Nichole!

Duty!

Nichole!

Duty!

The conflicting notions volleyed away in his head for a few seconds, and then he managed to pull himself together and croak out a question.

"Did you give her an answer?"

Which was pretty good, under the circumstances, though his normal line would have been, *Did you favor her with a reply, sir?*

"The matter," Maijstral said, "is still under discussion."

"Hrrrr," said Roman, a sound of frustration much like a growl.

Couldn't his employer make up his mind about *anything?* The Duchess was clearly a perfect, brilliant match, but if Maijstral was *determined* to be feckless and irresponsible, then running off with an actress was the perfect way to do that, and Nichole, to Roman's way of thinking, was the perfect actress.

Pick one or the other! he wanted to roar. *Either one will do!*

He stifled these thoughts, though the effort cost him. Hence, "Hrrrr."

He would have apologized, but Maijstral seemed not to hear. Maijstral rose from his chair and held out his arms.

"The supper costume, please," he said. "The white suit tonight, with the gold braid. If I must spend the evening mirroring Nichole's glory, I may as well wear the most reflective thing I've got."

The Shrine Room featured stone tablets of intricate workmanship that prescribed the rite now being performed by Prince Hunac. There were chants, the drinking of ritual intoxicants, offerings of quetzal feathers, flowers, and fruit, and blood drawn via a silver needle in the shape of a stingray spine—the genuine article would have been used by Hunac's ancestors, but fortunately the concept of hygiene had entered the life of humanity since then.

It was difficult to see Hunac, partly because of his short stature, partly because he was enveloped by a feathery ritual costume. Fortunately, media globes floated overhead at all the best angles, and the results were transmitted to screens set in the back of the room.

The crowd watched respectfully from the sidelines, facing either toward the ceremony itself or the handy video screens. Nichole stood in the very front of the crowd—it was her due as a member of the Three Hundred—and Maijstral stood at her side and paid as much attention to the crowd as to the ceremony itself.

He was beginning to develop a morbid interest in ritual bloodletting.

Alice Manderley hovered in the back of the room, watching neither the monitors nor the ceremony itself. Perhaps, Maijstral thought, the sight of blood was unappetizing to her. He felt a certain sympathy for a kindred soul.

Or perhaps she was looking for her husband Kenny, who was not present. Doubtless he was advancing his career somewhere else in the palace.

Aunt Batty stood opposite Maijstral in the front row and watched with an expression of polite attention. Maijstral could only guess what a Khosali gentlewoman would make of this sort of ritual. Probably, he concluded, nothing very positive.

Standing next to her in his green suit, Paavo Kuusinen watched everything very carefully and, as was his wont, let no detail escape his eye.

Midway back in the crowd, Maijstral could see Major Ruth Song, who still looked very like Elvis Presley. Next to her was a red-faced man in a uniform that Maijstral didn't recognize. As he glanced over the crowd, Maijstral accidentally locked eyes with the man and received a glare of hatred and defiance, a stare of sufficient emotional violence to cause a chill of alarm to travel through Maijstral's nerves.

Maijstral looked away. He didn't even know the man. Perhaps, Maijstral thought, he had intercepted a glare meant for someone else.

Laurence and Deco, Maijstral observed, were purposefully making their way through the crowd toward him, or rather toward Nichole. Maijstral sighed. Introductions, at this stage, were inevitable.

The intoxicants, whatever they were, had Hunac fairly loopy by the end—he was swaying on his feet and there was a broad, white, lopsided grin on his face. As the ceremony concluded the crowd tapped their feet in the pattern for reverence, though a few of the humans in the group banged their hands together in applause, a startling sound that the Constellation Practices Authority recommended as a more human custom than the Khosali practice of foot-tapping. The uniformed man with Major Song, Maijstral observed, was one of the more insistent hand-bangers.

Nichole turned toward Maijstral. "That was most enlightening," she said. "Did Hunac get up to all that at school?"

"Legend says he did. I never knew anyone who saw anything, though."

"Maijstral," said Laurence, who, now the crowd was dispersing, had finally reached his goal. "That was enthralling, don't you think? A link to our barbaric past."

"Odd to think of the universe being maintained in such a manner," Maijstral commented, and then turned toward Nichole to do his social duty. "Nichole, may I present—"

At this point a large fist filled Maijstral's eye and he went down. He blinked up from the floor in amazement and saw the large red-faced man standing over him and glaring at him. Major Song tugged at the man's uniform sleeve.

"You're a dirty rat-lover!" the man proclaimed. "That apology—hah! I've never seen anything so insincere."

"Milo," Major Song said, tugging, "don't do this!"

Maijstral could think of nothing better to say than, "Who *are* you?"

"What you said was an insult to everyone who died in the Rebellion!" the man went on. "I challenge you, you rat-loving thief!"

Major Song gave up her tugging. "He's drunk," she said apologetically to the crowd at large, accompanying her comment with a hands-up boys-will-be-boys gesture.

"Who *are* you?" Maijstral asked again.

"Robert the Butcher was a disgrace to humanity, and so are you," the man opined.

At this point the crowd, which had been agitated, suddenly fell silent. Prince Hunac had arrived, surrounded by his assistants. Maijstral observed that the assistants were dressed in full-feathered regalia and carried wooden swords edged with obsidian as well as large clubs consisting of a suggestively shaped stone lashed into the crotch of a stout stick.

The assistants were rather short, but their demeanor was of an intense, ominous, and unfriendly nature.

"Who profaneth the rites?" Hunac demanded, speaking—oddly enough—with the full majesty of High Khosali.

Maijstral knew a cue when he heard one. He pointed at Milo. "*He* profaneth them!" he said.

Prince Hunac snapped his fingers, and Milo, whoever he was, was promptly engulfed by Hunac's feathered entourage. Thumps, thuds, and yelps of pain accompanied his exit from the Shrine Room.

Major Song followed, waving her arms and asking them, please, to stop. Which, it should be pointed out, they did not.

Kuusinen and Aunt Batty broke through the crowd. Maijstral looked at Prince Hunac.

"Who *was* he?" he asked.

Prince Hunac grinned broadly and giggled as the intoxicants caught up with him. His pupils were wide as saucers. Considering what he'd been drinking, it was a significant accomplishment to have managed High Khosali at the height of the crisis. He dropped into the simpler forms of Khosali Standard. "Never saw that man before," he said. He offered a hand. "Would you care to stand?"

"Thank you."

Maijstral accepted Hunac's hand, but Hunac was unsteadier than Maijstral, and there was a certain amount of tugging back and forth before Kuusinen intervened to help Maijstral rise. Nichole's welcome arms steadied him as he found his feet.

"Are you all right, sir?"

"A *complete stranger!*" Maijstral complained to the world at large, and then, "I'm getting tired of being punched."

"So is your attacker, I imagine," Hunac said cheerfully. "You'd best get some patches on that shiner."

"Yes, I suppose." Media globes were swooping in, and it was clearly time to leave.

"Let me go with you, Drake," Nichole said.

"Gladly."

"I say. Maijstral," Laurence began, submerged in the crowd, "I believe you were about to introduce me—"

Maijstral and Nichole were already gone.

"I wonder if you underestimated the strength of public feeling," said Mangula Arish, "in regard to your controversial statements yesterday."

"What controversial statements?" Maijstral snarled.

Now that he was physically safe, Maijstral found himself with the luxury to grow angry. How *dare* these people? Who did they think they *were?*

He and Nichole were hastening down a palace corridor to his rooms. Only a reporter, it seemed, would have the nerve to interrupt them. She had to hop alongside in order to keep up with their rapid pace, a form of locomotion that made the bell-shaped skirt look as if it were being rung repeatedly.

"Your alleged apology for the acts of your grandfather. There are those who have found it wavering and insincere, even mocking."

In truth, Mangula's editor had done an outstanding job with the unpromising material—it had been a slow news day, otherwise he wouldn't have bothered. He'd edited Maijstral's words to maximize their potential, then sent the edited versions to the usual political hotheads, who were always eager to get their faces on video.

He had succeeded beyond his own cynical expectations, though he didn't think the controversy was good for more than a day's play. If Maijstral actually ended up in a duel and got killed, however, he could count on running the story for at least two or three days.

By then there might be some *real* news to broadcast.

"There are those who claim that you should be forced to apologize again for the nature of your remarks," Mangula went on.

"Apologize for my *apology?"* Maijstral said.

Everyone, he realized, simply *everyone,* was trying to kill him. He was going to get a few necessities from his room, he decided, and move into Nichole's suite and never come out. He would be surrounded by Diadem security until he left the planet. And then he'd recruit his own guards, a solid wall of muscle to stand between him and an inexplicably hostile universe. . . .

"Perhaps in view of the fact that you've been set upon by an outraged citizen," Mangula led on, "you might consider an apology of greater depth and sincerity."

"He was set on by *one drunken man,"* Nichole pointed out. "That's hardly a lynch mob."

Maijstral turned the corner just before his room, intent only on escape from this inquisitorial nightmare, and then saw, silhouetted against the distinctive, intricate design of the hallway's Bludarsian Seawood panelling, a peculiar shift of light, of color, of pattern. A perfectly familiar shift, though usually he only saw it when he was stealing something and caught a glimpse of himself in a mirror, cloaked by his darksuit. . . .

Triumph sang in his nerves. *Got you!* he thought.

Anger and exultation mingled in Maijstral's nerves, a perfectly dangerous combination. The spitfire slid from his armpit into his hand with practiced ease. He flung himself prone on the carpet, and —as Nichole and Mangula yelped in alarm—Maijstral opened fire.

Got you got you got you!

Stylish energies flamed off invisible shields and scorched the walls. Alarms clanged. Bright purple fire-retardant foam poured from the ceiling fixtures. Whoever was in the darksuit fled as Maijstral poured fire after.

"What . . ." Mangula got out, and then there was the hum of a stunner—the burglar returning fire—and Mangula flopped to the carpet, suddenly unstrung. Her sculptured hairstyle was melting rapidly. Her silver media globes thudded to the ground like overripe metallic fruit. The mystery figure disappeared around the L-intersection at the end of the corridor.

Mangula spoke with great effort and severity as Maijstral rose to his feet.

"Gleep," she said.

"Call security!" Maijstral told Nichole—perfectly pointless after all this, but it would give her something to do and keep her out of the line of fire—and then he sprinted after the intruder, for all the world like the character that Laurence played in the vids.

His feet, slicked by the foam that was pouring from the ceiling fixtures, promptly slid out from under him and he crashed face-first onto the purple billows.

Laurence's character never had these problems. Especially not when he was wearing a white suit.

"Fnerg," Mangula said with satisfaction.

Maijstral rose and slid, slipped, and skated down the hallway. Presumably whoever was in the darksuit could fly, and would have got a good lead on him by now.

"Snerk," Mangula commented.

As he approached the L-intersection he wondered whether to charge ahead or slow down and proceed cautiously in case the stranger was waiting there with a weapon. He opted for the better part of valor, but then to his alarm found that the slick foam under his feet wasn't about to let him put on the brakes. His momentum carried him inexorably out into the intersection, and so he raised the spitfire and squeezed off a few more shots—suppressive fire, he hoped desperately—and then he slammed into the wall hard enough to make his teeth rattle.

"Yibble!" Mangula shouted triumphantly.

The intruder had long since fled. Maijstral's shots had only caused more foam to rain down. He charged down the corridor, banged through a series of doors that looked suspiciously ajar, and then found himself in the submarine pen, a cavernous dome built on a plateau of white sand, with a tunnel leading downward and opening onto Palancar Wall.

There was a small private submarine diving into the tunnel amid a gush of bubbles.

Maijstral fired, causing a cascade of steam but no visible effect on the submarine other than to vaporize one of its running lights. The villain was getting away! Desperately he looked about for a submarine he could call his own.

"Submarine!" he shouted. "Open!"

Three unlocked canopies obligingly popped open, all small subs that Prince Hunac kept for the convenience of his guests. Maijstral hopped into the nearest, a colorful green two-seater with a transparent canopy.

"Power up!" he said. "Close hatches!"

"Very good, sir," said the submarine. The instrument panel flickered to life. The controls seemed similar to an aerial flier—not surprising, considering that a submarine was just an aircraft adapted to another medium.

"Follow the submarine that just left," Maijstral said. "Top speed."

"Flank speed is not possible in the docking area."

Maijstral clenched his teeth. Hard-wired safety mechanisms, in his experience, always led to frustration.

"As fast as possible, then."

"Very good, sir." The submarine cast off and thrashed toward the tunnel entrance. Air bubbled out of ballast tanks as it began to submerge.

"Do you carry any weapons aboard?" Maijstral asked hopefully.

Artificial intelligences are incapable of surprise.

"No, sir," it said.

So much for the cheerful fantasy of a volley of torpedos to precede the submarine out of the tunnel.

The surface closed over Maijstral's head. The submarine angled down toward the brightly lit tunnel.

"Hurry," Maijstral urged.

"I am proceeding with all possible speed in view of necessary safety precautions."

Maijstral could only hope that the intruder's submarine was as obstinately safety-minded as his own.

The submarine entered the tunnel. The engine noise, magnified by the close quarters, throbbed in Maijstral's head. He wiped purple foam from his white dinner jacket.

"Is there any possibility of establishing communication with the palace?" he asked.

"I could surface to extend a radio aerial," the submarine offered.

"Never mind. Is there any way I could keep the palace informed of my location?"

"I could use active sonar."

"Please do so."

"It would be unsafe to use sonar in the tunnel. I will commence pinging as soon as we reach open water."

"Where is the other sub?"

"I have no readings on my sensors."

The submarine floated effortlessly from the tunnel and into the astonishing blue of the open water. A horrid groaning noise ensued, causing metallic objects in the submarine to rattle alarmingly. Maijstral's nerves leaped.

"What was *that?*"

"A sonar ping, sir. Shall I discontinue active sonar?"

"No. Follow the other sub and keep on pinging."

"Very good, sir."

Another groaning noise rumbled through the sub's frame. Why, Maijstral wondered, was it called a ping when it sounded more like a cetacean in the depths of some unmentionable gastric agony?

Running lights appeared ahead. "I see a submarine!" Maijstral said. It was getting closer.

"That is the craft you have asked me to follow. It has suffered damage to one of its running lights, violating safety regulations, and its autopilot is returning it to the docking bay."

Delight filled Maijstral. He had never felt like cheering a hard-wired safety mechanism before.

"Follow the sub into the dock, please," he said cheerfully.

"Very good, sir."

The two submarines passed each other, Maijstral's sub groaning in welcome, and Maijstral peered from his cockpit for a glimpse of the intruder. He was disappointed: the stranger was still wearing a darksuit, and all Maijstral could see in the other cockpit was a camouflage hologram the color of the blue ocean, marred here and there by clumps of purple fire retardant.

The submarine itself was the same two-seater sport model as Maijstral's, bright blue. Apparently the intruder hadn't planned to make an escape by submarine and had been forced to grab the first sub available.

Then the intruder's submarine gave a lurch, banked in an abrupt change of course, and sped off in a northward direction, increasing its speed.

"What happened?" Maijstral demanded. "I thought the other sub was returning to dock."

"Someone must have overridden the submarine's safety mechanisms. I will report this violation as soon as we reach our destination."

"Follow that sub!"

"Very good."

The stranger presumably had a full complement of burglar tools and the ability to override the programming of artificial intelligences. All Maijstral had were his pistol and a couple of knives he hadn't as yet removed from their sheaths. Still, if he could keep the enemy in sight, marking his location with active sonar, he should be able to attract rescuers who would help him overcome the intruder.

Maijstral's submarine appeared to be gaining on the intruder. Perhaps the intruder was not as good a pilot as Maijstral's autopilot. Maijstral's heart cheered.

Then the intruder sub peeled away from the reef, diving and circling simultaneously. "Follow!" Maijstral commanded. Diving planes made adjustments and the submarine heeled over like a falcon stooping, in slow motion, on its prey.

The submarines spiralled down into the deep, one after the other. Blackness surrounded them. Maijstral had to crane his neck left or right to keep his target in sight.

He peered out to starboard and saw the other sub slip under them, still heading for the bottom, and then leaned out to port and, after a few seconds, saw the intruder reappear. But its orientation seemed different somehow, and Maijstral's brow furrowed as he tried to work out what had changed.

"It's coming up!" he said.

Maijstral's own submarine lurched as diving planes moved to a new attitude. "The other submarine is not following safe proximity procedures," the sub said. "I will report it at the first opportunity."

Maijstral's heart gave a lurch. "What do you mean by safe *proximity*—" he began, desiring clarification.

"We are in danger of collision," the submarine announced.

The other submarine's silhouette narrowed as it presented its bow toward Maijstral. "It's trying to *ram* us?" Maijstral yelped.

"Yes, sir," the sub remarked conversationally. "I am commencing evasive—" Its tone changed radically as a clanging alarm began to sound. "Collision alert!" it shouted. "Prepare for impact!"

"Prepare *how?*" Maijstral demanded, his heart flailing as he saw the other submarine's bow growing larger. "What am I supposed to—"

Bright yellow foam exploded suddenly into the cabin from a dozen inlets, covering everything and hardening almost instantly. Maijstral was frozen in mid-complaint, mouth half-open. Frantically, he tried to gulp air. There was a hideous crash and jarring that ran up Maijstral's spine, and he felt the submarine roll alarmingly.

Maijstral tried to move, but he couldn't. The foam had frozen him in place. He couldn't see anything, but his sense of balance suggested that he and his submarine were inverted and heading for the bottom.

"Collision foam has been deployed," the submarine said, voice muffled by foam. "It should be possible to breathe through it with effort, but it will dissolve in a few seconds."

"Hwa hoing hon?" Maijstral demanded, mouth frozen with foam. The submarine nevertheless seemed to understand his demand.

"We have suffered damage to the diving planes," the submarine said. "We are compelled to continue at a downward angle until we reach the bottom."

Terror clawed at Maijstral's heart. *"He're hinking?"*

"Hull integrity is at one hundred percent," the computer reported. "We will wait at the bottom until rescue can reach us. Please try to remain calm."

"Halm?" Maijstral demanded. They'd been rammed by the enemy and were sinking, and Maijstral had been frozen into a block of quick-hardening foam, and he was supposed to remain *calm?*

"Halm?" he demanded again.

The foam was beginning to loosen its grip. Maijstral fought to free one arm, then tore away bits of foam until he could remove the pieces around his mouth.

"What about the other sub?"

"It has also sustained damage. It has undergone an emergency blowing of its ballast tanks, and has made an uncontrolled ascent to the surface." The computer adopted a bitter tone. "Its pilot will be severely disciplined when word of this reaches the authorities."

Maijstral could only hope so.

For himself, he suspected that the first person he was going to see would be Colonel-General Vandergilt.

TEN

The first person Maijstral saw, as his submarine was towed back into dock, *was* in fact Colonel-General Vandergilt. The second was Prince Hunac, still in his feathered costume, and the third was Mangula Arish, who seemed pale and unsteady but whose media globes gleamed bright and ferocious.

Nichole was not to be seen. Probably Diadem security had her under lock and key.

The sub nudged up to the dock, and the canopy hissed open. Maijstral stepped onto the dock, and Prince Hunac ran up and hit him on the chest. The clenched hand bounced off without making much of an impression.

"Yes?" Maijstral said, puzzled.

Hunac thumped him again. He kept bounding up and down on the balls of his feet, and his bright pupils looked bigger than his fists. "You abused my hospitality, you thief!" he screamed. "I challenge you!" He had lost his grip on High Khosali and spoke in Human Standard.

Maijstral realized that Hunac was only hitting him in the chest because he couldn't reach his face. "Thief?" Maijstral said. He turned vaguely and pointed at the submarine. "But you got your sub *back,*" he pointed out.

Hunac kept bouncing up and down. Somewhere in his mind Maijstral registered the fact that he had never before seen anyone who was literally hopping mad.

"I'll cut you to pieces!" Hunac said, and punched Maijstral's chest again.

Everyone, Maijstral was reminded, was trying to kill him. Or marry him. Or maybe both. There didn't need to be a reason, it was just this *thing* everyone had agreed to do at some secret meeting to which Maijstral had not been invited.

"You'll have to stand in line," Maijstral said. He picked Prince Hunac up bodily and moved him out of the way, and then began his weary trek to Nichole's quarters.

It was safer than anywhere else he could think of.

Nichole's household, of which Maijstral's soon became a subset, moved within the hour to an exclusive resort hotel outside Havana. Diadem security, appalled at their precious human commodity becoming involved in a firefight in a presumably secure place like the Underwater Palace, had called in the reserves, and soon squads of large, grim humans and even larger, grimmer Khosali were patrolling the corridors, the roof, and the public areas doing the things that security people normally do—talking into their sleeves, patting the hidden pockets that concealed their weaponry, and scrutinizing hapless tourists who were left to conclude, from their somber and ominous appearance, that there was some kind of international crime convention in town.

Maijstral, once he'd showered off the foam and changed into a dressing gown, merely lay on the bed in the darkness of his room and stared at the ceiling. He'd slammed down three brandies, but never felt less drunk in his life. Adrenaline had burned off the alcohol the second it reached his system.

He was, he realized, doomed. Three challenges in three days, and all for things he hadn't done, and there was no earthly reason why the challenges should stop now.

The stranger, of course, had got clean away. Summoned a waiting flier once the submarine surfaced, and was last tracked over the mainland, flying low to avoid detection.

Maijstral had, eventually, found out why Prince Hunac was mad at him. One of Prince Hunac's priceless prehistoric steles had been found under Maijstral's bed. The intruder had planted it there, clearly, just before Maijstral arrived and began shooting. Maijstral had encountered the perpetrator making an exit, not as he'd assumed during the break-in itself.

Prince Hunac, whose reasoning faculties had not been at their best following his consumption of whatever was in his ritual beverage, had assumed that Maijstral and the stranger were partners, that something had gone wrong with their plan, and that Maijstral and the stranger had been attempting their getaways when their submarines collided.

There were any number of problems with Prince Hunac's theory, but he wasn't in any condition to make a more logical construction, and Colonel-General Vandergilt, happy with seeing Maijstral again in trouble with one of his hosts, had not been inclined to change the Prince's mind.

Three challenges, Maijstral thought despairingly, in three days.

He was the Hereditary Prince-Bishop of Nana! he protested. How *dare* these people challenge a man of the cloth!

He tried vainly to visualize a strategy that could get him out of at least some of the fights. But every thought was interrupted by the chilling image of Joseph Bob raising the bladed end of a dire staff for the coup de grace.

The dire staff. He was going to have to do something about that.

He sprang from the bed, ready to don his darksuit and head for his burglar equipment, but at that moment the phone chimed. He went to the service plate and touched the ideogram for "phone," then another for "image."

"Hello, Drake." The Duchess looked at him with level violet eyes. "I hope I'm not interrupting your rest."

"I wasn't sleeping."

She didn't seem surprised. "I had a hard time finding where you were. And then I encountered some functionary who didn't want to forward the call."

"I'm hiding out. Nichole has much better security than I do, and —well—it seemed the best thing to make use of it." He stepped toward the bed and sat on it so as to make it clear to Roberta that if he was not-sleeping tonight, he was not-sleeping alone.

It wasn't that he was immune to the thought of Nichole's comfort, but he had never felt less erotic than he did right now. Plus, he needed to be alone in order to skulk.

"I'm sorry if I neglected to communicate with you," he said. "My life has been . . . overwhelming . . . of late."

"So Kuusinen told me. It's obvious that you are the victim of a conspiracy."

He forced a haunted smile. "I would like to think so. If these are all random occurrences, then the universe is far more erratic than I'd ever suspected."

Roberta showed no sign of amusement. "Kuusinen said that you suspected the Bubber."

"Yes."

She gave a little shake of her head. "I don't think your theory holds water. He can't be responsible for what happened at the Underwater Palace."

He can if I *say* he is, Maijstral thought, but there was too much sense in what Roberta had just said.

Roberta's look softened. "Besides," she said, "he's been working constantly to prevent the duel. I've seen him try, but Joseph Bob won't see reason. Will's terrified that his brother will be hurt."

"A good sociopath would be able to imitate those emotions quite well," Maijstral pointed out.

The Duchess looked doubtful. "If you say so," she said.

"I'm open to any other theories," Maijstral said.

She bit her lip. "I don't have one. And we've only got a few hours."

"Yes."

Doomed, Maijstral thought. The word, rolling about in his brain, had a certain orotund majesty, like a tolling bell.

Doomed, doomed, doomed.

Roberta cleared her throat. Her eyes were shiny and she was blinking hard. She tried to make her tone businesslike. "I've arranged for a medical team to be present. There will be media globes recording the event to show that it will be fair. Kuusinen said that you accepted his offer to practice with the staffs, but that there wasn't an opportunity."

Roberta's tears were beginning to have their effect upon Maijstral. His own eyes stung. He wanted to sit in the dark and have a good long cry.

"I'll pick you up half an hour before sunrise," Roberta said.

"I will look forward to seeing you," he said.

For the last time, his inner voice added.

They both rang off before the call got too soppy. Maijstral dried his eyes and got his darksuit from the closet. He put it on and felt better at once.

He'd fixed one duel, he thought, and by the Active Virtues he'd fix a hundred if he had to.

The Bubber frowned into the phone pickups that were transmitting his image to Joseph Bob. "I think Maijstral has a good case," he said.

"For stealing from me?" Joseph Bob asked. The Prince was in the act of practicing with his weapon. Light glinted off the wicked blades of the dire staff as he advanced, whirling the staff before him.

"Maijstral's got two more challenges in the last two days."

Joseph Bob halted, frowned, grounded his weapon. "They're not going to fight him first, are they?"

"No. Of course not."

"So what's the problem?"

"It bolsters Maijstral's case that there's some murderous conspiracy involved."

Joseph Bob hoisted his weapon again. "Well, *I'm* not a conspirator," he said.

"Of course not. But if it were to turn out that you were the *dupe* of a conspirator, it wouldn't look good for us."

Joseph Bob thought about this for a moment, twirling the staff idly.

"I'm just looking out for our interests, J.B.," the Bubber added.

Joseph Bob nodded. "You've a point there," he conceded. "But it also doesn't look good if I let people steal from me." He gave another brisk nod as he came to a decision. "Tell you what—if it turns out there's a conspiracy involved, I'll challenge the conspirators, too, for daring to use me in their plans." He gave a boyish grin. *"That'll* take care of it."

Still grinning, he lunged with the weapon, meanwhile giving out the paralyzing Yell of Hate recommended by the best combat instructors.

The Bubber sighed. "Well," he said. "If you're *sure."*

"Of *course* I'm sure," Joseph Bob said, falling briefly on guard, and then he attacked again. *"Yaaaaaah!"* he shouted.

The Bubber terminated the call and walked into the other room where Her Grace of Benn waited. In order to have neutral territory in which to conduct negotiations, they had rented a room in Key West, and the place suffered from an overindulgence in the rustic and picturesque: woven palm frond lampshades, fishnets drooping from the ceiling, an ashtray made to resemble a starfish.

"Didn't work, I'm afraid," the Bubber said.

Roberta made a face. "It was worth a try."

"It was a good argument. *I* would have been convinced. But J.B. is having too good a time to really pay attention to quibbles." He sat next to Roberta and patted pockets for his cigaret case. "He's enjoying this belated discovery of martial ardor far too much," he said glumly. "It's being brought up in a house full of weapons, I suppose, and early exposure to all the stories about our ancestors' prowess . . . the warrior spirit was bound to break out sooner or later. I'm just sorry it's wrecking your engagement."

"If it *is* an engagement," Roberta said, equally morose. The Bubber produced his cigaret case and then looked at it for a moment as if he couldn't remember why he'd been searching for it.

"Could I have one of those?" Roberta asked. "It's bad for training, but occasionally one has cravings."

He handed her a cigaret and began a search through pockets for his lighter, but Roberta found hers first. They puffed in somber silence for a moment.

"He's run off to Nichole," she remarked. "I suppose there's nothing in it—she's an old friend and everything—but I'd much rather he'd run off to *me.*"

The Bubber did his best to be helpful. "Well, he couldn't, could he? I've been taking up all your time."

Roberta rose from her cane chair. "There's nothing left to arrange, is there?" she said, and walked toward the door. "I might as well try to get a few hours' sleep."

"You think you can sleep?" the Bubber asked in surprise. "I know I won't catch so much as a wink."

She hesitated by the door. "Well," she said. "I suppose you're right."

"There's an all-night bistro down the street," the Bubber said. "Perhaps we could have some coffee and a pastry."

"Oh." Roberta tilted her head and considered. "I suppose I might as well join you," she said. "The coffee will be welcome, but I don't think I could eat anything."

The Bubber flicked ashes into the starfish ashtray and rose, then hesitated on his way to the door. "I say," he said. "Would you mind if I asked you a question?"

"Go ahead."

"I haven't—er—bungled this horribly, have I? I haven't got my brother killed without realizing it?"

Roberta smiled and patted his arm. "You've done very well," she said.

"Oh." A surprised look crossed the Bubber's face. "Well. That's all right, then."

Maijstral left the hotel after telling the security people he needed some time alone, and flew off with the impression they were happy to see the back of him. Once in Tejas, he scouted the perimeter of Joseph Bob's estate, then left the car, activated his darksuit, and flew on silent repellers to the Prince's huge manor house.

His plan was simple. He'd sabotage the stunner on the one end of Joseph Bob's dire staff so that it wouldn't work at all, and then take care of the bladed end through the use of a resonance ring, a clever bit of burglar's paraphernalia intended for use on barred windows. The ring would snap around the bar in question, then find the frequency of the metal. A resonance effect would be set up that would shatter the crystalline bonds holding together the metal's molecules. The metal would weaken, then come apart.

Maijstral planned merely to weaken Joseph Bob's staff near its bladed head. Then, first thing in the fight, he'd take a swipe at the blades, and the thing would come off.

Everyone, he hopefully presumed, would believe that the old weapon suffered from metal fatigue, or perhaps just conclude that Maijstral was a far stronger warrior than he looked.

After disabling Joseph Bob's weapon, Maijstral would keep hitting away until he'd either won or the seconds put an end to it. Either way, honor was satisfied, and he would decline any challenge to a second encounter.

Maijstral broke into Joseph Bob's house easily enough, then headed for the exercise room, where Joseph Bob might have been practicing with his weapon. No dire staffs were to be found. He went to the study, in case the dire staff was hung on the wall with Joseph Bob's other weapons, but it wasn't there, either.

Good grief, Maijstral thought, is he *sleeping* with the damned thing?

He floated up to the regal apartments and glided to the door of the Prince's room. He deployed his scanners, but the audio scanner failed to report the sound of breathing, and the infrared scanner detected no body temperature.

Maijstral peeled the lock and entered. No one sleeping here: the bed had not even been turned down. No dire staff.

An uneasy feeling began to creep up Maijstral's spine. No, Maijstral thought, the Prince was just spending his last night with his Princess. Where was Arlette's room?

Arlette's room proved empty as well. Maijstral felt his mouth go dry. He flew along the corridor, peeling locks and entering rooms. The whole family had left, and Maijstral didn't know where.

Terror beat a tattoo in his heart. He wiped his forehead and tried frantically to guess where the family might have gone. Somewhere closer to the site of the duel, perhaps, Key West or Miami or even Havana. They might be in the same resort as Maijstral and Nichole!

The point was, he didn't know. He had no knowledge of what holdings the Prince or the Bubber might have in the Caribbean, and he had no idea, on such short notice, how to find out.

What, he considered, would happen if he just got back in his flier and zoomed off to continue his life as if nothing had happened? Live off his loot, or perhaps check into a New Puritan monastery and announce that he'd found God.

He would be disgraced, of course. Most if not all of his friends would drop him. There would be no question of marriage to the likes of Roberta or Nichole—they'd flee in disgust at the very mention of his name. He would no longer be able to float about at the top of society, picking his scores and earning a good living from commissions. The Imperial Sporting Commission might well revoke his license, which would mean that he could be arrested much more easily. If he ever needed money, he'd have to sneak about, travel incognito, and take down vaults and storehouses just for the money, and he'd be very, very vulnerable to the police.

And all because he didn't want to get killed. How fair was *that?* he wanted to know.

But the thing that really chilled his blood was the realization that Roman might leave his employ. Roman had standards. Roman was devoted to all the ideals implied by that scroll he'd created: family and honor and nobility. Maijstral didn't believe in any of these things, but Roman did, and if Maijstral betrayed them all in one fell swoop, then Roman, he was sure, would be compelled to leave him.

How could he survive without Roman? Roman was his prop, his anchor, the one certain, unequivocal thing in his difficult and equivocal life. Roman was *home.*

Roman had saved Maijstral's life a dozen times. If Roman left, Maijstral might as well be dead anyhow.

And if he was going to die, the duel was as good a place as any.

But still, there had to be an escape. He gave desperate thought to the matter.

Well, he thought, he was here in Joseph Bob's house; he had

sufficient gadgets to get him access to Joseph Bob's computers; and they could very likely get him a list of the family holdings. It might be possible to find that dire staff yet.

He might as well get busy. He had nothing else to do than die.

"Roberta?"

"Yes?"

"It's time to get in our aerocars and pick up our duellists."

"How far do you have to go?"

"Only as far as Key Largo. My brother's staying at the estate of Lord Pony. J.B. wanted to be able to practice with the staff and not have to deal with any interruptions. He hasn't told anyone he's there except family."

"Well, I don't have much farther to fly myself."

"Havana, yes?"

"Yes."

"A lovely place. You might stop there on your honeymoon, if things work out."

Beat.

"Was that a really tactless thing to say?"

A sigh. "I don't think so. But I'll give it further thought, if you like."

Doomed, doomed, doomed.

The word rang through Maijstral's head as he stood wrapped in a cloak on the verge of the sea.

Doomed, doomed, doomed.

He had found a list of all of Joseph Bob's possessions in the Caribbean. He had flown to every single one of them, his desperation increasing with the cumulative realization that neither Joseph Bob nor his dire staff was in any one of them.

Doomed, doomed, doomed.

Finally he'd run out of options. He had nothing to do but return to Havana, pick up his staff, head out to the Dry Tortugas, and die like a gentleman.

Doomed, doomed, doomed.

He shifted his weight on the sand and gazed out to the dark, predawn sea, hoping that someone would sail over the horizon to his rescue—smugglers, pirates, Colonel-General Vandergilt, anyone.

Doomed, doomed, doomed.

After his return to Havana he'd figured he might as well give fighting a chance, and he'd had Roman give him a lesson with the dire staff. It had been a disaster. The staff was solid steel and immeasurably heavy—every movement seemed to take forever and left him panting for breath. The wicked nest of interlaced blades on the end of the staff were appallingly sharp. He'd fired off the stunner once by accident and put his own foot to sleep.

He could not rely on martial prowess. And his only chance to rig the outcome had failed.

Doomed, doomed, doomed.

"Drake? It's time."

Roberta touched him lightly on the shoulder.

"I need to do your hair."

He gazed at the sea while Roberta tied his hair back with a ribbon. Then he turned and followed her to the designated spot. He took off the cloak, and Roman approached and handed him his staff.

"Remember," Roman said. "Get inside him. Hit left and right."

Maijstral didn't understand a word of it. It all sounded like the most inane babble in the world. "Yes," he said. "Thank you."

"Don't forget the Yell of Hate."

Maijstral nodded.

Roberta squeezed his arm. He felt the moist touch of her lips on his cheek. "Come back to me," she said.

Doomed, doomed, doomed.

Joseph Bob marched toward him confidently, the rising sun gleaming on his perfect blond hair. He looked utterly at home in this circumstance, and he carried his dire staff with confident ease. His lips were turned up in a slight smile. He looked as if he were on his way to a game of cards.

The only imperfection was the slight swelling around the broken nose—he'd removed his semilife patches so that they wouldn't interfere with his vision during the fight.

Doomed, doomed, doomed.

It was at this point, viewing his opponent, that resentment rose in Maijstral. How *dare* the man smile! How *dare* he look so perfectly at ease, so *sans-peur-et-sans-reproche,* so damned *happy to be here!* The man was a *fool.* A dupe. He was being used as a puppet by a legion of conspirators, and he neither knew nor cared.

"Ready!" The Bubber's voice broke and squeaked on the second syllable.

Combats with the dire staff begin *corps-a-corps,* with each staff held crosswise in both hands and touching, so that neither side could get off an easy shot with the stunner right at the start. Maijstral braced himself and pushed his weapon forward, felt Joseph Bob's weight as the two staffs came into contact.

Joseph Bob gave a little grunt of satisfaction as he leaned his mass into Maijstral. He was bigger and stronger and had longer arms, and the advantage was all his. Maijstral felt Joseph Bob's weight driving him into the ground like a tent peg, and dug his heels into the sand to arrest his backward movement. His arms were already tired.

"Begin on the count of three!" the Bubber shouted. *"One . . ."*

In the corner of his eye Maijstral could see media globes winking in the sun. This whole fiasco was being recorded in order to demonstrate to the authorities that it was fair.

Fair. The whole notion made Maijstral's blood boil. What was fair about a big, strong idiot being permitted to butcher a smaller, far more intelligent man?

"Two!"

Joseph Bob was a *moron!* A *simpleton!* How *dare* he be so casual about this?

"Three!"

Maijstral's resentment and indignation burst from his throat in a shattering scream.

"Yaaaaaaaah!" he yelled.

ELEVEN

Maijstral opened his eyes and blinked lazily at the ceiling. He yawned. He stretched. He rose from his bed and planted his bare feet on the floor and clenched his toes in the thick nap of the carpet.

He looked down at his knuckles. They were reddened and swollen and a bit sore. He flexed them in time with the clenching of his toes.

Voices were heard from the drawing room adjacent. Maijstral padded to the door, opened it, and entered the room.

Roberta, Nichole, and Kuusinen were watching a video and chatting. Glasses, bottles, and dirty dishes were strewn on tables. It was perhaps the twentieth time they'd seen the video, and they hadn't tired of it yet.

"Do you know," Roberta said, "I believe this is the first time I've ever seen one human being climb another."

In the video, Maijstral and Joseph Bob were facing each other, each with dire staff braced. The Bubber called out commands. And then, before Joseph Bob could move, Maijstral screamed, batted the Prince's dire staff out of the way, then threw down his own weapon and launched himself at his foe.

"Clever," Kuusinen commented. "Butting His Highness on his broken nose that way."

Maijstral couldn't remember any of it. He could view the video almost as if he were watching Laurence play some Maijstral-analogue in a fictional adventure. He was fairly certain that his head butt to Joseph Bob's nose was an accident, but he couldn't swear to it.

On the video, the Prince lurched as Maijstral climbed his front like a squirrel climbing a tree. Maijstral bit, punched, butted, and gouged. He screamed aloud the entire time. The Prince staggered, dropped his staff, and fell backward to the sand with Maijstral on top. Maijstral, still screaming, sat on his chest and hammered his head into the sand with his fists until Roberta and the Bubber dashed in to seize him and drag him off his prey.

"That's quite a Yell of Hate," Roberta observed.

"Drake looks like an *animal,*" Nichole said, a bit wide-eyed. Despite their long acquaintance, this was clearly an aspect of Maijstral that was new to her.

"Is it feeding time at the zoo?" Maijstral asked. They all turned to him in surprise. Nichole flushed with embarassment at being overheard.

Silent entrances were a signal feature of Maijstral's profession.

"Slept well?" Roberta asked.

"I think I can safely say it was the sleep of the just."

He sat beside Roberta on a settee and she took his hand. "We've been discussing you," she said. "And we've come to some conclusions."

"Other than the observation that I'm an animal?"

"That, too."

Maijstral flexed a hand and wondered a bit at the video he'd just seen. His astonishment at himself was still in a very tender state. He had some years before concluded that he no longer possessed the ability to surprise himself, and over time he'd managed to reconcile himself to the idea that he was incapable of facing physical danger; but the video was clear evidence that his notions of himself needed an overhaul.

If only he could *remember.* He couldn't recall a thing from the moment the Bubber counted three till Roberta and the Bubber hauled him off the Prince's splayed and hapless form.

Nichole turned to Kuusinen. "Mr. Kuusinen, I think, can outline the substance of our conversation."

"Could you call for dinner first?" Maijstral asked. "I'm starving."

He hadn't, he realized, eaten in days. His meals kept getting interrupted.

Maijstral's dinner was ordered from room service, then he poured himself champagne from a half-empty bottle that was sitting convenient to hand in a silver bucket. Kuusinen frowned, settled himself in his chair, and began his summary.

"It's obvious enough that you are the victim of a conspiracy," he said. "Our difficulty is that, while we can eliminate any number of suspects, we still have no firm idea who is behind it all, or what that person's motive might be.

"The conspiracy would seem to be aimed at getting you challenged by those people who have consented to be your hosts while you've been staying on Earth. The first attempt, at the home of the Prince of Tejas, was successful—"

A memory bubbled, like champagne, to the surface of Maijstral's mind. "It wasn't the first," he said suddenly. "When I was staying with Lord Huyghe, Conchita Sparrow saw someone in a darksuit hovering outside my window. The intruder fled, and I've assumed all along it was a police spy of some sort, but now it seems likely the stranger was a member of the conspiracy."

Kuusinen nodded. "That datum somewhat alters the time scheme," he said. "Your enemies are very well organized. Perhaps we should begin by itemizing their knowledge and capabilities."

He held up a finger. "First, they're aware of your travel schedule, and have laid plans in advance." Another finger. "Second, they include in their number a burglar of considerable prowess—Roman informed us that he had booby-trapped your room in the Underwater Palace such that it would have taken a burglar of no small competence to break in undetected, and of course it would have taken an extremely capable burglar to have stolen Prince Hunac's stele in the first place."

"That leaves out the Bubber," Roberta said. "Will probably could have stolen and planted the pistol, but he wasn't anywhere near the Underwater Palace, and nothing in his background suggests he could at any point in his life have acquired any competence as a thief."

Maijstral frowned into his champagne. "I have given some consideration to the notion that Drexler might be responsible," he said.

"Roman informs us," Kuusinen said, "that he and Drexler were dining together in the servants' hall of the Underwater Palace when you came across the burglar."

"Oh."

At this point the door chime gave a soft, shimmery noise; and three individuals, uniformed as splendidly as fleet admirals and operating in efficient silence, delivered Maijstral's dinner and swept away the dirty plates. The conversation suspended itself while they were in the room. It was always possible that one of them had been corrupted by the media.

As the grand potentates of room service bowed their way out, Maijstral applied himself to his plate. Sea lion Provencal, one of his favorites, mixed vegetables in season, and little heads of khronkh, fried crispy.

Kuusinen frowned and looked at his hand, with the first two fingers extended, and quite visibly rewound his summary, mentally replayed his earlier remarks, and then, once he located himself, recommenced. He thrust out his third finger.

"Three," he said. "The conspirators seem possessed of an undying, obsessive, seemingly irrational hatred toward you yourself, Mr. Maijstral. Who do you know that hates you so much?"

Bewilderment settled about Maijstral. "I can't think of anyone I've offended that badly," he said. "Fine, I've *stolen* things from people, but *still* . . ."

"*I* still wonder," Nichole added, "if perhaps the two burglaries are unrelated. Perhaps the first was planned for some perfectly rational reason—by the Bubber, say, as a scheme to get his brother's property—and the second was planned by someone who had heard about your problem with Joseph Bob and wanted to exploit the situation somehow."

"Who?" Kuusinen asked.

"Alice Manderley, perhaps?" Nichole ventured. "She *is* a first-class burglar and is, I presume, capable of breaking into Drake's room. . . ."

"But why would she do it?" Roberta interrupted. "What could her scheme have been?"

"Who knows? Drake interrupted it. Perhaps she wanted to steal a whole lot of steles, and planted one under Drake's bed so he'd be the one to bear the blame."

Kuusinen looked at Nichole levelly. "You pointed out, I believe, that she was in attendance at Prince Hunac's ceremony, and therefore unable to break into Mr. Maijstral's room."

Nichole's face fell. "Oh. I *did* say that, didn't I? I forgot."

Maijstral cast his mind back to the ceremony. "I wouldn't write her off entirely," he said. "I saw her at the ceremony, but she was wandering in the back of the room, away from everyone. And her husband was not with her."

"You believe her husband capable of taking the stele?" Kuusinen asked.

"I don't believe Kenny is capable of tying a bootlace without her help," Maijstral said. "But Alice might still have planted the stele while Kenny wandered about the ceremony wearing a hologram of Alice. It's misdirection, a basic element of magic. The fact that Alice wasn't a part of the crowd, and wasn't talking to anyone, might serve as evidence."

"It's a common tactic burglars use to mislead people," Nichole added. "Drake used to do it all the time."

"I still do."

"I'll keep my researchers busy regarding Alice Manderley," Nichole said. "And her husband."

"You might check again the list of high-rated burglars on Earth," Maijstral added. "There can't be many who are capable of leaving something the size of a Mayan stele in my room without setting off at least one of the traps I'd set."

"We're also checking everyone at Prince Hunac's party."

"And speaking of the party," Maijstral said, and felt his injured eye give a twitch. "Who was that Milo person?"

"Captain Milo Hay," Kuusinen said promptly. "He is the fiance of Major Ruth Song, the Elvis impersonator."

"I didn't steal anything from *him,*" Maijstral said. "Is he a participant in this conspiracy or not?"

The others looked at each other. "We don't know," Kuusinen admitted.

"He called me a 'rat-lover,' " Maijstral said, "and this was the second time I've heard about rats, the first being from Kenny Chang, of all people, and in connection with the Security and Sedition Act. What is a rat exactly, and why is loving one supposed to be so bad?"

The others looked at each other uneasily again. "A rat," Kuusinen said finally, "is a scavenging Earth animal widely regarded as a destructive pest. On account of a fancied resemblance, certain organizations in the Constellation have applied the term to the Khosali."

Distaste narrowed Maijstral's heavy-lidded eyes. "The 'prohuman' element, I presume," he said, deliberately inserting the quotation marks in his tone.

"Indeed," Kuusinen agreed. "Not coincidentally, the same people who are the most loud in support of the Security and Sedition

Act, which will prevent nonhumans from advancing past a certain rank in the military and civil service, and subject the rest to random, intrusive investigation."

Roberta smiled grimly. "Investigation, one gathers, at the hands of our friend Colonel-General Vandergilt."

Kuusinen nodded. "Her among others."

Maijstral fingered his diamond ring. "Is Captain Hay another pillar of the Constellation's security establishment? I didn't recognize his uniform."

"Captain Hay did not in fact receive his rank from the Constellation military," Kuusinen said. "He is a member of something called the Human Guard, a paramilitary organization devoted to protecting the Constellation from alleged enemies foreign and domestic."

Maijstral nodded. "And Captain Hay—*Milo*—perceives me as an enemy of the domestic variety."

"As we can detect no connection between him and you or your family, we suspect his aggression toward you may have been motivated by ideology, yes."

"And drink," added Nichole.

Maijstral ground his teeth. He had encountered this sort of fanatic before—on Peleng they called themselves Humanity Prime—and he had found them a severe and constant trial.

Of course on Peleng he'd also got a lot of money out of them, so the encounter hadn't been all bad.

Maijstral looked down at his plate and realized that his meal was gone. He didn't remember eating it.

Perhaps he was beginning to suffer from random outbreaks of amnesia.

He was still hungry. He ordered another dinner identical to the first.

"Do I really have to fight this Milo person?" Maijstral asked. "I'd think ax handles in a dark alley would be more his style than a fair combat."

"He hasn't been heard from since his challenge," Roberta said. "Nor has any second. He may have sobered up and decided not to pursue the matter."

Nichole's face settled into a satisfied smile. "Or," she added, "Prince Hunac's guards are still pursuing *him.*"

"Major Song tried her best to excuse Milo's actions," Maijstral said. "I take it she is also a member of the Human Guard?"

"No," Kuusinen said. "She is in fact an officer in the Constellation Marines, though she is on extended leave to prepare for the

Memphis Olympiad. Her grandfather, incidentally, was the late Fleet Admiral Song, hero of the Battle of Neerwinden."

As celebrated a military hero, Maijstral knew, as the Constellation's brief history offered. Neerwinden had been the first great victory for rebellious humanity.

"You'd think, with a grandfather as famous as all that, she'd know the difference between a genuine military and a false one," Maijstral said.

"She's a false Elvis," Nichole shrugged. "Her purchase on reality may not be of the highest order."

The discussion of Milo and Major Song had brought Maijstral's mind back to issues of personal survival. "Has Prince Hunac been heard from?" he asked.

"No," Nichole said, "though that's not surprising. Considering what he ingested yesterday, we suspect it will take him a lot longer to sober up than it will Captain Hay."

"I'd appreciate it if you'd appoint me as your second for both fights," Roberta said. "I'm experienced at it by now, and I have a tack I'd like to try with each of your foes."

"Yes?" Maijstral asked.

"My plans are different for each. With Hunac I'll try reason—all the arguments that *didn't* work with Joseph Bob, but might well work with someone less hungry for glory. I will simply offer him the evidence of a conspiracy and ask him to postpone things until we can find out who's responsible. He may prove amenable, though since his challenge was offered publicly, he may have a difficult time withdrawing entirely."

Maijstral's nerves gave a little wail at this conclusion. "Very well," he managed. "And how do you intend to handle Milo?"

Roberta looked at him levelly. "I plan to frighten the daylights out of him," she said, matter-of-fact. "And for that, I would like your permission to release to the media the video of your encounter with Joseph Bob. Milo may *really* want to reconsider when he sees it."

Maijstral showed his teeth. "When he sees my animal nature, you mean."

"Exactly."

"Besides," Nichole pointed out, "there's an army of media swarming just outside our hotel's perimeter. It's like an armed camp out there. We'll never be able to do anything unless we give them *something,* and I think the video and perhaps a press conference, with you, Drake, at your most outgoing and genial, if you please."

"I will try to summon such bonhomie as remains."

"It's only after we get rid of most of the press that we can enter into our plan."

Maijstral's eyebrows lifted. *"Our* plan?"

"Quite," Roberta said. "Since we don't know as yet who is responsible for your misfortunes, we've decided to go on a fishing expedition. Right now there's a wall of Diadem security around you, and it's unlikely anyone would try to penetrate it."

Maijstral felt a warm glow of inner gratification at this sentiment.

"But if you leave," Nichole added with a smile, "the conspirators may strike again. And that's exactly what we want."

A chill wafted up Maijstral's spine. "We want *what?"* he asked.

"We want to lure them into trying to frame you a third time," Roberta said. "And when they come, we'll be ready."

"We will?" Maijstral asked.

"Oh yes. We'll catch them, force them to confess, and get you off the hook. Nothing easier."

Maijstral had an intuition it was all going to be more complicated than that.

He looked from Roberta to Nichole and back again.

Taking dead aim, he thought. Magician's cant, and also what had been happening to him.

The conspirators, whoever they were, had taken dead aim at him in hopes of getting him killed or slammed away in prison.

Roberta had taken dead aim at him for her marriage scheme.

Nichole had done much the same.

Now the two of them together were about to put him in harm's way once more.

And Maijstral had the horrid, queasy feeling that he had no choice but to let them do it.

TWELVE

The meeting with the press was going rather well, Maijstral thought. Media globes winked in the sunlight overhead. The courtyard of the hotel was filled with reporters. Most of the questions concerned his encounter with Joseph Bob—his "strategy" for victory, his "feelings" during the fight.

Since he hadn't possessed the former, and couldn't recall the latter, he was free to invent something that cast himself in a suitably noble light.

Because their quarrel was based on a misunderstanding, he said, he didn't want to kill Joseph Bob; and therefore he resorted to fists.

His feelings, he reported, were such a mixture that it was difficult to define any of them very well. He then let the reporters suggest emotions to him, and he picked the ones he liked best.

Determination to win at all costs?

Yes.

Concern for Joseph Bob's welfare?

Naturally.

Fear?

"Well," he said, laughing, "of *course.*" And the reporters laughed with him.

One smiling young man waved a hand. "Have you heard of Laurence's offer to stand as your second for your other two fights?"

"Sorry?" Maijstral said. "Who?"

"Laurence. The video star who—"

"Oh yes! Laurence! Of course." Maijstral winced inwardly. "I'm sorry, I didn't hear—"

Somehow he knew he was going to pay for this.

Maijstral was mistaken in reckoning that the payment would not come immediately, however. At that moment an elderly man, white of hair and erect of bearing, strode from the crowd and brought his cane down on Maijstral's head.

"Dastard!" the old man cried in a passion. "I had the honor to serve under your grandfather, and I counted your father as a friend. How dare you disavow their cause? How dare you disavow your Emperor?"

Maijstral, from his position on the ground, rubbed his head and looked at the old man in amazement.

"Who *are* you?" he demanded.

"I am Baron Sancho Sandoval Cabeza de Vaca," the man said grandly, and pointed at Maijstral with his cane. "And *you,*" he added, "are a dastard! I challenge you to single combat."

Rage exploded in Maijstral. He jumped up, snatched the cane from the Baron's grip, and snapped it over his knee.

The Baron glared at him. He glared back.

"Perhaps," cried the voice of Mangula Arish from somewhere in the crowd, "you should again consider apologizing for your controversial remarks the other day. . . ."

Maijstral observed that Arish had her hair firmly lacquered back into place. On the whole, he preferred it limp and covered with purple goo.

"I think," Maijstral said, blood boiling, "this meeting is over."

He stalked back to the hotel and made his way to Nichole's suite. She looked up in surprise as he slammed the door behind him.

"Have we got *another* plan?" he asked.

Well, no, they didn't. So Maijstral and his suite flew on to Memphis, where they were to stay at the home of Tvar, a well-known art collector and an old acquaintance for whom Maijstral had performed several commissions. Tvar had been contacted by Nichole ahead of time and, no less immune to certain forms of glamor than the public at large, had been so dazzled by the call from one of the Three Hundred that the warning that she was likely to be burglarized by Maijstral's unknown enemies had only provoked in her a casual flick of her pointed ears.

"How *exciting,*" she'd said, her tongue lolling in a Khosali smile. "Perhaps I will have a chance to *shoot these conspirators down like dogs.*"

When this comment was relayed to Maijstral, the sentiment could not help but meet with his wholehearted approval.

On the horizon, Maijstral saw the minarets and domes of Graceland as he came in for a landing at Tvar's estate. He hadn't realized Tvar's place was so close. Before he'd stepped from his flier, Tvar emerged from the front door, arms outstretched in welcome.

She was a Khosalikh of medium build—a head taller than Maijstral, who was slightly above average height for a human—and was dressed extravagantly in a gown of rainbow texture that made her seem rather larger than she was. Her pointed ears peeked from a particolored turban ornamented with flashing gems. Chiming on her wrists were the bracelets that she'd commissioned Maijstral to acquire for her: they had once belonged to Lady Scarlett, the patroness of the poet who went by the name "Ptarmigan"—the bracelets were not very valuable, but Tvar coveted them for their associations.

She also had Lady Scarlett's liver in a cryonic reliquary on her mantel. She'd bought it at auction and hadn't had to use Maijstral as an agent for that one.

Tvar embraced Maijstral and sniffed his ears. "How pleasant to see you again!" she cried, and cocked her ears toward the boundaries of her estate. "I see you brought a flock of birds with you."

"Carrion crows, I'm afraid," Maijstral said, and glanced over his shoulder at the media fliers dropping to a landing outside Tvar's property.

"Hoping to follow you to your next duel, I imagine."

"And hoping you'll punch me while the cameras are looking," Maijstral added.

He turned as another, larger flier settled onto the lawn, and opened to reveal its passengers. "May I present Her Grace Roberta Altunin, the Duchess of Benn? And her aunt, the Honorable Bathsheba sar Altunin. Mr. Paavo Kuusinen."

There was a formal sniffing of ears. Tvar gestured toward the flier's roomy storage compartment. "Who's in the box?"

"My father, the late Duke."

"Shall we put him in the crypt, or give him a room?"

"A room, please," said Aunt Batty indulgently. "I'd like to have someone to talk to while the young people are going about their business."

"Anastasia?" the late Gustav queried. "Is that you, Anastasia?"

"No, Dad," Maijstral said. "Mother's not here."

"Anastasia isn't here?" The ex-Duke sounded disappointed. "I thought I heard her voice."

Maijstral maintained a grip on her patience. "You don't even like her, Dad. Remember?"

Ex-Dornier paused for thought. "Oh. Yes," he said. "That's right. I forgot."

"Isn't Nichole coming?" Tvar asked.

"Not at present," Maijstral said. "No." Tvar's ears drooped in disappointment.

The cold-coffin was shown to its room, and Roman and Drexler were set to work booby-trapping Maijstral's suite for the anticipated descent of Maijstral's unknown enemy. Maijstral, Roberta, and Aunt Batty were given a tour of Tvar's collection, which featured sensational artifacts mixed with sculptures and canvases that inclined in their subject matter toward the lurid. Probably the best was Mixton's *Baroness Kharniver Eating the Heart of Her Lover,* though Maijstral had a sentimental fondness for Actvor's *The Dying Ralph Adverse Gazes on the Shard,* which artfully balanced in its composition the glowing face of the dying burglar, the crystal glass of poison, and the fabulous, shining gem whose original, more luminous than any possible representation, Maijstral had first seen about Roberta's throat, and which he had in short order removed therefrom.

If Maijstral had an appropriate wall to hang the painting on, he might have acquired it for himself. But from his father he'd inherited practically no property at all, no wall, no mantelpiece, no alcove—nothing suitable for displaying anything fine, anyway. His entire domestic establishment consisted of Roman, Drexler, and a large assortment of luggage. If any great artworks came into his hands, they passed out as efficiently as they'd come.

Maijstral looked at Roberta and, with a start, realized that this situation might soon change. Roberta had walls and mantelpieces in abundance. If he married her, he could probably put anything he wanted on them.

What *would* he want on his walls? he wondered. And what steps would he have to take to make certain that none of his colleagues removed what he put there?

"And here," Tvar said, pointing to an instrument glittering in a case, "is the spoon that the Marquess of Tharkar used to remove his heir's eyes during an argument over dessert." Her tongue lolled in amusement.

"What was the argument about?" Batty asked.

"Dessert, as I said."

"I thought you said it was during dessert."

"The argument was *over* dessert, not *during* dessert. They fought over what flavor of sherbet to serve, I think." Tvar's eyes glittered with amusement. "You know, it is generally believed that the Khosali are a lot more steady, reliable, and law-abiding than humans . . . but I must say that when we go bad, we *really go bad.*" She cocked one ear toward Maijstral. "You know, Drake, you might consider spoons as weapons in your next combat."

Maijstral grinned with forced jocularity.

"I will if the other fellow will."

Roberta gave him a superior look. "Oh," she said. "And as to weapons, I have a much better idea than *that.* And by the way, if Captain Hay ever calls, may I borrow Roman for the meeting?"

"Hello?"

Roberta smiled as she saw who had telephoned her. "Will!" she said. "I hadn't expected to hear from you."

"I just called to let you know that J.B.'s been released from the hospital. He broke a cheekbone, and rebroke the nose and lost some teeth, and there are bruises and some nasty cuts—I think from that diamond of Maijstral's—but it's nothing that can't be repaired."

"I'm glad to hear it."

"Yes. He'll soon be good as new—better, once the teeth are replaced with implants." Pause. "You and I are still friends, aren't we? I mean, we can still speak to each other and everything?"

"Of course we can."

"Good. I'm relieved. Because I'd like to express my thanks for your part in forming Maijstral's strategy and keeping everything non-lethal."

"Well," a smile, "I'm afraid I can't claim credit for that. It was all Drake's doing."

"Oh. Well. I suppose I can't exactly call him and thank him, can I?"

"I don't see why not."

"Really?" Brightening. "Do you think it would be good form?"

"Certainly. It wasn't your fight, it wasn't your grudge. If we can all be friends again, so much the better."

"Wonderful. But I don't suppose . . ." A long pause.

"Yes?"

"I don't suppose I can resume my magic lessons."

"Well," laughing, "I think Drake is rather busy now."

"Yes. Of course. But still, it would be very nice to see you—to see you all again."

"I will look forward."

There was the sound of a chime.

"I've got to go, Will. I've got another call."

"Well. Talk to you later, then."

"I'll look forward to it."

Roberta switched to the other call and found herself gazing into the shaded eyes of someone who looked remarkably like Elvis Presley.

"Your grace?" the Elvis said. "I am Major Song. Captain Hay has asked me to act for him in the matter of his fight with Drake Maijstral."

"Ah," Roberta said. "I see."

She took a breath and steeled herself.

She knew exactly what she wanted to do.

Conchita Sparrow blinked in surprise when she saw who had phoned her.

"Miss Sparrow," Maijstral said, "are you busy?"

"I'd imagine that *you'd* be," she said. "What is it, three duels left?"

"I have no intention of keeping track," Maijstral said.

The score would be too depressing in any case.

"The media are full of the story," Conchita said. "Several of the broadcasters seem to have converted to twenty-four-hour Maijstral channels."

That, Maijstral reflected, was too depressing all by itself.

"I was wondering if I could hire you for a few days," he said.

Conchita looked puzzled. "You need me to build some gear?"

"No," Maijstral said. "Not really."

She grinned. "I can't imagine you want to hire me for my burglarizing skills."

"No. Not that, either. I want you to do a tail job."

"It's not really my line of work," she said, ears cocked forward with interest, "but I'm willing to give it a try. Who do you want me to follow?"

"Alice Manderley."

Conchita pursed her lips and whistled. "Well, now *that's* an interesting assignment."

"I thought another burglar would be more likely to understand any countermeasures she'd use. Are you willing?"

"Only too! Where do I find her?"

"The Underwater Palace for the moment, though I expect she'll be leaving in the next day or so. There's only one exit, not counting submarines, so I imagine she'll be easy enough to pick up."

"Sounds right as Robbler."

They spoke about fees and communication protocols for a while, then said their adieux. Maijstral turned away from his suite's phone pickups, a subdued green glow in his lazy eyes, and smiled.

Nichole had provided Diadem security's watch a list of all known burglars in the vicinity of Earth. Of those named, Maijstral judged that only Alice Manderley possessed the skills necessary to have neutralized all the alarms and traps in Maijstral's booby-trapped room at the Underwater Palace.

Which in itself wasn't conclusive, but it was something like a large pointing finger floating in the sky over Alice's head, inscribed with the ideogram for "inquire within."

If in the next few days, Alice took a little detour in the direction of Memphis, then Maijstral fancied he'd know what to do.

Captain Milo Hay looked as if he were battling a hangover in addition to his numerous contusions and bruises. His face was dotted with semilife patches and he moved uneasily, as if it hurt to exert himself.

Or perhaps he was made uneasy by Roman, whom Roberta had brought with her. Hay was apparently a professional xenophobe, and might therefore be expected to be wary of Khosali—but he might be indulged in this instance, as Roman was a sight guaranteed to produce unease in anyone with even the faintest grasp of sanity: skin wrinkled and gone from normal grey to bright pink, nose cracked and bleeding where the new age-ring was coming in, eyes starting from their sockets in a barely repressed psychotic glare.

He was the worst molter Roberta had ever *seen.* But apt, she concluded, to her purpose.

Captain Hay, despite his injuries and the effects of alcohol on his tender system, had nevertheless made an effort and donned the full dress uniform of the Human Guard, as splendid in its way as the white bejeweled outfit of Major Song, who—as ever—was dressed as Elvis.

"A *what?*" Major Song asked.

"Caestus," Roberta said, and fingered the studded leather straps she'd dropped on the table in front of Captain Hay. "It's an ancient Earth weapon, dating, I believe, from the time of the Romans. You strap one on each hand. I was surprised to find the caestus in the Khosali weapons lists, but there you go. They're a very inclusive sort of people."

Unlike others, her tone implied.

Hay picked up the straps and looked at the metal studs designed to crush bone, the hooks meant to tear flesh. He swallowed hard.

Immediately after Major Song's call, Roberta had flown to Alaska to meet with her in person. She wanted to handle this face-to-face.

Major Song hiked up her wide wrestler's belt. "Let me understand this," she said. "You *insist* on using this weapon."

Roberta straightened her spine and flashed a cold look at Captain Hay. "Your principal chose to strike mine with his fist. My principal insists he be allowed the chance to reciprocate."

"But this isn't according to form," Song protested. "You can't just dictate which weapons are to be used. It's up to both seconds to decide."

"Hitting someone without warning isn't according to form either," Roberta pointed out. She flicked her ears carelessly. "Of course, if your principal is afraid of facing the consequences of his behavior . . ."

Hay looked up sharply. "Hey. We never said that."

"We want to follow form," Major Song insisted.

"Let me point out that my principal has already fought one duel—just this morning, in fact. I assume you've seen it on video. He won a complete victory, of course, and with his bare hands." Roberta permitted herself to smile. "Of course, his antagonist was a friend whose continued existence my principal wished to preserve." She looked at Hay. "He doesn't know *you* at all."

A growling noise filled the room. Song and Hay looked in alarm here and there to find the source, and then seemed even more alarmed when they discovered the source was Roman.

Hay turned pale. "Say," he said. "Now, about these weapons . . ."

"That's why we insist on the caestus," Roberta went on. "It might be said that Captain Hay chose fists himself, when he struck my principal, and my principal chose the, ah, *intensity level* of the combat. If it's a formal duel, of course there has to be a chance of death. I'm informed that quite a few ancient Romans died in fights with the caestus, though of course there's a decent chance that, with those heavy studs and hooks, the loser will just be *mutilated* so severely they will be unable to continue . . ."

"Wait a minute!" Hay said.

"We *insist* on another weapon!" Major Song said, turning as red as her principal had turned pale.

Roberta looked at her. "Do you have another weapon in mind, or will just *any* other weapon do?"

Major Song opened her mouth, closed it, opened it again.

"I remind you," Roberta said, "that my principal has *nothing to prove* in the matter of his courage, while *your* principal, whose introduction to my principal was by way of a cowardly attack, has everything at stake—either he is a polite individual, fit to be seen in society, or he is not, and so far the evidence is not in his favor."

"Hold on here," Hay said. "All I did was *hit* the man. After what he said the other day, I couldn't help myself once I saw him. It was just . . ." He groped for words.

"A form of political protest," Major Song concluded.

"That's right," Hay said. "I don't see why it really *needs* to go any farther."

Roberta frowned, straightened herself, and looked at Hay. "Is it your contention that striking people is an acceptable form of political protest? And that there is no need for a fair combat as a consequence?"

"Well," Hay said, "yes, I suppose."

Roberta frowned, then shrugged. "If you insist." She turned to Roman and smiled. "I believe, Roman," she said, "that you have several political points to make with Captain Hay?"

Hay's eyes widened. He got out one word—*"Wait!"*—before Roman reached him.

Roberta closed her eyes during the worst of it. The meaty sounds of fists on flesh, the grinding of cartilage and the crack of bone, were quite graphic enough without her having actually to *watch* it.

Once a day for this sort of thing was enough.

Throughout the fight Major Song backed up against the wall and stared at the proceedings with horror. After Roman had finished, Roberta looked at her and nodded.

"I'm pleased we reached an understanding," she said, then took her caestus and left, fingering the media globe in her pocket through which she'd recorded everything.

The next visit would be to Prince Hunac. Unfortunately she anticipated that, with the Prince of Quintana Roo, she'd have to adopt a different strategy.

"Hello?"

Two perfect blue eyes gazed at Maijstral from the video. "Drake. I have some information."

"Oh yes?"

"Concerning the Baron Sancho Sandoval Cabeza de Vaca."

"Oh. Yes."

"He did in fact serve as a junior officer under your grandfather in police actions in Malaysia and on the Indian subcontinent. There is no indication that he and your grandfather ever met."

"I see."

"He and your father seem to have crossed paths on several occasions. They had an assortment of political groups in common."

Maijstral sighed. "No need to go into detail. I can imagine."

"I expect you can."

"The point being," Maijstral said, "*I* never met this man until he walked up to me and started hitting me with his cane. No glory is going to be won by thrashing an elderly nobleman in a fight."

And even less glory, Maijstral added to himself, if it was the elderly nobleman who happened to be the winner.

"I have been looking through the Imperial Sporting Commission's *Manual on Approved Formal Combat Systems,*" Maijstral went on, "hoping to discover if there is some way I can avoid fighting Sandoval, but all I've discovered is that if I object to Sandoval on account of age, the Baron is then allowed to find some strapping young brute as a substitute, and then I have to fight *him.*"

The blue eyes narrowed in concern. "How long is this manual?"

"Over two thousand pages, not counting all the statistics in the appendix. And, as I've discovered, it's not very well indexed."

There was nothing in the index, Maijstral had discovered, along the lines of *Fights, weaseling out of.*

"Continue your researches, then. Perhaps I will assign several of the Diadem's people to it."

"The Diadem doesn't mind you using their resources this way?"

"Gracious, no. The research boffins love work that has a *real* application. They got all these degrees and things, and here the Diadem sets them to research fashion trends, dig out old video star gossip, and find out which exotic fish rates as a 'must-see' off Cozumel. They *love* having work out of the normal run."

Maijstral smiled. "Well. Thank you."

"And another thing. I've arranged things at Graceland. You will be granted use of the Jungle Meditation Room tomorrow afternoon and all night, beginning at sixteen o'clock."

"Thank you."

The blue eyes looked at him frankly. "I must confess that I was of two minds concerning this business of sending you on to Memphis instead of keeping you here. I may have thrown you into the arms of your young Duchess."

"I haven't forgotten our time together."

"Well," grudgingly, "see that you don't."

There was a gentle chime. "I have another call," Maijstral said.

"Au revoir, then. I'll talk to you tomorrow."

"It's been tomorrow for a couple hours."

"Later today, then."

The blue eyes winked out, were replaced by eyes of violet. The eyes looked very weary.

"Good news. I've settled with Captain Hay, and there won't be a fight. I recorded our entire conversation, so that if he tries to recant or make untrue claims, we can release our version and make him look ridiculous."

Maijstral's heart warmed. "Splendid!"

"I'm sending Roman back to you. And I've just spoken to Prince Hunac. He's still under the influence, a bit, of the stuff he took last night—and I think that's fortunate, because it made him quite suggestible. He has agreed to postpone any confrontation until the situation clarifies."

Maijstral's already-warm heart sparked to a furnace glow. "My dear, if the phone permitted it, I would kiss you full on the mouth."

"I'm too tired for kisses right now." With a yawn. "Prince Hunac has offered me a room here, and I'm going to take it."

"Sleep well."

"What you must do is speak to the media tomorrow and let them know that the Hay matter is settled, and that your quarrel with Prince Hunac is on the verge of being composed. That will force our opposition to make another move—they've *got* to try to frame you again, or give up their plan."

"Nichole just told me that Graceland has become available."

"Excellent. Then you must tell the media of your plans for a religious retreat."

"I will. I'm a hereditary prince-bishop after all—I'll tell the media I'm going to spend a whole night praying for peace."

Laughter lines formed about the violet eyes. "I keep forgetting you're a bishop. You're not very ecclesiastical."

Maijstral composed his face into an expression of piety. "I prefer to keep my devotions private, thank you."

"Well. I'm a hereditary abbess, so I suppose I should not criticize."

"Really? Which order?"

"The Reformed Traditional Hospice Order of the Blessed Spatula."

"Oh. The Spatulans. I've seen their abbeys scattered here and there."

"Yes. And since I'm an abbess, I've got to see the Spatula itself, in a vault in the City of Seven Bright Rings. It's supposed to be an emanation of Gulakh XII the Well-Versed, who is alleged to have ascended bodily to heaven after he retired from the throne."

"An emanation, is it? I wondered why they worshipped a bit of kitchen equipment."

"They take it out of the vault once a year and make a holy omelette with it, and then the celebrants all swallow a piece. The ceremony is quite moving."

"I'm sure."

"My piece was a bit leathery when I tasted it, though." Another lengthy yawn. "I really should turn in. It's been a long day."

"You've more than earned your rest."

"So have you. But you got a nap." Another yawn. "I'll think about Baron Sancho tomorrow."

"I have every confidence in you. Good night."

"Good night."

Maijstral sat for a long moment in his darkened room and contemplated the remarkable women, the galactic superstar and the nobly born Spatulan abbess, who seemed to have taken command of his life.

Not, considering the alternative, that he objected. Not exactly. But he found himself yearning for that blessed time when he had been convinced that he was captain of his fate. That time seemed very remote now, though it had only been a few days ago.

This conviction had been an illusion, as the past days had shown. What had happened? Had he ever really been in command of his life, or had he always been the victim of mysterious forces who had, just recently, turned malevolent and mysterious, whereas before they had been content to permit him to live in illusive ignorance?

He shook his head. He was too tired and beleaguered to work it all out now.

He yawned and picked up his copy of the Sporting Commission's *Manual.* It lay heavy in his lap as he flipped the pages: the sort of reading guaranteed to send him straight to sleep.

And then he encountered, purely by chance, a paragraph that brought him fully awake. Carefully he read it. And, even more carefully, read it again.

Very nice, he thought.

This might just do the trick.

THIRTEEN

Media globes winked on high. Maijstral stood beneath the arched gate of Tvar's estate and smiled benignly at the assembled reporters.

"Furthermore," he continued, "I wish to announce that I accept the chastisement of my superior. I refer of course to the Baron Sancho Sandoval Cabeza de Vaca. I hope to reform my behavior, and I thank the Baron for calling my error to public attention."

Take that, Maijstral thought.

A sea of blank faces gazed at him. "What exactly does this mean?" someone asked.

"It means that I accept the Baron's assault as justified, and that I choose not to resent it."

"So you won't be fighting?"

Maijstral detected a tone of outrage in Mangula Arish's voice.

"No," Maijstral said.

There wouldn't be a fight unless Baron Sancho managed another attack, and Roman and Drexler, standing at Maijstral's side with arms folded in the capacity of bodyguard, were there to prevent just that, as well as keep away any other senile delinquents with violence on their minds.

There was a *very* respectful distance between Roman and any of the crowd of reporters. Just *looking* at him caused any number of people to go pale.

And in the meantime, the Diadem's publicity people, at Nichole's behest, would whisper among the media that Maijstral had chosen this humiliating option out of respect for the Baron's age, and out of concern for his mental health, which—as was plain to observe—was not quite of the best.

But *Maijstral* would say nothing of the sort—nothing for the Baron to object to, nothing that could cause him to issue another challenge.

If Maijstral couldn't have it both ways, what was the point of being a celebrity?

Another reporter scowled up from the mass. "So with the Hay fight cancelled, and the Hunac fight postponed indefinitely, this means you won't be fighting any more duels in the near future?"

Maijstral managed a smile. "Once a week is enough, don't you think?"

The reporters' mood was surly. They'd come for blood—they *depended* on the spilling of blood, and plenty of it—and now it looked as if they were about to be deprived of their feeding frenzy.

"Do you think," Mangula Arish called, "that your opponents are having second thoughts after your victory over Prince Joseph Bob? Do you think their withdrawal might be a reflection on their courage?"

Maijstral resisted the temptation to bounce a rubber ball off Arish's hair, and on reflection judged the question an act of desperation. She was trying to reignite the duelling frenzy through name-calling.

"I have absolutely no reason whatever to question the courage of any of these gentlemen," Maijstral said, "and I hope that if any of my erstwhile opponents chooses to resent the insinuation, they will remember it was you, Mangula Arish, who made it, and not I."

The other reporters chuckled while Arish turned pale at the thought of three enraged, bloodthirsty duellists stalking her.

"I have only one other announcement," Maijstral said. "The nearness of death in the last few days has caused me to reevaluate the condition of my spiritual health. It has occurred to me that I have neglected the religious duties implied by my status as the Hereditary Prince-Bishop of Nana, and I have decided to go on a retreat for the purpose of meditation, fasting, and prayer. The administration of Graceland has very kindly made one of their meditation rooms available for the purpose. I will be going on retreat this afternoon, and will remain in seclusion for an indefinite period. Thank you."

Ignoring shouted questions, Maijstral made his way back to Tvar's manse. Roman and Drexler followed slowly behind, their purpose plain—to pound like a stake into the rich Tennessee soil anyone who might feel the urge to pursue Maijstral and hit him with a fist.

Maijstral entered the mansion and found Tvar waiting for him.

"How did it go, dear?" she asked.

He gave her a Khosali smile, tongue lolling.

"Very well, I think."

Later that day a tailor appeared for Maijstral's fitting. Maijstral didn't travel with his ecclesiastical garments any more than he carried the formal court dress to which he was equally entitled—both were designed for the Khosali physique anyway, and tended to make humans look stunted, aswim in a sea of fabric and ceremonial implements. The tailor managed the complicated ritual garments in jig time, and then Maijstral posed for a long time in his bishop suit, while Drexler thoroughly recorded his image with a holographic video camera.

Later that day one of Tvar's servants—a second footman—stepped out onto the lawn wearing a hologram of Maijstral's image, stepped into a flier piloted by Roman, and was carried off to the Jungle Meditation Room in Graceland. The media waiting before the gate duly followed, thereafter to wait like pilgrims outside the gate of Elvis's city.

The footman would be amply compensated for any fasting, meditation, and prayer he might, in the course of his impersonation, be compelled to undergo.

In the meantime Maijstral, wearing his darksuit and armed to the teeth, sat in ambush in the room next to his suite. Roman, Drexler, Tvar, Kuusinen, and Roberta were arrayed likewise. Tvar's estate now contained a remarkable number of passive detectors—nothing that would broadcast an alarm, for they didn't want any intruder to hear it and run away, they wanted the intruder to come right in and make herself at home.

Alice Manderley, or whoever else was responsible for Maijstral's dilemma, was going to have a nasty surprise in store.

The hours passed slowly. It was after twenty-six o'clock when Maijstral received a phone call on his shielded lines.

"Yes?"

"Mr. Maijstral, this is Conchita."

"Go ahead."

"For some reason I'm not receiving a picture—should I call again?"

"I'm not transmitting a picture. I don't want to activate any pickups."

"Are you on a *job?"*

"Something like that. What news?"

"I thought I'd let you know that Alice Manderley and her husband have left Quintana Roo, and they're flying north. I'm on her trail."

Triumph hummed in Maijstral's nerves. "Very good. Do nothing to alarm her."

"Everything's right as Robbler. She's not evading or anything."

"Excellent. Call again when you have an idea of her destination."

"Right."

Gleeful, Maijstral relayed this news to his confederates and told them to be ready.

Alice was going to have *such* a surprise.

The intruder was delayed only briefly by the screamers on the perimeter of Tvar's estate—they were neutralized by black boxes deployed by an assistant. The approach across the back lawn was made swiftly—a hint of recklessness there, Maijstral thought, there were potential detection problems flying across an open space wearing a darksuit, and the intruder was ignoring them.

Steal from my *friends, will you?* Maijstral thought fiercely.

The intruder flew to the second floor and began peering in windows. Maijstral restrained the impulse to huddle into the holographic camouflage of his darksuit. He was perfectly well screened from anything the intruder was likely to be carrying with him—energy detectors for the most part, intended to locate alarm systems.

Ram me *with a submarine, will you?* Maijstral snarled in silence.

The intruder located Maijstral's room without difficulty—some of Maijstral's gear had been left in plain sight to make it easy—and then the window alarms were neutralized swiftly with a black box. The window glass was sliced out and floated skyward on antigravity repellers. The intruder entered, darksuit automatically pulsing out minute compression waves that cancelled the minute compression waves caused by a body floating through the air.

Set me *up to get killed, will you?* Maijstral demanded.

The intruder floated into the center of the room and hovered, apparently making a survey. Then floated toward the wardrobe that stood in the corner.

Sending a mental command from the proximity wire in the collar of his darksuit, Maijstral triggered his ambush.

Hidden force-field generators slammed invisible walls across the windows, blocking the escape route. The intruder could neutralize them, but it would take time, more time than Maijstral planned to give him.

Roman lunged from the wardrobe, where expert devices had been concealing his body heat, respiration, and very existence. He had a stunner in one hand and a spitfire in the other. He used the stunner first. Energies splashed off the intruder's shields.

More doors crashed open. Micromedia globes deployed in formation, recording everything for scrutiny later. Roberta, Kuusinen, Tvar, and Drexler opened fire. Maijstral slid through his door somewhat less promptly, wary of stray bullets.

"Surrender!" Maijstral commanded, and opened fire with his Nana-Coulville spitfire rifle.

The intruder's form, outlined by blazing energies, bounced around the room as if buffeted hither and thither by the blasts of its attackers. Maijstral's detectors showed that its shields were clearly weakening.

"Surrender!" Maijstral shouted, firing as fast as he could.

The outside detectors showed that the intruder's assistant was soaring across the back lawn, zooming to the rescue of his employer, setting off a lot of alarms in the process.

The intruder seemed to gather itself as if to spring, then flew swift as an arrow straight for the open window. The arrow hit the shield headfirst with an awesome, meaty thud, then bounced back and drifted toward the floor as if stunned. Drexler, stray fire bouncing from his shields, leaped forward and slapped a palm-sized energy vampire onto the form.

The vampire began sucking energy from the intruder's darksuit and equipment. The holographic camouflage began to shimmer, vanish in places.

"We surrender! Don't shoot!"

The voice came from outside, from the intruder's assistant. Kuusinen sensibly turned his attention toward the newcomer, pointing his heavy chugger toward the window.

The last of the camouflage drained away, revealing the glassy-eyed, twitching form of Laurence, the actor.

"We wanted to teach you a lesson," Deco said, "after you were so mean to us."

"I *was?*" Maijstral said in surprise.

"You *ignored* us," Deco said. "You said you'd never even *seen* Laurence play you on video—and that *had* to have been a lie. A deliberate insult. What sort of person wouldn't watch himself on video?"

Maijstral tried to remember whether he was ever rude to Laurence and Deco, and came up blank. "I never saw the other fellow either," he said. "Anaya."

"It's as if we didn't *exist!*" Deco said. "And you wouldn't even introduce us to Nichole!"

"I wouldn't?"

Maijstral tried hard to remember. He couldn't recall anything about Laurence and Deco at all, other than the fact he'd spoken to them briefly once or twice in the Underwater Palace.

Actors! he thought. They were each a universe unto himself, invincible little egos oblivious to anything but their own boundless need.

"And then," Deco continued, "Laurence called a news conference, announced that he believed in you, and publicly offered to stand as your second for your duels—and what did you do? *You forgot his name!* You didn't even call us!"

Laurence, stripped of his gear and searched for weapons—he hadn't been carrying any—was lying miserably on the carpet in Maijstral's suite. Deco, his assistant, knelt next to him, vocal as his friend was silent. The others stood about them, weapons still in hand.

"It's just that kind of indifference that made us angry," Deco said. "So we decided to teach you a lesson!" He looked at Laurence. "It was my idea, actually. 'Why don't you just sneak into Maijstral's room and steal something?' I said. 'Show him that you exist! Show him that you're *important!*' " He nodded toward Laurence, then looked at Maijstral again. "That's what I said, and that's what we did." His expression turned resentful as he looked up at Maijstral. "You weren't even supposed to *be* here!" he said.

Kuusinen, sitting on the scorched divan with his chugger across his knees, frowned at them both. "Are you claiming," he clarified, "that you aren't responsible for the robberies in Tejas and Quintana Roo?"

At this suggestion, an angry growl emanated from Roman. Deco and Laurence were aghast at this sound, but Deco soldiered on.

"Maijstral is to blame for those!" he insisted. "They were *his* robberies, and they went wrong," he nodded primly, "just like ours."

"Confess!" Roman roared. "You were jealous! You tried to get Mr. Maijstral killed!" He seized Laurence by the collar and flung him into the air like a rag doll. He caught the actor before he hit the ground and shook him vigorously. Deco, protesting, jumped to his feet and tried to grab Roman's arm, but Roman only seized him with the other hand and shook him, too, then banged his two captives together.

Maijstral, observing, believed that he could watch this forever.

"Fine, fine!" Laurence shouted, speaking at last. "I confess! We did it!"

"But we *didn't!"* Deco protested.

"I confess!" Laurence affirmed. "Let us go!"

Roman dropped them both to the floor at once. "Details!" he demanded. "And make them convincing."

"Whatever you want," Laurence said, a huddled picture of misery and defeat.

At this moment there came the chime of a communications system, and a voice.

"Gleep," it said, somewhat muffled. "Fnerg."

Maijstral listened in puzzlement. He couldn't quite make out the identity of the caller, or the meaning or import of the words.

"Snerk. Yibble."

Roberta, eyes wide, leaped up from her seat. *"Batty!"* she cried, and ran for the door.

Maijstral, following at a run, felt his heart sink. Somehow, he knew, it had all gone wrong again.

He was right. When he ran to Batty's room, he discovered the old Khosalikh lying on the rug, floored by a stunner blast. The padded supports that had held the late Duke of Dornier's coffin were empty.

Maijstral's father, the late Duke of Dornier, had been kidnapped, and his coffin with him.

FOURTEEN

Colonel-General Vandergilt was pleased, so pleased that a half-dozen loose strands of hair had escaped her helmet without attracting her notice. A victorious smile played about her lips as she watched a team of Memphis police collecting forensic evidence from Aunt Batty's room.

Aunt Batty herself had been taken to the hospital by Roberta. Stunner blasts could have unfortunate consequences for the elderly.

"It looks as if your gang is falling apart under the pressure," Vandergilt said.

"I don't have a gang," Maijstral pointed out.

"You're connected to all of these people that you're accusing. Laurence glorifies your crimes on video. Alice Manderley is a fellow professional." A superior look crossed her face. "Criminal gangs fall out—it happens all the time."

"Nevertheless," said Paavo Kuusinen as he frowned at Vandergilt, "a crime has been committed against Mr. Maijstral. Do you intend to investigate?"

"Of course," Vandergilt said. She noticed her dangling locks of hair and began methodically stuffing them back into her helmet as she spoke on, her voice cheerful and matter-of-fact.

"We'll do everything possible. Search the room for forensic evidence, put out an alert for the coffin and its, ah, contents. But of course, if we don't find the coffin by tomorrow midnight, it will legally become the property of the thief." Vandergilt looked at Maijstral and smiled. "An element of the current law which I believe you have often used to your advantage, Mr. Maijstral."

"But it isn't as if my father was a painting or a statue or a piece of jewelry," Maijstral said. "He's a *person.* There's no statute of limitations on kidnapping."

Vandergilt considered this. "Your father was declared dead, was he not?"

"Ye-es." Reluctantly. "Almost two years ago."

"Well then, he's not a person. He's inanimate—an *it.*"

"He may be in a box," Maijstral said, "but he still talks. Thinks, after a fashion. Isn't he a dependent, like a child?"

"I'm afraid not," said attorney Kuusinen. "The Constellation follows Empire law in this regard. After being declared dead, the elderly are considered keepsakes—like Lady Scarlett's liver, downstairs. Otherwise there could be no Imperial succession—no one could be crowned Emperor if his precedessors still retained their legal existence."

"Admirably put, Mr. Kuusinen," Vandergilt said with a thin smile. Her eyes glittered as they turned to Maijstral. "Another of those archaic Imperial laws causing trouble for you, Mr. Maijstral. What a pity that the Constellation Practices Authority hasn't got around to fixing that yet—but with the Burglars' Association putting up such resistance to the Authority's efforts to remove protections from Allowed Burglary, their other vital work has been delayed."

Another lock of hair was working its way from under the shiny brim of Vandergilt's helmet. Maijstral wanted to grab it and yank it out by the roots.

"Perhaps," Kuusinen said, perceiving perhaps the dangerous look in Maijstral's eye, "we should let the authorities do their work."

Maijstral withdrew, his blood simmering. Stealing his *father!*

It wasn't as if he'd exactly miss Gustav Maijstral if the late Duke dropped out of his life once and for all. But the theft itself was as vile an insult as he'd ever experienced. It wasn't as if Maijstral's father was in any way valuable property. The entire theft had been aimed at Maijstral himself. *Take this,* the theft said, *and suffer.*

The necessity for action coursed through Maijstral's veins. In another type of personality—the Prince of Tejas, say—the action might be to stand in fair combat on a distant beach, dire staff in hand.

Maijstral's character demanded another form of action.

He didn't want to fight. He wanted to *get even.*

"We need a council of war," Kuusinen said.

"Yes," Maijstral said.

"Perhaps at the hospital. Miss Batty may be able to give us some clues."

Maijstral could have said that she wouldn't—the most she would have seen would have been the vague outline of a darksuit against the window before the stunner blast rendered any perceptions unreliable—but he assented anyway.

He needed to get away from Colonel-General Vandergilt while he was still master of his passions.

It wasn't as if he would ever assault Vandergilt, but on the other hand the mental image of Vandergilt's home—a home stripped of all furniture, all clothing, all possessions—was floating insistently before his mental eye. But robbing Denise Vandergilt would be a very, very dangerous thing to do.

And it wouldn't help a bit with recovering Maijstral's father.

Where am I?

A sinister laugh. *Welcome to . . . Hell!*

I don't recall being on a planet called Hell. I was—it was Earth, wasn't it? Yes, I'm almost certain it was. I was going to have cocoa.

There's no cocoa in Hell, Dornier!

Isn't there? We must be in the provinces. I will have some nice warm milk, then.

You can't have milk, Dornier. You're dead!

Oh . . . You're right. I forgot.

You won't forget it anymore, Dornier. You're in Hell—the afterlife designed for punishment.

Oh . . . ? Really . . . ? That sounds like a most unpleasant place.

It is. It's meant *to be unpleasant.*

Take me home at once. No—not home, take me to Earth.

You're in Hell, Dornier!

. . . There was some reason why I was on Earth. I forget.

Hell, *Dornier!* Hell!

I forget so much these days.

I said you're in Hell!

Yes, you keep repeating that. I wish you wouldn't. I heard you perfectly well the first time.

You're going to be here forever and ever! You're going to undergo eternal punishment!

Are you . . . . Jacko?

Jacko! Of course I'm not Jacko!

Oh. I thought perhaps you might be. I thought I heard his voice.

I'm not Jacko, and this is Hell!

My dear fellow, I wish you wouldn't keep repeating that. You're becoming quite a tiresome person really.

You're going to be here forever and ever. Your punishment will never end.

Gracious, you do go on. Beat. *I don't suppose you'd know if I could get a nice cup of cocoa, could you?*

"Stealing Drake's father was a particularly malicious touch," Aunt Batty said. "I suspect we are looking for a person who is not entirely rational in his hatreds."

"Well," Maijstral wondered. "Who is?"

Batty was propped up on pillows and seemed reasonably comfortable in her hospital bed. Roberta's servants had brought her an embroidered nightdress and cap from her own wardrobe. The cap had two holes in it for her pointed ears.

If Batty was suffering any ill effects, they were well concealed. She lapped tea delicately from a saucer and seemed, on the whole, fully recovered.

Maijstral, Roberta, and Kuusinen sat in a respectful circle around her. Roman and Drexler were back at Tvar's place, making certain that the police neither stole anything nor planted any evidence. After the police finally left, Roman would fetch the false Maijstral back from Graceland and rescue the poor fellow from his regimen of fasting, meditation, and prayer.

Laurence and Deco were in police custody. Tvar, the householder, of a more practical and vengeful bent than the Princes of Tejas and Quintana Roo, had announced she intended to press charges.

Kuusinen dropped his teacup noiselessly into his saucer. "The thing that is beginning to signify," he said, "is the motif of the family that plays throughout Mr. Maijstral's recent experiences. The media demanding some sort of apology for the behavior of his grandfather, the late Duke Robert. Hay challenging him on account of his grandfather's behavior while Baron Sancho challenges him out of a misplaced loyalty to the same grandfather. And now Maijstral's father, who spent his life defending Duke Robert's behavior, has been kidnapped."

He looked levelly at Maijstral. "I think whoever is responsible for your predicament has a grudge against your entire family. Perhaps any hatred for you is incidental to hatred for your grandfather."

Roberta looked puzzled. "Who would hate your grandfather?"

"Thousands of people," Maijstral sighed. "*Tens* of thousands."

Roberta was startled. "Good grief. I know he was a famous Imperialist, but what exactly did he do to raise such ire?"

"Your question demonstrates that your education was on the Imperial side of the border—the Empire was so embarrassed by my grandfather that they don't talk about him much. He's barely mentioned in the official histories. But here in the Constellation, he's the bogeyman—the ultimate oppressor, the ultimate traitor, the ultimate bad example."

Roberta's eyes widened. "But what did he *do?*"

"Killed," Maijstral said, "tortured, threw people in prison without a hearing—here in the Constellation he's known as Robert the Butcher. He was far more excessive than any Khosali in defense of the Khosali Emperor. The Khosali were so appalled by his excesses that, after he fled to the Empire, they never employed him again—just let him live on his pension. They disbanded the Green Legion so that he'd never get the chance to use it in another war. One reason that I don't use my title is that I don't want to be called *Dornier*—it's a term of loathing here."

"*Tens* of thousands," Roberta repeated. "That's a lot of suspects."

"Mr. Maijstral's problems didn't begin till he arrived on Earth," Kuusinen observed, "so I think we can narrow our investigations to Earth residents."

Maijstral wanted to grind his teeth. "I *meant* tens of thousands of Earth residents," he said.

"I think I may be able to narrow your range," said the voice of Conchita Sparrow. Camouflage holograms shimmered off, and she appeared above them, hovering near the ceiling. She flashed a grin at her own ingenuity and then dropped to the floor. Her grin froze as she observed that Roberta was pointing a very businesslike pistol at her.

"Am I interrupting something important?" she asked.

"Roberta," Maijstral said, "may I introduce Conchita Sparrow, a colleague. I have hired her to perform certain investigations on my behalf."

"I would have dropped in earlier," Conchita said, "but there were cops all over Tvar's place, and I preferred not to call attention to myself."

"Very wise of you," Maijstral said.

Roberta put her pistol away, folded her arms, and looked severe. "I wish you had told me that you were employing an agent," she said.

Maijstral, having seen that stern expression before, decided to tread warily.

"My apologies for not telling you," he said. "But you were on your way to Cozumel at the time and since then, well, we've been busy." He looked at Conchita. "You have news?"

Conchita eyed Roberta warily. "Can I talk in front of these people?"

Roberta's eyes flashed.

"You may," Maijstral said hastily.

"Well," Conchita said, "I was following Alice Manderley, but I lost her."

"Is that *it?*" Roberta demanded. "That's all you have to report?"

Conchita flashed her an annoyed look. "As a matter of pickles, it ain't," she said, and then turned to Maijstral. "She was in this bright orange Iridescent flier, a real flash job, and got in the flier with her husband. She opaqued the glass as soon as she took off, so I only had the Iridescent to follow, but the flier is so distinctive that there really wasn't any problem. I followed her flier to a garage in Albuquerque. A medium-sized cargo carrier flew out a few minutes later, followed by Manderley's flier, and so I followed Manderley. But when the flier landed in Vancouver, only the husband got out. Manderley had given me the slip."

"Was the cargo flier large enough to carry, say, a coffin?" Maijstral asked.

"You bet," Conchita said. "And there's more. After I lost Manderley, I thought I'd fly to Memphis and see if you had any more instructions for me. And as I was coming in for a landing, I saw the cargo flier taking off from that patch of woods just north of here."

"The *same* cargo flier?" Kuusinen asked. "You're sure?"

"Photon Twelve, brown with white stripe, registration number HHD458772N," Conchita said.

Kuusinen nodded. "Very good, Miss Sparrow," he said.

"I figured something was up, so I followed the flier. But it didn't go very far—it just hopped over the trees to Graceland and landed there."

"Graceland?" Roberta said in surprise.

"Graceland?" Maijstral wondered.

"Graceland?" said Kuusinen.

"Oh my," Batty said, her ears cocking forward with interest. *"Graceland."*

"Graceland," Conchita smiled, and then continued. "She landed in one of the central landing stages, right in the middle of the whole complex. The airspace was restricted and I couldn't hover overhead indefinitely, and anyway the flier moved under cover almost at once. I tried to find some place to observe from, but I couldn't see anything, so I thought I'd better give you a report. But when I got to Tvar's, I saw the place swarming with cops, so I waited until you came out, and then I followed you here."

"My compliments, Miss Sparrow," Kuusinen said. "You have done very well indeed."

Roberta produced her pistol again, twirling it around her finger. "I think it is time to get our hands on this Alice Manderley," she said. "Perhaps we can lay an ambush near Graceland and wait for her to leave."

"She could be anywhere by now," Conchita pointed out.

"We should get ahold of Kenny Chang," Maijstral said. "Alice will do anything to keep us from damaging her husband. For some inexplicable freak of character she's devoted to him."

Get even, he thought, and a little triumphant hum smiled its sinister way along his nerves.

He rose from his chair and turned to Batty. "If you'll forgive me," he said, "I'd like to set Roman and Drexler to work." The thought of Kenny Chang in Roman's hands caused him to smile. "We have a long night's work ahead of us," he said.

"Have a lovely kidnapping, dear," Batty said. Maijstral and Batty sniffed ears, and Maijstral left, followed by Kuusinen. Roberta remained behind to comfort the invalid.

From the hospital lobby, Maijstral called Roman to ask whether he'd gone to Graceland to pick up the false bishop, and was told that the police were just leaving: Maijstral told him to wait. He then called Nichole. When her hologram appeared, her face showed concern.

"Well timed, Drake," she said. "I was on the verge of calling you. My researchers have come up with some alarming news concerning Alice Manderley."

"That she stole the stele, and took my father's coffin this afternoon?"

Nichole received the news without surprise. "Indeed yes—or so the information implies. Your . . . *losing* . . . your father in such a way distresses me."

"You've heard?"

"Of course."

"Have you heard that Alice took him to Graceland?"

She looked thoughtful. "No. I hadn't heard that. But it makes sense in light of what I'm about to tell you."

"Indeed?"

Nichole's admirable brow wrinkled. "Are you speaking privately?"

Maijstral glanced over his shoulder. "Mr. Kuusinen is here."

"Could you engage the screen, please?"

Maijstral hesitated for a moment, then nodded. "If you wish." He turned to Kuusinen. "My apologies, sir."

Kuusinen acknowledged the apology with a graceful wave, and Maijstral activated the privacy field. He turned to face the phone pickups.

"Yes? Why the urgency?"

"I have some financial information, gathered quite illegally, and I would prefer not to have to admit how I got it before any third parties. Particularly an attorney who seems to be infamous for remembering odd facts and who may have some professional obligation to speak honestly in front of a judge."

"I recall your mentioning that Alice had received a sum of five hundred novae," Maijstral said.

"Yes, though all that information cost me was an inscribed recording of my last play. The *next* mass of data is going to cost me a private dinner with the Chief Auditor of the Constellation Bank."

"I am sure anticipation has him all aquiver." Maijstral laughed. "Nichole, have I mentioned lately my exceeding admiration for you? Your resources never cease to amaze."

"Oh, my news is amazing all right. Alice was paid five hundred novae just before she arrived here from Qwarism. She was paid another five hundred within hours after the stele turned up under your bed. And she was paid a third five hundred earlier this evening, after your father was stolen."

"Fifteen hundred," Maijstral said. "That's a pension generous enough to support Alice for life. Or Kenny for a month. But who can afford to pay them sums that large?"

Nichole looked at him levelly. "The money came from the account of Major Ruth Song."

Maijstral was staggered. "The *Elvis?*"

Nichole gave an incredulous laugh. "That explains Graceland, doesn't it?"

Maijstral tried to rein in the astonished thought-imps that seemed to be running amuck in his brain. "Here I thought she was merely a political crank. Now I discover she's fanatic enough to spend a fortune to kill and discredit me."

"Remember her grandfather, the Fleet Admiral? The Nelson of Neerwinden?"

"Yes."

"Well it turns out his *first* wife, no relation to Miss Song at all, died in police custody in a roundup of the relatives of rebel leaders."

"A roundup ordered by my grandfather."

"Exactly. Though it appears that her death was an accident, a mistake by the doctor called in to treat her for some long-standing condition."

Maijstral tried to work this out. "So Major Song has organized this complex and highly expensive conspiracy in order to avenge the death of some stepgrandmother she never met and isn't in any case related to?"

"So it appears."

Maijstral shook his head. "There's got to be more to it than that."

Nichole looked exasperated. "She's just *crazy,* Drake! You don't need any other explanation than that. She not only inherited her political convictions from her grandfather, but her religious ones as well. The late Fleet Admiral Song became a convert to Elvis late in life, and he endowed Graceland with one of its showiest pavilions. He's buried in the mausoleum and sleeps forever in the Arms of Elvis. Major Song is one of the most important lay sisters in the faith, and she has an apartment in Graceland itself."

Maijstral stiffened. "I have a feeling she's got something in that apartment that I want back."

"Very possibly."

"I'll go there directly. But in the meantime I need you to call Kenny Chang and arrange an appointment with him. Tell him you've got a part that's just right for him, and that you'd like to meet him as soon as possible. Tomorrow morning would be nice. Can you do that?"

"Of course. And I take it that it will be you and Roman who keep this appointment, not me?"

"Naturally."

She gave a sigh of relief. "Oh, good. Kenny's so utterly dreary I'd hate to have to really meet him. The phone call will be bad enough."

Maijstral bowed toward the pickups. "Thank you, my dear. I'll call you tomorrow."

He made as if to leave, but Nichole fixed him with an urgent look. "One more thing, Drake. This is important."

"Yes?"

"Major Song has made other payments."

A warning hum sounded in Maijstral's mind.

"To whom?"

"Drexler. Three payments of twenty novae each. The first a few days before you arrived on Earth, then just after the Tejas theft, and again just this afternoon."

Maijstral looked down at his hands and found they were miming the act of closing around Drexler's throat.

Taking dead aim. That's what Song and her conspirators had done to him.

And he was about to take dead aim himself.

"*Thank* you," he said. "I will deal with this at once."

"I know you will, Drake. Give my love to Roman, will you?"

"Oh absolutely." He smiled. "Once he's finished giving *my* love to Drexler."

Maijstral hastened into the servants' parlor, followed by Tvar.

"Roman," he said. "Drexler."

"Sir. Miss Tvar."

Roman and Drexler rose hastily. They had been monitoring Tvar's security gear on the unlikely but hopeful theory that the mystery burglar might return.

"Oh. Sorry." Maijstral, bustling into the room, had brushed against Drexler.

"My fault, boss."

Maijstral smiled at him thinly. "Yes. I'm afraid so."

Drexler's ears cocked forward. "Boss?"

Maijstral stepped back and regarded him. "I confess a certain surprise to discover just how cheaply you work."

Drexler's fingers twitched, advancing toward the opening of his jacket. His sturdy body seemed to inflate slightly. "Boss?" he said.

"Alice Manderley was paid more than you by a factor of more than twenty, and all for doing the same job. Stealing, I mean, and planting the goods in my room."

Drexler made his move, his hand diving into his armpit. His eyes widened and his ears cocked forward.

"Looking for this?" Maijstral said, and produced the pistol he had just snaked from Drexler's holster.

Maijstral's next line would have been, "Roman, secure this traitor!", but he never got it out.

Roman had anticipated him. Drexler barely had time for a yelp of dismay before Roman had seized him by his crotch and throat, upended him, and dashed him skull-first to the floor.

There was a horrible crunch as vertebrae compacted. Drexler collapsed, his limbs atwitch. Maijstral frowned down at him.

"Roman," he said, "I wanted him in a condition to answer questions."

"Sorry, sir."

"Well." He shrugged. "As long as he's unconscious, search him for further weapons and any communications or flight devices. Then—" He turned to Tvar. "If Miss Tvar will provide us with the room in the house most resembling a jail cell?"

Tvar's tongue cheerfully lolled from her muzzle. "Lightless?" she asked. "Airless, dark? With stone walls to prevent any escape by burrowing?"

"Something like that, yes."

"I believe I have a place suitable to the purpose. It's the room in which Savage Simon used to confine his victims—I bought it entire and had it shipped here from Kualu." Her expression brightened. "I also have a number of his original instruments. For atmosphere."

Maijstral turned back to Roman. "Secure Drexler and put him there. We'll talk to him when he's conscious."

"Very good, sir." Roman took a detector and began patting Drexler down. Finding nothing suspicious, he picked the other Khosalikh up by the collar and dangled him like a child's doll.

Maijstral turned to Tvar. "Miss, if you could show Roman to the dungeon?"

"Delighted."

"Roman, after you've secured the prisoner, I will require you to take me and Conchita Sparrow to Graceland."

Roman paused in the act of carrying Drexler from the room. "Miss Sparrow, sir?"

"We're going to need a tech," Maijstral said, "and she's available."

"Hrrrr," Roman growled meditatively. Then, "Very good, sir."

"Carry on."

Maijstral, busy though he was, paused for a moment to enjoy the sight of Roman carrying away the unconscious Drexler.

Though he could not realistically consider himself the captain of his fate once more, Maijstral thought, he'd at least managed a self-promotion. To warrant officer, perhaps, or maybe even lieutenant.

FIFTEEN

You were a spy for the Empire, Dornier!

A spy? Oh don't be silly. What do you take me for, a member of the Secret Dragoons?

You belonged to the Imperial Circuit. The High Custom Association. The Nostalgia Party. The Imperial Armed Forces Relief and Reunion Society. The Empire Party. The Old Nobles' Association. . . .

Oh yes, the Old Nobles. What a splendid bunch of fellows they all were.

You conspired with them! Conspired against the Constellation!

We had such splendid plans for when the Emperor returns . . .

You admit it!

Of course. None of it was secret. You can read our minutes in our publications. . . .

It's the secret parts I want you to confess. Who gathered the information? Who were the spies?

I don't know what you're blithering about. . . .

The Old Nobles' Association! Who were the spies?

The Old Nobles . . . so jolly. So jolly.

What were their names?

You aren't Bertie, are you?

Bertie? Who's Bertie?

Such chums we were. We went to school together, you know.

I'm not Bertie!

Such a fellow for pranks he was. This is just like one of Bertie's jolly games, you know.

This is no game, Dornier!

He'd sneak up on you at night and shout 'Boo.' What laughs we had. You're just like him, you know.

I'm your inquisitor, and this is Hell!

Oh yes. I forgot.

This is going to last forever, *Dornier. Forever!*

Oh, surely not. I'm sure I've got an appointment somewhere. . . .

Dornier! Listen to me!

. . . Now was it on Earth, or someplace else? I wish I could remember.

The two Graceland security guards, making their rounds, quailed visibly as Roman loomed out of the darkness. "Halt!" one of them squeaked.

In Roman's shadow was Conchita Sparrow, dressed in a hooded cloak against the night air, and carrying a tray on which rested some pieces of fine porcelain. Roman approached the guards, growling ominously.

He was having a hard time controlling his growl reflex.

One of the guards cleared her throat. "What is your business?"

"I am bringing a pot of restorative tea to the Prince-Bishop of Nana in the Jungle Meditation Room."

The guards both looked relieved that Roman's answer hadn't been something to the effect of, "I am here to yank your spines out through your necks."

"Pass," one of them said.

Roman passed, growling.

Their wide eyes fixed on Roman, neither guard noticed the slight distortion in the air over their heads that marked the passage of a well-known thief in a darksuit.

Maijstral entered the Jungle Meditation Room and paused for a moment to let his eyes, and his staggered sanity, adjust. He had known that Graceland was renowned for the extravagance of its decor—all the minarets and domes made that clear enough—but he had never seen anything like *this.*

The ferns and the full-sized palm trees that reached toward the domed ceiling, the dome itself covered with an allegorical fresco of Elvis Vanquishing the Blues, its principal figure glittering with sequins, crowned with stars, and with its feet planted on a sunset pink cloud. The animal skins, most with heads attached, that covered the floor in layers. The fall that poured silver water, like a stream of mercury, into a pool lined with lava rocks. The shields, spears, and more exotic weapons that massed on the walls, enough to outfit a barbarian army. The stuffed rhinoceros—at least Maijstral *assumed* it was stuffed. The elephant tusks planted in rows. The furniture covered with hide.

The most normal thing in Maijstral's view was the sight of himself, Drake Maijstral, dressed in ecclesiastical robes and snoring on one of the hide-covered couches.

Maijstral floated toward the couch, dropped to his feet, and turned off the darksuit's holographic camouflage.

"Martin."

The snoring Maijstral awoke with a start.

"Sir!" He jumped to his feet and turned off the hologram that made him look like Maijstral, revealing himself as a smallish human with a shock of blond hair. "I hadn't expected you."

"Has anything occurred, Martin?"

"Just after I got here one of the Elvii—Elvis XXIII—called to offer you a personal tour of Graceland tomorrow. I thanked him for his kindness but explained that I was not certain my schedule would permit."

"That was well said, Martin. Thank you."

Martin smiled. "It was interesting being a celebrity for a few hours, at least."

"I'm afraid your moment of fame must come to an end." He gestured toward Conchita and Roman, who had silently entered behind him. "I need you to don Miss Sparrow's cloak and leave with Roman."

Martin bowed gracefully. "Very good, sir. Would you like me to instruct you in the workings of the sound effects and video?"

This statement was sufficiently intriguing that Maijstral, though pressed for time, agreed. Martin led Maijstral to a service plate and touched the ideogram for "sound." Immediately the dome began to echo with howling monkeys, birdcalls, and the distant roars of hunting beasts.

"A bit overwhelming, I'm afraid," Martin explained. "They were interfering with my, ah, meditations, so I shut them off."

"Please do so again."

"Yes, sir."

"And the video?"

"There are a great many projectors under the dome, so you can watch several videos at once."

"What videos are they?"

"Oh—a wide selection, sir. You reach the catalogue by touching this ideogram. There are several of Elvis himself—gathered from primitive media, one gathers—but I'm afraid I'm somewhat Elvis-deaf, if I may coin a phrase, so I haven't sampled them."

"Very good. Thank you, Martin."

Maijstral passed Martin the agreed-upon sum, plus a bonus. Martin smiled, pocketed the cash, and offered, first, his thanks, and second, his conge.

Maijstral turned to Roman. "Return Martin to Miss Tvar's, then stand by with the vehicle. If I find my father, I'll probably need help in getting him away."

"Yes, sir," Roman said.

Martin and Roman took their leave, Martin looking nervously over his shoulder at the continual sound of Roman's growling. Maijstral looked at Conchita.

"Are we ready?"

She grinned. Beneath the cloak she'd been wearing a silver-grey darksuit, and now she triggered the holographic camouflage.

"Fingo all right, boss," she said.

As he flew off into the darkness, Maijstral made a note to himself to find an opportunity to ask Conchita just what that piece of cant actually meant.

"Pardon me, sir," said the Baron Sancho Sandoval Cabeza de Vaca, "but is there a Mangula Arish here?"

Graceland glowed on the near horizon, astonishing, fabulous, and perfectly at one with itself. Outside the gates clustered the vigilant and faithful media, hoping for a glimpse of Maijstral, though an earthquake or a bloody riot would have worked just as well. One of the reporters nodded.

"The lady over there," he said, pointing. "With the high-impact hairstyle."

"Thank you, sir."

Baron Sancho squared his shoulders and marched toward his target. Mangula was preoccupied with controlling the media globes she'd deployed around the Graceland perimeter, and paid little attention to the approach of the erect, elderly figure until the Baron, who was too gentlemanly to use his cane on a woman, slapped her neatly across the face with a silk-lined glove.

"Call me a coward, will you?" he demanded. "I demand satisfaction!"

Mangula stared at him for a moment, and then, both to his surprise and hers, turned and fled into the night.

No luck. No luck at all.

There was no sign of Maijstral's father in the apartment that Major Song kept here, and no sign of Major Song either. There was no apartment assigned to Alice Manderley, but she could have been hiding or using a pseudonym, or hiding Maijstral's father in the apartment of an unknown confederate, so Maijstral and Conchita were faced with the tedious prospect of checking every single apartment in the blocks assigned to visitors. And with the Memphis Olympiad coming up in a few days, the greatest orgy of Elvis impersonation in all civilization, the apartments were almost all full.

"Did Elvis actually *live* amid all this?" Maijstral asked. "Legend would have us believe he was a simple country lad."

"Oh no," Conchita said. "The original Graceland wasn't very large—well, it was small compared to Tvar's place anyway—but it was destroyed in the New Madrid Earthquake centuries ago. Since then Elvis's admirers have built what I believe are termed 'creative reinterpretations' of the original."

"I wish they had been less lavish," Maijstral said.

Conchita looked glum. "I wish they had been less numerous."

Fortunately there were few places in any given apartment where something the size of a cold-coffin could be hidden, so each apartment could be checked fairly quickly. But even so the eastern horizon had turned pale by the time Maijstral and Conchita had finished.

"There's only one set of apartments we haven't checked," Maijstral said, speaking over their coded communications link. "The Elvii themselves."

"Oh no." Behind her holographic camouflage, Conchita sounded shocked. "They wouldn't, would they?"

"All it takes is one fanatic."

"I suppose." She sighed. "But the place is so *huge.*"

"Let's do it quick, the sun will be up in a minute."

"Right."

They soared off to the extravagant Pavilion of the Elvii, the nerve center of Graceland, where the Clones of Elvis, all reconstituted from the original's remains and genetically identical to the King Himself, administered the huge empire that was in their charge.

There was the cult center, with its priests and temples. (Elvis had not yet been added to the official Khosali pantheon, but there were hopes.) There was the vast acreage of Graceland itself, a giant center for tourism. There were concert halls and auditoriums. There was the Memphis Olympiad, where Elvis impersonators from all over the galaxy competed for the prize of the Championship Belt. And there were royalties to collect, licenses to grant, and concessions to administer.

No one in Graceland was in danger of going broke.

The security was formidable around the area: guards marching in pairs, and the place was studded with detectors that required the full complement of Conchita's black boxes to overcome. Peering in the windows with their detectors deployed, Maijstral and Conchita observed the Elvii—old Elvii, young Elvii, fat Elvii, and thin Elvii, Elvii sleeping and Elvii meditating, Elvii eating and Elvii fasting . . . Elvii, Elvii everywhere . . . but no coffin could be found.

"Thagger," Maijstral swore. "I've had it. The sun's up, let's get out of here."

He was sweating, but not as a result of heat from the rising sun. The distortion caused by their darksuits was much more apparent in full daylight than at night, and there were more people about to observe them. Detection was an ever-increasing possibility.

"There's an Elvis coming," Conchita warned. "Better wait."

The Elvis in question was an elderly one, with thinning white hair. He was mounted on an imitation panhead Harley (training wheels extended) that gave a gentle electric whirr as it coasted up to the gate of the Residence. The Elvis parked the bike, then walked to the gates (ornamented with old human-style musical notes covered in gold leaf) which parted silently in his path.

Maijstral's mind snapped to attention.

"Wait a moment," he said. "How did the gates know to let him in?"

The elderly Elvis ambled up the path (huge slabs of emerald and ruby cut from asteroid material) and toward the doors (trefoil wood from Canther, carved with reliefs of Elvis Healing the Deaf), which likewise parted without a challenge.

"He's got to have some kind of identification that takes him through security," Conchita said.

"If we can get one, we can enter anywhere."

"Especially if we look like Elvis."

"Let's steal one."

"Right, boss."

As they reached this decision, the elderly Elvis became visible again, rising to the top of one of the Pavilion's towers (sheathed in green jade and carved with dragons) in one of the Pavilion's exterior glass elevators (in the boxy form of an antique microphone). Maijstral and Conchita flew to the top of the tower (carved in the shape of a giant lotus), where they watched through window glass (inscribed with an image of Elvis Negotiating a Peace with the Aborigine Geronimo) as the Elvis yawned, removed his vestments, and headed for the shower. Maijstral swiftly neutralized the tower room's various alarms—easily spotted because they were in the shape of grimacing demon masks—opened a window, and flew in to pass his detectors over the Elvis's discarded clothing. A diamond-studded pin in the shape of an ancient Cadillac ground vehicle responded with a complicated energy pattern, and Maijstral removed it.

"Are you certain that's it?" Conchita asked, as he closed the window behind him.

"No. We'd better test it."

He flew down to one of the Pavilion's doors and dropped the pin onto the stoop. No alarms rang. The doors silently opened. Maijstral dropped to retrieve the pin and then made a careful, zigzag flight back to the Jungle Meditation Room.

"I want you to analyze this pin and duplicate it," he instructed as he pulled on his clerical vestments over his darksuit. "If that Elvis has the seniority I suspect he does, it should get us in anywhere."

"We'd have to move fast, boss," Conchita said. "Once the Elvii find out this pin is missing, they'll reprogram their computers to call security instead of open doors."

"I suspect the old fellow just got off duty and is heading for bed. So we'll have some hours, anyway."

"I hope he's due for a long rest." She took the pin, looked at it for a moment, and then put it in a pocket. "Well," she said, "I'll fly out of here."

"Thank you, Conchita. You've done very well."

"Yeah." She grinned. "I usually create a catastrophe by this point, but I haven't embarrassed myself yet, have I?"

"No, you haven't."

"I'll try to keep it up, then."

She turned on her camouflage and flew toward the doors, which opened at her touch. She gave a yelp, and then the doors closed and Conchita reappeared.

"Guards, boss! Hundreds of them!"

Maijstral's heart crashed in his chest as he hastened to the doors. He opened them a crack and peered out. Uniformed guards were, in fact, pouring into the open square outside. But they were forming ranks and facing to Maijstral's right, not assuming assault positions, and they were dressed in fatigue uniforms, not armed and armored for battle. He closed the doors and turned to Conchita.

"It looks like a morning formation," he said. "They'll probably disperse after receiving their instructions."

Relief flooded Conchita's face. "For a minute I thought I'd done something horribly wrong again."

"Wait until they disperse before you leave. All it takes is for one of them to look in your direction as you fly out, and the jig's up."

"Right, boss."

He sat on the meditation couch and looked at the tea that Conchita had brought earlier. "Is there real tea in here?"

"Sure. Shall I tell the pot to warm it up again?"

"By all means."

Conchita sat next to Maijstral on the couch and gave the pot its instructions. Maijstral stretched and yawned.

"I wonder how long it's been since I've slept."

"You look tense, boss. Why don't I give you a massage? It'll perk you up."

"That would be nice. Thank you." Maijstral offered her his back. Conchita's small hands proved surprisingly strong and effective in finding the knots in Maijstral's muscles and dispersing them. He straightened, his back tingling with pleasure.

"Thank you," he said. "That was very considerate."

He glanced up, saw her looking at him.

"Oh," he said. After a moment's thought, he put his arms around her.

"It's about time you noticed," Conchita said. "I haven't been hanging around in your air ducts just for the fun of it."

"Sorry," Maijstral said. "But I've been distracted."

"I'll forgive you," she said, "if you'll kiss me right this second."

"Very well," Maijstral said, and did so.

In the matter of being captain of his fate, he thought, perhaps he could just leave the tiller unattended for a while.

SIXTEEN

Let us review your sins, Dornier.

Excuse me?

Your sins, *Dornier, your* sins!

Oh for gracious sake. Why do you keep repeating yourself?

Because you don't seem to comprehend your position!

Oh, I understand it perfectly well. I'm in this, ummm, Hell place, and I'm supposed to, to . . . oh, what is that word again?

Atone, Dornier! Atone!

Oh yes. That's it.

I call to your attention the League for Imperial Youth.

Ah yes. We had the most jolly meetings.

An attempt to corrupt the children of the Constellation with alien ideas!

Oh, what rot. You talk the most amazing brand of stuff, do you know? Stuff and . . . what's the other word?

I'm here to force you to confront your past! To admit that you conspired against the Constellation by corrupting its children.

We had sing-alongs at our meetings. And nice little cakes that Miss Ginko sent up from the bakery.

You conspired, Dornier! Conspired!

Lovely little cakes with strawberries on them. And those creamy sort of buns that have that, you know, filling. And then the kind with the little nuts on them. I wish I could have a taste of them now. . . .

Confess your crimes, Dornier!

. . . What are those nuts called again?

Never mind the nuts, Dornier! You must confront the reality of your crimes and confess!

I can almost taste those buns . . . You wouldn't have one or two in the pantry, would you?

No! You're dead and in Hell! There'll be no more buns for you!

No buns? What a pity. Perhaps a little biscuit with jam, then?

You're dead! *You're* dead! *You can't have a biscuit!*

Oh that's right. Sorry.

Now, Dornier. We'll begin again. And pay attention this time.

If you just keep repeating yourself, my dear fellow, I don't see why I should.

I'm not your dear fellow!

Well, yes. That's obvious enough, I should think. But there's no reason not to be polite, even in Hell.

"The guards are dispersing. You'll be able to leave in another moment."

"Fingo all right, boss."

"I'll call Roman and have him bring me out in the flier. It looks as if he and I will have a busy morning. But I want you to get started on breaking the code of the Elvii right away."

"It'll be a piece of cake."

Beat.

"Conchita?"

"Yes?"

"You wouldn't mind answering a question, would you?"

"Only too, boss."

"You're not planning on marrying me, are you?"

"Why? Are you about to pop the question?"

"Frankly, no."

"Well, that's only sensible. You should get to know me first. Besides, I think I'm a little young for all that."

A smile. "Ah. Thank you."

"No prob, boss."

"No, as you say, prob."

* * *

Darkness loomed. It was a darkness that yearned to be broken by a flash of lightning, or perhaps by a stabbing organ chord, but instead it was broken by a voice.

Not, one must admit, a *nice* voice either.

"Drexler, you may as well admit you're awake. The neuromonitors make that clear enough."

Drexler's eyes, which had been determinedly shut, now shifted to determinedly open. "I want a doctor," he said. "I've been injured."

"What makes you think I'm *not* a doctor? You find yourself on a standard surgical table, with all the appropriate restraining straps, blood gutters, and so forth. You will observe I am wearing a doctor's apron—a bit spattered, unfortunately, from the last operation, but it's still perfectly functional."

"If you're a doctor, why are you wearing a mask and electronically altering your voice?"

"Because if you refuse to cooperate with me, I may be compelled to commence a surgical procedure that the Medical Association might not sanction. You will observe that I have my instruments sharpened and ready."

Drexler's body gave a leap within its restraints. *"Aagh!* What *are* those?"

"Custom instruments. *My* instruments. *Nice* instruments."

Drexler stared. *"Nice?"*

"This is my favorite—you will observe that it is a pair of scissors designed to cut *outward,* not in toward the center. And *this* instrument, originally designed for pulling teeth, but which has been found perfectly suitable for extracting, well, just about *anything* . . ."

"Let me up! Let me up!"

The masked figure put out a calming hand. "Not until you've had your *operation,* Mr. Drexler."

"What *operation? I don't need an operation!"*

"It's best to let doctor decide, don't you think? I believe we need to *extract* something. Either information, or *something else.* . . ."

"What do you want to know? I'll tell you!"

"Why are you conspiring with Alice Manderley against your employer?"

"Because I was *paid,* of course! It more than made up for the money that Maijstral cost me!"

"Cost you? How did Maijstral cost you money?"

"On Silverside, I was working for Geoff Fu George. Chalice and I had a bet against Gregor and Roman about whether Fu George or

Maijstral would steal the Shard first. I bet all I had, all my savings, and I lost. I wanted to start my own career as a burglar whenever Fu George retired, and I couldn't. *Now let me up!*"

"I don't believe your operation is quite over yet."

"Put that thing down!"

"Doctor knows best, Mr. Drexler."

"Just put it down! I'll tell you what you want to know!"

"Very well. Who was it that contacted you?"

"A human named Commander Hood. He's a free-lance leg-breaker, works the circuit."

"When did he first contact you?"

"About three months ago, just after I'd started working for Maijstral. On Kobayashi."

"Who did he say he was working for?"

"He didn't."

"I'm not certain I believe you, Mr. Drexler. . . ."

"Put that down!"

"But if you won't let me extract the *truth,* I'll have to extract . . ."

"I'm telling the truth! Put it down!"

"I think I'll just leave the instrument right here where you can see it. Now what exactly did this Commander Hood tell you to do . . . ?"

"Drake! Welcome back."

"Thank you." Sniffing Roberta's wrist. "I hope your Aunt Batty is well?"

"Oh, she's fine, thank you. Just tired. The hospital will be releasing her later this morning."

"Splendid. Any news?"

"Well, that short person—the one with the hair—flew in about an hour ago, demanded a room, and has been at work ever since."

"Very good."

"And I just finished watching Tvar's interrogation of Drexler on a video link."

"And . . . ?"

"Drake, it was the most uncanny thing I've ever seen. She put on Savage Simon's apron and became *another person.* She was terrifying."

"She got results, I take it?"

Roberta shuddered. "Yes, but . . . you know, I think she's been around all these macabre objects far too long. They've gone to her head."

"I recall her remarking to the effect that when Khosali go bad, they go *really* bad. I'll have to take care never to get on her wrong side. What did Drexler say?"

"He says he was hired by someone named Commander Hood."

"Hood? I've met him—he got into a scandal years ago and was thrown out of the navy. Since then he's been making a living as a thug for hire. No style at all—couldn't ever get into a sanctioned form of larceny."

"Drexler claims he doesn't know who Hood was working for."

"Fortunately we do, so that doesn't matter."

"Drexler admits that it was he who put Joseph Bob's pistol in the air duct, but otherwise he just transmitted intelligence to the other side, telling them where you were going to be, and what defenses you'd installed. He gave us the number he'd called to report, and it *is* registered to a Mr. Hood."

"Does Drexler know where they took my father?"

"He said not. I am inclined to believe he was telling the truth."

"Well." Maijstral's heavy-lidded eyes closed to slits. "I have a pair of tasks remaining for Drexler—perhaps I had better ask Tvar to keep wearing Savage Simon's apron so that he will perform them willingly."

"What do you have in mind for him?"

"First, I want him to call Commander Hood and tell him that I've decided to flee to Tasmania and go into hiding."

"To allay their suspicions."

"Exactly."

"And the other is to transfer his—sixty novae?"

"Sixty. Yes."

"Transfer it into my account. There's no reason why he should be allowed to profit from all this. And anything else in his account should go as well."

"I commend your sense of justice."

"Thank you."

A door banged open. Roberta jumped.

"Boss!"

"Conchita. You have met Her Grace of Benn, have you not?"

Conchita barely spared Roberta a glance. "Last night, yeah. I just wanted to tell you that I've broken the code and we can get into Graceland anytime. How many coded badges will you need?"

"One for me, one for Roman, one for yourself . . ."

"And for me."

"Thank you, Roberta. It's not necessary, of course."

"I think I would enjoy being in on the kill, so to speak. And Kuusinen will come, too."

"Five copies, then, Conchita."

"Right, boss."

"And then go into Memphis and purchase five holographic Elvis disguises."

"You bet, boss. Is that all you need?"

"For the present, yes."

"Right, then. Bye."

The door banged again. Roberta frowned.

"Roberta. You seem puzzled."

"I am marvelling at the breadth of your acquaintance, Drake. I was barely aware of the existence of people such as Miss Sparrow, and now it would seem I am involved in an adventure with her."

"You should broaden your circle, Roberta. After all, there are far many more of Conchita's sort than of yours, or mine. I hope you will consider the experience an enriching one."

"I am dubious as to the nutritive value of this brand of enrichment. Why are you smiling?"

"A private thought, regarding enrichment. Nothing with which to concern yourself."

An image flickered to life. A shifting image, difficult of aspect.

"Miss Manderley?"

"Who's that? I can't see. Are you wearing a darksuit?"

"Let me adjust the angle of the camera. There. Is that better?"

"*Ahh!* No! What is he doing to Kenny?"

"Dangling him upside down over the Grand Canyon, Miss Manderley."

"Tell him to stop! I'll pay anything!"

"I'm afraid I can't tell him to stop just yet, Miss Manderley."

Alice Manderley shrank back into her seat. "Why is that Khosalikh bald? Why has he painted himself all red like that? He must be mad!"

"He's just a bad molter, Miss Manderley."

"*Nobody* is that bad a molter!"

"Kenny will not be harmed if you agree to our demands."

"Anything!"

"Within the next minute, I want you to step into the flier that just landed on your front lawn. You will not carry any arms, communications equipment, or locator beacons."

"Yes! Yes! Just don't hurt him!"

"Miss Arish?"

"Yes."

"My name is Copac. The Prince of Quintana Roo has sent me to —wait! Come back!"

The flier's door hissed closed. Earth spiralled below as the machine took flight.

"Take me to Kenny!" Alice demanded.

"Not just yet."

"Drake!"

"Now, now, Alice," Maijstral pointed out from behind the controls. "I am wearing a darksuit and am camouflaged. You don't know who I am, nor do you know my companion, likewise disguised, who is pointing a pistol at you."

"Who was that freak who was dangling Kenny off the canyon wall?"

"An acquaintance of mine who can be trusted to fling Kenny to the gravitational constant if you should disobey my instructions in the least iota."

"Well." Muttering. "You've obviously got the goods on me."

"Exactly. And what I require is the absolute, perfect truth."

"Fine. Just don't hurt Kenny!"

Behind his camouflage, Maijstral smiled. "Firstly, how long have you been engaged in this conspiracy?"

"With those fanatics? Virtues, it seems forever—but they first contacted me a few days ago, after I got off the liner from Qwarism. By that point Kenny had acquainted me with the results of his financial speculation, and I desperately needed the money they were offering."

"Who contacted you?"

"Major Song. What an *unpleasant* woman."

"That has been my impression."

"She just ranted on about the Empire and some conspiracy of which you were supposed to be a part. I didn't take any of that seriously, of course, but her money was good, and—well, I didn't have any choice. I was desperate. I tried to keep Kenny away from her, though, when he suggested having her finance one of his productions."

"I recall that."

"Her fiance, that Captain Whatsisname, isn't a part of the plot, by the way. I was told never to mention it in front of him."

"So when he challenged me, he was doing it all on his own?"

"Absolutely. Song was appalled."

"Where did you take my father?"

"They ordered me to take him to Graceland."

"What did they do with him then?"

"I have no idea. They paid me off, took possession of the coffin, and then I called for a flier and left."

Maijstral thoughtfully twisted his diamond ring. "So you didn't even try to keep the coffin in your possession until midnight tonight? It will never be yours legally, and you can be prosecuted for the theft at any time?"

"Well—yes."

"That's awfully careless of you."

"You weren't supposed to find out I'd done it."

"Ah. Sorry not to have been killed in a duel as planned."

"I'm sorry, Drake. I truly found this job distasteful, and my employers appalling. I've been motivated by fiscal desperation, not by any personal animus toward you."

"Ah. And I suppose it never occurred to you that once I'm out of the way, you'll have a better shot at being rated number one?"

Silence.

"Do you have any idea what they intend to do with my father?"

"No, not really. Major Song babbled about a vengeance that would last an eternity, but she talks like that all the time, so it's hard to say whether or not it was hyperbole. She's truly insane, you know. It's lucky someone else was planning all this, I don't think she's capable."

"Wait a minute. *This wasn't all Major Song's idea?*"

"No. Not at all. She's following someone else's orders. She has it all written down for her—otherwise she'd forget something." Alice shuddered. "She's not a very rational person, Drake."

"Who's behind this?"

"I don't know. I didn't *want* to know. But whoever it is, he hates you with the most perfect hate of all time."

"Mr. Maijstral."

Maijstral looked up from the table where he'd placed his gear. Pistols, knives, restraints . . .

"Mr. Kuusinen," he said. "Please sit down."

Kuusinen did so. "I've been thinking. I think your father is still, ah, intact, and still at Graceland."

"I'm pleased to hear you say so. May I ask your reasons?"

"If Major Song and her cohorts intended to destroy the coffin and its contents, there was no need to take it to Graceland in the first place. They could much more easily have built a bonfire out in the countryside somewhere, and destroyed the coffin in perfect privacy. I imagine it would be difficult to find a place even in such a large place as Graceland where a burning coffin would not go remarked."

"Yes, I follow."

"So they took your father to Graceland for a *reason.* I must admit I have not discerned what that reason may be, but possibly it is related to the upcoming Memphis Olympiad. Perhaps Major Song wishes to use the coffin in her act—I've never known Elvis impersonators to use anything so eccentric as a coffin in a performance, but I gather she is an eccentric person."

"An understatement if ever I've heard one. Do you have any further thoughts?"

"Somewhat, sir. Though we cannot know the reason the coffin was taken to Graceland, we can know that whatever it was that Major Song intended to do with it, she may have done it by now. In which case the coffin and your father may be shipped out and destroyed."

"Time is of the essence, then."

"I fear so, sir. With this in mind, then, I have called up from computer files all the available architectural plans of Graceland, and I have asked my computer to perform an analysis of the data in order to determine all the places in Graceland where something the size of your father's coffin may have been hidden."

"I imagine there must have been a very great many."

"The resultant number was dismayingly large. Somewhere in excess of fifty thousand. But the *probability* of a coffin being hidden in many of these places was not very large—one could hardly put it anywhere public—and so I have further analyzed the data and come up with something in the neighborhood of three thousand possible—sir?"

"Yes?"

"You look startled."

Maijstral's green eyes glittered, and he smiled thinly. "An inspiration, Mr. Kuusinen. I just realized where the coffin is hidden. I believe we may go ahead and rescue my father now."

"Ah—very good, Mr. Maijstral."

"But keep your architectural plans in reserve. I may be wrong. And—do you have a few moments?"

"Yes."

"I wish to employ you in your legal capacity, if I may. Would you mind accompanying me to my room?"

"Mangula Arish, I've tracked you down! *Stop! Come back!*"

SEVENTEEN

Torment, Dornier! Eternal torment!

Eh? Eh? You were saying?

Long have I planned my vengeance, Dornier! Years have passed while my plans grew to fruition!

What are you going on about?

And now our minds have been wired together. You can't escape me—you're at my mercy! My mercy, Dornier!

Are you . . . Quigley?

Who is Quigley? Is Quigley a spy?

A spy? Oh, Virtues, no. Quigley is an old school chum.

Enough of your school chums, *Dornier! You're in* Hell *now!*

Hell. Oh, yes. I remember now.

Contemplate your sins, Dornier. . . .

Quigley's cook used to make the most perfect little omelettes. You couldn't have her make me one now, could you, Quigley?

I'm not Quigley!

You're not?

Get this through your head, Dornier! You're dead, you're in Hell, and I am not Quigley! *Can't you get it straight?*

Oh, of course. I'm being so silly. Of course *you're not Quigley.*

Just remember that, Dornier!

You're Jacko. I remember now.

I'm not Jacko!

Of course you are. You're Jacko, and this is one of your jolly little pranks.

I'm not Jacko!

Ha ha ha! I've found you out at last!

Aaaaah! I give up! I can't stand it!

Most amusing, Jacko. Your best yet, as far as I'm concerned.

Your brainlessness! Your endless drivelling! I refuse *to spend eternity with the likes of you! I'm cancelling Hell, and I'm cancelling it* now!

No need to get upset, old man. After all, I was bound to guess your identity sooner or later.

It's over! I'm going to call Major Song and have you disconnected!

Oh . . . I say, tell the Major to bring tea and cakes. I've worked up quite an appetite.

"Roman?"

"Sir? You called?"

"Please sit down. I have something to say."

The red-eyed, fiery-skinned giant seemed uncomfortable as he sat in Maijstral's presence. In addition to the obvious reason for his discomfort, Roman wasn't used to being seated in the presence of his social betters.

Maijstral frowned down at the table before him, where his genealogy, so carefully assembled by Roman, had been unrolled. He looked at his ancestors running back thousands of years, and thought of Roman's own genealogy, which went back even farther.

He cleared his throat. He wanted to be able to pick the right words for this.

"Roman," he said, "before we go off to rescue my father, I thought I would acquaint you with some of the contents of my will."

"Sir!" Roman barked. "Not necessary!"

This was hardly Roman's usual form, Maijstral knew, but then he reminded himself that this was hardly the usual Roman.

"I am certain," Roman added, more in his usual style, "that any dispensation which you have chosen to make is more than adequate."

"Well. There's a little more to it than endowments and so forth. Something special."

"Sir?"

"Your family has been in service to mine for hundreds of years.

Never in all that time has there been a single instance in which your family has failed to give its utmost for mine."

Maijstral was startled as Roman gave a brief roar, but it proved not to be anger, but rather something more in the nature of clearing the throat.

What Roman said, finally, was, "We endeavor to gratify, sir."

"And you have. You have. And in recognition of that, I placed in my will the intention that, on my death, the City of Seven Bright Rings be petitioned that one of my titles—that of Baron Drago—be given to you, or your heir. I also made provision for the transfer of sufficient funds to support any reasonable pretensions to which a member of the nobility might aspire."

"Sir!" The arm of the chair came loose in Roman's hand. His reddened eyes almost leaped from his head.

"But *then,"* Maijstral added, "I reconsidered."

A twitch danced across Roman's countenance. "I understand, sir," he said. "It is hardly fitting that I—"

Maijstral tried to repress a smile. "Roman," he said, "please let me finish."

"Very good, sir."

Roman observed the chair arm in his hand, and looked at it in surprise, not knowing how it got there.

Maijstral cleared his throat. "I reconsidered," he repeated. "I thought, why should all this wait till I'm *dead,* when by all rights you should have your reward *now.* So I have just now instructed Mr. Kuusinen to draft a petition to the City of Seven Bright Rings, and as soon as the Imperial Recorder in the next room copies it with his jade pen, and I sign it, the petition will be sent by the Very Private Letter service to the Emperor. And since we did the Empire that service on Peleng, as I'm sure you remember, I have every reason to believe that my petition will be granted. . . ."

His voice trailed off as he saw that Roman was simply staring off into space, the chair arm in his hand, his mouth fallen open and his tongue lolling.

"Well," Maijstral said. "Soon you'll be Lord Drago, so I thought you'd better be prepared. That's all, Roman—you may go."

"Sir—"

Maijstral rose and held out his hand. "Thank you, Roman. You have always given complete satisfaction."

Slowly Roman rose from his chair. He held out his hand, recollected the chair arm was still in it, switched the chair arm to the other hand, then took Maijstral's hand and clasped it. Maijstral winced as bones took the strain.

"Thank you, sir!" Roman bellowed.

Maijstral winced a second time at Roman's astounding volume.

"You'd best go and prepare," he said. "We'll be leaving in a few minutes."

"Very good, sir!" Roman roared, turned on his heel in formal military fashion, and marched out, the chair arm still in one hand.

Maijstral massaged his wounded hand, looked down at the genealogy, and smiled.

He had always thought that Roman would make a good lord. Every so often he and Roman were compelled to travel incognito, and Roman had on occasion operated under the name of Lord Graves, a perfectly genuine person who happened to be Maijstral's distant cousin. Roman had been so splendid at being Lord Graves, at adopting the proper mix of lordliness, condescension, and noblesse oblige, that Maijstral had often found it very odd of the universe that he, Maijstral, was the lord, whereas Roman, who was so much better at it, was the servant.

Of course Roman also *believed* in lords, and emperors, and so on, and Maijstral didn't. Perhaps conviction added something to Roman's performance that Maijstral, for all his birth and training, lacked.

There was a knock on the door, and then Tvar entered. Maijstral sniffed her ears.

"How fare our guests?"

"Drexler, Manderley, and Chang have been safely locked in Savage Simon's dungeon. Drexler has also been persuaded to forfeit his sixty novae and change."

"Very good." Maijstral would make the sixty novae part of Roman's—Lord Drago's—endowment.

It wasn't enough to support a lord for *very* long, but it would make a good start, and Roman could always steal some more. And it was more than Maijstral had to his name when he joined the nobility at his father's death.

"We'll leave as soon as Conchita gets back," he began.

"Right here, boss."

The camouflage holograms dissolved and Conchita floated down from the ceiling.

"Conchita," Maijstral said, "you must some day allow me to introduce you to the concept of a *door,* and of the *doorframe,* on which you may *knock.*"

"Sorry," Conchita said, "but the window was open, so I just flew up and came in. It seemed quicker than going the long way."

"Do you have our disguises?"

"Well—mostly."

"Mostly?"

"You asked for five, boss, but I could only find four."

Maijstral raised his eyebrows. "You could find only four Elvis holograms in all of Memphis?"

Conchita looked apologetic. "There's a high demand, boss, with the Memphis Olympiad coming up next week. And there's some kind of big ceremony going on right now, pre-Olympiad, with pilgrims from all over. You know how much Elvis's admirers like to dress up like him, right? Well, I called all over Memphis and I only got four holograms."

"Well," Maijstral sighed. "Can't be helped, I suppose."

Conchita brightened. "But I got a fifth hologram. It was the last one the store had."

"What does it look like?"

"Ronnie Romper."

"Ronnie Romper?"

"Yeah. The puppet from the children's videos. I really liked him when I was little."

Tvar lolled a Khosalikh smile. "I *adore* Ronnie Romper!" she said. "I used to visit the Magic Planet of Adventure every week."

Maijstral, it is apropos to remark, did *not* adore Ronnie Romper. He believed that the little puppet, viewed by everyone else as a harmless vehicle for juvenile delight, was in fact a horrid omen of doom.

This was not precisely superstition, but rather a product of some dubious inductive reasoning: a maniac assassin had once tried to cut Maijstral in half while wearing a Ronnie Romper disguise; and therefore Maijstral always viewed any close association with Ronnie Romper as an invitation to homicide.

If not precisely logical, the view has a certain consistency. That's inductive reasoning for you: it's sneaky, but at least it's based on data.

"How are we going to sneak Ronnie Romper into Graceland?" Maijstral demanded.

Conchita gave it some thought. "Well," she said, "if Ronnie's with *us* . . ."

Maijstral surrendered. Obviously it was his fate to take Ronnie Romper into battle.

"Very well," he said. "But let's leave at once, before I think better of it."

The main gates of Graceland were jammed: pilgrims, both human, Khosali, and otherwise, a great many of them either dressed as Elvis, wearing Elvis masks, or disguised by Elvis holograms, were swarming up against the stanchions, trying to get into the festival. Music boomed indistinctly in the distance, all bass notes and rhythm. The far-off roar of an audience rose and fell.

"Why you are Ronnie Romper disguising?" asked one Troxan. The tiny alien, who normally would have stood about as far from the ground as Maijstral's navel, was floating through the crowd on an a-grav harness ornamented with rhinestones, a cape, and a standing collar.

Maijstral found himself devoutly wishing he'd given the Ronnie Romper disguise to someone other than Roman, who by virtue of his height was far from inconspicuous.

It occurred to him that, insofar as Roman's answer to the alien's question might be to remove the Troxan's head from his shoulders, he should answer the question himself, and quickly.

"We're coming from a party," he said.

"I am climaxing this system my unbusiness journey," the Troxan said. "Most event making, friend finding grand tour."

To his horror, Maijstral realized that he *knew* this particular alien—his name was Count Quik, and Maijstral had met him on Peleng.

It really wasn't Maijstral's fault that he hadn't identified the Troxan immediately. Identification of Troxans is one of the minor arts, as they all have the same bodies, multilayered onion heads, and more or less fixed expressions. Sound resonates between the various cartilaginous layers of their heads and gives Troxans the most acute and discriminating hearing in the galaxy.

Maijstral cleared his throat and lowered his voice, afraid that his speech would prove fatally recognizable to the Troxan.

"I'm afraid we've run out of time," he growled. "So sorry. Good-bye." He began to elbow his way back to the rear of the crowd.

"Farewells, Mr. Maijstral," the Troxan said politely.

Maijstral clenched his teeth and continued his progress to the rear of the crowd, the others in his party following.

"Was that Count Quik?" Kuusinen asked.

"Yes."

"Do you think he will give us away?"

"He didn't last time."

"Last time he didn't catch us in the act of breaking and entering."

"Either way we've got to act swiftly, and crowding in front of the main gates is the least expedient way I can think to deal with the situation. We'll find a side entrance, and our identification codes should get us in. Once past the perimeter, we'll go straight to our destination. Very likely we'll get the business over with before Count Quik even gets to the main gate."

"Very good."

Out of the blue, a woman marked by a stiff, distinctive hairstyle charged right through the midst of them, knocking Roberta to the ground in her haste before she disappeared into the crowd. Media globes circling the woman's head marked her position in the crowd as she ran on. Kuusinen and Maijstral bent to pick Roberta up.

"Are you all right?" Maijstral asked.

"I'm fine. Wasn't that Mangula Arish who just knocked me down?"

"I don't know," Maijstral blinked. "Was it?"

The party scattered before a flying wedge of Mayans, who likewise disappeared into the crowd at a run.

"What's going *on?*" Roberta demanded.

"I haven't the vaguest . . ." Maijstral began, and then his blood froze at the sight of the Baron Sancho Sandoval Cabeza de Vaca bearing down on him, waving his cane.

"Are you sure my holograph is functioning?" Maybe, he thought, all these people were *recognizing* him.

"You look fine," Roberta said.

"Let's get out of here anyway."

They made their escape before the elderly Baron Sancho could hobble up to them, then circled around Graceland's perimeter until they discovered a gate, the entrance that led to Love Me Tender Street.

"If we'd had time to develop a plan," Maijstral pointed out, "we would have come here at the start."

Assuming the dignified mien of the Elvii, Maijstral led his group toward the gate, which obligingly rolled open at his approach. Two guards stationed behind the gate snapped to attention, and a third presented a portable log-in scanner and pen.

"Please sign in, sir."

Nothing for it but to continue, Maijstral decided. He reached for the pen and signed "Elvis Presley" in what he hoped was a bold hand.

The guard looked at Roman. "Why the Ronnie Romper disguise?" he asked, then turned pale at the sound of Roman's answering growl. His hand automatically rose to the pistol at his belt.

"We've been to a party," Maijstral said, in what he hoped was the voice of an old man. "My friend has a bad case of indigestion."

"Hrrrr," Roman agreed.

The guard's suspicion dwindled, but didn't vanish entirely. "And why are *you* disguised?" he said. "You're one of the Elvii—you *already* look like Elvis."

Inspiration struck Maijstral. "Ahhhhhh," he said, drawing out a world-weary sigh. "Even I sometimes yearn to be young again."

"Oh," the guard said. "Gotcher."

Maijstral led his group through the gate. The guard looked after Roman as he passed.

"By the way," he added, "my kids love your show."

Maijstral discovered, once inside, that Love Me Tender Street was crowded. Several concerts were going on at once in the various auditoriums and open-air concert venues, and more visitors were entering every second. The sound of music and the roar of the crowds were much louder. Maijstral's group found it slow going, but they made steady progress until a group of children spotted Ronnie Romper and ran up to join the party.

"Do your Pumpkin Dance!" one of them demanded.

"Take us to the Magic Planet of Adventure!" said another.

"The Pumpkin Dance!"

"Where's Cap'n Bob?"

"Sing the Pangalactic Friendship Song!"

Graceland, Maijstral realized, was a tourist mecca; and the tourists, seeing a holographic video character, were assuming that this was part of the *entertainment.*

Maijstral was on the brink of explaining that Ronnie was very busy now, in the midst of an adventure that was taking him from the Magic Planet of Adventure on a mission to Graceland to rescue Elvis from danger, but he found his explanation preempted by Roman himself.

Roman leaned over the children, raised his arms, and bellowed *"Buzz off!"* in a voice that froze the entire crowd in their tracks.

The children turned pale and fled, all except for the youngest, who wet himself, sat down, and began to cry. The child's mother rushed up to the child and picked him up in her arms.

"Beast!" she shouted at Roman's retreating back.

"Perhaps we'd better fly," Maijstral said. "We'll be more conspicuous, but we'll make better time."

They triggered their a-grav harnesses and rose into the air. Maijstral led them onto shade-lined Big Hunk O' Love Boulevard toward the center of Graceland, triggering as he flew his darksuit's sensory enhancements that increased his range of hearing and vision. An unforeseen consequence of this decision was that he could hear with unusual clarity the comments of the crowd below.

"What's this on my shoe?"

"Look! It's Ronnie Romper!"

"Hi, Ronnie!"

"Hrrrr!"

"My kids love your show!"

"I didn't know Ronnie was so *huge.* He's so little on vid!"

"Hey, Ronnie! Where's Auntie June and Uncle Amos?"

"Sing the Pangalactic Friendship Song!"

"What's this on my shoe?"

And then, lurching down the avenue, came a sight that Maijstral scarcely required enhanced vision in order to detect. It was a frightening figure, horribly disfigured, as tall as Roman and as powerful as a colossus.

It was Milo Hay, the fiance of Major Ruth Song. After the double thrashing he'd received from Prince Hunac's bodyguard and then from Roman, he'd been strapped into an exoskeleton to enable him to heal while moving about normally—if, that is, being strapped into a humanoid-shaped collection of gleaming, articulated metal can be called "moving normally."

Hay marched onto the boulevard with a hiss of hydraulics and a clank of metal. His face was covered by the semilife patches that were sopping up his bruises. Despite all his injuries, he had a strange, dreamy smile on his face, doubtless a side effect of overeffective painkillers.

Hay turned and began clanking down Big Hunk O' Love Boulevard in the same direction as Maijstral's party. Maijstral's blood turned cold.

"Faster," he said, and increased speed.

Hay looked up as Maijstral's group passed over his head. His dreamy smile widened. He waved.

"Ronnie Romper!" he said. "I love your show!"

At the geographical center of Graceland, surrounded by a company of guards in full dress uniform, stands the monument known as the Heart of Graceland. The huge gold-sheathed obelisk, in the shape of a giant torch, is by far the tallest freestanding structure in Tennessee, and on clear nights the Eternal Flame surmounting the structure can supposedly be seen from Pikes Peak. Long reflecting pools stretch from the monument in each of the four cardinal directions.

Maijstral dropped to the ground and his entourage followed suit. Moving with the dignity of authority and old age, he approached the main gate. A guard captain pointed a detector at him, read the display, and promptly saluted.

"How may I be of service to the Elvii?"

Behind his holographic camouflage, Maijstral smiled.

"Could you check the directory and remind me of the location of the resting place of Fleet Admiral Song?"

"Right away, sir."

The captain went to a service plate, consulted it for a moment, and then returned.

"Level Three, Row 300, number 341. He has a freestanding monument that will make the location plain. Do you wish me to escort you to the vault?"

"No, thank you. That won't be necessary." Maijstral nodded regally and led his group through the entrance.

"It is my constant joy to serve the Elvii!" the captain said fervently, and saluted again.

Maijstral entered and found himself in a huge room panelled in marble and draped in red velour. As he walked toward the center, the flagstones under his feet lit up one by one as he stepped on them, and an invisible organ began to sigh "Are You Lonesome To-night?"

The Heart of Graceland loomed ahead, a huge slab of polished black marble beneath which lay the mortal remains of Elvis Aaron Presley, lying forever with members of his family.

"Of *course!*" Kuusinen said. "I don't know why I didn't see it."

"I feel the same way," Roberta added. "Now it seems perfectly obvious."

"Beg pardon?" Conchita said. "It's not that obvious to *me.*"

The party approached the King's final resting place and came to a stop against the polished brass rail that circled the monument.

"Alice Manderley said that Major Song was just following orders," Maijstral said, "Which means she isn't behind the scheme. And Mr. Kuusinen was right when he suggested that there had to be a reason why my father's coffin was taken to Graceland, and not somewhere else."

"He was taken here to meet his chief adversary," Kuusinen said, "the man who headed the plot against him. It was *necessary* that Gustav Maijstral be brought here, because otherwise the meeting couldn't take place."

"Who is it?" Conchita demanded. "One of the Elvii?"

"Fleet Admiral Song," Kuusinen said.

"Admiral *Song?*" Roman roared. "But he's *dead!*"

"So is my father," Maijstral said. "But my father retains a kind of tenuous existence in his cryocoffin, and I suspect the same is true of Admiral Song."

Roberta nodded. "The late Duke—I hope this observation does not cause offense—is not always in a rational state. I suspect the same is true of Admiral Song."

"Long freezes rarely benefit the rational faculty," Kuusinen pointed out.

"Admiral Song was one of the Constellation's greatest heroes," Maijstral said, "and I suspect his granddaughter obeys his slightest wish without question. My grandfather caused the death of the Admiral's first wife, and he's been hungering for revenge ever since. Since his death, I suspect his vengeful desires have overwhelmed his reason."

Conchita whistled. "That Admiral's a sad case."

"Yes," Maijstral said. "And it's high time we deprived him of his prize. To the vaults!"

The elevator was lined with mirrors shot with gold veins, large enough to carry any number of cryocoffins without crowding, and played a cheerful arrangement of "Bossa Nova Baby" as it rose with a certain deliberate grandeur to the third level of the structure.

As soon as the doors opened, Maijstral's amplified senses began to hear a high-pitched, hectoring voice that rose and fell over the cheerful elevator music. He used the proximity wire in his darksuit to open his private communications channel, and subvocalized as he gave his instructions, inaudible to any eavesdroppers but clear enough to his own party.

"Something's up," he said. "Quiet now . . . and let's be certain to find the right vault. And if you have to talk, remember to subvocalize."

The others, silent, nodded.

The entire level consisted of the long, solemn marble rows of those who lay for eternity in the Arms of Elvis. An invisible chorus of angel voices sang a dirgelike, minor key version of "Mystery Train." Tasteful gold flashing neon signs directed Maijstral to Row 300.

The hectoring voice grew louder.

"Ridiculous drivelling fool!" it said. *"All my years of planning, and for this?"*

"Now, now, Bertie. Don't get upset—it will injure your digestion."

Maijstral stiffened as he recognized the voice of his father.

"I'm not Bertie, you maniac!"

"Admiral—don't get upset." Major Song's voice, a female baritone.

Maijstral drew his spitfire from its holster and set the charge to maximum.

"Why shouldn't I get upset?" said the first voice. "My vengeance is ruined! This fool is too thick-witted to appreciate the Hell I had in store for him, and you've bungled the other part of your assignment!"

"Sir—"

"When will Maijstral die in a duel, that's what I want to know!"

"He's still supposed to fight Hunac, sir," Major Song said weakly. "We just don't know when."

"Robert the Butcher's offspring must die! That's what my vengeance demands!"

"Yes, Admiral."

Maijstral reached Row 299, just before Admiral Song's resting place. He looked at the others—with his enhanced vision, he could do it without turning his head—and subvocalized.

"Roman, take Mr. Kuusinen down this aisle. Prepare to fly over the row of vaults and aid us on my signal."

"Hrrrrr, sir!"

"All of you, be careful when it comes to shooting. I don't want my father's coffin hit."

Roman's party drifted down the aisle and positioned themselves.

"I'm tired of waiting for Hunac to do the job," the Admiral ranted. "Go out and have Maijstral killed!"

Maijstral's blood froze. His pistol trembled in his hand.

"Have Hood do it," ranting on, "or have him hire someone. Just blow the monster's head off!"

"Yes, sir."

The Admiral's voice turned smug. "There is no guilt," he said, "in extinguishing vermin."

"I say, Bertie," ex-Dornier said reproachfully, "this prank is going a little far, don't'ee think? What if someone takes you seriously with this killing business?"

"Shut up, you—you—"

While the late Admiral spluttered in search of an appropriate epithet, Maijstral heard Roman's voice subvocalizing on his communications channel.

"These people intend to assassinate you, sir! We should eradicate them!"

Maijstral reflected how cheerful it might be to simply order *Roman! Kill!* and then sit back until it was all over.

But no. Something in him cringed from ordering a cold-blooded murder, even with all the provocation in the world.

His heart thrashed in his throat, making it difficult to subvocalize.

"Save my father first," he said. "If they resist, that's one thing—but if they don't, it's another. We have plenty of witnesses to their plan—we can have them arrested later. A crazy man in a coffin and a woman surgically altered to look like Elvis won't get very far."

"Hrrrrr!" Roman replied, his tone resentful. And then, "Very good, sir."

Maijstral turned to face the others in his party. (He could have seen them without turning, but they wouldn't have known he was talking to them.)

"Keep large intervals," he said. "If we clump up, we're just one large target. Keep your weapons ready, but no shooting unless I shoot first."

Where, he suddenly wondered, were these phrases coming from? He'd never been in the military, and he'd done his best to run away from any dangerous situations in his life; but now here he was lecturing the others on tactics like some wizened Death Commando sergeant in an action vid.

Probably it was all bubbling up from his subconscious. Maybe he'd watched too many Westerns.

He holstered his pistol, wiped sweat from his palms, took his pistol in hand again.

"I say, Bertie!" ex-Dornier said cheerfully. "You wouldn't have any of the bubbly about, would you?"

"Shut up! Shut up, shut up, shut up!"

For some reason the sound of the deranged corpse shouting at his father set Maijstral's blood boiling, and the anger set him marching around the corner and down Row 300 without conscious thought. And immediately he knew this business was going to be a lot more difficult than he'd expected.

There wasn't just Song in the aisle, for one thing. She had three companions disguised as Elvis. Maijstral recognized one of them as Commander Hood, the ex-naval officer turned bully, whose burly form was unmistakable even in a wig and paste-on sideburns. The two others looked like hired muscle. And a fourth companion, unless Maijstral missed his guess, was one of the Elvii himself, a sullen-looking youth in black leather vestments.

A pedestal bust of Admiral Song had been moved aside to permit access to his vault. The marble front of the vault, with his name and a patriotic inscription, had been removed. Two coffins were visible, both for the moment suspended in the grappler beams of a kind of cartlike lifting apparatus that itself hovered on its repellers a few inches above the ground. One of Song's henchmen was sitting in the cart's seat, operating the controls. Apparently both coffins had been jammed into the same vault, and it was necessary to remove both at once in order to sort them out.

That was the one piece of luck that Maijstral could see. He had brought straps and a-grav repellers to help carry his father's coffin from Graceland, but instead, if he worked things right, he could just commandeer the cart and drive it off.

Maijstral tried to summon authority and dignity as he marched toward the group. He held his pistol behind him, because he wasn't certain if the commercial hologram would conceal it or not. His enhanced vision showed Roberta and Conchita marching out behind him, spreading out as per instructions. One by one, Song's party noticed his approach and stared at him nervously while the late Admiral raved on.

"Do we have a problem here?" Maijstral's voice sounded faint over the crashing of his own heart.

"Who the hell is *that?*" Admiral Song snarled.

"I am of the Elvii," Maijstral said. "I heard a disturbance."

Maijstral was terrified that someone would simply ask, *Why's he wearing a hologram?* but it didn't happen. The young Elvis—the genuine one—stepped forward. Sweat glazed his brow. "There is no problem, sibling," he said. "Two of the deceased have been arguing, and we've decided to move one of them to a different vault. There's no reason for you to concern yourself."

Maijstral affected to consider this as he peered down his nose at the young Elvis. "I do not believe you are authorized to make these decisions," he said, making a hopeful guess.

The Elivs looked abashed and mumbled something. Song and Hood exchanged glances. Maijstral looked at the vault, at the two coffins.

"Two coffins in a single vault?" he said. "This is quite irregular."

Major Song stepped forward. "Sir? If you will permit—"

Maijstral looked at her. She was devout, supposedly, and perhaps would be disinclined to harm or question one of the Elvii.

"I do not recall that I gave you permission to speak," he said, and Major Song fell back in confusion. Maijstral cleared his throat. "I believe I will have to take the coffins downstairs and sort this all out with the proper authorities. Follow me, please."

For a moment he thought they'd actually do it—he could see the inclination in their eyes, the automatic impulse to obey the voice of authority when they had no plan of their own. But then the worst thing possible happened.

Maijstral's father spoke.

"Drake?" he said. "That's you, isn't it, Drake?"

There was a long moment of horrified paralysis. Maijstral could see calculations running behind all the others' eyes. Then Hood went for his gun and without thought Maijstral raised his spitfire and fired. *"Yaaaaaah!"* he shouted, the Yell of Hate coming to his lips unbidden. Flame fountained off Hood's shields, which apparently he'd managed to trigger in time. Slugs from Hood's chugger whanged off Maijstral's shields.

"What's that noise?" asked Maijstral's father. "Is it fireworks?"

And then things got confusing.

In a surge of terror Maijstral realized he was not accomplishing anything standing there and yelling, and that furthermore he was in the line of fire. He flung himself to the ground. Hood and one of Song's henchmen dived behind the coffins and began shooting from behind cover. Gunfire roared in the enclosed marble space. Spitfire charges fountained bright fire. Alarms began to ring, and purple fire-retardant foam began to pour from hidden reservoirs in the ceiling.

The Elvis, caught in the middle of it all, patted the pockets of his leather jacket frantically, looking for a weapon that wasn't there.

"I'm not shielded!" he shouted as bullets cracked by his ear. "Help!"

"Cease fire!" the late Admiral roared in a voice of thunder. *"Cease firing, you fools! You could hit me, and I'm not shielded!"*

The shooting dwindled away as this line of reasoning penetrated the startled combatants. Each side wanted at least *one* of the coffins to survive.

"Fireworks!" exclaimed Maijstral's father. "Is it the Emperor's birthday?"

At this instant two figures appeared, silhouetted against the ceiling—the flying holographic Elvis that was Paavo Kuusinen, and a giant roaring Ronnie Romper, both stooping on the villains like falcons on their prey.

Roman went for the burly Commander Hood, recognizing a fellow professional when he saw one, but on his way clotheslined the henchman who was sitting on the cart and knocked him into Song and the other henchman. Hit hard, Hood went down but dragged Roman with him into the growing river of purple foam. Kuusinen, acting with perfect logic, dropped into the cart's seat and seized the controls. As the cart spun on its heel, the coffins knocked the bust of Admiral Song to the floor and revealed Major Song and one of her henchmen, deprived of cover, struggling to their feet in the froth. Maijstral fired at the targets while he had the chance, his spitfire charges bouncing off shields but raising a huge purple cloud of steam.

Kuusinen got the cart pointed in the right direction and accelerated, running smash into the back of the leather-clad Elvis, who was flung forward into the foam, sliding along on his stomach until he cracked heads with Maijstral. Seeing stars, Maijstral grabbed the Elvis's collar, prepared to beat him senseless with the butt of his spitfire, but observed that the Elvis was already unconscious.

Maijstral looked up just in time to see the cart careening toward him at top speed. His heart lurched. He dropped his face into the foam as the cart, supported by its a-grav repellers, passed harmlessly over his head.

He looked up again. Dimly visible through a haze of purple mist, he saw Hood and Roman locked in combat. Hood's wig was badly askew. Roman aimed a kick at Hood, slipped in the foam, and crashed to the ground. Hood tried to stomp Roman while Roman was prone, but his support leg slid out from under him and he crashed to the ground as well. Both combatants rose, dripping foam, lunged for one another again, grappled, and fell.

"What's going on?" the Admiral shouted. *"What's happening?"*

Song rose from the foam, looking frantic, but promptly slipped and dropped into the purple with a mighty splash.

It looked as if Maijstral's side was winning. And winning, to Maijstral, had always meant getting while the getting was good.

"Follow the coffins!" Maijstral ordered, forgetting to subvocalize, and then he triggered his own flying harness and zoomed into the air after the retreating cart, flying backward and navigating through his enhanced, expanded vision. As he passed, Roberta and Conchita triggered their repellers and rose out of the foam themselves.

From behind the curtain of mist came roars and meaty thwacks as Roman and Hood pummeled each other. Major Song staggered upward and gaped after her disappearing grandfather. Her two henchmen likewise rose unsteadily to their feet.

"They're getting away!" she said. "After them!" But as they started to run they tripped over the bust of Admiral Song, hidden deep in the foam, and they tangled and crashed heavily to the ground.

Kuusinen's cart reached the end of the row and he tried frantically to make the abrupt right-angle turn demanded by the room's configuration. He failed and ran both coffins straight into the wall. Maijstral hadn't anticipated Kuusinen's abrupt stop and he sailed backward into the cart, sweeping Kuusinen off and slamming him against the far wall.

"Ouch!" said Maijstral's dad. *"What just happened?"*

Maijstral came to a halt, the breath hammered from his lungs by the collision, stars flashing in his eyes. He looked up dazedly just in time to see Roberta flying straight for him.

The impact bent a few ribs. And then Conchita crashed into the pile, making a surprising impact for someone her size.

"I believe we were supposed to turn," Roberta remarked.

Major Song and her henchmen slowly rose from the pile again. "They're helpless!" she called, pointing. "Get them!"

They began loping toward the stalled cart, foam splashing at every step. Maijstral and his group tried to get untangled. As the pack loosened, Kuusinen fell unconscious into the foam. Maijstral wondered where his spitfire had got to. If it was in the froth, he'd never find it.

And then Roman, who had finally choked Commander Hood into submission, rose from the foam and took flight, arms outstretched.

He rammed Major Song with his head, and his extended arms clipped the others as he passed. All three dropped, landing hard. Roman floated to where Maijstral's party were still trying to sort themselves out, picked up the unconscious Kuusinen, and set him at the cart's controls.

"Shall I drive, sir?" Roman said.

"By all means," Maijstral mumbled.

"Don't take the elevator," Conchita said. "Guards will be responding to the alarms by now."

They took the stairs, the cart thudding down the risers on its repellers. Turning the cart on the landings took time, and Ruth Song and her henchmen were closing on them by the time the cart crashed through some door and began moving down a long tunnel.

"Where does this go?" Roberta asked.

"I don't know," Maijstral said. "Kuusinen has the maps, and he's out of action."

"What's that *noise?*" Conchita wondered. There was a distant, powerful sound, a roaring like a distant ocean. It was coming from dead ahead.

The cart smashed through another pair of doors into a large, dark place, and the noise was suddenly much louder. Startled people darted from out of the way of the cart. And then the darkness fell away, and to Maijstral's horror he realized what was making the roaring sound.

Thousands of people . . .

Garvikh really had them rocking. He had the audience in the palm of his furry hand.

He had heard it said that he was the finest Elvis ever to be born Khosalikh. Certainly he was among the best Elvises now alive. As part of his apprenticeship he had mastered the difficult, antique Earth dialect, a dead language no longer spoken anywhere, in which the King had recorded his masterpieces. Garvikh had devoted thousands of hours to a series of special exercises designed to limber his sturdy Khosali hips and torso, never intended to move with the fluidity more natural to the human form, so that he could perform the demanding, difficult hip thrusts, the stilted, pigeon-toed walking style, the sudden knee drops and whirling assaults on the microphone that characterized the rigidly defined Elvis repertoire. This was High Custom, and High Custom performances required the utmost in precision. Each step, each gesture, each twitch of the hips or twist of the upper lip, was performed with the utmost classical perfection, the most rigid attention to form. There was no room for accident, for spontaneity. All was performed with utmost care to assure that every nuance was subtly shaded and subtly controlled, in the tradition of the great Elvis Masters of the past.

And now all the work, all the dedication was paying off. Garvikh was performing live in front of an audience of thousands, and he was wowing them. A Memphis audience was said to be the most knowledgeable, the most demanding; but if you could win them to your side, you had a place in their hearts forever.

He had opened with "All Shook Up" and "Jailhouse Rock" to get the audience on its feet. He'd made them swoon with "Surrender" and "One Broken Heart for Sale." Then he'd jumped into "Good Rockin' Tonight," to which he had choreographed jets of water from the fountains in the ornamental pond at the foot of the stage, the leaping water turned into a fantasy of color by spotlights. Now he was ready to wail on his best song, "Heartbreak Hotel." He had worked on the refrain for months, to get precisely the right tone to the mumble of the "I'll be so lonely" section.

But before he started, he wanted to drive the audience into a frenzy of anticipation. He carefully assumed the Sixth Posture of Elvis, cocking his head at a precise sixteen-degree angle and looking at the audience slightly sidelong. *"Well . . ."* he drawled, and the audience roared. He shifted to the Seventh Posture, the provocative "Undereyed Stance," difficult for a Khosalikh to pull off because it required him to look at the audience in a challenging way, as if from under his brows—but of course the Khosali have no projecting forehead the way humans do, and the whole movement had to depend on careful effect and illusion.

"Well . . ." he said again, and seven thousand hypercritical Elvis fanatics roared with approval.

He waited the prescribed six seconds for suspense to build. *"Well . . ."* he began again, and then perceived a movement off to his right. Not daring to change his posture, he turned his eyes in that direction, and almost immediately wished he hadn't.

Three flying holographic Elvises, trailing purple foam, were zooming onto the stage at high speed, accompanied by a hovercart that carried two long metal boxes covered with purple goo. A fifth Elvis lolled on the cart, drunk or unconscious, while a sixth figure—a preposterous red-haired giant with a fixed grin—sat behind the controls.

Ronnie *Romper?* Garvikh thought, but discipline demanded he not move a muscle, that he stand in the "Undereyed Stance" for the five to eight seconds necessary to provoke the audience to an ecstasy of anticipation.

The cart bore down on him, showing no sign of stopping. Garvikh was struck with the full horror of his dilemma. If he stepped out of the cart's path he would be making an unscripted move, defying thousands of years of performing tradition and probably ending his career on the spot. And if he didn't move out of the way, he would be run over by the cart, its cargo, and its redheaded occupant.

Garvikh decided to tough it out. He held the Seventh Posture, clenching his teeth in a snarl. The audience held its breath. Then the impact came, and Garvikh felt himself cartwheeling across the stage . . . and as stars exploded before his eyes and the stage came up to meet him, he heard the roar of audience approval.

Garvikh had not trained all his life in order to cave in easily to misfortune. He staggered upright, his hand still triumphantly clutching the microphone, and automatically assumed the Eleventh Posture, the one called "The King in Glory."

"I—" he began, the world swimming around him, and then through his confusion observed that three more Elvises—and wasn't one of them Ruth Song?—had just charged onto the stage and were engaging the first set of Elvises in battle. Fists flew. One of the first group of Elvises was knocked down.

The fans could hardly blame him for *this,* he concluded. Trying not to break character, he stalked forward and tapped one of the Elvises on the shoulder. "What's going on here?" he demanded, unconsciously speaking in the dead language he'd been performing all night.

The other Elvis whirled, punched him on the muzzle, and dropped him to the stage. The audience roared.

Garvikh decided to crawl to safety, but this proved more difficult than he anticipated, because first one, then another of the Elvises tripped over him and crashed to the stage.

Garvikh shook the stars from his head and rose cautiously to his feet again. Someone new had joined the fray—a ghastly-looking human in a clanking mechanical suit, trailing water as he climbed to the stage. Apparently he had crossed the ornamental pond in front of the stage. "Ruth!" the human shouted. Despite his apparent desperation, his face bore an odd, unfocused grin.

"Milo!" cried one of the Elvises. "Help!" It *was* Ruth Song, Garvikh saw, being held down and pummeled by a pair of Elvises.

Garvikh concluded that he should come to her aid—at least *she* was an Elvis he recognized. But as he ran to Ruth Song's assistance, Milo seized him from behind by his standing collar.

"Rat!" Milo yelled. Garvikh's teeth rattled as Milo shook him back and forth. Hydraulics hissed as Garvikh was flung across the stage.

The lights went out for Garvikh for a while, but when he cleared the cobwebs from his head the battle was still going on. Elvises were battling back and forth, but Milo held center stage, engaged with Ronnie Romper. Roars, thumps, hydraulic hisses, and clangs marked the blows of fists, feet, stage equipment, and Milo's armored shell.

One of the Elvises hit another Elvis so hard that he knocked his wig off. Another Elvis smashed an Elvis with the microphone stand. Yet another Elvis was trying to strangle a different Elvis.

A youngish human female with rocklike hair dashed across the stage, artfully weaving among the battling Elvises. Media globes orbited her head. Then a group of short, copper-skinned humans ran across the stage as well, scattering Elvises but exiting after the female.

The short humans were followed by an elderly human who hit several of the Elvises with his cane as he made his way across the stage.

The audience was going mad.

Milo's forearm thudded into Ronnie Romper, knocking him back into the cart. But Ronnie was undeterred—roaring like a demon, he picked up one of the boxes from the cart—was it a *coffin?*—and then used it as a ram to smash Milo in the chest. Milo staggered back. Ronnie pursued his advantage, hammering Milo again and again. Milo's arms windmilled as his heels stopped at the edge of the stage.

"Kill them all!" screamed one of the coffins.

Roaring, Ronnie apparently intended to do just that. He thrust one last time, and Milo gave a despairing wail as he went off the stage. A giant splash rose as the man struck the ornamental pond. And then Ronnie raised the box above his head, roared once more, a terrible sound, and flung the box down after Milo. There was a horrid clanging noise followed by a bright flare, as if some electronics had just short-circuited, and then Ronnie stepped back, his posture one of satisfaction.

Four Elvises were sprawled on stage, incapacitated. One of them, Garvikh perceived, was Ruth Song.

The Elvis still on his feet, plus Ronnie Romper, picked up two of the unconscious Elvises, then flew from the stage, followed by Ronnie Romper and the cart. Three wounded Elvises were left behind. The audience screamed for more.

Dimly, Garvikh realized that this was his cue. He dragged himself to his feet, staggered downstage, and found the microphone. He picked it up and assumed the Seventh Posture again.

"Wellllll . . ." he repeated, and the crowd went wild. He held his pose for ten seconds, then for another six, then for another six. The audience's excitement knew no bounds. Garvikh had probably achieved some sort of record. Finally he waved his arm, signalling the downbeat for "Heartbreak Hotel," then stepped back into the powerful "Wailing Stance" to cry the opening lines. Unfortunately his

foot landed on a pile of the purple foam that seemed, unaccountably, to have been smeared around the stage.

While the opening bars to "Heartbreak Hotel" rang out Garvikh performed a crazed, whirling dance for a few brief seconds, then fell to the stage.

From his prone position, he heard the roaring sound of audience approval. *Immortality at last,* he thought, and then he surrendered his hold on consciousness.

Maijstral and his party made their way to the stage door, which parted automatically for Maijstral's coded badge. As the doors rolled open, Maijstral gazed out into the combat-ready eyes of a platoon of well-armed guards, led by the same officer who had admitted them to the Heart of Graceland.

Oh dear, he thought, and prepared to surrender.

In his imagination, dungeon gates yawned.

The officer looked up from his portable scanner. "Are there any instructions, sir?" he asked.

Maijstral's thoughts brightened. "Why, yes," he said. "Some false Elvii have just disturbed the concert. Take your men to the stage and put them in custody."

The man saluted. "It is my constant joy to serve the Elvii!" he proclaimed.

Maijstral's stunned party left the amphitheater, trailing purple ooze, and the guards filed in to do their duty.

"Are we having a good time, Drake?" ex-Dornier asked. *"I can't really tell."*

EIGHTEEN

Colonel-General Vandergilt walked into Tvar's northwest drawing room, and Maijstral observed that she looked different from those occasions on which she was swooping down on miscreants, her eyes alight with fanaticism and hatred for all that was unEarthly. At the moment, having made her way past the pack of reporters at the gates of Tvar's estate, and having had to request admittance from the servants instead of stalking through the door with a uniformed group of bullyboys at her back, she seemed quite altered.

Even her hair was less threatening, with more disobedient strands than usual sabotaging her dignity.

Maijstral couldn't help but be pleased with the change.

"General Vandergilt," he said, "the butler told me you had news?"

Vandergilt's voice was a carefully pitched monotone, concerned only with the facts. "Major Song has confessed her part in the plot to have you killed by provoking a series of duels, and she has also confessed her scheme to steal your father's coffin."

Maijstral nodded. "I should congratulate you on your interrogative technique," he said. "I had thought she would prove sterner stuff."

Vandergilt reached a hand up to twine a strand of hair around her finger, then realized what she was doing and disciplined the hand promptly. "I had little to do with it," she said. "The Elvii ordered her to confess."

"Ah. Very good of them."

"The Elvis involved in the plot—Elvis XIV, by the way—has also confessed. I gather the other Elvii will formally expel him."

"The Elvii," Maijstral smiled, "are surely the reservoir of wisdom."

Vandergilt flushed slightly. "As for the instigator of the plot—" she began.

Maijstral's smile, like Vandergilt's flush, expanded. "You mean Fleet Admiral Song?" he asked. "The Nelson of Neerwinden? The Hero of the Human Constellation? Vigilant defender of the human race from all wickedness and alien contamination?"

Vandergilt cleared her throat. "Yes," she mumbled. "Admiral Song. As someone already declared legally dead, he is immune from any legal penalty, but it appears the matter is moot. There was some damage to his coffin, apparently due either to collision or to stray gunfire, and when he fell into the water he, ah, short-circuited."

Maijstral had wondered what that flare of energy implied. "Admiral Song is no more?" he said.

"Such existence as remained to him has been terminated, yes."

"Such a shameful end for a great man," Maijstral smiled. "Involved in a mean, sordid little conspiracy of theft and murder." He successfully resisted an impulse to snap his fingers and laugh out loud.

Maijstral directed her attention toward her boots. She cleared her throat again. "It appears that Captain Hay had no part in the conspiracy," she said, "and was acting in order to defend his fiancee from assault. He was severely damaged by the discharge of energy from Admiral Song's coffin, and is currently in hospital."

"What a shame," Maijstral grinned.

"Of course," Vandergilt said, and a bit of steel entered her glance once more, "there remains the problem of who entered Graceland illegally in order to liberate your father, and engaged in illegal gunplay within the sacred precincts." She looked hopeful. "These people, if discovered, could almost certainly be arrested."

"I'd love to help you, General," Maijstral said, "but I'm afraid I have no idea who these individuals might be. All I know is that my father reappeared in his room. If I were you," he suggested, "I might inquire among the Elvii. Perhaps they discovered the plot and acted to quell it on their own."

Vandergilt's look darkened. She tossed her head to get hair out of her eyes. "I will investigate the possibility," she said.

"Of course," Maijstral lied, "my information suggests that the Elvii were so appalled by the goings-on within their sacred precincts that they would never prosecute anyone who acted to expose malfeasance within their ranks."

Vandergilt's expression was sour. "Your information suggests that, does it?"

"Alas for justice," Maijstral said, "it does."

"The question remains," Vandergilt said, "of your intent to prosecute. If Major Song is to undergo a trial, of course it would require you to alter your schedule and remain on Earth for an indefinite period, with enormous inconvenience to yourself and your career." There was a subdued but hopeful glint in her eye as she spoke.

"And there would be such enormous publicity," Maijstral said.

"Yes." Leaping at her chance. "Very troublesome for you, I'm sure."

"And of course much of the publicity would be aimed at exposing the moral bankruptcy of the pro-Human movement, with unforeseen consequence for the Security and Sedition Act, which would legalize forms of discrimination against nonhumans and vastly increase the power of, among others, the Special Services Corps, to which you belong."

Vandergilt's face was a mask. "I'm sure I couldn't make those judgments, sir."

Amusement glowed behind Maijstral's lazy eyes. "I don't see why I should be inconvenienced by a trial at all," he said. "My presence probably won't even be required, not with Major Song's confession. And, of course," smiling thinly, "an abstract consideration for justice requires me to prosecute."

"As you say, sir." Stonily.

"Do I have to sign anything?"

"Right here, sir."

Maijstral signed with a flourish. "Very well, then, General Vandergilt," he said. "I leave you to your job."

"Yes, sir."

Maijstral waved a hand commandingly. "Go forth and arrest the miscreants, officer!"

"Yes, sir."

Colonel-General Vandergilt marched out, furiously stuffing loose strands of hair back under her cap.

Maijstral, pleased with this little scene, made his way from the northwest drawing room into the southwest drawing room adjacent.

Nichole looked up from the documents she was reading—information concerning the very best place to eat Fleth a la Normandie at Luna City, her next destination.

"Did it go well, Drake?" she asked.

"I believe it did, yes."

He sat next to her on the sofa. "It is in large part thanks to your researches that everything has gone as well as it has," he said.

"It was my pleasure. Those people were absolute *poison.*"

"Indeed they were. And now they've not only been thwarted, they've been exposed and humiliated."

She looked at him with her famous blue eyes. "You lead a surprisingly dangerous life, Drake."

"Perhaps. But at least I'm lucky." He took her hand. "Most of all, I am lucky in my friends," he said.

"Thank you."

"I will always be grateful for our friendship."

She cocked her head and regarded him. "I sense a *but* somewhere in this stretch of conversation."

"I regret it, Nichole."

"So do I." She blinked and looked thoughtful. "You are the only man ever to turn me down, Drake, do you know that? And now you've done it twice."

"Even with these disappointments factored in, I think your percentage of conquests remains admirably high."

She gave a smile. "Perhaps so."

"I hope this won't stop you from asking at regular intervals. I may yet change my mind."

"Well." She disengaged her hand and rose from the sofa. "Perhaps it was a foolish notion, anyway."

"I trust not, my lady." He stood, escorted her to the door, sniffed her ears.

"Next time you're in mortal danger," Nichole said, "I hope you won't forget to call."

"I won't. Thank you for everything."

"Give my love to Roman."

"I will. Thank you again."

A pang of regret touched his heart as he watched her leave. If only, he considered, there were two of him, or perhaps three, so that he could explore all the choices available to him.

He'd managed to duplicate himself in his magic act, he thought. Pity it had been a trick, and hadn't lasted.

Prince Hunac's unblinking dark eyes were still a bit unsettling. Maijstral was brought to mind of obsidian knives and bloody altars.

"I called as soon as I heard," Hunac said.

"That is very good of you."

Hunac blinked. Finally. "It is my part to apologize, isn't it? I misinterpreted events."

"Some highly intelligent people took very good care that you should."

"It is good of you to say so. Still, I should have seen that there was something wrong."

"You allowed Her Grace of Benn to persuade you to delay, and that enabled me to deal with the situation. For that delay I should thank you."

The obsidian knives flashed again in Hunac's eyes. "It strikes me that those responsible for the situation should be compelled to atone for their crimes. I have sent out emissaries in quest of Major Song and Alice Manderley, who so abused my hospitality."

Alice Manderley, Kenny Chang, and Drexler had been released as soon as Maijstral and his party returned from Graceland. Maijstral suspected that Alice and Kenny would book passage on the first liner leaving Earth.

Drexler, deprived of funds, would have to steal something in order to make an escape, a task made difficult by the fact that Maijstral had kept all Drexler's burglar equipment in his own possession. Maijstral was certain that Drexler would never be employed by any high-ranking burglar again, not once Drexler's treachery had been thoroughly aired by the media.

"Would you happen to know," Hunac inquired, "where Miss Manderley might be?"

"If she's not at home, I'm afraid I have no idea." Thoughtfully, Maijstral fingered his diamond ring. "I would appreciate it, by the way, if you postponed any encounter with Major Song until after her trial. I would very much like to make certain that her cause is publicly and thoroughly discredited."

Hunac nodded. "I will take your request under serious consideration."

"Thank you."

"My emissaries have had no luck with Mangula Arish—she keeps running away the second they appear."

Maijstral repressed a smile. "That is unfortunate indeed, Your Highness."

"Now I learn that she has resigned her post and fled outsystem."

"Perhaps this is a victory in itself."

"I will have to consider it so—after I give her flight the maximum possible publicity."

"I hope other journalists will bear it in mind."

Hunac permitted himself a flintlike smile. "So do I." The smile warmed a bit. "I hope you will accept my hospitality in the Underwater Palace again. I think I can promise you that you will have a much better time."

Maijstral nodded. "I will accept, if I can. My plans are a bit uncertain at present."

"Good-bye, then. Thank you for being so understanding."

"Farewell. Give my best to the toadfish."

"I will."

The Prince's image faded, leaving Maijstral with an aftertaste of pure satisfaction.

Things had worked out well.

"Dad?"

"Drake? Is that you, Drake?"

"Yes, it is."

Maijstral sat on a chair and signalled to his father's guards to leave the room.

He wasn't about to let his father become the hostage of yet another political lunatic. He had hired a squad of well-armed, well-equipped bodyguards—well, *coffin*guards—simply to sit in the room with him and keep him safe from any further adventures until ex-Dornier could be shipped back to the family crypt on Nana.

If the guards had to spend their time listening to the corpse's prattle, at least they were well compensated for their efforts.

"How are you doing, Dad?" Maijstral asked.

"Well," the late Duke remarked, "I seem to be dead."

"Yes." Trying not to smile. "I had noticed. I meant, you're not suffering any ill effects from your adventure?"

"With Bertie? Oh no. I had a *splendid* time!"

"Bertie?"

"Oh yes, my old school chum. He had this most elaborate *prank* worked out. It had to do with, oh, metaphysics and things."

Maijstral worked for a moment at understanding, then gave up.

"I'm glad you enjoyed yourself," he said. "Is there anything you'd like now."

"A cup of cocoa and a biscuit would be nice."

Maijstral sighed. "Well," he said, "I'll see what I can do."

"Nichole sends her love."

"Thank you, sir."

"Is there anything you need?"

"Thank you, sir, no. I am provided with all the necessities."

Maijstral smiled as he left Roman's hospital room.

Roman was recovering swiftly. His flesh had lost its alarming scarlet color and was approaching the normal, healthy grey. Black stubble covered his skin where his fur was growing back. The new age-ring had healed.

Roman's molt, thank the Twelve Passive Virtues, was over.

It wasn't the molt that had put Roman in the hospital, however. When he raised Admiral Song's coffin above his head and flung it down on Milo Hay, Roman had strained his back.

It was the part of a lord, Maijstral thought, to retire to bed when his back pained him. Roman might as well get used to such privileges while he could.

He walked down the hall to Roberta's room, knocked, and entered. Roberta was propped up in bed, smiling and chatting with Will, the Bubber, who had come to pay a visit.

Roberta had broken some ribs in the fight at Graceland. She had committed herself to the hospital less because her medical condition required it than because the rest of her household, Batty and Paavo Kuusinen, were already inmates, and she thought she might as well make a party of it.

"Hello, Roberta. Hello, Will."

The Bubber rose from his chair. "Hello, Drake."

"It's good to see you, Will." Maijstral sniffed Roberta's ears and kissed her cheek.

"How are the ribs?" he asked.

"Well enough."

"And Mr. Kuusinen?"

"Well, he *was* knocked unconscious. The doctors want him under observation. But so far no serious damage has surfaced."

"Very good."

The Bubber shifted his feet awkwardly. "I should push off. But first—" He smiled. "Drake, would you like to see a card trick?"

"By all means."

Will's trick was a complex one, involving a force, a shift, and a back palm. When he produced at length the three of rovers, Maijstral and Roberta both affected amazement and offered congratulations.

"Very well done," Maijstral said.

"Thank you." The Bubber beamed. "Is there any room for improvement?"

"Well, your patter could use a little work. And I could see the little finger break from this angle."

The Bubber's face fell slightly. "Oh."

"I'd advise working the trick in a mirror."

"I will. Thanks." He looked thoughtful. "You know, Drake, I'd like to ask your advice in another sphere, if I might."

"Certainly."

"Joseph Bob is wondering if he should challenge Alice Manderley and Major Song for their part in misleading him."

Maijstral gave the thought his consideration. "Well, it was Drexler who stole the pistol, not Alice."

"J.B. wouldn't challenge a servant."

"I shouldn't think so. And Major Song is about to undergo a trial that will discredit her forever, I expect."

The Bubber nodded soberly. "True."

"And—just between the two of us—" Maijstral touched the Bubber's arm and smiled. "Duelling is a perfectly silly custom, don't you think?"

The Bubber looked surprised. "Uh—if you say so. I suppose it is." He shuffled his feet. "I've taken up enough of your time. Good-bye, Drake, and thanks. See you later, Roberta."

Roberta waved from her bed. "Good-bye, Will."

The Bubber left. Maijstral sat on Roberta's bed. "I suspect I have not thanked you enough," he said. "You kept me out of Hunac's clutches, and you risked yourself in my behalf yesterday. You've performed superbly, and I'm thankful you suffered no more than some cracked ribs."

Her violet eyes warmed. "I'm glad it's over."

"So am I." He smiled, took her hand. "I've had time to think."

"At last." Her look turned serious. "And your conclusions?"

"You've made the most attractive offer—"

Roberta's face hardened. "But you're not going to take it."

"My life is too unsettled at the moment for me to consider marriage. If you'd made the offer at another time—"

"It can't wait." Shortly.

"Or if it were possible for us to spend time together normally, to get to know one another before making any decision—"

She sighed. "I had a feeling this would happen. Ever since our night together."

Maijstral's ears cocked forward in surprise. "Beg pardon?"

"Well. That night wasn't—well—it wasn't what I'd expected. Perfectly *pleasant,* you understand, you were very nice, but somehow —I don't know—the whole experience was somehow lacking."

Maijstral was surprised. "It was our first night together," he said. "A certain amount of awkwardness is to be expected in the early stages."

She waved a hand. "Oh, it wasn't that. Just—well, I'd been thinking about being with you for *years,* understand. And it wasn't what I had anticipated."

Maijstral felt a touch of annoyance. He could hardly be blamed, he thought, for any failure to live up to Roberta's lush schoolgirl fantasies.

"Perhaps," he ventured, "your expectations were a trifle unrealistic."

"What do you think of Will?"

Maijstral's eyes lifted. "Sorry?"

"Do you think I should marry Will?"

"Er—"

"If I'm not going to marry *you,"* tartly, "I've got to marry *somebody.* And I've spent a lot of time with Will in the last days, and he seems suitable enough."

Maijstral gave it thought. "Speaking dynastically, it would be a good match."

Fire flashed from her violet eyes. "He's a little green," she judged, "but I reckon I'll be able to make a man of him."

Maijstral found himself thoroughly glad he had not consented to the engagement. The result might be admirable enough in the abstract, he thought, but hard to live with in the long run.

"If I may be permitted to make an observation," he said, "it would be that men are not *made,* but make themselves. A partner can make the task easier, but cannot drive a person to it."

Roberta frowned.

"Will's problem," Maijstral added, "insofar as he has one, is that he has nothing to do that his brother, or someone in his circle, has not done before him. If you marry him, you should encourage him to be something other than a consort."

Roberta seemed a little amused. "You think I should give him a hobby?"

"You are a very well-known racer," Maijstral pointed out. "And I think you'd be a lesser person without *your* hobby, no?"

"Hm," Roberta said, and frowned.

As Maijstral left, he cast his mind back to the night he spent with Roberta, and felt a cold little anxiety gnawing at the back of his mind. She had seemed enthusiastic enough at the *time,* he thought. He had thought he had behaved rather well.

And then he wondered if the whole comment had been some small attempt at revenge. Very possibly, he thought.

He dropped into Kuusinen's room and found him asleep. He would thank Kuusinen later.

The next room was Aunt Batty's. He dropped in, spoke generally of his admiration for Roberta, and then mentioned he had decided with regret to decline her offer of marriage.

"Indeed," Batty said, and her ears flicked forward in disapproval. "This will not improve my standing with the family. Most of them thought Bobbie's schemes highly unorthodox, and I supported her. When recriminations are handed out, I will receive more than my share."

"If it is any consolation, I believe she has replaced me already. With Will, the Bubber."

Batty considered this. "Well," she said, "she could have done worse."

"I hope this will not prejudice your biography."

Batty looked down her muzzle, her face severe. "Some in the family might consider this rejection an insult, though I suppose I should take a more charitable view. I will try to do my historian's duty and avoid any reflections—on your character, say, or your valor —which may seem to me unwarranted."

Valor? Maijstral thought, a taste of panic fluttering in his throat. He really *would* have to get a look at that manuscript.

The last room was that of Conchita. She, like Kuusinen, had been knocked unconscious in the fight, and likewise was being kept for observation. He opened the door, peered inside, and saw Conchita watching a video.

"Hello," he said, and knocked.

She brightened. "Hi! I was just watching the vid."

Maijstral looked at the screen and saw people in Stetsons racing across the prairie on horseback. "Are you fond of Westerns?" he said.

"Only too. They're my favorite."

Better and better, Maijstral thought.

Conchita smiled and patted the bed beside her. Maijstral closed the door behind him, stretched out next to her, and put an arm around her.

Their kiss was very long and very pleasant.

"Why don't you stay awhile?" Conchita said when it was over.

"I have no other plans." He contemplated the situation for the moment. "Perhaps," he said, "I should lock the door."

"Can you lock a door in a hospital?"

"If the top-ranked burglar in the galaxy can't figure out a way to rig a door," Maijstral observed, "then he isn't worth his title."

Some time later, Conchita curled up next to Maijstral, pillowed her head upon his shoulder, and closed her eyes. Maijstral gave thought to the situation.

"You haven't experienced any disappointment, have you?" he asked.

"Disappointment? Why should I be disappointed?"

"No feelings that, say, your fantasies haven't been in some slight way, ah, completely fulfilled? Your expectations haven't been in any way disappointed?"

"Don't be silly," she said, and yawned. "You don't mind if I take a nap, do you?"

Roberta, Maijstral concluded, was simply *wrong*.

Experience told in these matters.

"There is only one thing I have to request," he said.

"Mm?"

"The hair," he said. "You'll have to change it."

"The fin? It makes me look taller!"

"I think your height is perfection itself."

"Well. Thank you for saying so."

"The fin goes, yes?"

"Oh." Sleepily. "If you insist."

As Conchita drifted off to sleep, Maijstral noticed that the video was still on. He looked for the service plate to shut it off and saw that it was too far to reach without disturbing Conchita.

He looked at the image. The Western had ended, and instead Maijstral saw a red-haired puppet with a fixed smile.

Ronnie Romper, Maijstral thought. *Oh no.*

He looked in despair at the service plate, still out of reach.

"Gosh, Uncle Amos," the puppet was saying. "I sure was scared. My knees were knocking together like anything!"

"Those dinosaurs were intimidating, that's for sure," Uncle Amos said, puffing his pipe. "I was getting pretty anxious myself."

"I was so afraid I almost ran away."

"But you didn't," Uncle Amos said. "That's the important thing."

Ronnie batted his eyes. "I don't understand, Uncle Amos."

Uncle Amos gazed at Ronnie from beneath his wizened white eyebrows. "Bravery doesn't mean that you don't feel fear," he said. "A fellow about to be run over by a herd of dinosaurs would have to be pretty stupid not to feel fear, now wouldn't he?"

"Gosh. I guess so."

"A brave person is one who feels fear, but who overcomes it and goes on to do what he has to do."

"Wow, Uncle Amos," the puppet said, "I never thought of that."

Maijstral stared at the screen. *I never thought of that, either,* he thought.

A sense of wonder overcame him. He lay back and reviewed his life. Based on a conclusion he'd drawn at sixteen, when he'd fought his first duel, he'd always assumed he was a coward.

But he *had* fought the duel, and another just a few days ago, and in between he'd been in a number of situations in which either he was shooting at people, or they were shooting at him, or both were happening at once. And yesterday, during the raid on the Heart of Graceland, he'd been giving orders as if he were an experienced warrior instead of a sneak thief with a sinking heart.

It wasn't as if he hadn't been afraid the whole time. But, just like Ronnie Romper, he'd done what he'd come to do, and not run away. Or rather, he hadn't run away until it was *time* to run away.

And of course his profession involved breaking into other people's homes. Preferably when no one was there, of course, but maybe that was merely common sense rather than a reflection on his bravery.

Perhaps, he thought, his sixteen-year-old assessment of himself had been overharsh.

He looked at the screen and blinked. *Thank you, Ronnie,* he thought.

The puppet had his uses, after all.

He lay back, Conchita peacefully sleeping on his shoulder, and gazed upward, past the hospital ceiling, into a universe of expanding possibility.

Some months later, when she and Roberta had returned to the Empire, Aunt Batty went in search of her notes and failed to find them.

They were missing—all the information she'd gleaned from Roman's genealogy, from her interviews with Joseph Bob, from her long conversations with Maijstral's father. All gone.

She had packed them most carefully, she knew. And now the entire package was gone.

She considered this for a long moment. *Most foolish,* she concluded. Her memory was perfectly good, and of course she could draw on the pages of notes and manuscript that had never left the Empire. Most of the second volume was completed. It was only the third that would be delayed.

It was never wise to annoy a biographer, she thought. They—*we*—have ways of getting our revenge.

If there was anyone who was an expert in the matter of interpretation, in the slight distortions of the facts necessary to cast aspersions on a person's character or ability, on an individual's motivations or worthiness—well, that person was a biographer.

She would take *very good care,* she thought severely, with her study of Maijstral.

And if he regretted the outcome—well, Aunt Batty thought, whose fault was it anyway?